IN REGALIA

May 2019

To Becky,

Happy Retirement!

Yours,

Erin McCormack

IN REGALIA

ERIN L. MCCORMACK

LONGTALE PRESS
BEDFORD, MA

This book is dedicated to the following people:

Claudia Fox Tree, friend, educator, activist, inspiration; and her family, for sharing their home and celebrations

Twins everywhere, including Laurel and Sarah, Savannah and Indigo, and their special relationships

Others who sing at the drum with me: Claudia, Jennifer, Laurel, Sarah, Bridget, Jan, Linda, Dana, Carolyn, Deb, and all others who have come and gone over the years

Massachusetts Center for Native American Awareness (MCNAA)

Hawk (Harry) and Braveheart (Lee) Edmunds

Pastor Brent, for his story and his perspective

My Native American ancestors, those known and unknown

Indigenous people everywhere, for persisting and remaining themselves on this planet, in spite of oppression, and for all they have contributed to our common humanity

My mother, Patricia Maloney McCormack, for her courage, endurance, and faith in me

Acknowledgments

Many thanks to those who've helped me on my way:

Katie Robinson, content editor and guide

Carolyn Haley, editor to the rescue

Sara Ellenbogan, valuable writing assistance

Carol Trio, sister-in-law and careful reader of text

My book group friends, for being the kind of readers I aspire to reach

Leonard Rose, who gave me feedback I could get nowhere else

Jennifer Wolfrum, for last-minute catches and a boost of confidence

Mary Jane St. Amour, stalwart friend and supporter, in good times and bad

Donald, Dylan, and Derek Koundakjian – aka Team Koundakjian

Chapter 1

Renee. Even dead, her sister led trouble to Helene's door. Helene put down the letter and picked up the photograph, blurred and taken at a distance: six children in costumes at a picnic near a lake. Two of those children were Renee's – twins, Helene's niece and nephew she had never met and did not recognize. She looked more closely; surely the youngest two were Renee's, although they did not look much alike in the picture. The toddlers in the front, one darker, one lighter, were about the right age, say around three years old in the picture. The other girls and boys, all with long black hair, were the twins' cousins on their father's side. Indian – Native American. Or so Helene understood, from what her brother had told her.

About a year ago, Denis brought the news that Renee had died, appearing on Helene's porch with a black Lab at his heels. No phone call, no warning. No smile of greeting, either. He stood under the porch light at her tidy, dignified colonial, dripping of rain and smelling like dog, to tell her that their sister had died, at twenty-nine, of the same fast-moving breast cancer that had killed their mother. And then he left, never stepping inside. Denis, the middle child who was always just passing through. A musician with no permanent abode, as far as Helene knew. He gave her no details, no explanation, just the facts of Renee's death. It was the first Helene had heard Renee was sick at all, never mind cancer.

Helene's eyes ran over the simple block printing on the letter again, still unsure exactly what the words meant – a notice or request from someone named Malvina, apparently the twins' aunt on the father's side. She knew their father's name was Louis from the birth announcement, the one communication from her sister in – what, almost ten years? Moving from the table to the counter where she kept her address book, Helene pulled out the card from Renee from four years ago. A printed photo announcement with a few words. The picture showed two babies wrapped in "naming blankets," according to the card, welcomed by their parents, Renee and Louis, along with family, friends, and clan members. Below were the babies' names – very ethnic: Wishi-ta, and Tana-na – but it didn't say which was which. Helene had sent a card and some cash without telling Kenneth. She had received a simple thank-you in return and then there had been no more contact between them, she remembered now with a flush of heat.

She brought the address book to the kitchen table and sat again, picking up the letter that had just arrived.

To Helene Roy Bradford,

I am Louis's sister, who has been taking care of the twins with my husband in our home. We also have my mother, brother, and three children. Louis is not here with us due to some problems he could not avoid.

Wishi-ta has allergies, very bad. She has been several times to the emergency room for rash, swelling, and trouble breathing. The doctors do not know the cause. They want to test her, which will require many trips to the clinic. Also, she needs medications.

We live next to the house of Renee and Louis. The phone number is 999-555-2314.

Malvina Marshall (Lopes)

What did the woman want?

Helene put her hand to her face, taking a couple of slow, deep breaths. Misty, the ghost cat of 23 Meadow Lane, whispered by her ankle, silent and soothing. Even the tick of the wall clock was muted. All seemed at peace in the well-ordered kitchen in a peaceful, well-ordered house. The furnishings were contemporary and good quality. There was nothing from her old home, the Roy household, because nothing from that past was likely to bring good memories, or had managed to survive the bad memories. Mom's illness and passing at forty-three. Dad's quiet drinking and tight-lipped decline until he, too, passed, at fifty-five of a heart attack, with no desire to see sixty or grandchildren. Renee and all the commotion of her teen years with the drinking, drugs, petty theft, detox, and disappearing for weeks at a time. Only occasionally had there been a sprightly note from Denis's fiddle down in the basement while Helene, at the sink or at her desk, was toiling on, toiling on – trying to get away.

Helene got up; dinnertime. She put on the light in the waning spring day and busied herself in the familiar routine, preparing dinner for herself and Kenneth, who would be home promptly and faithfully at six o'clock, and then going through her tote bag in preparation for the next day. She was a school nurse at the nearby elementary school.

But after the stir-fry was readied and the table laid, Helene was back at the counter, pulling out her cell phone from her purse. What did Denis know about this business in the letter from Malvina? He seemed to have had regular contact with Renee and her family. He was not estranged in the same way, and he'd never had the same issues or responsibilities as Helene. But he also traveled a great deal with his band and could be anywhere in the Northeast (or farther, for that matter).

She hesitated, looking over her kitchen. It was full of good smells and sights, including the Scandinavian-design table and chairs, light wood cabinets, granite counters, and recessed lighting. Calm and harmonious. She had fought for all that, earned it, after the chaos of trying to keep together a family that was bent on falling apart. She had been fifteen when her mother died and not prepared to be the woman of the house, or a mother to the two younger children. It might have been different if her father had not fallen into such a stupor, stuck in a job that meant little to him and marooned without the love of his life, all his other family back in Canada. And there was Renee, five when their mother died, acting out every bit of anger and heartache, trying to get a reaction of some kind from somebody.

Helene found her hands clenched and the familiar pressure in her chest, even after all these years and all that therapy. She called Denis's number. Ring, ring – and then to voicemail, of course. She would have been lucky to have him answer, surrounded as he was in that world of constant music, his hands occupied.

"You've reached Denis, but not really. Leave a message, if you like – after the music." And then a clip of recorded music, a Cajun tune, followed by, "Let the Good Times Roll."

"Denis, it's Helene," she said, slowly, thinking. "Do you know what's going on with Renee's children – well, one of them, anyway?" She hesitated. *What else?* "I got this letter from Malvina, Louis's sister, out of the blue. Going on about allergies, health problems." A quick decision. "I don't know what she wants from me. And where is Louis, anyway? If you know anything, get back to me – soon, please." And then, just about to click off, "Hope you're doing OK these days."

It was about quarter of six, half dark outside, and a light breeze was rippling the sheer curtains at the open windows. In a few minutes, Kenneth's car would swing into the driveway. Helene could feel her pulse quicken and began drumming on the table. Suddenly, without further thought, she had Malvina's letter unfolded in front of her with the photo of the kids. A body of water in the background. A blanket spread with coolers, chip bags, a gallon container of juice or something. The oldest was a girl bent over one of the toddlers. The other kids, not the twins, looked like boys, even with the long, almost waist-length hair. They were looking at the camera but not posed, not even really smiling – they were certainly not told to say "cheese" – and donning quite the yard sale of outfits with nothing particularly coordinated. But there was something in how they looked, their expressions, that was different from what Helene saw in the first and second graders at her school. It was like they were already fully themselves, not simply childish innocents, and she could not shake the impression that they were looking at her.

She pressed the number from the letter into her phone. It rang only a couple of times before it was answered by a young voice. "Marshalls." Helene almost ended the call before realizing it was the family name, Malvina's married name.

"Hello, may I speak to Malvina, please?" she heard herself say.

"Ma!" the high-pitched voice yelled into a distant room.

There was a slight delay, while a scuffle of voices, footsteps, and other noises came and went in Helene's ear.

Then, "This is Malvina."

"Malvina, it's Helene, Renee's sister – you wrote me a letter."

"Yes."

"So, I understand there's a problem with…an allergy problem."

No reply. "Well," said Helene, "I was wondering why you wrote me. That is, what do you want me to do?"

"I don't know," said Malvina.

"Hm…well, I'm really not sure what I can do from here. Unless you want me to consult with a doctor. Try to find out more about what's wrong…"

"If you come here, you'll see what's wrong," Malvina said flatly.

"Hm…" Helene's heart beat faster, part of her recognizing that now was the time to say, No, I'm sorry. I can't do that.

"If you could give me some details," she prompted.

"There's a lot of papers, forms, in a folder. The doctor at the clinic doesn't know what's causing the problem. We don't know, either. You're a nurse; maybe you can find out."

Helene felt a flush, or more a wave of white light – shock. Every instinct was to stay away, far away, from the bottomless pit of trouble and uncertainty that was Renee's life. And yet, there was a child with a serious health problem, no fault of her own, and she needed help. Her sister's child, Helene's own blood relation. Even now, in the back of her mind, she was thinking anaphylactic shock, antihistamines, steroids – her professional training kicking in.

"I…I…"

There was a slapping sound or a clang, maybe metal, over the phone line.

"I'm making dinner," Malvina said. "You can call me back."

"Wait," Helene said. "This weekend, maybe, I could come."

"Sure. Anytime. We'll be here."

"OK. I'll have to check. I'll let you know."

Helene had the address and knew where the town was; maybe two and a half or three hours away. She put the phone away.

A car pulled into the driveway – Kenneth, a few minutes early. She went to the door to meet him.

"Hi."

"Hi, there." He smiled broadly, warmly. Bright eyed, even after a hectic day at the real estate office. Fortunately, regular business ended by five thirty, and Kenneth was faithfully home for dinner, except on those nights he had to socialize with clients; that was his promise to Helene. Today there was an extra bounce in his step; they were almost ready to open the new branch in a neighboring town, two years coming.

She kissed him on the lips before he walked past to the front hall, where he put his briefcase on the bench and slipped off his jacket to put away in the closet. His button-down shirt and tie were still neat after all that running around to closings and open houses.

"So," he started, and then stopped, cocking his head to the side. "What's up with you? Something's up. I can see it in your face."

She held back a sigh. "Yes, something is up." She wavered a moment. "Renee. Well, her kids. There's some big crisis." She didn't mean it to come out quite so dramatically.

Kenneth's smile contracted. "Oh, boy. That sounds like a story. You'd better fill me in."

"I got a letter," she said, "from the aunt." A short laugh escaped before she caught herself – "their other aunt, the husband's sister. One of the twins, the girl, has some serious medical issues, apparently."

"Ah." Kenneth's eyebrows rose, crinkling his forehead. At forty, he had a full head of brown hair that was only just starting to silver and dark, expressive eyebrows over hazel eyes. He kept fit with a serious routine of running and weights at the gym; if his face and torso were a little fuller these days, he was no less handsome than when they'd met in their twenties, and he still had the same full, confident smile.

"The aunt, Malvina…she wants me to come."

"Then I guess we need to talk about this," Kenneth said. "Dinner can wait." He took Helene by the arm, gently, guiding her to the kitchen.

"Sit," he said, taking his usual chair. "I want to make sure I understand. You got a letter from a woman you've never met, Renee's sister-in-law, who is asking for help with one of Renee's children because of medical issues?"

"Yes."

"This is somewhere in Massachusetts, as I recall."

"Western Mass., two or three hours' drive."

"And what about the father, Renee's husband? They did marry, right?"

"Yes, they did. I don't know what's up with him. Malvina, the one who wrote the letter, says he's not there, for some 'problem he couldn't avoid,' as she put it."

"Hm…" Kenneth said. "That doesn't sound good."

He reached a hand across the table, and the pale hairs on the back of his fingers caught the light next to the solid, reassuring gleam of the gold wedding band. "You know, and I know, we have to be very careful with anything that has to do with Renee, even now. It was a long struggle for you to get to this point. Right?"

Helene nodded.

"And the medical issue is what, exactly?"

"Allergies, I guess. Pretty bad ones. She has had severe reactions that sent her to the emergency room – swelling, trouble breathing, basically life threatening. But they don't know the causes, and they want to do more testing."

Kenneth nodded. "Hm…so, the idea is maybe you can rush out there and take care of this?"

Helene looked away at the familiar warning note in his voice. "I would think she maybe wants help with the doctors, appointments, that kind of thing. She knows I'm a nurse."

Kenneth nodded again. "Maybe. Or, money. I hate to say it, honey, but they could be looking for money. I'm sure these health problems can be expensive and time-consuming, and it was never clear to me, at least, what the father did for a living – if anything. Maybe now Renee is gone, they don't have her paycheck anymore."

Helene shrugged. "Maybe. Who knows?"

"Or," Kenneth continued, "It may be a matter of managing their money properly. My father used to say Indians got monthly checks from the U.S. government, but I'm not sure that's true. I really wouldn't know."

Helene shook her head doubtfully. "It couldn't be much, if they're living in old base housing."

"I wonder why the aunt is writing and not the father, anyway?" Kenneth straightened the silverware around his plate.

Again, Helene had no idea.

They sat a moment in silence.

"We have to be careful about this, Helene. We can't afford you getting pulled into that kind of chaos again. I can't help but think they're fishing around a little here. Why not tell you on the phone what she wants? We don't really know if the problem is all that critical."

Helene spoke quietly. "But it might be."

"Yes. But it's not your problem to solve. It's Renee's life, and Renee's choices. Let them deal with the consequences."

"She's gone," Helene said. "It's not the child's fault there's a medical problem, or that the father can't manage this himself. The aunt – his sister – has three children of her own."

Kenneth gave her a long look. "If it really is financial hardship, we can give them some money – just give, not a loan. A one-shot deal, nothing ongoing, or it will never end." He spread his arms. "A thousand? Two thousand? And then it's out of our hands."

Helene got up to bring the water pitcher to the table. *Yes. Yes, we could do that. But...*

She returned, standing by her chair. "I said I might go up, on Saturday."

Kenneth's eyes widened. "No, Helene, don't do that. It's not a good idea, for so many reasons. Once they get you in person, they'll play on your sympathy; they'll guilt you into something you should never feel guilty about. Come on, honey, you know what I'm saying. People like that..." He blinked rapidly a few times. "Not that I really know. But it seems like they're just barely hanging on. I mean, I didn't even know until you told me that there were Indians around here; seriously, I thought they were all out west, whoever was left. I understand that they have a lot of problems – maybe some from the past, but probably some of their own making. The drinking and so forth. Who knows, maybe that was the connection in the first place."

When Helene didn't answer, he went on, "If you get involved, on any level, then you'll have all that crap to deal with – again – and I'll have to deal with it too. You agreed that cutting off contact with Renee was critical for your own mental health. And look, it worked – for you and for her. We got life back on track; and, apparently, from what your brother has indicated, Renee stayed sober, no matter what else is going on."

Still Helene didn't speak.

"Is that true, or not?"

"It's true. But I am a nurse, and I want to find out what's wrong. I believe I'm strong enough to handle it; I have moved on. If the little girl dies, because I haven't at least tried to help, then I will find it hard to live with myself, sister or no sister."

Kenneth inhaled sharply, and his face took on that look, like he was about to yell, like he used to sometimes, out of concern or frustration. But he didn't.

"It's up to you. But remember what the therapist said: no more rescue missions. It's not good for you, or for anybody." Then he sighed. "I can't go with you Saturday or Sunday – too many open houses. What about Denis? Is he anywhere to be found these days?"

"I have a call in to him."

"OK," Kenneth said. "But we're in this together, right? Anything – anything – they say or ask goes by me too."

"OK," she said.

Then Kenneth's stomach grumbled and he smiled apologetically. "OK, then. That's quite the surprise out of nowhere. But, hey, it's dinnertime and I'm starving. Let's eat."

Chapter 2

Helene swiveled from the tow-headed boy standing in front of her to the form on her desk and checked "No signs of scoliosis."

"OK, Brendan," she said. "Send the next one in." He scampered out through the office door. Her cell phone dinged in her purse from a text.

"Just take a seat, Maria," she said to the seven-year-old in purple leggings and a long pigtail. "I'll be right with you."

She shouldn't be checking her phone, not during work hours, not with students in the office. But if it was Denis returning her call, she wanted to know.

Turning her back to Maria, Helene read the message: "What's up, darlin'?"

Denis, indeed. Quickly she texted back, "Ten minutes. Don't go anywhere. Important."

She finished with Maria and then two more students, all of them sticky with the end-of-the-school-year heat wave and no air conditioning. Ten days left and counting, Helene as much as the kids and the teachers. As the last of the second graders straightened his T-shirt, in no great hurry to leave, Helene guided him gently out the door, closing it firmly behind.

She punched in Denis's number on her phone. To her surprise he answered.

"I'm right here," he said in a warm tenor voice. She wondered if he had a beard these days. He had the dark coloring of their father's French-Canadian ancestors; Helene and Renee had been fair and blond from their mother's Nordic side.

"And where might that be?" Wherever it was, it sounded like he was talking from a pit or a cavern – somewhere big and echoey. She heard voices in the background, strumming, and occasional musical notes.

"Tennessee. With the band. Bluegrass festival. We're getting ready to rehearse, but I've got a few minutes."

"Hallelujah, lucky me."

"So, what's up, big sister?" Denis was always quick with a deflect. "Something on your mind, I guess."

"Yes. I got this letter from Malvina Marshall out in western Mass. – you know who she is, right?"

"Yup, Louis's sister – the in-laws."

"Yes, and a photo of a bunch of kids, including Renee's. One of the twins, the girl, apparently has bad allergies, even though they don't know the cause. According to Malvina, she's ended up in the ER a few times. Do you know anything about it?"

Helene heard footsteps outside the door but they passed by. "Can't say I do," Denis said. "Although there's always something going on with those kids, one way or another. Nothing serious, just usual kid stuff. Broken finger, sprained ankle, that kind of thing." He paused. "So, she wants your medical advice?"

"I don't know what she wants. She just sent the note and the picture of the kids. On the phone she said I should come. That's it. But she wasn't very clear about it."

"Ah, the mysterious Native American…"

"That's not helpful, Denis. She probably wants me to see the situation, all those kids running around underfoot. I could hear them in the background."

"They're good kids, all of them," Denis said. Like he'd know. "A bit active. But the twins are real sweet, the two of them. Just like little kittens, you know."

Helene didn't know. Over the phone she could hear a man's voice shouting, "Five minutes." And a drumbeat. And the screech of feedback through the speakers.

"Can you hear me?" she said.

"Yup, go on."

"I said I'd go out there on Saturday. Kenneth's not too happy about it. He thinks there might be something up. And he doesn't want me to get involved."

"Right. Of course. So what are you going to do?"

"That's why I'm calling, Denis. What do you know? And how come Malvina is the one writing me, not the father? *Some unavoidable problem.* That's what she wrote in the note. What's that mean? Is he in jail or something?"

Denis let out a wry laugh. "Actually, yes. But it's complicated. He's in a federal prison in upstate New Hampshire…"

"Oh, for God's sake!" Helene started, but Denis cut her off.

"Wait, let me talk. There's a story, and you should hear it first." He cleared his throat. "Some young Native guys tried to blow up a dam on a river in Maine, something to do with water rights, and somebody got killed, accidently. They didn't even know the guy was there. Louis had nothing to do with the explosion, but I guess he helped the guys when they tried to get away."

Helene snickered. "You must be kidding."

"No, I'm not. The trial ended in March, sentenced twenty years. So now the lawyer is working on an appeal."

"Sorry; that still sounds terrible."

From all those miles away, a few more notes of music; a banjo, it sounded like. Or mandolin?

"No, listen," Denis rushed to get the words out. "He's not some bonehead derelict. He's forceful and outspoken, but he's not violent. I've talked with him over the years. He's a smart guy; went to law school for a while, knows what he's talking about. He's been involved with Native American activism for a long time. This was part of a greater protest, and some of the younger guys got carried away. Louis didn't know about it. That's what he told me. If he had, he would have tried to talk them out of it, just because shit like this always happens. He wanted them to go through legal means, even though it takes such a damn long time."

"Twenty years is a long time."

"Yeah, well. Louis had a gun in the back of the truck – the so-called getaway vehicle. It was a hunting rifle that belonged to his father, but they say it was part of the crime. So something went the wrong way, and now he's got to deal with it."

"And his family," Helene said, trying to keep the disappointment, or really disdain, out of her voice. "They have to deal with it too."

"You don't know, Helene. He's devoted to those kids, all of them. Nieces and nephews too. He's good to them, trying to raise them up right."

"Denis, how can you say that, when he's not even around? Prison and then a record. How could he let that happen, when their mother is dead?" Helene sighed. "I don't know what to do, Denis. It doesn't sound good at all. Kenneth's right, I don't want to get in over my head with this. Let it be on him, this Louis; he's the one who's made his choices."

There was a rush of voices, shouting, and more snatches of music.

"OK, OK, on my way," Denis said, muted. "Sorry, Helene," he said into the phone. "Got to go."

Helene was sorry too. She wanted to know more. Denis's information hadn't helped her decide. If anything, the signs were bad, warning, "Stay away."

"OK, thanks anyway," she said. "Call me sometime, would you? Just so I know what's going on with you. I'm either at home or school; you can always reach me."

"I will. No, I will, seriously."

He ended the call. Helene sat back at her desk, gazing at the pictures of Kenneth and Misty, her real family, her now family – besides Denis and those ghosts from the past. She got up from the chair with a "humph," dissatisfied with the conversation and herself, for not knowing what to do.

Thelma Silberman in the Counseling Office – that's who she needed. If Thelma was even around, since she covered other schools, as well. She was somewhere between an older sister and an aunt to Helene – not a mother, though. Late fifties, divorced, one son, Jewish but not very observant, as far as Helene could tell. A former flower child, so she said, and Helene could believe it. Some people at school thought them an odd pair, but Thelma was the closest friend Helene had ever had, even with their separate lives and Thelma's occasional digs about Kenneth the Great.

Helene closed the door, taking the key with her – not so much for her purse, but because of the medications she stored and sometimes administered to students. The Counseling Office was in another wing of the building and she could have called over first, but she just wanted to get out of the room for a few minutes.

No Thelma. The secretary said she had a meeting at the Superintendent's Office. Did she want to leave a message?

No message. Maybe she could reach Thelma at home tonight, although she'd rather see her in person. Helene returned to her office just as the bell rang for the end of the day. A small stack of paperwork sat on her desk. She should finish before she left, but this other thing was nagging at her. Maybe she would call Thelma and leave a message. As she took out her cell phone, she was surprised to see a voicemail message.

Denis again!

"Something's wrong with the mixing board, so here goes – one more thing. I should have said this, but you caught me off guard. You should go see them, Helene." Denis's voice had an urgency to it. Something new and unfamiliar to Helene, who only knew the mild, soft-spoken, charming brother who had hidden away in the basement with his music and slipped away as often as he could. "The kids are loving and beautiful. You didn't get to see her after they were born, but Renee was a great mother – like our mom, I think. I know it's surprising but she really turned around her whole life, taking care of herself and the kids and their home. Louis had a lot to do with it, and his family. I can't really explain. She was as happy as she'd ever been, since Mom died..." He took in a long breath, "And that was a long time ago. She wanted to see you, Helene, I know she did. Not when she was sick; she thought it was asking too much."

He paused, then Helene heard another long intake of breath. "I know how hard this is for you. How all the shit fell on you. By that point, Dad was useless. You were the one taking Renee to rehab or out looking for her on the streets. I was just trying to keep my own shit together. I really think you should go, for your own sake. There's so much that would be good for you to know." More background noise. Then, "Sorry. Bye."

Helene wasn't prepared for this – not his sympathy, and not his pushing her. As if he had any right. She put her phone away, blindly packing then repacking her tote for home. She headed out the side entrance, away from the bus loop to where her car was parked. As she put the car into Drive, she found that her heart was thumping painfully, and she wished again she could see Thelma's face – not Kenneth's – before heading home.

She still lived in her hometown but in a newer, more upscale section. Her commute brought her through the center of town, crowded in the later afternoon with the buses and traffic from a couple of companies that let out work early. At the red light she reached into her purse, fishing out the phone. And then, at the next intersection, she pulled over into the big municipal parking lot that connected the town hall, library, and police station. There were plenty of empty spots, and she parked under a tree. For a moment she just sat with the phone in her lap, wondering if she could catch Denis again – or if she really wanted to. Her thoughts went to the current crisis in addiction – opioids – something not much present ten years ago when Renee was at her worst. Thank God for that. How much easier it was getting drugs, and more prevalent in white suburban towns like this. Most likely, there was Narcan inside the police station nowadays. No, Renee would not have survived this epidemic, Helene was sure.

A uniformed police officer walked out of the station toward one of the patrol cars parked in the lot. Helene's eyes widened: Officer Heming, older and grayer, but the same guy from the three – or was it four? – times she'd gone to pick up Renee from the holding cell. The slight stoop, white-blond crew cut and eyebrows – it was him. Reflexively, she looked down at the phone in her lap. He had been nothing but patient and helpful, but for that kindness she could not bear to see him again.

He got in the car and drove away. She called Denis, who answered.

"I can't believe I got you again."

"Still working on the mixer." She heard a slight belch. "Just finished a burrito."

"So, you think I should go, huh? Based on what, exactly? Are you saying you've been seeing them – Renee's family, the extended family?"

"Yeah, on and off. Hold on." He took a swallow. "More so in the last year when Renee was sick, and for her service, of course. That's before all that dam business. Now Louis is gone. The twins are living with Malvina and Noel and the cousins, next door. The grandmother and brother are there too, in the same duplex." He paused. "I was there a few months ago."

"But you didn't come here," Helene said. "I haven't seen you – we haven't seen you – since Christmas."

"Come on, Helene," he said. "Let's not go there. You know Kenneth is not crazy about me, or my dogs."

"Dogs?" she couldn't help asking. As if one weren't enough – the one who'd torn through Helene's house one early visit, chasing the cat, breaking the end table.

"Yeah, Max and Crash. Well, yeah, they're active. They stay with a friend in central Mass. when I'm touring."

"Oh, I see."

"Besides," Denis said, unexpectedly. "I've been doing some music with Izzy."

"Who?"

"Izzy – Louis and Malvina's brother – the youngest, maybe twenty or so; he plays the flute. Great guy. Very creative."

There was really nothing Helene could say to that. The music that he loved so well, and that had taken him away from home.

"Great," she said. "Anything else you can tell me?"

"Well, I can tell you the girl twin, Wishi-ta, the one with the allergies, she looks so much like Renee, it's unbelievable." Helene tried to recall the fair-haired toddler in the picture, but the face was too shaded. "Like you, for that matter," Denis said. "You have to see for yourself. Just go, Helene. Then you can decide."

"Hm…" she murmured. "So, when will you be back this way?"

More background noise on his end; a telling pause.

"Hard to say, probably later in the summer." There he was, the brother who was so good at slipping away. "The manager is trying to book us at some clubs in the Boston area. Maybe you can come." And then, quickly, "And Kenneth."

"Hm…maybe."

"I'll send you the dates," Denis said.

Right.

Helene heard the strum of a guitar, raised voices. "OK, I'll let you go. Take care of yourself, Denis."

"You too."

Something stirred in Helene's chest. Jealousy? And anger. Denis had clearly made connections; he'd been in touch with Renee's family more than with her. And he was making a kind of living for himself as a musician, his dream and passion. That was the very thing that had put Dad over the top – that Denis had started college, the degree in engineering his father always pushed for, and then he had dropped out to play music, living hand to mouth, an itinerant. Not that he had asked Dad for money or for anything. And the tuition at the state university was reasonable back then. But that had been Dad's whole reason for staying at a dead-end job in a dead-end industry, as round after round of employees was let go. All of it was pointless if the kids didn't at least try to reach further, as Helene had done. But no, Denis went back to his fiddle – he never really left it. And the kicker was that it was Dad's fiddle, and Dad who had taught him how to play. Funny, Helene thought; she loved that music, too, even missed it.

Her gaze had returned to the police station, and she pictured again the windowless holding room with a lightweight table and gray plastic chairs. And then she saw a younger Officer Heming leaning over Renee, who was doubled over in her chair, to see if she was OK. And how Renee had vomited on his heavy black shoes, just missing Helene's. It had been deliberate aim, Helene was sure. Anything, anything, to offend rather than accept pity. Helene's stomach twisted with the impossibility of that terrible time. And the very worst time, the last time she'd ever seen Renee. Like a heavy gray cloud, the memory descended – what had transpired between them, which Helene had not spoken of to anyone, ever, and never would.

She put down the window, taking in air, and then turned on the radio.

She exited the parking lot, focusing on what was to come: home, cat, dinner, Kenneth. And, it looked like, plans for a trip west to meet some improbable family members, including a little girl who apparently bore a strong resemblance to her dead sister.

Chapter 3

Helene sat in her car, taking in the view – a street of former base housing
in muddy spring was not an inspiring sight. Round, yellow forsythia
bushes brightened the small yards between units, and a few tulips poked up
next to the sidewalk. Otherwise there was little color, the squat, rectangular
buildings uniformly dull white, all in a row. Some were duplexes, and
many had cars in the driveway with no garages. Not so bad, Helene
thought. But not so good, either. She had driven three hours, with one stop.
It was her first time to this area of the state, the flattish open land bordering
the hills of the Berkshires. A breeze kicked up grit from the pavement,
while the sun peeked out through fast-moving clouds.

She heard raised voices and excited shouting before she saw a group
of children passing between yards, all ages. One of the older boys was
carrying a small child piggyback with long hair flapping behind. Another
youngster, maybe seven or eight, according to Helene's experienced eye,
flew by without a shirt, even in the cooler temperature, although he was
wearing boots and a bright-orange knit cap, also with long hair streaming.
They disappeared out of sight, and Helene got out of the car.

The unit was numbered 4312 Patriot Road. It was part of a duplex
with two front doors, but no names and no mailboxes. In the driveway to
the right was an older white minivan, a cargo unit secured on top. In front
of the door on the left, a men's red bicycle was propped against the railing.
Helene squinted at the note on her passenger seat; hopefully, she had the
right address. Then she noticed a plaque, hand drawn, of a lumbering bear
with a fish in its mouth and a chime made of metallic feathers snapping in
the wind; surely this was it. From the back seat, Helene took out the bag of
gifts she had brought: LEGO Toys for the boys and Polly Pocket dolls for
the girls – "in," popular items – part of the incidental knowledge of her job.

At the right-hand door, she knocked and stepped back, hearing again
the voices of children, but none came into view and no adults were outside,
either, as far as she could tell. She was knocking again when the door
opened. A woman stood in front of her in a maternity dress, green and red
like an unlikely Christmas tree adorned with dangling earrings, a long
silver pendant, and a jumble of bracelets. Her lips parted slightly as she
took in the sight of Helene with something like wonder and perhaps
apprehension.

"I'm Helene," she announced brightly. "Renee's sister, that you
called."

"Yes," the woman said, nodding slowly. "I know." Still she didn't
move, blocking the doorway. She was on the short side, with a heart-

shaped face and hazel eyes, black hair pulled back in a ponytail. Helene thought she must be a mix – not all Native. Almost immediately, Helene picked up the smell of smoke, herbal, incense-like. Not pot, or cigarettes, though; she knew those. She frowned, without intending to. The smoke, the pregnancy – she was not expecting either of these things.

She *didn't want to tell me on the phone,* was her first thought. *She wanted me to see her this way.* And then, despite herself, *No wonder she's looking for help.*

"Come in. I guess you found us OK." Malvina turned sideways – very pregnant.

"I did. It…it wasn't far off the highway. I got a little turned around when I got on the base – those signs are confusing."

"Yup," said Malvina. Then, after a moment, "Thank you for coming."

Helene stepped into a hallway and followed Malvina toward the light at the back, the kitchen. It was warm and smelled of recent cooking – grilled cheese and soup, by the look of the leftovers.

Malvina saw her looking. "You want a sandwich?" she said matter-of-factly. Helene pictured herself in front of a plate of sandwich quarters with a sippy cup of milk, like one of the kids.

"No, thank you. All set."

"Water then, or soda?"

"No thanks."

Malvina started clearing the table, putting dishes on the counter and in the sink. When Helene moved to help, Malvina waved her away.

"Sit, please. I just want to make room."

Helene sat in a cleared spot, putting the toy bag in the corner behind her chair. Her glance traveled down a passageway along the back of the house, connecting the units of the duplex, she assumed. Light came in from a door to the backyard, and there appeared to be a small room, closet or toilet, off the hall. At the opposite end of the hall was a closed door – where the grandmother lived, and this Izzy.

From the backyard, they heard a shriek of laughter and shouts of aggrieved protest. Helene couldn't make out the words.

Malvina peeked out the window over the sink, scanning the yard. She must have seen something, because she rapped on the window and made a gesture. In a moment, the outside door into the back hall opened and a dog scampered into the kitchen, a mutt of some kind, circling Helene's feet excitedly, before heading to Malvina. He retreated into the hallway, where they heard a child's voice, "Come here, Yellow Dog." After a moment, a trickle of liquid sounded in a bowl, and a soft, breathy humming came through an unclosed doorway.

"I have some papers," Malvina said, walking toward the back hall. And then, "I had to put them away, or they'd have food all over them. Just give me a minute."

She left, and Helene could hear her talking to the child in the bathroom, then walking away, another door opening.

Helene got up to look out the window to the backyard, which ran directly into the neighbors' lawns, marked with occasional bushes. A good-sized garden stood in one corner, fenced in with chicken wire, next to a shed and a compost container. Past the deck on the ground was a ring of stones around a pit of charred wood and ashes. A couple of the kids had come into view, the boy with the boots and a smaller fellow whose jeans were caked with mud. The older boy stopped at the fire pit and bent over, reaching into the ashes. As he stood up again, he turned to the smaller boy and rubbed the ashes on his cheeks and forehead. He stopped to examine his work and then added another stripe. Then they were gone.

There was an exchange of words in the back hall, the flush of the toilet, running water in the sink. Then a skittering of footsteps as the child exited through the other unit. But Helene didn't hear a door close. Malvina reappeared with an envelope and a folder of papers. Someone had written on the front in big block letters, "WISHI-TA LOPES." Malvina handed the envelope to Helene and sat down.

"It's from the preschool," Malvina said.

Dear Mrs. Marshall,

Re: Wishi-ta and Tana-na Lopes

We are writing to request a meeting with the legal guardian of Wishi-ta and Tana-na Lopes regarding recent health concerns. We do not have in our possession the required documents for these students in case of emergency. We know that Mrs. Lopes is deceased. In trying to reach the father, Mr. Louis Lopes, during a recent emergency, we got no response to the phone number we had. Your name, Malvina Marshall, was listed as alternative, but the listed number is no longer in service.

This is a serious matter. The preschool director had to take Wishi-ta to the emergency room without a guardian or up-to-date insurance information. If these cannot be provided, we can no longer accept the students at the preschool. For their sake, it must be clear who will handle any further emergencies that arise.

Helene looked up, saying nothing.

"There is no legal guardian," Malvina said. "Louis is not here." She stopped, waiting for Helene, who sighed before she spoke.

"Because he's in prison."

"There will be an appeal soon," Malvina said.

"And there's no one else? Not you?"

"My baby is due in the summer. The doctor says my blood pressure is too high; I should be lying down." Malvina made a sound like crazy idea. "Izzy can't do it – my brother; too young. No experience when it comes to things like that. Doesn't drive, either, just rides his bike. He comes and goes, in and out – work, college, powwow. Not him."

There was a stirring, Helene thought, at the other end of the hallway, the other unit. Some kind of motion, out of view.

Malvina pushed the medical folder toward Helene, who leafed through it. Annual physicals for both twins. Height, weight, vitals, immunizations – all normal. Then the reports, one for a cat scratch, of all things – Tana-na. And an ear infection. And Wishi-ta's pink-eye. All of them signed by Renee. Helene stared at the signature, the handwriting so familiar.

Then a set of four reports, all of Wishi-ta's care for the allergic reactions, one at the hospital and the others at a health clinic, noting that the EpiPen had been used effectively and the reactions had subsided.

Then the recommendations for follow-up: testing of various allergy agents over a matter of months, and then a series of shots to "desensitize" against the source of Wishi-ta's allergies. For medications, Benadryl at night and Claritin at signs of any symptoms.

Helene closed the folder and looked at Malvina, unexpressive across the table.

"That's pretty concerning," Helene said, nodding.

"Take these." Malvina pushed the papers back toward Helene. "I made copies."

Left to herself, Malvina was not going to elaborate. Tempering her frustration, Helene asked evenly, "So, what do you want me to do?"

Malvina shrugged. "I don't know. What do you want to do?"

Helene hadn't expected that, and she wasn't sure how to reply. Of course, she'd been thinking all week, since she got the letter. What was she prepared to do, if anything? And how would she do it? Clearly the problem was real, and now she also knew about the lack of a guardian. Plus Wishi-ta needed the tests. Was that something Helene could commit to from three hours away?

She closed her eyes. She could do something, but she had to set limits, firm limits. Earlier in the week, Kenneth had Helene call an attorney friend of his, who was involved in family law. The lawyer had suggested health-care proxy, an easy form to complete. And, if needed for the insurance forms or any kind of financial business, she could get power of attorney. When she had told him that the father's family was Native American, he mentioned that he believed the Indians had their own health program – she should find out.

"I can look over the reports again, and make sure I understand what they're saying. I'm a nurse, as you know. So I can at least explain what's going on, and what needs to be done. If you can tell me about the insurance, I can see what's covered." She paused. "Isn't there health service for Indians? My husband's lawyer told me to ask."

Malvina blinked a couple times before answering. "It's not like that, for us. We're not a federated tribe, the Pemaquots, at least not yet. So we don't get any benefits, not health, or education, gaming rights, nothing."

Helene tipped her head. "Why not? You're Indian on both sides, right?"

"Always and always," Malvina said with a small smile. But her hand was smoothing a paper on the table, over and over, some unexpressed emotion. "It has to do with treaties, census rolls, and documents, I guess. You must prove that you're an intact tribe, continuous for generations, staying on the same land. But Pemaquots traveled from the coast to the lakes, across Maine and Canada, and the treaty to stay on that land was given by the British, not the Americans."

Helene was still puzzled. "So there is a written record."

Malvina shrugged. "That's Louis's fight – what he's been trying to do, prove we're a nation. But it's not done yet, so we don't have any of those kinds of things. My family has insurance through Noel's work. But Louis and Renee, they went on MassHealth, so that's what the kids have. Pretty good, I guess. Maybe you can check there."

"I can certainly do some research," Helene said. "And see about specialists in the area. I can help you set it up, and after that you can always call me."

"Wishi-ta needs someone close by to help her through this," Malvina said softly. "Or she could die."

A warning bell went off in Helene's head: close by? Malvina couldn't be suggesting that Helene commute there, to the old base? Or to stay there? That was beyond reason.

"Are you asking me to take charge of her? To...take her?" Helene tried to keep her voice calm.

Malvina's forehead wrinkled before another look crossed her face – a flash of anger? Or more like pity, Helene thought.

There was a hiss from the other room, startling both women. It was no cat, for sure. They were being watched by someone, a person. The grandmother, perhaps, or the younger brother?

"Not that," Malvina said, shaking her head. "Her home is here with us, with her family."

Without a thought, the words came out of Helene's mouth, "I'm her family too." She never meant to say it. She'd never even let herself think it. But it was true.

"The house is empty, next door where your sister lived, and Louis, a single home. We're making the mortgage payments for Louis. You can stay there as long as you need." She was gesturing to the left, where the house must be, but there was no window to see through. No doubt similar space and layout, Helene thought, except not attached. *Renee's home.*

"Malvina, I have a home, and a husband, and a job – and a cat. I can't just up and leave. People depend on me. You understand that, right? I'm not sure what Renee told you, but we have an active, involved life."

"Denis told us."

Helene had to laugh, because Malvina didn't seem to realize what a crazy idea it was. But neither did she seem prepared to argue, instead rising and crossing the room to a slider to the back deck. She turned back, beckoning.

"The children are outside."

Helene tucked the papers into her purse and got to her feet. She eyed the bag from Toys"R"Us and couldn't decide – take it or leave it? Why had she even bothered? Good will – of course, remember? But she did not want to appear like some kind of good fairy or Mrs. Claus, bestowing gifts. She thought she'd be sitting in the living room, and all the children would be called in, one after the other, so she could learn their names. She would say hello, hand them their gifts, and then the cousins would leave, only the twins remaining behind, shy and gentle children sitting quietly on the sofa.

But it wasn't to be like that. From the back deck, the two women watched a group of children in the next yard playing a chase game. *Cowboys and Indians* came to Helene; she couldn't help herself. They'd played that game as kids, but it was long out of fashion and these days politically incorrect. Certainly no more guns and bows and arrows. The yellow dog ran between the children, along with another, larger dog, a homely mutt who barked a lot. Malvina's backyard was full of balls and toys. Bikes and scooters lay across the grass, abandoned for the moment.

"Kiowa," Malvina called. In a few seconds came an answering call, and a girl popped out from behind budding lilacs separating the houses and waved.

"Call them in," Malvina shouted, and the girl disappeared again.

In a matter of minutes, a pack of kids ran into the yard, eight or ten of them, until Kiowa turned and said, "Everyone, go home now; take your things." She was probably the eldest, eleven or twelve, and she had Malvina's sturdy build, round, coppery face and small chin. Half the children moved on, dragging bikes and scooters, grumbling over the end of their fun.

Slowly the remaining children assembled by the picnic table. Kiowa lifted a smaller girl onto her hip, and a young boy was being pulled along, hand in hand, by two other boys, a strong resemblance between them. He was the one with the ash on his cheeks and glowing eyes.

Five sets of eyes were focused on Malvina and the lady next to her; all talking came to a stop and all movement. Helene could feel their gazes on her face, neither friendly nor hostile, just puzzled. A kind of awe settled over them. Helene's gaze traveled one to the next. She knew right away which were the twins, even apart, even so unalike: the blond girl on Kiowa's hip and the ash-faced boy. And then she met eyes with the fair-haired, blue-eyed girl and was struck dumb. The likeness to Renee at that age was so great – her facial features, her build, her neck and arms and legs. Helene's hand began to rise to her mouth until she forced it down by her side.

"They want to meet you," Malvina said, nodding at Helene. "Renee's family." She turned back to the children, "Her name is Helene, but her married name is Mrs. Bradford – maybe she likes that better."

Still Helene couldn't speak; the children's silence was unnerving.

The biggest boy spoke up, "Are you her sister or her mother?"

Helene swallowed. "The older sister, by almost ten years. Our mother, the twins' grandmother on our side, is…she is…no longer living."

"From breast cancer," said Kiowa, knowingly.

"Yes, that's right."

"You look like her, Renee," Kiowa said. "I think the twins might be confused."

Then the bigger boys began to murmur. Kiowa put the girl down, and one of the boys, the one with no shirt and orange hat, pushed the small boy forward. Both twins hung back – spooked perhaps, by this woman who was like their mother, but not.

"Wait," said Malvina. "This is Kiowa, the oldest," she said, indicating the tallest girl, just starting to develop, the helper.

"This is Pawnee; he's eight. Then Cree, with no shirt, who just turned six."

She picked up a T-shirt from the table and threw it at him. "Put it on."

"Why don't you sit," Malvina said to Helene, indicating the picnic table. "I'll bring the twins to you." She went first to the girl, holding an edge of the table and bending down heavily to whisper in her ear. And then she took her by the shoulder, leading her to the boy twin, speaking quietly to both. Holding each child by a hand, she brought them over to Helene.

"She is your family too," she said to the twins. And then, to Helene, "What should they call you?"

How had she not thought of this before? What was she to them? Not Mrs. Bradford, the school nurse. Not Auntie, either. A distant, never-seen-before relative who looked like their mother.

"What do they call you?" she asked Malvina.

"Malvina."

"OK. Helene is fine, I guess."

"Helene," Malvina spoke carefully, almost a formal introduction. "These are the children of my brother, Louis, and your sister, Renee, who has passed over. This girl is Wishi-ta, the kind; and this one is Tana-na, the brave."

"Hello," Helene said. She bowed her head to each. "Wishi-ta. Tana-na. Such nice names."

No one spoke until Malvina said gently, "Each named after water, which is sacred to us."

"I see. Well, I love water too, so that's good." Helene smiled.

Still they were serious, hesitant, Wishi-ta holding on to Malvina's side.

"Ah," said Malvina, softly. "But does Helene know who came into the world first?"

"Me!" said Tana-na.

"And who stayed within her mother the longest?"

"Me," said Wishi-ta. "Three more minutes."

"And tell Helene, where do you live?"

"Massachusetts," said Wishi-ta. "On Turtle Island."

"Which is the nation of your grandfather?"

"Wampanoag."

"And the nation of your grandmother?" Malvina asked.

"Pemaquot," they answered in unison.

"Very good," exclaimed Helene. *They certainly have that down.* A declaration of some kind. Although who would ever guess that Wishi-ta, light as she was, was part of any kind of Indian nation?

But Malvina was not done: "And the clan of your grandmothers?"

"Wolf!" shouted Tana-na, grinning broadly and howling to the sky, until the cousins, watching from the deck, joined him.

Then smiles broke out, and the other children started to laugh and tease. Suddenly the spell was broken, and they were just kids in a yard, interrupted from play. They were physically beautiful children, just as Denis had said. Helene wanted to pull the twins closer, to really examine them, to feel them with her own hands. Tana-na was bigger and stronger-looking, with medium-black hair and the same coppery skin tone as Malvina. He bounced on his toes and played with his long hair, regarding Helene with mild curiosity. He was one of them, who clearly belonged in this family group.

Helene tried not to stare at Wishi-ta – her blue eyes, and pink and white coloring, more delicate looking, perhaps because of her illness. The impression of Renee as a child was so strong that Helene felt a blurring in her vision, shadow images of people – Denis, their parents, and Helene herself as a young teenager, who loved her baby sister like another mother.

And then Malvina sent the children back off to play. She said a few words to Kiowa, and then headed back inside through the sliding door.

"I realize it's a lot, taking them on like this," Helene said to Malvina's back, as she followed. "And with all this extra...I can meet with the doctor, if you want..." Malvina had already crossed the kitchen into the hallway, leaving Helene behind, wondering if she heard anything she'd said.

Malvina returned with a young man in tow, tall, lanky, with thick dark hair spilling over his shoulders, and a few sparse whiskers on his chin. His gaze was slightly unfocused, like he'd just woken up or had been sitting at a computer screen. Even rumpled, he was striking looking, with the long, graceful build and chiseled features of a model.

"Izzy," Malvina announced. The younger brother, Helene deduced, quite a different specimen from his sister.

Helene walked over, extending her hand. "Helene Bradford. Renee's sister."

"I would know you anywhere," he said, with an easy smile.

"Oh, well," Helene said, both pleased and slightly taken aback. "And you must be Louis and Malvina's brother."

"That's me," he said. "My name is Isidore, but you can call me Izzy, seeing as you're family, or at least bear a crazy resemblance to other members of this family."

He was a bit of a character, Helene thought, and realized this was the fellow Denis had been talking about, another musician.

"Take her over to the house," Malvina said to him. "Unless you want to stay and watch the kids."

"I'll go. Where's the key?"

Malvina handed Izzy a key, already in her hand.

"I'll call you," Malvina said to Helene, "after I talk to the doctor. We will make an appointment when you can come back. Next week?"

"Um…yes. I think so. Friday is a teacher's workshop day; that might work."

Malvina nodded and then turned back to Izzy. "Give her the box."

The box?

Helene followed Izzy out of the house, frowning in puzzlement. They walked next door across a patch of grass and up the driveway past a camper truck starting to rust. The box must have something to do with Renee – her personal records or medical history? Helene took a breath, wondering if she really wanted to know.

"Don't let the cat out," Izzy said from the front step, holding open the door. Helene was surprised to see a big orange tom, watching from the end of the hallway. His back lifted slightly and he let out a low hiss.

"Red Cat," said Izzy. "Won't leave. Thinks he's a dog, or at least a guard cat."

"He lives here alone?"

Helene pulled the door closed, following Izzy through the front entry, turning left into the living room.

"Yes, he prefers it. We feed him and change the litter box. I bring the twins here to visit. He was Renee's cat."

"I see."

The house was humble, the furniture worn, but it was full of color and homemade decorations, pictures of the twins and other family members.

The sofa and upholstered chairs were covered with Southwest-pattern blankets and pillows. On the shelves were Native American figurines in all manner of dress, fishing, hunting, dancing, tending fires, carrying children – a whole village of mix-and-match people. Clear plastic bins filled with fabrics and art supplies were stacked in a corner. Next to the bins stood a work table with a couple of straight chairs. And on the table sat a large cardboard box.

"This is where she kept her crafting stuff." Izzy gestured. "The E-Z Up canopy and most of the display stuff for powwow are still in the truck. We never unpacked." And then, unexpectedly: "I still come here sometimes, to study or read. It's quiet, you know. Compared to over there." He jerked his thumb toward the duplex. "Especially after Noel put in the passageway between the two sides."

Helene reached out a hand toward the box.

"Hold on," Izzy said. "Let me show you the rest of the house first."

Not that Helene had asked. Not that she expected any kind of house tour from this most unusual sort of Realtor.

The kitchen was much like Malvina's, only with less clutter. Maybe someone had cleaned up after Renee passed. Or maybe Renee had been a tidy homemaker, like Helene, like their mom. That was hard to imagine, from her messy bedroom at home and her messy life. There was a dark, heavy pine table, beautifully crafted.

"My father made the table," Izzy offered. "He was good with wood; I think he liked his woodpile more than he liked people. No, I mean, he liked making things with his hands. He made a canoe when he was young, back at the Home Camp in Maine. Just to see if he could do it. It's still up there. He wouldn't bring it down here. He never really liked it as much here, anyway. Or my mother, either." A wry smile flashed across his face. "But she's stuck here now. Except in the summer when we go back."

He had a lot to say, this young fellow, compared to Malvina. Perhaps there was some family resemblance, the coloring and features, but he was stretched out taller and thinner. And he had dark-brown eyes and a beautifully formed mouth, very expressive.

"What happened to him?"

"Passed over. Lung cancer took him a couple years ago. He was seventy, older than Neesa. They had me late – sort of an 'oops' baby. Up north, they call me the 'caboose papoose.' That's Indian humor."

Helene had to laugh, even while thinking that maybe he was the public relations guy, trying to win her over.

From the kitchen, Izzy moved to another room, on the right. A children's room, clearly. The twins' room. Two of everything, except the one double bed, the blankets still in a nest and covered with stuffed animals of every kind. And Barbie dolls.

"But they're not staying here?" she asked.

"No, they sleep with Kiowa, on a mattress in her room. And the cats, except Red Cat, of course. He stays here."

It was not a pink room, or blue or yellow. It was gold and green and brown with murals on the walls: rabbits, deer, an eagle, and a raccoon.

"Someone is a good painter," Helene murmured, taking in the artwork and the smell of young children.

"Neesa," Izzy said from the doorway. "She does this stuff all the time." He lifted a shoulder. "She told the twins she would paint more animals and birds, when they learned their names."

Nice, Helene thought. That was nice.

Then Izzy left, through the kitchen again and into another room, a bit larger and darker – the parents' bedroom. Helene stopped, hesitant to enter. She was not sure she wanted to see this private space. But Izzy was gesturing around him, talking away. She took a step inside, only to be hissed at by Red Cat at the foot of the bed.

"Mainly, I wanted you to see the regalia," Izzy said, turning from a dark corner of the room. The walls were blue-black, just past twilight, and thick drapes covered the windows – like a cave. Over the bed was a heavy plush blanket, black and gray and white of two wolves with golden eyes. This room too had a mural on one wall, a night sky with a half moon, clouds, and stars.

Talented, this Neesa, Helene thought. But not talented enough to dispel the still air and the hush of the room.

Then Izzy turned on the light, and two costumes came into focus: Indian dress, male and female, placed on hangers on hooks in the wall.

"One for Renee; one for Louis," Helene said, nodding.

"Renee made this herself." Izzy lifted the sleeve of the woman's outfit. "Well, with help, mainly Neesa. She really worked at it, though, determined, you know?" His fingers traced some beading, and he added softly, "She started on something for the twins, but then she got too sick. I thought you would like to see."

The dress was made of leather, simple in cut and design, fringed on the hem and sleeves. The beading across the chest and down the front was not quite even, a bit childish to Helene's trained eye. Despite imperfections, it would have taken a lot of time and focus to do this, beyond anything she had known Renee to do. Helene understood that Renee had married into a Native American family, one that lived in contemporary Massachusetts, who drove cars and had jobs. She had not expected to find that her sister had "turned Indian."

She nodded. "Our mother was a seamstress; she was very good with a needle. I didn't know Renee had the patience; good for her. For the powwows?"

"Yes. And the wedding and the naming ceremony for the twins. The special occasions."

Helene felt her throat constrict. A wedding dress for a bride, and one Renee had made herself.

Izzy walked over to the bureau, taking up a framed picture. "Here they are, at the wedding ceremony. And me, in the background." It was Izzy, indeed, in his own finery, plumage like a peacock. A beautiful boy. And the married couple, somber and dignified in the clothing she saw hanging before her. Louis in a feathered headdress and Renee with silver jewelry at her ears, neck, wrists. Louis was shorter, wider than his younger brother and not as handsome, except for his full, dark hair worn long and his intense gaze.

Helene felt a sudden desire to leave, drawn toward the familiarity of her car and the roads leading back home.

"Thank you for showing me, Izzy," she said. "But I think I better get going. I told my husband I'd be home before dinner."

Izzy nodded, padding in his worn sneakers back to the living room. "Don't forget this," he said, pointing at the table.

The box.

"Mostly we just threw a bunch of her stuff in the box," Izzy said. "There was a leak in the ceiling and water damage behind the bookshelves where Renee had all her folders and pictures. We just grabbed whatever we could and put it in there. Some of it was ruined," he added softly. "I'm sorry we couldn't save it all."

"Fine; I'll just put it in the trunk and go through it at home."

"It's pretty heavy; let me take it. Unless you have time for a quick look. Maybe there's stuff you don't really need, old bills or something."

Helene put down her purse to glance through the contents. Mostly papers and photos, folders, a couple books, notepads, and a bag of bracelets and earrings – Mom's old costume jewelry. There were a lot of loose-leaf pages that had been dated and written on, perhaps once bound, but now creased and out of order, in Renee's handwriting. A journal, it looked like. Helene flipped through a few pages and saw a sentence: "When Helene saw it, she…"

She closed the folder quickly; it was something she could read later, in privacy, hoping it was nothing too negative.

She picked up an overstuffed file, creased and bent, with a rubber band around it, and met Izzy's eyes.

"Medical records," he said. "From the cancer, and the births, and from before that too – some of the places she stayed – detox." He spoke without expression. "In the cloth bag, those are photos, but we don't know who they are, so we can't tell the twins – later, when they're older, I mean."

Helene took out a small photo album – her family, the Roy family, their parents, and Helene, Denis, and Renee when they were children. On the steps of their family home; at a birthday party; Christmas. Renee at three or four, the duplicate of Wishi-ta. One of Denis with his fiddle. And one of Helene, in her graduation gown, standing next to Dad and Renee; Denis must have taken the picture. Even shadowed by the cap and tassel, Helene could see the pained, angry look in her own eyes. No Mom there to celebrate. No celebration, really. It had not been a fun time.

She closed the album and slid it back into the bag. "OK. I've got this." Then she paused to take Wishi-ta's records and the letter from school out of her purse to add to the box. When she moved some of the folders to make room, she saw the death certificate for Renee Lopes. Date of birth and date of death; not quite thirty. Place of death: at home.

She looked up quickly at Izzy. "Renee died here, at this house?"

Izzy's expression changed; he seemed to retreat from Helene, from the here and now. He leaned against the wall, his words slowing.

"The hospice came the last couple weeks," he said. "The hospital bed was here" – he indicated the place – "close to the sofa, so the twins could climb up with her or sleep there, them and the cats."

Helene was feeling pressure behind her eyes, the sadness that she had worked so hard to dissolve and let go of. "I don't want to be a weeper," she had told her therapist. "I'm done with crying. It's embarrassing, and makes me look weak. And it doesn't help."

But there they were, tears stinging her eyes.

Izzy was saying, "She wanted to be here, so everyone could hang out. She wanted to be in the living room, while she was still living. And it's brighter out here, the light is better so she could work when she felt up to it. She wanted Louis to sleep in the bed, except when he fell asleep on the sofa. Or sometimes we took turns." He pointed at a chair, an upholstered recliner. "This is where I sit and read, or whatever. Sometimes I played my flute for her; she liked that."

He paused, looking into Helene's eyes. "It wasn't good," he said, "her dying so young. But it wasn't terrible. We were here with her; it was in the evening, maybe ten, and we were all dozing: Louis, the twins, and me. We didn't think the time was that close. Denis was coming, but not until the weekend. Then Neesa came to check on us, and Renee was gone, passed over, as we say." He paused, remembering. "She was cremated, and we took the ashes to Maine, the tribal land."

Helene nodded slowly. She had not wanted to know how Renee died; but she had, really. Truthfully, she was shocked. She had pictured a bad end: cold, dark, smelly, messy, disgusting, alone. Or, possibly, in a hospital room hooked up to lines and tubes with blinking monitors, like their mom. Helene would not have predicted this, death at home with family and her own small children.

She went to pick up the box but it was heavy. Izzy took it from her, as she went to open the door, Red Cat watching from the hallway. Izzy was quiet now, his face closed. She was glad he had no parting words, no amusing observations.

Just as she started the car, Kiowa came out of her house, waving.
What now?

Helene opened the window as Kiowa approached the car.

"My grandmother would like to speak to you," she said. On the front step, Malvina stood facing them, an older woman next to her.

"Just one minute," Malvina called. "We will come to you."

The other woman, Neesa, was short, dark skinned, and unsmiling in an oversized T-shirt and leggings. She wore glasses and her eyes were hard to see within the folds of her lids. She strongly resembled Malvina, especially the shape of the face; but her hair, surprisingly to Helene, was cut short. Neesa too wore long earrings and a lot of jewelry, mostly beaded or with semiprecious stones.

At the side of the car, they stopped. Helene shut off the engine.

She wanted only to depart with the box and time to herself to figure out how she felt and what she wanted to do.

"Allo," Neesa said.

Helene nodded.

"I want to tell you something," Neesa said. When she leaned closer, Helene could smell smoke, but not on her breath. Not cigarettes.

"She was family to us," Neesa said.

"Yes. I know."

"She make a good mother and wife." Neesa patted her chest. "In here, she have good..." She stumbled for the word.

Malvina said, "She doesn't speak much English. She speaks our language and French. *Spirit*, she means; Renee had a good spirit."

"Thank you," Helene said. What else was she supposed to say?

That was the message, apparently; Neesa was done. Helene restarted the car. As she drove away, she caught Neesa and Malvina in her rearview mirror, staring after her. Strangers to her, but not to her sister. *Family*, Neesa had said, like they had staked a claim to Renee, some kind of power that had somehow redeemed Renee from her earlier life with that other family, the Roy family, who was not able to save her or value her enough.

Helene had to remind herself to slow down as she exited the base: the posted speed was twenty miles per hour. Once on the highway, she found herself hurrying east, away from the clouds that seemed to descend on the horizon behind her, blocking the sun and the afternoon light.

Renee's journal – 1

I've never been one for keeping a journal, but I'm going to try. Some of the counselors at rehab suggested it, but I never wanted to. I didn't believe anything would come of it. Alice with the frizzy hair told me to find "something" – writing, painting, knitting, crafts, that kind of stuff. She said everyone needed a creative outlet. I remember thinking, Like that's going to help? But here I am, trying to write and doing crafts, making bracelets and earrings to sell at powwow, not that they're very good. Some things for the baby too. That's the real reason for writing – this baby on the way. It's the weirdest thing – I'm totally scared out of my mind, but I'm excited, too – like "I won the lottery" excited. The best, biggest thing that could happen to me, which I didn't think would ever happen because of all the ways I screwed up my body over a lot of years. That scares me and being a mom scares me, but in a good way, I think. I hope. I pray.

So, writing away. Write, write, write. Alice said to try for a page a day, not every day but most days; I think I can do that. Now I have a few things to say, some good things going on, happy things, about the baby and Louis, and things around here. I see no point in going back to all the bad stuff, even though they said to put your feelings down, try to get at what drives you to do things. Maybe later. Or maybe not. The thing is, I kind of like writing. I'm pretty sure I wrote a couple stories before – for school, I think. One was about blue jays – so beautiful but so loud and noisy and complaining. Something like that. Who knows? Maybe I have a few more stories in me.

Now I've started. I think I'll go back to when I first met Louis, how that came about in such a strange way. And then getting to know him and his family, things about Native American culture that I learned. Then our road trip, him and me. I think that's what did it, changed me. I say it was Louis, and it was. But I relapsed after him, that time. So, really, no one person can save you from yourself, if you're not ready. But that time on the road, camping, eating lousy food, the truck breaking down, the people we met. How we turned to each other, and how I helped him when he struggled too. That's a pretty good story, I think.

Chapter 4

Just a week after Helene's first visit to the base, the grass had come into the yards, and all kinds of people and their pets were outside with the warm weather, although she couldn't spot the twins or their cousins. At Malvina's house, Izzy had met her at the door, flute in hand. Malvina was in the living room, her feet on a hassock, clasping a bag in her lap; she looked even bigger with pregnancy, uncomfortable, more puffy-faced than last time. Helene noticed that her ankles were swollen – blood pressure. But she had agreed to go with Helene to see the pediatrician without Wishi-ta, leaving her husband, Noel, in charge of the kids. From the file of papers, Helene knew that Noel worked for the phone company; Malvina said he had taken off early to work on some projects at home. He stopped in briefly to say hello, a hefty, big-boned fellow with an easy affability, unlike his so-serious wife. His black hair was pulled back into a short tail and his face was shiny and weathered from time spent outside, the picture of strength and health. She liked his relaxed, soft-spoken manner, a simple "We're happy to know you, and thanks for coming."

Inside the car with Malvina, Helene again detected the smell of smoke, that same herbal scent. But she didn't want to ask, not yet. Instead, she inquired about allergies in the Lopes family: not many. Helene was about to say that childhood allergies were common when it hit her that she and Denis both had peanut butter allergies as kids, and she still had plant allergies in the fall. It had not occurred to her that Wishi-ta's allergies might be from her side of the family. Perhaps it was best to let the doctor take the lead on this, she decided, and try not to conjecture.

The pediatrician at the clinic, Dr. Gregorian, seemed competent and up to date, a dark-haired woman in her forties with a warm manner and keen observation skills. Helene took notes, asking a few questions to clarify the doctor's comments. Malvina reported the latest developments at home: Wishi-ta had had one allergic reaction since Helene's previous visit – late at night, and with no idea of the trigger – food or otherwise. She had recovered, but then developed a worrisome wheezing she had not had before.

Right away, Helene recognized it: asthma, brought on by the allergic reaction. Tricky. She had encountered it before with children at her school, and she knew the game plan: an inhaler for the asthma. Then a series of tests, looking for possible triggers, followed by immunotherapy to build resistance to the allergens. This was what Dr. Gregorian recommended, referring them to the desk to make the appointments with an allergist. The preferred schedule was a four- to six-week series of appointments, two or three times a week. Malvina looked at Helene, who asked the doctor, "Can we call after we check our calendars?" and then, "What if I'm the one who brings Wishi-ta? Do you need a consent form?"

"I believe so," said Dr. Gregorian. "But let me check with the office manager – right to privacy and all that. Most likely it's a simple form that, uh, her father could sign and mail to us; or, fax, if that's possible." She seemed to know that Louis was absent.

In the car, the two women were quiet. The appointments were a big commitment of time, no matter how they looked at it. And there was no benefit to waiting. In fact, waiting would only prolong the risk of a serious reaction. Malvina was not likely to offer any suggestions, so it was up to Helene what course she was willing to take.

Back at Malvina's, Noel was waiting for them with Kiowa and the twins, spilling out the front door to meet the car.

"Come in," Noel said to Helene. There were traces of flour on his forearms and blue frosting under his fingernails. "We made cupcakes," he said. "And iced tea."

Helene smiled at their obvious excitement, and she was touched. She checked her watch quickly, thinking of the ride home. But it was such a nice offer, and she could use a quick bite.

"Thank you," she said. "That sounds very nice."

Malvina had already gone inside; Helene followed the little troop, and was met by the sweet, buttery smell of baking. Passing through the kitchen, she stepped onto the deck and saw the picnic table set with cups and plates, the basket materials set aside. Helene took a seat while the children waited, finally seating themselves around the table. The grandmother, Neesa, did not join them, and Helene was glad. It might be awkward, since Neesa apparently didn't speak English well and didn't seem to welcome Helene's presence, even if she was supposedly there to solve a problem.

A tea party was the last thing Helene had expected. But the cupcakes, moist and gloppy with icing, were delicious, and the iced tea welcome. Then Izzy appeared, again with the flute, ready to perform.

"This is song of thanks," he said, "for the Creator. It's about the bears awakening after winter." And then, tossing his long, gleaming hair with an affected air, "I'm pretty happy with it, myself."

He played a song both playful and somber, while the children listened without talking or fidgeting, even the two older boys who had come up on the deck to join them, helping themselves to the cupcakes.

"Lovely," said Helene, when the song ended. "I mean, stirring, if that's the right word. I could almost imagine the bears waking up and finding a bright, sunny world again. Thank you, Izzy."

"Lovely," one of the boys snickered, but he went right back to licking the frosting off his cupcake.

Helene asked the kids a few questions, about sports and friends and school, the usual stuff, and they were not shy to answer and volunteer observations in an almost adult way – wanting to know if she had pets and if she lived in the city. They also wanted to know if she was going to the Spring Moon powwow the following weekend – obviously trying to see where she fit in. They seemed to know she was family, sort of, but not the kind they were familiar with.

"Probably not," she told them. "It's pretty far from home."

From down the street came the sound of a chainsaw cutting wood, a high-pitched, startling sound that jolted Helene, reminding her again of the time. But something else came to her, something she wanted to see.

"Thank you so much for the treats," she said, motioning to the sticky mess that remained on their plates and faces. "And for the concert, Izzy."

He smiled, but shook his head. "Not really a concert; just an honoring song for the spring."

"That, then." She paused before adding, "I was just thinking I might like to take another quick look at Renee's house. Would that be OK?"

Malvina shot her a shrewd look.

"No problem at all," said Noel, rising slowly, joint by joint. "Izzy, can you take her over while we clean up here?"

Helene got up, taking her purse and saying good-bye. She met Izzy at the front door, waiting with the key.

"I'll have to keep an eye out for that cat," Helene said, more relaxed with Izzy, feeling she could joke.

"Oh, yeah, he's fine," Izzy said. "He's just a very loyal cat, you know. He was always with Renee, up to the end. Maybe he still feels her presence here. Cats know things."

"Ah."

Inside the house, Red Cat was curled on the sofa in a patch of sunlight, waking to yawn slowly as he watched Izzy and Helene enter. The room was as golden and sandy as Helene remembered; she noticed that some of the paintings on the wall were canyons and mesas – the American Southwest. And a depiction of that peculiar figure she'd seen elsewhere, a humpbacked man playing a flute. Curious. Indian.

"Mainly, I want to see the kitchen again," Helene said, "If I needed to make a meal…"

"Everything's still here," Izzy said, facing her. "Nothing's changed. We try to clean and dust, keep it ready for when Louis gets back – maybe sooner, maybe later, we just don't know. Come."

Helene set down her purse on the kitchen table, opening cabinets, checking the water pressure from the faucets, and turning on the burners of the gas stove. Everything clean; everything in working order. And little of the clutter from Malvina's house – of course, no one here to make a mess, except the cat, and Izzy when he came to read or play his flute. She remembered that and wondered if he would be put out if she ended up staying over a night or two, requiring some privacy.

She passed by the master bedroom; she didn't even want to look. There was another room, next to the twins' room, at the front of the house, more like a study or den.

She stood at the open doorway, thinking, then said to Izzy, "I could stay in here."

"You wouldn't sleep on the big bed?" he said behind her shoulder.

She turned to look at him. "No, I couldn't do that." She was surprised at her own honesty.

"She didn't die there, you know. It was in the living room."

"I know. You told me." Then, with a helpless look: "I don't know why, exactly. I just can't."

"Then you can't," he said. "We've got plenty of sleeping bags and pads and such, from camping – at the powwows."

"Thanks, but no; I've got an inflatable mattress at home. That should work – if I decided to stay overnight. Three hours is a long drive, each way."

"Right." And then his eyes narrowed in a rather catlike way. "I wouldn't know, because I don't drive."

"Oh? Why is that?"

He shrugged. "Haven't gotten around to it. Haven't had the need. I'm a bicycle Indian – my faithful steed is a red Raleigh, gets me most places most of the time, except if the snow's too deep."

He was disarming; Helene found it hard not to smile. "OK, then, if that works for you." And then, because she hadn't really given an answer to Malvina, she said, "Well, I've got a lot to think about. And I'll have to talk things over with my husband. But I'll give Malvina a call this week, see what we can work out; please tell her. Oh, and how long until she's due?" She hadn't been able to ask Malvina that directly.

Izzy screwed up an eye. "Beginning of August, maybe? Something like that."

At the door, as they were leaving, Wishi-ta and Tana-na met them with a paper plate covered with foil. More cupcakes.

"If you get hungry," Tana-na said. "Or Malvina said we'd eat them all, and throw up."

"Thank you, Tana-na," Helene said, wanting to say the name again, try it out on her tongue. "And Wishi-ta." Wishi-ta was hanging back a bit, still bewildered, perhaps, about Helene. But the sun was shining in her hair, giving her a kind of radiance, and her eyes were light blue, the eyes of Helene's mother and sister. And Helene herself.

On the drive home, a plan came clear to Helene. Really it emerged as soon as she got in the car, after a last look at the twins in the front yard – dark-haired Tana-na and blond Wishi-ta – the incarnation of Renee – though Kenneth wouldn't know that. Helene knew what to do; it was just a question of how to present it to Kenneth. For sure, he would have some objections, but even he could see the sense of it. Short term. The timing was right; school was out shortly for the year. There was no cost, a place to stay, and she could work on her professional nursing credits when they weren't otherwise at the allergists. There was something really very important at stake – a young child's health, and even life. As soon as school ended, she could spend weekdays up at the base, going to the appointments, coming home for long weekends. There was no reason to make the three-hour trip each way every day, or every other day. Finite. Manageable. Just for a few weeks, until they found the triggers, started the shots, had a solution.

Renee's journal – 2

So the first time I saw Louis, he was full-on Indian, including the face paint. He walked into the health clinic where I was working, like he stepped right out of a movie. I thought maybe they were filming in the area, and he had been injured in a stunt. His right hand was wrapped in a mound of gauze. But no; he was in regalia, as he told me right off, when I asked why he was wearing a costume. The braids, the feathers, leggings, moccasins, and a vest kind of thing with all sorts of emblems and designs. His chest and abdomen were in plain sight, big old tattoos on his forearms. He was a sight, I can say that for sure. Brown skin, muscles, not a big guy, but sturdy; handsome in his way, with those nice lips and a surprising dimple. Not much older than me; I was about twenty at the time and staying at a halfway house. This was my first real job, not bad while it lasted.

Anyway, I did the intake, giving Louis the forms to fill out. But he had to wait for his sister to come in from parking the car, since he couldn't write with his burned hand. The sister showed up a few minutes later – Malvina, of course; she looked like him. She was pregnant, in a long shapeless dress with an Indian print, a toddler at her side – Kiowa. I know all that now. She filled out the forms for Louis, and he brought them back to me at the counter. A burn, it was clear, and he seemed to be running a fever, but she didn't put much detail, so I asked him.

A previous burn on his palm had become infected. We were alone at the counter, only a couple old folks in the waiting room, and Malvina, occupied with Kiowa. As Louis explained it, he had just come from an event, a powwow. His hand had begun to throb and was so sore he couldn't drum, which was what he was there to do, so his sister had brought him here to the clinic. The burn was from a week earlier, at another powwow in Mashpee on Cape Cod.

"But how did it happen?" I asked. I wasn't supposed to, probably, but I was curious. I had heard about powwows in various places around Massachusetts, but I never thought there was anything dangerous about them.

"Fireball," Louis said, holding my gaze.

"What's that?"

"A game we play, the men of the tribe, with two teams trying to get a ball between two posts. But the ball is on fire. And sometimes we burn our hands or feet."

"Really?" And I thought it been turning over meat on a grill. "But why would you do that, if you might get burned?"

"That's the medicine," he said.

"That makes no sense at all." I was a kind of fresh girl in those days.

"Then you lack understanding," he said. He was about to turn away.

"But I'd like to understand," I said, mainly to keep him there.

"Really?" He sounded gruff, but I knew I'd caught his eye.

"Really."

"It's a way of healing, both physical and spiritual. We take on the suffering of our people, our tribe."

"And does it cure anyone?"

He shrugged. "If they think it does, it does. Like prayer, right? But most prayer is private and doesn't cost anything. We play medicine ball in a big arena front of lots of people under the sky right as the sun is setting. When we're playing, we don't even feel the pain, or just a little."

I nodded. "OK. But now you've got this." I pointed at the bandaged hand. "So you're right back where you started."

He leaned in, close to my face. "No, whatever else it does, Fireball cures the suffering of being alone, isolated, alienated from other beings. It's about what you would do for others, and what they would do for you."

And the he added with a smirk, as I stood there blinking: "No, this is me trying to be badass. I wouldn't go to the first aid tent, and then I worked all week with it like this, getting worse and worse. And now I'm here."

"And now you're here," I said. "And you probably need an antibiotic for that, I'll bet you."

"Damn right," he said. The nurse called his name, "Louis Lopes," and he took back the clipboard and followed him in, the young guy right out of nursing school who used to smoke with me on his breaks.

Malvina was slumped in the chair, resting her eyes, hands across her middle. Kiowa was talking to a stuffed giraffe.

I figured that was the last of him, Louis. I was in the back when he left, so I didn't see what they did for him, or if I was right about the antibiotic.

Renee's journal – 3

The second time I met Louis was also a surprise, a few weeks later. Funny thing, it was only a couple blocks away from the health clinic. A Monday night, at an AA meeting at the church. I was waiting on the sidewalk for Jessica, my ride back to the halfway house. And there stands a scary-looking dude in jeans and a tank shirt, a big bad wolf tattoo on his arm, shell earrings and a necklace with teeth. Louis!

I knew his name from the intake, but he didn't know mine.

"Louis," I called out. "We meet again."

Of course, I couldn't help but think, So much for the medicine. He was there, just like me. Kind of sad how those stereotypes could be true.

He didn't know me right away. So much for that excellent tracking skill of the Indians.

"From the clinic," I said. "Your burned hand."

He nodded. He remembered.

"How is it, anyway?"

After a moment, he lifted his hand to show me, tender pink flesh, but healing.

"Back to drumming?" I asked. Cheeky, it's true. But I never thought I had anything to lose. And I liked men's attention that way too, especially in the party scene. I could get pretty much what I wanted from them at the time, weak souls all of them, without giving much away. I did some terrible things for drink and dope, but sleeping around was not my usual operating style. If I was fast enough with my mouth, I didn't need to use my body.

"Maybe I am," he said, wondering, I'm sure, what business it was of mine. The thing is, I often remembered things people told me, and sometimes it spooked them.

"Running a little late," I said, pointing toward the church basement windows, where folks were still milling about inside.

Again he looked like he was not planning to answer, but he did. "If I were coming here, I'd be on time. I'm picking up a friend, who currently cannot drive."

Ha! I knew what that meant. I lost my license two years earlier. "I see." So he was not chasing sobriety himself.

I realized that he was maybe waiting for me to offer something about myself. I was not going to say that I was five weeks sober and living at the halfway house with a bunch of mixed-up young adults like me. For the fourth – or was it the fifth? – time.

"And I'm waiting on a ride home," I said. "And working hard at my next pin." I looked out the corner of my eye to see his reaction. Nothing. But I was pretty sure he knew about the little rewards for weeks and months of sobriety. Anyway, it was my way of saying, "Yes, I'm an addict."

Problem was, I wasn't really working at my next pin. I had no true *interest in sobriety. I preferred being high to the times in between, except of course when I got in trouble. Not so much with the law, although that happened occasionally – no big deal to me – maybe to Dad and Helene. By trouble I mean the hassle of being out of money, or out of a place to live, or losing a job. And then it was all such a pain in the ass, for a while. The thing is, with that little allowance I got from home, I could go long and far on my adventures.*

Except that I was starting to not feel well. And not look that good. And a couple of times I sort of lost myself, ending up places I didn't mean to be, without a plan. Like that time at the Walmart parking lot, where I passed out under a streetlight. It might have been OK if the police had come along, but I came to when some guy was trying to stuff me in his car. That wasn't cool. And when I tried to get away, he punched me in the face, loosened a tooth. And the girl with him took my watch, Mom's watch. Other addicts, probably. Not nice people.

Louis's friend appeared through the church door, with a wave and nod. He'd already lit up a cigarette. A scrawny guy with baggy jeans and a do-rag.

"Cuz!" he called to Louis, ambling slowly in our direction. "Good as your word." He didn't look like a cousin; he didn't even look Indian – more black, with a few kinky curls escaping the do-rag. Then he looked in my direction.

Louis glanced at me, and then at his friendly cousin. Then back to me.

"I don't know your name."

"Renee. Renee Roy."

"Take care, Renee," he said. "And good luck." He nodded toward the church.

Then I saw Jessica on her way out with Mickey, a guy she liked, who was nothing but bad news. I knew it would be a matter of days before they'd be partying again, maybe hours. And maybe me too, if I went with them.

"Oh, Louis," I say, before he moved off. "I was thinking maybe I'd like to go to one of those powwows. What do you think?"

He stopped, tipping his head. "Sure, if you want to. Everyone's welcome."

"But how about the Fireball?" I was talking fast, not wanting him to get away just yet.

He held up a hand to the cousin, who was standing next to him with an amused sneer; he thought it was a pickup thing, clearly. Which it kind of, sort of was, in a weird way, if I didn't blow it.

"Nah, you missed it. It's a once-a-year thing. They don't do it at most powwows. But there's a powwow somewhere most weeks in the summer, on the weekends. You can find them online, easy."

"Right," I say. "How about this weekend?"

"Sure. Middlefield, up towards Boston."

"Yeah, I'd like to go. See what it's all about. Could learn something new, right? They've got food?"

"Yup."

"What about the tickets? How much is it?"

"Not a ticket, really. Entrance fee; five dollars maybe."

I give him a big smile. "I could swing that." And then, "Are you planning to go?"

"Yup." He could see where this was going. "My family sets up a booth; we sell jewelry, rattles, fans, baskets, T-shirts, that kind of stuff."

"Cool," I said. "I'd really love to see that. And music too, right? Drumming?"

"Yup." I had him; I could tell. And he knew I wasn't even all that interested in the powwow, or the stuff.

"Trouble is, I don't have a ride. Any chance you could take me?"

His smile broadened, and that's when I knew he saw what he was getting himself into. God help him.

"I might. My truck is packed; you might have to sit in the back."

"I'll keep the baskets from flying away. Just tell me what time. I can wait for you at the Dunkin' Donuts on Main Street." The pink-and-orange coffee meet-up place in just about every New England town.

"Eight o'clock too early for you?"

"Damn, that's early. I'll be ready. With my coffee."

"OK."

"Don't stand me up."

"You, either."

His cousin was enjoying this, I could tell. He was an addict too. He knew all about manipulation, and had to admire my clever way of working the Indian culture angle. Probably a victim of the wheedling white girl too, in his time.

Jessica shouted for me. She was frowning, but no Mickey. I was out of danger, at least until powwow. But not Louis; he was in it now.

Chapter 5

The weekend before school let out, Helene and Kenneth were invited to a birthday cookout for Kenneth's sister the next town over. Brenda's husband and their two teens would be there in their recently expanded, totally renovated home. It had become unseasonably warm for spring in New England, and Helene had changed into a summer skirt and top, touching up her makeup. She could hear Kenneth shaving in the bathroom, waiting until after his Saturday workout to shower and change. She had packed a tossed salad and a loaf of artisan bread. As she took the salad dressing bottle from the refrigerator, Misty darted past her ankle, silent as always. Never a mew; never a purr.

"No, kitty; no time for a rub," Helene said, a bit wistfully. Part of her didn't feel like going. The food would be good, but the questions and the comments, the pointed jostling between family members – sometimes those were hard to take, especially those of a personal nature or which had to do with Helene's past.

As expected, the conversation with Kenneth after her return from the base did not go smoothly. Helene waited until after dinner was cleared, and Kenneth listened attentively as she laid out the plan, nodding from time to time, only interrupting for clarification. And then he frowned. He could be supportive about her reviewing information and helping to make medical decisions, but for her to uproot herself and go stay there for days or even weeks at a time was too much to ask.

"They didn't ask," Helene said. "I thought it would be best for me and for Wishi-ta."

"You'd be marooned up there," Kenneth said, leaning back in his chair. "And if I know you, you'd get to brooding, being surrounded by all those reminders of Renee. For your own sake, it's not a good idea." His smile was tender. "And I would miss you. Me and the cat."

Helene thought, *You work all the time, anyway. And you're a grown-up; she's a child.* But all she said was, "I'd be home for long weekends, if there are no Monday or Friday appointments."

"If only things were that simple," Kenneth said, a slight flush in his cheeks. Under the table his knee fidgeted, but his voice stayed even. "You know how often things don't work out, and then you'd be entangled in their lives, and it would be so much harder to leave."

That was a hard point to argue.

"And what about vacation?" Kenneth said, sitting upright. "I thought you wanted to rent a cottage on the Cape for a week. I've been looking for some open spots on my calendar."

Not likely. Kenneth was a man who had a tough time giving himself a vacation; even when they were away, he brought his work with him.

"Good," she said, lightly. "I'm glad to hear that, anyway. Let me know what you find."

Ken balled up his napkin and Helene got up to bring the coffee pot to the table, pouring for them both.

"Thanks," he said, and then, with a calculated expression: "What about that armoire you were planning to refinish? You always enjoy your summer projects."

Helene shrugged. "Certainly nothing urgent."

Kenneth sipped the coffee and sighed. "Well, just think about it some more. I can't say I think it's a good idea, because I don't. And I really think if you just said *No*, they'd have to find other options. Maybe you want to prove to yourself that you're stronger and above all that old family stuff. But you don't have to prove it to me, and I sincerely hope you'll think twice before putting us through that turmoil again. OK?"

"OK."

They hadn't talked about it again, and Helene had the impression Kenneth thought it was a done deal – off the table.

On the way to his sister's house, Kenneth was commenting on how everyone had a long summer vacation, except him. His sister was a teacher at the community college; their high school kids had summers off, of course; and even his brother-in-law was a high school gym teacher and athletic coach. The family had a place on a lake in New Hampshire, where Kenneth and Helene would go occasionally. They pulled into the driveway, between weeded mulch beds, everything ship-shape as ever.

While the steaks were on the grill, the two couples sat on the back deck in the late-afternoon sunshine with drinks and appetizers.

"So what are your summer plans, Helene?" Brenda asked. Her sister-in-law was three years younger than Kenneth, ambitious and energetic like her brother. Also like her brother, she was good-looking, a natural dirty blond who had gone with a platinum look for years. She made a point of dressing well, in an unfussy, well-tailored way, and followed a vigorous fitness and beauty regimen, perfectly made-up even on casual occasions. Helene couldn't see the point of foundation and lipstick when sitting in the heat. She was a minimalist, at best.

"Will we be seeing more of you at the lake house? I don't know why you don't just come and stay a couple weeks, leave Kenneth behind. He's a big guy; he can fend for himself."

"Thanks, Brenda," Helene said. "But I don't know yet what I'm doing for the summer."

"Hold on," said Kenneth, making a comic face. "Don't be tempting my wife. I've got big plans for Helene this summer."

Both women looked at him, Helene with genuine surprise.

"We've got this new townhouse development, thirty units – some condos, some rentals. I need Helene to work with the interior designer to pick out light fixtures, sinks, faucets, all the bells and whistles – she's great at that, a natural."

"True," said Brenda. "But she still deserves some summer fun, right Helene?"

Helene nodded, a tight smile at her lips. *The town houses.* Yes, she knew about them, but the development was still in the permitting stages, working out things with the Conservation Committee, not likely to start construction until the following year. Of course, they could be looking at catalogs, visiting showrooms – which she had done for a previous project. Kenneth liked the interior designer, but he trusted Helene, especially for function and cost. And she enjoyed the work, but it certainly wouldn't take weeks of her time.

"I don't see why I can't do both," Helene said.

"Oh, Helene," said her brother-in-law, Carl, sitting across from her in a sports team T-shirt, nylon shorts, and spotless athletic shoes. His hair was buzzed short for the summer, like the high school basketball star he used to be. "Always so agreeable. That's what we like about you; no fuss, no muss." That was likely directed at Brenda, bossy and practical, recently made head of the Business Department.

Kenneth had gotten to his feet. "She's the best, Helene. Top marks in every category."

"So unfair," Brenda put in, petulant, making a face. "Naturally beautiful, with practically no effort. I don't see a strand of gray in that hair. Perky boobs and the world's most perfect eyebrows."

Kenneth smiled, his lips drawn back. "Just like the day I met her."

"Like a model," Carl said, a beery note in his voice, egging.

"Yes, indeed," Kenneth went on. "At the photo shoot for Bullocks catalog fall season of…" He ended with a cough, obscuring the number of years.

Helene looked down into her wineglass. It came up every time they were together, her one-time modeling experience. Part of this weird, unwanted rivalry between the women, along with Brenda's complaints about the effort of staying youthful-looking, not to mention the cost. How she hating getting older, and hadn't found any upside yet. And how it was so much better for Kenneth, who was considered in his prime, even though he was older than she was.

"So unfair," repeated Brenda. "While I've got crow's-feet and stretch marks. Done in by motherhood." They all laughed, but there was a flash of pique in Brenda's remark, directed at Carl or maybe Helene, who was, of course, not a mother. It looked to Helene like Brenda had had some work done to fill in the lines across her forehead and from nose to mouth, but

Helene was not about to comment or to ask.

Kenneth left with Carl to replenish drinks. Brenda turned to Helene expectantly.

"What's up? I sense something brewing."

Helene hesitated. "Yes, well, there's this thing, and I haven't decided what to do about it."

Brenda leaned in, almost spilling the wine out of her glass. "Sounds intriguing. From the deep, dark past?"

Helene sighed. "You know about my sister, Renee, right, and her problems when we were growing up?"

Brenda nodded. "Yes, with the drugs and all that. Then she took up with an Indian guy, had some kids, and died young, not long ago."

"That's the story. One of the kids, the girl, has some serious medical issues, and the husband's family has asked me – us – for some help."

"What's wrong with her? Not cancer?"

"No, she has allergies, which can be life threatening, and also asthma."

"Yeah, so?" Brenda shrugged. "That can be dealt with, those EpiPens and such. I don't know why they would need you personally." She cocked her head, hair falling to the side. "You think there's more to it?"

The two men arrived back on the deck carrying more wine and beer, in time to catch the end of the conversation. The wine bottle was open, a premium chardonnay, and Kenneth leaned over to refill wineglasses.

"What Helene is not telling you is that the father is not in the picture – he's in jail, trespassing on federal land, abetting criminals, and having a firearm in his vehicle. Some kind of Indian protest in Maine." At least he didn't mention the explosion at the dam or someone being killed. But it still sounded bad. "Totally irresponsible, if you ask me – when his wife is dead and he has two small children at home."

"No way," Brenda said. Pink patches appeared on her cheeks – either the heat or the wine. Her forehead, very smooth, was shiny, like someone in need of a fan.

"It's true," Kenneth went on. "And the rest of the family lives in housing on an old military base, and apparently goes back and forth to their homeland in Maine, when the spirit moves them." He made a wavering motion with his fingers – the spirit moving. "It's not clear to me what their source of income is. A federal subsidy, I suppose, like they all get."

Helene didn't think so, but wasn't absolutely sure. If they didn't qualify for Indian insurance, they wouldn't get federal aid, either. Isn't that what Malvina had said?

"Louis was working for a nonprofit," she said quietly. "And doing construction work. The brother-in-law is a telephone line repair man – a pretty good job, I think."

"Oh, and they make arts and crafts to sell at the powwows," Kenneth said, which was also what Helene had told him. "I doubt that's much of a moneymaker."

"Sounds like a made-for-TV movie," said Brenda, rolling her eyes. "But I don't know about getting involved. It could be a real mess. I know those people have had a tough time of it, but they don't seem to be able to move beyond their problems and give their children a better chance. It can be done; millions of immigrant families have done it – risen out of poverty and gone on to make good lives. Look at us." She gestured around the deck. "It was nothing but hard work that built this house." Then she laughed. "And the lake house – well, that was a small inheritance, and a second salary."

Helene took a small sip of wine, and then another. She allowed herself only one glass of wine, because of health, because of past experience. Because of Renee and their father. She wished they would drop the subject.

Fourteen-year-old Zach came out to the deck to grab some chips and salsa and a swig of his father's beer. When he passed, Helene got a whiff of smoke – pot, she was pretty sure. She recognized it from Renee, and from Denis in the basement. But Zach's folks were oblivious or for some reason were ignoring it. Helene liked Zach, and he seemed to like her. But she also knew him to be a slippery character, easy with white lies, and not particularly respectful to his parents. Her niece, Ashley, two years older, was in a challenging, resistant stage, withdrawing to her room most of the time. She didn't seem to have a social group and openly expressed dislike for school and her teachers, which was hard on her educator parents – or maybe the point. Still, they had the lake house.

"When will the steaks be ready?" Zach asked. The munchies, thought Helene. When he smiled at her, she wondered how no one else noticed his bloodshot eyes. Thankfully, the steaks were ready to come off the grill. Ashley was called, and large platters of salads and side dishes appeared; all from the gourmet catering store, all very good. The talk turned to music and movies, sports and stars. Ashley occasionally joined in, mostly sniping at her brother, not always good-naturedly. Helene recognized teenage angst when she saw it, but it all seemed at a distance, another level from the turmoil in the Roy household, mostly centered around Renee. This family drama would pass, focused on some new object or changed into other kinds of discontent, none of them very serious.

Later, as the day was winding down, after the cake and candles and a new charm bracelet for Brenda, the conversation came back to vacations and plans.

"We'll be expecting you for July fourth at the lake," Brenda said. Her voice was breathy, a bit slurred. Eyeliner had seeped into the creases of her eyes and the foundation looked sticky – after all that effort. It reminded Helene of something Renee had once said – in a face-off at court with a tough lady lawyer, polished, dyed, and groomed to the max. "All that war

paint doesn't frighten me." Oh, she had been fresh, Renee. Terrible. "And
it doesn't do a thing for you. You know bleach is a poison, right? And
you'll never get those eyebrows back." All very inappropriate, including
the war paint reference. It wasn't funny at the time. But tonight it brought a
smile to her lips, remembering.

"Of course," she replied to Brenda. "That's the tradition."

"And any other time you want to come up. Please don't say you're
going to be away and trying to fix up that mess your sister left. You work
hard during the school year; you deserve some R and R."

"You're probably right," said Helene. "I can't quite picture what I'd
do with myself up there, aside from appointments, of course. In any case,
thank you for the invitation."

Brenda was giving her a certain look. Helene wondered what her
sister-in-law really thought of her – a little condescension, she thought.
Pity? Probably perplexed. It was funny how she seemed to want so much
for Helene to come – to value what she valued?

"You better come." Brenda tossed her hair expressively, like a
teenager.

"Thanks again, and good night."

Helene had several sleepless nights, lying still not to wake Kenneth,
who needed his sleep and would probably chide her, anyway, for still
wrestling with the issue. She had spent the last couple days trolling the
computer to find out as much as she could about allergies, asthma, tests,
and shots. Some of it was quite frightening, but it did seem manageable.
What would they do if she didn't come? Malvina was due soon, Izzy
couldn't drive, Neesa couldn't drive, and Noel went to work every day – or
watched the kids. He could take some time off, but then he had to take time
off for Malvina too.

A social worker – that's what they could do. A social worker would
help them coordinate services, and maybe arrange rides. She wondered that
no one had suggested it to them. And then, in a flash, she knew – probably
they had, and probably they were worried that social services might
investigate the situation and possibly take the children away, especially
one with an urgent medical problem. She had encountered the situation
before, a few times, at work. Once, a social worker had come to the Roy
home to speak to their dad about Renee, who was eleven at the time. Her
father had little to say, leaving it to Helene, who spoke convincingly and
reassuringly that Renee had supervision and structure, and love. For the
next couple years, Helene had done her utmost to keep Renee in line, and it
mostly worked, until it didn't work – and Helene had gone away to nursing
school. That was the turning point.

At night in bed, she tried to tell herself, *What will be, will be*. It could
be for the best if social services intervened – a mother dead and a father in

jail, not enough resources. And then she thought of herself, Denis, and Renee – a mother dead and a father lost in depression – and how she'd wished someone would come to their aid, just for a while, to help them cope.

Then one morning on her way to work, Helene found herself breathing hard and shaking. She pulled over to calm down – maybe Kenneth was right. Maybe it was too much; she wasn't strong enough. And fate would sort itself out. Certainly, she could research on the computer and share the results, by mail or by phone call. She could plan another trip in a month or so, to see how things were going. But by and large it wasn't realistic for her to manage the problem from here. She had enough on her plate. Continuing Ed credits. Her summer projects. And some preliminary work for Kenneth's town houses – that could be fun. And a trip or two to the lake. Soon enough, September would roll around again.

But as she sat staring into the morning light, she saw Wishi-ta's golden hair and Red Cat and the cupcakes and Izzy's flute. And something else pulled at her, pulled her in that direction, even though she couldn't say what.

Chapter 6

On the last day of school, an early-release Friday, Helene was startled by a face at her office doorway. Her brother, Denis, with a full reddish beard, his brown hair pulled back in a ponytail. The amulet at his neck and tattoos on his forearms made him look like a small-framed Viking, yet with none of the fierceness. She rose from her chair, surprised by how glad she was to see him. Then her arms spread open, although they had not been a family to hug or kiss.

"The wandering musician," she exclaimed.

"In the flesh."

"I am...very happy to see you. I thought you were..."

"I am," he said, "supposed to be with the band. We had a day off, and I'm basically AWOL. I drove all night to get here, and I'll probably drive all night to get back."

Helene frowned. "To see me?"

"And Kiko and my dogs. But yes, you. Can we talk?"

"About Renee and the kids?" She lifted a hand defensively. "Denis, really? You want to send me in on a rescue mission, so to speak, to fix things, since you're not around? Is that it?"

Denis nodded, holding her gaze. "That's pretty much it. Have you decided what you're going to do?"

Helene stared back. "No. I haven't decided. I have been up there, twice, in person. I thought I could maybe bring Wishi-ta back here on a temporary basis, and get her back on track, back to health, but they wouldn't agree to that. So then I considered spending time up there on a limited basis, but Kenneth really dislikes the idea, and I have my doubts. Whatever I can do, I can do from here. It really is asking too much for me to uproot myself."

Denis stroked his beard. "Yes, right, that's what I figured. But the situation remains. Wishi-ta has a serious health issue, still not completely understood. Her mother's dead; her father's in jail. Her support system is overextended. They need help."

For a moment, Helene couldn't find words to reply. *Some nerve, to ask me – again, to take responsibility for a such a difficult situation.* But he wasn't wrong. She turned to look out the window at an almost empty parking lot. Finally, she turned back. "You know what? I'm all done here; let's go. Do you want to come to the house?"

She could see his reluctance. Some discomfort with Kenneth, although Kenneth had always been considerate and reasonable with him, if not exactly supportive or welcoming. And Kenneth had been her only support after Renee had disappeared; for that alone, Denis should be grateful.

"How about we take a ride out to the old house," he said. "Some weird part of me wants to see it, especially now that you guys got it all gussied up."

Helene cocked her head. *What was that about?* But it wasn't far, and she hadn't been by in a while, although she and Kenneth were landlords and had tenants staying there. At first she and Kenneth had planned to manage the place, but it ended up being a headache finding tenants, responding to the problems that cropped up, and so they'd hired a property manager.

"Hardly that," she said. "But it needed a rehab, badly." She got her purse and tote bag.

"You want to ride in my truck?"

"With dog hairs? No thanks. I'll drive."

They drove past the former Roy house twice, turning and slowing to get a good view. It was now gray instead of white, and they had taken down some of the maples in the front that shed so many leaves each year. But it was mainly the same, spruced up, with the addition of a climbing structure and an assortment of colorful molded-plastic playthings. Helene pulled past the house and parked on a grassy spot off the road where the house was still in view: the same porch, the same driveway, the same bushes.

"Looks good," Denis said, nodding. "They've got kids, I guess."

"Yup, a couple with three kids; two girls and a boy." She raised her eyebrows. "Just like us."

Denis considered a moment. "Well, hopefully, not just like us."

They saw movement inside the house and someone let a dog out the front door, a small mixed-breed dog, also like a toy. It didn't go far in the yard; the electric fence they had asked to install.

"Mom would not have gone for that," said Helene. "A dog."

"You never know," said Denis.

After a pause, he went on, "I must admit it was an excellent idea on your part, you and Kenneth – to keep the house and rent it, instead of selling right away when Dad died. At the time I thought you didn't think I could handle my share of the money – or Renee, either. But having the extra income each month is a real help. What would I have done? Bought a condo? I'm hardly ever in one place for more than a couple years."

Helene looked at her hands in her lap, the wedding ring, and the subtle signs of aging over the years.

"Renee, well, who knows what she would have done with the money?" Denis went on. "Maybe she would have blown through it too. But how much can you spend on drugs and alcohol? Or maybe she just wouldn't have to work, or even try to work. A car, maybe?" He looked at

Helene. "I don't think she ever had a car."

"Probably not." For some reason that brought a pang of sadness. "We put her share in a CD, not that it was so much."

Denis looked out the window, open to the soft warm air. "Remember that gazebo Dad built, or arbor, whatever you call it – in the backyard? The poles and canvas covering, with a bunch of lawn chairs; so simple, but Mom really loved it."

"She'd take her knitting out there, or needlework, even after she got sick."

"And how Renee used to create all those little scenes with acorns and pinecones and what-have-you?"

Helene sighed, leaning back against the seat. "All gone now." Her chest felt full, like something pressing down.

Denis turned to her. "I know you think I bailed on you and Renee. And maybe I did. But I had to get out, or I would have ended up in trouble myself." He looked at his own hands, smiling wryly. "Did I ever tell you my plan to run away to that cabin in Vermont where Dad used to take us?"

"The cabin." Helene nodded slowly. "Gosh, I haven't thought about that place in years. No one goes there any more, that I know of. Maybe one of Dad's cousins. I have a key and some directions…if the place is even still standing. But no, Denis, you never let me in on any plan."

"Well, in any case, I never got there," Denis said. "No, it was not good after you left for school; and there were times Dad was out of control. Not just Renee – Dad himself. You know, we always thought he was a quiet drunk, but he could get physical."

Helene looked at him, skeptical. "Dad?"

"It happened. With Renee, of course. Remember she was a teen, and she was always a bit reckless, especially after Mom died. But she would do things just to provoke him. Not only coming home late or drinking his booze. She would mouth off – silly, stupid stuff. You know how you and I used to tiptoe around to not bother him, just leave him in peace with his vodka? She was loud, and she would say these ridiculous, stupid things, like, 'Mom's watching us from heaven, and she doesn't like what she sees.' Or, 'If your boss knew you got drunk every night, he would never let you operate that equipment.' She was fresh, I'm telling you, so fresh."

"She wanted attention," Helene said flatly. She knew that now. The therapist had helped her to see that. "Any kind of attention, even negative. But I thought Dad just tuned her out, like us."

"No," said Denis. "She had a way to get under his skin. She could really irritate him. To the point he lashed out."

Helene turned in her seat to face him.

"Are you saying he hit her?"

Denis shrugged. "Well, he tried. She usually got away. Sometimes, though, he pushed her; pushed her away. And one time…"

He paused. Helene wasn't sure she wanted to know.

"I was home for the summer after freshman year. We were having dinner, the three of us. Renee was wearing sunglasses inside the house. For no good reason, you know? And then Dad told her to take them off, and she wouldn't. She said she was a celebrity in disguise, just waiting to be discovered so she could get away for good and start her real life. So he got up from his chair and slapped her; hard enough to knock the glasses off, hard enough to split a lip. But she just laughed and put the glasses back on, broken, the blood running down her chin."

Helene set her face. She reminded herself it was all in the past; that both Dad and Renee were gone now. And yet anger welled up – at Renee as much as Dad.

"I got between them," Denis said. "And I said if he hit her again, I'd hit him back. So he stood there, wavering on his feet. But then Renee said she could fight her own battles, thank you very much. And I thought I might hit her too. I took off right then and there, for parts unknown. End of college, et cetera."

"I'm sorry," Helene said, evenly, breath controlled. "I knew things were not working out, but not the details. So Dad called me and asked me to come home – made me, really. He said that Renee was out of hand, you were gone, and that he had to earn a living or none of us would have a roof over our head or food on the table. So I came back, not that it did much good."

Denis raised a hand. "It was Dad – he let us down. He just..." He shook his head, helpless. "He gave up on everything altogether. It's like he deflated, like a balloon."

Helene couldn't argue. It was true. And she'd asked the therapist how a person could just give up like that, when they had a family to take care of.

"That was the depression," she said to Denis. "That's what overtook him, after Mom died. And not just that. The medical bills he was trying to pay off. And the changes at work; those kinds of jobs were just disappearing. And all that overtime he used to get was gone."

"You think that's what did him in?"

She shrugged. "My therapist says he lacked resources, a support system. He had no family around, no friends outside of work, he had no faith, really – he only went to church for Mom's sake."

"And there was Renee."

"Renee."

For a moment they sat in silence, except the rumbling from Denis's stomach; Helene had just run out of the granola bars she usually kept in her tote.

"You know what's wild?" Denis said suddenly. "Dad never knew that she did OK after all. That she had a family – kids – more than you and I have." He must have seen the look on her face. "I'm sorry. I didn't mean…"

She waved it away. They sat silent a few moments, the shadows getting longer, until two kids came out into the yard with a ball. Helene started the car.

"Anywhere else?" she asked. "Or back to the school?"

With a wag of his head, Denis said, "I was thinking ice cream. How does that sound?"

"It sounds good," she said, smiling. "Are you trying to sweeten me up?"

"Nah." Denis's good-natured smile spread across his face. "Just hungry. I like the soft serve at Jelly's Roll." His eyes crinkled, "That's a good memory, isn't it?"

Indeed, it was.

The day was so fine and the ice cream so tasty, they sat on one of the benches, in unspoken agreement to leave the past behind. Instead, Denis described his latest trip – the band members, the clubs, the hotels, his impression of parts of the rural South – "quite enjoyable, in their way. And they love our music." At the moment, the music life was good to Denis. He was still with the massage therapist who watched the dogs while he was on the road, and was perhaps more than a dog-sitting friend. When the band returned to Massachusetts, he expected to be in the area for a couple weeks, and then another gig on the road; this one to Pennsylvania and Ohio.

At another picnic table, a pregnant woman sat facing out, with three children coming and going from her side. She was probably close to forty, with more than a few gray hairs. The woman called out to the children a few times in a voice that was vaguely familiar, perhaps the mother of children who attended her school. Just as Denis and Helene finished their cones, the youngest child, a girl around three, screamed and began to cry loudly. The older two were off playing hide-and-seek in the bushes with other kids. The pained crying continued for some time, even after the mother had pulled the girl onto her lap, hushing her; Helene and Denis turned to look.

"A bee sting," the woman said loudly, apologetically. "Right on her finger." Another woman, older, went to the ice cream stand and came back with a bag of ice. After a few moments, the child was quieter, but still whimpering. A girl in an apron from the ice cream stand had joined them, standing over the mother and child, speaking in a low voice, her forehead creased.

Denis was wiping off his fingers and gathering the used napkins and wrappers when Helene saw the pregnant woman get to her feet, the toddler in her arms. She was speaking to the teenage girl, who disappeared into the bushes, calling out for Thomas and Owen. Denis returned from the trash barrel, ready to depart, but Helene gestured at the woman and child, shaking her head.

"I'm just going to see if everything's OK," she said.

"Sure," said Denis. "I can tell you from experience, they're a son of a bitch, bee stings."

Helene approached the small group. "I'm a nurse, if you want me to take a look."

The child was burrowed into her mother's shoulder, while the woman held the bag of ice over her hand. The girl's skin was flushed and sweaty. When Helene leaned in to take a closer look, the little girl pulled away, hiding her face. But not before Helene saw red splotches on her cheek.

"We need to go," the mother said, both anxious and annoyed. "I'm just waiting for my kids; someone's gone to find them."

The older lady turned to Helene. "I'm a nurse, too, retired. It looks like she's having a reaction; it could be serious. I'm going to call 911." The woman took out a cell phone and asked the girl in the apron for the street address of the ice cream stand.

Helene turned back to the mother and child. "Can I see?"

The mother angled the girl toward Helene, before lifting the ice bag off her finger. Denis stood behind, watching. Even as Helene inspected the sting, which was bright red and hot, she could see the hand swelling, and the little girl's breath had become quicker and more labored – definite signs of allergic reaction, needing epinephrine. She'd seen it in five or six children since she'd started working in the school; one of them had been severe, dramatic, life threatening. But the EpiPen had worked, every time.

"Do you have an EpiPen?" she asked the mother, who shook her head.

"No. I don't even know what that is. This has never happened before. Why? What's wrong with her?" Her voice had started to rise, sounding a hysterical note. "Where are the boys? I can't leave them."

Helene saw the teen employee making her way back with the two boys in tow.

"They're coming; they're fine. Listen to me," she said firmly. "I have an EpiPen in my car. It's a quick prick. The injection can really help. I've done this before. Do you understand what I'm saying?"

The woman, blinking rapidly, looked from Helene to the older woman. "I...I..."

"It's safe and it works quickly," the retired nurse said. "It's probably what the paramedics would use, anyway."

"OK, I guess," the woman said.

"So, you consent?" Helene thought to ask. "You want me to go ahead?"

"Yes, yes. Please, whatever you can do, help her."

"Denis, can you get my tote out of the car, in the back seat? Bring the whole bag."

While he hastened off, Helene put a hand on the woman's shoulder. "I need you to sit down here, with your daughter on your lap." Then, more softly. "What's her name?"

"Olivia."

"OK, Olivia, I'm a nurse, and I have some medicine that will make you better, pretty quick. I need your mom to help, and you too." Helene doubted the little girl could take anything in at this point, so she turned to the mom. "I'm going to administer to the thigh but you need to hold her tight." The woman nodded.

Denis had returned, opening the tote bag and taking out the EpiPen in its case, handing it to Helene. She opened it and prepared the needle for injection. The woman set her jaw, wrapping her arms around the girl, binding her movements

"It will be quick and sharp, and then we count to ten, all of us, loud as we can. Quick as that, it will start working."

She plunged the tip in, eliciting a howl from the girl. But it was properly delivered, and Helene started the count, Denis and the mother joining in. A few moments later, as the mother rocked the child, crooning to her, they heard a siren's low blare, still at a distance. A crowd had gathered, although Denis held them back, explaining it was an allergic reaction to a bee sting but that they'd already given the medicine.

In the minutes between when Helene gave the shot and they saw the ambulance in the distance, Olivia had started to breathe more easily, less flushed and agitated. It was a few more minutes before the ambulance pulled into the parking lot, and the paramedics emerged.

"Over here," Denis shouted, waving. The small crowed cleared for them, and the two men, one older and one younger, came up to the mother and child at the picnic table.

"Allergic reaction?" the older man said.

"Yes, I guess so," the mother answered. "It came on suddenly after she got stung by a bee."

Helene spoke up. "I gave her the EpiPen," She recognized the older paramedic, Ray; he'd been to the school on a couple of occasions. "I'm the nurse at school."

"Right," he said, nodding. "Thought I knew you. Glad you were here. Looks like she's doing OK now." He turned to the mother. "We'll check her out, and make sure she's stable and hydrated. If it is an allergic reaction, you should talk to your pediatrician; they'll probably tell you to see an allergist, get a scrip for the EpiPen."

At that point, most of the crowd dispersed. Someone had taken the boys to another table, giving them water, and wiping their hands and faces with wet paper towels.

"Thanks for your help," Ray said to Helene. "It made a difference. We've got it from here."

"Sure. That's great. I guess I'll go, then," Helene said.

The mother had put a hand on her arm. "I can't thank you enough, all of you," she said. "Life savers, truly. Wait, before you go, you're not Helene Roy, are you?"

Helene smiled uncertainly. "Was. Now Helene Bradford. Do I know you?"

"We were in high school together," the woman answered. "Emily Gardner. History class."

"Ah." She did remember Emily. Not the brightest bulb on the circuit. At least, no lover of history. A nice enough girl, at least a normal girl with a normal life.

"And this must be Mr. Bradford?"

Helene laughed. "No, my brother, Denis. Just visiting. He was a couple years behind us."

"Oh, yes," Emily said, forehead crinkling with effort. "I remember. A brother and another sister, a little one."

"That's us. Good memory." Helene turned away, ready to leave. "Well, we'll be going."

"Wait," Emily said. "Any children? I've got a flock of them, as you can see. Maybe we can get the kids together or something."

Helene kept her smile in place. "No, no kids. Just a cat. But it's nice to see you, and I'm glad it all turned out well. You're in good hands now. Danger's passed, right, Ray?" she called out to the paramedic.

"Yeah, we'll stay a few more minutes, but everything's pretty much back to normal."

"No emergency room?" the woman asked.

"Not unless you want to. Just see your doctor, like I said."

"Hallelujah," said the mother, and Helene found herself responding, "Amen."

In the car, Helene waited for Denis to say something, about Emily's comments, or the heroic rescue. But he didn't. They started down the road. Finally Denis spoke into the silence. "I have something for you," he said. "From Renee. Back in my truck. I was supposed to give it to you a long time ago. I just forgot."

"What is it?"

"I don't know. It's wrapped, not too big."

Helene pursed her lips, without a clue what it might be.

They drove the short distance back to the school, where Denis's green pickup truck sat by itself in the lot, teachers and staff gone for the day.

Helene parked next to the truck and got out, following Denis to the passenger side of the truck. He opened the door and lifted a jacket that had been covering a small package, wrapped in a cloth with a string. He handed it to Helene, watching as she opened the cloth to reveal a beaded leather pendant, maybe four inches long and across, on a leather cord. A bluebird in blue, orange, and white.

She looked up at Denis. "Did she tell you what it was for?"

He half smiled. "The bluebird of happiness? You know, like Dad used to say."

"You think?"

"Who knows? I know she made it herself after the twins were born, when you sent a card and some money. She sent another letter, but you never replied, so she figured you didn't want any further contact."

"I didn't get a letter," Helene said, shaking her head. "I'm sure of it."

"She said she wrote it."

"No," Helene said. "No letter. You know, though, I have this box of her stuff Izzy gave me, including pages from her journal."

Denis laughed, raising his eyebrows. "That must be interesting reading." Then the smile faded. "Our Renee."

Yes, our Renee, Helene thought ruefully, *whom we lost for ten years, now forever*. At least she had.

"The pages are loose," she said. "All jumbled up, and I'm still sorting through them." She stopped, exhaling slowly. "I'm a little afraid what I'll find, what she says about us – about me."

Denis shifted in his seat, ready to get back on the road for that long drive.

"No worries," he said. "Renee had nothing but good things to say about you." He squinted an eye, recalling. "The twins knew about you; they've seen pictures from when we were young. I think Renee just said that you lived far away, and that you had important work that kept you busy, like Louis. You know, taking care of sick children, helping them to get better." His hand was resting on the door handle. "No, I just think she wanted you to know that she was OK, that she was happy."

Helene's cheeks were burning, but Denis was already in good-bye mode.

"Bye, sis," he said. "I've got to hit the road." He leaned in for a hug.

"Bye," she got out, her voice raspy.

Denis had made his argument. No wheedling; almost casually. How could she help a stranger's child, and not her own sister's child? But even more so, how had it come about, Renee's escape from addiction after so many of her formative years had been spent in such bad, unhealthy ways? What had she found that could make her change like that?

In that moment, it was decided, decided for her. She would go.

Renee's journal – 4

That first powwow I went to was loud, colorful, dusty, and damn hot. How did these people not think about shade in the middle of the summer? Inside the vendors' booths, there was shade, but no breeze whatsoever. I was a dripping mess. And not dressed right for the occasion, either. I thought I'd get in the spirit of things with a skirt and a fake-leather vest with fringe over a camisole. Without the vest, I'd look like a sleaze in a wet T-shirt contest, not the impression I was going for. I braided my hair and wore the Mardi Gras beads that some former resident of the halfway house had strung over the lamps. Louis picked me up, a few minutes late. Apparently he had to drop off his cousin at a construction site where they were both working over the summer – and the reason Louis was staying at his aunt's house on the Cape.

First thing I noticed when we got to this powwow, I was in the minority. There were many people of color, as they say, all shades of black, brown, and white. They didn't all have that straight, dark, glossy hair. I saw a lot of frizzy braids and ponytails. And some blondes like me. Later I learned that many had mixed heritage – European or black, Cape Verdean off the coast of Africa, speaking Portuguese – descendants of sailors and fisherman. Whalers, even. But the thing was, with all these Indians walking around in regalia, as I now know it to be, they all wore glasses or sunglasses. And some of them wore baseball caps, because it was so hot and sunny. I guess that was a new kind of tradition.

Louis left me in front of a tented area with four big drums, six or seven men seated around each. He had to talk to somebody before "Grand Entry" and he didn't want me along. So I wandered a bit, just to see what was what. Not a large crowd, really, some kids running around, most of them dressed for the occasion. A big circle of lawn chairs around a roped off grassy area with an entrance to one side. A front table by the drums and a set of flags on poles mounted in a stand. I could smell before I saw the food booths: burger stands with drinks and a few special items, such as fry bread, Indian tacos, and bison burgers, along with regular burgers. And something called "wohape," a bright-red pudding served warm. One stand was selling clam chowder, of all things, and stuffed quahogs – just like at those little Cape Cod diners.

Then, suddenly, someone was on the PA system announcing Grand Entry, and slowly, in no hurry at all, folks made their way to the opening in the grassy circle. There was a welcome, a prayer, and some announcements. That's when I saw Louis at one of the front tables, talking into a microphone about petitions and protests about water rights somewhere. It's lost on me now, but I do remember hearing his voice, slow and clear and businesslike, surprising me to see him in this kind of role, public speaking and all. He told me he was usually at the drum, but his hand wasn't completely healed, so he was a little freer to do other things.

After that, they called the veterans. There was a special song at the drum for them, serious, and it made my heart jump. My dad was a Vietnam vet, but he had nothing to say to us kids about his military service – just something closed off in the past. But here they were honored, and first. Then they had everyone enter the circle who wanted to, elders, men and women, and children step-dancing to the drum. Following that was dancing of other styles, men and women separately, some of them wearing numbers for prize money.

Louis came back to find me.

I said, "You didn't tell me you were a celebrity here."

And he said, "I'm not. I'm just speaking my truth." He said things like that, just waiting for a comeback, but I didn't have one, not that time.

"OK," I said. "What's next?"

We went over to where Malvina and her husband, Noel, were tending a booth – jewelry and T-shirts, like most of the others – and some small woven baskets, very carefully done. I was taken with those right away; I would have liked one, but starting at thirty dollars, it was too much for me. Grass or straw, I thought, that's way too pricey – well, that's what I thought at the time.

"My mother makes those," Louis said. Malvina, seated in the shade fanning herself, gave me the once-over. She was big as a whale by then; the baby due within a week or two. No Kiowa; home sick with Grandma. Noel was friendlier, a gentle giant, relaxed and enjoying himself. The heat didn't bother him, he said; he was used to all kinds of weather. When he wasn't at powwows, he worked for the phone company, line maintenance.

"How do you like these?" he asked me, pointing at the T-shirt selection. "Homeland Security" said one with a group of armed Indians. Or the one he was wearing, "Fighting Terrorism Since 1492." Kind of radical on such a cloudless, summer day.

We visited a few more booths, where everyone seemed to know Louis, and some of them got into intense conversations about rights this and rights that. He just said, "This is Renee," but no one had anything to say to me. It was OK, and after a while, I asked, "How long does this go for? Think you could drop me off back at the bus station?"

He gave me a quick glance, twitching his lips.

I started fanning myself. "No. Really, thanks for bringing me. I'm glad I got to see it. I'm getting kind of overheated here – too much sun. White girl, you know?"

It was meant to be a joke, but Louis's forehead wrinkled in concern. "Yeah, I can see that. You should have worn a hat. Here, have a drink." He pulled out a water bottle from his string bag, and handed it to me. Just for a moment, I wondered if it might be more than water and whether or not I even wanted that. Which I always wanted, always, and didn't really care, sobriety or not. I sucked it down – cool, wet, and nothing but pure water.

"OK, let's go," I said, handing back the bottle.

But Louis was looking me over in a certain way. I knew there was some interest, attraction, but something else, too. He knew I had an addiction problem, since he'd met me coming out of an AA meeting. But I wasn't sure what that meant to him.

"There's someone I want to say hi to before we leave," he said. "Actually, two guys; elders – they're twins. They're dancing soon, but we can catch them."

I considered. "Hm...two old guys, twins. Identical?"

"Yup."

"And they're still dancing?"

"Like teenagers."

"Could be interesting. Let's go."

I had seen the men earlier in their full and elaborate regalia – it was hard to miss them. And just alike. As we got closer, I had to shake my head; these guys were really into it: leggings, breast shields, feathers, shell earrings. In fact, take away the glasses, they could have walked out of the past, even long hair in thinning ponytails. Senior citizens, with dark, narrow eyes and smooth brown skin with few creases. Still good-looking, handsome.

Louis greeted them, one after the other, with that one-arm hug they like to give.

"Good day for powwow," Louis said. "How are you doing?"

"Fine," said one.

"Elbow's a little creaky," said the other. "I played nine holes of golf before we came this morning."

Honest to God, I had to cover my mouth, not knowing what would come out. Imagine!

Louis introduced us, and they were all smiles, the two brothers: Falcon and Spirit Warrior.

"Red and yellow," Falcon said to me. "That's how you can tell us apart;" He lifted the red medicine bag off his chest. "Except when we want to fool people, we change them. If we're not side by side, no one can tell. Not even our mother."

"God rest her soul," said Spirit Warrior, with the yellow bag.

"You're dancing, right?" Louis asked.

"You bet," they said together.

"It must get hot," I said. "With all that stuff you're wearing – the regalia."

"Yeah," said Spirit Warrior. "It's a good sweat."

"Good if you don't pass out or get a nose bleed," said his brother.

"That's only happened once."

I could see the detailing on their vests. "Who made those for you?"

"Made them ourselves," Spirit Warrior said.

"They're really nice; fancy."

"Yeah, our mother got us started, long time ago. Made us do it; she thought sewing and beading would keep us boys out of trouble."

"Did it?"

"Some of the time." Falcon shook his head. "Then we went off the wrong way for a while, quite a while – drinking, fighting, up to no good, all that kind of stuff."

My breathing got faster; I glanced at Louis, wondering – was this a setup? But the identical faces were easy, not self-conscious at all.

"Not being responsible," chimed in Spirit Warrior.

"Took a toll on our health," said Falcon.

"And on our family."

They stood silent, reflective, nodding at me or at the past.

"So what happened?" I had to ask.

"Well, I'll tell you," Falcon said. "We got back on the Red Road, both of us, at the same time. Our mother came to him, Spirit Warrior there, in a dream and said we should go back to the old ways, the traditional ways – as much as we could. She said our spirits had gotten lost. So we did, at least, what we could. Our kids thought we were crazy, at first, but I think they can see now that it's better."

"Yup."

All this time Louis had been quiet. Still, I had a sense what he was doing, pushing me this way.

"So what makes it better than anything else – church or AA or whatever?"

Falcon smiled, shrugging. "Couldn't say. Nothing else worked for us, that's all. That's why we're here today, wearing all this fancy stuff and getting ready to dance."

A voice on the PA system had called for the next dancers, and Falcon and Spirit Warrior nodded farewell, joining the other men entering the circle.

"Still want to leave?" Louis asked me.

"No," I said. "I want to see this."

The drum began, and the dancers danced, mostly older, mature men. Some were slow and shuffling, others more rhythmic. But Falcon and Spirit Warrior were like boys, full of life and fun and energy. It was so clear how the music was moving them, each arm and leg. It was strange to see, someone older like that, so loose and free, and strong too. In bodies that were once beat up and neglected, like mine was. But they were beyond all that stuff now, I could see it. I could see health and happiness. I saw peace. I saw joy. I saw all those things that always seemed so far away in my life, until I wondered if they really existed at all.

After that, Louis drove me past Dunkin' Donuts, all the way to the halfway house. By then I was sleepy and sunburned, ready for a cold shower. I didn't invite him inside, but he could see what it was. He didn't kiss me or anything, but I knew he liked me, and I wasn't sure how I felt about that.

"Well," I said. "Now I've been to a powwow."

"Want to go again?"

I considered. "I don't know. I liked it, but it's not like I really belong there, or anything."

"Everyone's welcome."

"Hmph."

"Anyway, there's one in New Hampshire in a couple weeks. I'll be back at the drum by then. It's up near my folks' place, so I'm planning to stop by there."

He wrote down his number on the back of the powwow program. "Call me if you want to go."

"OK. I'll let you know."

Renee's journal – 5

Two weeks later, I was ready to go – to powwow or New Hampshire or anywhere away from my current place. I was struggling again, God knows why. As much as I liked the powwow, it bothered me too. Or, at least it got something going inside of me, the old battle of good Renee and bad Renee. There was nothing terrible that happened; no big issues or conflicts. Things were going OK – my little job, no real distractions. Things were quiet at the halfway house. Jessica had gone home, and Mickey disappeared. But the closer I got to good Renee, the more I knew I'd soon be running the opposite direction.

Louis picked me up in his truck, the bed loaded with folding tables, plastic bins, and display cases. We drove almost three hours out to western Mass. to stop by his folks' house. That's where Malvina lived too, and Noel. And Izzy, the younger brother, who was only ten at the time.

I knew we were going to a former military base, the cookie-cutter houses lined up in rows. Not that there's anything wrong with that. Louis had explained to me that Native families from a number of tribes had gravitated to the area for jobs, moving into the inexpensive homes. Gradually they had taken over the old officers' quarters for a community center and formed an intertribal association, a place to gather and keep up parts of their culture. There was even a chief, or a guy they called Chief, although not the chief of any nation, just their little group.

As soon as we pulled up to a white, one-story duplex, a little brown face popped out the front door, and then disappeared back inside. In another moment, as we were getting out of the truck, the child reappeared, making a beeline for Louis: skinny as a rail in oversized shorts, a tank shirt and moccasins, a purple and pink shawl draped across the shoulders. Long hair in back and bangs in front. All eyes and ears, a sweet smile.

"Izzy," said Louis, pulling the child in for a hug that was warm and fierce. It was that moment I knew I wanted something from Louis. I wanted that hug too.

"Can I come? Can I come?" asked Izzy. "Neesa wants me to stay home."

"What's up, little man?" A boy, then. Until that moment it was unclear to me.

"Amos, he's back on the oxygen. And Neesa says I'm still sick, but I'm not."

"We'll see," said Louis, tucking Izzy's head into the crook of his arm like a ball. "Let's go inside. This is Renee."

Izzy's gaze turned to me, taking his time. Then he stepped away from Louis, spinning so that the shawl flared out around him.

"Do you like this shawl? It was my mom's."

I paused before speaking. "Those colors look good on you."

He smiled before turning to Louis. "Maybe she could watch me at powwow. I can take her around while you sing at the drum."

You might have thought he was working the charm, but not in someone so young. I felt my heart clench – that he liked me, in that moment, when I was nervous, a bit shaky, skinny and pale. Very pale.

We went through the front hall into the kitchen, which was not occupied. Izzy pushed through the screen door to the back deck, where two people sat at a table spread with grass and reeds in piles. Neesa, the mother, was short, plump, and middle-aged with cropped hair, still black, and glasses. She was weaving a basket, nearly done, very intricate with stripes and geometrical patterns. Careful, clever, creative, like my mother had been, good with her fingers, making something beautiful from next to nothing. A kind of magical power.

Across the table, hooked up to an oxygen tank, was an older man, Louis's father, and Izzy's. His eyes were closed, his face to the sun, until he heard us and opened them. Green eyes.

"This is Renee," Louis said. "She's going to powwow with me."

"Hello, nice to meet you," I said, thinking that was the polite thing.

"Good day," said Amos, wheezy. A small smile creased his face, which was framed with a grizzle of hair. He was tall and skinny, like Izzy grew to be, but with a small, round stomach resting on his thighs. "Good day for powwow." That was the only time I ever saw him. He died soon after that, lung cancer, not quite seventy. He was a good twenty years older than Neesa, the only marriage for both.

Neesa didn't part her lips. She looked up from her work, staring at me, holding my gaze until her face darkened.

She hissed something, in a language I didn't understand.

Louis shook his head, but still she scowled, continuing to look at me. She did not like what she saw. I don't know if Louis had said anything about me, about my problems and my living situation. Either way, she saw something bad; something she didn't want around Louis – or Izzy, either.

And then she went back to that beautiful basket; and something pierced my heart. She could create something like that. And she recognized the poison in me that even clean hair and a pretty smile couldn't hide.

"Have you priced any baskets?" Louis asked his mother.

Neesa gave a quick shake to her head – whether she did or not; she wasn't sending them with us.

"Can I go?" Izzy asked again.

Louis looked at his mother, waiting for an answer.

Again, she shook her head.

"But..." said Izzy. "She can take care of me." He pointed at me. "And I can take care of her too." He came closer to his mother's side. "She could get lost; you know, like a lost cat."

Strangely, his mother did not snap back, but looked steadily at Izzy.

Finally she spoke. "No." But it was gentle.

We left after Louis loaded more things into the truck. Izzy came out with us, carrying a little orange cat against his chest, a kitten. Izzy was a beautiful boy, with high cheekbones and dark, expressive eyebrows.

"Do you want to hold him?" he asked. I took the cat, soft and practically boneless, nipping with sharp little teeth.

"I'm not sure he likes me," I said.

"Yes, he does," Izzy said. "He's playing with you; he thinks you're just a big cat."

"I see," I said, giving the cat back.

"Next time," he said, "we'll go together." He sounded so confident. "And I'll play the flute for you. I'm teaching myself."

"We'll see." I don't like to make false promises.

"No," Izzy protested. "You have to come back, so you can hear a song I'm making for you."

"For me?"

"Yes, I can already hear it in my head."

Just then Neesa came to the door, motioning Izzy back inside. She didn't look at me, even when Izzy turned to say, "Then you can see my regalia." An expression came over Neesa's face that I later learned to recognize – her lifelong struggle with this strange last child who was so loved, and so unknowable to her.

Right after that powwow, I returned to addiction, probably the worst time since I'd left home. It was Neesa who drove me to it; that truth in her eyes. And it was Izzy who danced ahead of me in the light, as I sank into the dark, with his shawl and his flute and a way of seeing me with his heart.

Chapter 7

Helene arrived at the base on Monday in the midafternoon, her car packed with clothing, books, her laptop, and groceries she'd picked up at the store. Noel had given her a key to the house on Saturday, when Kenneth had come up with her, taking precious time off on the weekend. He had softened somewhat after hearing the story of the child at the ice cream stand and how she had rendered aid. It was his nature to be helpful. He was just worried about Helene herself, he explained, her sensitivity, and the idea of being taken advantage of. The turning point was when Emily Gardner, mother of the child who was stung, called the house to thank Helene again and report that Olivia was doing well and they'd gotten the EpiPen. Helene had been at the library, but Kenneth got the whole story firsthand, and heaping praise for Helene. After that he relented, saying only, "Let's just be clear on the when, the where, and the why. Short term only; a month at the most. Home on weekends. And we'll make some plans to get away later this summer, just me and you."

Helene was glad Kenneth was more open to the idea and appreciated his decision to make the trip and see for himself. But to herself she said, "I won't know the end date until they finish the testing; it may take a while." Now was not the time to say it. And, for reasons she didn't understand, she had not mentioned Denis's visit at all. As for vacation, that was chancy at best. Always, something turned up at Kenneth's work. It was like that, she supposed, when you ran your own real estate agency, and got involved with development projects. Instead of a fish, it was "the house that got away." The default was a few days here and there at his sister's lake house.

On Saturday, when they'd arrived in the afternoon, it was Noel who met them at the door, ready to play host. He was wearing a leather apron, tool belt, and goggles on his head, in the middle of some home project. As before, he had a relaxed, almost jovial manner. He brought them into the kitchen, where Malvina was sitting at the table. Noel brought over the coffee pot and sliced blueberry bread.

"Malvina's got to take it easy," he explained. "Doctor's orders."

Noel had written up a paper that he slid in front of Helene. "All you need to know. House phone, trash pickup, post office. Electricity's on, and phone. There's a room air conditioner if you need it, and I got out the fans."

"Thank you."

Then he put down a second paper, in a marigold color, that said "Intertribal Community of Western Mass." News on top, a calendar or schedule.

Helene picked it up to look at.

"What we're doing at the Intertribal Center," Noel said. "You know, workshops, ceremonies, and socializing. There's usually some food. You're welcome anytime or we can take the twins with us." He flipped the paper over. "It's just down the street." He pointed at a little map, four blocks down and one block over. "You can't miss it."

She took it, nodding silently.

As Helene turned to Malvina with more questions about the twins and the house, Kenneth asked Noel about his projects. Noel was back on his feet quickly for a big guy. "Come on, I'll show you."

The project was a covered porch for Renee and Louis's house, where Helene would be staying – something Louis had started but not had a chance to finish. Helene had barely noticed; apparently it was almost done.

On the car ride home, Kenneth said, "Noel does excellent work. That was solid workmanship. And the whole home is in pretty good shape." He had expected something run down, which some of the places around the base were. He seemed reassured by Noel, at least, and found him a reasonable person that he could talk to; they spoke "the same language," which was square feet and load-bearing walls.

Kenneth merged into the passing lane. "I asked him how Louis had ended up in so much trouble. It's quite a story, this water rights business, some river up in Maine. They were building a dam for hydroelectric power, but it would interfere with the flow of the river and the spawning of the fish. Some of these young Indians, hotheads, used dynamite to blow up the foundation. They didn't know there was a guard on duty until they checked the rubble, and then they ran. I guess they called Louis, asking for help. He said he'd drive them across the border to Canada, and that's when they got caught. It was Louis's gun in the truck, actually, his father's hunting rifle. They're all in prison now."

Helene nodded. She had wondered about the details of Louis's situation, but didn't really want to ask. Or know who to ask. And now Kenneth had gotten the story himself, man to man, so to speak. He had formed his own impression: Noel was friendly and capable; Malvina, quiet but on top of the medical questions; and the kids all lively and good-natured, occasionally loud. Only Wishi-ta had been reserved, playing with Polly Pocket dolls on the porch with a friend. Kenneth commented later that she appeared very sweet and well behaved, with such pretty hair.

"How does that work?" he asked Helene, driving away from the slanting sun as lights began to come on. "She looks out of place, like some Scandinavian princess."

Helene shrugged. "Louis has some European in him and so did Renee – I guess it's just genes."

"I don't know," Kenneth mused, tapping the steering wheel. "Those twins don't look at all alike. Not even the same size. Are you sure they have the same father? Maybe there was someone else before Louis?"

Helene bristled, staring out at the passing tree line. With all Renee's faults, she was not promiscuous; she'd been fussy that way. "No, they're twins," she said flatly. "Same father. That's how it turns out sometimes."

At home, Kenneth walked into the kitchen and flipped over the months of the wall calendar. "Mid-July should do it; if it lasts that long. Give you some time before you go back to school. It's not fair to ask you to give up your summer. Or," he added with a wink, "fourth of July at the lake."

Then he was on the phone for an open house the next day. After that, the developer called with news on the proposed town houses, a problem with siting, so all plans were put on hold. There was, however, a new idea under consideration, that Kenneth might need Helene's help with, but not yet. But since meeting Noel, and seeing his sturdy construction methods, he had no more real arguments about helping out at the base.

On Monday, Helene had expected to spend time setting up in Renee's house, maybe taking a walk around the neighborhood, and then visiting with Wishi-ta and the others, just to get herself more familiar. Already she could see that Wishi-ta was the more elusive of the twins, a bit of a ghostly presence at times, hanging in the background, like Misty, the cat.

When she knocked, Neesa opened the door, to Helene's surprise.

"She sick. Lie down," Neesa explained. Helene followed her into the kitchen, then into the bedroom, which was stocked full of baskets, dolls, fans, and clothes along each wall. On a double bed, Malvina was sitting up, doing needlework.

"I'm not sick," Malvina said, carefully putting her work away. "It's the swelling from blood pressure. The doctor said bed rest for now."

"Oh, dear," said Helene, sympathetically. "That's a challenge."

Malvina cocked her head. "It's OK. Except no driving. But everything is close by. Store. Playground. Intertribal Center. Just appointments."

"Well…I have a car, if you need something," Helene said, but Malvina just shrugged. "I'm getting set up next door. And I thought afterward the twins can come over; I got a few things – games and puzzles. And a couple dolls." She'd noticed a handful of Barbie dolls scattered around the house.

Malvina called out to her mother in that other language they spoke, and Neesa appeared in the bedroom. Then she called for Izzy, who likewise appeared, giving Helene a cheerful tip of his head. As before, his shiny hair was long and loose, and he wore both a pendant and earrings of silver and bone, or maybe even animal teeth. Other than that, he was dressed in skinny jeans with a zip-up sweatshirt. He carried a large clamshell and a bag of plant material, what looked to Helene like herbs or weeds, something perhaps to help Malvina.

But no, it was not for his sister.

"Izzy, call the kids," Malvina said. He loped down the hall to shout out the back door. Helene could hear upraised voices, and then a shrill whistle, human. They had to come, whether they wanted or not. Soon after, footsteps and voices sounded in the kitchen, and Izzy reappeared with children in tow, Kiowa, the two boys, and the twins. Plus Neesa.

"Go to the house and smudge," said Malvina. "The whole house, and yourselves, too."

"Can I light the sweetgrass?" the older boy – Pawnee – asked. "I'm good with matches. The lighter never works."

Malvina barely nodded, but it was settled, and they all turned to leave, except Malvina.

"Should I go?" Helene asked. "Are they going to light a fire inside the house?"

Malvina gestured her out of the room. "Izzy will tell you."

They trooped together from Malvina's house to the front steps of Renee and Louis's house, waiting for Helene to unlock the door. Inside, they went directly into the living room, standing in a circle, fidgety with expectation. Neesa stayed silent, standing next to Kiowa, who was almost the same height, and Helene was struck by the resemblance. They looked for a moment like twins themselves, only one old and one young.

"I have to explain to Helene," Izzy said, placing the clamshell on the coffee table. It was seven or eight inches across, shiny and iridescent inside and pierced with a few holes.

"I got this at powwow," he said, holding out the plastic bag. "Sweetgrass. You can keep it here, and the clamshell, too. Use it whenever you need to. I mean, when it could help you with cleansing and good energy. It helps take away bad thoughts and feelings; like cleaning, except with smoke."

Helene nodded. "I guess so. But could we do it outside? I don't know if I want the place full of smoke," and then, without thinking, "It might be bad for Wishi-ta – you know, her asthma?"

"No!" Wishi-ta protested, indignant, taking Helene aback. "It's good for me." So much like Renee.

Izzy stood thoughtfully. Neesa was staring at her; but Helene could never tell her thoughts. The kids seemed to hear but not pay much mind. This was just a thing they did; how could it be dangerous?

"You know," Izzy said, "we've never had that problem with Wishi. But I see what you mean. No, we want to smudge the house itself. You know – like a fresh start, or a blessing. But we can open the windows and doors." He stopped, examining Helene's face. "The house has its own spirit. The smoke can take away some of the pain, and the sadness from before. From when we lost Renee; when she was sick and when she died."

There was a stir in the air, but silent. The children were listening; they understood what he meant. Neesa went to open the windows in the room.

Slowly, Helene nodded. "Well, all right, then."

"It smells nice," Pawnee said, helpfully. "Sweetgrass."

"Sweetgrass, sweetgrass," echoed the twins.

Helene had to smile. "Then sweetgrass it is."

Izzy took a book of matches from his pants pocket and handed it to Pawnee. Good as his word, the boy got the plant material in the shell to catch fire after a couple strikes. Then, carefully, he blew on the tiny flame, until it began to produce smoke, both sweet and acrid. *Ah!* That smell she remembered, from the first time entering Malvina's house.

Once the embers were glowing, Pawnee used his hand to fan the smoke around himself.

"Like this," he said. He waved up and down, around his back and even under his feet, stepping out of his sandals. He closed his eyes, inhaling, and then handed the shell to Neesa, who repeated his motions, taking more time and blowing again to revive the faltering smoke. One by one, the children smudged themselves, casually but thoroughly, whispering a few words among themselves. Izzy got the clamshell back, and poked at the flame.

"It's still good," he said, taking his turn and then handing the clamshell to Helene.

"Me, too?" She began the fanning with a little giggle. "I suppose I could use some good thoughts and energy. Let go of all that stress from the school year."

Izzy nodded solemnly. "And the pain you hold inside. The smoke will take that too."

Helene looked down at her feet. Why would he say that? It was a bit presumptuous, hardly knowing her at all. Then she wondered, again, how much they knew about her from Renee, the years she had lived here with them. Izzy might have learned things from the months that he had sat with Renee in this same room as she was failing.

The flame had taken again, and the smoke was thin but steady. "Good," Izzy said. "Now follow me. I'm going to use a feather to spread the smoke." He turned to Neesa and the kids. "You can go now." But the twins wanted to stay and play with the animals on their old bed.

Just Izzy and Helene went from room to room, fanning the smoke into the corners, up to the ceiling, and even in the closets, where clothes were stored. A detour to the back porch which was almost complete, Noel's handiwork. In the kitchen, Izzy opened cabinets and shelves, chatting all the time about a column he wrote for an online magazine, and certain ideas he was trying to share about modern Indian life – like how they wore jeans and went to McDonald's, that kind of thing.

"Louis told me to do it, actually. He said I should be useful to our people, besides playing my flute." A bashful smile spread across his face.

"I'm not out there, like him. But I like to write. About other things too, like video games, or music or movies. I wrote a review about Star Trek for the school newspaper."

"Good for you," Helene said, leaning against the kitchen counter. "That's quite ambitious. How often does your column appear?"

"Supposed to be once a month, but sometimes I miss. And when we're in Maine, the Wi-Fi is pretty spotty." He turned to her, his eyes bright. "So, check it out at Nativenewsandaction.com. You might like it."

Helene tried to keep back a smile. "I will. I'm sure it's very interesting."

They returned to the living room, where Izzy snuffed out the embers in the shell. He handed the shell plus the bag of sweetgrass and the book of matches to Helene.

"I'm not sure I'll use them," she said. "I mean, it's fine, but it's not something I'm accustomed to doing."

"No problem. But they should stay here at the house, anyway. You know, for when Louis gets back."

"Oh, right." *When?* That was optimistic.

Izzy left, taking the twins with him, and Helene was on her own, the aromatic scent hanging in the air, not unpleasant. She unpacked the car and the cooler, putting groceries away in the pantry and refrigerator, leaving out fixings for a quick sandwich. She had decided to sleep in the twins' room for the time being, until she could set up the air mattress in the den. The closet of the twins' room was crowded with linens and winter clothes, old toys and decorations. The only real closet space available was the in the front hall, with a few jackets left hanging. Clearly one was for a woman, a petite-sized winter coat, in a bright red – her sister's. The leather jacket must belong to Louis. Helene closed the door quickly, shutting out the personal smells and the images.

She wanted to organize a work space in the living room, which was the largest room and had the best light. She took out textbooks and workbooks, pencils and office supplies, putting them on the repaired shelves. Izzy had said that he would come back later to help set up an Internet connection, so she left her laptop, mouse, and keyboard on the crafts table, which would do for a desk with a chair.

By midafternoon she was ready for a break and wandered to the back porch, cool and shaded, enclosed with screens to keep out the bugs. It was quiet, no kids out playing. She stretched, yawning – catching up, really, from the busy school year and all these new developments. She sat in a canvas folding chair, leaning back, closing her eyes. First came the sound of children's voices and dogs barking. Then it turned night, and dozens of cats and dogs were running in the yard, agitated, alarmed. In the bushes, in a dark corner, two glowing eyes looked out at her – yellow-gold, like a wolf. And then, it grew into a human figure, a man. *Louis!* She startled awake in daylight, hearing only the buzzing of insects outside the screen. Such a strange dream, she thought, before slipping back into a half-dozing state, her arms and legs too heavy to move. It was almost five o'clock when she heard a noise at the door, and a voice calling her name: *Izzy*.

"Coming," she said, scrambling to her feet. "Be right there."

In the living room, Izzy was looking over her laptop with interest. "So, you ready to get this going?" he asked.

"That would be great, Izzy," she said, covering a yawn. "I hate to say it, but I'm so dependent on that thing for my news and e-mail, and all my little business things."

"Oh, yeah," Izzy agreed. "Me, too. I can spend way too much time online, for the dumbest things, but I always fall for it. On the other hand, I've learned a lot, and I'm basically the IT guy around here."

"For the family, you mean?"

"The family, other folks at the base, over to the intertribal office. I'm the one who got the website set up."

"Those are good skills to have."

"I guess so. Anyway, let's see what we have here."

It didn't take him long to type in some passwords and get a connection to the Wi-Fi that was set up in the house. "Renee was pretty good too," he commented, "great at researching stuff. Not Louis, though. Too impatient. When he wanted a PowerPoint presentation or something, he always came to me. I guess he didn't use computers much at college. And then he started law school, you know, but he didn't finish."

"So he never took the bar?"

Izzy looked across the table at her. "He probably could have passed it – he's that smart. He knows all that stuff, but he just wouldn't take it, on principle."

"On principle?"

"He says the Constitution has been no help to us – I mean, Indians. The 'rule of law' is interpreted however those in power want it to be – mostly not in our favor. That's his conclusion."

"I see." That did say quite a lot about Louis, she thought. "Many thanks, Izzy, for your help. Can I get you a lemonade, some cookies?"

"Sure."

Izzy sat down at the kitchen table, surveying the new furnishings: a coffee pot, a juicer, and Panini maker. Cute towels and cutting board.

"Like to cook?" he asked.

"Well enough, I suppose," Helene said, smiling. "The basics. My husband pretty much likes the traditional foods." Then she stopped herself. "I mean, meat and potatoes, veggie and salad."

"We're going to the Intertribal Center for spaghetti supper," Izzy said. "Do you want to go? Five dollars a person, and it's not bad, if they don't overcook the pasta."

Helene had driven by the Intertribal Center, the two-story brick and concrete structure that Noel had told her about. It looked like an Elks building, or an oversized gym. The grass out front was worn, but there was a welcoming sign and colorful flags by the entrance, the American flag, and others she didn't recognize.

"I don't think so. I have soup and a sandwich here. But thanks, anyway."

"Sure thing. Or just come for ice cream. Maybe around six, before they start the movie."

That perked her interest. "What are they showing?"

Izzy lifted his shoulders. "Something Indian, maybe, or an action film, or something for kids."

He got to his feet, stretching.

"Thanks again, Izzy," she said. "For getting me set up here, on the computer."

"No problem. My pleasure. And don't forget, check out my column – online – One Little Indian – that's me. Just Google it."

"Oh, I will. For sure."

After he left, Helene found a piece of scrap paper and wrote down "One Little Indian," Isidore Lopes, at www.nativenewsandaction.com. She was curious just what kind of writer Izzy was. And, who knew, maybe she'd learn something.

1. This Land Is Our Land – by One Little Indian

Coming at you from the great state of Mass-a-chu-setts. An Indian name, naturally. And a commonwealth, actually. They say (whoever "they" are) some ideas in the U.S. Constitution came out of the Massachusetts constitution, which borrowed from the Iroquois Confederacy to the west, which already had the notion of democracy. Well, that's for the historians to fight over. Me, I'm just an observer.

In actual fact, my brother, Louis, put me up to this – writing a column for the online journal, Native News and Action for the enlightenment of cyber readers – Red and not. Big Bro' has always been a mover and a shaker, out in the world doing things, while I've been more of a homey. So, as Louis is currently tied up in matters beyond his control, he told me, "Do something useful, Indian. Turn off the damn video game and write about your views and experiences – what's going on now, in today's world." He gave me a whole list of suggestions, in case I got stuck. No excuses. He also reminded me, "You're just one little Indian – not spokesman for all nations." And, "Check your sources. No bullshit."

No Native casinos, though. You'll learn nothing here from me. I've never been inside one. There's already so much written out there by others far more informed than me. Some places it's a hot button issue: those who think casinos bring nothing but debt and debauchery. And those who think they've succeeded only too well. My take.

By way of introduction, call me Izzy. I'm a Pemaquot out of Maine on one side and Wampanoag on the other; plus a smattering of this and that, some French back there. Family story is that my father's gr-gr-something was a Portuguese sailor on a whaling ship, settled down on Cape Cod and married a Wampanoag. Could be true. I'm a flute player, video-gamer, huge fan of sci-fi and fantasy, biker (pedal type), part-time student at the C.C., and employee of the local Costco – which is a blessing upon my people – that is, my mother and large extended family. Riding single in the saddle (this from someone who's never been on a horse). And no kids, either.

Every couple weeks or so, I'll be sending up the occasional smoke signal to you all, what's happening here and there, now and then, in Our Land – not "My," not "Your." Our. All due respect to the dude who wrote that song, but I don't know that he had Indians in mind. The thing about *Our* is that it applies to pretty much everybody who lives here on this land. We all have a say, right, not just the folks with the most or biggest deeds. So tune in for more, as I figure out what I'm going to write next. Now, off to play flute and then it's time to stock the shelves.

Chapter 8

The next morning, Helene was ready by eight fifteen to pick up Wishi-ta
for her first set of allergy tests at the regional medical center. She had slept
surprisingly well among the twins' menagerie of stuffed animals, but
closed the door on Red Cat. Her dreams were vivid, kaleidoscopic images
of cats and beads and smoke, the clock on the kitchen wall, and children's
voices at play, calling out to her – *Helene! Helene!* The water took a while
to heat in the shower, and she found only one bath towel in the closet,
wondering where the others had gone.

Her purse was on the kitchen table, and the folder with the
appointment information. She heard voices outside, and then a knock on
the door.

"We're here." A girl's voice.

"Coming."

In the front hall stood Kiowa with two booster seats for the car, and
the twins with a backpack each.

Helene looked at them, perplexed. "But the appointment is for Wishi-
ta only," she said. "We're not going anywhere except the doctor's office."

"She won't go without Tana-na and me," Kiowa said, "And I'll make
sure they listen."

"Oh." Helene had not expected an expedition and she didn't want to
mind three children while trying to focus on the doctor's words. She could
understand that Malvina was not up to going, and was glad that Neesa was
not there.

"Where's Izzy?"

"Gone to work."

"And your dad, too, I suppose." That elicited a doubtful look from
Kiowa. Maybe it was her tone.

Helene glanced away, not wanting to meet Kiowa's eyes. Was Helene
just being used for babysitting purposes, with Malvina's pregnancy issues,
and so forth? But she couldn't see herself trooping them all back to the
other house and making a scene about it, either. Plus the two other boys
were still at home. And Kiowa seemed a sensible girl.

"All right," she said with a sigh. "Let's go."

At the doctor's office, Helene went to the front desk to check in,
where the receptionist asked for a twenty-dollar co-pay. She made sure to
get a receipt. It made her wonder how the twins' expenses got paid – by
Malvina and Noel? Or had Louis left money in an account? Helene turned
in the already completed form to become Wishi-ta's health-care proxy.
There were several children and parents in the waiting room ahead of them,

none there too long before others came and took their place.

When Wishi-ta was called for the tests, all three children rose, ready to go in. For a few moments, Helene stood in the waiting room speaking in a low, firm voice: only she and Wishi-ta were going into the examination room. Wishi-ta would not budge, hanging on to Tana-na's shirt and trying to stay behind Kiowa. With mounting agitation, Helene realized that she could not get Wishi-ta to come without bodily removing her, making a scene. And maybe trigger an asthma attack. She felt a prickling along her neck, frustration and annoyance. She was a school nurse, after all, and was used to getting children to acquiesce to things that were sometimes uncomfortable. Yet, she couldn't help but see how they stuck together, these three, in support of Wishi-ta.

A nurse came out to entice Wishi-ta to go with her, without success. Finally, the doctor himself appeared, Dr. Wang, short and trim in his white coat, with tufted gray hair. Behind the glasses, his eyes were smiling; this was nothing new to him. The twins in turn were keenly interested in the doctor, exchanging a whispered few words.

"Come one, come all," Dr. Wang said, waving them inside, and so they filed into the small room after him. On the examining table, holding Kiowa's hand with Tana-na in sight, Wishi-ta didn't make a sound as the doctor pricked the skin of her back over and over, even when her eyes were wet with tears. Helene was impressed at her quiet fortitude.

After the tests, they returned to the waiting room until the preliminary results were available, Wishi-ta with her shirt back on. Helene took a seat next to Kiowa, who had taken out juice boxes, one for each of them, including Helene, who declined. The twins were occupied with a train set, while Kiowa sat quietly, sipping her juice and twisting a band on her wrist imprinted, "Water Rights are Human Rights." Helene picked up a housekeeping magazine, dog-eared and out of date.

"So, Kiowa," Helene said, putting the magazine down. "What do you do during summer vacation? Any special plans?"

There was a long pause before Kiowa spoke, sparing with words, like her mother. "I play in the summer basketball league."

"That sounds like fun. And, what else? I'm really very interested – so I can learn what goes on around here."

Prompted, Kiowa was too polite not to reply. "And I take care of the kids, especially since Mom has to stay in bed." Another sip. "We go to powwows, at least the ones around here. I'm working on my jingle dress. One of the ladies is helping me. Neesa says I can make baskets with her."

"That's plenty to keep you busy. Probably no vacation this year, though, because of the baby?"

Kiowa gave her an odd expression. "We don't really go on vacations. We're going to Maine, to the Home Camp. But that's not vacation, because we live there too, besides here."

"Oh, really? You have a house there?"

"Kind of. Neesa's house, and her family's. Sometimes we go the whole summer. We stay up there with Neesa, and the others come and go."

Helene had that sensation that there was a lot more going on than she knew, that wasn't made clear to her, although it was important.

"What about the baby?"

"We'll go after the baby is born, for the naming ceremony. And then we'll stay until school starts. I can't wait," Kiowa said, her face lighting up. "It's great there; well, except for the bugs. But we see all our cousins, and swim and canoe, play games and sing, and have all these big feasts."

In Helene's mind, an alarm went off but she maintained a calm expression. "But Wishi-ta won't be able to go," she said, evenly. "Or least, she can't stay. She's got to finish the tests, and then get some shots, if she needs them. And someone has to be here to take her."

Kiowa shrugged. "You'll have to ask my mom. But Wishi-ta will come for the naming ceremony, anyway." And then, with an encouraging look. "You can come too."

Helene's first thought was, *That was not part of the plan. That is certainly not part of the deal.* But she couldn't yet decide what she would do about it.

It was time for results, at least from the first set of tests.

"The doctor is ready for you."

Again, they all marched in, Kiowa and Tana-na standing along the wall, out of the way. Wishi-ta hopped back onto the examining table.

Dr. Wang stood between Wishi-ta and the wall, consulting a chart and then fingering one and then another of the bumps on Wishi-ta's back. Out of the fifteen, it looked like six or seven had reacted.

"The usual suspects," said Dr. Wang. "Mold, mites, dust, and dander. Wasps and bees. We've only looked at a few of plant allergens, but pine pollen could be a problem."

He sighed, looking at Wishi-ta. "Those are a few of the things that bother you, young lady. But there's a good chance you could outgrow some of them."

And then, to Helene, "We haven't looked at the food allergens yet. They tend to be the real troublemakers, producing the extreme reactions. So we'll have to set that up, and meanwhile I'm going to ask you to keep this food record." He handed a folder to Helene, who wondered how she would keep track of those meals she was not there to see.

"Here's a list of things you can do to make the environment a little easier on Wishi-ta..." Another list of things to do, clean, replace, get rid of. Away from animals. It was already looking tricky to make all these changes in a crowded house with a lot of people coming and going, not to mention pets. Helene had another thought – which she kept to herself, mulling it over.

"Thank you, Dr. Wang," she said, signaling to the children it was time to leave. Helene had to admit things hadn't gone badly at the appointment, after the bumpy start. In fact, very well.

"Good job, you guys," she said when they got to the car. She put a hand on Wishi-ta's thin shoulder before opening the door. "We should call you 'Wishi-ta, the Brave'," she said, recalling Malvina's words. It was meant as a bit of a joke as well as a compliment, but Wishi-ta swelled with pride, and Helene felt an unexpected pang of tenderness. There was now a clear path to help Wishi-ta with her condition. But the only way Helene was going to carry through Doctor Wang's orders was if Wishi-ta lived in Renee's house, with her, or someone. And if Wishi-ta, then Tana-na…

Suddenly, Helene, like Renee, had not one child to deal with, but twins. It had to be. There was no other way.

"Here we are," she said, as they pulled into the house on the base. "Now I have to talk to Malvina and Noel about a few things, so we can make a plan." She had turned to address the twins in the back seat. "Looks like we're going to have a sleepover." That only created more confusion. "What I mean is, you two are coming to stay back in your old house for a while. Doctor's orders. OK?"

Their eyes opened wide, but no one spoke, just nodding in silence.

In fact, it wasn't so bad making the changes for Wishi-ta's health. Within a day, Helene had cleared out the rugs and old linens in Renee's house, replacing them with new "hypoallergenic" versions, and done a thorough cleaning and dusting with the approved products. Noel came over with an industrial vacuum to clean vents and even used it on the furniture upholstery. He and Izzy found wooden-frame chairs to replace the two worn ones in the living room and den, to be fitted with hypoallergenic cushions. Out with the Southwestern blankets, at least for now. The hardest part was telling the twins that their stuffed animals had to be stored while Wishi-ta was having problems. And sadly or not, Red Cat had to be relocated to Neesa and Izzy's part of the duplex; out of his age-old territory, nothing left to defend.

Helene had gone next door to meet with Malvina, Neesa, and Izzy about the food issues. Malvina said she would keep track, turning to explain things to her mother. Apparently, Neesa was the cook during Malvina's convalesce. They called Kiowa into the kitchen, also explaining to her about keeping track of any food or snacks that Wishi-ta had eaten and showing her the chart, which she would bring each night to Helene. Mainly the twins would continue to eat lunch and dinner at Malvina's, but sleep, bathe, and breakfast at the house where Helene was staying. On the weekends when Helene was gone, Neesa would take her place.

By Tuesday evening, preparations were complete.

The twins came over in the evening, already in sleepwear – oversized

T-shirts — teeth brushed, stories read. All ready for bed. Kiowa had come too, planning to spend the first night with them. After saying good-night, they went off to the bedroom without a murmur, although she could hear whispering from time to time.

Helene washed up and changed into her own long sleep shirt. She got her pillow and a blanket from the den and stretched out on the sofa, with its freshly vacuumed cushions and a couple of new throw pillows. She read only a brief time before she too was asleep, turning fitfully through the night, until finally a deeper sleep overtook her. She never thought to set an alarm, always waking so promptly by six in the morning, all through the year. But she was fast asleep when something touched her cheek, soft, warm. It felt like Misty, at home. But as her vision cleared, she saw Wishi-ta before her in a long pink T-shirt, barefooted, her head illuminated by slanting morning rays. It wasn't yet six, she decided, and nothing else stirred.

"Wishi-ta!" Helene said, rolling to her side. "Are you OK?" She didn't see signs of swelling or rash.

"Yes."

"Then what is it?"

"Can you come, so I can show you?"

Helene was surprised to see Wishi-ta alone, without her robust and energetic shadow. She looked even paler in the morning light, except her hair, which was golden.

Helene pushed herself to a seated position, straightening her sleep shirt. It was only slightly cool in the room. She thought that Wishi-ta was going to bring her to the kitchen to ask for something she'd seen in the pantry or in the refrigerator. But she led her straight to Renee and Louis's bedroom, passing the open doorway of the twins' room, where Kiowa and Tana-na still slept, splayed across the double bed, all covers on the floor.

Helene switched on the light in the back bedroom, which faced west, and had its drapes pulled closed in lasting darkness.

Wishi-ta pulled her to the corner where the regalia was hanging on its posts.

"This is my mother's," she said, fingering the fringe on the dress. "And this is my father's."

"Yes, I know, Wishi-ta," Helene said. "Izzy told me. They're very nice. Someone worked very hard to make those."

"I helped her make this," Wishi-ta said, holding out a sash. "I found every color of bead that she needed, and the thread too."

"That's wonderful," Helene said, hearing the pride in Wishi-ta's voice.

"My regalia isn't done, and neither is Tana-na's."

"I see. But what about those other clothes you showed me, for the powwows?"

Wishi-ta raised her shoulders and gave a long sigh. "From Kiowa and Pawnee, when they were little. But that's not ours, not really. Mine is going to have a cat on it."

"Oh, really?"

"For me, special. With water and turtles and squirrels and a cat." She shrugged. "It's just in a bag now. Malvina was going to do it, and Neesa, but they're too busy."

Helene was starting to understand. "Well, maybe I can help you. I'm pretty good at sewing. My mother taught me." And then she paused. "Your other grandmother."

Wishi-ta looked more doubtful than curious.

"Even a shawl, with fringe?"

"Does it have to have fringe?"

"It has to." Wishi-ta stepped away and began to turn and twirl an imaginary shawl. "For the dancing." She stared hard at Helene, willing her to see. "Like a bird or a butterfly."

Helene nodded. "I see. OK, we can have fringe. And a cat and a squirrel and a turtle."

"And water."

"I'll have to write it down."

Wishi-ta had hopped onto the bed, curling against a pillow.

"And then we can make something for you," she said. "I'll help you, and Neesa will too, after the baby."

"Oh, well." Helene was completely at a loss. How to explain that she would not wear regalia, that it wasn't even appropriate? And that she was not going to be Wishi-ta's mother or a substitute for her mother. "I'm not much of a dancer," she got out, rolling her eyes. It was feeble, but maybe it would get her off the hook.

"Doesn't matter," Wishi-ta insisted. "Just come in the circle and wear your regalia, that's all. We'll be there, me and Tana-na, and everyone."

Helene felt a rush of blood in her face, a little light-headedness, and dropped onto the bed next to Wishi-ta.

"Oops." She tried to laugh, blinking her eyes. "I guess I'm not quite awake yet."

Wishi-ta patted the bed by her knee. "You can sleep here," she said. "It's OK. I can stay with you sometimes, if you want."

Her voice was so solemn and her words so unexpected, Helene could not reply at first. But she took Wishi-ta's hand in hers and rubbed it, giving it, finally, a kiss. "That is very kind of you."

There was a scampering in the kitchen, a breathy pant. Then Tana-na was in the room with them, and leaped in one bound onto the bed. "Ah-oooo!" he howled, rolling on the wolf blanket. "We are wolf clan," he cried. And then Wishi-ta was on her knees and they howled together, but friendly, wavering howls, until Kiowa walked in, rubbing her eyes.

Renee's journal – 6

We have a due date and a schedule for the prenatal visits. There's an option to see a midwife, but only if I'm cleared by the doctor. The next thing is the ultrasound – to get a picture of the growing fetus, and to find out the sex, if we want.

I'm not sure what I want – more information, or less. There are tests they can do, at certain points. And, given my history, I think they're keeping a pretty close watch on me. God knows, I wouldn't be the first to drink or drug while pregnant, no matter the vows or promises, but I don't think that's going to happen, and I can't say exactly why. The craving is not there, or maybe the pressure. Louis doesn't drink at all anymore, and his family doesn't drink much, either. At the Intertribal Center, they have a lot of events that are alcohol-free, and that makes it a lot easier to go without, if it's not there to try to ignore. Malvina told me they hold dances too, where they serve alcohol, but there mostly oldie-type music and dancing, and no one seems to go overboard.

I feel so different. Maybe it is giving up the booze and drugs. Or maybe the pregnancy itself. I'm sure the time we spent on the road made a difference. That's not to say I haven't had moments of wanting the high, or wanting not to think about things, future or past. When we returned from the road, Louis and I, for a while I got the cold shoulder from Neesa, and from Malvina too. I could tell they didn't trust me. Of course, Amos had just passed, and they were in mourning; I understand that. But some of that sorrow and anger was directed at me. Even though I was making my way, slowly but surely, back into the world of work and responsibility, helping Louis fix up the house he had purchased next door. All that was good for me. And in the present moment, I was OK. But the old stuff had followed me into my new life – even though no one from the old bad times knew I was here. Dad was dead, and Denis had gone. Helene was in the house, but she had no way of knowing where I ended up – not a clue except the time I called from the road, just to let her know I was alive.

I could blame it on Mom being in pain, and Dad with his anger and depression, all of that. But it was how I lashed out and hurt people, and disappointed them, and made so much more trouble and worry than anyone deserved. Except I couldn't help it; I never could help it. Somehow, it was my nature, a compulsion to beat my fists against some terrible, dangerous monster. Only now I can see, there was no monster – it was a void, a pit, something missing. I think now it was grief, my own and all around me, like a cosmic hole sucking us in and I was fighting to get out.

It doesn't matter now; only that I could never stay ahead of it, the grief or the trouble. It was only after the time I failed here, in front of Louis and his family, having the first drink, and then another and another, until I passed out, lost in the dark, did I know how much poison was in me, drunk or not.

That's when they did the sweat for me, at the sweat lodge with the big stones, and the fire and water, entering with Neesa, Malvina, Elsa, and Bernice – a few of the other women. I wanted to melt away, dissolve, leave all that behind, and just become an empty vessel. I just about fainted. But as I took in the heat and the steam, I felt my energy shift, a weight lifting, and a shadow passing out from me, leaving behind another Renee, a clean and undamaged one that I didn't even know was there.

Funny, this business with morning sickness, nausea, and sometimes light-headedness; it's not new at all. It's pretty much how I lived for years, since I was at least fourteen. But it's so different, knowing about the baby, knowing that it's what normal people feel.

I do think about this baby inside, and I wonder what it will look like, me or Louis, or any of our relatives. Or some blend in between. And how it will talk and walk and develop – all that a mystery. But I'm getting more comfortable with the uncertainty. It may sound crazy, but I think that's part of why I would get high – the certainty, the familiarity of it all. How none of the other questions, decisions, problems mattered much beyond the next fix – simple, really. And when the counselors would ask me, Didn't you know the risks – the quality of the drugs, the people you were with, where you would end up, and was there even a safe place to go to? I had to say, No, I was comfortable with it all. That part didn't scare me much; I didn't expect much. Not from others, and not from myself. It was easy, until it was something I had to deal with again, which I was used to. Or I died, and then it would be over. There were times, I admit, I did ask God, if there was a God, please, let it be over. Just so I wouldn't have the trouble of starting all over again, of what to do with myself, and how to avoid having to deal with my family.

Renee's journal – 7

Well, here's a shocker, or more like a cosmic joke – twins. Two of them inside of me. I knew something was up when the girl doing the ultrasound paused and her eyebrows went up. But she wasn't going to give it away. They got Dr. Gonzales in there, and she's the one who said, "Renee, Louis; there are two heartbeats. You're having twins."

"Oh my God," I said. "You've got to be kidding me."

But Louis raised his hand in a fist pump. "Yes! More of us." By which, of course, he meant Indians. So there we were – instant family, I guess. I still have a hard time believing it, and if anyone asked me, I would have said I didn't want twins, but now I'm getting used to the idea. And there's something nice about it too. Like regular siblings, but even closer; someone you know you belong with, even after you grow up. We don't know the sex yet, because of their positions. But probably next time. So they might be identical or might not. Might not even be the same sex.

You should see Louis strutting around like a proud peacock. I overheard him talking with Erik, that ne'er-do-well, about being a father. Erik, of course, is trying to downplay it. "That's another way to reel you in, buddy." He has a kid himself, but rarely sees him, as far as I can tell. So he's trying to influence Louis, just like old times. But Louis isn't buying it; he's ready to be a father. And that doesn't mean he's stuck in one place; his work is his work, I know that. But he wants the responsibility of being a father; he wants these kids; he wants family.

I was surprised Louis made it here in time for the ultrasound; he was traveling from Canada, up in New Brunswick – another rally, another meeting. But that's a long drive. After we found out I was pregnant, and dealing with all the morning sickness and stuff, I decided I'd stay home for a bit – feather my nest, like they say. I was still in bed this morning, not due in the store until nine, and then the appointment after lunch. I heard something in the front room, but I figured it was Red Cat on patrol. I turned over to my other side, squished the pillow between my knees, kind of dozing. I was looking away from the door when Louis came in – quiet, stealthy. And then he sneaked up on the bed behind me, not touching, but breathing on my neck. Of course I knew, and gave him the elbow.

"Ow! I thought you were sleeping." He burrowed his face into my shoulders.

"No, you didn't." But I was smiling. Red Cat jumped up next to the pillow. "My God, this bed is getting crowded."

"You bet," Louis said, coffee breath in my face, and his hand sliding over the mound of my stomach. "We're breeding a nation of warriors here, you and me. Now you are the mother of nations."

I kissed him. "In your dreams. If I survive this, I'm done. Besides, when are you ever around these days to do the dirty deed?"

He was smiling full face, more than I was used to seeing. "Oh, I'll do my part. Or we'll go on the road, all of us. A baby in every state. We'll repopulate this country."

"God help us. I'm tired already." But I hugged him mightily, because of how he wanted more of me, and that I was part of his dream. Who else but Louis saw me this way, loved me this way?

Who else but Louis could stand up to his mother, and Malvina, both – the day I showed up at their door after I left home and Helene, shaking like a leaf, still nauseous, bony and bruised, at my absolute worst?

I'd left the house when Helene went out for milk and bread, twenty minutes to get dressed, take cash from the drawer, right where Mom used to keep it, and go. I took one of her coats too. It was late winter, raw, and I'd left my jacket behind when I got out of the car in the night. Or maybe they pushed me out, because I was puking. I'd come up from the Cape with some people to a house party close to home, in the town next to mine. I had money and scored some drugs. But then I passed out on the back deck. Someone was shaking me, trying to slap me awake, but I couldn't stay upright; the sky was spinning.

They put me in the back of a car, and drove me over the town line. The cold air had woken me a little, so I could recognize the main road. "There," I said, and they let me out, speeding away, happy to be rid of me. I thought I could get home; I thought I knew the way. I turned down a side street where I saw a big white house with green shutters, so like my house. I mounted the steps, two, three, four and stopped. We have six steps. It was not my house, not my door. I stood there thinking I could ask to come out of the cold. But I didn't. I didn't like the picture of me knocking on the door and trying to seem nice, and asking to use the phone because I was in trouble, again. I didn't want to face that look, whatever it was. If it was kindness and pity, all the worse. Because I should really tell them not to worry, nice people, this has happened before, and will happen again. But I was so damn tired of it. So I left the house, left the yard, trudging along the road, because I didn't want to go back and do it all over again. Because, really, nothing worked.

That's where Helene found me, on that side street, in a snowbank.

The hardest part of leaving Helene was getting from the house to the bus station. I wanted to get out of town before anyone saw me, and my best chance was to get to the transit center the next town over, maybe three or four miles. To say it was an ordeal is an understatement; because I had a will of iron, and I could barely get my legs to move. But once I got on the commuter bus, it took me into Boston where I could get a Greyhound bus out to the base, which was one of their stops. And then just another mile or so to the base housing.

I didn't know if Louis would be there, even though he came back a lot of weekends between construction jobs, which were not many this time of *year. If he hadn't been there, I would have just turned around and kept walking, somewhere away...from people and drugs and rehabs and all of that. Out to the country, I suppose.*

But I saw Louis's truck, with a pop-up camper on the back. He's not the one who opened the door. It was Malvina, a baby on her hip, and a doubtful look on her face. She seemed to recognize me, but wasn't sure.

I asked for Louis, and she said he wasn't in. Her mother came up from behind, and I knew she recognized me, and was there to keep me away from her son.

"He's busy," said Malvina, but then she stepped out of way to let me in, out of the cold. She could see I was shivering. She said something to her mother, who disappeared into the kitchen, where I heard her rattling around.

"Can I leave him a note, then?"

Malvina shrugged, but she led me into the kitchen, pointing to a chair, and then pushed a pad of paper and pencil toward me.

There was a sound at the front door, and Louis appeared as if out of nowhere, in a T-shirt and jeans. No jacket. But I was sure that he hadn't been in or near the truck; where else could he have been?

He came into the kitchen, bare arms and a kerchief over his head. There was white powder on his cheek and on his hands. "Renee."

"I tried calling you at the other place, but they said you were gone."

He nodded. "I'm going on the road, for a few months. I just stopped here to load up and take care of some things. Why are you here?"

The three of them stood around me at the table, watchful.

"I didn't know where else to go. I had to get away from — that life, from myself. I thought you could help me, uh, find a place for a while."

"She can't stay here," Malvina said. "Not like this; not around the children. She should go to the clinic."

"No." I said. "I can't go to another clinic. I'm OK now, clean, physically. I'm past the withdrawal. I know I look bad; I haven't been taking care of myself. But I'm not actually sick." I paused, trying for the right words. "I'll leave if you want me to but I won't go there."

Malvina and the mother hissed words at each other that I couldn't understand. But it was Louis that mattered; I wouldn't look away until he answered.

"No, not here," he said. "Next door, for the night. You can stay there."

The kettle whistled and Malvina brought me a cup of tea, something reddish that smelled of berries, I remember that. And a piece of bread with peanut butter, like a kid.

I looked around for Izzy, the boy. But he was still at school, and the only movement was the little dog that wandered about, and the ticking of the clock.

Louis washed up, wiping the plaster off his face, and sat down at the table with me. Malvina brought him a cup of tea too, but she didn't join us. She and Neesa looked at each other and left us alone in the room.

Louis cupped his hands around the mug and stared at me, this problem at his doorstep.

"I'm a mess, I know. I have no right to ask anything of you."

"Why me? I never came on to you."

"No. You were too smart for that."

"Then why? You don't know me, or really anything about my family or culture. What makes you think I can help you, or will?"

"I don't know," I said, even though I did know it had something to do with Izzy, and Neesa's baskets. The twins at the powwow.

"I'm leaving tomorrow," Louis said. "I'm traveling cross country, meeting with people in various places, working on water and land rights. I won't be back for weeks, maybe months. I'll be living out of the camper or even a tent sometimes. No hotels, no restaurants."

"There must be room for two in that thing," I said, suddenly sure that's what I wanted, that's what I needed.

He laughed. "You're not my girlfriend. You're not even my friend."

"But I have some money. And I can make myself useful. I can drive, and follow directions. I'm a pretty good cook."

He cocked his head. "Really?"

"No, that's not true. But it could possibly be true. I've never really tried."

He smiled again, softening.

"And I'm loyal," I added. "And if anyone gave you a hard time, I'd back you up all the way."

He laughed, throwing his head back. "All twenty pounds of you?"

I narrowed my eyes. "It's a different kind of power."

Then he was quiet, and I let him think.

"You have no idea what it's like, life on the road."

"Maybe I do. A little. I haven't really had a home in a long time, years, just moving place to place. I don't need much, and I don't even mind being dirty sometimes."

We heard a man's voice in the back of the house, and then the two women, talking quickly, explaining, complaining.

"Please," I said. "Let me come with you. I want to go on the Red Road."

He stared at me, not laughing now.

"You don't even know what that is."

"But I want to know."

"Because?"

"Because nothing else works."

And then, like that, he was decided. "The Red Road," he started, and then shook his head. "I'm just going on "The Road" Road; streets and highways. But OK, you'll go."

It was the first time in a very long time I felt wetness on my cheeks, and I knew they were tears. I never cried, ever. I wanted to say, "You won't regret it." But I couldn't say that, not for sure. But I did say, "Thank you."

Louis got up to go into the other room, and Malvina followed him back, with Noel, her husband, carrying the baby.

"Renee's going with me," Louis said, and, surprisingly, there was no more argument. "We'll leave tomorrow, as I was planning, but she can stay next door tonight. Malvina, do you have something she can wear?"

"Nothing will fit her," Malvina said, but she turned and went out again.

"Noel, let's talk after I take Renee to the house. I got a punch list all made up here, what else needs to be done. And I gave Malvina a check for the work you've already done and for materials."

Noel nodded, looking me over in a thoughtful way.

Before we left, Louis pulled a cell phone out of his pocket. "I got one of these," he said to Noel, "so I can stay in touch on the road."

"Hi-tech Indian," Noel said with a smile. "Here, let me see." Louis gave him the phone, and we left to go next door.

"My baby," Louis announced, and I wasn't sure if he meant his truck with the camper or the house, which looked dingy and forlorn in the gray landscape. Inside was a small-scale construction site, with cloths on the floor and a paint tray and caulking gun on a small table. He brought in a sleeping bag from the camper, along with a folded blanket and a pillow.

"You can sleep here," he said, putting the stuff in a back room and closing the door behind him.

Even with the noise in the front, the hammer and electric screwdriver, I slept the sleep of the dead. And when I woke, later that day, it was like I'd crawled into a cave, somewhere in the dark underground, where no one else existed. But then I came to, and stayed under the covers, listening to the sound of the work, men's voices. Louis coming in to ask if I wanted something to eat; Neesa had made stew and sent some over. When he quit for the day, he brought the heater into the back room, with instructions to keep a safe distance. Where he slept, I don't know – maybe in the camper, or maybe with Izzy. I didn't sleep much in the night, but lay still on the floor, never more alone. Yet there was a calm I hadn't felt in a long time.

The next morning, we were getting ready to leave, me with my ID and some cash, a bag of women's clothes in my arms. The camper was stocked and ready. As we got prepared to leave, the whole family came out to say good-bye. Izzy was in a snow jacket with a fur cap and earmuffs, but I would have known those eyes anywhere.

"They wouldn't let me come over last night," he complained. "But I *knew it was you. We can go to powwow when you get back."*

"Maybe," I said.

"I got something for you," he said. "Neesa said you were sick."

"We'll, I'm getting better" – as if saying it could make it true.

He gave me a tatty brown bear, about the size of a cat. "Louis said Red Cat can't go with you, so you can take this instead. Don't worry; I have a lot of animals, a whole pile of them on my bed."

"Thank you, Izzy."

"I wish I could go."

"Maybe when you're older."

Then it was time to leave. There was a long, boring stretch as we headed west into New York state, and then south. I slept a lot. But every mile we traveled, I was cleaner, farther, safer. And I had hope.

Chapter 9

The next days at the base went quickly, although Helene could not really say where the hours had gone. She came across more signs of Renee's family life: cups and plates, pots and pans, magazines and books, old mail and handwritten notes scribbled by Renee and Louis. There were a couple of Renee's unfinished craft projects, jewelry, and a book of law cases marked at a section on water rights. She'd brought with her the journal pages that Renee had written, worked into a rough timeline, starting when Renee met Louis met and her first time at a powwow.

The day after the first appointment, Noel had come over with an envelope of cash – two hundred dollars. That was for the co-pays and for what was needed to make the house more dust and mold-free, which meant a trip to Walmart and then to a pharmacy.

The second appointment was Wednesday, and this time Wishi-ta came right away, alone, from playing with Tana-na and her boy cousins in the backyard – under Neesa's watch.

"Don't you want Tana-na to come too?" Helene asked. But Wishi-ta scoffed and took her hand. "It hardly hurts at all. And Tana-na got mud all over his shorts."

"OK, then let's go."

They were in and out of the office in less than forty-five minutes. This time the results came back clear and strong.

"Peanuts and tree nuts, which we suspected; they could be fatal in the worst scenario," Dr. Wang said, kindly but matter-of-factly. It was old hat to him, a long career of screening for deadly reactions. "Those are some of the worst offenders. No almonds, walnuts, cashews, or pecans; not even in the proximity. Sometimes sesame falls into that category, so I'd stay away from that too. We'll do more food and plants next time."

Not good news, but not a surprise. Malvina had been told to keep peanuts and peanut butter away from Wishi-ta since the last episode. That was the worst of it; Wishi-ta loved peanut butter – and it could be a hidden ingredient. But she didn't love allergic reactions and she was more than willing to give it up.

"We'll see you Friday," Dr. Wang said, as they left with the new report.

Helene visited Malvina afterward, to update her on the appointment.

"How are you feeling?" Helene asked. She pulled a chair up to Malvina's bedside to go over the reports, holding up the papers to show. Malvina had trouble grasping things: her hands were swollen, the fingers like little sausages. The plain gold wedding band looked painfully tight.

"OK," she said. "It's only a few weeks now, anyway. I think the doctor will induce me, if it goes over due date."

"Another baby in the house," Helene said, getting to her feet. She was careful to hide that note of envy. Malvina already had a houseful of children that she was watching over – with her mother's help, granted. But none for Helene. After the second miscarriage, she couldn't get it out of her head that it was not meant to be, after all the trouble in her own family, including the hereditary breast cancer.

Malvina told her that everyone was going to the Intertribal Center the following night, Thursday, and Helene was welcome. There would be pizza and salad available for five dollars, and potluck to share. Neesa would be sure to bring something appropriate for Wishi-ta to eat. After that came workshops and music. This week was a birchbark horn and fan-making class for the kids. Kiowa was going to work on her basket with Neesa.

Helene was about to decline when Malvina added, "You might like to see them dance. The twins always join when the men sing at the big drum, and Cree and Pawnee too."

"I would like to see that," Helene said after a pause. "Will they wear their costumes…er, regalia?"

"No, not for this; it's just for fun, for us."

"All right, then, I'll try to stop by."

Late Thursday afternoon, Helene poked around a few minutes in the refrigerator and cupboard. She didn't have anything for potluck. She could take five dollars for the pizza or for the salad if the pizza was inedible. Or she could always eat after she got back. Then she returned to the novel she had started, a historical romance she was beginning to enjoy.

Just before six o'clock, she heard voices outside on the sidewalk and peeked out the window to see Noel, Neesa, and the kids heading toward the Intertribal Center, Kiowa carrying a pot and Neesa her basket-making materials. The children hopped and skipped, no feet dragging. Once again, Helene wondered at the pediatrician's question, "Did the twins show signs of anger or fear or anxiety after the death of their mother and absence of their father?" But she had to say "No," not that she could see. Was it their age perhaps – three, when Renee died, and four, when their father left in the late winter? They would be five soon, in September. Was it that, their developmental stage, or something else?

She let them pass, and went to freshen up and change. Back in the living room a few minutes later, she caught Izzy speeding by on his bike, hair flying, carrying a backpack with a bag of chips poking out the top. She smiled at his part of the potluck. Then she walked out the front door, careful to lock up – not that there was much of value inside except a small TV, the laptop, and her purse.

It was less than a five-minute walk to the Intertribal Center, four blocks up and one to the left. Noel had told her that it formerly had been an officers' club, complete with dining hall, an elevated platform, and a commercial kitchen, with an assortment of small meeting rooms and office space on the second floor. The heavy window drapes were likely original, according to Helene's practiced eye, faded gold with a few drooping hems and probably harboring quite a few years of dust.

Entering the Intertribal Center, she heard a buzz of voices. Some people were already seated at long tables set end to end with an assortment of folding chairs – more like an indoor picnic than an officers' club. But there were green tablecloths and glasses of pink tulips, adding bright color. Children scrambled between the tables, chasing and hiding, until a grown-up called them back. On the walls hung blankets and quilts with animal designs or patterns of stripes, triangles, and spirals. At the front of the hall was a low platform with several flags on poles to each side. In one corner, a circle of chairs was set up around a large mound covered by a blanket: the drum, Helene assumed. There was a kind of head table on the platform, in front of a screen. An older man was at the table, tapping a microphone, while Izzy bent over fiddling with electrical cords.

Helene spotted Renee's family at a table at the front, and made her way over, passing a bulletin board next to a display case of photos and banners. The bulletin board was covered with flyers for events at the Intertribal Center, as well as powwows throughout the area. There was a special program for veterans in a couple weeks, a fundraiser for a family in need, and a guest speaker who was a Native American educator and activist. Helene recognized the woman on the flyer from a recent TV news program about a gas pipeline crossing Native territory: a tall and commanding presence with cascading dark hair, glasses, and a serious agenda. Every time the interviewer, an academic, expounded on his own views, sucking up airtime, the activist returned politely and doggedly to the topic: the Native American perspective.

Just as she was about to move on, a picture in the display case caught Helene's eye, a young woman amid the mostly older folks in faded black-and-white photos. She stopped, looking closely at the caption: "Renee 'Shooting Star' Lopes," with the dates of her birth and death, standing alone in her regalia. It was a memorial display, and to Helene it was beyond strange; it was crazy. Her sister had gone over to this whole new way of life, this other identity, in the years since Helene had last seen her. Even a Native name: Shooting Star, a little silly, perhaps, but appropriate: fast, hot, flaming out. Did Denis know? What would Kenneth say – if she even told him?

Across the room, Noel was waving her over to the table, as a voice came over the microphone urging folks to take their seats. They had kept a chair for her between Kiowa and Wishi-ta, and a glass of water had already been poured from a communal pitcher.

An older, barrel-chested man with a full, broad face and glasses spoke into the microphone, welcoming the crowd to sit and listen. His white hair was pulled into a ponytail, although his eyebrows were jet black, and he sported a surprisingly large gray mustache. He said something in another language, and then said in English that it was a prayer of thanks in the Micmac language. He introduced himself as Jerome "Wandering Moose" Bernard, and then acknowledged the organizers of the evening and went over the activities that would follow the meal.

"That's Chief, or Big Chief," Kiowa whispered. "But he's not really a chief. Not through his family. Just for all of us here."

"I see," said Helene, but really, she didn't.

"I know you're all hungry," Chief said. "And we will enjoy this food together. But before we do that, a few important announcements. Ray Martin is still in the hospital, and they are looking for a blood match, if you haven't gotten yours checked yet. The Caron family lost their house in a fire, as you know, and have been staying with various friends and neighbors. They are looking for an apartment or temporary housing, where they can be together until they decide what to do about the house. On the bulletin board, you'll find some of the items they need. Also, there's been some break-ins in town, and the police sent a reminder to 'lock doors when you're away' – for those of us not in the habit, and that's most of us, I guess.

"And now, Izzy 'Birdsong' Lopes has a report for us about his brother and our brother, Louis, who is incarcerated at the federal prison in New Hampshire for his actions related to protecting our water rights in Maine. Izzy, can you come to the microphone."

Izzy got to his feet and walked to the table, lifting the microphone out of its holder to speak.

"Iz-zy, Iz-zy, Iz-zy!" The voices rose loudly, especially the children's, and Izzy smiled and gave a little bow.

Izzy waved a hand to hush the voices. "There is news," he said, "and some of it is good. There's a hearing coming up. Louis and his lawyers have made progress on his part of the incident related to the explosion at the dam and the death of the security guard. However, the judge will not reconsider the gun charge, even though Louis told her it was in the truck for hunting purposes, and never meant to be part of the crime or the escape. In the meanwhile, Louis says that the plans for the dam are being held up, and it's possible they'll find some case law to support the Indian water use rights, or even some documents that show that the surrounding lands were deeded to Indians way back, hundreds of years."

"A-ho!" Helene heard. Cheers went up, and applause.

"Louis is in good spirits, going crazy with all that research, still bugging me, even from there. He says he's staying strong and healthy. He appreciates everyone's thoughts, and especially those who have written to support him. That's all."

Izzy left the table, and Chief returned, taking the microphone. "Thank you, Izzy. And know that we honor Louis for his work and sacrifice, and all your family."

"A-ho!" from the crowd.

"Now let's eat."

Lines formed on two sides of a buffet table for the pizza and salad, various side dishes and drinks. Most people already had their meal tickets, but Helene had to stand in a short line to get one.

"Welcome," said the woman who took her money, a late-middle-aged lady in glasses with piercing blue eyes and remnants of blond in her exuberant, frizzy hair, along with beaded earrings and a bright circular medallion, also made of beads. More Irish than Indian, thought Helene. But she had learned a lesson just from being with the twins: looks could be deceiving.

"Glad you are joining us," the woman said, a trace of Boston in her voice, but certainly not Beacon Hill. "I know you're Renee's sister; they said you were here. You look like her."

"I suppose so," Helene agreed. "Well, thank you. I'm glad to have the chance to, ah, meet everyone."

The woman tapped her broad chest. "I'm Elsa, Jerome's wife – the Chief." Then she lifted a fleshy arm to gesture at two older women at the table with her, more Native-looking than she was. "This is Charlotte and Alberta."

Charlotte looked up with a slight smile on her full, dark-skinned face; her hair was still mostly black, secured with a decorative barrette, and she wore earrings made of feathers. Next to her sat Alberta, bony and sharp-featured with thin gray braids, like some emaciated bird of prey. No smile there; more like permanent frown lines. When Alberta sat up straight in her chair, Helene saw the front of her T-shirt: "Homeland Security," under a graphic of four Indian warriors with guns. Not exactly a warm welcome.

"She was a good mother, Renee," Charlotte said, still holding on to the ticket.

"That's nice to hear. I…I'm sure she was surprised having twins."

"Yeah, a shock. But we helped her out, us women. She got a lot of help with Malvina and Neesa right there."

Helene wasn't sure how to reply. She settled on, "It's nice to meet you all," and reached for the ticket. "And I'm sure –"

"Never saw you before," skinny Alberta said, fixing an eye on her. "The brother; we used to see him sometimes. But not you."

There was an awkward moment before Charlotte said, "That's not our business, Alberta." She turned back to Helene. "Lots of people have a rough start in life, not just Renee. She turned herself around and had those beautiful children; that's what matters."

Helene's face started to burn. Clearly, they knew about the addiction, and whatever other problems Renee might have talked about. And about the big sister who was three hours away but not part of her life. Helene wasn't going to be pulled into that discussion. It had been Renee's choice to leave and not tell anybody. Just a call from a pay phone to say she was alive. All the notice Helene got about Renee's new life.

"I'm glad she found a place here," she said stiffly and then turned to leave. "Thank you."

The pizza was fine; the salad was OK. Helene didn't take any of the potluck side dishes since she hadn't brought anything.

The kids ate quickly and got up to play. At the table, some older women and a man were sitting in a group on the other side of Noel: friendly Charlotte and her husband, Robert; scowling Alberta; and a tiny, round-cheeked woman named Bernice, with long, loose hair threaded with gray, and bright dark eyes behind her glasses. Another man, younger, maybe in his thirties, with long hair and a neck tattoo, had taken a seat next to Alberta, saying hello to all the others, but not Helene. He didn't even look at her, although he could hardly miss her, diagonally across the table. At one point he turned to Alberta, calling her "Grandma," and then Helene could see the resemblance, the wide forehead and pointed chin, plus the sour expression. An apple right off the family tree.

The conversation turned to the family who had just lost their house in a fire. Several people at the table had gone inside the burned house to help salvage whatever they could. Noel had been driving rescued items in his van to a storage facility in the area. But he was not there the day the insurance investigators had come, sending a small crew of young men throughout the house, into the attic, and up on the roof to make assessments of the damage.

Robert was speaking: "The one fellow, him with the camouflage pants, he was on the roof with another one, and we could hear them laughing. They were passing stuff up through a hole in the roof, and saying what junk it was, all the holiday stuff, and the blankets and regalia. The one said, 'Better we put a match to it and get rid of the rest – total loss.' And the other said, 'I have a better idea: you light it, and I'll put it out.' Then he pulled down his pants and pissed into the hole. Charlotte could see from where she was standing in the driveway, and she shouted up at him, but he didn't hear or he didn't listen. Our niece was inside, just going to tell them that she found a bin of documents, when she saw the piss coming down – thought it was rainwater or something."

"Terrible," muttered Alberta. "Local kids, I heard. From that Catholic high school. Hah! What do they teach them there, anyway? Where is the respect? Who cares what people's stuff is like – it's important to them."

"Where's their self-respect?" Robert said, somberly. "That's what I want to know."

Noel said he would find out the name of the supervisor and report it. Maybe they'd get a talking to, or let go from the job. It might even be a misdemeanor.

Alberta's grandson, Wilton, spoke up: "Fat lot of good that will do. You know as well as I do, white justice is no justice for brown people; just a system for keeping us in our place."

Helene caught a wave of reaction passing from person to person, but no one spoke further. She hadn't said a word, fidgeting in her seat. She found Alberta's eyes on her. *What for?* Like she was judging her and all white people for those youths' stupid action. Helene excused herself, getting to her feet.

"Well, I came to see the dancing. When will they start?"

Six pairs of eyes looked up at her.

"Could be any time," Noel said. He, at least, always seemed pleasant and reasonable, never that cold stare. "The men will take the drum out after coffee for a few songs. The kids might come, or they might not."

"I see." Helene pushed back her chair. "Maybe I'll run along then. I have some course work to catch up on." Her words came out a bit stuffy, even to her.

"Hold on a second," Noel said. "Izzy's going to play his flute soon. You might like that."

Helene closed her eyes, deliberating; stay or go? It was such a tug-of-war. Yes, it was good for her to know something of the world Wishi-ta was growing up in. But more than that, she couldn't see the point, as she'd be back in her own comfortable home with Kenneth and her cat and her OK job within weeks.

But there was something about Izzy; she liked him.

And there was something here that had worked for Renee, whatever it had been. She couldn't ignore that, either.

She sat down again, smiling slightly. "Yes, I would like to hear Izzy play."

He came to the platform area again and sat cross-legged on the table, turning off the microphone. Without preamble, he began to play; the room got quieter and then almost still. His music had Native influences, but then other parts sounded Western, almost jazz or folk or even classical. The twins had come back, leaning into Neesa and Noel, who were still seated, until the songs were done.

Helene needed to use the bathroom – in the back hallway, toward the kitchen. On her return, she stopped in front of the "Wall of Warriors," another display of pictures with captions explaining how each was a "warrior for the people in the war of oppression and genocide by Western Europeans." No sugarcoating there, Helene thought. She recognized some of the warriors: Sitting Bull, Geronimo, Tecumseh. Others she didn't know: Metacom, Weetamoo, John Trudell, Winona LaDuke. None of them smiled.

When Helene got back to the dining area, a group of men, maybe six or seven, mostly older with a teen thrown in, had gathered next to the drum, pulling off the covering blanket. They passed a smudge bowl, a large clamshell like Izzy had brought over to the house, and waved the smoke over themselves, their sticks and the drum. Then they sat, passing a small basket between them and sprinkling something over the surface of the drum. When Helene looked at Noel, he said, "Tobacco."

They began a song, and the twins ran over immediately, along with some of the other children, mostly younger. Their movements were not coordinated in any way, except they moved in a circle, some of them turning in circles. Tana-na, especially, stepped high, quick and light on his feet, transported by the beat. He seemed to forget about the others in the large hall, which was starting to dim with twilight. Wishi-ta danced more delicately, holding hands with another girl, and occasionally giggling. Maybe a dozen children danced and a couple of elders, others coming and going into the circle.

"It's nice how the kids seem to enjoy it," Helene remarked, at the end of one song.

"They grow up with it, you know," said Charlotte. "But some of us are just learning the songs now, because we didn't have much of this around when we were young."

"We have a women's hand drum circle," Bernice said, her eyes crinkling. "Just started two years ago. The woman who leads us is Micmac, from Nova Scotia; she sings all kinds of music, professionally. But she's learned a lot of Native songs so she can teach us. Anyone can join."

Helene supposed that "anyone" included her. That is, some wannabe outsider looking for an interesting cultural experience. Or, she chided herself, maybe it was just an open invitation.

"If you feel like coming," Bernice said, "just show up. She's got extra drums. It always works out."

"Thank you," said Helene. "We'll see. I won't really be here long. Ah, anyway, good night – and it's nice to meet you."

On her way out Helene told Noel and Neesa that she was leaving.

"We'll bring the twins by in a bit," Noel said.

"Thanks," she said, checking her watch. Probably time for a phone call or two; check in with Kenneth, see what Denis had to say.

The singers at the drum started another song, melodic and repetitive.

"Wishi-ta, do-ya, do-ya, do-ya." That was the main part of it. Wishi-ta – like her niece – named after a song! If their mother, hers and Renee's, could see them now, or even their father, what would they make of it all? In their wildest dreams, could they have imagined that their grandchildren would be raised as Native Americans, surrounded by a community of

Native Americans, more connected to that than their Swedish, Irish, or French-Canadian backgrounds? Which, come of think of it, Helene didn't know much about, either. Except that her father used to drop hints, occasionally, that they might also have Native American blood – his mother had told him so. But that was from a long, long time ago, if it were true at all.

She stopped at the door, looking back at the drummers and dancers, following the rhythm of the song. A man in a leather jacket entered the hall, pausing next to Helene to look around. He was maybe fifty, with graying dirty-blond hair pulled back in a ponytail and a scruffy beard. Well built, except for a few extra pounds in the middle. Blue eyes. Small silver earrings. She noticed a scar down the side of his neck, an old one. *But not Native*, she thought. Her puzzlement must have shown, because he gave her a friendly once-over, raising his eyebrows.

"This song," Helene said, trying to cover. "What's it called, do you know?"

He cocked his head, listening. "I'm going to guess 'Wishi-ta.' But don't quote me on that."

"Oh."

"Name of a river, maybe?" He squinted, as though trying to recall. "That's secondhand or thirdhand info. Not Native," he said. "But I've got Native in-laws. That's why I'm here, looking for my sister."

He gazed at her longer than was comfortable. "You're Renee's sister, I'm guessing."

"Yes."

"I knew her, through her husband, Louis, mainly. I kind of come and go around here. But I'm sorry for your loss. And that of the family."

"Thank you," she said a stiffly. Who were his in-laws? Who had told him about her – that she even existed? "And you are…?"

"Erik Norling," he said. "Elsa's brother. Chief is my brother-in-law, almost thirty years now."

She nodded. Elsa, big bosom, frizzy hair at the ticket table. "Oh, yes. I met her earlier; she was taking money."

"That's her, in the middle of the action, always."

Helene didn't mean to appear like she was interrogating him, but she couldn't help herself.

"So, you're not Native. What about Elsa?"

"Nope, Swedish and English, just like me. But as you see, she's part of all this now, and one way or another, she kind of brings me along."

Helene had to smile. Right, like this big, tough guy could be led along like a puppy.

He was smiling too. A broad, relaxed smile, that of someone who had time and maybe not too many worries. Then his gaze went back into the room and he lifted a hand to wave at Elsa, who was looking at them.

"Well, good luck," he said. "And nice to meet you…"

"And you too."

His eyes crinkled, amused. "I was looking for a name there, Renee's sister."

"Oh, yes. Helene. Bradford." And something made her add, looking down at her wedding band, "That's my married name. I was a Roy, like Renee…before she married…uh…Louis." That didn't come out very smoothly.

"I see. Well, so long, Helene. I'm being summoned."

She watched him stroll away. Curious.

On her way back to the house, Helene replayed the images and sounds of the evening. All she had learned about Renee and Louis. People she'd met, Native and non-Native. The bristling anger at those insurance workers who had been so disrespectful about the house that had burned. Alberta's hostility – toward her or all white people, she wasn't sure. The Chief. His non-Native wife, Elsa. And the wife's brother, Erik, an aging hippie, perhaps. The music, and the dancing, and, above all, the beating of the drum.

She let herself back into the house, thinking about the next day, Friday. She would call Denis, and pack up her few things in a travel bag for tomorrow afternoon. An appointment at the allergist at ten, and then Helene was done for the day, for the week, free to return to her own home and husband, and Misty. But she wasn't as anxious to get back as she would have thought.

Renee's journal – 8

The thing is, we don't have any pictures from the trip – our time on the road. Neither of us had a camera, and besides, we weren't really thinking that way – saving up memories. Like I'm trying to do now.

So when I say road trip, I mean it. A lot of miles on the highway – I'm trying to add it all up and come up with a total. Back roads too. But what I don't mean is hotels, motels, or even people's houses. It was the back of the truck on the side of road all the way, besides the time we spent in Phoenix and a place in Oklahoma where they had rooms to put us up. When we left Massachusetts, I didn't really know our destination, or our route. All I really heard was "Phoenix," one way or another.

After a day of travel, we had to find a place to park the truck with its pop-up camper, and then "set up," so to speak, which was mainly a kind of awning coming away from the back of the truck, with a couple of chairs, a gas ring burner to cook on. There was room for two to sleep in the camper, but mostly Louis took his sleeping bag outside. At first.

As we headed south, it got warmer. After that cold snap in March up north, mostly it was just turning into spring. A fair amount of rain, but no snow or frost. On the way back, a tornado in Kansas, but we dodged it. Just like in The Wizard of Oz. We heard the warning on the radio, and could see the sky getting darker. But we couldn't tell where it was coming from, so we had no idea where to go. Just kept driving, me at the wheel, Louis peering through the raindrops. We never did see the funnel.

I had said I would help with the driving. Initially, that was not true, because I pretty much slept in the camper bed for the first few days, so Louis had to drive. I wasn't shaking anymore, or feverish, but I was dehydrated and pretty much skin and bones from not eating right while I was drinking and drugging. I also didn't do any cooking. But Louis didn't say anything, just nudged me now and then to sit up and eat something, which he prepared. Like I said, there was room for both of us in the camper, but he took his sleeping bag outside under the open sky, or the awning if it rained. Which I thought for sure was his Indian nature. Or that he was resisting his male instincts. But then he told me that it was because the camper smelled bad, and I personally smelled bad. The smell of bad stuff coming out of my system through my pores and hair and breath, everything. Even though I brushed my teeth, and sponge bathed, even put on deodorant.

"Is it that bad?" I asked, since I really couldn't tell myself. I was sitting with him in the cab of the truck. In my absence he had spread maps and papers all over the passenger seat, which I had to move. I saw that he had drawn a route on the map leading through the Carolinas then west toward Arizona.

"Pretty bad," he said.

"Oh, well, sorry. Are we going to get a shower anytime soon?"

"We can stop at the next truck stop."

"So where are we?"

"Virginia."

"Hm...that's pretty far." I stretched and yawned. My hand waved out the open window, where the air was soft and warm. *"I am kind of hungry. Anything to eat?"*

"Beef jerky."

"Oooh."

He gave me a side glance. *"Is that delight or disgust?"*

I shrugged. *"Not sure. Never tried it. Doesn't sound appealing."*

He shrugged. *"Indian staple, especially on the trail."*

There was a cooler between the seats with plastic gallons of water, some fruit and chips. And the jerky. I didn't want to press my luck. I took the chips and poured water into a plastic coffee mug.

Louis still didn't have much to say; and yet he was always calm and agreeable when I spoke to him. He must have been wondering what kind of situation he'd gotten himself into with me. It's not like we had a lot of conversation when we left the base. I know Neesa had given him an earful in their language, which I had to assume was about me, and not very encouraging.

"I want to make myself useful," I said. *"There must be something I can do."*

"We'll see."

"After we eat and shower, I'll be up for some driving."

"Got a license?"

"Um...not at the moment. Is that a problem?"

"Not if you don't make it a problem."

"The safest driver you'll ever meet."

"Hmph..."

"And," I added, *"If we stop at a store, I'll pick up some groceries. I can heat up a can of chili or cook a hamburger as well as you can."*

"Sure."

I turned to look at him, studying his profile. As indifferent as he looked and sounded, I could tell there was some agitation under all that. Who was better than me at hiding what I really felt? I thought I should try to make things clearer as my mind was starting to clear.

"So, Louis, there's nothing up with me and you, right? I mean, I don't expect anything, and I don't think you do, either. I'm just your traveling companion, and I'm happy to assist you in any way I can, at any of your meetings. Whatever. You have your business to take care of, and I have no clue what I'm doing, except for getting as far away as I possibly can from trouble with a capital T. Change of sky. Fresh air. Right? You get that. Indians are used to moving around, place to place, nomads. Well, that's

what I'm doing now. Trying to pick up some new thoughts and ideas."

Louis didn't speak, but I knew he was listening.

"So, there's no reason you can't sleep in the camper, if you want, after I wash up and we air it out a bit."

There was there barest shrug of his shoulders.

"Besides," I added, "I may have a vaginal infection. I'll pick up some cream at the store. I just hope it's not a UTI – urinary tract infection – that's a bitch. And I'd have to get antibiotics for that. But don't worry; there's no danger to you."

His lips tightened; that steadfast calm was starting to crack; it was all I could do not to laugh. I couldn't help myself; I could never help myself. The worst that could happen was that he'd put me out on the side of the road, and that was OK with me too. So he was stuck with me, unless he could be that guy who turned his back on someone like me, a walking, talking mess. It was all true what I said, but I'm still not sure why I said it.

We did stop for showers and food at a truck stop in North Carolina. Two memorable things from that: Louis stayed right outside the ladies' room while I showered and changed, on the lookout for danger I guess. And second, while I did cook a nice dinner that night, I threw up most of it – too much, too fast, after not eating for a long time. So he got to witness that too. Not in the camper, though, or in the truck. On the side of the road, and I felt much better after. Still, he chose to sleep out under the awning, if we were outside city limits. When it poured, or if we were caught too late in a built-up area, he slept beside me in the camper, each in our own bag. I knew that he often woke with an erection, like most guys I'd been with. Once, during those early days, he turned over in his sleep and landed next to me, his arm reaching over my waist. Then I felt his breath on my neck, and sensed his eyes blinking open.

"Turn the other way," I said, taking his hand off me, which he did, settling back into sleep.

A kind of routine developed as we went along, and I noticed that Louis was never really in a hurry. Things took as long as they took, and some places we stayed on for a while. When I asked him about getting back for his construction job, he just shrugged.

"This is more important," he said. "And I have no great plans for getting rich, so what does it matter?"

This was when I learned that the Red Road was not even a road at all. I knew it was a metaphor about a concept, a way of life. But silly me; I thought such a place had existed, and it was somewhere that Indians went to worship, or make a pilgrimage, like Jerusalem or Mecca. Turns out, there's no ancient place; it's not even an ancient term; someone just made it up. And, come to find out, the idea itself was kind of vague and different from place to place, person to person. Even Louis was not a hundred percent sure. It was an "evolving idea," he said. Or, as he put it, "Sort of universal guidelines, pretty specific to the tribe and place. Some call it Walking in Beauty; that's a Navajo term, or 'Diné.'"

"What kind of guidelines?"

"Mostly about respect. Respect yourself, respect others, respect the Earth; that kind of thing."

"OK, I can go with that."

"Thankfulness."

"Well, yes, when I have something to be thankful for, which isn't that often."

I could see his dimple form and fade, but he didn't counter me.

"Not hoarding wealth, when others don't have enough."

"No problem there."

"Generosity."

"Yup, when I have it, I like to share. For the most part."

"Bravery."

Was I brave? "I'm not quite sure what that means. But I'm not afraid of much."

"I see," he responded. "How about kinship – loving and honoring family."

"I might have to work on that."

I could see him looking at me out of the corner of his eye. "Striving for purity and strength in body and soul."

I wriggled in my seat, looking out the window. "Maybe not so good." And then, more challenging. "So then, it's like the Ten Commandments?"

"In some ways. Not really. There's no threats about hell or vengeful gods. It's mainly about living now on this earth, rather than promises for a future in heaven." He shrugged. "I guess that's what it is. And I'm not always sure I'm on the Red Road, either. I have a temper. I am not very patient. I've been known to be angry and hurtful. Try as I might, I'm not always very peaceful or accepting."

"That's good. Otherwise I'd have to think I'm traveling with a saint."

"No saint here," he said with a wry grin.

We rode for a while in silence, looking over the landscape. "So, just to be clear, Red Road is not a place, and we're not going there on this trip."

"Correct."

In that moment I could say aloud what had always been between us, but not acknowledged.

"I was hoping it was somewhere to go to get help for recovery. I'm clean, but I could relapse, any time. That's what I always do, and I need to do something different."

He nodded, looking ahead. Then he took a deep breath, gesturing to the flat, sunbaked earth, and the wide-open blue sky all around us.

"Well, this is different, isn't it? You never did this before."

I had to smile, filled with a kind of gladness I hadn't felt in a long time. "You bet. I never dreamed of doing this before, and certainly not with someone like you."

"We'll see." He had to have the last word. "It's a work in progress and there's no guarantee we're going to make it, you or me."

I thought he was teasing, how we'd put up with each other, or not. But it was more than that; he actually meant "Make it alive." That's a thing I never could have guessed, the danger of driving down the road while being Indian.

Renee's journal – 9

Funny thing, now I've gotten started on this writing, I can't wait to keep on. And funny thing, it's Helene's face I see when I'm telling the stories – the ones that I know will shock her, and the ones that help to explain. I'm still at it – waving my arms – Danger! Danger! And then, "Just kidding." Just for attention, just to knock her off balance and pull her down with me; just the only way I knew how. But this is a different story, and I wish she could hear it.

Only once on the road did Louis raise his voice to me – and then just a single word, "Stop." It was a long stretch of highway in a sweltering nighttime landscape – somewhere in the middle of the country, headed west. I was sick with the heat, nauseous. All I wanted was to stop somewhere with good air conditioning so I could feel human again, or almost. A cold drink, a popsicle; it didn't seem much to ask. But all he did was shake his head, staring ahead. No. Each time, until the last time, when he pulled over, the headlights disappearing into black dust.

"Stop!"

Worse, he turned off the engine, and my voice got sharp. "For God's sake. We could die in this heat! I'll pay for a hotel room."

So this is what he did: he turned on the dome light and pulled his T-shirt off over his head, turning to show me his back.

"Count them."

Scars, he meant. There were several dark stripes, raw-looking, and a number of smaller scratches and bumps of hard white tissue. One, at least, showed the remnants of stitches. I'd seen his back before, and the marks and bruises; old fights, no doubt, or construction injuries. He had no tattoos on his back, only his arms.

"Seven? Eight?" I said to appease him. "So what? You've had some knocks; I have too. That's what happens living rough on the streets, right?" I lifted my chin. "At least you're a man."

He nodded, then waited a moment. "That one, on the left, about halfway down. Feel it."

I traced my finger over a deep pit in the skin, an inch or so round.

"Bullet hole," he said. I hadn't expected that. Not where we came from; not in the kind of quiet backwater where his family lived. In all my time on the streets, I'd never seen a gun. Knives, yes. Not a gun.

"Forty miles back," he said. "Three years ago, traveling with another Indian. We stopped for a meal and a drink. But it was the wrong place, at the wrong time. When we didn't get up right away, guy pulled out a gun; and when we didn't move fast enough, he pointed the gun. And just as I was getting to the truck, opening the door, someone took a shot. We drove almost a hundred miles to the next rez, to get medical help from someone who might care to save me."

"OK, OK," I said, looking down at my lap. "I get it. We can go. Just go."

He wasn't done with the lesson, his back the textbook.

"Right shoulder," he said. "Look close."

Smaller, sharper, deeper pink.

"Knife?"

"Yup. Twenty-five miles ahead. Service station. Taking a piss. I came out and a man was standing in front of my truck, blocking me. I guess he didn't like the decals or maybe the dream catcher on the mirror. I was going around to the other side when he grabbed my arm. I had to throw a punch to get him off me. He held on, and we locked arms, wrestling like bears."

I could picture it, but how was he stabbed in the back? His eyes crinkled; he was reading my thought.

"Not him. The other guy; the one that came up from behind with a war whoop and planted the knife. But when the blood spurted, he jumped back. Then they both disappeared, and the man inside the station locked the door, waving me gone."

We sat in silence for a moment until he said, "Renee," more gently, "this is no America the Beautiful family road trip – you have to understand that it is not possible for me to travel from one place to another in this country without threat of violence. There are some people in some places who hate me, and all us brown people, for reasons they probably don't even understand. But it is not safe, and we are not welcome. And you are not safe being with me, no matter how white you are. In fact, worse for both of us. You get that?"

I squirmed in my seat, beginning to think we were going to melt to death, right there and then.

"Yeah," I finally said.

It's not that I hadn't noticed earlier, now and then, disapproving looks or unfriendly manners, but I was used to that from my runny nose or grimy fingernails, general lack of grooming. I thought the problem was me. Or me and Louis not looking like great customers.

"So be prepared for a little inconvenience," he said, "or worse. Don't worry, I stand my ground when I have to. But I'm on a mission here, and I'd rather not die on the road – or in the fucking toilet. So I don't provoke, and I get the hell out as soon as I see trouble. You, too. Watch your mouth. Whether or not you care what happens to you, I've got shit to do."

The cab was baking, even in the dark, and we were both dripping sweat. I glanced at the final gallon of water, getting low. Finally, he relented and turned the engine back on, and the cool air.

Afterward, of course, I got plenty of chances to see just what he was talking about – the man at the ATM machine: "What's taking you ladies so long? You're holding up the line." Louis's hair. Or the woman at the *information center, who handed me a pamphlet for the Pioneer Homestead.*

"Everyone's in such a hurry to the outlets or the theme park. So few tourists take time to appreciate our history, how difficult it was for the pioneers to survive here, with all the terrible hardships they had to face." I didn't think Louis heard; then he appeared at my side and took the pamphlet, tossing it on the counter. "I'm not a tourist. This is my home, and nobody knows my history. What about our hardships? Where's the pamphlet for that?"

She wasn't happy, that lady. Yes, he came across pretty badass, although he was just making a point. Still, she asked us to leave, and waved across the room to one of the security guards. It was a quick stop; good thing I used the restroom first.

Then I could see it, the distrust, the dislike, over and over in so many ways, large and small. And I could see, too, when he put on his "warrior" face, the warning mask that said to leave him be. But what I didn't see then was the cracked heart behind the muscles of his chest, protected by the tattoo of scars on his back, his yearning to move freely about this land, his only homeland. Not enemy, not tourist, not guest. Simply at home.

Renee's journal – 10

Our route wound through Arkansas and Missouri to Oklahoma and New Mexico, and finally Arizona. Each stop was to meet with representatives of some Native group about a legal issue they were involved in, mostly to do with land and water rights, where the goal was to get updates on current matters, and exchange information about legal cases and precedents. Often, the meetings were scheduled at the same time as a local powwow, where Louis would speak at the microphone as an invited guest.

Louis had said I could come with him or not to these events. Or most of them. A few did not include non-Indians; and a few, I think, did not include women. I wanted to go, partly for something to do and partly to find out what they were talking about. At the meetings I started taking notes, because I thought it would be helpful, a record of the information, suggestions and decisions that were made, and a running list of who was involved and their contact information. No one ever questioned why I was there, at least not openly. Louis introduced me as a friend, but I took to saying I was "assisting" him. People would think what they would. Louis had met several of the representatives before at different conferences and powwows. Some of the gatherings, like in Oklahoma, were huge compared to the ones I'd been to in New England. I remember thinking I didn't realize there were that many Indians still alive, and I hope they're not still mad at white people.

At the powwows, we camped out like everyone else, and I enjoyed eating and visiting with some of the people we met there, who were curious about things back in the Northeast. What was Boston like? Or Cape Cod? The casino situation, the weather, sports, all that kind of stuff. Mostly there was no alcohol allowed, and I was glad about that. I had achieved more days of sobriety in the past – angrily, unwillingly, jumping out of my skin. Each hour, each day a trial. But now days passed without me really wrestling with the problem, time evaporating on the road or the meetings and events we attended.

Our time on the road had become more routine as we settled on the kind of music we liked – '80s and '90s rock, and talked more about family and growing up. I gave him an edited version of my story – such as it was. I told him about the drinking and drugging, starting at thirteen, and full blown by seventeen, the trips to detox, the halfway houses – which he already knew about. I told him about the time I overdosed in Taunton and ended up at the hospital. The endless times that Helene had to rescue me, especially after our father gave up and refused to take my calls. Most everything, but not about the last time just before I left for good, what happened there at home, and what I put Helene through. When I thought I had no more shame, and nothing I really cared about, there was still that.

Louis told me about his life growing up with extended family at the

Home Camp in Maine, and regular trips to the Cape, before the move to western Mass. His mother and father had met at the Mashpee powwow, when his mother was fancy-dancing as a girl. She had traveled from Maine to visit relatives outside Boston, and they'd all gone to the powwow. Louis's father had grown up in New Bedford, where he had become Americanized in a Native, Portuguese, and New England Yankee sort of way. He'd spent time in the military, and had been working in the fishing business, but decided to move with Neesa to the Pemaquot land in Maine, where her father was from. Her mother was part Maliseet, which was another tribe in Maine, not far away, but more French and more Catholic – so it was kind of a Romeo and Juliet kind of romance. Only they didn't call it that.

Sometimes on the road, I would read aloud to Louis, some of the legal material he had brought with him, or information on the tribe we were about to visit – there was a lot he didn't know, and room for intercultural misunderstandings, even with the best of intentions.

But then we got into stories. I read from books I picked up along the way – whatever I happen to find – used or donated books, some Native, some not. And that got Louis on to some of the horror stories that he learned growing up, and used to tell Izzy to scare his pants off.

"Natives have some badass monsters," he claimed. "Some of the spirit stuff is really frightening – ghosts and shit. And then there's Chenoo, or what some people call Windigo...you won't sleep if I tell you."

"Try me."

"Cannibals. Windigo is the spirit that enters people if they eat other people, even during starving times. Then they come back, looking like just regular folks, and do their evil."

"And you believe it?"

"That's the problem. I believe it and I don't believe it, both."

"Yeah, I know. Being raised Catholic is kind of like that. And even though I rejected most of it, I can't help thinking some of it's true."

"Don't disrespect Mother Mary around my mother," he warned. "She's got her own private little combo-religion, but she takes it seriously."

"Oh, I would never."

On the way back from Phoenix, we made a return visit to Santa Fe, which surprised me. No unfinished business that I knew of. But I had an idea of what it might be, and I didn't like it. When we stopped the first time, we stayed three nights, a long time in one place. There were people he knew from previous meetings. And one of them was a woman, in her twenties, nice-looking, outspoken, driven.

On the third night of our first stop in Santa Fe, Louis never returned to our campsite. The meeting had run late and I was pooped. Louis was still engaged in intense conversation, and I heard talk about going out for *food and drink. I left, walking the short distance to the truck. When I woke in the early morning, he wasn't in the camper and he wasn't outside either.*

He didn't say anything, when he returned the next morning. That's what made me think he was with that woman. If it was something else – falling asleep, or somebody had a problem, he might have said. But not a word. I kept my fresh mouth shut. I had no right to say a thing if he wanted to be with someone else. He said he'd had different girlfriends over the years, all Native I assumed, but he didn't want the work or bother of a relationship while he was focused on his activism. Still, he was a guy, not bad-looking. Smart, well spoken, direct, serious but he could be funny, with a kind of intensity about him that was powerful, attractive.

But after that time in the desert areas with the Navajo, the Hopi, and the pueblo peoples, something had changed in me. I was clearer in the head and more willing to try toward something that might be important.

When he told me that we were going to stop again in Santa Fe, I felt a jolt. I asked why.

"I have to get something," he said.

"So we're not staying."

"We'll stay over."

"Tonight?" It would have been a real push.

"Tomorrow."

OK, so he wasn't going to tell me. He had a certain look about him; maybe the stress of travel and meeting so many people, the challenge of his work. Maybe it was me. Something in him wanted an outlet, a letting go, maybe a forgetting. Or maybe it was the other way, wanting contact, connection. I had a day to think about it, and one night, before we arrived in Santa Fe.

It was a long and boring day on the road, under a hot dry sun. By evening we were still in the desert, miles and miles between towns and gas stops. I was driving, and found a spot not far off the road, near a stand of cottonwood trees, for a little shade and privacy. We spoke very little during supper; that tension he carried inside him had gotten to me as well.

Funny thing, I wasn't even sure then what I was going to do. Not like a conscious decision or trying to manipulate the situation. But something was directing me, something like that urge to survive; and then the fight against it, that craving for not caring. There I was watching me watching him as he put out his sleeping bag under the awning, letting down the netting for the bugs. And then he was in the bag, not zippered all the way, and it would be moments, maybe seconds, before he was asleep. I wondered if he even noticed me in the folding chair, just sitting as I sometimes did. I got to my feet, realizing that I was committing myself, that I was letting it matter. That it was just plain me, Renee, and no drugs or alcohol to excuse my actions.

Then I was next to him, squatting by his head.

"Louis," I said.

His eyes flickered open, widening as he saw me so close. He blinked a couple times and then tried to roll on his side, pushing up on his elbow.

"What do you want?" He was tired, I know, and I'm sure he was uncertain about me, to say the least, or about getting more involved with someone like me. But he didn't look away, and he knew what I meant.

"I want to be with you."

He sighed. But I saw the flame flicker in his eyes, interest, desire. Me. And I had in that moment the idea that he had always seen something in me, something both good and bad – dangerous – like a drug.

"I'm better now."

Louis's smile said maybe, maybe not. But he was more awake now. I lay down on my side, facing him, and I could feel the heat that radiated from him. And my own heat.

"And clean."

His smile widened, and I put my hand on his cheek. He put his hand on my hand, lifting it away, and then replacing it. Then he touched my fingers to his lips, drawing them across his eyes and cheeks. He let go, bending to unzip the bag, and I helped him, until it was fully opened. Then we stretched out again on the sleeping bag, front to front. I waited for him to kiss me; his decision. Then he closed his eyes and took a breath, like someone going underwater. When he opened them again, we kissed, and he pulled me on top of him. The spark was lit, flickering, growing. Still, he was slow, deliberate. He kept watching me, never taking his eyes off me, even when desire had spread and become more urgent, the fire beginning to burn.

"Louis," I said. "I never did this before when I wasn't high, or the guy wasn't high."

"It's OK," he said, stroking my arms, my back. "We'll figure it out."

"Sure?" It was hard for me to admit the doubt. But I was still pushed on by something bigger than me, going forward blindly. That this was what I wanted, and it was good for me. He had been good to me, all this time, when he could have hurt me or abandoned me. What I saw was that he cared for me, for my pain, and that he respected my striving to find a better way.

We peeled off our clothes, naked by the side of the road, under the branches and the stars. Louis knew something of women, sexually. I could tell by the way he touched me, and let me explore his body. Then everything built to a pitch of heat and feeling and gladness that I had not known before, and I let it take over me, all defenses down.

"Woman," he said, breathing heavily. "You're strong for a little thing. What you do, you do all the way, and then some."

"I know, that's my problem."

"It's no problem."

Not here, not now. It was everything.

We put our sleeping bags together for the night, but I hardly slept. How did such a thing happen to me, after what went before? The stars were low and bright in a blue-black sky with no moon, and I felt like we were alone on another planet. I knew there was a lot ahead of us, good and bad, and some little kernel of fear stayed inside that I would somehow manage to spoil it, too.

When he woke, I was staring him down, once again.

"Louis," I said. "Are we still going to stop in Santa Fe?"

He gave me a long look. "Yeah, I have to pick up a file from Scott." Then he sighed. "And I really should let her know, Melanie, that I won't be seeing her."

"I guess so."

"I don't want to be an asshole. It's happened before."

"But you're not bound to me, you know that. This might be good for now, for on the road, but after that, who knows?" I had to shake my head. "I'm not sure I'm family material."

"Slow down, Shooting Star. One thing at a time." And then he pulled me back next to him and rolled on top, breathing, talking, kissing. That's when he gave me that name, and it stuck. I was nine weeks into sobriety, and almost believing change was possible. Which it is, although not always like that, like magic. If it takes time to build addiction, it takes time to relearn old ways and feelings. And that's why Neesa didn't trust me at first, on our return. It took some doing to move beyond Neesa's suspicion, and some pain.

It was only later, shortly before our marriage, one night in bed in the dark that I learned that Neesa had given Louis words of warning against me – that I had a power that could be good or bad. She thought I might be a sorceress to have turned her son's head in that way. Those were the words she called out to him as we were leaving on the trip.

"But you let me come, anyway."

"Well, I was twenty-five; she couldn't really tell me what to do."

"Oh, right. Big man and all."

"I thought she might be right," he said. "I couldn't explain it myself. I never wanted to be with someone like you. I wanted to marry a Native woman, have Native children, and live that lifestyle. Or at least with someone who valued our way of life. I still do."

"I've come pretty far, I think."

"Yes, but I didn't know it at the time." He shifted next to me, onto his back. "I was embarrassed at first – blond girl, blue eyes – just the symbol of what I didn't want in my life."

"And yet here you are."

"Here we are. I guess some part of me recognized that warrior spirit could be inside someone like you. Little but fierce, like a weasel, or a fisher

cat."

"Gee, thanks."

And I could tell there was a smile on his lips, a dimple in the dark.
"But I should give thanks to Izzy too."

"Izzy?"

"Yeah, but he liked you from the start. And my mother could see that.
She always trusted his, well, vision, insight, whatever you want to call it."

"I always knew he was special. But I didn't know he was in my court
way back then."

"Special is right. Definitely one of a kind."

"Sweet and colorful. And funny and gentle. A beautiful child."

"And still in your court."

2. Still Here, Not Gone, On the Rebound, Rising – by One Little Indian

A memory from growing up – actually, after we moved from the
Indian township in Maine to this former military base in
Massachusetts for housing and jobs. Fifth grade, maybe. My teacher,
Miss P., a local woman, young and earnest, was curious about me and
my family.

"Izzy, what's your background? I mean, your ancestry?"

When I told her we were Pemaquot and Wampanoag, it didn't
mean much, obviously.

"Well, where are you from?" she asked.

"Here," I said.

"But when did you move from out west, and why?"

Because, out west – maybe Arizona and New Mexico – was where
the Indians lived, those who were left. And only on reservations. So I
told her, "Never been out west. More north – Maine, Canada. Oh, and
Cape Cod too." Trying to be helpful left her totally confused.

"But where did you come from, *originally*?"

That was beyond me to explain. Another teacher, middle school,
wanted us to do family trees, as far back as we could get. We were told
that Emily's ancestors had come here the earliest – in 1620 with the
Pilgrims. I had to raise my hand. "My family's been here maybe ten,
twenty thousand years, something like that." But no one believed me, I
could tell. Including the teacher.

Thing is, it's hard to convince some people we're still here, alive,
and don't live in wigwams or tipis. It's true, diseases wiped out
millions of indigenous people, like the big plagues in Europe; wars
took a toll – *the* Indian Wars, never mind bounties and scalping. For
some, killing off the buffalo was the end of food and shelter, not to
mention our brothers of the plains. Reservations were usually crappy
land, bad water, no game; and large-scale livestock farming wasn't
really our deal. Cows and pigs in barns, not so much – especially if you
traveled like we did. Then and now, not everyone ended up on
reservations, anyway. Some Indians stayed near their homelands,
maybe keeping a low profile, just going about their business, not
calling attention. Can't blame them, either. One thing to be a "ghost"
– left over from another time. Another thing to be a curiosity that
belongs at the county fair or Wild West show.

And lots and lots of other Indian folks moved to the cities – not by
choice, thinking "Bright lights and car exhaust – can't wait!" In the
1950's, the Indian Relocation Act was meant to assimilate Natives and
give them urban jobs and homes, taking them away from home and
community. For some, it was a crisis of identity. You could say they
died of despair – suicide, drinking, violence, bad health, diabetes. But

others kept on keeping on…and still do to this day, having families, working jobs, trying for education, and having some say in how their lives go, and what's important.

Some good news, however. Louis, my brother, has his fingers on the pulse of Indian Country. He's the one who told me, "We're on the way back. The Native population is increasing, slowly, almost reaching what it might have been before bleep-bleep." Well, before Western contact. Let's just leave it at that. Natives are on the rise, raising their voices, and sharing their stuff: art, books, music, movies, fashion, media of all kinds. Pushing back to recover land and water rights, fishing rights, hunting paths, developing new urban programs for those who've left the reservation to renew traditions, keep the culture going and growing. Today, the calendar is full – powwows, marches, and protests, Talking Stick circles, language classes, cultural and educational programs of every kind year-round. Not dead, not gone, not quiet. Just look around; you'll see.

Chapter 10

Denis didn't return Helene's call until Saturday morning – from the road. Ohio. He was gone again, on a tour that had come up unexpectedly but was a good opportunity for the band. Prime folk venues, working with talented musicians and promoters; and another fiddle player, well known in the field, who wanted to talk to him about recording together.

Good for Denis, Helene thought. But that left her high and dry, dealing with Wishi-ta and her allergies. And whatever else she might have pried out of him, which he wasn't going to share from a noisy bar in Cincinnati.

Misty was well and Kenneth was fine, trim and neat and groomed as ever, even preparing Saturday breakfast for the two of them. A haircut during the week too; the little gray at his temples added character, maturity, as her sister-in-law liked to point out. He bounced from the stove to the counter, talking all the while. The new branch office was opening shortly and he was in discussions with a contractor to buy and "flip" some of the older, smaller houses around town for something bigger and better – and pricier.

"I have a one o'clock appointment with a seller, but I should be done by four. How about I swing by here and pick you up, and I can show you some of the properties we have an eye on?"

"Sure," she said, smiling at his boundless energy. He'd already been out for his morning run, showered and shaved, letting her sleep in. It was hard to say why she was so tired. Maybe she just had a lot to take in with all these new developments.

"And then," he said, "maybe drinks and dinner someplace not too shabby. How does that sound?"

"Sounds good to me."

"Rick says that new steakhouse is good – worth every cent."

"OK, then, let's do it."

"And after I've wined and dined you, maybe time for a little romance. I've missed you, coming home to this quiet house night after night. Misty will have none of me; she just hides when you're away."

Helene laughed. "Oh, come on. You told me you had business dinners Wednesday and Thursday."

"Yes. But that's business."

"Fine, I'll put on a dress."

He leaned in to kiss her. "But I have a little business to talk to you about also."

"Really? I thought the town-house development was put off."

He put the pan down on the stove, turning off the burner, and came to sit with her.

"It is. But this is even better. We'll need someone to 'stage' some of these new homes – that is, put in some basic furnishings and make the place look attractive, inviting. Basically like a professional shopper, except some of it we lease. Top-end stuff, baby. You'll be in your element."

"I will?" She had to laugh, although she was flattered. What she had done with their home, she had done on a budget. She was raised that way and couldn't get away from it. But it was nice-looking, good quality.

"I thought my element was giving school kids Tylenol and tissues for runny noses."

"Well, here's a new opportunity."

"It sounds like fun." And then she added, "But I won't have much time right away, the way things are going up there." She gestured vaguely toward the west.

"Really, you think so?" Kenneth looked a little disappointed. "I thought it was going smoothly. You understand what's going on and pretty much how to manage the problem, or handle it, if it comes up. Right? That's what I understood you to say. No crisis; everyone cooperating."

She scratched her neck. "Well, yes and no. There are still more allergens to test for, and then addressing the asthma part of it. Plus Malvina's due in a few weeks – that's the real reason I'm there."

Kenneth was back on his feet, stacking the dishes in the sink.

"Well, if there's any way to wrap things up, we could definitely use you." Then he glanced at the clock. "I have to go by the office before my meeting. Busy, busy, busy. But busy is good, right? Ka-ching!"

Helene, nodded, sipping her coffee.

He paused dramatically in front of her – handsome, athletic, hers. "I'm sorry I have to run. Weekends are the busiest time in real estate, you know that. We have our date tonight."

Helene finished her breakfast, thinking that she would get a walk in and maybe a trip to the library. But first, call Thelma Silberman.

Thelma was home when she called. "Helene, I got your messages, and I've been thinking of you. A lot. So you're home?"

"For the weekend. I was thinking of taking a walk. Want to join me?"

"Not so much. I'm working on a shawl. But come after you're done. I'll give you a cold drink. You can fill me in."

Helene got to Thelma's just a little after eleven. Thelma was almost twenty years older than Helene, prematurely white-haired, short and bosomy. Like Helene her schedule was lighter in the summer. Her great passion was knitting and crocheting, and she was involved with the Arts and Crafts Society. Her college-age son, Jacob, was rarely home, off now on a summer internship. After a slow start, she had proved to be a good friend, especially when Helene was coping with the aftermath of all that had gone on with Renee.

"My dear, my dear," she greeted Helene with a hug. "You look like a person who has undertaken a strange and mysterious journey. Is that true?"

"Kind of."

"Tell me all about it, and have a cookie and some lemonade."

They chatted, catching up on Helene's new situation. Helene also mentioned things at home with Kenneth and his summer plans for her.

Thelma did not look particularly pleased. When it came to Kenneth, she had a tendency toward sarcasm, one time calling him "a modern-day knight in Brooks Brothers armor and Rolex chain mail." She thought he didn't find her up to snuff, socially, for Helene, not the kind of friend he would have preferred for his wife

But Thelma stayed on the subject. "You're talking about teardowns, right?"

Helene shrugged. "I guess that's the term for it. Sounds terrible, but I'm sure whoever Kenneth works with would do good work."

Thelma's lips twitched. "Hold it there, missy. I want to show you something."

She left the room and came back with a postcard, handing it to Helene. "Is that who he's going to work with? Apparently they have their eye on my house."

The card was a solicitation for homeowners looking to sell their house at a competitive price to a developer to be torn down and rebuilt into something else – better.

"I'm not sure if it's a compliment to my location or an insult to the state of my house. I know it's not the best-kept house in the neighborhood. I'm just not Tina Tidy-Home, and my ex gives me such a hard time about home improvement projects, even though I house his son ninety percent of the time."

The name on the card was Daniel Clarke. Helene didn't know if that was the developer Kenneth had in mind, but the name seemed familiar.

"You're not moving, are you?" she asked in some alarm.

"Wasn't planning to. But such an incentive they're giving to get me out of here. Maybe it's time to go to New Hampshire, follow the other retirees."

"No!"

"No, no, honey. Just kidding. I'm not ready for retirement. And I have way too much going on here; I'm not going anywhere."

Helene found her heart was pounding. She would not be happy if Thelma left, especially if she left because she was pushed out of her home. But that wasn't the case. And that's not exactly what Kenneth was planning to do. Was it? All of a sudden, she wasn't so sure that she wanted to drive around with Kenneth looking at houses like Thelma's with the idea of getting people to leave so that great big new houses could be built.

"Well, you better not," Helene said.

Thelma reached across the table, touching Helene's hand. "Never mind. So you are otherwise OK? I know you're making progress with your niece. But how does it feel dealing with all those people and places from Renee's life? It must be a bit strange, even if your parting had not been so...abrupt. Probably kind of interesting, in its way."

"You're right – it's weird. But not bad. I mean, so far everyone seems to have liked Renee and thought well of her. I assume that she stayed off drugs and alcohol while she was there. It's just so bizarre that she had to become like another person from a whole different culture to do it."

Thelma sat back in her chair, head tilted, her therapist pose. "Maybe that was part of her transformation. But don't forget, she was still evolving, and who's to say that she wouldn't have eventually been ready to make contact with her own past. And, from what I understand, the Indian culture is also evolving, holding on to some traditions and taking on parts of the modern world, like computers, cars, all that good stuff."

Helene wrapped her hands around the drink glass. "I guess so."

"We are all human, after all, with a lot of things in common."

"I know. I know. But I don't see how I could commit to that, just for the sake of being an aunt."

"Who says you have to? Just be yourself. They reached out to you for help; that doesn't mean they're trying to bring you in – like Renee."

"She rejected us, to be with them."

"You see it that way, but maybe it was something else – opportunity, survival. You know about her addiction, but you weren't an addict. That's something Native Americans know something about and maybe have more understanding of, or at least acceptance. That's all."

"I don't know." Helene got up to bring her glass to the sink. "Enough of that. But thanks for listening, Thelma. I sometimes wonder if I'll ever get past all that stuff."

Thelma smiled, a bit sadly. "You don't really get past it; you just learn how to live with it and carry it with you."

After Helene left Thelma's, she ran a few errands and then returned home. There was a message on the answering machine, a number from the base. Malvina, she was pretty sure. And, then she had a brief, bad moment: maybe it was about Wishi-ta – another episode. It was not all clear and easy; things were still being worked out. And then another moment of anger; why had they had to interfere in her life in the first place?

When she called back, Izzy answered.

"Hi, Helene," he said, in his light, breezy way. "The message is that Wishi-ta and Tana-na are going to be dancing at the Summer Moon powwow in Upham tomorrow. In regalia. Neesa's staying home with

Malvina, but Noel's bringing the rest of us. It's only forty-five minutes from where you live, so we thought you might want to go."

"Oh, well," Helene said, relieved but a bit flustered. "Yes, I might like to, at some point. But I'm not sure about tomorrow. I'll have to check with my husband."

"Sure. We just wanted to let you know."

"We'll see you Monday, if tomorrow doesn't work out." Which she doubted it would.

Then Kenneth was back with much to discuss on their ride around town: changes on the Zoning Board; new properties on the market; and mainly, the progress at the new branch office, which he really wanted her to see. They also went to see a couple of the properties that were being targeted for teardown. Not Thelma's house, thank God, Helene thought. The places Kenneth took her to were all derelict, kind of eyesores in the neighborhood, older but without charm. One of them she thought kind of cute, a ranch in a neighborhood of modest family homes not far from the school. But Kenneth said there was no safe way to preserve anything that was there – it was better to knock it down to the foundation.

At the restaurant, Kenneth didn't care to hear more about Renee's family, or things on the base, and Helene didn't feel like talking about them, either. Or how she felt about them. But he did mention that he was playing nine holes of golf early in the morning, and then would be gone through midafternoon – a couple of open houses he needed to check in on.

"It's this time of year," he said, apologetically. "Spring and summer are just crazy. I thought you'd just be resting and relaxing. I mean, you just finished the school year, and then all this." By which he meant Wishi-ta's health and related issues. "It will be just you and me for supper. My sister invited us, but I thought you'd rather skip that. I know it can be a bit much with those kids and all the questions sometimes."

That was true, she conceded. All of it was true. Kenneth's career and his business opportunities had grown steadily since the last recession, when things had come pretty much to a halt. No question, the real estate business was cyclical and seasonal. Yet she'd thought there would be a leisurely Sunday morning and then maybe a hike or bike ride with Kenneth in the afternoon. Apparently not.

So she called Thelma the next morning.

"I have an invitation for you," she said. "How would you like to go to a powwow?"

"Is this a game we're playing?"

"Not at all. I know it's a change of tune, but I got a call yesterday that the twins would be dancing at the powwow in Upham. And it turns out Kenneth has a full day without me. So here I am, 'Free Bird.'"

Thelma laughed heartily. "Then let me put on my feathers and I will be 'Hummingbird.' Sure, I'd love to go; always up for a new experience. And I'd be happy to meet your niece and nephew, and the whole tribe – oops, I guess I shouldn't say that."

"Probably not." Helene paused. "And there's another reason…"

"Go on."

"Well, your professional eye – what you think of the twins when you see them, how they're doing, adjusting, all that."

"Emotionally, you mean?"

"And physically, everything – are they well taken care of?"

Helene heard a long exhalation, and then her name from the other end of the line.

"Yes?"

"You know I'd do that anyway, don't you? Kids' welfare, that's my job – and yours. And if I see something amiss, I do not keep it to myself."

"I do know that," Helene said, a bit plaintively. "But, honestly, with some of their customs and traditions, it's kind of hard to tell."

"Got it," said Thelma. "When do you want to leave?"

"Izzy said to get there for the Grand Entry around noon. Can we leave around eleven?"

"I'll be ready."

When she picked up Thelma, who emerged from the front doorway, Helene had to smile. Thelma had dressed for the occasion in a long black skirt, white blousy top, and a great big silver-and-turquoise necklace hanging from her neck like a bib. And matching earrings. With that striking outfit and Thelma's olive complexion, dark eyes and eyebrows, she might blend in with the crowd. Or not.

"That's quite a necklace," Helene remarked as Thelma got into the car.

"Navajo squash blossom," Thelma said, fingering the stones. "I got it on a tour to the Southwest, Arizona and New Mexico, at one of those trading posts."

"Very nice. But I don't think that's the kind of stuff we're going to see at this powwow."

Thelma waved that away. "Maybe. Maybe not. No matter. I wanted to show my solidarity with Native American causes."

"I see." She knew Thelma supported several organizations dedicated to social justice and change. But not Native Americans, necessarily.

"Actually, it's my first powwow," Thelma admitted. "I'm always interested in cultural events, but I never heard much about these until lately. Who would have thought in our own backyard?"

The directions to the powwow that Helene had gotten online led them down a long, winding suburban road, not far off the highway. Parking was in a grassy field, rather bumpy, that was part of a historical state park, small but quaint with barns and streams and walking paths through mature groves of trees. A few boys were assisting with the parking, and one of them pointed the women toward the entrance to the powwow. The field was not crowded, but across the way was a little village of vans and campers, with more cars and trucks pulled up.

The entrance was simply a table under an awning where a couple of women collected a fee of five dollars. Beyond them was another field of grass, lush with recent rain, a pavilion at one end and a ring of maybe twenty or thirty booths surrounding a central area roped off with stakes and a small fire pit in the middle. Against a background of trees coming into full foliage, with wooden picnic tables and lots of folding chairs, it had the feel of a summer picnic, rather cozy and casual.

"Is there a map or directory?" Thelma asked the women at the table.

"Just walk around," said the younger one in jeans and a T-shirt; her manner was brisk, businesslike. "You'll find everything. Or ask."

"Okey-dokey," Thelma said. "Any rules we should know about? This is my first powwow, so I don't know and I don't want to offend anyone."

Helene's brow puckered. Thelma's question seemed unnecessary; a line was forming behind them.

The other woman at the table looked over. She was not young but still handsome with waist-length hair hanging loose down her back, jet black. Other than her jewelry, she wore no regalia, just a tribal T-shirt and sensible shoes; she had prepared for a long day running the event. She smiled at Thelma, her dark eyes sparkling. "No rules, but a few guidelines. The emcee will say something before the Grand Entry. Thank you for asking."

As they entered they heard crackling noises on the PA system; tuning up for the day's program of events. People of all ages were walking around in regalia, in groups, laughing and talking. Some folks were setting up chairs; others stood outside the inner ring, where Helene presumed the dancing would take place.

"Testing. Testing." Helene recognized the voice over the PA system: Izzy – apparently the tech guru for all kinds of events. She could see him standing near the head table, not far from the tent that covered two groups of singers, the drums already in place. Izzy was in regalia too, except that his sunglasses were sitting on his head, holding his hair back like a headband.

She placed her hand on Thelma's arm. "That's Izzy, the tall, thin guy over there at the table. See – tapping the microphone."

Thelma looked. "Well, that's a rather lovely young man, I must say. The outfit suits him very well."

"Regalia," Helene said, automatically. "It's called regalia."

"Yes," Thelma said, comfortably. "Much nicer. Should we go over and say hello?"

"I don't want to bother him while he's setting up. But I want to find the twins, and the others." She scanned the area, which suddenly looked much fuller of bodies in motion. "I'm pretty sure they're all in the Grand Entry parade, so we'll see them then, and we can catch them afterward. Like I said, nobody knows I'm here."

"I'm sure they'll be very happy," Thelma said.

"Gray Owl here," the emcee's voice announced. "Ten minutes to Grand Entry. Can all dancers please proceed to the entry area. Before we begin, we will observe the sacred circle ceremony and a special honoring song for our vets. I want to take a moment to remind everyone, no photos during the ceremonial parts of the powwow; everything else, pretty much OK. If you want to take a picture of someone outside the circle, it's always nice to ask first."

"OK, we're coming along, now…" The voice faded, and there was a pause away from the microphone. Then he resumed. "Almost ready. A few more veterans to the front, please."

Pause, muttering, static. The voice continued, "Meanwhile, I want to start, as always, with thanks and acknowledgment of all that is good, and the power that has brought us here together on this most wonderful day in a place called Upham by the settlers, but which is Setaug to us, our homeland for thousands of years. We give thanks to all relatives, two-legged, four-legged, those who swim and those who fly. We give thanks for the abundant wealth of Mother Earth." There was another pause, and it sounded like a chuckle. "OK, not wealth. We don't do wealth. That's not our thing, stockpiling stuff, while anyone else goes without. Maybe the better word is abundance, the abundance of Mother Earth, which we celebrate here with glad hearts."

Helene and Thelma exchanged glances. The emcee had such a casual, friendly tone, but there was a bite in his commentary, as well.

The Grand Entry started with the veterans, then the elders, and Helene saw a few faces from the base, the Chief in an impressive headdress and a couple of the older women with shawls, and blankets folded over their arms.

Then it was the adult men and women, and she was tickled to see Noel in his special ribbon shirt, with a headdress of feathers and moccasins on his feet. She didn't want to wave at him, but he saw her and nodded as he shuffled past. Others entered the circle, few that she recognized, until one woman, tall and serious, passed close by – the Native American activist from the TV interview. Helene quickly scanned the powwow program, remembering the name, Carolyn Red Fox, and saw that she was presenting a workshop later, "Indian Givers: global contributions of indigenous people of the Americas."

When Helene looked up again, the dancers were starting to fill the circle, and suddenly Izzy appeared, bare chested, braided, and resplendent in feathers and beads. He swayed and dipped side to side, fluid and graceful, in a trance of quiet joy, so different from the gawky, thrown-together young person hurrying by on his bike. Here too he had his followers: a colorful group of young adults, school friends and work friends, cheering him on outside the circle. Helene elbowed Thelma, whispering, "That's him; that's Izzy."

Then came the children, all of them. Malvina's boys were right up front, leading the dancers in a practiced, assured manner. The twins followed with Kiowa, Tana-na emulating his boy cousins, moving energetically in rhythm with the drum, while Wishi-ta stayed close to Kiowa and stepped along delicately, a small imitation of the older women who had passed by.

"There they are!" she whispered loudly to Thelma. "Those kids in the front. The little ones are the twins."

"They're beautiful!" Thelma said. "Such wonderful clothes. That little boy, how proud he looks. Isn't that something?"

As they came closer, Wishi-ta looked up and saw Helene. First her face clouded, and then she was jumping and waving, until Kiowa looked over too, giving a friendly smile.

"Oh, my! She looks like you," Thelma said. "The little girl. Same coloring, same features." She turned to Helene. "I guess you must have noticed that."

Helene pressed her lips together. "More like Renee, but we did look alike as girls."

"It's marvelous that so many of the children are taking part. Some of them don't look very Indian, do they?"

Helene had to agree. Although the majority were "people of color," some appeared black or Hispanic. And many were blond or blue-eyed, showing European ancestry.

"I wonder if that's ever a problem," Thelma remarked in her school psychologist voice. "I mean, with being authentic and belonging to a tribe, that kind of thing. I imagine it could be awkward for those kids who look white, if they grew up in this culture and identify this way, even if they have Native relatives."

"I don't know, but that's a good question."

The Grand Entry procession had come to an end, with many folks dancing within the circle, and then, when the drum ceased, starting to exit.

"Maybe we can catch them now," Helene said. She spotted Kiowa's yellow dress, adorned with hundreds of small metal cones, jingling with every step.

"Kiowa!"

Kiowa, stopped, looking around, and then gestured toward a place outside the circle and drumming tent.

By the time Helene and Thelma arrived, Kiowa was chatting with a woman, while the twins were dancing excitedly around two older men, both in bright purple shirts and leather leggings, with magnificent feather headdresses. They both wore glasses, and looked just alike. They were no younger than seventy, and might have been eighty.

One of the men scooped Wishi-ta into his arms, while the other teased Tana-na that he had something hidden in his hand. An old joke, a familiar routine.

Just as Helene and Thelma arrived, Kiowa gave the other woman a hug and turned back to the twins and the elders.

Thelma strode up to the group.

"Hi, there. I'm Thelma," she announced, not shy. "This looks like a happy reunion."

One of the men smiled with utmost good nature. "It is a reunion – the old twins and the young twins. That's kind of special, don't you think?"

"Very special," Thelma said. "Do you mind if I get a picture of you, together?"

Thelma had the gift of inserting herself into all kinds of groups and situations without the least embarrassment. But Helene winced a little when Thelma asked their ages – the young – four and a half. And the old – seventy-eight. But she was glad that Thelma had brought her camera and had asked first. She realized too that Thelma was watching the children, asking questions and listening to their answers as she snapped away.

The rest of the afternoon passed quickly. Helene and Thelma had a lunch of hot dogs and Indian tacos with the family at the picnic tables under the trees, and then made the rounds to all the booths. Thelma chatted up the vendors, discussing yarns, beads and patterns, or the uses of the herbs and teas. Kiowa took the children to get fitted for new moccasins, an annual event.

Helene found herself on her own, drifting along with the crowd, booth to booth, stopping once for a lemonade. As she stepped away with her full cup, she spotted a young man in full dance regalia, just ahead, and watched as a feather fell from his headdress onto the ground, which was a patch of mud and grass.

"Wait," she called out, but he kept walking, unaware. Helene took a few steps forward and retrieved the feather. It would be a shame for anyone to step on it and break it or grind it into the mud. She shook off a few particles of dirt and hurried after him.

"Excuse me," she said, coming alongside him. "You dropped this."

He turned toward her and glared as she held the feather toward him. "You should have left it and let me know so that I could get it myself. It has to be cleansed."

Helene was surprised. "It's not that dirty. It was only there a second."

He frowned. "But you handled it, and you haven't smudged, have you?"

"No," Helene said, still confused, and now feeling accused. "I was only trying to help."

"Well, you didn't," the young man said, taking the feather and shaking his head. "And if it was an eagle feather, we'd have to do a special ceremony with the vets; the whole powwow would have to stop." His lips twitched side to side. "That might be good to know, if you're coming to a powwow." He turned and walked away.

Helene was left standing there with her lemonade. "Not even a thanks," she muttered. Clearly, she had offended, without meaning to. But where were these rules posted, anyway? Or was it just the insiders' way of keeping others out? Like, *You can visit the powwow and spend your money, but you're not one of us.* At least that's how it came across; or, in fairness, how he came across.

She continued looking for Thelma. There was one booth she had stopped at before; the jewelry on display was more abstract and contemporary in design, a few pieces that she liked. She came up to the booth, standing next to a petite, middle-aged woman with long hair looking at shell jewelry, who looked vaguely familiar. She was not in regalia but wore a pendant of a walrus, carved in ivory or bone.

"Bernice?" Helene said after a moment. The short woman took off her sunglasses, her face almost perfectly round, and eyes that seemed almost Asian. "It's me, Helene, from the base – you know, Renee's sister. We sat together at the potluck dinner."

"Oh, yes." Bernice's smiled widened, taking over her whole face, making her eyes almost disappear.

"Do you dance?" Helene asked.

"Just the intertribal. It's all kind of new to me. I didn't grow up with any of this."

"Really?"

"I'm Inupiaq – from Alaska." She paused, waiting for Helene's response.

"Eskimo?"

"We don't use that name for ourselves. Anyway, I couldn't wear my ceremonial clothes to a place like this; I'd sweat to death." She laughed, merrily, and Helene did too, after the image of Bernice in a fur parka flashed by.

"I suppose you would. But how did you ever get here – I mean, this far from there – where you're from?"

Bernice shrugged. "My dad was military; we moved a lot. He was white; my mom is Inupiaq. I still go back sometimes, but it's a long trip."

"I'll bet."

Then Bernice went back to the jewelry she was looking at, rather simple, stylized earrings. "These will work," she murmured. "I'm trying to match a certain blue."

"Don't you make your own?" Helene asked, surprised.

Bernice looked up. "Not really. I've made a few things, but I'm never happy with them. Not my thing. I'm much better with chalk." Now she was smiling cheerfully. "That's my medium. Chalk drawings, mostly portraits, some animals, nature. I could do that all day."

"Oh, I see," said Helene, rather impressed. "Well, good luck, then. I'll see you around."

Thelma was at the crafts booth, watching a weaver. She was well loaded up with new purchases. After the demonstration, Helene was thinking it might be time to say good-bye and get on the road. As they walked back to the picnic table, the emcee announced the intertribal dance; everyone was invited to enter the circle. Kiowa waved across the ring to Helene and Thelma. Helene declined with a shake of her head, but Thelma went without hesitation. Wishi-ta had run over to the side of the circle, looking up at Helene, one of her braids coming loose and her shawl dragging on the ground. "Come on, don't you want to?"

It was tempting, but Helene couldn't do it. "Not today. Some other time, maybe."

"OK," Wishi-ta said. "I know you'll like it." Then she spun, making the fringe fly, and ran off to join the others.

As Helene watched from outside the circle, someone stepped next to her, she thought to get a better view.

"Ah, Helene Bradford, from the base," a man said, a light baritone. Helene turned to see the fellow she'd met on the way out of the Intertribal Center, Elsa's brother, Erik. Not in regalia, but somewhat dressed for the occasion, with a kerchief at his neck and a large silver belt buckle. A backpack hung over his shoulder.

"Oh, yes, hi. I didn't expect to see you here."

"Yup, me. I can't get away from it. Whenever I'm in town, Elsa's got me helping in some way or another. We're doing a big feast after the powwow, and I'm on the grill crew."

"Oh?" Helene turned toward him, interested. "I thought it ended at five. I didn't realize that it went on at night too."

"Yeah, the feast. Lots of folks are staying overnight, camping out, so they like to eat together, without all the..." He gestured at the milling crowds.

"The guests?"

"You could say that. You interested?"

Helene shook her head. "I haven't been invited."

"It's not that kind of thing. Everyone knows the Lopes family; that's why you're here, right? If you don't have something for the potluck, throw in a few bucks." He cocked his head, appealing. "It's a good time – relax, kick back, we'll get out the board games, old school, new school, any kind you can think of." His smile widened. "OK, that can get pretty intense."

She laughed briefly. "No, I really couldn't. I'm here with a friend, and we're leaving shortly." She pointed out Thelma in the dance circle with Wishi-ta and Kiowa.

"Well, maybe I'll see you another time," Erik said, but he remained at her side. "Back around the base. You can't help running into folks there. You should really come out to some of the socials. We even have a beer or two, not like here. Dancing to the oldies; that's a lot of fun." He paused, taking a breath. "If you don't know the steps, I'm a pretty good teacher."

Helene smiled, forced to be upfront. "I'm sure it's nice, but I am married, you know, as I said before. I'm only there during the week. On the weekend, I'm home with my husband."

"Oh, yeah?" he said, looking around. "Where is he? I don't think I saw him."

Helene sighed, putting a hand to her mouth before she said something heated. He was pressing his interest a little beyond what was friendly. But she didn't want to tell him off, being the brother of the Chief's wife. And she was kind of flattered that he was paying attention. Or was it something else, some signal she was sending that she wasn't aware of?

Then he said, leaning in, close to her ear, "Renee said you were beautiful – well, like her but more beautiful – that's what she said." And then, as she startled, he stood back, smiling. "And taller. She always thought that her, uh, troubles, stunted her growth, that she should have grown a few more inches." He laughed as Helene's mouth fell open. "But in her pregnancy, she was beautiful – in full bloom, as they say. Damn big, though, carrying those twins."

Helene swallowed her first reaction – *Who do you think you are?* She was stunned. Not that she hadn't dealt with unwelcome come-ons over the years; she had, plenty, and sometimes in the most inappropriate places, like out at a restaurant with Kenneth across the table, a client rubbing her knee – but she hadn't expected here, not like this, invoking Renee.

Then Thelma was back with the twins, Pawnee, and Cree. "Kiowa's in line at the bathrooms," she announced. "Oh, hello!" she said, noticing Erik with obvious interest. "I'm Thelma, an old friend of Helene's friend. And you must be a new friend…"

Helene started to say "someone from the base." But the kids had surrounded him, shouting, "Erik! Erik!"

"Say hello to the Candy Man." With a sly look, he slid off the backpack and unzipped a front pocket, revealing a stash of candy. He brought out chocolate bars, packs of gum, and bags of M&M's, brown and yellow. Wishi-ta reached out for one of the bags.

"No!" Helene stepped forward. "Wishi-ta, you can't have those!" She snatched the M&M's away, returning them to Erik. "Sorry," she said, in her strict nurse's voice. "Nothing with nuts or made in a plant with nuts – allergies, they're quite serious."

Wishi-ta had pulled her hand back, chagrined. Erik lifted his shoulders. "OK. Did not know. No problem. We'll find something else for Wishi." He poked around the pocket of the backpack. "How about Life Savers? Will that do?"

Wishi-ta did not look like she wanted Life Savers, but she took them with a soft, "Thank you." Meanwhile Tana-na was halfway through a chocolate bar and the other two boys were sucking on Tootsie Pops. To Helene's surprise, Wishi-ta sidled up next to her, leaning against her thigh, just under her elbow.

"For you ladies?" Erik offered his candy selection. Another strike against him in Helene's mind, offering junk food snacks, especially at a powwow. Neither healthy nor authentic. But no one else seemed to hold it against him.

"No thanks."

Izzy's head appeared behind Thelma, and he walked up next to Erik. "Hey."

"Hey, yourself."

"Anything there for me?" He selected a Mounds bar, munching on it incongruously as he twirled the end of a braid, festooned in leather wraps and feathers.

"Aren't you glad you came?" he asked Helene and Thelma.

"Wonderful! Quite the cultural experience," said Thelma.

"Yes, very nice," Helene said, less effusive. "But we've got to get back, I mean to town, to our homes. I'll be at the base tomorrow, but not until after lunch. I'll see you all then." She turned to Erik. "We'll be going along, then."

"Nice to see you again," he said, all polite. "And nice to meet you, Thelma."

As they made their way back to the car, Thelma was humming in a kind of rhythmic manner, snatches of the drum songs, keeping a running commentary.

"Great kids, all of them. They've come through their losses pretty well – the twins, but the cousins too. It must be hard on all of them to lose such important family members. The cousins seem very close, like they really look out for each other. That Noel, solid as a rock." She stepped daintily around a mud puddle. "And Izzy; what a character. I love it! You really can't put a label on him, can you? And yet he too seems very grounded, centered, kind of a happy-go-lucky type."

"So you think they're OK?" Helene asked, unlocking the car door. "The twins, I mean."

"I do. Except that Wishi-ta seems a little less lively than the others.

Maybe pacing herself a little, holding back. And I thought she sounded a little breathy at times. Maybe it's the asthma – or fear of another asthma attack. When you've been short of breath like that, it can be quite frightening."

"Hm…" Helene nodded. "That's helpful, thanks, Thelma."

As they departed the parking field, Thelma added, "Nice guy, that…ah, Erik. Great with the kids. And nice-looking, too. Fifties, do you think?" She chuckled. "Looks like he could be a fun time."

Helene choked back an exclamation.

"Oh, come on, Helene. A woman can dream, can't she? I didn't see a ring on his finger."

For all her psychological insight, Thelma had not picked up on the strange vibe. Helene decided not to mention the strange conversation after all. That could be difficult, even with Thelma.

But another awkward thing did come up on the drive, as they were getting closer to home. Thelma had been quiet a while, thinking.

"You know, Helene," she said, in her more serious mode. "You're good with kids, that's clear. Has there been any discussion of adoption?"

"Oh, no. Never."

"Don't say it like that, like it's totally crazy. I mean, if the father is going to be in prison for twenty years, it seems reasonable they might consider it a long-term option."

"Kenneth is adamant that we limit our involvement. I really don't know how it would work at this point in our lives."

Thelma batted the air.

"What! You're still young enough, and fit. Don't talk like an old fart before you are one. No, I just wondered if it had come up."

Helene found her heart beating fast at Thelma's words: prison, adoption. Maybe not such a fantasy, not so unreal.

They exited the highway, only minutes from home. Thelma had been watching her, evaluating.

"Those genes are strong," she said. "Now I can imagine what you were like as a child, you and your sister. Wishi-ta could pass for your daughter."

"Hm…" Helene murmured, taking it in without comment.

But later she had a terrible, restless night in bed with Kenneth, unable to settle but not wanting to disturb him. The powwow had been fine, nice in its way. But those conversations, with Erik and with Thelma, had gotten to her. It was one thing for Erik to remark on her looks – big deal. But then, what he said about Renee – the intimacy of it – she couldn't help picturing the two of them in a room somewhere back at the base, probably Renee's house – and Renee saying that to him, and talking about her – Helene. That was bad enough, but then, what Thelma had said – "adoption" – when that was the thing she and Kenneth had been trying to steer away from, that level of entanglement. And worse: "could pass for your daughter." Worse because it was true. And, if true, what did that mean?

Renee's journal – 11

Now that the time is approaching, I'm fighting that old impulse to run away, get out. Only thing, I can't get away from my own body, and not from these two little squirming creatures inside of me. It's ridiculous how pregnant I am. Totally uncomfortable. Totally awkward. Kind of useless for many things. If there was a fire, I might not escape the burning building. Slow, slow, slow. And not good on stairs, either. Can't run; can't hide. Varicose veins and high blood pressure; not in fighting shape any more. All I do these days is sit on the sofa, reading or writing. When the panic comes over me, I take deep breaths and hide under the blanket.

But really, I'm fine. I think so. I've looked at some of those childbirth manuals, but I know none of it really helps when push comes to shove. I have to accept that I do not have total control over my life or my body. And maybe that's not a terrible thing. All I have to do is try to stay healthy and rested; the rest is just kind of happening to me. And, scary as it is, it's thrilling too. I can say that it's a blessing to have these children; it's also a blessing to go through childbirth. Pain itself doesn't scare me. I've always had a high tolerance for physical pain; maybe that's why my life in addiction went on for so long. There was hardly any kind of noisy, dirty, cold, terrible place I couldn't take, if I was high, or looking to get high. It's the mystery of it all that I've been pondering; and the idea of my mother born to her mother and all those generations going back and back.

So it's going to be a matter of trust, and that was probably the hardest lesson to learn. But I do trust, in Louis, Neesa, Malvina, Noel, Elsa, Charlotte, Bernice, all those who have been here for me during this pregnancy. I was disappointed that the births would not be as I hoped: at home, a midwife, no drugs, etc. Well, having twins and hypertension changed that. So to the hospital I will go. And, if it ends up a C-section, so be it. I begged and begged for no drugs, but they said it depends how things go. But not something addictive – that's what they said, and I have to trust them.

Louis, of course, is not here at the moment. He's in Montreal, but that's not far, if things start earlier than expected, which they say is likely. But I'm OK with all that now; I get it. When he has to go, he has to go. I know he'll be back, because his home and his heart are here, as he says, or wherever his family is, and that's me now too.

Denis says he'll be here as soon as he hears the news – that the babies have been born. Part of me wishes that Helene could be here too, through the birth and to greet the babies when they come into the world. But I just don't see how that could happen – like magic, we forget about all the bad things that happened, to both of us, in our family growing up, and then at the end – the grand finale, so to speak. The end of that life and beginning of this one; my rebirth. And even if that could be so – that we could get beyond that – what about Helene herself – the fact she never had kids – can't, as far as I know. Now here we are with twins! Like rubbing it in their faces. Not that I even know Kenneth, but Denis is not too crazy about him. Calls him a striver, an achiever. Says he built the perfect trophy case to keep his trophy wife in – Helene! I said that he was talking crap. No one has more heart or deserves more peace than Helene. Denis says Kenneth is very protective, making sure Helene's got everything she needs. Is that love? I wouldn't know about that kind of love. With Louis and me, it's different, but I don't know if I could ever explain it to anyone.

The truth is, no one really expected me to stay, most of all Neesa. I know she was biding her time until I left, like a blowing leaf. I get it; I really do. How could a mother like that want someone like me for her son? I think I surprised her, though, lasting as long as I did, almost a year that Louis and I were living together, getting along, building a life, talking about a future. Poor Neesa! And the rest of them. Well, not all. Izzy, of course, my guardian angel. And, in fairness, Noel; he's never given me a hard time. I keep telling Louis that if something ever happens to him, I'm going to take up with Noel – either get Malvina out of the way, or become wife number two. The problem is, I wouldn't be a good wife number two; I'd have to be number one. So look out Malvina! I'd take the kids, too. And of course Neesa, now that you mention it; she's part of the package. Now, that is.

Now it's a different story, because of what we went through, that trial of fire, so to speak, that finally changed things between me and Neesa. So Neesa was proved right in the short term and me in the long term. I didn't leave, but I did fail; that is, fall off the wagon – that stupid old expression. Just as weak and untrustworthy as she always thought I was.

It was just over a year since our road trip, and Louis was busy with his advising work. Sometimes I went with him; but I had started a job here, at a little general store near base, plus taking a class at the community college, starting to think about a degree. Then one day Louis announced he was going cross country again, for a month; but I couldn't go. What was worse, he was traveling with this guy I really disliked, who also didn't think much of me, at least in part because I was white. I was angry with Louis, for announcing this out of the blue, not even waiting until the end of the semester, only a couple weeks away. And knowing he'd get an earful of "whites this, and whites that" just didn't make me happy. I remember saying to Louis, "So this is your full-time cause now? It can't wait, and they can do nothing without you? So important! Just tell me, who are you when you're not being an Indian all the time. Do you have any idea at all?"

It wasn't nice, and he wasn't happy with me, either. I sometimes felt that he was embarrassed about me; that it was a weakness on his part that he had taken up with me, and he wouldn't be taken seriously. And why *couldn't he be more like Noel, who enjoyed his golf league and rock music concerts? Or Izzy, who was into science fiction, and loved to play with computers?*

Our first big fight. He left. I was in the house by myself. Not that we had any liquor, because we didn't. But I went that night to one of the socials, this one with a '60s theme. Again, no drinking. But I was dancing and socializing, and one of guys there, not a regular, he just showed up now and then, said to me, "So, me and some friends are going to Jackson's Bar up the road a couple miles. Want to come? You can ride with me."

Of course I wanted to go. More than anything. So I did. I had one drink, then another, and then began drinking with a vengeance. And, to my surprise, I really had lost tolerance for drinking. Soon I was nauseous, slurring my words, and had to throw up in the toilet. But that didn't deter me; I was dedicated to ruining things as best I could. There was dancing; the same guy put an arm around me, but even he could smell the puke, and said, "Maybe enough for you, sweetheart." But it wasn't enough. And when he said he was leaving, did I want a ride home, I wouldn't go. Finally, when they were closing, another guy took me by the elbow, steering me to the door. Maybe he tried to get me in his truck; maybe he was yanking at my pants; but I wasn't going anywhere with anyone.

"The North Star," I cried, and pulled away from him, stumbling into the darkest shadows of the trees outside the bar, the light fading quickly beyond the parking lot. My plan was to walk; my plan was always to walk, away. There was, in the way back of my mind, this idea of a run-down cabin in remotest Vermont that belonged to my dad's family, where we went a couple times when I was very young, so I hardly remember it at all. Except the isolation, the farthest place I could think of.

I walked toward the wilderness. But it wasn't too long before I began to think of my cozy bed at home with Louis and the wolf blanket we pulled on top of us when it was cold. And the sofa where I liked to sit and study, or even the backyard where I'd take a chair out next to Malvina and watch the kids play. I turned, and my feet got going a little quicker, in the direction toward the base. If I got back, and I drank a lot of water, and I fell asleep, no one would know. Except me.

I got on the road, and followed the yellow lines, one foot in front of the other, stopping once to rest, and once to vomit. I got to the base, the big sign at its entrance, and I could feel the warmth in my heart, the desire to get home and safe, and get this behind me, hidden away, no worse for the wear.

But it was not meant to be. The streets looked too similar with the same kind of homes. My head was aching, and I was thirsty. I found myself out at the end of a street that led into a field surrounded by a barbed-wire fence, a DEP toxic waste site. I was turned around, lost. I tried to get back to familiar ground; I tried. Finally, there was a house with a swing set like the one on our street. I crossed into the backyard, thinking it was a shortcut. But it wasn't, and I sat down on the swing, exhausted. It began to swivel and sway, and off I fell. And there I stayed until the next morning, waking to a mutt of some sort licking my face. And, following the mutt, a woman I did not recognize, but who apparently recognized me.

It was Noel who came to get me, with Izzy. They got me in the truck and drove me home.

I was in bed for the day. Malvina came over and wiped me off and gave me broth and water. No one spoke to me, but I heard them talk about me, and I know a phone call was made to Louis. After school, Izzy was by my side, and he brought his flute to play while I lay on the sofa, an ice pack on my head.

"So are you on guard duty?" I asked him.

"Nah, I just wanted to hang out with you and Red Cat."

I tried to smile. "I guess I made a mess of myself. Not the first time, either."

"They're going to do a sweat on you," he said. "You need some strong medicine."

I knew what he meant; they had built a sweat lodge on the edge of the base, near the woods. Louis had gone a couple times, and some of his friends when they visited.

"Hm...think it will work?"

He shrugged. "I think you should try."

"When?"

"Tomorrow night, if you're ready."

I sighed. "But Louis won't be back."

"Nope. It's just the women, anyway."

"Oh, boy," I said. "Just what they've been waiting for; a chance to steam me alive." I was joking, but Izzy looked worried.

"No, I'll go. I want to go."

Thing is, I don't remember much of that experience, either, my first sweat. It all seemed so strange, foreign, the rituals, things I now know as medicine and that are beautiful, meaningful: the four gates or doors; how we enter and leave; the teas we drink before and after; the cold water poured on hot stones; the prayers. I knew nothing then of the sacred roles: firekeeper, pipe carrier, and drummer, all of them singing through the night for the one who is suffering.

That night I only knew I was inside the lodge with seven or eight other women, including Neesa and Malvina, pitch black except for the glowing stones in the fire pit. Neesa was in charge, giving directions in that way of hers, with a telling gesture and a few words. She waited for us all to smudge before entering. She ladled the water onto the stones to make steam, and she said when it was time to take a break or to change the stones. Malvina was her main assistant, and Izzy was there, outside, for part of the time. He helped the others bring hot stones in on a shovel, while Noel stayed home with Kiowa and baby Pawnee.

There was singing; some of the women beating on their hand drums. There was talking too, about life and problems, not just mine. I remember clearly a story that Bernice told us about growing up on the Alaskan tundra, and how one day she fell through the ice while skating with her brother, and she thought she would die while her brother went for help. But in those cold minutes, just after twilight, the northern lights had started to shimmer in the sky, and with them came a humming sound, like music. She had thought it was death, until her brother came back with her dad, and they hauled her out.

I was light-headed, not entirely myself. I dozed. I was weak from lack of food and the alcohol, even though I had sucked down water during the day. I might even have passed out at one point. But they got me back outside, revived me with cold water, and sat with me until it was time to go back in.

But this I remember: the sweat down my back, and my abdomen, my arms, and face, the stickiness of my pits and groin; the melting and evaporation of the toxic waste in my system. All of us inhaling the steam and one another's breath, exhaling pain and stress and fear. For the first time in such a long time, I didn't fight, but gave in. I was not alone in a sterile room with only my shame and defeat for company. Except for Helene, coming and going at my bedside, sick with fear, without hope and alone herself in the suffering I caused her.

That's how I know that the birth – or births, I should say – will be all right, no matter what happens. That is, we'll get through it, all of us: me, the babies, Louis, and the family. So what, it will be the hospital with a doctor checking on me. I can deal with it. Louis will come, if he can get here. Neesa and Malvina will be at my side; my coaches, so to speak. Now that they saved me, they're stuck with me on their hands. Something changed since that time I fell off the swing and into the sweat lodge. I had stayed ahead of addiction with avoidance and willpower, and still I slipped. But when I slipped, the women were there for me, without holding it over my head. In a weird way, I think it made Neesa more comfortable with me after that happened; maybe just that it had come, as she expected, and we moved on from it. Not that she ever, ever wanted me for a daughter-in-law. But Louis loved me, no matter how impossible that seems to anybody. And she loved Louis. So there we were. And here we are, awaiting her grandchildren who may end up as much like me as Louis. But I think she'll love them too.

Renee's journal – 12

I have ten minutes, maybe twenty before one twin or the other needs me. No one told me that breastfeeding was so constant, that babies woke so often, and we have two!

Well, it's a mess. I'm a mess. It's all a glorious mess. And I can't believe that these two babies came out of me, and that I'm still here to tell about it. The births were a story, like I'm sure all are. Even at the hospital, there was the drama of whether Louis would make it in time. I was scheduled for a Monday, but the babies were ready to come before that, at thirty-seven weeks – not bad for twins, and they're good weights: baby boy, the first out, at four-and-a-half pounds; baby girl, three minutes later, at five pounds. Everyone was so pleased – like I'd won the contest for biggest pig at the country fair. But I was happy too. And shocked that they came out so perfect, and with so little trouble – well, once the doctor made the incision.

Neesa stayed with me and Malvina came later. They said Louis was on the way, almost back. He started at midnight for a seven-hour ride, but the doctor was ready to begin the surgery first thing in the morning. Well, Louis made it, and he was a mess too. In a state – not about me, but about their names. He begged me to hold off, and to wait for him, which I did. But those babies have come into the world without names, and we're still waiting on Louis for a final decision. He says it takes time; he wants American Indian names for them at school, and in the public; but they must have their Pemaquot names, as well, which they'll get at the naming ceremony. I said if he doesn't come up with something soon, they will be Sally and Freddy. It's funny, I never was a girl who played a lot with dolls, or dreamed of my own children someday. Maybe because I was so young when my mother got sick, it wasn't part of my growing up much; we didn't have many other little kids around. By then, Helene had outgrown dolls. So I never named anything, not even Red Cat, who was gifted to me by Izzy as a kitten, years ago, before he became the big, orange, watchful fur ball that he is today.

I hear a bleating from the basket, and I think it's the boy. He's such a busy one, and hungry all the time. Even after this long pregnancy, sometimes I can't believe they're here, in the world, as separate little beings, our own little family. They don't look much like either one of us, or anyone; just themselves. Everyone says they're beautiful, and I think they are, even though I never thought babies were beautiful.

Yup, somebody's stirring, and I'm on my own for a couple of hours, because I wanted to be, to see what it feels like. There's almost always someone around, someone to get one baby or change the other one. But I needed this, quiet time, just us, so they can know I'm their mom. It's hard for me to say it, that I am. Because I can hardly believe that this could happen at all; or, not a mistake or worse. We are a family within a family, and we're all fine, at least for the moment. In another week or so, we're headed up to the Home Camp in Maine, all of us, for the naming ceremony. Looks like we're packing for a year.

I'm being summoned. I'll write when I can, but not like before, I don't think.

Renee's journal – 13

Twins asleep. Diaper bag packed, ready to go. Another day, another doctor's appointment. It seems like we're running over there every other day. The twins are fine, actually great, for being premature. But the doctors want to check out every little thing that comes up, so if I call the office, I know they'll say, "Bring them in." And if I'm bringing one, I'm bringing both. The respiratory stuff is what concerns them. A bad cold for another kid could be serious for Wishi-ta or Tana-na. Their immune systems are still developing. The breastfeeding helps, but now that's become a problem. Not so much with them; one of my breasts has become blocked, the nipple tender and sore. Something else to check out, down the line. Meanwhile, it looks like we'll have to supplement with formula. Then I say to myself. So what, big deal? But sometimes I get rattled.

When I'm having trouble getting back to sleep, after the babies wake and feed, I think about my mother and Helene too. I wish they could see me and these babies. I think how, in another life, it would be so nice for them to share this happy time. And nice for me to share my thoughts and worries with them, because they understand more where the fears come from. Well, that's pie in the sky. I'm lucky, I know, that Louis is so good with me and the babies, far more patient than I thought he'd be. But he's still gone a lot too. I don't resent that commitment, but I miss him, because he's the only one I can really bitch to, and who will understand and not take it wrong.

I have no reason to complain, really. Malvina's been great, very helpful and supportive. She's more at ease with me now, and she's so happy with these twins, dotes on them like they were hers. But she's not much of a talker, even on good days. And Neesa, God bless her, has been like a private nurse and home health aide to me and the babies, since the day we came home from the hospital. She does everything before I even think to ask. And she's like the guard dog at my front door – she sets the visiting hours. Elsa comes most every day, and, sometimes Beatrice or the others. They just want to see me and the babies, they say, and then somehow they're drinking coffee in the living room, which Neesa has already made. And after a little while, Neesa shoos them out the door again. They always offer to come watch the babies for an hour or so, if I want to go out, but they have no chance with Neesa around. The only one who can slip the barrier is Izzy, who comes and goes as he likes, no matter what his mother says.

Chapter 11

The following weeks passed quickly, settling into a regular routine of appointments, time at the playground and at the Intertribal Center, evenings at Renee's house reading or watching TV after the twins had gone to bed. Quiet hours cooking, baking, cleaning, arts and crafts with the kids, taking walks in the neighborhood. On a few mornings, Wishi-ta asked to braid Helene's hair, humming as she worked. "This ties us together," she explained, tightening the strands. "And gives you strength. Neesa says prayers when she braids, but I don't understand the words." Helene figured it was a good bonding activity, and she didn't mind leaving the braids in for a few hours, brushing out her hair at night.

On Fridays, after lunch, Neesa came to stay at the allergy-proofed house, while Helene bid a rather wistful farewell to the twins, always with bear hugs. On her return home, Kenneth embraced her warmly, pouring a glass of wine and asking for "the report," since they didn't talk at any length on the phone during the week. He was going at breakneck speed on his projects and had collected catalogs for her to look through, planning fantasy kitchens, dining rooms, and living rooms.

Wishi-ta seemed fine most of the time. Now that they knew better what some of the allergens were, there were few serious incidents. Once, following a visit to a neighbor's house, cleaning chemicals may have set off a prolonged wheezy cough. And one evening Wishi-ta reacted to the sesame paste in a hummus dip that someone had brought to Thursday potluck. She only had brief taste, but Helene noticed a flush and panting breaths, more than running around. But by the time they had figured out the trigger, the reaction had receded, never requiring the EpiPen. There was no longer any threat from Red Cat; the very week that he had been relocated, he took off outside and had not returned. Perhaps he never would, although the children held out hope.

Over the same period, Helene observed behaviors in Tana-na that made her think he might be hyperactive – the constant activity, jumping and skipping, the lack of focus before going on to the next thing, fidgeting while waiting or watching TV. And that other little boy behavior, the oblivious groping of his privates whenever he was excited. Maybe. Or maybe not. She wanted to ask Thelma about it, but she was away on a conference one weekend, and visiting her son at college the next. Of course, when Thelma had seen him at the powwow, Tana-na was dancing, truly in his element. Helene decided to wait and watch; it was summertime with less structure, but kindergarten might be a different story.

There was an oldies' dance at the American Legion hall near the base on Friday, and Helene decided she'd like to go, something fun for her and Kenneth. At the playground she had run into Bernice, who was watching her grandchildren, visiting from out of town. According to Bernice the dance was a chance "to dress up, go out with grown-ups, and hear some of that great old music, with none of the nonsense of bars." Some of the older folks were accomplished couples dancers. Helene enjoyed dancing; she and Kenneth had taken ballroom dancing lessons before their wedding. A plan was made was for him to come up and stay overnight, to spend some time and meet more of the community. Helene found herself looking forward to the night out, doing something different.

But Friday afternoon Kenneth called to say there was a flood in the basement of the new branch office, and he needed to be on hand. He was deeply apologetic, truly sorry to miss the dance, but she should go and enjoy herself. At the last minute, she tried Thelma, leaving messages on the answering machine. She was a bit disappointed, wondering if she would get onto the dance floor after all.

Thelma couldn't make it, either, and Malvina and Noel would not be going. But Bernice told her on the phone. "There's no reason not to go. Come on; I'm driving." So, Helene put on a beige skirt and red short-sleeve top with a long necklace; the best she could do with the clothes she had on hand. It was a short ride to the hall with plenty of parking. The dark, low-ceilinged room was brightened with strings of lights and sparkly centerpieces on the tables that ringed the dance floor. She smelled the food in warming trays on the buffet table, as well as beer and smoke from the adjoining bar area. But there was a cheerful buzz of voices in the room, women in skirts and men in ties, some with Native touches.

Erik was there, spiffed up, his beard trimmed and his hair tied back, black vest and bolo tie. The self-proclaimed dance instructor. When he saw her, he smiled, but then turned back to the man he was talking to. He took a seat with Elsa and Chief's family, at a table diagonally across the dance floor. Early in the evening, he stopped by Helene's table, but only to say hello and to chat with Robert and Charlotte a few minutes.

"Bernice, what about Erik?" Helene asked, after Erik had moved on. The others had gotten up to get in the food line. "You're widowed; he's single, I guess. I assume. Close enough in age. So what do you think?"

Bernice was nursing a gin and tonic. "What I think is, he's a charmer."

"Yes, but is there a serious side? I know he's not Native, but he's been around a long time, it seems, so he kind of knows the drill. And his brother-in-law is the Chief."

Bernice smiled into her drink, Sphinx-like, mysterious. But still good-humored. She must once have been beautiful, and now her beauty had wrinkles and laugh lines. "He's not really the Chief, since we're not one tribe or nation. Just a group of us that get together, intertribal."

"Right, I get it. But what about Erik?"

Bernice looked up, eyes glittering. "Not for me. He's one to come and go, never stays for long. I have to keep an eye on him and my daughter, the younger one, when she visits; she's got no sense at all. Not that he's a bad man. But I had a man who made me coffee every morning and rubbed my feet every night. Good or bad, he was there." And then, her smile spreading: "He's a good dancer, Erik, and he asks all the women to dance. Are you hoping for a dance too?"

Bernice seemed so simple and straightforward, but Helene realized she was sly – and observant.

"No," Helene protested. "I'm an old married lady – almost ten years."

"Old, no. But married is a funny thing, especially around here."

"Stop! I don't want to hear any more."

Bernice made the signal like zipping her lips, and Helene burst out laughing; it was so funny to see coming from a modern-day Eskimo – or rather, Inupiaq. What a kidder Bernice was.

Helene thought for sure she'd say no if Erik asked her to dance, but she got to her feet at once when he did. The song was a slower one, and couples chatted as they moved about the dance floor. Helene found herself focused on the scar on Erik's neck instead of looking over his shoulder. Suddenly, out of nowhere, she blurted, "My mother wasn't tall. I don't think that theory is correct – what Renee said." And then, as he nodded, she said, "I think it's mainly genes." He didn't reply, and that was the extent of their conversation. But Helene had to remind herself to step back from him, making space. She could feel warmth coming from him and coming from her, and it surprised her. He wasn't drunk; she wasn't drunk. It wasn't like when some of Kenneth's colleagues laid a hand on her thigh or bottom at a party; that was automatic, removing the hand or slipping away. But Erik? Even cleaned up, he was a bit scruffy around the edges. He didn't hold a candle to Kenneth.

And yet, unaccountably, when the song ended, she was still holding his hand. For a brief, puzzled moment – maybe light-headed, maybe the one glass of wine – she was reluctant to let go. There was something she wanted to get straight with him – but had no idea what it was. When she didn't move, he slid a hand under her elbow, and that snapped her out of it. She pulled away and turned toward the table. But not before he caught up to her.

"Thank you for the dance," he said politely, walking with her off the dance floor.

"You're welcome," she managed to say.

Then he danced with another woman at a different table, and Helene sat with Bernice and the others. Soon the evening came to a close. There was no second dance with Erik. Helene found herself strangely fatigued as she left for the parking lot. It was an odd moment, for sure, but it meant nothing, only that Erik had spooked her with his comments at the powwow about Renee. And that scar.

When Helene went home Saturday morning, she mentioned the social to Kenneth, and how much she had enjoyed dancing.

"Fine, fine, good," he said, absently. "We'll go sometime – soon." He was keyed up about the new office, and wouldn't leave it alone until they made a trip to check on the site, taking dozens of photos to record the flood damage. The last words she remembered before going to sleep were carpet, square feet, mold remediation.

Helene returned to the base Monday afternoon, prepared to talk about what would happen after Wishi-ta completed the last of the tests. And after Helene stopped coming on a regular basis. Wishi-ta would need a regular ride to get the allergy shots, once they knew all the allergens; they could work on a roster of drivers. For the longer term, Neesa could stay at Renee's house with the twins; she was willing, now that they understood the problem. But only after the new baby was born, and Malvina was OK. Izzy might manage with the twins at night, with some support. It would be a patchwork of care, at best.

Once inside the house, Helene put her things away and walked over to let the others know she was back. She'd seen the kids running through a sprinkler in the backyard, but they had not seen her. The boys were doing something active and messy in the mud and grass after the big rainstorm. Wishi-ta was with another boy and girl in a corner of the yard.

Helene called through the screen door at the front, and then let herself in. "Malvina?"

"In here."

Malvina was sitting up in bed, a fan directed at her face, looking bloated and miserable. The due date was couple weeks off, but there was talk of an early delivery.

"Hey," Helene said, walking into the room. "How are you doing?"

Malvina shrugged. "OK for now, I guess."

"Where's everyone else, besides the kids?"

"Neesa and Izzy, they're gone up to Louis's hearing. They left yesterday; not sure when they'll be back."

Helene pursed her lips, trying not to scowl. "I didn't know they were going. No one told me."

"They just got the date."

Helene nodded. And then it struck her: "How did they even get there? They don't drive, right? Either of them?"

"Nope. Elsa's brother gave them a ride. Like a taxi service; you pay him, he'll take you, if he's around."

"Ah, Erik." Helene almost rolled her eyes. "Well, that's helpful." She paused, calculating silently. "So how's that going to work with them gone? I know Noel is here at night, but what if you had a problem in the day, after school? Or if I'm out? You could call 911 for an emergency, but then the kids would be here on their own, right?"

There was shouting in the backyard, and Helene went to the window to see one of the neighbor kids wrestling lacrosse stick away from Pawnee, who would not give it up. Meanwhile, Tana-na was slipping and sliding in a big mud puddle, rather too close to a cement wall.

"Tana-na!" she shouted. But before he could even respond, a woman appeared, some kind of needlework in hand. She must have been watching from somewhere out of view. To the right, on the porch, Kiowa was bent over a book – summer reading. She was watching but didn't get up.

"Oh," Helene said, still at the window, watching the woman lean over to speak to the two boys playing tug-of-war. "There's Elsa."

"She's watching the kids this afternoon," Malvina said from her bed. "And Alberta or her sister will come other days. I don't know when, but they wrote it down somewhere. They have a schedule for dinners too – they'll bring them to the house."

"That's good of them," Helene said, somewhat stiffly. "I suppose they have cars and can drive. But I'm here too, for now – except when we're at the doctor's, of course."

So that was a bit of a fuss for nothing, but it still rattled Helene that key members of the family were away while Malvina was confined to bed. Kiowa was like a clone of her mother, quiet, resourceful, practical, but it wasn't right to make her the one in charge, either. Like Helene had been when she hadn't wanted to be. Her father had come home sullen and angry at night, not like good-natured Noel, who loved playing with the kids. And Malvina didn't have a wild child like Renee, already sneaky and defiant at nine or ten – the product, Helene realized, of a family that did not want to be a family anymore with their mother gone. And, she realized, here there were helpful neighbors, and that was something the Roys never had. If anything, the neighbors had stayed away.

A week later the whole elaborate system was put to the test – and failed. Helene realized immediately her plans for the next stage of Wishi-ta's care would not be adequate; something had to be done. Izzy and Neesa were still away when she arrived back at the base to find Wishi-ta in a full-blown anaphylactic shock in Malvina's kitchen. No one else was there, except Yellow Dog, skittering around her on the floor. Wishi-ta was collapsed against a cabinet, red-faced and panting, a box of cookie mix torn open and spilled. She followed Helene with her eyes, helplessly beating her chest.

"Wishi-ta!" Helene cried, crouching next to her. Closer up, she saw the signs – the puffy lips and wheezing, and immediately got the EpiPen out of her purse, taking time only to push up Wishi-ta's shorts and jab in the thigh, holding the count to ten. Then she sat on the floor, cradling Wishi-ta in her arms.

"Just a few minutes; it will be better in few minutes." They waited together, the dog circling back and forth, yapping. Other than that she heard nothing in the house. And then, distantly, children's voices outside.

"Malvina," she called out. And again, louder, "Malvina." But there was no response. Finally, though, Wishi-ta's color began returning to normal, and the swelling became less evident, though the girl still panted for breath.

Where were Alberta or Elsa, or any of the women? Where was Kiowa? And how could Wishi-ta have been left like this, unattended? She wanted to ask Wishi-ta, but her instinct was to stay calm and let Wishi-ta recover without causing more distress. Soon enough, Wishi-ta's breathing evened, and then a few tears began to slide down her face. She turned into Helene's stomach, and Helene wrapped her arms around her.

It was only when they had gotten up again and let the dog out that they heard voices closer by: Tana-na's and Cree's, arguing.

Wishi-ta was seated at the table, drinking water as Helene swept up the floury mess. She was in a hurry to bag the mix and remove it, to be examined later. They heard footsteps on the deck and the back door slider get pulled open. No one looked more surprised than the three boys, followed by Kiowa coming into the kitchen. Tana-na held his hand in the air, wrapped with some kind of towel or bandage.

"What are they doing?" Pawnee said, pushing in from behind.

In a second Kiowa had sized up the situation. "To your room, you two," she said. "Tana-na, go in Malvina's room. I'll be right there."

As soon as they left, Helene turned to Kiowa. "Where is Malvina?" she asked, working to control the edge in her voice. "Why isn't she here?"

Kiowa was shaking her head, stunned, frightened. "She was having some sort of pains...contractions...the doctor said to bring her in. We couldn't reach my father, so Elsa took her."

"Just leaving you here?"

Kiowa was slow to answer. "Alberta is coming, but she couldn't get here right away. Maybe at three o'clock?" Kiowa looked at the ceiling, disoriented. "I forget. But she's coming. And I was in here with Wishi-ta; we were going to make Jell-O." She pointed at the boxes on the counter. "But Tana-na got his arm stuck in the fence, and they couldn't get it out." The look she gave was so much like Neesa, for all those who do silly and foolish deeds. "They were only making it worse, until I finally had to get help. I never thought it would take so long."

Her eyes took in the mess on the floor and Wishi-ta at the table. Then she looked back to Helene, who said, "Wishi-ta had an allergic reaction, full blown, from the cookie mix, I think." Her voice was gentler now, resigned to the inevitable. Not happy, but relieved the crisis was past.

Kiowa stared wordlessly.

"I used the EpiPen, so she's OK; at least the reaction has subsided. She was pretty shaken up." Helene couldn't help herself. "We both were."

Kiowa's brow furrowed. "I wouldn't think Wishi-ta would do something like that."

"I didn't," Wishi-ta breathed out. "It was Yellow Dog. From the pantry. He got it down, all by himself. He was doing like this." She imitated a dog with a chew toy, waving it about and growling.

"And you tried to pick it up?"

Wishi-ta smiled bashfully. "Yeah, and I tasted it, too, on my fingers."

Helene considered. There was no reason to take out her wrath on Kiowa; she had been busy with those three active boys. And she couldn't blame Elsa or Malvina. But it was as she had feared and predicted. They just didn't have enough coverage for all the needs of everyone in this house; especially now, while Malvina was so close to her due date. Wishi-ta looked mostly normal; calm and trusting, considering that she had survived another frightening attack that might have been fatal. And then Helene felt the pinch of tears in her eyes, because it had almost been a terrible, awful thing.

There was a sad bleating from Malvina's room, and Kiowa turned to go: Tana-na.

"His hand," said Kiowa. "The wrist. It's bleeding."

Helene took a deep breath. "OK, send him out here." Kiowa was gone like the wind, only too happy to escape the room and Helene.

In a moment Tana-na came into the kitchen, holding his injured paw. He sat in the chair next to Wishi-ta. Helene took off the towel, sizing up the injury. Pretty routine, not requiring stitches; Helene had years of experience fixing up scrapes and bruises like this. She asked Kiowa if there was a first aid kit in the house: hydrogen peroxide, antibiotic cream, and some gauze and tape. Kiowa nodded, returning in a couple minutes with the supplies in a basket, which Helene took with a nod of approval. That was a good sign, at least.

She treated the wound and believed it would heal quickly – if Tana-na didn't pull the bandage off. The twins were quiet, watching her, on their best behavior. Helene shook her head and smiled. "I think it's time for chocolate milk, don't you think?"

From the front hall came voices: Kiowa speaking, and then a female adult; no, two. It sounded like Alberta and Frances, aka the Sourpuss Sisters. Helene glanced at the clock on the stove: three o'clock, right on time, as promised. Kiowa was filling them in, explaining what had happened. All was well now, so it appeared. But the uneasiness did not leave Helene as she studied the dates on Malvina's wall calendar: Malvina's due date; everyone's appointments; and the time in Maine. She flipped the pages to September, the beginning of the school year – for

Malvina's kids, the twins starting kindergarten, and Helene herself.

She told Wishi-ta and Tana-na to get ready to go with her next door. The women had walked into the kitchen, gazing about without expression. Helene said hello to them, and assured them the twins were both OK. She would take charge of them from here. The women nodded silently, unsure, it seemed, of what Helene might be thinking or feeling, and not wanting to engage. Helene and the twins left through the front hall, pulling the screen door closed behind. They were just entering the other house when Helene remembered a bag of books and papers she'd left in Malvina's living room from the previous week, more research on Native American health and welfare.

"Go ahead," she said to the twins. "I'll be right back."

On Malvina's front steps, through the open doorway, she picked up voices from the kitchen – not loud, but not soft.

"I don't know why they want her here. We can deal with this; we always have. Let her go back to wherever she came from."

Alberta.

"Uh huh," came the other voice. *Frances, the follower.*

She realized they were talking about her. She didn't enter or leave, but stood listening, unable to help herself.

"Renee was bad, too, when she first came. But at least she came around, you know; she understood something. Not this one. Something not right."

"Fake," said Frances, "phony."

"Yeah, but we know some folks like that. She's, I don't know…"

They pondered a moment, as Helene balanced on the top step – caught between getting away and hearing more.

"Too good for us."

"No, not that. She doesn't care nothing about us, just like squirrels in a tree to her. Something else…"

Another silence.

"She knows nothing about our history and things our people went through; and I'm sure she doesn't care. But what about the traditions? The ceremonies?" She made some rude noise. "That's nothing to her, just mumbo-jumbo. Same old, same old white ignorance."

That was all true, and Helene could not deny it, but did it really matter in a health crisis? Wasn't there something to be said for modern medicine? The two old cranks; why weren't they at least grateful for what she had done?

"Thing is," Alberta went on, ominously, "she got something inside of her. I don't know – is it dark or maybe it's just empty?"

Helene's hand went to her mouth, to keep from speaking out. And yet, and yet…something buzzed and vibrated in her chest.

Helene walked down the steps, leaving the tote. As if it hadn't been a bad enough day, to find Wishi-ta in such a state with no one in charge? She knew there were others, besides these two, who did not like her, for whatever reason. But dealing with this small-mindedness didn't help the situation. And it revealed a lot about who these people really were – at least some of them. And she wasn't so sure herself if it was best for the twins, or any children, to be raised around those negative attitudes.

Back home on the weekend, Helene tried to explain the situation to Kenneth. Dinner was cleared, and the dining room table was covered with pamphlets and catalogs relating to house layout and design. They had been at it over an hour when Helene suggested a break for coffee. She made them each a cup and brought it to the table with a plate of nonallergenic cookies she had made earlier in the day, putting aside a dozen or so for Kenneth and herself.

"That situation I was telling you about," Helene said, referring to the conversation at dinner about Wishi-ta and the emergency in the kitchen. "I had a couple more thoughts." She saw that he had reached out to pull a paper closer to read. He paused, looking up, preoccupied, reluctant to switch gears.

"Yes?"

"I was thinking it would be good if you could spend some time with Wishi-ta. I could bring her here or we could meet you someplace close by, for lunch maybe. I've been thinking about scheduling an appointment with an allergy specialist at Children's Hospital, one with training in asthma."

Kenneth nodded, a finger in place on the page. "Sure, that's fine, but why? I trust how you're handling things, and I believe you that she's a sweet young girl who deserves your help and attention. But you've already done so much."

Helene sipped the coffee, thinking about her words. "I'm wondering if we should consider adoption," she said finally. "Make it permanent, so that she has some real security, and to take some of the burden off Malvina's family."

"Whoa, there," Kenneth said, straightening up. "You're jumping way ahead of things." He closed his mouth and then opened it again, struggling for the right response. "I'm sure you're charmed with her, and feel good about what you're doing, but have you really thought things through?"

"I have." She was calm, prepared. "She'll get the care she needs. We have the room, and we're not too old to be parents of a kindergartener. She can attend the school where I work. It could work out very well."

Kenneth blinked a few times. "It's one more thing to take on right now. You know how busy I am, and how I wish you could be part of this too. You have your job, which I always thought you found rewarding. Plus I don't see how we can just take her away from those people she's always known."

"It's only three hours; we can certainly get together with them."

"Helene, you know it's not just distance; it's the world she knows."

Helene felt herself getting worked up, resenting Kenneth's unwillingness to even consider the idea, which wasn't so crazy, which had some real merit.

"We're her family too. Her mother is dead; her father is in prison. I'm the closest relative who has the ability to really make sure Wishi-ta is taken care of."

Kenneth sat looking at her a moment before he spoke. "I can't say I think it's a good idea, but I'm willing to wait awhile longer to see where things stand. The way I see it now, you're doing them a great service while they're in this current situation. But let's hold off until they are back on track; the baby's born, the kids are in school. I think it will be a much brighter picture, and you can come and go as you like, and have the twins stay here on occasion. Like what aunties and uncles do, right?"

He sounded so reasonable. But Helene was not satisfied. He had not seen Wishi-ta in shock. He did not know about the cheerful chaos of their lives, and how easy it was to lose track of someone.

Kenneth shrugged. "What can I say? This is just the sort of agitation we need to avoid, getting yourself so worked up like this. Let's table this for now. Meanwhile, you can go ahead and schedule that appointment with the specialist. I'll be happy to see Wishi-ta again." He got up from his chair, circling around to the back of Helene, bending down to press his face against her neck, and kissing her cheek.

"OK, sweetheart?"

And she heard herself say, "OK."

But really, she wasn't. The next morning she told Kenneth she wanted to leave in the afternoon, Sunday, since Wishi-ta had an early Monday appointment, which was partially true – they were to drop in for a quick check after the "episode" at any time. She tried calling Denis, who, as usual, didn't answer. She hated this feeling, not knowing what to do; if anything she did made a lasting difference; if Wishi-ta would be OK when she was not in her sight and her care. There was a mystery at the center of all this, Renee and her life at the base, all that Helene had learned from the journal entries. How had Renee regained a sense of hope, when Helene recognized so well that black cloud of hopelessness that shadowed her still, no matter how good her husband, no matter how safe her life?

A fit of impatience sent her to the car, driving through the back streets of their hometown, looking for the "white house with green shutters on a curvy road" where Renee had told her that friends from Boston had dumped, thinking it was the Roys' house.

She had always wondered just which house it was and how far Renee had walked on that cold March night. She passed the spot where she had found Renee on the side of the road, almost frozen. Later one of the police officers told her that the people in the house had called in a prowler, someone outside their house; they'd seen car lights driving away. But Renee had left by then. The police never saw her, either. But once again Helene could not find the right house. Years had passed; houses were bought, sold, repainted, re-sided. Perhaps she would never know.

Back at home she phoned Thelma. "I brought up the idea of adoption to Kenneth, and he doesn't think it makes sense."

"Well, how did you bring it up? Was it because of that incident with Wishi-ta?" She had talked to Thelma during the week, soon after it happened.

"Yes. In part. It was kind of a catalyst for the idea, especially if I do end up bringing her here, taking her to a specialist in Boston. What she has is life threatening."

"Kenneth knows that. How did you come across? You know he is so quick to put out any fires, especially concerning you."

"I just said what I thought, and what I felt."

"Well, that's a good thing. So."

"So...what?"

"Do you want me to tell you what I think?"

"Yes! That's why I called."

"Well, you know I'm a child psychologist, not a marriage counselor. I think Kenneth likes things just as they are. He's got enough on his plate, and doesn't want to worry about you or anyone else. He still sees you as fragile, and he wants to protect you, and keep things on an even keel. To put it more plainly, based on what you've told me, he seems to think he's already got one dependent, and that's enough for him."

"That's not fair."

"Fair? What's fair got to do with it? People see things how they see them. And you are, I think, his little princess in her very nice castle. At least that's how it comes across to me. Maybe I'm wrong."

Thelma wasn't wrong, Helene knew. That's pretty much how it was, what it had evolved to, with Helene's complicity. But it didn't have to be. Kenneth could be convinced. She realized she would need to get agreement from Malvina's family, and Louis, of course. But this was important, and this was right. They had room in their house and in their hearts for a poor suffering child.

Yet there was still a sting in Kenneth's words, and Thelma's. Kenneth had not thought much of her potential as a mother, it seemed to Helene, especially after her miscarriages. He never encouraged the idea of infertility treatments or adoption. Because of that catastrophe with Renee, all those years ago, when anyone would have been knocked off-balance. Evidently everything she'd done wasn't enough – the talk therapy, the medication, all the self-help methods. She'd tried everything, really, except to tell the whole and complete truth. The fact that Renee had rallied, had survived the addiction and the misery – that wasn't Helene's doing. She had failed Renee, despite her best efforts. She at least owed it to her sister to make sure her child was safe.

She would show Kenneth, show both of them, that she would do whatever was necessary for the sake of this child, who was her sister's daughter, and who needed someone looking out for her.

Renee's journal – 14

A stolen, quiet moment. Louis out, just for the evening. And the twins asleep. All put away for the day. No visitors. Just me and Red Cat.

The other night, I found myself praying – a quick Hail Mary – getting into bed, Louis snoring. It just came to me, out of the blue. Of course I remember the words – mass every week until Mom was too sick to go. Then the priest came to the house, Father Gerard: old and gray, tired and dried out, without much comfort to offer – except my mother's release from pain in heaven – where we'd join her eventually. After Mom died, none of us went back, ever.

Hail Mary? I can't explain it. A prayer of thanks, I think, for the blessings in my life. And maybe a tiny prayer of hope – that things will be OK now, whatever happens. And for strength, for when it will be needed.

It might be from when I was at Neesa's recently, her part of the duplex, the twins with Malvina. I asked if she had anything for a skin irritation that just won't go away. She went to look through her herbs and ointments, leaving me alone in the living room. I had a few moments to look around – old family pictures, some of her baskets. Native crafts and decorations. And all that religious stuff, Catholic. Crucifixes and rosary beads. A picture of the Sacred Heart, surrounded by thorns, dripping blood, just like the one my grandmother had over her bed. But most of all, images of Mother Mary. Statues and pictures, a painting on a black velvet background, always with that same expression – somewhere between peace and pain.

It hit me for the first time how serious Neesa was, how deeply spiritual in her unique way. She was not one to talk about personal things, not to me. Over time, I'd come to learn that she had faced a lot in her lifetime. There was an uncle who'd run away from a boarding school, killed a man in a fight, and ended up in prison; an older brother now close to seventy, sometimes homeless, sometimes at the Vets Home. Louis told me that his mother had cut her hair short a long time ago, as a sign of mourning for a sister who'd gone missing as a teen and was never found. She took up with a hot-tempered lumberjack, and just didn't come home one day. A wild girl, I guess, like me. I was beginning to understand more of Neesa's distrust – of me, of the white world. And her need for comfort and for strength. Maybe she was hedging bets, holding both kinds of faith.

So there are choices, I guess. God. Mary. Jesus. Creator. Manitou. Many forms. But I see now something to give thanks for, something to pray to, when times are uncertain, and something to praise, for making this wondrous world. I might not see all the patterns, I'll never know all the meanings, but I believe there is something. Amen. "A-ho."

Chapter 12

After the next set of Wishi-ta's appointments, Helene was feeling more and more confident that she was the one best in charge, who knew the most about Wishi-ta's health situation and what was to be done. At the moment the focus in the family was on Malvina and the baby in the womb. It was also on Louis. Izzy and Neesa had returned from the hearing with not very good news. The appeal had not succeeded, and the sentence of twenty years stood. The lawyers were considering another appeal, but they were not overly optimistic.

Malvina and Noel had no objections when Helene told them she was going schedule an appointment with a Boston specialist for Wishi-ta. But they were less enthusiastic about having Wishi-ta stay for a longer period at Helene's home. Mainly, they said, because of all that was happening at the base: the new baby coming, getting ready for the trip to Maine. Plus there would be no other children. Helene secretly wondered if they suspected Wishi-ta might like it too much, and start to compare to life at the base.

Wishi-ta had become accustomed to the appointments, and enjoyed their excursions together to the store or post office or library. And more and more, she nestled in close to Helene on the sofa when they read stories. Even at the Intertribal Center, she ran back and forth from the roving groups of children to Helene's side, to show her what she had made or tell her something. Tana-na too accepted Helene more readily, turning increasingly to her for what he wanted or needed. She had introduced a few ways to help him focus – chewing gum or squeezing a foam ball – that seemed to help without need of medication, at least for now.

Meanwhile there was a growing buzz about the trip to Maine, commencing as soon as Malvina was cleared to travel after the birth of the baby. The women and children would stay in Maine until school started, while Noel and Izzy would commute on weekends after their vacation time was spent. It wasn't just the Lopes/Marshall family that was going, either. A number of families, some distantly related, were planning to go for different lengths of time, a big, sprawling camp-out. Much of the talk was about people they would see, the fishing and boating and swimming. And the feasts, which Helene understood to mean cookouts, including a legendary clambake. After some discussion it was decided that Helene and Wishi-ta would drive up for the naming ceremony and stay until the next set of shots. Then they would return to the base for the next weeks to complete the appointments. Finally, assuming that Wishi-ta's immunity was significantly strengthened, she would make the drive to Maine with

Izzy and Noel until the end of summer. But not Helene.

Helene was now occupied with things other than running the household, Wishi-ta's appointments, and the continuing credits for her nursing license. She was researching adoption law, specifically concerning a jailed parent. Already she had assembled a thick file of notes as well as books from the library. Out of curiosity she asked Izzy if the twins had been to visit Louis since he'd been incarcerated. They had not. According to Izzy, the prison was sterile and depressing, nowhere for them to picture their father. Plus they were used to him being away for long periods on the road. Louis was awaiting word on a transfer to a facility closer to home. Meanwhile, Helene wanted to know, had there been any discussion about Malvina and Noel legally adopting the twins? With a dubious shake of his head, Izzy said, "No, we still hope an appeal will work and he'll be back."

The meeting with the Boston asthma specialist was scheduled for early Thursday morning, requiring Helene and Wishi-ta to drive down on Wednesday, staying at the house overnight. Following the appointment they would meet Kenneth for lunch, somewhere fun and kid-friendly, then either return to the base or stay a second night, depending on the time. As it worked out, Kenneth didn't get home until after dinner on Wednesday; Wishi-ta was already asleep.

"Perfect angel," Kenneth said to Helene, standing at the doorway of the guest room where Wishi-ta was sleeping with one of her hypoallergenic stuffed animals. "But I suppose they all are when they're asleep. It's when they're teenagers and awake that they're so much trouble."

Helene didn't respond, not sure if his comment was directed at Renee or their teenage niece and nephew, who had been causing his sister and her husband such worry and aggravation in recent years.

"Still on for lunch tomorrow, after the appointment?" Helene asked.

"It's on my calendar," he said. "Just call when you're done, and I'll meet you at the restaurant – Rainforest Café, right?"

"Yes. I know it's hokey, but it will be a treat for her and they offer allergy-free children's meals."

"Can't wait," Kenneth said, smiling.

The allergist at Children's Hospital was young, female, and Harvard educated, and essentially confirmed all that Dr. Wang had told them. She seemed optimistic that Wishi-ta would outgrow at least some of her allergies as she got older and gained more weight and strength. The asthma, besides being allergy related, could also be brought on by cold air and exertion. Those were conditions that her family, caregivers, and Wishi-ta herself would have to learn to manage. She was to have access to an inhaler at all times, and learn how to use it herself.

The appointment didn't last as long as Helene had expected, and they were done by ten thirty. Still too early for lunch. As they were walking toward the parking garage, the cell phone rang in her purse.

It was Izzy. Malvina had gone into labor early in the morning, and was at the hospital now because of the high blood pressure. Neesa was with her, and Noel was on his way from the work site.

"That's great, I guess," said Helene, a bit nonplussed. "Hope all goes well. Are you calling me just to tell me, or for some other reason?"

There was mumbling at the other end, voices speaking over one another.

"Oh," Izzy said. "I thought you would want to know. And Wishi-ta. I thought she would want to be here."

"Wishi-ta?"

"When they come home. To welcome the new baby."

"I see. Hmm…we're still at Children's Hospital. We're going to meet my husband for lunch, and then maybe stay another night."

There was a pause.

"Tana-na is asking for Wishi-ta," Izzy said. "And for you too."

Wishi-ta had been staring at Helene since she had spoken her name, probably guessing it was family.

"About the baby," Helene said aloud – and then wished she hadn't, since she had hoped to have more time here, at home, with Wishi-ta and Kenneth. And that nice luncheon out. But Wishi-ta's eyes had widened with excitement.

In that moment Helene decided – they would go back to the base. What was lunch, after all? And they could come back another time, so Wishi-ta could get to know Kenneth. She would resent being kept away from the big events they'd been waiting for through the summer – and that, Helene didn't want to be responsible for.

They would need to go by the house before leaving, after a call to Kenneth to cancel. Just a quick stop to get their bags, and maybe a few more clothes. A picture flashed in front of Helene's eyes – clothes for the new baby or even a swaddling blanket – simple gifts that she could make herself on the sewing machine. Their mother's old machine, which Helene hadn't used in years and ended up putting back in its case in the closet. She could pack that too, as long as they were going to the house. Sometime in the future she could show Wishi-ta and Tana-na how to sew on a machine…when…well, that was not so clear. The future was like a swirling cloud, but certainly there would be opportunities to do more things together. Fun things. And important things. As she and Wishi-ta took hands, skipping toward the car, Helene found that she was happy and excited too.

After dinner that Neesa had prepared, Helene went back to Renee and Louis's house, the twins in tow. They slept through the night, and the next day awakened to hear there was a new baby girl, Tewa. Kiowa had come to the door to tell them; the baby had been born at four in the morning, and both baby and mother were fine. They would stay two days at the hospital, unless the blood pressure did not come down.

All of the kids were excited, running back and forth between the houses, peeking into Malvina's room where the basket was ready for the baby, along with a corner full of clothes and supplies, many borrowed or donated from friends and neighbors. They began packing their own belongings into duffel bags, which Helene gathered was the custom for their trips to Maine. It was no use for her to say it would be a few days yet, at the least.

"But we're going too, right?" Wishi-ta asked her more than once. "You and me?"

"Yes, we're going. We have to be there for the baby's naming ceremony, right? But we'll come back here afterward, you and me, to get more of the allergy shots. If there's time before school, maybe we'll go back again. Maybe." The word just came out: we. Helene was considering the possibility, more time together – if it all worked out.

Wishi-ta nodded, her serious nod. But her look was so trusting, and for the first time, Helene thought she saw real happiness behind the girl's eyes: looking forward to something, knowing she was part of it all. She might have to give up something, but it was for a reason, and she was in good hands. Helene felt her heart pushing into her lungs, knowing she was the object of that kind of trust and faith.

Then Malvina was home; the baby was home; Noel was home; Neesa was busy cooking. Izzy had started his time off from work. It was like a holiday with all kinds of cakes and goodies from the neighbors and members of the Intertribal Association. And more baby stuff, and equipment. The already crowded house was almost impossible to walk through without stepping over things, including the kids' bags and backpacks and all manner of groceries and supplies. Wasn't there a supermarket up there at the Home Camp? Helene wondered.

Then the serious packing began. Helene was not sure what was needed for this style of camping, but Bernice assured her that there were houses or cabins enough to put everyone up. Those who wanted to could put up tents. She should take her summer clothes, a bathing suit, good walking shoes, and plenty of bug spray.

Izzy had made a special trip to see her at Renee's house, catching her alone. While in Maine, he needed to see Louis again, less than two hours away in New Hampshire. They had some new materials to go over. Also, Izzy said, Louis wanted to meet Helene in person and talk about the twins. They could go sometime after the naming ceremony. Izzy would make arrangements for the visit, registering ahead of time.

"You can drive," he said, seated barefooted at the other end of the sofa. He smelled fresh out of the shower, wearing a black-and-yellow Bruins T-shirt. "Otherwise Erik or Robert will take me."

"No, I'll go. I want to meet him."

"It's no picnic, you know." He wagged his head, wet hair splashing across his shoulders.

"I realize that."

"I'm just saying because you don't look like someone who has been to a federal prison before."

"No, I have not."

"And Louis is a trip, if you know what I mean. Intense."

"I get that idea."

"OK, then." Izzy's familiar smile broke out; he had accomplished his mission, whether or not he was the one who had chosen it.

The journey to Maine was like a military convoy with the number and order of vehicles departing. Izzy was in the vanguard, along with Erik and Neesa, going to open up the houses and set things up. Elsa, the Chief, Pawnee, and Cree were in the next vehicle to leave, stopping along the way where the boys could get out and run around. Next were Noel, Malvina, and Kiowa, with the baby – in the quiet car, or van actually, with all the baby equipment. And then finally Helene with Bernice and the twins. Charlotte and Robert were arriving the following day with several members of their extended family. Other cars and trucks were rolling out, as if the whole base was decamping for another place.

The drive was long but not unpleasant, and the twins slept off and on in the back seat, not complaining much about the long stretches. Helene had packed a picnic lunch with drinks in the cooler, and pulled into one of the roadside rest areas with a shaded pavilion and a sparkling stream tumbling down a hill near the parking lot. Bernice was easy to be with, and happy to talk about her life's travels, the first fourteen years in Alaska, and then in several different parts of the United States with the Army. She had two grown daughters with children who lived outside of Boston; and a son, who was also in the military. Only one of her sisters had returned to Alaska, and Bernice went back every five years or so to visit. Her younger daughter was thirty, but kind of a "wild child"; she had a toddler, but no husband currently.

It was twilight by the time Helene and her carful arrived, following Izzy's scribbled instructions and peering at not very clearly marked signs along the unpaved road. But when she pulled into a clearing, there was no question they were at the right place. Neesa was watching out for them, or at least for the twins. As soon as they were released from their car seats, they ran to her for a quick hug and then scampered through the open door of the house where she waited, the only actual house. A dozen or more cars, trucks, and campers were parked in a grassy area in front of a ring of small wood-frame structures, very basic cabins.

Helene and Bernice got out slowly, stretching, and then walked over to Neesa. She directed them to one of the cabins, and told them to take the room with two beds. The twins could sleep in sleeping bags in the front room. Other than a table and a few chairs, there wasn't much else inside: a bench or two and open shelves for supplies. The overhead light came on with the pull of string. And then Helene came to realize that there was no bathroom and no toilet. Behind her she heard Bernice chuckling.

"What, are you going to turn around and go back now, no running water?"

"But no one said…"

"No, they got it at the big house, you can go there. Or behind this camp, there's another camp, where the Boy Scouts come for part of the summer. It's part of Neesa's family property, but they rent it out, and then we can use their dining hall, toilets, and showers when they're not here. There's usually someone at the camp office, and a pay phone too, if you get desperate for contact with the outside world."

Oh, boy, thought Helene. Boy Scouts bathrooms; she could hardly imagine. But she held her tongue, just raising her eyebrows in response to Bernice.

As they unpacked, Helene noted the truly rustic nature of the place, including the chinks in the foundation where plant life had started to grow, and the corners where the spiders had hung their webs. Although she expected it was probably quite old, darkish and a bit musty smelling, it had been recently swept out and wiped down, no scat or animal residue. The work of Neesa, she surmised. There was very little to do; everything was as ready as it was going to be, including for the upcoming naming ceremony, which she had little to do with. In one of her travel bags, Helene had packed a gift for Tewa, what she hoped was appropriate: a small wooden plaque with hand-painted birds. It was the best she could do from a quick stop at the little gift shop outside the base. Her sewing projects would have to wait.

What she didn't realize was that they would be traveling, all of them, some forty-five minutes to the seacoast for the naming ceremony the next day. A sacred place, she was told. A place where the Pemaquot had lived, hunted, fished, and worshipped as long as anyone knew. Some said ten thousand years, some said fifteen; some said more than that. It was a blustery day, and when they arrived at the rocky cliff, waves were crashing below, sending cold spray into the air. Back from the cliff, in a more sheltered area, Izzy, Noel, Erik, and some of the men built a fire in a pit, which smoked fitfully in the wind.

Everyone was to gather in a circle, with four elders waiting to welcome the baby and give prayers for her family. Chief and one of Noel's brother's were elders, as well as Neesa's sister, Wen, who still lived in the area. The fourth, to Helene's surprise, was Erik. Izzy played the flute and one of the women sang along with her hand drum. Each elder had a gift for the child, rattles and fans, a piece of jewelry. Wen offered a traditional Native American story and Erik produced a child-sized flute, likely suggested by Izzy. At one point the elders stepped out of the circle to confer on the new baby's name, while everyone else began to move in place or step side to side so not to shiver.

Presently the elders rejoined the circle, smiling and relieved, wrapping their arms around themselves for warmth. Chief cleared his throat, speaking in his deep bass: "She Moves According to the Wind" was the baby's Native name, in the Pemaquot language. Helene thought the ceremony was lovely and strangely moving. Like a baptism, in a way.

Finally it was time for the feast, which Charlotte and Neesa had organized. Plenty of hot coffee, hot cider, hot chili, and venison stew, a specialty.

"Well?" said Erik, taking the folding chair next to Helene, with a bowl of stew. "Did I do OK?"

Helene shrugged. "I think so. I don't know. I was kind of surprised..."

"That they asked me? Yeah – me, too. Trying to lay some responsibility on me, I guess." Erik laughed, and Helene noticed drops of moisture in his beard. "No, I've known this family a good part of my life. Good people. I would do whatever they asked me. And," he added, "I'm good with children."

"The Candy Man."

Then he looked sideways at her. "At least with other people's children. Not so much my own."

He told her about his middle-school-aged son, Connor, who lived in New York state with his mother, whom he helped support but didn't spend a lot of time with.

"I see." Helene wasn't sure what else to say. He was middle-aged; she was not shocked that he'd had a previous relationship, or that it didn't work out.

Erik looked down, wiping a spill from the front of his jacket. "Renee said you were like a mom to her." He looked up. "After your mother died."

Helene was nonplussed, confused, again, why he would say such personal things about her life. It was disconcerting to learn that Renee had talked about her at all, and to someone like Erik. And that she had said, "like a mom."

"I'm not sure what to make of that," she said finally, tense. "Our...relationship wasn't easy, for so many reasons; it would be hard to understand."

He kept spooning stew into his mouth, waiting.

"I wasn't really much like our mother," she said. "Renee probably told you all we did was fight, her and me, I mean – not our mother."

Erik smiled. "Some royal battles." His forehead scrunched as he summoned the words. "'Locked in mortal combat' – that's what she said."

The Styrofoam cup fell out of Helene's hand as she jerked away, blinking tears. *Mortal combat.*

She recovered the cup from the ground, sitting stone-faced on the chair, the wind whipping her hair. She was glad the children were away, occupied; she wasn't sure she could bear to see Wishi-ta right now. Then she heard Erik's words coming through, undeterred.

"She was a big fan of yours, Renee. All the crap you had to deal with, because of her. And she thought you would have been a good mom, if you had children of your own."

"Stop it," Helene hissed. "Just stop talking, please. I don't appreciate it."

His eyes narrowed, puzzled. "But who's going to tell you? Renee's dead; Louis is gone; Izzy was too young to really understand."

"I'm going to get some tea," she said, getting up. First she looked around to check on the children, hunkered down near the fire pit, crumpled plates and dropped food everywhere.

He was wrong, Erik. There were things that Renee could tell her – things from Renee's journal, that she was reading bits at time. But she wasn't going to tell Erik that. No way would she would let on that she possessed a source of information about Renee's life she wasn't even sure she wanted to know herself.

Two days after the naming ceremony, Helene and Izzy were getting ready for the drive to the prison. No one had told the children the purpose of the trip. The older kids wanted to know if they were going to the store, which was a distance away and full of treats. Helene said No, they had some business to take care of, that was all. Only Wishi-ta asked if she could go too. And when they said No, she wanted to know when they would be back – for lunch or for supper?

"It might be after supper," Helene said gently, hating to disappoint. "But we'll be back sometime today. I promise."

Still Wishi-ta looked sad. Her hair, though clean, was a mess; but there was no time to fix it. Maybe Neesa would braid it for her.

"You don't worry about us, and I won't worry about you, OK?" Helene said. "The best way to make the time go faster is to go have fun with your cousins and all the kids. That's why we're here. So, go on." She gave her a hug, and Wishi-ta ran off.

Izzy was just coming out the door, a backpack over his shoulder. He had chosen to wear some of his more Indian-themed clothing – a T-shirt with a thunderbird image, a choker necklace and earrings made of wampum, with his hair hanging loose. Not regalia, though. Whether it was in solidarity with Louis, or so that Louis wouldn't give him a hard time, she couldn't say. The T-shirt was a kind of light cranberry, almost pink, unisex, if not his mother's.

The ride was slow and rather featureless on a secondary road that meandered west through Maine into New Hampshire. More and more they came across signs in both French and English. And more and more there were stretches between little towns with nothing to show human presence besides the pavement. However, there was always the hope of moose, Izzy told her, or bear.

"Wouldn't that be something?" Helene said.

They couldn't listen to the radio, since reception was so poor. And, that made Helene expect that cell reception wouldn't be great, either. They rolled on, surrounded by endless woods, with occasional clearings and fences marked with "Keep Out" signs, or bold announcements declaring the land to belong to one paper company or another.

"About your brother," Helene said, glancing at Izzy. "What's driving him in all of this, and what, exactly, is going on?"

"He's always been a leader," Izzy said from the passenger seat, one knee bent and a foot on the dashboard. "And he learned a lot from our grandfather, Neesa's father, who was involved with the land claim cases in the 1970s. The tribes felt they had a right to land that had been taken from them by the state of Maine and given to others to own and develop, while tribes felt they should have federal protection from an agreement that went back to 1790, the Non-Intercourse Act."

Helene flinched at the name: non-intercourse sounded so strangely intimate, in a weird sexual way, like the two cultures should never meet or intermarry.

"Anyway, there was a huge law case about it that went on for years, and there was a lot of bad feeling against the Indians that they would be reclaiming property some of the big companies owned, or private citizens owned, even if it had been taken unjustly. The situation got nasty, or so I'm told. But our grandfather was one of the people on the council who were working on the settlement; he went to Washington, D.C., a few times, and down to Bangor and Portland – that's when they were all living at the Home Camp.

"It was all a lot of legal stuff I don't really understand, but Louis grew up on it. Learned everything there is to know about that kind of law. And then he went off to U. of Maine, and after that he started law school. But it drove him nuts, for some reason, so he left. Now he's kind of an expert on that stuff, and he goes around – well, he did – advising other tribes on their status, their land and water rights, and what legal recourse they have."

"To get their land back, you mean?"

Izzy wagged his head back and forth. "Not so much, not the original land. Little bits, here and there. But more about compensation, money to buy land with, if they can, or use it for other things, education, business, different kinds of investments, so to speak."

"That's quite a battle he's engaged in."

"Louis – he won't stop," Izzy said. "Even in prison, he'll keep fighting," And then a funny smile crossed his face. "With words, I mean."

About halfway, they made a rest stop at Marty's Quick Stop, the first gas station/minimart they came to in fifty miles. Helene had gotten the key to use the restroom outside the shop, and was on the way back inside, when she looked through the plate-glass window, peering between ads for Marlboro cigarettes and Coca-Cola. A big burly guy, the one at the counter who'd given her the key, was gesturing at Izzy, who stood with slumped shoulders and no expression.

"What is it?" she asked as she pushed through the door. The burly man turned to her, a disgruntled expression under his weathered, faded baseball cap.

"Izzy?" she said, when no one replied. "What's the problem?"

"This…this – person," the man started, "was trying to shoplift; I saw him…er…" – his lips drew back – "…whatever, over by the candy. Which is now in his hand, as he was walking out the door."

"Izzy?"

"I was just looking around, waiting for you."

Helene looked back at the man. "I don't think so," she said. "We've got money; I was just coming in to buy coffee. He can have whatever he likes; I don't know why he would just take it."

"For fun." The man glowered. "Some of them, just for sport. What was I supposed to think, the way he's slinking around the place?"

"That doesn't mean he was shoplifting."

"I didn't know he was with you, did I? I see you pull up and get out of the car, regular, normal-looking lady. Next thing I look up, this…person is in the shop. How am I supposed to know you're together with this…this freak? Just look – wearing those crazy clothes and everything."

Helene had no idea how to reply. She looked at Izzy, who stood impassive.

"You don't know what you're talking about," she said, shaking her head at the man. She heard her voice quavering, but she knew better than to get into an argument; it would only get uglier. "Come on, Izzy. Let's get out of here. This man doesn't deserve our business."

But Izzy didn't move. "But you wanted a cup of coffee." He spoke in a light, soft voice, stopping her steps toward the door.

She turned back. "Not from him I don't." The words came out shrill; she couldn't help it. All she wanted was to get away from the man and his stupid store. So why didn't Izzy?

"You should have your coffee. I don't know when we'll find another place." All of a sudden, he was adamant, stubborn. And, then he looked up; not at Helene, but at the man. They all waited. The man gave the barest of shrugs.

"OK, OK, I'll get the coffee. One dollar."

"And some Tic Tacs." Izzy put the money on the counter before Helene could stop him. "I changed my mind," he said to her.

In silence, the man handed Helene her coffee and made change for the two items.

Just as they were leaving, she heard him say, "Freaking queer." They kept walking, not looking back.

In the car, her hand with the coffee cup was shaking.

"You want me to drive?" Izzy asked.

"No, just hold the coffee for me; I'll be all right. Besides, you don't drive."

"Sure I can, if no one's around."

She took a couple of deep breaths before pulling back onto the road. They passed a sign for the next town and one for the prison, thirty miles. Izzy popped a couple Tic Tacs in his mouth, the minty smell blending with the coffee aroma.

"What a terrible man," Helene muttered, more to herself than to Izzy. She glanced at his profile, so smooth and lovely and seemingly unruffled. Too pretty. Maybe that was the problem.

"What would you have done?" she said. She heard anger in her voice. And fear.

Izzy thought a moment. "Well, I wanted those Tic Tacs. I would have thrown the money on the counter and run, probably."

"But if he caught you, or wouldn't let you out the door?"

"He could look in my pockets; there was nothing to find."

She drove on another mile before she spoke again. "That wasn't really it, though, was it?"

"No, he just didn't like me, or the look of me." He was slouched in his seat, his head against the window. "I might have gotten a bloody nose out of it."

"Or worse," Helene said, hands tight on the wheel.

"Or worse," he agreed. And then, so softly she almost didn't hear. "Wouldn't be the first time."

They arrived at the prison gates just before noon, well before visiting hours. They could go wait in line, with the other visitors, or, suggested Izzy, "Maybe we should eat first. It might be a while before we get in; depends what's going on in there and how full the visitor room is."

"But we drove all this way."

"Doesn't matter if there's a lockdown or anything else that might be going on. Let's eat; I'm hungry, anyway. There's a good spot that way; it's on the water."

So they drove a bit farther along the road, ending up near a large lake, sparkling in the late-morning sunshine, ringed with tall pines. There was a grassy spot where they could pull up and park. The prison was out of sight behind the trees. A few other people were there, eating or smoking, taking walks, employees from the prison, Helene assumed. She and Izzy found a bench in partial shade with a soft breeze off the lake. Neesa had packed lunch for two: ham-and-cheese sandwiches on white bread, with chips, pickles, and apples.

Helene lifted her face, inhaling the scent of the trees and the water. "This reminds me of the place where my father used to take us in northern Vermont, where the first generation stayed when they came down from Canada, working in the logging camps." She laughed. "Talk about isolated. My dad thought he could sell us on the cabin for a vacation place – no water, no electricity, no TV! We couldn't wait to get home."

Izzy shrugged, his face still a bit closed. He bit into the apple.

"Which do you prefer," Helene asked, "being at the base or being at the Home Camp?"

He chewed thoughtfully. "Both," he said, "for different reasons, depending on the time of the year, and things like that. But sometimes they both drive me nuts too." He made a face. "Nothing much changes. Same old, same old."

"Really?" She didn't expect to hear that from him.

"I wouldn't mind seeing the city lights," he said with a crooked smile. "More action, more diversity, more...well, people. Everyone thinks I'm the homebody, but that's not completely true."

Helene mulled it over, gazing out over the water. Izzy was young. And, well, different. Maybe it was the urban life he was attracted to. Or maybe he just wanted a little more independence. She started packing the remains of lunch.

"But you like the great outdoors, right?"

"Right, but I also like the great indoors. I don't want to live in a world without lights, computers, and the Internet, at least not for long. You know," he said with a sly look. "Some Indians that say that the Internet is just the manifestation of Spider Woman's web, connecting us all, like it or not."

"Wow," said Helene, mock-slapping her cheek. "Pretty far out. Izzy, you're a trip."

"I've been told." And then, just like an Indian of old, he seemed to look at the sky to tell the time. "Let's go."

Finally, after a half-hour wait, they were cleared to pass through the locked entry doors into the visitor room, where they had to undergo yet another screening. Several guards stood around the room, which was large and already full. Children were playing on the floor with toys marked

"DOC Property."

Finally there was Louis in a khaki prison uniform, being checked at another door by another guard. He was shorter and stockier than Izzy, and not as handsome, but clearly a brother. The hair at the back of his head was in a small tail, and he had a few gray hairs.

The guard led him to their table, where they sat in a square of light from high-up windows – like being in a basement, only it was the ground floor. Helene could see only the tops of the trees that had given her such pleasure at the lake. She tried not to look at the other inmates and their visitors, but it was hard not to notice that many of them were non-whites, even this far north in one of the states that had a small minority population.

For a moment no one spoke. Louis held Izzy's gaze a long moment, not allowed contact, and took some time looking over Helene, a play of emotions on his face. She was sure that part of it was her resemblance to Renee, and the version of their family story that Renee had told him, maybe even how they had parted. A glimmer of pain passed over his taut face. Yet he bowed his head in greeting.

"You had a good trip?" he asked.

Helene looked to Izzy to answer. His eyes flicked away.

"Clear weather," he said. "Compared to last time with Neesa, that crazy thunderstorm that came up out of nowhere. Erik, that guy has nerves of steel, didn't bother him at all."

"No one else on the road," Louis said.

"True that."

"I think you grew another inch since last time." A dimple formed and disappeared with Louis's quick smile.

"It's been a month." Izzy smiled back. "And you're still the same."

"The new baby, Tewa?" Louis asked. "And Malvina?"

"Good. The baby's good. Malvina's OK now, I guess." He looked to Helene, who continued. "She's fine. The high blood pressure resolved after the baby was born, but they're going to monitor her for a while, see if she needs medication. But my guess is that she's past it now and shouldn't have more problems."

"And my children?" Louis asked, looking directly at Helene. "How are they?"

She gave him the rundown as succinctly as possible, up to and including Wishi-ta's visit with the Boston allergist. And then, without intending to, she mentioned the question of Tana-na's attention issues, and some of her methods to help him focus without medication, but that it might be a concern when he started kindergarten.

"They're great kids," she concluded, "all of them, really." She found the words gushing out and reminded herself to stay businesslike, the professional nurse that she was. "And adjusting well – all things considered."

Louis nodded, acknowledging her meaning. He had listened without interruption.

"We are grateful to you," he said simply. "I am grateful to you. Renee wanted you to know the children. It was her plan to invite you to meet them and be part of their lives." He stopped, then swallowed. "We just didn't think it would be like this."

It was the time, she saw, to put out the idea she been contemplating after some research – if not for an answer, at least to think about.

"I know the two of you have some business to talk about that doesn't concern me, the legal case and all. But before I leave, I have something to ask you, or at least ask you to think about."

A look went between the two brothers.

"About Wishi-ta," she said. "Her future. I think that it might be in her best interest to live with me and my husband, near to the specialists in Boston, where we could really give her all the attention she needs for her medical problems. I've spoken to my husband about this, and we want to know if you would consider letting us adopt her and raise her, since you will likely be gone for such a long part of her childhood."

Louis first looked confused. "Just Wishi-ta?" he said. And then he looked shocked, angered. "How could you think of that, separating her from her twin?"

Oh, she saw quickly, that was the objection: the issue of twins. Or the condition. Both or nothing. That was his agenda, of course, if he were in control of the whole situation. But he was not, now that he was in prison.

She thought carefully before responding. "Well, the reality is that we're only prepared to take on one child, my husband and I, and it is Wishi-ta who needs the special attention. Tana-na's issues are not life threatening." Louis's face grew harder as she spoke. "Malvina and Noel would have more time to address Tana-na's needs, rather than both of them. And he fits in so well with the cousins."

Izzy seemed to have receded into the background, watchful witness to a growing conflict. Across the room a little boy began to wail inconsolably. A cloud of sadness overtook the room, until his was the only voice. Then he was hushed, and the low conversations resumed.

"The twins must be together," Louis stated, his face deepening with color. "That's what's best for them; for both of them. Already they have lost a mother and a father." He gestured with his arms to the room and further. "And now to be separated from each other – don't you see that pain?"

"Yes," Helene said, clenching her hands under the table. "Maybe there has to be some lesser pain, in order to avoid a greater pain – or death."

"No. The pain of the spirit is worse."

"Worse than death?"

"We take care of our children."

"How can you say that?" Helene found her voice rising. "When you're sitting in here, hundreds of miles away from your children, all for the sake of a cause? How could you risk such a thing when you're a father to young children who need you?"

She could see Louis's anger, and also his struggle – staring at Izzy who would not look back. She too gazed at him; it calmed her to see the rise and fall of Izzy's chest, to see the softness of his face.

"You think I'm a bad parent," Louis said, "because I'm trying to make the world a more fit place for my children, my Indian children, to live in? It is for them, and all the children, the elders, all of us, that I do this. You think I've abandoned them, the twins? But they are with family, and family is me. Izzy is me, when I am not with them. And Neesa, Malvina, all of them. And we are part of a community and our Native nations. They are surrounded by family and love. What other security is there?"

Helene had always acquiesced to stronger opinion, worked around strong personalities or avoided them as best she could. Yet she could not back down from this, compelled by some unfamiliar force.

"All fine and good, Louis, from here," she said, a coolness in her tone. "But try to look beyond your own agenda and your noble mission, to a sick little girl who needs help now. At worst, she could end up in the foster care system. Think of what I, we, could offer Wishi-ta – two parents, a nice home, good education, advantages to getting ahead in the world."

This time Louis shook his head. "No. You think those things are so important, but they're not, not to us. All that striving for something better means there's something wrong with you, you're not good enough. In our way, you are born whole and complete, and our welfare is as important as any other human, or animal for that matter. Right, Izzy?"

Izzy nodded.

"OK, OK," Helene said, seeing that Louis was going to hold the line, no matter what. As Izzy said, he was one for words, and he could use them well, like weapons. She was ready to fight, in her own way, but wanted to avoid an onslaught of Louis's frustration with the whole world.

"I am her aunt, you know," she said finally. "And I do have some say in her welfare. There are means I could use to press this forward, but I don't want to do that. It could make things ugly that don't need to be. I was hoping we could work together on this; that you could see another perspective, beyond yourself and your philosophy. It's not like she'd be so far away, or that she wouldn't see Tana-na or her cousins on a regular basis; we could do that."

Louis shot Izzy a look, raising his eyebrows. "I think you'll find things are a little different in Indian Country; there are laws that apply to Native adoptions, keeping the children connected to the community. You might want to check that out. Or –" Louis paused, blinking, calculating.

"You could move to the base. The house is available as long as you would need it."

Helene laughed sharply, trying not to scoff. Izzy turned away, his face drawn.

"I can't do that!" she said. "Our life is elsewhere: our house, our work, my husband's business."

"So he couldn't change jobs or commute, work remotely, if this is so important to you?"

In that moment Helene knew that what he said was true; Kenneth would never consider it. Never. Or that alternative lifestyle.

"He can't," she said tersely. "He's in real estate, and he's tied to the market in our area. He's got all kinds of projects going on and holds the deed to a number of properties. He's pretty much tied to the land."

And just as she said it, she heard how the words came out, making that claim. It was not what she wanted at all. The tide was turning against her; all her caring, noble attempts to help, to understand, to communicate; all the sacrifices she had made were being diminished. She clamped her lips shut, determined not to get more upset.

Louis heaved a sigh, clearly done with the discussion. Helene shifted, picking up her purse, getting ready to depart. Izzy stirred, but he didn't get up.

Louis stayed planted in his chair, measuring her, judging her. "You look like her. Renee," he said, taking her by surprise. "But you're not like her, in your heart. She had a warrior heart and she fought for everything or against everything, with everything she had, not holding back."

Helene's face twisted in frustration. *Wasn't that what she was doing now? Fighting for Wishi-ta?*

Louis continued, "You can't fight for others if you can't fight for yourself. Renee lost her fear, but you seem to fear all the things that could go wrong in the universe so you don't really live in it. We have had our apocalypse, as a people, and she understood that, what it's like. She understood when you're pushed to the extreme, you have to be honest and you have to risk all or you lose everything."

"She was an addict," Helene exclaimed. "She ruined things." Her voice had risen; others had turned to look at them, and the guard made a disapproving face.

Louis answered quietly, "Sometimes you have to burn down to ashes to rebuild."

Helene got to her feet, taking breaths to recover herself.

"I'm going," she said. "I'll be in the car, Izzy, when you're ready. Take your time. But I told Wishi-ta that we'd try to be back around dinnertime. Good-bye, Louis. I think you're wrong about this, and it's too bad Wishi-ta will have to suffer."

"She doesn't have to suffer," Louis said, shaking his head. "You're the one who's suffering." And then, to her surprise, he went on, "And I'm sorry about that. I won't agree to you adopting Wishi-ta and taking her away. But you should know I don't hate you, and I can't hate you because Renee loved you."

That's what made Helene turn and stride to the exit. She swallowed the sobs that threatened to escape while the guard checked her back out again. Her vision blurred as she followed him through the locked doors. She wept in the car, but her tears were dry by the time Izzy reappeared, not more than half an hour later.

The ride back was quiet. Izzy offered to play his flute as Helene drove.

"You brought it with you?"

"Always."

"Thank you, but no. I don't think so, not now."

After a while, Izzy said, "I could tell you some stories."

It was dusk when they arrived back at the Home Camp. A bunch of folks were sitting around a campfire and the kids were roasting marshmallows on sticks. As Helene got out of the car, the murmur of voices came to a halt, all faces turning in her direction. That told her the word was out: a call from the pay phone, somebody checking in with Louis, who told them how he had rejected her proposal for adoption. She felt a crushing weight on her chest. Fate had ordained that she would not accomplish what she felt she needed for the sake of another. So many of her efforts in life had led to dead ends. And what she had achieved didn't seem to hold much significance here. For a moment her feet would not move.

Then a small body broke out of the circle and ran to her: Wishi-ta, her hair golden in the flickering fire. She wrapped her arms around Helene's waist, burying her face.

"You're back," she said. "I've been waiting and waiting."

All eyes were on the two of them, as Helene stood rooted in disappointment and pain.

"Come on," Wishi-ta said, taking her hand and leading her to the fire pit. "Here's a seat for you." Then she looked back at Izzy with an impish smile. "And you too. We saved you both some food, and then Izzy can play his flute."

Helene was powerless to resist. She joined the group, looking into the circle of faces who gazed at her with a certain sadness and not without sympathy.

3. Nightmare at the Museum – by One Little Indian

My mother refuses to go to museums, especially museums of natural history or anthropology. She says they're haunted, and full of angry, sorrowful spirits. It's shocking, she says: obscene. From what she's heard, of course. She's never actually stepped inside. There's no way my mother would agree to chaperone a middle-school trip to the museum of anthropology in Boston, the one run by Harvard. She wouldn't sign the permission slip, either; and my dad had to do it on the sly. I wanted to go so bad – all the kids were going; it was Boston, the city. What could be so bad, anyway? Turns out my mother wasn't so wrong. I got spooked in that place; it's not a happy memory for me.

The bus ride was great, and seeing the city. We saw the natural history museum first, and then the anthropology section. Even natural history made me a little queasy – all those dead, stuffed creatures, big and small. Then there was the part about us: all kinds of Indian stuff set out in these nice glass cases. Some of it was beautiful, but none of it was ever meant to be art. It was our stuff – what we made to live with, some of it special, sacred: kachinas from Arizona and clan poles from the Northwest. Genuine stuff, taken from the places where it was displayed or buried. It was embarrassing, not right, and made me sad. Even then I figured out if it was in a museum, it was not where it was supposed to be, and that whatever meaning it had to some real person was gone.

I appreciate learning about the past and history. I liked the dioramas of village life, weapons, and canoes at the museum. How accurate were they? I couldn't tell you. It's someone's interpretation, and probably not someone who lived at the time, or was even Indian. To me it was like space beings in the future trying to explain what life is like for us today, in the good old USA. Bound to get a few things wrong. I get science too, and "hard evidence" – but that's not perfect, either. Somehow it's not cool how Indians tell their history – stories and songs, information handed down generation to generation. If it's not "documented," it can't be real, even if it is real. Well, who says so, anyway? Wampanoags have a pretty clear idea of Norsemen stopping by their shores around 1000, and accounts of Indian explorers from tribal nations to the west. But if there's no paper, or metal, or ceramics, that's not history, I guess. And not taught. Just the other version, if at all – Indians safely in the past.

Now there's NAGPRA – Native American Graves Protection and Repatriation Act, thanks to pressure from indigenous people. Returning bones, relics, ceremonial objects to the nations where they came from. Giving some nations a chance to rebury their dead, hopefully not to be robbed again. It may be part of this bigger movement – to return "loot" that was stolen by collectors, some of it for science, some for wealth and fame. But it was big business for many years, suggesting that either robbing graves is no big deal or some humans are not quite human enough to actually care about their dead. Well, let me tell you, that's dead wrong, on both accounts.

So, my mom's not all wrong about museums – and not all right, either. But personally I think a little bit of her is curious to see what's in the anthropology exhibits for herself. I just bet she thinks she might recognize a pipe, a canoe, a basket, decorated in some familiar pattern that she's pretty sure belonged to someone in her family, our family, from some time ago. Or maybe her great-great-grandmother's shell necklace that went missing. I suspect she thinks she knows where some of that stuff belongs – and I told her recently, just maybe the people at the museum would be interested in talking to her and finding out. Who knows?

Chapter 13

It would be a seven-hour trip back to the base, just Helene and Wishi-ta in the car. They'd gotten a late start. After a stop for burgers and sundaes at Friendly's, Helene was feeling unaccountably tired. Almost on impulse she pulled into to a Ramada Inn off the highway. It wasn't safe to continue, she decided, and besides, they didn't have to get to the doctor's office until the afternoon. It would be a bit of a treat and a holiday, with a good bed and a hot shower.

Wishi-ta's eyes were huge as she looked around the hotel lobby. "Why are we staying here?" she asked.

"Just you and your daughter?" the hotel clerk asked, a middle-aged woman with over bright red hair. "I have two doubles."

Helene glanced to see if Wishi-ta had heard the question. "Yes, just the two of us." Of course anyone would think they were mother and child; it was entirely logical. But Wishi-ta was entranced with the vending machine by the counter – so many goodies in bright packages.

"Come on, Wishi," Helene said, holding up a key. "We're room 132." Wishi-ta followed Helene wordlessly to the first floor room. Helene held the door open as they stepped inside.

"Ooh," Wishi-ta said, holding her nose. "It smells funny."

It was not the response Helene expected. Though the room was not luxurious, it was spacious and clean, recently renovated. She'd loved staying at hotels as a kid, the very few times it happened. It felt different from home, special, away from everyday life.

"Just for tonight," she said. Then she sniffed, something a bit off: the rug, maybe, or cleaning chemicals? She cracked the window for some outside air. They washed up, put on sleep clothes, and watched TV together until falling asleep on the same bed, Wishi-ta folded into the curve of Helene's back. Around four o'clock in the morning, Wishi-ta awakened, tugging on Helene's arm. In the dark, Helene could hear the slight wheeziness, enough to turn on the light and look for the inhaler. Wishi-ta didn't say anything, but her face was a bit flushed and she squirmed about, making a mess of the covers.

"We won't go back to sleep now," Helene said, standing in front of the bed. "Let's get dressed and get out of here."

The night manager looked surprised to see them with their bags.

"Anything wrong?"

At first Helene only shook her head, eager to get on her way. Then she felt Wishi-ta's eyes on her.

"Something in the room," she said. "It smelled a bit funny, maybe an allergic reaction." She gestured toward Wishi-ta, who was now fine.

The woman screwed up her lips. "It's a clean place; we get high ratings."

Helene couldn't hold back her yawns: "Not complaining." Yawn. "The rug or the cleaning materials?" She shook her head. "I don't know. I'm just telling you. We'd like to check out, please."

The rest of the ride passed quickly, and they arrived at the base in full daylight with time for grocery shopping before lunch. On a hunch Helene suggested that they go by the Intertribal Center "to see if anyone is around." She wanted to be sure Wishi-ta was at ease, with some familiar faces. It was family circle time, parents and children sitting around for storytelling, and then an activity making drum sticks or "beaters" with deerskin pouches filled with animal fur, and decorated with leather strips and beads. After that it was time for the appointment, which ran long, and then home for dinner. Only then did Wishi-ta ask for Tana-na and the others. What she really wanted to know was when they were going back to the Home Camp.

"We'll see. It depends on how the shots go. That's very important, you know."

Wishi-ta's face clouded.

"But it won't be too long before they're all back home. You'll see. Meanwhile we've got lots of things to do here. There's a nice farm we can visit, with some lambs and baby goats. And Neesa wants us to take care of her garden while she's gone, and pick all the things that are ripe. Maybe we'll do that tomorrow."

After supper they played War and Match-Match cards on the new hypoallergenic rug in the living room, with a fan moving the warm air around. After dark a knock came at the door. Helene looked up to see Erik through the screen door, a halo over his head from the front door light – a bit of a specter if she hadn't recognized him.

"Come in," she said, surprised and a little hesitant. She hadn't heard his truck pull up, the red one with a black cover over the bed.

"I am the welcome-back committee," he said, making his entrance, slightly shiny and soiled with the work of a hot day outside. Wishi-ta scrambled up from the floor and ran over to hug him. He scooped her up, nuzzling the back of her neck. With his free hand, he dug out a pair of tiny plastic bubbles with figurines inside, a dog and a horse. She immediately climbed down to examine them. Then she disappeared into the bedroom, to return with a plastic doll castle – miniature, like the figurines. She settled in on the rug, next to Helene.

"Thank you," Helene said, a bit stiffly. "And Wishi-ta thanks you – right, Wishi?"

She nodded, forming the words, although no actual words came out. Erik loomed six feet above, seeming to glow with the light behind him.

"And also to check up on the two of you, make sure you made it back OK, and have everything you need."

"Obviously we're here, no problem," she said, gesturing around. "As you see, everything's perfectly fine."

"Great," he said with a smile. "I know you're a very on-top-of-things kind of woman. I wasn't worried or anything. But I started to wonder when I didn't see your car pull in last night."

Helene's mouth fell open. "You were looking for me…us?"

"I kind of was. Elsa called on the pay phone over at the scout camp, and she said you'd left late morning, so I expected to see your lights on at night. Then I saw the car out front earlier today, so I knew you'd made it."

Helene wriggled herself upright, rising to her feet, to be more on a level with Erik. "We stayed at a hotel; I was tired. Is something wrong with that?"

"Not one bit. Glad there was no trouble on the road."

"Nope." She knew her tone was cool, but she also knew he was watching her closely, only short feet away. There was a few days' growth of stubble on his chin, and his sideburns were overlong, not clean and trim like Kenneth's.

To her surprise his face relaxed into a smile. "Well, maybe I'm just happy to see you're here."

That, at least, was more direct. *How to reply?*

"I've got a six-pack in the truck." He gestured with a hand. "Would you like to join me for a cold pop?"

She blinked a couple times. "You mean here?"

"That would be nice."

She would enjoy a beer, but she didn't want him to come in, to stay, to drink in the house. But something had come over Wishi-ta, a kind of relief and excitement when he entered the house. That, she wanted to keep, and he seemed to know it.

"Wishi-ta wants me to stay, don't you?" She looked up, her hair falling away from her face, in full grin. "I think she's grown this summer," he added. "Look at that beautiful face, like a flower in bloom."

"OK, sure," Helene said. "Just one, though. I am in charge of this young lady." She felt the need to spell it out.

After he left, she got a couple of glasses from the kitchen and a juice box for Wishi. Erik came back through the door with the beer and a bag of chips, family size. Even though they'd just eaten a good healthy dinner, Wishi-ta scrambled up, bouncing on her toes for some of those salty chips. Erik opened and gave Helene a beer, declining the glass, and sat down.

"Are you going back to the Home Camp?" Helene asked, taking a seat opposite him, on the sofa. She tucked one of the new pillows into her lap. Wishi-ta had gone off the chips fairly quickly and was back to her world-building on the rug, humming softly. Suddenly she jumped to her feet, racing down the hall to the twins' bedroom as the adults looked after her, bemused.

"In a while I'll go back," Erik answered. "I'm here to get supplies, and I have a few things to take care of."

"Supplies for what?"

"Building. The pavilion by the lake – did you see it?"

She thought a moment, recalling a respectable pile of wood. "Oh, that stack of lumber, you mean?"

"It will be a thing of beauty once we're done," he said archly. "But, you know, they have these ideas about the design, how they want it built, et cetera. The Indian way." He sipped his beer, exhaling with pleasure. "Usually not the fast way."

"And you are the contractor, so to speak?"

"Kind of, sort of. They hire me to do some of the basic carpentry, since I've been in the construction business a long time." He lifted his eyebrows. "Like Louis. This was his idea, but now he's not here and I've inherited his grand plans."

Helene nodded, saying nothing. She drank so little in general, she could feel a tiny buzz already.

"It's in honor of your sister." He stopped – watching her.

Helene raised a hand, a warning. She glanced down the hallway, where Wishi-ta was still in search of some desired item.

But then Erik surprised her again. "I wasn't really her favorite person, not at first." He took a long drink. "We made our peace, at the end."

"Oh, dear," she said with a humorless giggle. She couldn't help it. He had no tact. Not that Renee had much. "What did you do? Something inappropriate?"

He smirked. "You might say that. We were buddies a long time, Louis and me, since he was a teen. Even though I'm older." He chuckled. "Maybe not any wiser. Anyway, I tried to get Louis to go out for a drink now and then, for old times' sake, you know – after a big job or just to unwind. But Renee did not approve."

Helene swallowed a small burp. "Well, she wouldn't, would she?"

"Hmm…" He took another sip of beer, settling back on the sofa. "How about you?" he said. "Would you go out for drink with me sometime, listen to some kick-ass music, shake out your hair and howl at the moon?"

Helene hissed, pulling her feet in beneath her. "How can you ask me that?" she said in voice just above a whisper. "You know I'm married."

He shrugged. "I guess I know that."

"It means I want to stay married. And I have a good husband. Why would I risk that?"

"Why, indeed? Maybe there's something you'd find out that you didn't know."

Her face was burning, but she kept quiet as Wishi-ta reappeared, a toy horse in hand. Back on the rug, she yawned as she played with her figurines, the adult voices making music in the background, the words meaning nothing to her.

"I...I..." Helene started. But Erik leaned over to tickle Wishi-ta on her stomach. "Someone's getting sleepy," he said. "Your bed is calling you, 'Wishi-ta, Wishi-ta,'" he mimed.

"No," she protested, but the sleepiness was in her voice. She pulled herself up by Erik's knee, looking into his face, one hand clutching her little plastic friends.

"Are you my father now?"

Helene's hand flew to her mouth. She saw the affection between them, but she had not expected that. Erik patted a spot on the sofa and Wishi-ta climbed next to him.

"Wishi-ta," he said gently, touching her arm. "Do I look like your father?"

"No," she said, rather sadly. "But where is he, again?"

"Up north," Erik said, leaning close and speaking softly. "Remember what Malvina and Noel said? He's at a great big place doing important work that only he can do. But it's just for grown-ups, so kids don't go there."

Up north. That was an interesting way to put it.

"So we can't see him, me and Tana-na? Or not our cousins, either?"

"I'm afraid not. But you know what he said to me, the last time I saw him?"

With a start, Helene remembered that Erik had also visited Louis in prison; he was the one who had given Izzy and Neesa a ride when they went up for the hearing.

"He said, 'I have to do this work for my family and my children. Every day I look at their pictures and give thanks for them.'"

Wishi-ta nodded gravely. "I pray for him with the tobacco, and Mommy, too." Slowly her gaze turned toward Helene, with a kind of longing and confusion. Then Wishi-ta sighed, looking back to Erik. "But Mommy is with the ancestors now."

"Right you are." Erik kissed his fingertips to Wishi-ta's forehead. "Good night, sweetie. You need to get to bed. And it's time for me to head out too."

Then he was on his feet, heading toward the doorway, turning back briefly to Helene. "Good night." And he was gone.

The next few days were quiet and peaceful. Yet Helene remained uneasy over nothing and everything. She found herself inexplicably watching out the window for a red truck, and wondered at the phone that never seemed to ring. It was as if she had taken a vacation from her own life, isolated here with Wishi-ta.

She had called Kenneth the day after their return. He was sympathetic about the conversation with Louis, but not surprised or particularly disappointed.

"If you want," he said, more to soothe her than with any real hope, "I'll call my friend who does family law, and see what he says. But I have to say, aside from the allergy and asthma problems, she seems fairly well taken care of. I don't think you'll get much traction."

He said he would come up to the base on the weekend for a little moral support, and to help assess the situation. He had to leave Saturday night, though, for a busy Sunday. And he'd asked a local interior designer to start coming up with a few ideas, as things were moving quickly and Helene was not available.

Almost immediately after she put the phone down, she called Thelma, keyed up and frustrated with Kenneth, although she couldn't explain just why. But Thelma didn't answer, and Helene's short message just asked her to call back. No answers, no relief, just this strange agitation in the pit of her stomach.

"I was away, at a crafter's show in Maine, didn't I tell you?" said Thelma when she returned the call a couple of days later. "Something on your mind?"

Helene took the phone into the living room and settled on the sofa to tell her what had happened. How Louis had rejected her idea and she had sensed a reaction to her visit from the others at the Home Camp.

There was a moment of silence, and Helene wondered if Thelma was working on one of her projects. Then Thelma sighed. "No, honey," she said, "that won't work. Louis was sure to reject the idea of you taking one twin and not the other. I didn't realize that's what you were thinking. We never talked the details, just the general idea. I agree with him on that. It would be one more loss; it's not fair to either of them. Don't you see that?"

Helene thumped the pillow next to her. "But it could be a matter of life or death. How would it be any less devastating if Wishi-ta died?"

"Oh, dear. I don't think that will happen," Thelma said. "I really think they must be fully aware of the problem now. That other circumstance was so unusual – Malvina's problem with the pregnancy, and Tana-na's accident. That will not happen again."

"But now they have this new baby. That family is already spread thin."

"Helene, be fair, they have done well by Wishi-ta, by both of them."

"But she's thriving with me, thriving. Like a flower in bloom; people have noticed, and said so."

"I'm sure she is. But you can still be in her life; still be her auntie. Clearly, that's important too."

Thelma spoke with kindness, sympathy, but she was unrelenting. Helene was ready to end the conversation. No one seemed to really understand what was going on, what was at stake.

Then Thelma's words came through. "I have to say, as a friend, you pursue this adoption at a risk. And not just for the reasons you might think."

"What, then?"

"I think maybe it's your marriage you should focus on right now. I really try not to interfere, but I'm not sure it could not sustain the stress of a child or children right now. Kenneth is just not buying into the idea, especially now, while he's totally caught up in his career and the real estate opportunities." She paused at the other end of the phone line, taking a breath. "Let me put it this way. While you've been away at the base, Kenneth has become quite the man about town, out most nights with a lively set of friends, all the movers and shakers. You know the kind of people I'm talking about – the smart set, those successful, well-heeled gentlemen and their lovely, agreeable wives." She chuckled. "Believe me, I know. I lost a husband to one of them. He didn't like me getting older, wiser, and more outspoken, and she was right there ready to swoop in."

"You mean people like me and Kenneth?" she asked, a bit of acid in her voice.

"Oh, no," Thelma exclaimed. "I'm sorry. I didn't mean it like that." For a moment, Thelma seemed flustered. "I mean, Kenneth has his share of admirers, some of them women, quite assertive, shall we say? Not that he's done anything wrong; I'm not saying that."

"No, Thelma! You're wrong. He's not like that."

There was a long sigh. "No one's like that until it happens to them. And who could blame him, for enjoying this kind of success and attention. I think he hoped for more, um, support from you, and appreciation."

Helene sucked in breath, upset and angry, at Kenneth – and at Thelma, for saying such things.

"Don't get me wrong," Thelma said. "I'm sure he loves you, in his way. But I'm afraid you're not part of the excitement in his life right now, and you don't seem particularly interested in sharing it. All those little projects, or not so little projects, are his babies, his children. And that's what's important to him right now, not so much your concerns or the twins. You need to think hard about your choices. I'm saying this because I care about you. You have to be realistic about the situation, and about what is important to you."

Helene closed her eyes. "Thelma, please. Stop." It wasn't that she didn't already understand on some level; she didn't like it spelled out in such a dire, absolute way. Like she had no rights or choices, except to go along with what everyone else was saying.

"I've said my piece," Thelma said. "But I'll be in touch. And remember, school will be starting again, and all that goes with it. You have options. And will you please, please remember all the good you've already done for Wishi-ta, and the others? It was a crisis, and you rose to the occasion. And there's plenty of time for a deeper, richer relationship in the future. Just remember that."

Helene hung up the phone, dismayed – was that what Thelma really thought? That Helene had not considered the larger consequences of fitting one child, or two, into their lives? Or that Kenneth was leaving Helene behind because she had not gotten caught up in all his new developments? She swallowed, looking through the curtained windows into the quiet street. It was a kind of test, she realized, for both of them, of their marriage, and what kind of person Helene herself truly was, something still not entirely clear to her at forty years of age. But she was clear about one thing: she was not giving up, no matter what Louis, Thelma, Kenneth, or anyone else thought. In her reading she'd come across the idea of a petition for adoption, when the biological parents were not fit or able to raise a child. She was as much family as Malvina and Noel. She could do this, with or without Kenneth's support.

The following day, there was a message from Kenneth. Denis had sent her a package. It was marked "Handle with care," he said, but lightweight, flat, and not very large. Should he bring it with him? Was there anything else Helene wanted or needed from home? When she called back, she asked Kenneth to open the package.

"It's a CD," Kenneth said. "A music CD. It has the name of the band, Frenzy and Firelight, and "Demo." There's a note here too. Do you want me to open it?"

"No, not now," she said evasively, thinking, Who knows what it may say about Renee or the folks at the base? Or Kenneth himself, for that matter. "But good for him, making a recording. No wonder I haven't heard a word from him lately."

"The Wandering Troubadour," Kenneth said, and Helene had to smile, but it was a wry smile. That was the romantic version.

"Nothing else," she said, "I'm all set here. Oh, actually there is one thing, the dictionary." She didn't explain that it was for the petition for adoption she was drafting, letting him assume it was for the coursework for professional credits.

"Got to scoot," Kenneth said. "So I'll see you on Friday, then. I'll let you know what time as it gets closer."

"Sure. Great. See you then."

Friday morning, Kenneth called to say he would be on his way right after lunch. Helene and Wishi-ta went midmorning to visit a local farm and orchard. Right away Wishi-ta found a friend to play with, a boy from the base who was a year older. Next to him she didn't seem so small. She was acting more like a fully developed four-year-old than Helene had seen at the beginning of the summer. The twins' fifth birthday was in September, and Helene had been thinking of what she wanted to get them.

After lunch and quiet time back at the house, Helene got another call from Kenneth. He was in his car and sounded rushed. Something had come up, so it didn't look good for tonight after all, but he'd make an early start on Saturday, and they should plan on an early dinner, before he left again Saturday night or very early Sunday.

Then Friday night, after Helene was in her pajamas reading a book in bed, he called a third time to say that there was a critical problem with one of the new construction sites, something to do with soil contamination from an old factory, and they would have to reassess and determine how to go forward. And it had to be tomorrow, Saturday, and he had to be there.

"I'm so, so sorry this had to happen," he said, and she was sure that he was. "It's the nature of this kind of work, dealing with the land, and construction. You understand that, right? Maybe you and Wishi-ta could take another trip down here? We can have that meal together. Let me know what you want to do."

"I will." But she already knew she wasn't going to make the trip. Not for five minutes of his time and a hurried meal.

"Good night, Kenneth."

"Good night. Wish me luck."

"Of course."

She felt fine on Saturday, energized. She and Wishi-ta spent time in Neesa's garden, and then Helene found a small bike with training wheels in the shed. Helene was amazed that Wishi-ta took to the little blue bike as well as she did, even with a creaky handle bar and uneven wheels. Helene found herself trotting behind, slightly out of breath, but laughing along with Wishi-ta as she finally stopped in front of the entrance to the Intertribal Center. To her surprise Bernice was headed inside from the opposite direction in a sleeveless dress, hair pulled up from the heat, carrying a covered dish.

"You better watch her good," Bernice said. "She flies like the wind."

"I know, I'm the one chasing her," Helene said. "What are you doing back here and what's going on?"

"My daughter and her family are visiting. One of my grandsons had a lacrosse tournament in New York state, and they decided to stop on the way back."

"How nice for you," Helene said. "Is it Josie?" That was the daughter she was curious about.

"No, thank God. Just as well she's not here, or she'd been mooning over that Erik, since he's back around." She gave her head a shake. "For goodness' sake, he's twice her age."

"Oh." Helene clamped her mouth shut, afraid what might come out.

Bernice turned to watch a woman and three young people, teens and preteens, coming up the block, also carrying platters and bowls.

"That's Elinor and her kids; come on, I'll introduce you. Do you and Wishi-ta want have lunch with us?"

"I don't want to impose."

Bernice stared her down. "You have some strange notions," she said finally. "If you want to come, come. And the next time, if you want to share a meal, maybe some of us will join you. Doesn't that make sense?"

"I don't have any..."

"Bring milk," said. "Or a loaf of bread or some ice cream. Whatever you have on hand. Or you can wash up after. Whatever suits you."

Wishi-ta was already off her bike, pulling open the door to go inside.

"Well, then, it looks like maybe we will join you." But then it struck her, Bernice being back from the Home Camp. "How did you get back here? Caught a ride with somebody?"

"Yup, Erik," Bernice said easily. "I had to sit next to his toolbox in the cab, for seven hours. He didn't want them getting wet in the back. Humph..." The picture made Helene smile.

At lunch she found out that a group of folks – including Bernice – was going to a fundraiser that night, two towns over, which included music, dancing, prizes, and raffles. And drinks. It was an organization that supported families in need, Native and other, including salvaging and storing of materials that had been burned in the Carons' recent house fire.

"Come with us," Bernice said. "Just for a couple hours. It won't be late."

"It's not for kids, though."

"No, they allow drinking at the VFW."

"What about Wishi-ta?"

Bernice clucked her tongue. "What about her? She can stay with my grandchildren. Tiffany is seventeen, and she can drive."

"But, but –"

"But nothing. About the allergies? Tiffany can handle it, just show her what to do. You better not make Wishi-ta afraid for her own self; there's no reason she can't stay with those kids. And no reason you can't go."

Helene looked down at her hands in her lap, her fingernails overdue for filing and clear polish. She had the idea that Bernice was trying to coax her out of herself. That Bernice, like all of them, knew of the standoff, so to speak, with Louis. Yet for some reason they still wanted her there, and not unhappy.

"OK, OK," she said. "But I only have the one skirt; everyone already saw it at the last dance."

"Oh, please."

Chapter 14

Robert and Charlotte were back from the Home Camp for a series of medical appointments, and they were going to the fundraiser, too. They gave Bernice a ride and stopped to pick up Helene, as well. She couldn't ask, but she was pretty sure that Erik would be there. Why wouldn't he be? He was all about music and dancing, and drinking and flirting; it was right up his alley, as far as she could see.

"No Elinor?" Helene asked Bernice, sharing the back seat with her.

"No, she's meeting a friend for dinner. Not into this stuff much." To Helene's blank look, she responded, "Doesn't get along with some of these Indians – too political for her taste."

Oh, well, then.

They were some of the first to arrive, as Robert wanted to get "a good table not too close to the speakers." They paid the entrance fee and went by the raffle table to check out the prizes: baskets of goodies, food, sports stuff, the kinds of things you might find at a parents' association fundraiser at Helene's school. Beyond that were a couple of Neesa's handmade baskets, some jewelry, a beaded pouch, and another gift basket, this one with pieces of leather, animal fur, and bags of beads and shells. Someone had made an effort to decorate, putting out centerpieces on the tables and streamers hanging from the ceiling, in the theme of an old-time sock hop.

Soon the room filled, voices rising to be heard and a line forming at the bar. Helene stood at the table with Bernice and the others, who were telling her about the family whose house had burned, when she saw the frame of a man with longish hair and a full beard walk through the doorway: Erik. He looked casually through the room, and then stopped when he spotted her, making his way over in an unhurried manner.

"Lovely ladies," he said to the group at the table, "and Robert himself. Let the party begin. There's nothing doing until this man hits the dance floor." The women tittered, as Robert was a quiet and restrained older man, who tended not to overexert himself much.

"And you're here," he said directly to Helene.

She felt herself blushing. "For the fundraiser; it sounded like such a good idea."

"Of course; but I want a dance with you."

With everyone watching, she nodded. "Sure, sure."

Then he moved on, stopping to talk to others and then finding a spot close to the bar, where he hung out in between visits to the buffet, landing only a minute to eat at another table.

There was a brief program: an appeal for the raffle items and a report about the progress on the burned house, and then it was time for dancing.

Helene had a number of invitations from the middle-aged men who were there to dance: bachelors, widowers, divorced men, and those whose wives watched placidly from the tables. These guys, Helene realized, liked to show their stuff.

"The Twist" came on, and a lot of folks got up, mostly in groups or on their own; it wasn't really couples music. All through the dance, Helene felt Erik's eyes on her, but when she looked back, he was always talking or taking a swig of beer. It wasn't until the fifth or sixth song that he strolled over to her table, reaching out a hand. The tune was something fast and swingy – so that she found herself breathless with spinning, while he seemed to enjoy seeing her off-balance.

Then he danced with Bernice, and with Charlotte, polite and easy. It was almost an hour later, when a slow song came on, that he returned for Helene. She felt unsure; she didn't want to make a big deal of it with everyone watching. She got to her feet and walked to the dance floor with him, letting him take her hand, and place his own low on her back.

They didn't make small talk, and Helene didn't look directly at him. But she had the curious sensation of floating, being buoyed in the water. She sensed that the others in the room had made a space for them, were circling them – those who knew them, and those who didn't. But she couldn't understand why. Were they waiting to watch her falter, crack, or fall; kind of like rubberneckers at an accident, unable to look away? Or did they see something invisible to her, some force of the inevitable? But that was ridiculous. No one wished her harm; why would they? She and Erik were doing nothing inappropriate or even out of the ordinary; just social dancing. But it was more than that, and she knew it. Mostly she felt the places where he touched her, and his breath on her cheek and neck, the melancholy of the song, and some other thing that kept her there in his arms.

Then the music changed to another song, a fast one, with the emcee calling dancers to the floor. They excused themselves passing Helene and Erik, standing motionless. He leaned in to say something, but she couldn't hear.

"What?" She still couldn't hear when he repeated. But then he beckoned her to follow him to a corner of the room, and then down a back hall that led to storage room. There was no one else there; it was quieter.

She knew why, but it was embarrassing to think he wanted to sneak away like teenagers.

"What did you say in there?" She pointed toward the function room.

"I want to kiss you," he said. Not that he really said that.

"You can't do that," she said, shaking her head. "Seriously. You know…"

"I can," he said. "And I will. Unless you tell me not to."

She was starting to vibrate with fear and with longing.

He made a face: "Is that what you're telling me?"

She shook her head. And he kissed her, long, sweet, and slow. And she kissed him back, full of wonder, but certain of herself, even though the lips were different and the smell. And she was a married woman who never strayed, had never wanted to stray.

"Why?" she said, pulling back. "Why would you want to kiss me, or be close to me? There's nowhere to go." She felt a painful thump in her rib cage. "And nowhere to hide."

He gave a wry laugh. "I don't go much by logic; you might have noticed that. You are a beautiful woman with a broken heart. The first time I met you, I could feel your longing and your…your sadness. I know what those things are."

She was abashed, shocked. "How could you possibly know that? How would you know anything about me?"

And then she knew: Renee – at least some of it, their history, the bad times.

He shrugged. "I know some of it."

"So," she said, breathlessly. "You want to be with me, even though you think I'm a mess? What, to take advantage of someone who is struggling? Is that it?" But she didn't think so. Yet she couldn't understand otherwise.

Erik put a hand to her face. "You're a beautiful mess. And I don't think you're weak enough to be taken advantage of. I'm pretty sure you've got some kind of toughness in there, if you're anything like your sister."

Helene turned away. "Do not talk about her, please!"

"But she's here with us, isn't she? In some shape or form." He drew her face back, and she couldn't look away. "I'm not afraid of your pain. It's just another form of passion, only you don't want to hurt yourself too much by it."

She pulled his hand from her face, summoning reason. "What about Kenneth – my husband? How is this not hurting him?"

"But he's not here, is he? He doesn't really understand this kind of pain, and he can't really help you, on a personal level. Only that he doesn't want it to be too distracting. Isn't that true?"

"This is some kind of sweet talk," Helene said, shaking her head. But she didn't step away. It was like being inside a force field. Certainly, there was danger all around, but right in this space she felt refuge.

"I'm looking for somebody too," he said.

"You barely know me, whatever Renee might have told you. And whatever this is" – she gestured between the two of them – "it's not love."

He shrugged. "I wouldn't know. I don't think I know what that is, real love. At least I've been pretty bad at it, keeping it going. I just know I feel something for you, Helene, something strong – desire, connection, need, whatever you want to call it."

"Humph…" It came out just like Bernice.

He smiled, a bit sadly. Or just a great actor, putting it on. "I love the best I can; and try not to do much harm – that's my motto. Simple but true."

She stared, perplexed. What was he saying? What did he want?

Then they were kissing again, and Helene felt the filters drop away and the fears. She felt something too, for this man. And she needed something from him – a guy that was not one to stick around. But he fit in here, somehow. And how he was with Wishi-ta…

Someone came to the top of the hall, looking for an exit or a bathroom. Helene pulled away from Erik, heart pounding, giddy, disoriented.

"Let's go," she whispered. "We can't let people find us here like this."

"No, that would be a shock, wouldn't it," he said, which bothered her, but not as much as she would have thought.

"You're a good kisser," she said. What she meant was that she was uncertain, off-balance, and drunk on emotion or lust. Then she put her hand on his arm, holding him back. "Wait a minute. So this is it, right?" Of course it was. They couldn't carry on an affair under all these noses, with Wishi-ta in the house, only a short time until Helene returned to her own home and Erik was off on his next trip. It was just that they had feelings for each other, under these strange circumstances. So what?

But he released her hand. "No more talk," he said. "No more."

They were back on the dance floor, and then separated for the rest of the evening until coffee and dessert.

But then the deejay called the last dance, a slow one, and Erik came back to Helene's side.

"May I have this dance?" he asked. But she couldn't answer, sitting dumb in her chair, looking at the table.

"Well?" said Robert. "Yes or no? Don't keep the man standing there."

She rose to her feet, moving on automatic pilot, until they were back on the dance floor, and their hands joined once again, his other hand lightly at her waist. But close enough to feel his warmth. He had beer on his breath, and she'd had two glasses of wine; one more than her limit. Not too much but enough. Thankfully he didn't talk, and he didn't press up close. She couldn't relax; no way. She was almost faint with desire and dread. What was this? What were they doing, and in front of all these people? At the end she pulled away, moving quickly toward the table, and safety. But he was right behind, stopping her before she got there.

"Do you want to ride home with me?"

"Are you even safe to drive?"

"Yes, I am. I made sure of it. Will you come?"

"Are you crazy?" she hissed. "I can't do that. They're waiting for me;

I've got to go."

He nodded, lips pressed together. "OK."

"That was one thing," she whispered, eyes directed to the back hall. "But that's the end of it; it goes no further. I'm not...not...a..." She fumbled for the word. "An adulterer." Even to herself, it sounded stupid, melodramatic.

By then his face had shuttered and he took out the keys from his pocket, preparing to leave.

"See you around," he said.

"Maybe."

But when he started walking away, she found herself at his heels and then at his side, talking quickly.

"Wait. I'm sorry. I didn't mean to sound like that. But I can't risk it. I have a good life, you know. And a marriage worth working on. You're a nice guy, but this was just a little slip, and then it's back to real life. You know that, right?"

He gave a half smile. "I don't know anything for sure."

But Helene didn't want to hear that. "Ah, right. You've got the best of both worlds. A family and community that loves and accepts you whenever you're here, and the freedom to go off where you want, with whoever you want, without real responsibility."

"Yeah," he said. "That's exactly what's it like. I'm one lucky fellow. So long, Helene. I know you have a lot to deal with. Let's see how it all works out."

The next morning Helene was up early She hadn't slept well, despite all the dancing. Maybe the wine; more likely the kiss, or kisses. She couldn't get it from her mind – the pleasure, and the guilt. And then Wishi-ta not being in the house with her; it felt so empty and alone. She kept looking for signs of movement down the street at Bernice's, where Wishi-ta had slept.

What have I done? What have I done? she kept asking herself. But the answer was not clear, and it felt like she was standing apart from herself, watching as she moved about the house.

At eight o'clock she went to collect Wishi-ta. Bernice was already out hanging laundry. She popped a clothespin on the line, watching Helene's approach.

"Hi, Bernice," Helene said, stifling a yawn. Her eyes were heavy with fatigue.

"You OK, Helene?"

"Don't I look OK?"

Bernice shrugged. "How do I know?"

But she was digging at something, Helene could tell. If not suspicious, Bernice seemed concerned.

Helene went inside to get Wishi-ta and then headed back to the house. In the kitchen she put together a picnic with some of the produce from Neesa's garden. They were meeting another family with children who were starting kindergarten along with Wishi-ta and Tana-na, and Helene was eager to hear their views on the school and the teachers. They wore swimsuits under their clothes and had brought towels, for a dip in the shallow river by the park.

The picnic was cut short by a sudden thunderstorm, which kicked up dust and created mud puddles, but didn't last long enough for a real soaking. Back home, Helene put on a kids' video for Wishi-ta, and opened a novel she hoped would relax her. Only she couldn't read and she couldn't relax. Not then. Not at dinner. And not while she was playing Candy Land with Wishi-ta after dinner. But Wishi-ta was tired from her sleepover at Bernice's and was ready for bed early, leaving Helene restless and fidgety on the sofa, unable to concentrate on her course work or the book. Even working on Renee's journal pages couldn't distract her, as strange and fascinating as it was to read about her life here at the base – as well as occasional references to Helene herself, and their own family. Maybe it was the closeness and humidity after the storm; she was so sticky and uncomfortable, even with the fan on. She found herself on her feet, pacing, wanting to go for a long, fast walk, but she couldn't leave Wishi-ta alone.

Then the phone rang, startling her. It was Kenneth, and she could barely talk to him.

He asked about the fundraiser, and she just said, "Oh, very successful, well attended; they raised a lot of money."

"Good," he said. "And Wishi-ta, how is she doing?"

"Very well; she had fun at the sleepover, and no problems."

"I feel bad about standing you girls up on the weekend," he said. "So I'm going to try to make amends. I've got nothing on my schedule the day after next. Does it make any sense for me to drive up tomorrow night?"

"Oh! Ah, no. Not really. There's no reason to do that, no need. You should just take time for yourself, relax – if you can."

"Then, how about next weekend? I saw that Disney On Ice is at the arena. A buddy of mine can probably get tickets. What do you think?"

"Oh, gosh," she said, a little breathless. "I don't know. Let me think about it. There might be something scheduled here for the kids; you know, with all of Wishi-ta's friends. She'd probably hate to miss it." It could be true, but she didn't know that for sure.

The line was quiet.

"So you're still pretty upset with me, then?"

"No, no. That's not it. I do understand, I mean, how busy you are." That was true. But there was this other thing, the reason why she didn't want to see him. It was just something she was not ready to deal with.

"All right," he said. And then, unlike him: "Well, I won't bore you with the details of this project we were having so much trouble with, but I can say we're back on track, and we have not one but two, potential buyers, and that means a bidding war."

"Oh, great," she said, so deeply uninterested that she could hardly hide it.

"Right," he said, and then a little more sharply, "Looks like I have to carry on building this real estate empire without you. You're so focused on everything up there these days."

"Just at the moment, yes," she said. "I have no choice."

"Don't forget. School is right around the corner. By the way, it looks like the new contract arrived in the mail. You probably have to sign and return it, right?"

"Yes. That's right. I do. Could you forward it to me?" Then on afterthought: "And maybe send Denis's CD, as well, since you didn't, well…"

He jumped in, cutting her short. "Sure, happy to. Anything else?"

"No, that's it. But I appreciate the offer about the ice show; that's very generous. Can I get back to you in a day or two?"

"Certainly."

They rang off, but Helene picked up the phone again right away. Her heart was beating fast. Something was going on with her, this secretiveness and evasiveness. She absolutely did not want to see Kenneth right now, or even think about school.

She called Denis; she needed to talk to him. He might actually understand, even if he couldn't help. But he was not there. And when she left a message on his voicemail, it was impossible to keep the resentment out of her words. "Why are you never there when I call? What if I actually needed you for something?"

She wanted to call Thelma, but she just couldn't. She didn't want Thelma's version of the truth of the matter, or her advice, which would be stay away from Erik, to get herself out of a situation that could change everything in ways she might not like, and which couldn't be undone. And she was still angry, maybe unfairly, at how Thelma had told her, ever so gently, that she was wrong-minded about pursuing adoption.

She would have liked to talk to Izzy. Not really about her problems with men, or with Wishi-ta or with herself. Just to hear his voice and his sort of otherworldly take on all matters that seemed to reduce stupid human emotions to something natural and passing, not to be taken too seriously.

But they weren't there, any of them. And Bernice, who Helene was sure still had her daughter and grandchildren. And it was getting late, too late to call someone out of the blue.

There was no one, really. She went back to her novel, but the minutes ticked so slowly, and she couldn't even stay seated. She started cleaning the kitchen cabinets and the refrigerator, although nothing was very dirty.

It was ten o'clock, then twelve o'clock, and then one. She had been in the backyard, looking at the stars, and then back for a shower to cool off. She even allowed herself a glass of wine. But nothing worked.

She found herself at the front door, staring out through the screen in the direction of Elsa's house, where the light had been on earlier. It was only four houses down across the street, on the corner of the next block, shouting distance, practically. Erik was there, she was pretty sure. His truck was parked on the street. Where else would he be on a Sunday night?

She opened the door, and then closed it. She'd rather not leave Wishi-ta sleeping alone in the house, but she wasn't going to wake her. None of these folks had monitors in such small houses. She could run over and be back in less than five minutes, with the house in sight all the way. Plus a minute to see if he was there or not.

She pulled a sweater around her long sleep T-shirt and ran barefooted across the street to the Chief and Elsa's house. At the door she knocked gently at first, and then louder until an interior light came on and she heard footsteps. The door swung open, and there was Elsa standing in a light robe, her gray hair loose. Her eyebrows lifted in the surprise of recognition. But she wasn't more surprised than Helene.

"Elsa!"

"Helene, what's going on? Are you OK? Is it Wishi-ta?"

"Ah, no, not Wishi-ta," Helene said, having trouble forming words. And then, from the back hallway, the Chief came shuffling toward the door, skinny legs sticking out of his lightweight pajama shorts. Helene was mortified, having no idea that they had returned from the Home Camp. And then, from the corner of her eye, she saw the end of Elsa's car under the carport at the far side of the house, and wondered that she had not noticed.

"Who is it?" Chief called out gruffly.

His wife turned to him. "Helene, from across the street."

There was no backing out now. Helene took a deep breath and plunged on. "I'm so sorry to wake you. I didn't realize you were here. I need to talk to Erik."

"OK," Elsa said slowly, looking Helene over and nodding. "You'd better go wake him," she said to her husband.

Helene made an apologetic face. "I've got to get back to Wishi-ta. I don't want to leave her alone."

Then Elsa gave her a sterner look. "Then go. I'll send him over."

"Thank you. And I'm sorry. Good night." Without further explanation, she was out the door and down the street, overtaken by such embarrassing giddiness, she had to laugh. She let herself back in the house, not closing the door, and then returned to the sofa, with the open book and the wineglass on the coffee table. Then she was on her feet again, peering out the window until she saw Erik, in shorts and a T-shirt, ambling toward the house. She met him at the door.

"Thanks for coming," she got out quickly. "And I'm sorry to disturb you. It's not exactly an emergency. And honest to God, I really had no idea that Elsa and the Chief were back. I don't know how I missed their car..."

"Hold up," he said sleepily. "Give me a chance here."

He came in through the doorway and followed her into the living room, both of them still standing.

"What is it?"

"I don't know, exactly," Helene said. "Something's wrong with me, but I don't know what it is. Like I'm not myself, and I'm very..." She paused, shaking her head.

"Upset?"

"Agitated. Like a cat trying to jump out its skin. It's so many things at once..." She paused, her mind a tumble of thoughts, people: "Wishi-ta, and my meeting with Louis, and this place, and going back to school, and my husband, my friend Thelma." She paused again. "And you."

"Yeah, me, huh?" But he didn't laugh, just nodded. His eyelids were still half-mast, but there was now a gleam, an interest and a knowing.

Her mouth felt dry. "I need somebody to talk to," she said. "And I can't reach my brother. You know Denis; who knows where he is? And Thelma, she doesn't really understand." She gestured with frustration. "I can't talk to Kenneth about..." She stopped. It was clear what she was referring to.

"So you woke me in the middle of the night to listen to your problems?" he said with a grudging smile. "Then you can at least offer me coffee." He wasn't looking at her directly, and she knew there was something else in his words.

"No. Not like that. I needed, I wanted some, you know, support or something."

"Something?"

"Company?" she said breathlessly.

"Helene," he said, his voice gentle but husky. "Can you not just say it?"

"I want to be with you," she said finally. Now, she realized, it was on her, whatever happened next.

His smile broadened. "That's good. Because I want to be with you too."

"And you're not worried," she said, the words rushing out, "that I'm falling apart, or losing control, and everyone's going to find out and it's all going to be a big mess?"

"Not worried."

It was like a weight had lifted, but she couldn't really believe it. There would be hell to pay, she was pretty sure. But she felt lighter now, and freer.

He held open his arms and she walked into them, hungry and glad. She kissed him like she hadn't been kissed before, although Kenneth, who was nothing if not ardent, had kissed her passionately many times. But now Helene didn't care about much of anything, not her lack of makeup, or the slightly ripe smell under her arms.

"Let's go back there," he said, gesturing with his head. "OK?"

She wasn't sure she would be OK with it: her sister's bed, where Renee had had sex and slept with her husband under the wolf blanket. But she was. None of that mattered tonight, except not waking Wishi-ta or scaring her.

"But quiet," she said.

"Like a mouse."

At the side of the bed, they kissed again, hands on backs and necks and waists. Shedding her T-shirt and her panties, she stood in front of him, only the second man in her life to see her naked, not counting her father when she was a baby. Erik kicked off his flip-flops and shimmied down his shorts, but stopped to let Helene help him with his T-shirt, taking a minute to finger some of the scars from the long-ago car accident and from using his body without much regard. He was not as fit as Kenneth, but his arms and legs were muscular, if his belly was a little soft from hours on the road driving a rig.

They lay on the bed, not needing to open the covers. She couldn't keep herself from pushing up against him with her hips and breasts, kissing and kissing the white of his neck.

"No hurry," Erik said, a bit breathless. "Ain't going nowhere. Besides, I'm no twenty-year-old, you may have noticed."

"Sorry. I'm sorry."

"No, not sorry. Just take a breath."

He grabbed her hands, moving them away from his crotch. "I'm taking my time," he said. Then he pushed her down on the bed and knelt over her, nuzzling into her stomach, and then to the top of her thighs. "And let me check this out. I'm going to do what I can for you, in my own humble way."

He worked his way up her abdomen and then to her breasts, stopping to trace his fingers up and down her skin. She was both shy and excited to have him touch her like this, all the while a gentle, silly patter – not about hot mamas or sexy bitches, just teasing and caressing. As he closed in toward the wet spot between her legs, she got the idea of what he was doing – the stimulating and the relaxing at the same time; the gradual build up, and then the backing off, just for a moment. She recognized that he knew what he was doing, had been at this kind of thing for a while.

And then he let her rub his penis, already firm but growing warmer and tauter. As she stroked harder, he stopped her with a hand on her head. "Hold off, for now; the show will be over too quick."

But he was ready to go down on her, which was not part of Kenneth's repertoire. She was trembling with tingles and sparks, the anticipation of what was to come. Then Erik got up from his knees and rolled onto his back, pulling her on top, his hands on her hips and moving with her, getting more focused and more urgent.

"Do we need something here?" he asked. He shook out his wallet from his pants pocket and retrieved a rather creased and faded condom.

"I guess," she said softly. "Just in case, even though it's not likely." As he put on the condom, the memory rose of Kenneth and herself, the anxious times of trying to get pregnant, the almost mechanical motions of having sex at the right time in the right position, and the underlying sadness of barrenness.

"No thinking," Erik said. Quickly he went down on her again. She felt herself letting go, knowing she was going to come, if not in moments. That's when he rolled her onto her back, entering her once more and arching over to lick a nipple, saying, "Work with me. We're getting somewhere, and no one can stop us now." As she moaned, he kissed her deeply, and then put his face next to her face as they thrust and thrust into orgasm. Helene's thoughts vanished, all of them; what she should do, what she should not do? And then, just jumbled images: the old house, her new rug, the twins, Yellow Cat, the lake, the cabin, the drum, from somewhere beyond speech.

And then the moments of recovery. She was still buzzing with sensation, but not with worries or misgivings. She only wanted to caress the hard-used body next to hers and plant kisses on his hands. He was still awake, but had to work at it. She rubbed her own face and arms and stomach, taking in the feelings.

"You need to go?" she asked.

"I can do what I like," he answered. "Grown man, supposedly."

"Yes, but Elsa, and the Chief, what will you tell them?" Then she giggled. "What will I say? I'm not good at lying, and there's nothing that's going to sound very good."

"I won't say anything, except to tell them all is fine; there's no problem and no reason to worry. They don't need to know more, and they won't ask me." He turned his head to look at her with a wry expression. "Anyway, they know."

"Really?" Her heart thumped, but it must be true; it had to be.

"Probably figured it out, those two; smarter than you think. But they won't say anything – unless they have to."

"You're probably right. But will you come again, tomorrow?"

"If you want me to."

"I don't know. Well, I do, I'm sure, but I know it's a risk, and…"

He put his hand on her hands, resting on her chest. "Don't overthink it. Really, it won't help. I want to be here, with you; I want this. But it's not the same for me, and I realize that. Just let me know."

"Then can you stay?"

"Do you want me to?"

"No, probably not. You know, because of Wishi-ta. And so other people don't…"

"Fine." He pushed himself up, yawning with a kind of catlike pleasure. Then he was on his feet pulling on his shorts and T-shirt, and another wave of excitement came over Helene, watching him, thinking of what he had done to her body, what she had done.

When he was finished, he sat again, turning to her. "The deed is done," he said. "We can't unring this bell," and he smiled. "Not that I want to. But we're going down a different path now, and you have to get ready for what's ahead, whatever that might be. And it's probably going to be more pain, for somebody – and probably us too."

"That's your advice?" She almost laughed.

"And keep the faith."

His tone was gentle, not teasing, and his look was so tender she almost couldn't bear it.

"And you'll come tomorrow – at night?"

"I'll be here, unless you turn me away."

"And Elsa and the Chief." She grimaced, shaking her head at all the things that took her by surprise. "I hope they're OK with….Why are they even here now?"

He yawned. "Medical stuff. Chief's having his knee fixed."

"Oh." Something so mundane, yet so unexpected – to her.

Erik slipped his feet into the flip-flops and left, closing the door quietly behind him, but leaving the living room light on.

Helene got up to go to the bathroom, and to check on Wishi-ta, curled around her stuffed turtle. Then she returned to the living room to put away the glass of wine, and turn out the light.

Wanton was the word that came into her head. And wild. There was, she perceived, danger ahead, of wrong moves and bad decisions, but she had started down the road, as Erik said, and there was no going back.

Renee's journal – 15

Try, try again. So much time has passed since I picked up a pen to write in my journal. I had to start another notebook, since I can't seem to find the binder. Or pretty much anything. I really wanted to keep going, but it just hasn't been possible. Such a full life these days, family and work, powwows and playgrounds, baths and storytime. Soon the twins will turn three, so busy and smart and healthy. Of course, there are little things, but it seems like despite my bad history, they are turning out fine. It's hard not to think that way sometimes – that there will be consequences for my past behavior on me or them. But then I think of Mom with her cancer and Helene unable to have children – that had nothing to do with their actions, just fate. So I appeal to Creator and to Mother Mary for strength if fate or consequences bring trouble. If worse meets worse, I remind myself, there's Fireball. And that makes me smile because of Louis's burned hand.

Sometimes I think they came just in time – Wishi-ta and Tana-na. Their presence fills me up so much, especially when Louis is gone. And he's gone plenty, called away more and more. I know it's important work, and I know that he's the one they turn to – an authority. I've edited some of his reports because it's something I can do for him, and because he's doing this for us, our family too, besides other Native Americans. It's amazing how much is happening right now, right in this area: new developments with the tribes in Maine about building a dam on the river. Some of the younger members are worked up, angry – according to Louis. Now, in his thirties, he's like the wise older brother, telling them to wait, get informed, and consider consequences before taking action. I can see it's tiring, and he says he gets short-tempered with people. But not with us – not with me. I can see that home is what he needs in order to do the work he does – these children, me, all his family are medicine to him when he is weary. And a seasonal sweat. And the two of us in our wolf bed – working on more babies, but maybe just one at a time.

When Denis was here, I told him about writing in a journal – all my feelings and emotions, the strange series of events that led me here, and my life since. He was happy about it and encouraged me to write whenever I could, including my own stories and poems, and that maybe I could write some lyrics and he would set them to music. I love that idea. So, for now, I'll mainly work through things in my head, and jot them down when I have a chance. The time will come when I can do more. But in the meanwhile, I have this new life, two children, part-time job, all that Louis is involved in, and this crazy, wonderful Native family and community – so much to remember and write about.

Renee's journal – 16

What a racket – those kids running wild in the backyard – the twins trying to keep up with their cousins on this beautiful spring day. I'm the one with some stupid virus, or whatever it is. The occasional puke – not like the old days, but enough to drop some pounds, not by plan. A while ago, a day in bed would have been the greatest luxury, but now I'm stuck here, away from the children, drinking Neesa's teas, no one to keep me company, bored out of my mind. Only good old Red Cat at my side. And a few minutes to write.

Earlier in the day, I heard Neesa and Izzy arguing in the front room. The door was shut and I couldn't hear well, except a couple times Izzy said "Raj", his friend's name, and then something about Boston or "the city". He'll be graduating soon, and I think he wants to explore the world a little. They were both upset, Neesa more than Izzy. And I knew, as I'd known for a while, that she was not having an easy time raising Izzy without his father. He is a kind and gentle soul, but a bit silly at times, and immature, and also a klutz and prone to breaking things. Maybe it's the way he's grown so quickly, tall and willowy – and he's not used to those long arms and legs.

In all these years, since I first showed up, Izzy has been on my side – welcomed me, saw the good in me – although I still don't know why. He's very intuitive; he knows things and understands things. Louis says so too. The kids adore him. The thing is that when he sees good in you, you start to see it in yourself. And, as far as I can tell, he sees good in most people, even the ones who have teased him or taunted him at school, for his long hair, colorful clothes, or his love of pretty things.

Once he was visiting as I was getting ready to go out to dinner with Louis, our anniversary. After I dressed, Izzy came into the bedroom to tell me about his latest video game while I put on make-up. I could feel his eyes on me as I applied mascara and eye-liner, blush and shadow. He sat on the bed stroking Red Cat, watching intently; I explained what I was doing because I know he wanted to know, though I'm no expert.

"I outline my lips first, then fill in, not too much." I winked at him in the mirror. "So, Izzy, are you making plans to fly the coop, so to speak?"

He sighed. "I just want to go to the city and have some fun. Raj has cousins we can stay with. We can take the train."

"Sounds like an adventure. But you need to learn some city smarts, if you want to survive there." I made a face, blotting my lips with tissue.

"I'm not going anywhere yet," he said with that sweet smile. "You're stuck with me. Like Red Cat, always by your side."

I had to laugh. That kitten grew up to be a fierce tom cat and self-appointed protector. Especially now, when I'm not feeling well, he's always with me, never out of sight.

Chapter 15

To Helene the next day seemed so utterly normal, a day without appointments, a couple errands with Wishi-ta, and a trip to the garden for zucchini, lettuce, and carrots, taking turns with the hose. Then Wishi-ta asked for a walk to the marshy area behind the base housing, where they had seen turtles and frogs and skittering water bugs. Helene was leery, having seen remnants of oil spills in the water, even though supposedly it had been cleaned up. She suggested a visit to a neighbor with new puppies. Most of the time, Helene did not think about Erik explicitly, but image after image, and the warm sensation in her groin, reminded her of what they had done.

After lunch Wishi-ta wanted a trip to the playground, hoping to find playmates, but the place was empty. There was not much to do after Wishi-ta had taken a turn on the swings, now perfectly capable of pumping herself. She was becoming so confident and eager, it warmed Helene's heart. And even that sounded a warning bell – had she taken a risk in her relationship with Wishi-ta, with all of them? The words single mother came into her head. She was shocked and pushed them out again immediately. When Kenneth called later, in a peppy, upbeat mood, she could barely hold a conversation, making apologies in the sweetest, most regretful voice – "Just a minute, I'm afraid; we're on our way to a music program at the Intertribal Center." And when he said he could get three tickets for the ice show on the weekend, she begged off again. "It's not necessary. Really. We're going to a state park with some folks here, a lake and some boats. You know, trying to take advantage of the good weather."

At dinner she hardly tasted the meatloaf and potatoes on her plate and chattered on, saying silly cheerful things to Wishi-ta, who looked at her askance across the table. In shame, she wished Wishi-ta would yawn and want her bath and bedtime story early.

So what if Erik comes over? Wishi-ta will love it; she seems to love him. There's nothing strange about that. Even after she goes to bed. But Helene wouldn't mention it; she didn't want Wishi-ta to ask, to get her hopes up.

Wishi-ta was in bed by eight thirty, and then the house was quiet as Helene sat reading, but not comprehending. Nine o'clock passed; nine thirty. She felt a stab of panic; maybe he wouldn't come. He had gotten what he wanted, and maybe that was the end of it.

She got out her folder to review the adoption notes, trying to list points that would convince Louis of the seriousness of her plan, a plan that now included Tana-na, no matter what part Kenneth had in it. For some time she stared at the pages, making no progress. Then she was up and down looking for Erik out the window. Finally she gave up and made herself a cup of tea. Just after eleven she heard footsteps outside and a quiet knock.

Erik came through the doorway, and she was at his side, trying not to look anxious or annoyed, which she was, a bit. But mostly she was glad, glad, glad, and relieved. And excited. And nervous.

"I thought you'd come earlier," she said, keeping her voice light. "After Wishi-ta's bedtime."

"I was trying to wait," he said, "until a more decent hour." He rolled his eyes, abashed. "And then I fell asleep."

She wasn't mad; she couldn't be. He was here. "Well, you're here now." And then, figuring she had nothing to lose by being honest: "I might have had a few moments of doubt."

His face clouded. "Whatever else I am, I'm serious about this, about you." And that made her both happy and even more nervous. "Anyway, may I come in and sit down? We can still say hello, and how was your day?"

"Hello," she said. "And, I've been thinking about you, about us, all day. But it still doesn't make sense."

"Right. At some point we'll have to talk, I suppose. But for right now, I'm here, I'm clean, I had a full day, a short nap, and I'm sure glad to see you."

That was it, and they went right to the bedroom. Helene tried, as Erik had said, to take it easy, take it slow. But it was hard; there was so much of her that felt to be pushing forward, so unbottled, without restraint.

This time, afterward, they returned to the living room, to have a dish of ice cream, sitting next to each other on the sofa. They froze in place when they heard whimpering from Wishi-ta's room. Immediately Helene was on her feet, standing in the doorway and listening for further noises, but there were none. That was it; just a calling out in a dream.

Then she was back in the living room, gazing down on Erik, just licking the last of his ice cream from the spoon, surprisingly delicate. And then she wanted him again, and the taste of ice cream in their mouths, and the coolness of their tongues on their sensitive, private parts. She put out a hand, and he looked up, smiling and cocking his head.

"Let's go," she said.

That was the evening he stayed, almost the whole night, slipping out around four, before the Chief was up in the morning.

And that's the night she learned about other parts of his life that she'd only had hints of, bits and pieces: growing up in upstate New York; time in the foster care system, mostly with Elsa; not much of a student; a brief stint in the Army, which he did not enjoy, but where he learned some of his construction skills. Attending college, until he decided there was no point in a degree in psychology, and then dropping out to make money. He did well enough to buy a cabin in Pennsylvania, which he still owned, and had lived there for a few years with a long-term girlfriend, until they broke up and she moved back home to upstate New York. And the son they had together, now twelve.

"What's his name?" Helene asked.

"Connor." Then Erik lowered his head. "I haven't seen a lot of him lately. Partly because of my ex's new boyfriend, but now he's out of the picture too."

Helene nodded. "And the cabin – you still have it?"

"I do." His eyes crinkled in a smile. "Some place to go when I want to get away, or run away, is more like it."

"We had one too," she said, musingly. "Up north in Vermont. Very rustic. I'm not sure it's still standing."

"Nice for you," Erik said. "I hope someday you'll see my place." For a while, he explained, the cabin had been rented, but then he decided to add on a woodworking studio, and he didn't want tenants messing with his tools or his materials, or getting hurt, so it was mostly vacant. He still went occasionally to make pieces for people on commission, which was not bad money. Otherwise, he was here at the base with Elsa and the Chief, as his center of operations for construction in season, or trucking jobs, which he had a license for.

"So, like a boarder," she put in. "Or a third child, perhaps?"

"Both, I suppose," he said, not at all offended. "Hopefully more than that. It started when I got in a car accident, about twenty-five years ago. A bad one, someone died, and I was in the hospital for months. When I got out, I was not doing a good job taking care of myself. Managed to get myself into a hell of a mess." He looked at her. "Pain pills – you know what I'm saying, nurse?"

"I do."

"Well, you sure don't want that when you're using power tools or heavy equipment. So they had to bring me back here and retrain me, I guess. And then I never left. I mean, I do leave, but then I come back. I've got their daughter's room now that she's grown and moved out. She gives me hell when she visits; I'm back in the den. I pay something to Elsa and the Chief, and that helps them out too. I like it here; it's easy, comfortable. Just one more brave in the tribe."

"Isn't that politically incorrect?" she asked, making a face.

"Not if it's true," he said.

The next day and the next were largely the same, until Helene allowed herself to be lulled into the idea that this was now her life, the new normal, what every day would be like. Erik came faithfully in the evening, and tooted as he passed in his truck during the day, busy with construction errands. They sat together, all of them, Elsa, the Chief, Erik, Helene and Wishi-ta, Robert and Charlotte, at the Thursday night community dinner. Bernice was there too, her daughter's family gone. Helene had prepared a salad of greens and vegetables out of Neesa's garden. The talk was general – the warm, sticky weather, Robert and Charlotte's plans to return to the Home Camp, Bernice happy to have her small home back to herself. Business as usual, Helene told herself, although she saw Elsa's eyes rest on her and Erik with a thoughtful look, and wondered what it meant. That evening, not an hour after they parted, Erik was back, full of plans to finish the pavilion, having recruited another guy to help.

"When are you going back?" she asked. They were in the living room, sitting on the sofa where the fanned air could reach them.

"Not sure," he said. "It depends. Looks like I've got another hauling job, going south, and that might be a week or so."

She was shocked. It was like she'd forgotten what he did for a living, and that taking private long-haul jobs was a big part of his income.

"Helene," he said, catching her look of disappointment, "you know I go sometimes; but I also come back."

"Maybe I don't know that."

"Well, that's how it is."

"I won't know what to do with myself, if you're gone," she said, only partly joking.

But instead of reassurance, he said, "Maybe I can put it off. But maybe not. We'll have to manage somehow." His tone was serious.

But that we got her as much as anything. She wriggled in closer to his side.

"You know, Erik, this is so different for me, so different from anything I've ever done before. I don't know that much about you; maybe you've had affairs with married women before, but I never thought it would happen to me."

He nodded, not saying anything.

"I feel," she said, the words tumbling out, "I feel a little bit like Renee, her behavior, just going ahead without thinking, and ending up in trouble – by which I mean disaster. I'm not putting this on you. It almost seems like something is pushing me, or pulling me, and I'm still not clear what. But now I can't see one bit ahead into the future, except how I keep looking for you, wanting you. Like an addiction." She was stricken by the thought, putting her hands to her face. "Like Renee!"

Erik took her hands into his, looking in her eyes. "Come on, it's not the same, not that kind of addiction. It's just, well, strong emotions coming through, for whatever reason, right now in your life."

"I hope you're right."

A car passed, and then they were back to the overwhelming quiet that came over the base at night. Erik kissed her hands, one at a time, putting them back in her lap.

"If it makes you feel any better," he said, almost bashful, "I have a confession to make."

She stared back, noting the long shadow across his face, deepening the lines of age and experience, reminding her there was so much of him she didn't know.

"What?"

"I was interested in you before we ever met," he said. And then, with a flip of his head. "Renee, of course. Some of the things she said. And the picture."

Helene pulled away. "What picture?"

"The famous model picture," he said with a sly smile, while Helene cringed, already embarrassed. "One day I stopped by, looking for Louis, who was running late; so I came in and sat, right here." He pointed to spot on the sofa. "We were chatting, Renee and me, shooting the breeze. She asked about my latest, well, love interest – a girl she knew. Apparently not the right girl, in her book. She said she wanted to show me something, so she went over there." He pointed to the repaired bookshelves. "She got out a picture of you, a proof from a photo shoot – you were modeling clothes: sweaters and skirts, that kind of thing. You know what I'm talking about, right?"

"Oh my God," Helene said, shaking her head. "The department store. Yes, I remember, but how did Renee get that picture?" She looked away, trying to think. "She had nothing with her when she left; that is, nothing except the money she took out of my bureau." It slipped out; she glanced at Erik to see if he caught it. "I guess she could have taken it then, when she left...but why? Why would she?"

Erik shrugged, and put his finger to her nose, then to her lips. "Some kind of model," he said. "Elegant, classy..."

She pushed his hand away. "Or maybe Denis brought it here, to her. I know he brought other family pictures, books, that kind of thing." That could have been it, but she was still confused. "I don't know why she would show you."

"She said you were beautiful; I guess she wanted to prove it." Erik raised his hands to each side. "She said they offered you a job at a modeling agency, but you didn't take it."

"Um." She fell back into the past, that room, the clothes, the camera. She was twenty-four, at home, working, dealing with Renee. That's when she had met Kenneth, a friend of the storeowner's son, who stopped by to say hello. She'd had the sense of a setup; things being put in motion. He'd pursued her, but very low key. And she held back for some time; but eventually he'd won her trust. Handsome, positive, respectful, respectable Kenneth. He wasn't deterred by the Renee's antics, or by the aftermath of her leaving, which was just as bad, although perhaps a relief from the drama.

"Renee waved that picture in front of my nose," Erik recalled. "She said that you would never go for a guy like me, so immature, irresponsible, and so forth. All that kind of crap." His voice pitched up. "'You're not worthy of someone like my sister, but you could be, if you tried.' Quote, end quote."

Helene smiled, but sadly. That lost time; the picture; Kenneth's courtship; and Renee singing her praises – to Erik, of all people.

"I'm certainly not that girl anymore," she said, eyebrows arching.

"Certainly not," he agreed. "Or you'd never have me now." And then he drew back, his gaze solemn. "But you're even more beautiful. And I'm trying to be a better man."

On Friday, Helene knew that Erik was going to be away for the day, unsure about his return. She was fine in the morning, in the routine, but by late afternoon she was jumpy. It was the weekend; she should at least call Kenneth. She did not want to talk to him; she did not want to see him, or even to go home. But she could picture the house, the kitchen, the bedroom, each of them clean, neat, tasteful. And she felt bad that he was in that large house without her. Even if he did have an active social life and plenty of folks to have dinner with, and was out so much of the time, anyway. It was not the same. And the cat, Misty. She'd left Kenneth in charge, since she couldn't bring Misty here, with Wishi-ta's allergies. There was no comfort there; Misty didn't even like Kenneth, and he didn't like her, either.

When her cell phone rang just before dinner, she about jumped out of her skin. Erik or Kenneth – whoever it was, she was afraid her words would come out garbled.

It was Denis.

"I'm sorry," he said. "I thought I told you we've been performing at night and recording in the day. And then I heard your voicemail, and sounded like I best call ASAP. So I've got a few minutes now. Talk to me."

Helene was so taken aback she didn't know where to begin, or what to say at all. She checked that Wishi-ta was still engaged in drawing at the kitchen table and then slid away into the living room. "Wishi-ta's fine and I'm, well, I'm OK. Everyone else is gone up to the Home Camp; you knew that, right?"

"Right. So what's going on, then?"

In the message, she had explained about the visit to Louis, and its outcome, and her return to the base alone with Wishi-ta.

"There is another problem." She was stumped how to continue.

"OK," he sighed. "What kind?"

"A big one."

"Get it out then, before I get called away."

"I can hardly believe I'm telling you this," she said, twisting away from the open, screened windows. "But, oh, trouble with the marriage, with my marriage." She stopped again, dry-mouthed.

"Kenneth, you mean?" Denis said on the other end of the line, far off in Ohio or Tennessee or wherever he was. She heard voices in the background, laughter and occasional harmonizing. "Has he cheated on you?"

She should not have been surprised that he was so quick to think the worst. Denis and Kenneth had never really liked each other, or they came from such different places, although in fact the same hometown. Different styles and priorities.

"No," she said. "It's me. I'm the one who cheated."

She heard an intake of breath. "What? You're kidding. How is that possible?"

"It's true."

He was thinking, processing. "Someone from the base?"

"You know Erik, Elsa's brother – the Chief's brother-in-law?"

"Him? That's who? Oh, man, Helene." He sighed loudly, and she could picture his face, that look of dismay at another fallen sister – the strong one.

"I can't explain it, Denis. I really can't. It just started, really, but I...I..."

"I what?"

"I can't seem to stop."

There was another sigh, a long one.

"Erik's OK, I guess, but he's...well...he's a truck driver and construction worker, gone a lot. He's got no home of his own, that I know of, and he's, well, not what you want in a guy. Right? I mean, who am I to talk about lifestyles, but that's not at all..."

"I know, I know. And it's not him. I mean, he showed his interest. But it's what I wanted, and so I just did it. But now I have no idea what's going to happen."

It was quiet on his end, the voices muffled; Helene wondered if he'd moved to a different room.

"Well, I did not expect this," he said finally. "Or maybe I did, at some point – I mean about you and Kenneth. But that's not what I thought you were calling about. From your message I thought you were all worked up about pressing for the adoption, and getting everyone behind you, why you're the best person for this because of, oh, you know, the big house, good job, stable marriage, all that. But now, what the hell, Helene? How does this make any sense?"

He was right. But she had done it. Maybe out of disappointment, or anger, or something else. And still she wanted to raise the children – separately, on her own if she had to.

"I do want that too," she said. "I mean, taking care of the kids, the adoption. This other thing, with Erik, that's different; that's not connected."

"Of course it's connected. Helene, come on. Do I have to spell it out? You want to petition for adoption, while you're going through separation, divorce – because of this guy, Erik?"

"No, wait. Listen. I can support them on my own with my own money and my own career. It doesn't matter what happens with Kenneth or Erik."

Another long pause. "Really? That's how you feel? So are you going to tell Kenneth?"

"No! Not now. I don't know when. I don't even know what I'm going to do next week, or when school starts."

In Denis's background Helene could hear a phone ringing, a door slamming. She imagined a bright room and a bunch of guys sitting around, all excited about making their music – and how wonderful that must be. And how, maybe, it really was the right choice for Denis, all those years ago. She heard him shout a reply, and then speak back into the phone.

"I've got to go." A big exhalation. "Shit. What a mess. No, I'm sorry, Helene, I can't be there with you. But after things are wrapped up here, I'll be back. And I'll try to take your calls from now on or at least get back to you as soon as I can…"

"Thank you, Denis," she said, feeling her throat tighten. "I think I might need help with this."

Then things moved along so quickly, Helene could not have foreseen any of it.

Erik came by that night with a couple beers for each of them, after Wishi-ta had gone to bed. As they sat in the living room, he said he would be leaving the next day on a job for about a week, but the trip could go longer, depending on what happened when he got there. A familiar route that paid well. Good relations with the owner, and so on. He didn't want to say no.

"Now you've got me in a state too," he said plaintively, drumming on the empty beer can. "I have no idea what I'll find when I get back."

"Me, either." But she did tell him that she'd told Denis, everything, that he was on his way north shortly and knew that she wanted to go forward with the petition for adoption.

"Great," Erik said, making a face. "He'll be thrilled to see me, I'm sure." Then he waved it away. "Never mind. But what is the plan? Where are you going to live? Around here?"

"Maybe. I don't know."

"But then you'll be on your own, won't you?"

"Maybe," she said, dropping her head against the back of the sofa, staring at the ceiling.

"Ah, well," he said finally, getting to his feet and offering her a hand up. "That's more than we can know right now. How about we put all that aside and just think about the here and the now." He held her eyes. "The you and the me."

With a sigh, she went with him to the bedroom, where he held her for a long time, placing small kisses until she began to respond. Even then, their lovemaking was quieter than before, but fierce, like a struggle.

"The thing is," he said afterward, "I don't want to go, but I have to. I'm sorry to leave you on your own like this to face whatever it is, but I also know it's not for me to say."

"Now you stop talking," she said, placing a hand on his mouth. "Whatever happens, we've had this time together." She rolled over to her side, facing him directly. "At least I feel like I can breathe again. And I didn't even know I was holding my breath all that time."

He stayed through the night, and woke just before dawn to leave, kissing her and wishing her luck, as he put a hand on her cheek.

"You have my number," he said. "If you need it."

"I'd only call because I want you back," she said. "Maybe it's better if I just try to sort things out while you're gone."

On one level, Helene was relieved at Erik's leaving, hoping she could think more clearly. While he was near, all she could think of was sex and desire. Was it true, what Denis had asked, could their lives ever mesh? And what kind of future could they have? Erik was good with children, in paying attention and giving affection, but could he be any more than that? At bottom, she knew she had to be prepared to do things on her own.

Mindlessly she fell into the daily routine with Wishi-ta, breakfast and wash-up, laundry and gardening, grocery shopping with a stop to feed the sheep at the farm. After lunch, working a puzzle with Wishi, looking forward to storytelling at the Intertribal Center in the afternoon. But then Helene heard the sound of an engine turning off, and jumped to her feet to look out the window. Noel's van had pulled into Malvina's driveway, and out climbed Noel and Neesa. A back door slid open to reveal Cree strapped in his seat, head dropped to one side. Noel went around to unhook the seat belt, picking up Cree and carrying him to the house, while Neesa unlocked the front door.

"Wishi-ta!" Helene called into the den. "Noel is back, and Neesa and Cree, over at the house." When Wishi-ta appeared at her elbow, barefoot, Helene said, "This is a surprise. I hope everything's OK."

She helped Wishi-ta find her sandals, and they headed next door, calling out and letting themselves in. They went to the kitchen, looking around. Noel was returning from the boys' bedroom, and Neesa was not in sight.

"What's wrong?" Helene asked. "Is Cree all right?"

Wishi-ta was bouncing on her toes, pulling Helene toward the back bedroom. "Come on, let's go."

But Noel shook his head, tired and strained. "Sorry, Wishi, not now. Better let him rest. He doesn't feel good, and the ride back wasn't too comfortable."

"Is he sick?" Helene asked.

Noel shrugged, rubbing his chin. "Not sure. He's got something wrong with him, almost like flu, but not sneezing or coughing. Tired, achy, feverish. A couple days now; he hasn't been himself. Not eating, kind of droopy – you know that's not like him."

They heard Neesa talking to Cree in the back, urging him, it sounded like, in a combination of English, French, and their language. Then Cree's cranky words in reply.

"Neesa's going to dose him with some medicine she has here; basically just a tea. She uses it for pretty much everything, colds and headaches. She's going to get some more of her herbs from the woman down the road. We'll try that for a while, keep him quiet, see what happens."

Helene looked into Noel's face. For a quiet, easygoing guy who was definitely not an alarmist, there were lines of worry around his eyes. Helene felt a pang of sympathy, to have to deal with this so soon after Malvina's difficult childbirth, and the worry about the twins, and Louis in prison. It was a lot on him; maybe too much.

"Do you want me to check him over?" she asked. And then she smiled, trying for humor and reassurance. "You know, I am a nurse. I see sick kids all the time."

"Yes, I know, and you've been so good with Wishi-ta." Noel considered. "Let him settle in for now, take some of Neesa's tea when it's ready. If he doesn't perk up, maybe that's a good idea." Then he lowered his voice so Wishi-ta couldn't hear. "That's one reason we came back, if we need to see the doctor at the clinic. Not much access to health care up there."

"Can we see him?" Wishi-ta asked. "Just for a minute. So he knows we're here." She was looking at items on the table that Neesa had taken out from her bag.

"Just for a minute, though."

Helene and Wishi-ta went into the room together. Neesa had drawn the curtains, so it was quite dark, and she was applying some kind of salve to the numerous bug bites on Cree's arms and legs. He lay with his long hair pulled back, revealing his thin neck. A pair of nail clippers was on the bed next to Neesa, and it looked like she'd trimmed his nails to keep him from scratching the bites. The boy still looked miserable, with none of his abundant energy, his will to resist Neesa's ministrations all gone.

They went to the bedside. Neesa barely gave them a hello, except to put her cheek up for Wishi-ta's kiss. Wishi-ta was suddenly shy of her cousin, so transformed from the loud and active boy that she knew.

"Hi, Cree," Helene said. "Sorry you don't feel well." The drawn expression of his face was more than she expected, and she could only think it was one of those miserable viruses that can be picked up any time of the year. His coloring also looked off, pale and gray, but maybe that was the dim light of the room.

Neesa shifted position, putting herself between them and Cree: a clear sign for them to leave.

"Hope you feel better soon," Helene said. Wishi-ta took Helene's hand, stricken by the sight of her sickly cousin.

In the kitchen Noel was drinking a glass of water by the sink, waiting for them.

"He's not himself," Helene said cautiously. "I would imagine that it's a virus he picked up somewhere, if you're pretty certain it's not what he ate."

"No. We all ate the same things, for the most part. But you're not saying he's allergic, are you?"

"Oh, no. I meant more like food poisoning, if he had been throwing up or had diarrhea."

Noel shook his head. She looked around the kitchen. "Is there anything I can do for you, in the meanwhile? We can run to the store. Or something for dinner?"

Noel smiled, but it was the smile of a weary man. "Thank you, but we're all set for now. I'm going to check in at work, so I can pick up groceries. Neesa can handle things here. Let's see how things are in the morning."

Unaccountably, Helene had an uneasy feeling about Cree. "And I mean what I said: call me if you need me or if you have any questions, any time."

"Thanks, Helene."

They decided to skip the storytelling, and Helene put on a video for Wishi-ta while she prepared the evening meal. Occasionally she peeked out the front window, watching for signs of activity. But after Noel went out in his truck, no one came or went until almost dinnertime, when Elsa walked crossed the street with something on a tray and a big canvas bag. Helene flinched as she saw her climb the front step, to be met by Neesa and invited in. What, oh what, would they tell each other – what's happening at the Home Camp and what's happening at the base. Not that she thought Elsa was a gossip, but she also thought that if there was reason for Neesa to ask anything about Wishi-ta and Helene, Erik's name might come up.

Then she moved away from the window and reminded herself that

that wasn't their main concern at the moment, and that for all Helene knew, her time with Erik might simply pass like a blip on a radar, meaning little to others. Back in the kitchen, at the cutting board, she gazed out through the newly finished porch to the backyard, so quiet without the voices of children, and she knew the connection between those women was long and deep, more than their concern about her.

She thought of calling Erik, and then decided not to. The point was having time apart to think. And then Kenneth called, and she told him about the return of Noel and Neesa and Cree. She realized that was an opening for him to ask her to return, with or without Wishi-ta, or to make a promise for the next weekend. But she couldn't initiate the subject. She stalled as long as she could, until he put the question to her directly.

"So, when are you coming back?" He had a right to be annoyed at her evasiveness. "Or is there something going on I should know about?"

"I need time to think things over," she said, quickly. "About us, you and me, and our priorities. I feel like having a child, or children, in our lives is not what you want right now. But I'm beginning to realize that I do."

He was quiet a moment, but not angry. "OK, I get it. That would be natural, spending so much time around them as you have. But that will all change for you, and for them, as soon as school starts, and your job and your activities here."

"I'm not so sure about that," she said vaguely. "That my feelings are going to change."

"Well, we won't know until time has passed, will we?" And then he cleared his throat. "I understand now that you are not interested in the house projects, the design and layout, all that stuff. That's fine. I've got someone else to help me now. But I really thought you'd kind of like it, something to do, a creative outlet. It's not that we need the money, or anything. Just something we could do together. Kind of like we did for our own house, and I know how much you loved that, and how well it turned out."

That was the thing. Maybe she did enjoy it then. Yes, she did. But she didn't now. Whatever it had meant, the large, gracious, tastefully decorated house, it didn't mean that anymore. Too much room, she thought. And everything was perfect, all the time, not littered with signs of children and family and crafts and powwows. Something had shifted by her being here, but how could Kenneth understand that?

They left it at that, she was not coming home for now, nor would he make a visit. Time to think. There was something in the way that Kenneth said good-bye that made her think that he was pretty sure she'd come around in time. That she'd realize the value of what she had, what they had, realize that this was just a pipe dream. But for the first time, she heard something more, something of doubt, not just about her, but about the marriage. Like maybe it was not so unfamiliar to him. Of course there had been a bad time in their marriage, after her miscarriages, and her prolonged grief and depression, all of which he blamed on her family and on Renee. He'd been worried then, and in charge, and pleased with himself when she rallied and things got better. But maybe too he saw other kinds of cracks but just didn't know what to do about them.

After she finished with Kenneth, she almost called Erik, seeking comfort, reassurance, even just to make sure he would answer the phone. But she didn't. She didn't call Denis, either. With a restless "monkey mind," she didn't think she'd fall asleep, but she did, after checking on Wishi-ta. Then at one o'clock she heard knocking at the door. She was awake immediately, thinking Erik, unexpectedly back early. And then there was the sound of the door opening, her name being called. She got quickly out of bed, turning on the light. There was a man's figure in the doorway, and she knew then that it was Noel, about Cree. What else?

In the living room, she switched on a light.

"He's worse," Noel said. "His neck is stiff, and he says he hurts all over. There are these strange red marks, not just bug bites." He thought it over. "Something's wrong when he looks at me, something wrong with his face."

Helene pulled her robe around her. "You took his temperature?"

"One hundred; not too high."

"And gave him Tylenol?"

She thought maybe that was not part of Neesa's medicine arts, but again he nodded.

"Seems like something more is going on; I don't know if I should take him to the hospital."

Helene nodded. "Let me see." She stopped at the front door. "But what about Wishi-ta? I don't want to leave her, even for next door."

"Neesa will come."

"I'll get my first aid bag."

They left together, and Helene went straight into the boys' room, where the lights were on and Neesa sat by Cree's side. The sheet was pulled off, but he was wearing a tank shirt and white underpants. This time, when Neesa looked at her, there was a mute appeal rather than her general suspicion; she too was worried. Noel told her about Wishi-ta, and she got up from the bed to leave without a word.

Helene sat on the bed where Cree could see her. "Cree, I'm a nurse at the school where I live, and I take care of lots of children. I know you feel sick; I want to look you over, OK?"

He nodded. And then Helene saw it, what Noel meant, the kind of droopiness of one of his eyes and his mouth on the right side She had never seen it before in a child, but thought it was a kind of palsy, a neurological disorder that came on from a virus sometimes, or from pressure on a nerve.

She looked into his eyes and mouth, but had no way to examine his ears. Then she felt around his neck, very gently, probing for swelling that might be mononucleosis, or some other infection.

Then she slid the tank shirt up to his armpits, and looked over his chest, and had him turn over to examine his back. There were plenty of bug bites, and some scratches. Those Neesa had treated, and they looked better. But there was a rash, or part of a rash that disappeared into his underpants – half of a red moon, and half of its orbit.

Her heart started beating faster, as she began to think she knew.

"Cree, there's something I need to look at. Can you push your pants down in the back for me?"

He rolled to his side, and Helene pulled the elastic of the waist just far enough to see the full moon and the circle around it. A bull's-eye rash.

"I think it might be Lyme disease," she said, keeping her voice neutral, professional. "From a tick bite. Do you see the shape of that rash, the red circle inside a circle?"

Noel was looking at her as if she were speaking another language.

"He's very..." She stopped herself. "He needs antibiotics, right away. He needs to go to the emergency room."

Noel was still staring.

"Now. The sooner the better," she said. "I'll come with you. Why don't you get him ready? I'll tell Neesa and get my purse."

"Are you sure?"

"I'm pretty sure."

"Lyme?" He shook his head, like something vaguely remembered. "How serious is it? He won't need to stay...?"

"I'll tell you on the way. It's important not to wait." She almost bit her tongue, keeping back the words any longer than you have already.

To Cree she said, "Do you know what an antibiotic is? A kind of medicine."

When he nodded, she went on. "If it's what I think it is, that will work, but you need it right away and we have to go to the hospital to get it. I'm coming too. I can help explain."

They went off into the night, following almost empty roads to an almost empty waiting room about forty minutes away. When Helene said, "I think it may be Lyme disease," the intake nurse asked immediately, "Is there a rash?"

"Yes. Red and very clear."

The doctor, a young man with dark, short-cropped hair and round spectacles, came right away and took them into a bay of the emergency room. He confirmed what Helene had guessed. At least, he was sure enough to start treatment, and would take some blood tests to find out what they could.

"Your son has a pretty classic rash," he said, speaking to the two adults, who didn't correct him. Funny, Helene thought fleetingly, how easy it was for people to assume. "When did it first appear?"

Helene looked at Noel, who shrugged. "Maybe four, five days ago? Hard to say, with all the bug bites. That's when he started acting sick, anyway."

The doctor looked down the chart, but in his brief nod, Helene felt that he thought they might have flagged it sooner.

"Yes, well, it's fairly developed at this point. We're going to give him IV antibiotics tonight, and rehydrate him. After this, there will be a month of antibiotics," he said. "Doxy." He paused, blinking twice. "Doxycycline – sometimes it's a little hard on the GI system. But he's young and healthy, so he should recover pretty well – if the whole course is taken. But I'm troubled by the palsy. He should be followed up with the pediatrician until that resolves."

Noel said yes to everything and agreed to make the appointment with the pediatrician as soon as possible, Dr. Gregorian, the twins' doctor.

The ER doctor gave them some literature on Lyme disease, and left them to wait for the nurse who would hook up the IV for the antibiotics.

Noel used his cell phone to call the office at the scout camp, waking the manager. He had to repeat twice what the situation was, and what to tell Malvina in the morning.

"Do you want to write it down?" Noel asked, and then repeated the information back in bullet points: "Hospital. Lyme disease. Antibiotics."

Noel said thank you and good night with a patient resignation. Then he called Elsa and the Chief, getting Elsa on the line.

"Sorry to wake you," he said. "It's about Cree...Lyme disease...Helene is with us...Neesa is with Wishi-ta...can you let her know?...that would be good, if you don't mind...we might not be back until sometime in the morning...he's OK, I think...we're OK...thanks."

In the visitor chair, Helene listened with one ear, the rest of her mind busy and upset, angry even, while at the same time sorry for Noel's troubles and glad that she had been there to help. It wasn't right, she thought, that they were so ill prepared to deal with the children's needs, that Cree should have become seriously ill. Who knew, even now, what the consequences might be? Lyme could take a toll for life, in some cases. How did they not see the unusual rash and at least seek answers? But help had been delayed while Neesa continued to treat with her teas, which did not work adequately for this condition.

Yet she could not find it in her heart to blame Noel. He'd had so much responsibility, along with Malvina and Neesa, since Renee died and Louis got locked up. And the new baby. Noel worked hard, she knew, and they lived a modest lifestyle. It just didn't seem to be enough to ensure the safety and well-being of the children, all six of them now. What if she hadn't been here for Wishi-ta? Or for this? It's not that she aspired to be an angel of kindness. But then, in fairness, they had brought Cree back early, looking for additional care, whatever it might be. And they had called her back in the spring when they knew they couldn't handle Wishi-ta's allergies. The situation was clear: they had asked for help, and if they needed it, they would have to take whatever she decided to do. No matter what Louis said, or Kenneth.

It was there, in the emergency room, that her plan was hatched, what to do and where to go – at least for the short term, while things were in crisis. Looking back afterward, she realized the elements leading her to this action had already been in place. Had things been otherwise, she never could have done it. She was not going back to work at the school, and she was not going anywhere without Wishi-ta.

Chapter 16

Helene went with Noel and Cree to the pediatrician the following day, and she felt sure that Cree was in good hands and there was a plan of action that would work well, though it might take some time. She also had her own plan of action, but that could wait a while longer. The main thing was to see Cree's palsy start to resolve, which it did after a few days of antibiotics; the droopiness lessened. His appetite was better, and with it some energy returned. In less than a week, Cree was much more like his old self, bouncing around inside the little home, until Noel, with Helene's approval, said it was OK to play outside, as long as he and his cousin, Wishi-ta, got their nightly tick checks.

After Cree's follow-up appointment, Noel came back to Renee's house with Helene, leaving Cree and Wishi-ta next door with Neesa. On the weekend he hoped to drive to the Home Camp with Neesa and Cree, now that the Lyme disease was under control. They wanted to take Wishi-ta with them; she seemed to be doing so well. Helene was welcome, also, but he understood that she probably needed time back home; a break before school resumed.

"Oh, no," she said, taken aback. "I don't need to go yet. And I'm not sure it's a good idea for Wishi-ta to go without me to supervise, with how busy everyone is."

Noel looked at her a moment, concern in his gaze. "Helene, you've been wonderful to Wishi-ta, to all of us, during this time. But the time is coming for you to return home – if not now, soon. Wishi-ta has come to depend on you, to some extent, because of her condition and because you're so much like her mom. But she's better now, and she needs to learn to separate from you too. Before the twins start kindergarten." His voice softened. "I know it will be hard for both of you."

"No," Helene said, trying not to let her voice rise. "No, not yet."

Noel placed a hand on her shoulder, warm and comforting. As tall and husky as he was, with heavy jowls and dark, glinting eyes, he was a mild man when he could have been so fierce.

"I know that Louis wasn't very welcoming of your, ah, proposal," he said. "And that he had a pretty strong reaction. That's Louis's way, the leader, the fighter, not known for compromise. But we've seen you more, know you more, and we've seen how you've been with the children. In time he'll come around, I think, to work with you in some way for the sake of the children. But for now, it's time to think about your own life."

"But Wishi-ta has another appointment Monday..."

"It can wait. I asked at the pediatrician's. I told them we'd call to reschedule." He sighed, lifting his hand away. "Wishi-ta asked to go back. She misses Tana-na, and everyone. She wants you to come too, but I explained to her that you have another life, with other people who are important to you – like her father and his work – and that you would have to go. But that you would be back sometimes to see us."

Helene could barely refrain from crying out. That was the last thing she wanted, with all her heart. But she couldn't say anything. Everything he said was true and reasonable, except that it wasn't true for her, not any longer. A kind of blind panic came over her. At the same time she felt a slowing of time, heard a strange, calm voice, saying, This cannot happen; I won't let it happen. There's got to be another way. What came out of her mouth was, "Yes, Noel. But I scheduled a follow-up for Wishi-ta with the specialist in Boston." She looked away. "Next Tuesday; it's important. After that, I'll drive her up to the Home Camp. OK?"

Noel nodded thoughtfully. "OK."

On the Friday afternoon, Helene spent an hour with an attorney, while Elsa watched Wishi-ta. The office was near the base, a sole lawyer, who admitted up front she had limited experience with family law. If Helene wanted an expert, she had to go to the city. In the meantime she could educate herself online and through some of the library's resources. The lawyer made it clear that the adoption process was very difficult without the cooperation of the living parent regarding health, education, and religion. Otherwise it was a matter of proving the inadequacy of the jailed parent, with court records or other kinds of negative evidence. It would be easier to become legal guardian, but that mainly applied to financial matters, not much else. Not good news; not what Helene wanted to hear.

As she left the office, Helene smiled automatically at the middle-aged woman at the front desk, who gazed up in surprise, like a start of recognition. She might have been from the base, but no one Helene remembered. Possibly Native American. In the car she sat a moment, weighing options. She could see the outlines of this conflict, and what needed to be done on her part. If only Louis were less narrow minded, he could see that her solution was right and just; but he would not give, she was sure. At this point she could research further, anything that could improve her case. She could engage a lawyer from the city. She could afford, with the money she had, to outlast and outpower Louis, if it came to that. But not now; there wasn't time. Despite what Noel had said, her fears for Wishi-ta's safety in an emergency had been validated by Cree's illness. Her contract with the school was waiting to be signed and returned, with a starting date. If she was going to take action, it had to be now. And then she saw the answer, in her mind's eye: the time and the place.

Just like that, she made a decision. She would go away with Wishi-ta to the cabin in Vermont that no one, except possibly Denis, knew the location of. Everyone else would be distracted, or at least not focused on her and Wishi-ta. It was more than a plan; more like a vision, a course of action which Helene could see in her head: this; then this; then this.

Her hands gripped the steering wheel – with a thrill of excitement and maybe danger. Not physical danger, but rulebreaking, secretive and risking a backlash of anger and disappointment from who didn't understand the whole situation. There was a risk, too, in not taking action, possible harm to Wishi-ta. Her heart pounded in her chest, and she felt a surge of purpose, energy – and wondered if it was what Renee had felt when she took chances and pushed the limits. Wild. Willful. Could those actually be forces for good?

But no, Helene told herself, shaking her head. Not like Renee; it was totally different. Helene would proceed as she always did, carefully, ensuring that there would be no harm and no alarm while they were away. It was just a chance to clear her own head, getting her thoughts straight, and protect Wishi-ta's health, of course. More time to bargain; for Louis to come around, and the community. A statement of her commitment and determination. It could only deepen her relationship with Wishi-ta, making the bond stronger.

She made a list of things they'd need to pack, with a quick trip back to her house while Kenneth was out. It was a challenge what to say to Wishi-ta about the plan, how to present this sudden development. She had to say something: a getaway; a special place where Helene had gone as a child, something special she wanted to share.

She knew the name of the town, not far from the Canadian border, and had a vague recollection of the roads leading out of the town center. She needed the key, and she needed the directions. Plus some camping equipment, as the cabin was unfurnished and unheated, without power. Denis had stored some things in their attic, and Neesa's family had a lot of supplies for powwows. What had Louis done with all that stuff he and Renee used on the long road trip – the stuff Renee talked about in her journal? Helene guessed it was still in the camper truck, parked in the driveway. The problem was to look when there was no one around to notice.

The next time Noel took Cree for bloodwork at the doctor's office, Neesa went along for some grocery shopping. That was Helene's chance to check out Louis's truck. Wishi-ta might well see her, so there had to be a pretext – something legitimate, in case Wishi-ta blurted something to Noel or Neesa.

"If we go camping," Helene said, "we'll need some chairs and coolers, stuff like that."

Wishi-ta was only too eager. "You mean the Home Camp? What about Cree?"

"No," Helene said. "Another place I want to show you. Where I used to go with your mother and Uncle Denis, when we were children. Cree can't go this time. Come on, let's see what we can find."

The truck was not locked, and nor did it look like anyone had attempted to empty it out. Packed inside was an assortment of camping equipment, most of which looked serviceable. Helene brought out the few things she thought they could use. Back in the house, she made a note of what else to buy on the way: food, more medicine, more batteries, that kind of thing. Soon they would be gone without fanfare for some undetermined length of time, not long, hopefully. But no one had cause to worry.

Neesa and Noel would depart believing that she was taking Wishi-ta to Boston for the follow-up with the specialist. Kenneth would assume that she was staying on longer at the base. She had written three notes: to Malvina, to Kenneth, and to Erik, which she would leave behind to let them know they were OK, and that she needed time to sort things out, for Wishi-ta's sake and her own. She would mail the note to Kenneth, buying time; and the notes for Malvina and Erik would be left on the coffee table at Renee's house, for when they came looking.

She had to make a couple of important phone calls: first to the doctor's office to cancel the upcoming appointment; she would "call back to reschedule." If there was a problem, no one knew better than she what to do, and she had EpiPens and inhalers. She had even looked online to find the nearest hospital, in case of a real emergency. Then she had to call her school to say there was a family illness she was dealing with out of town, and she would be delayed in her return – they should have a substitute ready. The contract, she said, "was in the mail." On an impulse, she picked up an application for a youth passport from the post office. But after she got home, and printed Wishi-ta's name on the first line, she couldn't bring herself to finish it, just to stuff it in her bag of papers, just in case.

After that, it was so easy. Except for keeping her cool. Saturday morning, they went to say good-bye next door. Helene had packed the camping gear and supplies at night in the trunk of her car. In the back seat, next to Wishi-ta's car seat, were just a few bags of clothes and toys, for a short outing. Inside another tote bag on the floor, she put a number of children's books and nursing journals, paper and writing utensils. Finally, as a last-minute thought, Helene got the cloth bag that held Wishi-ta's regalia, almost complete, and also the sewing kit, and stashed it out of sight. It might be something to do on long evenings.

The ride to Kenneth's house was quiet, almost relaxing, with little traffic on the highway. Wishi-ta played with her plastic figures in the back seat, finally nodding off. When Helene got to the block where their house was, she took a pass by first, to be sure there was no car in the driveway or movement inside the house. It was so odd to see the still house in the day, such a neutral dove-gray with little color or adornment – sleek and modern, and somehow sterile. "The trophy case," Denis had called it, according to

Renee's journal. Maybe that was apt. It was where things were stored and dusted, but little noise or activity had filled those rooms.

She let Wishi-ta sleep in the car inside the open garage as she went inside to find the key to the cabin and the directions, and hurriedly packed more things for herself, along with more toiletries and first aid supplies. She got two of Denis's lanterns from the attic, flashlights and a camp stove. And her passport from the bureau, not that she was planning to use it, but since the cabin was so close to the Canadian border, just in case. She really had no idea what shape the cabin was in, so she was prepared to stay at a hotel, temporarily, if needed. Their last stop was a branch of the bank in a neighboring town, where they didn't know her, to withdraw a few thousand dollars. She'd always kept her own account, where she deposited most of her paychecks, which were for major purchases or vacations. Or emergencies – like this.

"Big trip," she said to the teller. And then, shocking herself, "Heading west." It was so silly and unnecessary, but it was possible, she thought, that it might divert someone looking for them. The cashier, a young man in a green vest, smiled pleasantly, but had not the least interest in her real or pretend plans.

And then they were on the road, headed slightly east, and then north to Vermont beyond the Green Mountains, to a part of the state not known much for tourism, and still sparsely populated. Frenchman's Cove; that was the name of it. The cabin was on the shore of a cove that opened to a lake. Great fishing, so her dad had claimed, and she believed it to be true. Bare bones, for sure. But Wishi-ta wouldn't mind; in fact, she was used to it from the Home Camp; that was part of the appeal. And it was temporary, until Helene figured out what she was going to do. For now it mattered only that Wishi-ta would be under her care.

The weather held warm, even as they went farther north. They stopped for a picnic lunch and a stretch at one of the visitor rest stops, then continued on for another couple hours, until it was time to exit, now heading east through open, flat country, destined for an area which was lake-filled and densely forested. Finally there was the sign for the village, and finally the route number that led to the road which accessed Frenchman's Cove. There were a few other cabins along the cove, as she recalled, but none within view or within shouting distance. Unless things had changed over the years. When they had come in her younger days, even with lanterns lit, no one could see them; and even if they called for help, no one would hear.

The rutted road was wider than she remembered; someone had cleared trees to each side. Pulling off onto the winding gravel path, she saw that it was strangely light ahead, where the cabin had nestled in the dark of many evergreens. Surrounding the cabin were stumps of trees and a woodpile, evidence of construction: someone had added an open deck to the side overlooking the cove, which glittered in the late-afternoon sun.

Helene pulled up and parked. Her senses were on alert: someone had been here. But there was no vehicle and no tracks where the moist earth had been dampened. Grass had grown tall around the woodpile and around the flat rock path that led to the cabin's door. No one here recently, anyhow.

She got out of the car before waking Wishi-ta. She mounted the steps to the entrance, elevated a couple feet off the ground to make a crawl space under the cabin. She had a momentary vision of Denis behind Dad at the door, prancing to get in, while she and her mother, with Renee in her arms, approached more cautiously. She half smiled, thinking of the mice that skittered away when they entered or raced across the ceiling boards at night, keeping Helene awake – not frightened, but aware.

Then she looked at the top of the doorway with a kind of shock. Someone had installed a light fixture with a black cap and glass sides – electric. Electricity had been installed, and maybe more.

"Well, what do you know about that?" It was almost as if she'd spoken to Dad –thinking of his amazement and perhaps consternation. *Who had changed this old place, his retreat from real life?*

She wondered if the key she had would even work, but it did. It was, she recalled, the key that her cousin had sent Dad after they changed the locks. The key turned. It was the right cabin, in the right location, the woodwork stained dark with age, only someone had spiffed it up.

Inside it was warm with summer sun, despite the tree shade. It had been updated with light fixtures, a sink, and a very basic stove. Even an empty refrigerator that was not plugged in. She glanced outside at the car, deliberating. She wanted to know what else had changed; but she also wanted to discover the place again with Wishi-ta. She went back to the car to wake her.

Wishi-ta opened her eyes to Helene bending to release her from the car seat. The light shone through the trees, glowing translucent green. Like Oz, Helene thought for a moment. Not the Emerald City, but the Emerald Cabin.

"Here?" Wishi-ta murmured. "Home Camp?"

"No, the cove," Helene said. "Our old family cabin. Come on, sleepyhead. Let's check it out." And then, to herself, "I think Renee was your age, the last time we came."

Wishi-ta reached out sleepily to be lifted from her seat, and landed a little wobbly on her feet, taking Helene's hand to follow her into the cabin.

"What do you think?" Helene said, as they stood in the kitchen, looking through the big glass window.

"It's so bright," Wishi-ta said. And then, blinking rapidly, "and sparkly."

"That's the sun on the water," Helene said.

"But it's a house," Wishi-ta said. "A little house made out of wood."

"I guess it's not really that much like camping," Helene admitted. "I thought it would just be us and a fire in the woodstove, but somebody put heat in here, and lights. My cousin, probably." She was a little rattled over the signs of human activity and improvement, but she was also grateful. So what, if someone came along – she was an owner, an heir, and had every right to be here with her niece. And it wasn't like anyone had bothered keeping in touch after her father died.

"Maybe even a toilet," she said hopefully. "Let's see." There was a toilet now, with a sink, and even a kind of vanity to hold the cleaning supplies and extra toilet paper. "Fancy!" Helene exclaimed.

The bedroom had actual beds, a double and two twins on frames with blankets and pillows – no sleeping bags needed. It was all a little cushy, she thought to herself, like maybe a woman's hand had been at work here – either Uncle Al had remarried or their cousin had a wife or girlfriend. Yes, there was a mirror; she was pretty sure that would explain it. As expected, there was no service for her cell phone. And there was no landline at the cabin. Helene wondered how the uncle or cousin managed when they visited. Or maybe it was the cell phones they were trying to get away from. And no TV, although she had discovered a radio which got decent service out of Burlington and Montreal.

"A little musty," Helene said, "but not bad." She stood a moment, quiet. There was still the faint scent of the woodstove and something perhaps a little sour in the kitchen area – old food, or rodent droppings, maybe. She almost laughed recalling the time that six-year-old Denis had caught a mouse, showing it to Helene. Without his mother's knowledge, he'd put it into a bread tin with water and cheese, but unfortunately no air. The next day the mouse was unmoving when he took the lid off. Denis had been dumbfounded, crying out when he realized the mouse was dead. Their mother reclaimed the bread tin with few words and a shake of the head, and told Denis to take the dead mouse outside. But Helene knew Denis needed more than that; she accompanied him out to the woods, where they dug a hole and buried the mouse with a prayer and a little ceremony.

"Do you think that a mouse has a soul?" Denis had asked.

"I don't know, but it might," she replied.

"Then it's good we said a prayer. Just in case."

Back in the kitchen with Wishi-ta, Helene found that she had tears in her eyes from those long ago memories, still sweet.

"That smell," she said, covering the moment. "It could be a mouse, a dead mouse."

Wishi-ta nodded, looking at her curiously. Then her lips twitched. "We better smudge."

Helene's mouth opened in surprise. Of course: smudging, getting rid of the bad, welcoming the good. And getting rid of the bad smell.

"That's a great idea," she said. "But we'll have to do it later. I..." She tried to think of an excuse – the idea was still strange – then stopped herself. "I forgot the shell and the sage. We'll see if we can get them when we go into town."

Wishi-ta did not look convinced; in fact, she looked disapproving. Helene did not want that, a bad way to start off their time together.

"Or we can gather some pine needles, for now," Helene said quickly. "I have matches and a lighter; we can burn them in a bowl. How about that?"

"OK." Wishi-ta's tone wasn't enthusiastic. "What about tobacco?" she asked.

"We'll have to get that too, I'm afraid." She could see uncertainty in Wishi-ta's posture. "I'm sorry, Wishi-ta. I'm still new at this. And I need help to know what to do, and to remember." Then, taking a leap, she added. "What do you think we should do?"

After a moment, Wishi-ta brightened. "Are there shells here, I mean, at the lake?"

Helene considered. "Yes, I think so. Some freshwater mussel shells – kind of black. That what you mean?"

"That would be good. And we could burn the pine needles and a little grass, maybe. Or leaves, maybe."

Helene was surprised to find herself so relieved. "That's a plan. We'll do the best we can, for now. OK?"

"OK."

"Well, first we'd better bring the food in," Helene said, "Will it be hot dogs tonight? Or hamburgers? Your choice, young lady."

"Hot dogs."

"All righty, then. And we might as well bring in the other stuff, before it gets dark."

Wishi-ta nodded. "Then can we go to the lake?"

"We certainly can."

They unpacked quickly, and walked down to the lake, a whisper of breeze in the trees, and the water almost like glass. From where they stood, they could see dark shapes in the clear water along the shore, tiny minnows, and then some larger fish. Wishi-ta wanted to take off her shoes to get her feet wet, and Helene took hers off too. Within a few minutes they had spotted a number of the mussel shells, most of them closed tight. But there were a few that were open and large enough for a pinch of plant stuff to burn.

They returned to the cabin, gathering a handful of pine needles and a few brown leaves. The grass was green and moist, not likely to burn, according to Wishi-ta. The little fire took a while to catch, but a thin stream

of smoke was all they needed to fan around themselves and the rooms.
Wishi-ta's face was now open and bright, happy to have smudged, happy
to have shown the way.

After that Helene got the little stove to start right up. They pulled
chairs and a small end table onto the side deck to eat hot dogs, beans, and
canned corn, relishing the sounds and sights of the declining day until the
bugs sent them inside. Helene thought it best to keep close to routine, so
they played Crazy Eights and War, and then read stories before bed. Wishi-
ta said she wasn't sleepy, and was hesitant to go in the other room. Helene
settled her in the bed they would share, and left the door open. In minutes
she heard the change in Wishi-ta's breathing.

It was quiet in the cabin without human voices. Outside the windows
the air thrummed with crickets. The night was not entirely dark, with a
quarter moon and tiny pinprick stars. Helene went out on the side deck,
and then stepped through the screen door onto the ground between the
cabin and the lake. When she looked up, she saw a blurry streak of white in
the sky and remembered, after all these years, that it was the Milky Way.

There was, of course, her other life going on in that other place, or
rather two places, but she had the delicious sensation that no one yet knew
they were gone or wondered about them. She had managed to work out a
situation where they could essentially disappear for a bit, a few days,
anyway, before anyone even started to say, "But I thought they were at the
base," or "I thought they were in Boston to see the specialist." And who
would even say these things to each other?

And then she thought of Erik, on the road, or maybe at his destination
by now. They had agreed not to communicate until Helene had a better
idea of what she wanted to do. So he wasn't looking for her, either. Or
maybe he was. Or maybe he was thinking of her under this same quarter
moon.

The next day was full of the business of getting used to a new place
and exploring the lake. There were primitive trails through the woods,
leading to each side of the cove, and a narrow beach that stretched for
some distance before running into rocks or trees. Helene promised they
would take out the kayak stored on its side next to the cabin, and paddle
along the shore – when they were ready. She wondered if they could buy a
child's life jacket in town, or bait for the couple of old rods that were
stored on the deck.

They spent the next day around the cabin, setting up and working on
"projects" – Wishi-ta's regalia, and a woman's belt that Helene had started
on. The following day they were ready to go into town – for groceries,
sage, and a proper container of some kind for smudging. Also a child-sized
life jacket. She wasn't at all worried about being recognized. It had been so
long. No one would recognize the name Helene Bradford. But she decided,

anyway, to call herself neither Helene Roy nor Helene Bradford, but Ellie Bradshaw – a name that would not identify her, and that she could remember. She didn't think Wishi-ta would notice. She didn't like to lie, but found she could do it quite easily. A family trait, perhaps, like Renee.

The older gentleman at the counter in the general store wore a red cap with a moose, and a blue Northeast Kingdom T-shirt. He looked to Helene to be the kind of guy who didn't mind about the bristle in his nose or his ears; friendly enough, but not too friendly. He must have figured she was not "from here," but he didn't ask where she was staying and she didn't volunteer. They were visiting, she said; she wasn't sure how long. If pressed she would say they were at a cabin at Frenchman's Cove, friends of friends; and that "her husband couldn't get away until later." She wanted to be friendly, but not too friendly, and not too mysterious.

No one, not a soul would think of this place, except Denis, when he finally got word that Helene and Wishi-ta were gone. She wasn't even sure that Kenneth would recall the place existed – it was about the opposite of his sister's lake house – and he didn't have Denis's cell phone, although he was capable of tracking him down. Kenneth would have gotten her message by now, appealing for time to mull things over. She wasn't sure what he would do. There was a child involved. He already held strong views about what had happened to Helene early in their marriage, during those times that she struggled. It was possible he would feel responsible to take the lead. Or he might take it at face value – a getaway, time away. Maybe he was just too busy to piece things together.

Back at the cabin, they smudged again, the whole place: sage from a spice container, placed inside an ugly stone jar Helene had spotted at an antique/junk shop. They got the feather from Wishi-ta's regalia bag, and fanned the smoke in each room, including the bathroom and the deck, and themselves. Wishi-ta was quiet and businesslike, and proud of how she could strike a match herself.

It seemed to Helene that Wishi-ta fell into the new routine comfortably, even with pleasure. She asked about Tana-na and the others. Could they visit too? Would they be going to the Home Camp before kindergarten started? Were there other children here? Helene found out there was a playground behind the elementary school, which they visited. The tiny town library held a drop-in story time a couple of days a week. The weather was exceptionally fine, warm, clear days and cool nights, twilight and dawn suffusing the pine trees with light; vivid gold sunsets across the lake.

It was Helene who had a hard time winding down in the evening, no matter how active they had been in the day, walking, swimming, paddling. Memories of the time she'd spent here with her family came to her unexpectedly. As changed as the place was, so many things came back to her, songs, things said, the meals, the times at the lake, all of it. A rug, a teapot, some of the chairs, the box for the wood for the woodstove, all remained from when she had been there before. The windows looked out to the same views, although more grown over. And the night sounds: mice, pines branches brushing the roof, loons, and sometimes howling in the distance; her parents' voices talking after the kids had gone to bed.

Although she had not loved coming here, at least in her preadolescent years when she'd had to leave her friends behind and everything here seemed so backward, she also remembered when this world was enough for her and for Denis, something special; Renee had been too young to remember. Their parents had seemed more at ease, and their mother sang more. Their father talked about the fishing and about some of his old relatives from outside Quebec, "crazy Canucks" he called them. Crazy, maybe; but they sounded to Helene like a merry lot who loved to sing and dance and make music. That's when the fiddle would come out after dinner at the cabin, but in her family there was never any dancing.

Turning over in the bed, Helene had to admit there were times they had been happy, before it all went wrong with her mother's illness, and everything that followed. She wept into her pillow, missing her parents, and knowing that they had loved her and loved each other very much, despite the pain and anguish that followed. They were just not equipped to deal with loss and heartache, his family too far away in Canada, and her family having turned their back on her when she married beneath her and stayed in Massachusetts, while the others moved farther west. Her mother had said once that her own childhood had been joyless, and Helene could now see that was probably true.

One morning, almost a week after they arrived, Helene woke in a panic. *What if they never got my messages? What if they really don't know we're all right?* She had already planned a trip into town, and while she was at the store, she could find out about making phone calls.

At the general store, she asked the man with the moose cap, Ernie, where she might go for cell service.

"Oh, a ways," he said, hands resting on his plump middle. "Maybe twenty miles that way, they have the community college there. So they got to have computers of some sort, and the cell phones too. But you can always use the phone here, you got to reach someone. Just leave a dollar or two, whatever you think."

"Thanks," Helene said. "Not now. I just mean for the future, if I need to."

"Right," he said. "You need something, you come here. That's how we do it. If I'm not out front, I'm in the back. Me or the wife. Just walk in the door, anytime."

She was touched, and it was good to know, should there be any actual emergency. If the car didn't work, she could still walk the four or five miles into town, and Wishi-ta too, if need be. But it shouldn't come to that. Wishi-ta was doing so well, no issues at all. There were a couple of playmates for her at the playground, and they both enjoyed story time at the small library. The days were slipping by so comfortably, and Helene began to relax. No need to keep up such a guard: they were just on holiday, after all. She asked an older woman who'd lived all her life in the area if she remembered a family who used to come up summers and stay at a cabin on Frenchman's Cove – "cousins of mine."

"Yes," the woman had replied. "A jolly man, so friendly, and his sweet-as-pie wife. I remember. Two kids, I think, a girl and a boy. What a nice family," she said, nodding. "They always seemed so happy."

Chapter 17

On the next hot, sunny day, lulled by serenity and the beauty of the place, Helene proposed an outing a little farther than they'd been. Wishi-ta too had taken to the new surroundings, content and at ease – but she got excited about a little adventure.

They were at the shore of the lake, having walked north as far as they could, until stopped by a mound of rocks, tumbled by some ancient glacier. It rose perhaps twenty feet above the waterline. To go around the rocks meant wading into water over their heads. It was a comfortably cool and shady spot, the sun blocked by the rocks where they splashed about. A small twinkling up in one of the crevices lured Helene farther out onto the slime-covered rocks lapped by the water. Something metal, it appeared, with the ghost of red paint. And then it dawned on her: a fishing lure. She had a flashback – standing in this spot with her dad and Denis; somebody, either herself or Denis, casting out over the water, except that the lure got stuck in the tree branches, and they had to cut the line.

It might have been theirs, from thirty years ago. Or maybe someone else's who had discovered this sweet fishing spot. She drew closer, mounting the wet rocks, where the lure was just about in reach, saying to Wishi-ta, "Wait until you see what I found."

Just as she rose to her toes to dislodge the lure, one of the rocks she was standing on gave way and tipped sideways. Instinctively, Helene took a step back, seeking a more secure foothold, but her sneaker slipped on the slimy surface and she fell backward and sideward, one arm grabbing for the cliff face, and the other windmilling to regain balance. It was too late – she couldn't stop the fall, although she remembered, later, scraping her forearm on the way down. She was going to get wet; that was the last thing she thought before looking up into the blue sky, and the sudden dimming of the light. What she remembered afterward, or thought she remembered, was the sound of voices, men and women from across the lake, soft and sorrowful, murmuring in a language she could not understand. Then there was no light and no sound.

When she came to, Wishi-ta was beside her in the shallows, pouring water over the arm that was bleeding. Beside Wishi-ta was a clump of wet leaves; for weeks afterward that clump puzzled Helene, until she realized it had been a poultice to stem the bleeding. Her arm hurt first, throbbing, although it was not much more than a long scrape. But the pain in her head came later, along with the blurred outline of rocks and trees. And Wishi-ta's head and hair.

She never did know how long she was out. How long Wishi-ta had stayed there beside her, waiting for her to wake up. Not sleeping, but like sleep. She was pretty sure there had been a dream, a strange one. She was back at the house she shared with Kenneth, in her kitchen, drinking tea while Misty the cat wound around her ankles. Then there was a popping sound from inside the cabinets – the fine, light-blond maple wood that she had so desired. She got to her feet and opened a cabinet door to look – the glasses were breaking, one by one, into little heaps of glassy dust. All of them, gone. And then the cabinets began to crack and warp, the hinges rusting, and the granite counter fell in large, flat chunks at her feet. That was all she remembered. When she opened her eyes, the sun had shifted, no longer the heat of midday, and a breeze had come up, making her shiver now that she was wet. But her first thought was Wishi-ta.

She reached out. "Wishi-ta."

She was still there, now pale and shivering. Her hand in Helene's hand was cold.

"Oh, so cold," Helene exclaimed. "Me, too. Let's get into the sun."

Slowly, in pain, Helene pushed herself upright to sit. Again, a pain struck at the back of her head, the light was dancing all around her, even in the shade. Wishi-ta's eyes and mouth were blurry lines.

"Oh, dear," Helene said, feeling the back of her head. There was certainly a bump, which was not necessarily a bad thing. Her fingers came away with blood, quickly rinsed in the water, but at least it wasn't at least pouring down her neck.

"I guess I took a tumble," she said to Wishi-ta. "But I'm all right; just a little bruised. Are you OK?"

But Wishi-ta had begun to cry, a quiet weeping that devastated Helene, forcing her to fill her lungs with air and breathe slowly. How could she have let this happen? She who was so careful, always. The nurser of injuries, not the victim of them. How could she let Wishi-ta witness this, another adult failing her? But Helene hadn't left; she was conscious, and she would use everything in her power to reassure Wishi-ta that Helene was basically fine and still in charge. Although, she knew on some level, that the head injury was serious, probably a concussion.

"No, no, honey," Helene said. "Just a little accident like Tana-na has, or Cree. Right?"

Wishi-ta swallowed, making an attempt to stop the tears.

Helene peeled the leaf compress off her arm. "Look, no more bleeding," she said. "What a nice job you did. Now you're the nurse. See what happens when you don't pay attention. Pretty silly, huh?"

She made her voice light and turned away from the brightness of the sun on the water and slowly rose to her feet, holding on to the rocks. She felt a wave of nausea but fought to keep it down.

Wishi-ta was staring. Helene wanted to hug her, comfort her, but she was afraid that she might not be steady on her feet.

"We better go back to the cabin," she said. "Can you lead the way?"

Wishi-ta nodded, but still she hadn't said anything. Helene wondered if Wishi-ta had tried to call for help, or maybe even started down the path back to the cabin, but she could recall nothing at all. And she didn't want to ask. Besides the scraped arm, her ankle was a bit wobbly. She hobbled along after Wishi-ta, with rippling bands of light in front her eyes, just focusing on the next step and the next. She had to stop once, nauseous again, and this time she couldn't hold it back. She turned away from Wishi-ta, bending over the low blueberry bushes that lined the path.

"Sorry. I know that's not very nice, but at least I feel better now. Wait, let me get a mouthful of water before we go on." She bent over to scoop the water and almost toppled over. But she righted herself just in time. This time she said nothing; perhaps the least said, the better. The thing was to get back to the cabin.

They made it back without further incident, but Helene's head was beginning to pound. She got Tylenol from her medicine kit, and then put out cotton swabs and alcohol to clean the wound. Wishi-ta was at her side on the sofa, waiting to help.

"You know what you can do for me, honey?" Helene got out through gritted teeth, not wanting Wishi-ta to see her pain. "In the refrigerator, in the freezer down below, can you get me one of those blue ice packs?"

Funny thing, she thought; there had been a number of ice packs already in the freezer when they arrived – for food coolers, probably. But she brought ice packs with her pretty much wherever she went, an occupational habit. In any case, there were plenty.

"We'll get to the boo-boos in a bit," she managed to say, putting the ice pack between her head and the sofa. "Why don't you lie down beside me here, and be my little kitty cat. I can just touch your hair like this, and it will make me feel better."

Then she closed her eyes, while the world was spinning about. Slowly the whirling subsided, and slowly the ice and Tylenol began to kick in, and she felt some relief. Also a strange fatigue, which she fought off with cold compresses and silly chatter, knowing that was not a good sign. Later she washed off most of the blood, standing under running water in the simple shower stall, holding on to the back of a chair. At the kitchen table with wet hair, she watched as Wishi-ta put jam on bread for her supper, along with an apple. Helene herself couldn't eat.

The night was sticky warm; they slept off and on, side by side covered by a sheet. In the night Helene got up to vomit; afterward she kept a low light on, afraid to slip into a deep sleep. She was frightened, but at the same time apart from herself, instructing herself like someone else – a nurse, "do this, now do that." And using that same voice to talk to Wishi-ta. Awake in the night, she knew she should go for help in the day, but wasn't sure if she could, or should, drive. Not that there was much traffic, but it wouldn't do to have an accident on top of this. Mainly she tried to tell herself it was a freak accident, and that her head would clear in time. They had food and power, and Wishi-ta was not a tiny toddler in need of help for everything.

But still.

The next morning dawned overcast and a bit cooler. Helene's head was not much better, but not worse than before. The rest of her was achy and sore from the fall. She could see a little better: the top half of her field of vision was a bit blurry, whereas the lower half was clear. She rolled to her side to get up, swinging her feet to the floor, and then moved slowly in stages, determined to make coffee and have breakfast ready before Wishi-ta awakened. Still, she listed, feeling her way along the walls, as she made her way to the bathroom to examine the scrape on her arm and replace the bandage.

They had breakfast and tidied up. Then Helene felt her knees start to buckle, and a gray fog descending, forcing her to sit on the sofa again. She told Wishi-ta that she was tired because she didn't sleep well, because of her bruises; they would go out again when she was more rested. As she sat there, ice pack in place, resting her eyes, Wishi-ta went to retrieve her own small backpack from the bedroom. She brought out her people and animal figurines and made a little village on the floor, telling stories about her creatures' lives.

"She got hurt," Helene heard her say, "so they had to find the right medicine. And the women came around and sat with her while she was sick. And they gave the tobacco to send up prayers."

Helene dozed off, waking later with a start. Wishi-ta was still where she had been, on the floor, moving her little creatures around. But Helene was warm now, her mouth dry. Slowly, carefully, she made her way to the kitchen sink, where she poured a glass of water and took more Tylenol. In twenty minutes she felt stronger and a little clearer. She got up to put the ice pack back in the freezer, noticeably clearer now, and steadier.

"How about a snack, and then we'll head to town?"

"OK."

"We'll get some ginger ale at the store," Helene said. "And ice cream. That always makes me feel better. How about you?"

Wishi-ta nodded. They ate apple slices and cheese, with chocolate kisses for a treat, and for energy. Helene packed a couple of water bottles in a cooler to take with them.

The car was parked in a shady area, out of the summer sun that was starting to break through the clouds. Helene started the engine and backed up, heading down the track that would lead to the side road – not far, not long.

"Just roll along," she told herself. "Slowly but surely."

There was not another car in sight, and the woods were strangely quiet, the midday lull when the birds rested, and even the squirrels found a cool spot to rest. They had gone maybe half a mile when the path split, or so it seemed to Helene, who couldn't remember for sure which was the way to the main road. She turned to the left, thinking it was more familiar, and then decided suddenly she should have gone right. Twisting the wheel suddenly, she felt the car lurch in the direction of a sizable gray birch.

"No!" She jerked the wheel again and the car just grazed the tree, traveling past it over a berm, the front passenger wheel descending into a sizable rut, where they stopped. She put the car in Neutral, and then told Wishi-ta, "Hold on, I'm going to try to back out." The rush of blood to her head made her squint when she turned to look over her shoulder. "Here goes." She reversed, but they went nowhere. She revved the engine again and again, still not moving. Finally she got out to take a look; the car was tipped into the rut, one of the back wheels lifted off the ground; the car was truly stuck. She sighed, leaning against the car and forcing deep breaths to hide her growing anxiety. She went around to the back passenger side, opening the door with a wry smile.

"I got us good and stuck, I guess," she told Wishi-ta, unbuckling her from the car seat. "Back to the cabin for us. Tomorrow we'll try again, bright and early. I'll bring something to put under the back tire. If that doesn't work, we'll take a nice walk into town."

Her voice was so much the school nurse, serious, but not worried, conveying, All will be handled as it needs to be. She retrieved her purse and the two water bottles, handing one to Wishi-ta.

They made it to the clearing by the cabin with no trouble, although once Wishi-ta tugged at Helene's hand, saying, "No, this way."

With the heat, Helene began feeling light-headed.

"Let's stop here a minute," she said. "And rehydrate. I'm awfully thirsty. Aren't you?"

"But the cabin is right there," Wishi-ta said, surprised. "I see it."

"Of course, sure." Helene swigged down water. "Let's go."

It was cooler in the cabin, with a mild breeze coming off the lake and through the porch.

"How about we put the radio on?" Helene said. "Maybe we'll get some music. I'm just going to sit here on the sofa and enjoy this nice breeze."

Even before she said it, Wishi-ta had gone to the freezer for an ice pack. She handed it to Helene, who took it from her, kissing her fingers. Even more than usual, Wishi-ta looked like young Renee, albeit with all of the sugar and none of the pepper, Helene thought. In truth, she didn't know what they could do, except wait for her to get better, another night's rest. And yet, despite the shame and fear of failing Wishi-ta by getting into this situation, she felt herself calmer, even peaceful, and didn't know why.

Again she slept and woke to see Wishi-ta on the floor in front of her, now drawing with paper and crayons she must have gotten herself. Music played in the background, and occasionally there were voices speaking. Sometimes Helene thought they were talking to her. Then the day was cooler, and she was feeling a chill.

"Wishi-ta," she said. "Can you bring me a blanket from the bed?" Afterward she heard Wishi-ta padding around in the kitchen, opening the refrigerator, and taking out something, maybe fruit, maybe leftovers.

"Wishi-ta, can you bring me some water and the Tylenol bottle?"

Then, with the light declining, she was aware that Wishi-ta had spread sleeping bags on the floor next to the sofa, curling up around one of her stuffed animals, and burrowing in like a little animal. The night came on.

Helene slept, and then woke in the night, hot and sweaty. She wanted to get up for the bathroom, but her head was so pounding and her legs so unsteady, she had to crawl on hands and knees.

She was able to get to the refrigerator, opening it to get a bottle of orange juice from a low shelf, and then feeling around for the other ice pack in the freezer. Back at the sofa, she took more Tylenol and replaced the ice pack, slightly more focused.

She needed medical assistance. But there was no way to reach anyone, and no one knew, really, their location out here. She couldn't send Wishi-ta; it was too far. They had to wait, but she wasn't sure that was going to help, if the symptoms would recede, or the pressure in her head. Somehow, with all her knowledge and training, she had gotten them stuck here. Like Renee, she had taken a risk with her life; but unlike Renee, someone else was depending on her. She was no better as a caretaker, as a parent, than her own parents had been, keeping the children from harm. But she would try; she would make the best of whatever happened. If her head cleared soon, all the better. And if she was no better after she regained some strength, they would go back out on the road and get as far as they could, as long as they could.

The rest of the day passed, Wishi-ta bringing water and ice packs as needed, and making a kind of sandwich with bread and turkey breast. Helene nibbled a bit and praised Wishi-ta for her efforts. Wishi-ta had dragged a few more toys into the room, and then some books, falling asleep after lunch at the other end of the sofa. Later, through half closed eyes, Helene watched Wishi-ta wake in a room filled with the slanting light of the end of the day. The girl sat up, blinking against the radiance, her hair flying with static, truly golden.

"Do you think you can pull the shades down?" Helene asked. Then Wishi-ta went to pee, and Helene heard her humming in the toilet: not a children's song or TV jingle, but some tune that Izzy had played on his flute. When she came out of the bathroom, she disappeared immediately into the bedroom, where Helene could hear her rustling around. When she returned she had the cloth bag that held her regalia, and the sewing kit. She brought them to the side of the sofa, placing them on the end table. It must have been the song that reminded Wishi-ta of Izzy, Helene thought. Or, she just wanted to work on a project.

"Oh, honey, I don't think I can do that with you now; maybe in a day or two."

"I know," Wishi-ta said. Standing in front of Helene, she took off her tank shirt and shorts, down to her underwear. Carefully she took out the regalia, first the dress and shawl, then the leggings and moccasins, and finally the leather covers that held her braids, and a feather fan. Without speaking, she dressed herself and pulled her hair onto each side of her neck.

"Can you braid me?"

"How about I put it in a ponytail?"

"No," Wishi-ta said. "Braids." She shook her head at Helene. "It has to be. With these." She held out the leather wraps and a feather, giving Helene a meaningful look. "You know."

But if Helene knew, she couldn't remember, and shrugged.

"For prayers, for blessings." Wishi-ta's whole body was taut, insistent. Helene sighed and nodded.

"OK." She waited for Wishi-ta to turn around, presenting her back and murmuring so softly that Helene wasn't sure that she heard the word: "Mommy."

Helene made loose braids of Wishi-ta's fine hair, tying them off with the leather wraps, the bottom inches hanging free. At the very last, Wishi-ta placed a thin leather cord over her head, which held a small red pouch, her medicine pouch. All the kids from the base had them, and most of the adults too. Helene had never found out what was inside each pouch, or if they were the same or different.

"There," Helene said. "You look very nice. Are you going to dance?"

Wishi-ta shook her head. "There's no drum."

"Then what?"

"I'm going to put tobacco in the lake and pray," Wishi-ta said, quite matter-of-factly. "So you can get better."

Helene's heart began to thump painfully. She had never dreamed such a thing was possible, that a child could be so self-possessed. Wishi-ta was not even five, with such limited experience of the world beyond the base or the Home Camp. No Disney, few restaurants, none of the experiences of other middle-class families: a day at the beach, or a trip to the city, movies, amusement parks, any of that. To see her at home, she could have fit right in with all the other children at Helene's elementary school. But in the dimming light of the room, Helene realized that Wishi-ta was really and truly Indian, of that culture and mind-set, and inheritor of all that history, terrible and otherwise. It was a mistake to think that because she looked like Renee, she was any less Louis's child, and a product of that family and their traditions. She couldn't have looked less like Neesa in so many ways, but certainly Neesa was in her too.

"Will you stay on the path," Helene asked, "and not go in the water?"

"Yes."

"Will you call out so I can hear your voice?"

"Yes."

"OK, my sweet. You take such good care of me. Please be careful."

She heard Wishi-ta's footsteps on the stairs to the path to the beach.

"Are you there yet?"

"No."

"Are you there now?"

"Yes."

Wishi-ta was out of sight, but Helene could hear her voice, some of the words reaching her ears. "Take care of..."

And then, shouting: "Izzy! Noel! Neesa! Malvina!" Like she was calling to someone across the water, who could jump in a boat and paddle over. "Come on!" she said, as if hurrying them across the water.

When Wishi-ta returned to the cabin, she came right to Helene's side, showing her the empty pouch. "All gone," she said.

"You are a wonder," Helene said, stroking her head and drawing her in for a hug. "Just a wonder. Your mother and father would be so proud of you," she said. "And your whole family. Everybody. But especially me."

For supper they ate a small meal on the sofa of ham and cheese with pickles. Wishi-ta took her allergy medicine, and Helene took a couple more Tylenol, noting that her supply was getting low. But it helped, a little. And she was able to rest comfortably, dozing off and on, while Wishi-ta curled up on the sleeping bag again, their new way of camping out. Eventually Helene fell into a deeper sleep, waking to a moonlit room. She got up to go to the bathroom. Better, she thought. I'm a little better. On the way to the kitchen, her arm brushed against the bowl of fruit on the counter: apples, peaches, and plums. The bowl tipped and the fruit fell to the floor, scattering. She was afraid to bend down, and left it for the morning.

At the sink, gazing out the window over the lake, she spotted movement, a wide wingspread of some kind of bird. Not the flap-flap of ducks or geese, but a slow guide. Only she couldn't see the eyes, to tell if it was an owl, and it disappeared in complete silence. She started back to the sofa. She got as far as Wishi-ta and the sleeping bag, and knelt down, curling up on the outspread sleeping bag, putting a sofa pillow under the side of her head. And that way she fell back to sleep, very still and deep, as if she'd been drugged, although she hadn't taken anything more than Tylenol. But in this sleep she was in another bedroom standing over Renee back at the Roy house, and there was a struggle between them, an intense and difficult tug-of-war, completely silent, until it was over. Helene surfaced into wakefulness for a moment, just to remember what it was, and then fell straight back to a dreamless sleep.

It was not quite dawn when a slamming sound woke Helene. And then chatter, human, or so she thought. She listened again, and there was definite movement, snapping twigs, maybe an animal, a largish animal. She became more alert but didn't move. Man or beast, what was she going to do, anyway?

And then steps on the back deck, and low voices, male.

First she saw the bumpy beam of a flashlight. Then two figures crossed the deck to the screen door of the porch. The silhouettes were slim and hatless, carrying nothing. Uncle Alphonse, she thought, and cousin Julian. Who else could it be? Escaped bank robbers? And then they were at the slider between porch and house, also left open after Wishi-ta's trip to the lakeside.

The first man entered, searching with the flashlight; the second was right behind. In a moment Helene was bathed in a pool of light, blinding and painful, until the beam moved mercifully to the side.

"Jesus." It was Denis's voice. And then Denis's face, crouched down next to her, taking in the bandaged arm and the hair crusted with blood, even since the shower.

"Helene," he said. "Helene; it's me, Denis."

"Yes," and then she turned her head slightly. Before she could even see, she knew it was Izzy, the tall, thin frame and the long hair.

"Izzy's here too." Extending his arm sideways, he said, "Can you hold this?" and gave the flashlight to Izzy, turning back to Helene. "Can you sit up?"

Helene gestured to toward the sink in the kitchen. "There's a light over there. But don't wake Wishi, not yet." But even as she spoke the name, Wishi-ta stirred, murmuring.

Izzy went to turn on the light, and Denis put a hand out to Helene. "Can you get up?"

"If you could help me. I banged my head pretty bad." She heard the words coming out slowly, maybe a bit slurred, unless that was just from being awakened from deep sleep.

"You had an accident?" He had put his hand under her elbow, and supported her as she sat up.

"I slipped and fell on some rocks in the water. So stupid, just careless."

"When?"

She shrugged. "Two or three days ago?" But it could have been a week; it seemed such a long time ago.

Once she was upright, Denis helped her to the sofa. Izzy took her spot on the floor, pulling Wishi-ta into his lap, where she yawned sleepily. His long hair hung down, making a curtain over the two of them. Helene didn't need to see their faces; she knew how deep the bond was.

"You heard me?" Wishi-ta said. "I called and called."

"I'm here."

To Helene, Denis said, "We have to take you back, both of you." She couldn't miss the grave note in his voice.

"I know."

"Do you need to go to the hospital now, before we go?"

"I don't think so. No bleeding. Some pressure comes and goes. Not worse; maybe a little better."

"OK, then, we'll get you packed up, have a quick breakfast here, and then get on the road."

Helene nodded. Whatever, of course. It was no longer her say.

"But why? How?" Helene wanted to know.

"We can talk about it in the car," Denis said. He got up and crossed into the kitchen, where the fruit remained on the floor, stopping him midstep.

"What the heck? Did you guys have a food fight?"

For the first time in days, Helene smiled as she watched Denis pick up the apples and pears. He was family, and he had come when she needed him. He was here, with Izzy; they had found her and Wishi-ta in time. Izzy had scooped up Wishi-ta from the floor, carrying her piggyback around the room – what looked like fun. Yet, when he turned, Helene caught his look of sweet sorrow, pain, and near loss. So far he hadn't spoken to Helene, although he could see she was impaired, leaning on Denis for support. There will be consequences for this, she thought vaguely, and I will have to pay.

They ate cold cuts and bruised fruit. Denis went around packing what he could find and emptying the refrigerator, noting the improvements to the place.

"Pretty spiffy," was his offhand comment. "Maybe we'll come back another time. Wonder if the fishing is still good?"

There were streaks of pink in the sky over the lake, the beginning of another day. Of course they were leaving, but there was still something magic about their time here, perhaps sacred. The car was packed; yet they were reluctant to depart, Helene and Wishi-ta sitting wordlessly on the sofa while Denis stood out on the deck.

Izzy went outside and returned with his flute.

"I'm going to play for you," he said, standing by the open screen door to the deck. "As the sun rises. It's a beautiful day."

They were to return to the base in an elderly gray Buick, Elsa's car, since Denis's truck would not accommodate four. They stopped by Helene's car, stuck in the rutted track. Denis got out and removed the registration, locking up with her keys.

"We'll have to come back," he said, back in the driver's seat. Next to him, up front, Helene nodded. Not that she liked leaving her car behind, and her independence. But she might not be able to drive for a while, at least until her vision cleared and her balance was better.

"We'll go to the base first," Denis continued, looking ahead on the dirt track. "And drop off Izzy and Wishi-ta. We have to find a pay phone, though. They need to know we found you. Noel came back from the Home Camp, waiting to hear…"

Again Helene nodded.

"And then I'll get my truck and take you home." He glanced sideways. "To your house."

"No," she mouthed, not wanting Wishi-ta to hear. "I can't, I don't want…"

Denis cut her off. "That's the plan. I can't stay. I have to finish the recording; they can't do it without me." His voice softened. "I'll call Kenneth too. He needs to know about your concussion. Someone's got to take you to the doctor and be responsible while you're recovering. You understand that, right?"

"Yes." What choice did she have?

She sank lower in her seat, avoiding direct light. Kenneth wasn't really the problem. In fact, he was a good manager of situations, and was good with doctors, as she knew from previous experience. He would want to help at a time like this, no matter how strange the circumstances. As for Erik, he seemed almost a ghostly presence, not quite real. She would deal with him later, or maybe not. Maybe that was the end of it. The affair had been just a trigger for all of this, nothing more.

It was that "dream" house she didn't want to go back to, and all that it represented. And being away from Wishi-ta, by her own doing. For that she was too sad to even speak. But it had to be, at least for now.

Farther down the road, after the phone calls had been placed, Denis explained what had happened, and how they had come to find them at the cabin. After her last phone call, he'd had a bad feeling, and kept trying to call back, but there was no response on her phone; nothing for over a week.

"No cell service up here."

"Yes, well, then I got in touch with Izzy at the Home Camp. He said that you'd gone to Boston with Wishi-ta for a hospital appointment; that's what Noel said when he got back with Neesa and Cree. Then I called Kenneth, and he hadn't heard from you, either. He had a message that said you'd be away a few days; he thought you'd decided to go back to the Home Camp before school started, but your cell didn't work up there."

Denis's beard was shaggy. He also needed a trim and a comb. For the first time Helene saw a few gray hairs.

He cleared his throat. "I was not happy about it. That's when I guessed you might have taken off, but I had no clue where or when. I didn't want to say anything to Kenneth, not then. I wasn't sure, from what you said before, when we talked on the phone…" He paused, weighing his words and the back-seat passengers. "I called Izzy again, and asked what he thought." He looked in the rearview mirror at Izzy, who had his head back, eyes closed.

"Izzy's the one who mentioned what you said about the cabin, when you were together in the car to see Louis. Right, Izzy?"

"Right."

"So you can thank him for that. The moment he said it, I knew that's where you would go. So Izzy said he would help me find you. I told the guys at the recording studio it was a family emergency, and drove north. Izzy caught a ride and met me at the base. We saw the notes you left at Renee's house when we got there, so we knew you meant to go for a few days – but here it was, almost two weeks later – and no word at all."

"I'm sorry," Helene said tiredly. "Really. I didn't mean it to work out this way. I was going to get in touch soon, let everyone know where we were, and why. But then this happened. And I got us into this stupid situation." She touched her head. That was mostly true, but not completely. It didn't acknowledge the spell that kept them there, away from the other life, the conflict and confusion. "It's still not right…I'm not right; I've changed…I feel like, like…" But she couldn't explain, in the car with Izzy and Wishi-ta in the back, with her head all banged up. It was beyond her. Gazing out at the endless rolling greenery, achy and sore, with pain in her head, she longed for bed; not the big king bed with fine linens at the house with Kenneth, but the lumpy double bed covered with the wolf blanket.

Chapter 18

Kenneth was a good nurse; and Thelma, an able substitute when he couldn't be there. He expressed nothing but sympathy and real concern about Helene's injuries and the problems with her vision and balance. The "sick room" was the guest room where Wishi-ta had stayed, with soft morning light and tulips on the bedside table. There was a constant supply of water, ginger ale, and healthy snacks, regular and tasty meals, and a compress that she placed on her head that gave some relief. With Thelma's help she showered, shampooed, and got into clean, comfortable clothes. Kenneth had replaced the bandage on her arm and examined the head wound beneath the padding that the doctor had put on.

"Oh, that pretty hair," Kenneth said soothingly. "If you comb it right, it just about covers the wound."

The X-ray had shown a hairline fracture, but the doctor saw nothing further on the MRI. Signs of a concussion, definitely. There was brief talk about wearing a protective helmet, which Helene rejected. She was willing to use a cane for stability. The truth was, she didn't plan to go anywhere or see anyone. She talked to Denis and Izzy only briefly when they called. She couldn't read and wasn't interested in TV or radio. Even when Thelma was there, she preferred not to "talk about things," rather just to hear Thelma's voice, reporting on school matters, some of the staff and students she knew, or even Thelma's knitting and crocheting projects.

She missed Wishi-ta terribly, and suffered almost as much that Wishi-ta was without her, even if she was back with family members. She felt so apart from everything and everyone else. No one else had shared what she and Wishi-ta had shared, that time together, the blessed peace of nature, and the time of suffering and of prayer. No one could understand how deeply she was affected by the dream visions she'd had during that time, or how magnificent Wishi-ta had been, so full of strength and spirit. And beyond that she was homesick for life at the base, the people and their doings, that other way of being. She could never, ever go back to the old life with this husband in this house in this town. It was even hard to let Thelma in, who was devoting so much of her free time to the aid of a friend who had essentially left her behind.

"You really are much better," Thelma said one day in the bedroom, where Helene had retreated after lunch, not even bothering to shower and change for the day. Thelma sat in the rocker, knitting a bright fashion scarf: too cheerful, Helene thought. Something about the way Thelma wore her hair, and her vibrant, elaborate wardrobe made Helene think of Dolly, the matchmaker from the musical *Hello, Dolly!* – wise in the ways of humans and eager to provide solutions. But not so much for Helene, sadly.

"You're much steadier," Thelma said, knowingly, pulling at the yarn, "and I saw you looking at those old photographs. So what's the plan? I don't see much action here."

"I know," Helene said without energy. "What am I supposed to do? I don't really want to be here, and I really can't go back there, to the base."

"You can talk to me," Thelma said in that voice of hers, easy but insistent. "I am a counselor, you know, a shrink. Something has made you go way out of your comfort zone, and I'm not really sure what it is."

"I'm not sure, either," Helene said. "Don't worry about it, Thelma. It's not your problem."

"But you're my friend, and I am worried." The knitting needle came to rest. "You're in a difficult situation, and I'd like to help, if you'll let me."

Helene leaned her head back against the pillow, staring at the ceiling. "I don't think anyone can help."

Thelma didn't press further, but continued knitting while Helene closed her eyes. Perhaps she dozed, because she woke later to the sound of voices. Kenneth was home and talking to Thelma in the kitchen.

First she heard Thelma: "She wasn't dressed when I got here after lunch. I encouraged her, but she's just not ready yet."

"I'm afraid it's the same as before." That was Kenneth.

"What do you mean?" Thelma asked, but Helene knew all too well what he meant.

"Well, before you really knew her; she had a bad spell, like this. It was not long after Renee left, after her big meltdown, so to speak, and we didn't know where she was, or if she was even alive. She didn't bother to tell anyone until she was gone on the road halfway across the country, maybe five or six weeks later, a call from a phone booth."

There was a short silence. Then Thelma, in a measured tone: "Yes, I'm sure that was a trauma and it hit her hard. But this is different; it was an accident, after all."

"Yes, but it's the same – shutting down, no energy, no nothing."

"Perhaps." Another pause. "She may be depressed following the concussion; it's not uncommon."

"I'm telling you, it's more than that. She's going down that same road. I hate to say this, but in a way it's good that she got hurt and had to be rescued. They weren't gone too long – you could still call it a getaway or mini vacation, whatever. Really, we're lucky no one has threatened to bring charges against her – you know..." Here his voice dropped so she couldn't hear.

Surely not that, Helene thought. There had been no danger to Wishi-ta – or shouldn't have been. And there was the message she'd left that clearly stated, "We're having a getaway, while I decide what I want to do next. In a safe, comfortable place. I'll be in touch."

But Kenneth's mind was of the world where people fought things out in courts, with fines and punishments. Yet she could not deny that Louis's family must have doubts and misgivings, especially after learning she had injured herself – questions about basic competency. She wasn't happy about the situation she had created, but she was digging in her heels, unwilling to take up the old life, no matter the pressure.

"She's working her way through this," Thelma said in the other room. "It takes a while, but I'm confident she'll do it."

Helene blinked back tears. Thelma was holding out for her. She believed in her, if no one else did.

Only later did Helene find out that Kenneth had contacted the psychologist she had seen after Renee's disappearance. Only then did she realize how serious he thought the situation had become and how much he truly didn't understand her motivations. She agreed to meet with Dr. Stone, who was willing to come to the house; Kenneth wanted to be there also. Now the three were seated together in the living room, Dr. Stone little changed from when they'd last met, years ago, when Helene seemed to overcome her emotional turbulence. His glasses were different, and maybe the hair more sparse, but the eyes were just as focused and intent.

"Helene, when Kenneth called, he said he is concerned about you, after this injury – and from before that. He says you are pushing him away. From what I've heard, your recent actions are quite at odds from what you previously expressed to me – the desire for peace, normalcy, security. What's going on?"

"It's not Kenneth," Helene said quickly. "He hasn't changed. I have no reason to complain about him. I've changed, and I honestly don't know why. But I don't see how I can go back to the way things were – really and truly, in my heart. I don't know what else to say."

"Kenneth?"

Kenneth twisted in his seat at the other end of the sofa.

"I think she's deeply disturbed – not just by the injury, but what led up to it. How she got roped into taking care of Renee's children – and all the pain that brought up, of not having children ourselves and recalling the whole disaster of Renee's life."

"Not at the end, it wasn't bad," Helene said.

"Really?" Kenneth directed a sharp look at her. "How can you say that? After seeing how she settled for a life like that, in that remote place, with barely enough to get by? Very limited opportunities for the kids, or anyone. I don't see how that's acceptable."

"Probably not," Helene agreed. How could she argue, when that was clearly how he saw it?

"What do you want, Helene?" Dr. Stone asked. "I mean, when you're better again, fully functioning."

Helene sighed, tugging at the hem of her cardigan. A cool front had come through the last few days, rainy. "I want a life with Wishi-ta in it, and Tana-na and the others." She took a steadying breath. "I don't want to live here anymore. And I don't think I can be married to Kenneth anymore, either."

"Tell him."

Dr. Stone was aptly named, Helene thought. Never perturbed by the arguments or the emotion; a practical man, more referee than judge or counselor.

She turned to Kenneth, as handsome as ever, grave and worried. His tie had gone askew and he didn't seem to realize; but it was beyond her now to reach out and straighten it.

"It's not you. Well, it is you, and what is important to you. I know how hard you've worked for this," She gestured around her, the room, the house, the furnishings, the neighborhood, the town. "This success. And how you've always shared with me so generously, and tried to please me and take care of me. But I can't do that anymore. I just can't."

Kenneth looked suddenly panicky. "Do you see what I mean, Dr. Stone? This makes no sense at all. Does it, to you? I think she's trying to punish herself, or me, or both of us, but I don't know why. Maybe we're not perfectly matched in every way, but I know she cares for me, and I love her very much. I think it's illness, mental illness, I really do. I took care of her once, and I'll take care of her again, but how can she possibly leave in this state? She's not fit."

Dr. Stone took a minute to respond. "As I said, when she's fully recovered from this accident. We all agree on that."

Then Kenneth sat forward, the tie still askew, his hair tousled from running a hand through it. All his feeling was in his face, his manner more persuasive for being genuine – just like he was in his business deals.

"Her concussion may heal, but emotionally, I mean, she's still a mess. That was from before the accident. She was acting strangely, not wanting to come home, refusing to talk about her work. But for no reason I could think of. Unless she was just upset with me being busy all the time. And if that's true, I can change, and I will change to spend more time with her. But if she's upset about my success in life or jealous, she's just got to see things differently, try to put it in perspective. She can't go back there; that's the source of the problem. But maybe time away would do her good, a retreat of some sort, under supervision. I think both of us don't want to go back to when she was on those meds that made her so blank and dull. She's gotten so much better, so, so much better. And now, this."

Helene pressed her lips together not to speak, not to smile. That had been her very first reaction to Malvina's letter, with news of Renee's twins and Wishi-ta's allergies. And now, this. One more thing to deal with, one more problem. She thought for a moment of bringing up Erik, and the sex

– just to give Kenneth a clearer, more concrete reason to push her away or to let her go. No, that was not the right way to go about this. He would likely hear about it, the affair, before too long. She had no desire to hurt him, none at all. She certainly didn't hate him, and she wanted him to be happy, but not with her. Another part of her stood apart, saying, *I don't want that enough to not do what I need to do for myself. He's a grown man; I'm not responsible for him.* She wouldn't be drawn into it, and she wouldn't budge.

Kenneth had tensed in his seat; she could see his jaw muscles working.

"Maybe," he said, "she needs a more thorough evaluation at the hospital, where they can really check her out. Not just for the effects of concussion, but to really observe her mental status, and to find the right combination of meds. I'm sure she'll stabilize again, quite sure. We had a long period when things were going so well. It just cropped up again, with this trigger. Doesn't that make sense?" He was looking at Dr. Stone, not Helene.

"Ask Helene," the doctor said.

Slowly Kenneth's head swiveled toward her. "Does it?" he said. "Because it makes sense to me. It would explain all this – and why you would want to leave a life and a marriage that have been so good for so long."

Helene's answer came calmly, from someplace deeper than her active mind. "I can see how it appears that way – because it seems so out of the blue. But it's not. It's not just from the struggle with Renee, either. It's from before that. I don't think I'm out of my right mind, and I don't think I need that kind of help. I don't need to go to a hospital or a retreat or get back on the meds. I just need to change my life."

Kenneth looked from Helene to the doctor and back. "Then, God help me, I just don't understand." His head dropped to his chest and he exhaled deeply; it was a sound close to a moan. Helene ached to see him this way, this man who worked so hard and had done so well through life – to be rejected for something he couldn't understand. But it had to be this way. Helene tried to console herself, that there would be many future opportunities for someone like him to meet other women, maybe even have children with them, and share that life with someone who appreciated him and what he had to offer. She saw now, his friends and family had never been certain of her. "Lovely, yes, and very sweet, but not quite…" they might have said.

Dr. Stone asked to talk to Helene separately, to get a better idea of her status. She answered his questions plainly, not holding back even about Erik. When it was time to wrap up the session, Kenneth returned. The doctor said that Helene was not in imminent danger to herself or others, and couldn't be compelled to get medical treatment against her will. It would probably not work, anyway. But, he said, they should meet again, and see how things stood then, including Helene's physical recovery. It was, he said, a difficult time for everyone, adjusting to new, unexpected developments.

After Dr. Stone left, Helene excused herself to take a nap, while Kenneth went to the store. On the bed she was unable to relax, too hot, too cold, a constant stream of words and images swirling in her head. She tried to recall her earlier experience with Dr. Stone, the first time around when she'd gone for counseling. About the medication she'd taken. How much? And for how long? The first prescription hadn't worked well, and they'd tried another. Was that something she needed now? Or wanted? She remembered the drawer in Kenneth's desk where he kept the medical and insurance information in neat files; that would be the place to check.

The house was getting darker, the twilight coming earlier; she padded in her socks to Kenneth's home office, and pulled out the drawer with the medical information, both hers and his. She found the file easily enough, and it contained the receipts and instructions for the medicine: Prozac first, and then Buspar. Taking a seat in his chair, she remembered how they had softened her agitation and then dulled it, and then dulled her to the point of constant sleepiness, perpetually ready to take a nap. With a shake of her head, she decided, No, it wasn't the same, and it wasn't the route she wanted to take. As she bent to replace the file, she caught sight of another file, labeled "Misc." She took it out, recognizing the paperwork for her parents' burial plots, Kenneth's registration for military service, and even an expired passport. There was also a letter, unopened, addressed to her, Helene Bradford. The return address was R. Lopes at the base, and Helene knew right away it was the letter from Renee that Denis had told her about. It had come, and Kenneth had put it away in a file in a drawer where she was unlikely to find it. Holding it, her hand began to tremble as she felt a slow burn up her neck into her face. Her throat constricted with shock, anger, rage even – over Renee's unanswered message and Kenneth's deception. She ripped the envelope open, tearing a corner of the letter.

"*Dear Helene,*" it began. And the rest was a short and simple request: "*Please call if you can forgive me for what happened. There is another way. I'm so much better now, happy, and I want that for you too.*"

She had reached out. And Helene had never replied. Because she didn't know. Kenneth had made the decision to keep it from her – out of fear, she was sure. He hadn't trusted her, and kept her from dealing with what she needed to deal with, leaving her weak and dependent and apart from her own family. He had robbed her of a chance to see her sister alive again, well.   Like that, a door closed against Kenneth, against that life – with a startling bang. .

She took the letter back to the bedroom, hiding it in her purse, unwilling to let Kenneth know she had found it. There was no longer a point to staying out of Renee's life, no changing of the past. And yet it made all the difference. Now she was impelled to go forward, without him, into uncharted territory. And not even sure of her basic physical soundness – could she handle things on her own with her new impairment, never mind care for children?

She looked at herself in the mirror, and the image was clear. Her eyes were wide open, the pupils back to normal, and there was no more hazy band at the top of her field of vision. She could walk fairly normally now, only using a cane for uneven terrain or distance. Bright lights and loud noises still pained her, but less and less. She could not deny, as Thelma had said, that she was on the mend. She turned from the mirror to the chair near the dresser, with a recently completed scarf, the work of Thelma's hands. Helene was not alone; she had one enduring ally. Never once had Thelma spoken a word of reproach. She had urged Helene to regain her strength and to engage with the world, but never a hint of what she thought Helene should do. Only support.

That's what gave Helene the courage to ask Thelma if she could stay at her place for the next couple weeks, while she decided what she was going to do, and how she would do it. She wasn't an invalid now. The bandages were off, she was able to read a little, but still not drive.

"Of course," Thelma said, across Helene's kitchen table. "As you know, my house isn't so, ah, spacious as yours. You can stay in Jacob's room. I just cleaned it out after he left for the semester."

"Are you sure? He won't mind?"

"He may not even know. I doubt he'll be home before Thanksgiving. It's not like he and I are on the phone every day with constant updates. So..."

"Thank you, Thelma," Helene said, her hands working in her lap. It was so hard to ask for things, for help. Only Thelma made it possible. "For this, and for everything. And especially for not lecturing me."

"Not my place," Thelma said, drawing herself up. "I'm being your friend here, and not your therapist. If you want to ask my advice, I'll give you a straight answer. Otherwise I'm just here for you."

"All right, then," Helene said. "Now I am taking some action."

"But not before you tell Kenneth."

"Of course," Helene said firmly, although she felt like a weight was on her chest. "I'll tell him tonight." She took a breath. "Can I come tomorrow?"

"Yes. But..." Thelma drew out the pause, narrowing her eyes. "We're agreed; it won't just be a cozy nest to hide out in, right? Not girls' night out, sleepovers and pillow fights?"

"No. I mean, yes." Helene smiled sheepishly. "I just need a little time to make some plans, and I can't really do it here."

"Got it."

She was too good, Thelma, and more than Helene deserved – she was mother, sister, and friend all in one. All those things that Helene had tried to be but never really knew how. Tears stung her eyes, and she blinked them away, too choked to speak. Silently she watched Thelma at work on her project, clipping loose threads and tying off knots, not so different from the women at the base. Other staff at school sometimes teased Helene about her friendship with Thelma, and Helene had been surprised by it herself. But she shouldn't have been. Like Helene, Thelma was in some ways an outsider in the small New England town: a New Yorker, a Jew. There was growing diversity in the population, but still strong networks of old-time residents, many of them in town for generations with no need or use for new acquaintances.

Helene ran a hand through her hair, letting a finger trace the bumpiness of the cut on her scalp. Her hair had grown since the beginning of summer, past her shoulders, and she hadn't had a proper haircut, just a trim. She had played with the idea of letting it grow long, down her back, at Wishi-ta's urging. But not now; dealing with hair was too much effort.

"One more thing, Thelma."

"Yes?" Thelma looked up.

For a moment Helene couldn't get the words out. Too much emotion was bubbling inside – her decision, Kenneth's reaction, Thelma's support – and the pain that went deeper than all that.

"I need a haircut."

"OK, sweetie, sure." Thelma lifted her scissors, gazing speculatively at Helene's head. "I could probably trim it for you, for now."

Helene turned her head slowly side to side. Something Renee had written in her journal, how Neesa had cut her hair in mourning for a lost sister. Helene felt a warmth in her chest. The knot in her heart was radiating heat, melting. The old grief of family sadness and the searing grief of Renee's loss. It needed release, like molten wax.

"No, short. I want it gone." The words came out oddly.

Thelma gave her a shrewd look. "Are you sure?"

Helene nodded.

Thelma continued to stare, a puzzled furrow on her brow. "Are you OK? Really OK, not just putting me off?"

"Yes."

"All right, then." Thelma said. "That's what we're going to do. So you'll call the hairdresser? I can take you any afternoon this week."

"No," Helene said. "Let's go to QuickCuts; you don't need an appointment." She pushed the chair back to get up.

"Now?"

"Can we, please?"

If Thelma was unsure of Helene's deeper motivations, she did not say.

But the humor was back in her voice. "OK, then, not a second to waste. Let's hop to it."

Helene had told Kenneth not to pick up dinner, that she was feeling well enough to make spaghetti and meatballs. And that they could talk. He said less than expected about her new haircut, probably assuming it was easier to take care of while the wound was still healing. The new look was not bad, Helene decided, cropped on the back and sides, a little longer in front.

"I want you to know," she said, after telling him about the move to Thelma's, "if I do start over, on my own, that I really won't need a whole lot. I may need the basics for setting up an apartment, bedroom and kitchen stuff, but I don't need to disrupt this house. I can use some of the extras from my folks' house, what we put in storage."

For the first time, Kenneth looked stricken. "But I thought you loved this house. And all the things we picked out together."

She realized how her words had sounded to him. "I did. And I genuinely enjoyed putting everything together like this, with you."

He rubbed his chin. "So you can just leave it behind, like that? I thought it meant something to you."

She sighed. "That was then; now it's different; that's what I'm trying to tell you."

She watched emotions cross his face: still perplexed, but coming to some kind of resignation, at least for the moment. He wasn't going to argue. But in his mind, she was wrong, and everyone could see that – except her. Perhaps he thought that time, and letting her make other plans, might help her see what was really at stake. And what she stood to lose. He was that loyal, she knew. He would step back, but he wouldn't give up.

And so she left. Kenneth spoke only once, coming into the guest room in the morning to say he was sorry it had come to this, but he would not stand in her way. That he loved her, and wished her luck finding her way. That the door was open, but only so long before he too had to move on. Then he kissed her on the cheek and left.

For a moment afterward, Helene blinked back tears of pity, for him, for the first real failure in his life – his marriage – for no reason he could understand, and for doing all the right things as far as he knew. But then she was on her feet, ready for coffee and toast, packing what she needed for when Thelma came at eleven. She had a strong feeling that this was the last time she would stay in this house. Yes, she was sad, but she was eager to go, and to leave it behind.

Thelma's house was full of soft knitted blankets and quilted pillows, plus a virtual jungle of untamed plants as well as Misty, the cat, who now made this home. Helene was set up in Jacob's room with the twin bed and the music posters, including Johnny Cash giving the finger. She had Misty for company during the day when Thelma was out, and whiled away the time with music, cooking, television, and walks nearby. She could even read in short spurts. Denis called regularly, and she had talked to Izzy a few times, getting updates on the twins and the family. He couldn't tell her much detail, though, since everyone was at the Home Camp through the long Labor Day weekend, while he stayed at the base after his return with Wishi-ta and Denis.

"How come?" she asked. "If everybody loves it up there so much."

"It was great," Izzy said over the phone. "But I was ready to come back. Sometimes I need my space, you know. It's nice having the house to myself. And my friends missed me, getting pretty bored with themselves."

Helene laughed, but she did understand, quite well.

"I'm sorry you never made a trip here," she said. "It would have been fun to show you Boston." She sighed. "Oh, well, maybe there will be another chance sometime."

Erik didn't call, and neither did she call him. Part of her missed him, or the excitement that he brought, and another part told her to get her bearings first, and that meant staying apart. Izzy assured her that Erik knew she was back and she was recovering.

The first week passed in a quiet, comfortable routine. Helene was feeling well again, stronger. She even wondered about driving – although her car was still in Vermont at a garage where Denis had it stored. Someone, or two people, would have to go up in order to drive it back, and that was something she would not ask Kenneth. She would have to wait for Denis, or maybe someone from the base would be willing to go with her – well, Erik, if he was around. If she should even ask him. Not that there was anything wrong in asking, and she was sure he would do it. But what it might lead to, probably lead to…

Too bad Izzy didn't have a driver's license. She thought she might ask him, if he and a friend would go up with her – she would pay them. Then she didn't hear from him all week, and began to wonder why. Maybe there was a family conference, discouraging contact with her. Or maybe she was just imagining things. She had left him a voicemail saying she'd moved to Thelma's, but since then not a word.

On Saturday Thelma took Helene to refill a prescription and pick up a few groceries. She suggested stopping at a new café in town, but Helene shook her head, reluctant to run into anyone she might know, who'd be bound to ask questions about her head or her haircut, or the upcoming school year, which she did not want to talk about. Back at the house, Thelma put on the kettle for tea, sitting at the table to go through the day's mail, opening one envelope with interest. When the kettle whistled, she got up, leaving the opened mail on the table. Helene recognized the logo on one of the brochures: the developer that Kenneth was working with.

"You're not selling, are you?" she asked.

"Well, considering it," Thelma said at the counter, pouring hot water into mugs and steeping the tea bags. "It's a good offer, and this place needs more work than I want to take on. I don't need a house anymore, probably get almost as much room in a condo. Jacob could care less; this is just a stopping over place for him."

"But still," Helene said, taking the cup of tea. "I thought you were against it in principle – flattening these older, small homes just to put up big ones."

"True. I do feel that way, in general. But on a personal level, this makes more sense. Plus the rest of the street is going that way, so I'd end up the runt of the neighborhood. Anyone who bought this house would just knock it down. Sometimes you just have to go along with the times."

Helene held back her first words, not wanting to come across as shocked or negative. Slowly she stirred honey into her cup, and then squeezed a slice of lemon.

"We all do things we never thought we would do." Thelma's words were carefully neutral, but Helene knew they were directed at her. She looked up, wondering if Thelma knew about Erik. No; she could not know more about Renee than what Helene had told her, so she must be referring to Helene leaving with Wishi-ta.

"Yes," she agreed.

"If you want to tell me anything," Thelma said, "it might help you come to a decision. Get everything out on the table."

That was it, the opening. Thelma had pushed the mail aside; she ignored the tea.

Helene took a breath. "You know that guy we met at the powwow? White guy, bearded – he gave candy to the children?"

Thelma's eyebrows rose. "I remember."

"Well, he…I…"

As Helene related the story, Thelma nodded without comment. Maybe she was surprised at the guy Helene chose, but she didn't seem surprised about what had happened.

"I don't know what to think," Helene finished, flushed with heat, turning the cup in her hands.

This time Thelma shook her head. "Maybe you do, on some level. It can be a symbol of something, or a trigger for something else. Or it could even have been true feeling. That's for you to figure out."

"And you think I should tell Kenneth?"

"Don't you think it's fair that he should know? He's really struggling to make sense of it all, and this might tell him something in a way that words and explanations just can't."

Helene nodded. "I know, it's so weird. I never did anything like this before."

Again, no comment from Thelma, no attempt at humor. They finished their tea in silence, until Thelma got up to put away the rest of the groceries. Watching Thelma move about her kitchen, Helene was chastened by something more than gratitude. It was, she thought, the discovery of someone looking out for you and wanting you to be true to yourself. That experience was new to her, something she wouldn't have known if this crisis – the breakaway and the accident – hadn't happened.

A few days later, Helene and Thelma had finished dinner and were sitting in the living room enjoying the end of the day, the windows open to branches of yellowing leaves. On the side table were black-and-white photos of Thelma's family members whose names Helene had learned – and their fates: Thelma's grandfather, the tailor, in Poland, who wouldn't leave his sickly wife to flee the country. Her mother's cousins as children in Europe, now scattered to Israel and Australia. Her father's aunt and uncle, entertainers in the Borscht Belt in the 1950s in their vaudevillian costumes.

Thelma was working on a baby's blanket for one of the teachers who was expecting. Helene had started a few small sewing projects, just cleared by the doctor for close work and driving again. Except for occasional headaches, she was so much better, almost overnight. Or really, since she'd moved into Thelma's house. They heard a knock on the door, and Helene glanced out the window to see Kenneth, carrying a small gift bag.

"It's Kenneth." She scrambled to her feet. "I'll get it."

She met him at the door. He was in khakis and a polo shirt, so he must have gone home from the office to change. She was so used to seeing him in a suit; he looked so much younger this way, and more vulnerable.

"Sorry not to call first," he said. "It's a special occasion, and I took my chances."

"Come in," she said. "We're in the living room."

She knew right away what the gift was for: her birthday on the weekend. He had not forgotten she was turning forty-one. And, maybe, possibly, he was testing the waters. Though dismayed, she could not help but be touched.

"Kenneth." Thelma's surprise was in her voice. "What brings you this way?"

"Helene's birthday," he said. "On the weekend. I didn't want her" – he turned to Helene – "you, to think I forgot. No big deal. It's something I got a while ago, and you should have it. So, happy birthday." He held out the gift bag, and she took it. She had to; it would be unkind to refuse, churlish. From the look of it, she thought jewelry, which was something he liked to give.

It was a pin of a stylized cat for a top or a jacket. She looked up in pleasure. "Why thank you; it's lovely. And it's, well, it's me." It was silver, but not expensive fine jewelry with gemstones or pearls. Simple, feminine, and sweet.

"I'd say that was a hit," Thelma said. "Come sit, please, Kenneth. We're not in the middle of anything here." Thelma and Kenneth were not on the easiest of terms, but she too was extending herself. Or, maybe, thought Helene, just being a nice person.

"I don't want to intrude," he said, then turned to Helene. "I'm not trying to pressure you, you know. It's simply a birthday gift. And I'll be at a seminar on Saturday, so..."

"No, it's very thoughtful," she said. "Just a birthday, really – not a milestone or anything." She found herself blushing. "Thank you for remembering."

"You're welcome." From the easy chair, he looked around the room, interested, as he always was, in homes and construction, layout and design. "It's very comfortable here," he said to Thelma. "All very cozy and cheerful." Buzzwords, for sure, but true.

"Thank you." She gave him an impish smile. "Enjoy it now. In a few months, it will be a hole in the ground."

Kenneth perked up. "Really? Are you going with Daniel Clarke?" When she nodded, he went on, "I have to say, quite impartially, it's a good deal, what he's offering. And really not a bad idea for someone, at, uh your stage of life."

"Right," Thelma said. "As I was telling Helene." Helene sat back, wondering if there was some agenda here she wasn't aware of.

"Some of my neighbors are going to hate me," Thelma continued. "The holdouts."

Kenneth waved away her concern. "There are always those who resist change, but it's coming anyway, so it's to everyone's interest to look out for themselves. This neighborhood was starting to look run-down; new families were really not interested in this part of town."

"I see."

"No offense."

This was more like it, what Helene expected. She was just happy the attention was off her. She began thinking about what Thelma might do, and if she might end up relocating out of town. Helene frowned at the idea. Then again, it couldn't be too far, since Thelma would still be working in the school system at least for a few years, and tied to her local clients. Plus who the heck knew where Helene herself might end up?

Then, unexpectedly, there was another knock, and a man's voice calling through the screen door. "Helene?"

She sat up with a start. *Erik?* It sounded just like him, but it couldn't be. Could it? In her last call to him, a message, she'd asked if he would hold off getting in touch until she was ready; she hoped he'd understand. He had texted back: "OK." Besides that, how did he know where she was?

Thelma got to her feet, putting the knitting aside. "Just a second." Helene was pinned to her seat, unable to move. Her heart pounded like she had been running a race.

She glanced at Kenneth and then away, listening to the voices in the front hall. For sure it was Erik. What would Thelma do, Helene wondered? What would she say?

She returned, with Erik behind her. "Erik," she announced. "To see you, Helene."

In the doorway he looked large and bearish, slightly alarming. He was in work clothes, with a scruffy beard and undeniable beer belly. He was focused on her, serious, not seeming to register the haircut, the changes, or the other man in the room.

"Helene."

"Yes, right, I didn't expect…" She was gibbering, not sure which way to go. What was Thelma thinking, bringing him in here like this?

Kenneth was on his feet. "Kenneth Bradford," he said, extending his hand, which Erik took, barely looking at the man. "I'm Helene's husband. Is there a problem?"

Then Helene knew that yes, there was a problem, or Erik would not have come.

"What is it?" she said, now also on her feet. "Wishi-ta? Tana-na?"

"No. It's Izzy; there's been an…incident, and he's injured."

"Oh, no," she said. "An accident? In a car?" He was always catching rides with sometimes unreliable friends.

"No, his bike, actually. He was riding home from work and cut off a truck, by accident. Some kind of altercation, apparently. His nose is broken and a couple of ribs." He paused, releasing a sigh. "They cut off his hair too."

Helene's hands went to her mouth. "Oh my God." And then she was in tears, which came on fast and furious, so unlike her.

"How could they?" she said, wiping the tears with her hands. "He's no threat to anyone." Yet she recalled that moment at the store in New Hampshire, the man who was so hostile. "Did they catch who did it?"

Erik pressed his lips together, seeming to choose his words. "Not that I know of. You'll have to ask him. The thing is, he's clammed up and not saying anything. Well, actually, he is asking for you."

"Me?"

"Yeah, he asked me to come."

"For my nursing?" she asked, puzzled.

"I don't think so. For the family."

Kenneth started to shake his head. "Oh, no, no. Not another disaster for her to step into. She's just recovering herself. Besides, she's the one who went away with Wishi-ta, without telling anyone. Have they forgotten that already?"

That was a jab, but Helene hardly felt it. Thelma had come to stand beside her, right at her shoulder, like a shield.

Erik took a breath, glancing at Kenneth. "They haven't forgotten anything." Then he pivoted, his gaze on Helene. "This is what Izzy asked, and I said I would find you and tell you, Helene."

She knew right then that she would go. But how to explain to Kenneth? – who was upset, not unreasonably. Or even Thelma, who might also have her doubts.

"I'll go," she said, nodding at Erik. Then she turned to Kenneth and Thelma. "I'm OK. You have to understand, Izzy is something very special, to Renee's family and to me too. He's the one who helped everyone accept Renee, in spite of her problems, and me too. He came to my rescue, up at the cabin. I have to go, I really do."

Kenneth had to be so disappointed and confused, but his face showed resignation, or just maybe repugnance toward how she'd changed. Even, confirmation, if he'd needed it, of how impulsive she'd become.

"Well, you're not up to it," Kenneth said flatly. "How useful are you going to be? There's no way you're ready to go anywhere."

"Come with me, Helene," Erik said. His voice revealed an intimacy between them, and Kenneth blinked a couple times. Then Erik continued, as if there was no one else in the room. The truth was coming out, ready or not – not in the way Helene had wanted it – all because of Izzy.

"I want you to come back too," he said, holding Helene's gaze. The room went hushed; only the sound of a dog barking down the street. "And I hope you want that too."

Helene closed her eyes, tempted to turn and run, so giddy and full of emotions. She felt Thelma's hand on her arm – supporting or restraining? But she was there with her.

"OK," Helene said, simply. "I'll go with you."

"Helene?" Kenneth stared at her. She owed him an explanation. Only, he was quick and observant, and able to figure things out. "This guy?"

She nodded. "Yes. I was going to tell you, wasn't I, Thelma?" She waited for Thelma's nod. "I certainly didn't expect this to happen, and I'm sorry it happened this way."

Now his look was more of incredulity than anger – that such a thing could happen. Did it seem so impossible that she would want a guy like Erik, worn and rumpled, when she had been with someone like Kenneth?

"Are you OK?" Thelma spoke quietly, but everyone could hear. "OK to handle this?" When Helene nodded, Thelma released her arm. "Then maybe we should leave you and Kenneth," Thelma said. "I'll get Erik here coffee, if he likes, or a cold drink."

Erik said nothing, but followed her out of the room.

Helene and Kenneth waited until they were gone.

"I give you credit," Kenneth said, a sharpness in his voice she wasn't used to. "I never suspected. Never. I certainly didn't expect there was, well, opportunity, like that at the base. And I didn't think you were capable of it, Helene."

Her eyebrows went up. "I guess I am."

"But with him? He's not...you're too high class for him. I know you, Helene, and I know you're particular. That guy doesn't even look completely clean. What does he have to offer you or those precious kids?"

She shrugged, not knowing how to explain.

"You know I wanted children," Kenneth said, getting redder in the face. "But I accepted it when we couldn't have them. I might have come around to the idea of adoption, if you had acted reasonably. But kidnapping, running away like that? I really do wonder if you're in your right mind. I'm beginning to think there is serious mental illness in your family; either that or you're determined to ruin a good life, like Renee and Denis. Yes, I know there was trauma; everyone has trauma. But not everyone gets a second chance like you did, and then throws it away. For life with a ragtag bunch of Indians and misfits, who probably don't want you anyway, after what you pulled."

Helene knew some of that was designed to hurt. And maybe some of it was true. Whatever offense there was, however, slid away; she just wished she could help him understand.

"It doesn't seem that way to me. It's what I want."

He kept blinking in disbelief. "I don't think I know who you really are," he said finally. "Or I was sorely mistaken."

"I didn't know, either," she said, nodding. "That other me wasn't who I really am, even though I tried, I really did. But I never meant to deceive you. That is, I didn't know myself, unless maybe deep down – I think maybe I did."

"I thought we had a good marriage."

She paused, choosing her words. "I'm not saying that we didn't care for each other, or try to do right by each other. And certainly there were many, many good occasions. But I was never myself, never. And I can't keep that up any more, and I won't."

"OK, OK," he said finally, his shoulders hunched. "I can accept that whatever happened to you when you were younger, all that trauma, changed or damaged you in some way that I cannot help you with. But, then, what? Not that guy..."

He gestured toward the doorway.

"I'm not looking to him for anything, except being together. I have to make my own way, and I can't even say what that will be."

"That doesn't sound wise or reassuring," Kenneth said. "It sounds like you'll land yourself in another mess. And then, don't coming looking to me..."

All the words that had stumbled around her head now came marching out in an ordered calmness, like they'd been practiced and familiar, like they were true.

"I'm not looking to make any difficulty for you. We'll sell my parents' house, and divide the proceeds between me, Denis, and Renee's children. We can give the tenants a few months' notice. That would be a good start for me. Plus I can get a nursing job pretty easily, school or hospital or doctor's office; they're always looking."

"Please," Kenneth said, holding up his hands. "Enough. It hurts me to think of you planning a life away from me, away from what we both cared about and valued."

Helene spoke gently. "I know. And I'm sorry. But I care about other things now."

"But what about me? Don't you care about me?"

This was the hardest thing, to hear these words from a man who had been a strong supporter, so optimistic and full of confidence.

"Of course I do. You'll find your way without me, I'm sure. There will be plenty of people cheering you on. You've got everything going for you, everything on your side. You always have." She took a breath. "But if you ever get tired of all this – the houses, the projects, the business, the social life – you could start over too."

"Without you?"

"Without me."

"What about him?" He jerked his thumb in the direction of the kitchen.

"Who knows? Not him and not me, anyhow; we certainly don't know."

Kenneth shook his head, defeated. No, she realized; he couldn't see that other life; couldn't see himself in that life. What was the point of education and ambition and achievements only to hide away where no one aspired to the really big wins?

Finally, his last plea: "Helene, you were meant for better things; you appreciate them. I know you've had doubts, and self-doubts, but you can accomplish a lot more than you think you can – more than that other life...whatever it is."

She wouldn't answer; there was nothing else to say.

Kenneth got up to leave. "I don't think this is right, I really don't. But I'm not going to fight for you, again, if you are determined to go this way. And I can't pull you back out of the mire again, either, if it all falls apart. Don't think my heart isn't breaking over all of this. I just can't quite believe it – and I thought a birthday present would make a difference. What a fool, huh?"

"Not a fool."

She found it very hard not to approach him, and put her arms around him to comfort him in his pain. But she couldn't do it; it wouldn't work.

"OK, then, I'm leaving. I guess we'll be in touch." And then he turned back. "I am sorry about Izzy. No one deserves that." *Damn, the man is basically so decent!* – and that was hard to take too.

He left, and Helene went out to the kitchen to talk to Thelma. Erik had gone to get gas for his truck – and to stay clear while Helene and Kenneth talked.

"I guess Jacob can have his bedroom back," Helene said wryly.

"You're going now?"

"As soon as I'm packed. And you know that's not much." With a sudden gesture, she pulled off her diamond engagement ring and put it in the gift box next to the cat pin, handing it to Thelma. "Keep these for me?"

Thelma took box. "You're sure – about all of this?"

"Why, do you have doubts about me now, all of a sudden?"

"Not that." Thelma's expression was strangely subdued. "In an odd way, I think sometimes a bump in the head is just the thing to make you see more clearly. They say that about Harriet Tubman, you know, who led all those people on the Underground Railroad – she was bopped on her head with a brick. And Saint Paul, come to think of it." She smiled halfheartedly. "It's just that I'll miss you."

"It's not so far away. And you know how to get there."

"Right."

"And you're moving on too, remember?"

"Yes, well, not that far."

Helene put her arms around Thelma and placed a kiss on her cheek. "I cannot thank you enough, or repay you. But I'm going to save that for a later time. Let me just say that you've been the best big sister I could ever hope for, and I love you for that."

Thelma, who was never at a loss for words, blinked back tears and returned the hug in silence.

4. Dress Like an Indian Day – by One Little Indian

So, middle school, my first year at this large regional school. My social studies teacher was really into us learning about all kinds of cultures. We had Japanese day, Mexican day, African day – with the food and music, and – you guess it – "costumes" from those different places. Extra points if you came in a kimono or a sombrero, or I suppose an African headdress.

So one day around Thanksgiving, he wanted to go beyond the Pilgrims and turkeys, and make sure to include the Native Americans of the area – Wampanoag, Massachusett, Nipmuc, Narragansett, all those great folks...of the past. Or so he seemed to think. He was pretty much going for that back-in-the day kind of vibe with leather, face paint, feathers – not what you'd call up-to-date contemporary-type clothing. So me, being a bit of a wiseass as I was at that time, decided to come in jeans and a T-shirt, with basketball shoes. As did my buddy, Raj, who wore just what he always wears every day, same as me.

The teacher said, "Hey, Izzy, what's up? I thought you were a real Native American, right?"

"Yes, I am," I said proudly.

"Well, you missed some easy credit. I was sure you had a costume at home. Didn't you know today was Dress Like an Indian Day?"

"Why, yes, I did. And this is how most Indians dress, most of the time."

"Well, I'm sorry, that's not very authentic. I can't give you credit for that."

"I beg to differ. It is authentic – because I'm Native American and this is what I wear."

He turned to my buddy. "What about you, Raj? You're not Indian; well, not *that* kind." In fact, Raj was just as Indian as me, but the *other* kind – from India. Besides being friends, we were almost clones, tall, skinny, black shiny hair, and brown skin. For kicks, we sometimes wore hats and traded clothes; mostly, no one knew the difference.

Raj thought for a moment. "No, I'm not. But I'm dressed like him, and he's an Indian. So I should get credit too."

We got full credit for that – but what the teacher got: priceless.

Chapter 19

They arrived late in the night, with no one there to meet them, and Helene let herself into Renee's house, saying good-bye to Erik at the door.

"Tomorrow we'll talk," she said. "After I've had a chance to see Izzy and find out what's going on. You'll be here, right? Not leaving again right away?"

"I'll be here."

"And what will we say?" she asked. "Or do?"

He yawned, stretching, likely tired from the drive up and back. "I don't honestly think it matters. Some folks probably guessed, anyway – not that Elsa would say anything. It won't stay secret. Not around here."

"But the kids," she said, fidgeting at the doorway. "It might upset them, or not seem right somehow."

He took her face in his hands. "How is it harmful to them if two adults who care for them also care for each other?"

For that she had no answer. She watched him return to his truck and drive down the street and turn at the corner to Elsa and the Chief's house, making her feel like a teen again – not that she'd ever really had that experience. It had only ever been her mother's illness and then her death and school and chores. Helene lifted the suitcase at her feet, switching on lights as she went to the back bedroom. The house, every room, just as she'd left it, maybe a little dustier. Except…the ring from a glass on the coffee table, and a candle pushed aside where feet might rest. Izzy, she thought, in his desire for peace and quiet.

She showered, smiling a little at the slight stickiness of her skin, and her crotch area. Not long after they'd gotten on the road, Erik asked, "Can we stop?"

"Here? Now?"

"Some place quiet, off the road."

"So we can…?" She couldn't bring herself to say "make out," although that's what she meant.

He nodded. "You had me worried there for a while. And then you didn't want to talk to me. I just want to be sure it's you here, for real. I didn't imagine everything."

"No, you did not." She looked ahead on the highway, signs for gas, restaurants, and a Motel 6.

"We could stop there," she said, suddenly overtaken by a racing excitement. She had wanted him all this time, but made herself not think of him, or them together. That was a distraction and a complication. But now it just felt real.

Erik had pulled off the exit and they sat at a red light.

"Really?"

She nodded. "I know, crazy. But there's no putting this genie back in the bottle, for better or worse. No one's waiting up for us; I'll see Izzy in the morning. Let's do it."

They pulled into the parking lot, almost empty, and checked in under Erik's name. With the midweek special, the rate was less than forty dollars.

In room 203, they put on the lights and pulled open the bedcovers. Helene needed a moment to pee and wash up, and then Erik splashed some water on his face and hands.

They met at the side of the bed and embraced. He was already excited; she could feel his erection through his jeans.

"I don't think I've ever been so glad to see someone as I am glad to see you," she said, holding one of his hands.

"Really?" he said, in a way that was both elated and doubtful. "You didn't look all that happy to see me back at the house."

She laughed. "It was a shock, and I pretty much knew the gig was up."

He looked puzzled. "I don't know; it looked like kind of a friendly get-together. What was he doing there, anyway, if you were supposed to be in some kind of seclusion at your friend's house?"

Helene sighed, looking down at their joined hands. "For my birthday; he brought me a little present."

Erik pulled back, wide-eyed. "No shit. Even after you left him?" He shook his head. "He's a better man than I am."

"Probably," she agreed, and then, rubbing the back of his hand: "But not better for me."

"Are you sure about that?"

"I am."

"So you think I also have some good qualities?" He gestured between the two of them with his free hand. "Besides this, I mean."

"No more questions," she said lightly. "Are you ready, m'sieur?"

"Yes, ma'am, I am."

The next morning Helene headed next door; both front doors were locked. She went around to the back, finding the slider to the deck open, and walked into Malvina's kitchen. From there she followed the hallway to the other part of the house where Izzy and Neesa lived, through an open door. She'd never been in this side before, which was brighter and more contemporary than she expected, considering Neesa's traditional ways.

Then she heard the buzz and pings of an electronic game, and called out. "Izzy?"

No answer.

She had to call a second time, getting closer to the open bedroom doorway, but not wanting to enter – he was, after all, a twenty-one-year-old with some right to privacy.

Then the electronic noise came to a halt. "Yeah, here. Is that you, Helene?"

"Yes."

"Prepare yourself."

That didn't sound good at all.

Izzy was on the side of his bed, a controller in his lap, facing the screen. Over his shoulders he wore a large towel like a shawl. A few comic books and magazines were scattered on the bed, along with popsicle wrappers. When he turned she saw a white bandage tented over his nose, and two puffy purply-red eyes – from the broken nose. She should have known. His hair was a mess, cut in jagged shanks and clearly not washed for a few days.

"Izzy! Look at you."

She wanted to put her arms around him, but he held up a hand – protecting himself or resisting her pity, or both.

"Definitely not pretty," he agreed. He shifted on the bed, and the towel slid off, revealing the large bandage on one side of his rib cage. The medicine bag hung from his neck, a recent repair to the cord in front. He was slender to begin with, and she could see the bony outline of shoulders and ribs. Helene felt a sudden pang of pity and anger. She gulped back an exclamation.

Izzy stared back at her through narrowed eyes. "Look at you," he echoed. The long scar on her arm, and her new short haircut – she too had changed.

"I know," she laughed without humor. "The two of us, wounded warriors." And then, "Oops, is that OK to say? I should say 'bandage buddies,' or something."

He shrugged. "It's all good."

But it wasn't good at all.

She sat on the bed next to him, but not too close. He smiled but then winced as she helped place the towel back on his shoulders. On the wall behind him were posters: Star Trek, of course, the new series and the old. Captain Kirk, Mr. Spock, Sulu, and Uhura were some of Denis's heroes – and part of her childhood, too.

"Erik had his doubts," Izzy said, a bit smugly. "But I knew you would come."

"For you, Izzy, and that magic you cast over everyone. No, really, I know that you are part of how Renee fit into this family, and now me too. You're the guy who came up to the cabin with Denis, or I might not be here at all."

For a moment he was quiet, and then he gestured to his bruised eyes. "Purple and pink, right? You know that fancy shawl Wishi-ta wears?"

"Yes."

"It was Neesa's and I fell in love with it. I was wearing it when I first met Renee. She said to me, 'Those colors look good on you.' She could see me for who I was, even back then, without judgment. I learned to grass dance when I was young and I still love it. But I hope someday I'll wear a shawl and do the fancy shawl dance. Do you know what I mean?"

"I think so," she said. "Yes, I do."

"But now I need you to help me."

"Anything, Izzy, that I can do for you. Just ask."

"I don't want the family to fuss about this. I want them to think it was a just a bike accident, me falling off and hurting myself."

Helene was surprised. She knew Izzy would want to avoid conflict, unlike Louis. But this was an act of violence, likely a criminal matter.

"Izzy, that's not right. I mean, those people have to be accountable for what they did."

"It was a stupid altercation. They were mad at me because their truck got damaged, because of me."

"That's no reason to beat you up. An accident, like you said, on your part, but it's a crime what they did to you: assault."

"I'll recover."

"It doesn't matter. They could do it to someone else." And then Helene realized that maybe they wouldn't do it to someone else, maybe it was because of Izzy: his skin, or his hair, or his, well, style.

"But Izzy, it's not going to work. I can't help you cover, not really. Your hair, why would it be cut?"

"I know," he said in frustration. "I don't know how to explain that, not any way they're going to buy. The thing is, I'm ready to go, to leave here for a while, and it's going to be so hard for Neesa, and the rest of them, especially after this."

"Leave? Not really?"

"Not so far and not forever. And not because of what happened. I've been thinking about it for a while now, the last couple years. I want to experience something besides here and the Home Camp, to live in a city like Boston. I started making a plan and saving up some money. One of my friends has already moved, and I'd have a place to stay. But then I didn't feel I could go after Renee died, and then Louis went to prison, and then Malvina and Noel had so much on their hands. But things are different now, since the baby is born and Wishi-ta is so much better – and since you've been here."

"I see." Helene nodded, although she hadn't really taken it seriously before, this desire to take flight, just some of his wry banter. Maybe she should have.

"You understand what I mean?"

"I do. And I think your family would too."

He sighed. "Maybe they would have – but now, since this." He tapped the white beak over his nose. "Neesa will live in fear every day, wondering what will happen to me, being the way I am."

"Indian, you mean?" Helene started, and then stopped. "Or..." How should she put it? "Between, ah..."

"Gay? Trans? Bi-? Something like that?"

She blushed. "Bisexual." She tried out the word. It wasn't so hard to say, just so odd-sounding, clinical, like a diagnosis. How strange her world was becoming. Like a dream – or waking up from a dream.

"That's one word for it," he said. "There's others. Natives sometimes say 'two spirit'; and that's just another category, not bad or good."

She nodded, taking this in. "Izzy, I'll support you, whatever I can. I can make sure you get back to health and you get legal aid for this assault. But more than that...? Do you think the family can accept me back, after what I've done? They must hate me."

"No one hates you," Izzy said. "Yeah, the deception hurt. And it was a betrayal of trust to take a risk with no kind of safety net." He stopped, considering his words. "But the truth is, while you were gone, no one really worried; we didn't know to. By the time everyone knew, we had already found you. The kids never knew about it until Malvina told them – very simply – that you'd stopped for a few days on the way north, and you had an accident. Obviously it would have been different if things turned out differently."

"You really think so...that's how they see it?"

"The family, they understand, I think, how strongly you feel. And they can see how well Wishi-ta's been doing with you, and how much she loves you. She misses you now; every time I talk to her on the phone, she asks for you. They know that; they don't want to keep you from her. They're just afraid you might do it again, and disappear forever."

"I won't!" Helene said, twisting on the bed, knocking off a Star Trek fan magazine. "I don't want to take her away from Tana-na and you, and everyone else. I know her life is here, and I just want to be part of it, not the aunt at a far distance. I'm not completely sure yet what I want, just that there's something about this community that appeals to me, maybe like Renee." She sighed. "I just hope I didn't spoil it. I know there are people here who don't like me, or accept me. I can't even blame it on them distrusting white people; this is on me, what I did."

"I'll speak for you," Izzy said. "And Elsa will, and Bernice. And Erik too." He waited a moment to see her reaction.

"Ah, yes," she murmured. "Erik. There's that too." Then, quickly, a diversion. "So what happened, Izzy, with the bike? Can you tell me? The real story?"

He held up a hand. "Not now. I don't have it in me, the energy, you know?"

She couldn't argue with him, even if he was just putting her off.

"OK. But I would like to know, when you're ready. Before too long and…" She trailed off, seeing his face close up. "So what can I do for you now? Can I look at the dressings, see if anything needs to be changed?"

He smiled. "Sure. Why not?"

"After that, I'll leave you in peace. OK?"

Izzy slumped forward, letting the towel fall away. "Let's do this."

Helene went back to Renee's house, going through the files she had been gathering on adoption law. She had the papers spread across the kitchen table: paper-clipped notes and photocopies. Whatever the family's position, it would be good to know the law and to understand what was ultimately the best situation for herself, the twins, and the family. She opened the file on Louis: his background and character, as the lawyer had suggested; some early scrapes with the law and delinquent credit card bills. There were unpaid medical bills for Renee, but she couldn't find it in her heart to use any of it against him. Nothing in Renee's journals indicated Louis was anything but a good father, a loving father, if on the road a lot, absent physically from his family. Certainly he was not the only parent in that position; just think of the military families. Better that she negotiate in good faith, if it came to it. She turned to other files. After a short while, reading through case histories of children of the imprisoned or the insane, she found it too depressing to go on.

She peeked outside, looking for signs of life during the weekday, but it was quiet; little street traffic and no bikes or barks or children's voices. Clouds were hanging low in the sky, and a wind kicked up, tossing the branches of the few maple trees. She saw a red truck turn into the street, and exclaimed, "Oh, yes!" before she realized it was not Erik but Wilton, Alberta's grandson who lived with her on the base. As he passed she saw all the Native American bumper stickers – not the spiritual kind: "Illegal Immigrants since 1492," "Remember Wounded Knee," "The Only Good White Man Is…" and similar. She gathered he was involved in Native activism, as Louis had been, although his group was more overtly political. Bernice had told her that Wilton and Louis had butted heads a few times, but not lately. Wilton had become a Louis supporter since he'd gone off to prison.

The truck passed, Wilton staring straight ahead. Otherwise, nothing going on out there.

Helene took out the box of Renee's journal pages, sorted into in chronological order. She had made progress with the earlier entries, but others were more scattered and incomplete. Many entries jumped back and forth in time. With each new page, she had to steel herself to face whatever Renee described in such unflinching detail. A lot of it was not pretty. Part of her was on the lookout for whatever Renee might have written about their own family life growing up and about Helene herself.

After a while restlessness set in, and Helene thought about talking a walk around the neighborhood. Rain was threatening, but not for a while. It might clear her mind to get outside for a bit. She lowered the windows in case a storm came up, leaving just a crack for air. She was gone maybe half an hour when the sky began to spit. Almost as soon as she walked in the door, the phone rang.

It was Izzy, and he was waiting for her.

"I just stepped inside," she told him.

"I know. I saw you. I'm ready now, if you want to come over."

Helene glanced around. Papers were still spread out all over the living room and kitchen, but there was nothing to disturb them, no kids, no cats. No reason to delay – and risk Izzy changing his mind.

"OK, I'll be right over."

She grabbed her purse and phone and headed for Izzy's. She found him upright at the kitchen table, like a prince awaiting his audience. He had put out two glasses and a pitcher of iced tea. She took a bottle of Tylenol out of her purse and shook out two for him, since he wouldn't take Percocet. It was important that he take full breaths, no matter how painful his broken ribs.

"So," Helene said, taking a seat as he swallowed the pills. "Go ahead. Tell me about this so-called bicycle accident."

He took a long, slow breath, weighing words, his long fingers sweeping the table absently. "Like I said, it was more or less random, a couple of guys in a truck with out-of-state plates. I was riding my bike home from work, hardly any traffic, sort of weaving back and forth across the road. The truck pulled out of a side road coming toward me, and there I was wheeling away, having a good old time for myself. I guess I didn't get out of the way fast enough and they had to swerve around me. So they ended up hitting the guard rail pretty hard, scraping metal. Meanwhile I kept going on my merry way; didn't realize. Guess they didn't like that." He squinted to remember. "They turned the truck around, honking the horn like crazy and shouting out the window. By that time I figured out they were pretty mad, so I hopped off the bike onto the grass on the side of the road, ready to dodge. Then they stopped the truck and jumped out, the two of them, and caught up with me."

Now the words were flowing more easily; he was seeing it all again clearly, his battered face alight with the relish of storytelling.

"'See that?' one of them said; he was pointing at the scrapes and the dent on the truck. 'You're going to pay for that,' the other guy said. He had a knife on his belt. He took it off and opened it, going for my bike tires. But I was standing between him and the bike, and I said to him, 'Not my trusty steed. This was an accident, and no fault of his.' At that point the other guy grabbed me by the shirt. Very strong; I wasn't getting away from

him. He pushed me to the ground, while the first one slashed the tires."
Izzy made a slashing motion – just so.

"Then that guy turned on me with the knife, but he didn't actually
want to kill me. He started cutting off parts of my hair, while the other one
held me down. But I wriggled around so much that the knife slipped, and
the guy cut his own hand, so now there was blood on all of us. That's when
the second one stood up and kicked me in the ribs. I rolled away, getting
on my knees and then on my feet. I had an idea how to slow them down, so
I picked up my bike and flung it, hitting the first guy in the knees. Well,
that stopped him, but not the other one, who caught up to me and landed a
punch – on the nose." He paused, dramatically, lifting a finger to his nose.
"As you see."

He was in his element, editing and revising some of the story line, no
doubt. But who the men were and what they looked like, he didn't say.

"Poor Izzy," Helene murmured, gazing at the damage. But then she
rallied. "That's an assault, two of them on you. And battery, with the knife
and with a foot. But cutting your hair like that…" She shook her head. "I
don't know. That's something else. I can understand why it would be hard
for Neesa, for all them, to have you go off like that, and not be able to
protect you." Her hands worked in her lap, uncertain again.

Then he smiled, the pained Izzy smile. "But really, is there any
guarantee of protection, no matter where you are? Or what you do? This
happened here, between Costco and home."

She had to agree. Right in home territory.

"How did you get home without your bike?"

"I walked part of the way. And then the mother of one of my friends
drove by, and she stopped. She took me to the clinic, so I called Elsa. She
sent Erik to meet me there. That's when I asked him about contacting you."

"And you thought he'd know?" A leading question.

"I thought he'd find out, and he did."

"So right now no one up at the Home Camp knows this, the truth."

"Not the whole truth. They know I'm injured. We'll do a sweat when
they get back, when I'm a little better. That's part of the healing process."

"Will you go to the police?"

He averted his gaze, seeming to watch the fast-moving clouds through
the deck slider door "I don't know yet. I have…doubts. Doubts that it will
lead to anything good. A bit of my brother in me, I guess."

She stared, willing him to understand how important it was, how
necessary. But she couldn't force it. Better to leave it for the moment. He
looked so weakened, the flame of his spirit down to a flicker. In need of
care, protection.

"Are you OK, Izzy?" she asked. "Really?"

Hers had also been a physical injury, and to some extent she'd been
caught out for an impulsive, emotional decision. But he was attacked, at

least in part, for who he was.

He wouldn't take the bait, or the pity. "Are you?"

She couldn't hold back a wry grin. "Getting better."

"Me, too."

Helene got up from the table. "Will you let me take a picture or two?"

The brown eyes narrowed.

"For my sake," she said. "In case you decide later…"

He shrugged, reluctant. "All right, I guess."

"Hold up," Helene said, suddenly energized. "Here's an idea. I'll get my camera and a pair of scissors. We'll do a before and after shot. You need a trim just to even out your hair, give it some kind of shape. Not too short, I promise. And then I can shampoo you at the sink." She turned, looking. "We'll put a towel in front of your ribs and I'll use the spray nozzle." She paused, assessing the extensive bandaging. "How about that?"

Izzy didn't answer, but his shoulders rose and fell.

"Trust me?"

He nodded. "I hope so."

After a few quick pictures, Helene had Izzy lean over the sink, padded with towels while she washed his hair, a pretty wet affair in spite of being careful. After the trim she had to press for a couple more pictures, front and back, naked from the waist up. When they were done, Izzy looked exhausted, although he said he enjoyed the "head massage." She felt bad about pushing him. But it might be important; no, it was important. Finally she released him back to his room, while she cleaned up. Outside there was a sudden downpour, but it passed quickly, and was barely sprinkling when she left for Renee's house, hoping to catch a rainbow where the sun was streaming through the parting clouds.

Once she stepped inside, she was puzzled to see the adoption files she'd left on the kitchen table scattered and spread out, not as she'd left them in a pile. She had closed the windows most of the way before leaving. If the papers hadn't been blown by the wind, then what else? She stacked them again and put them away, feeling her neck prickle. Someone had been in the house while she was out. The living room confirmed it, as she went to gather Renee's journal pages. Most of them were paper-clipped in bunches and ready to go in the box, with one stack unclipped, some of the pages on the floor – she wouldn't have left them that way.

Spooked, she looked around the rest of the house. Nothing out of place that she could tell. Only the papers. But who would have done this? Rapidly, she went through the names of anyone who might have reason, might be looking for something. No one. Yet, she could not dismiss the feeling of violation. No matter the custom on the base, she would start locking up when the house was empty. And, from now on, the papers would stay out of sight; one of the craft boxes would work.

Later Helene called Erik, just back from his workday. She needed to talk to him, about a number of pressing things. But not about the mussed-up papers. People had been known to walk into an unlocked house. Someone could have been looking for her and just peeked at the papers out of curiosity. Maybe it was better to hold off on saying anything, not to look for trouble where it might not exist. A voice whispered in her head: not paranoid, not some crazy person.

"Can you come over?" she asked. "I'll make supper."

"Supper?"

"Yes, actual food on the back porch."

"And then?"

"We'll see. I have some business to talk about."

"Ah, business."

He came to the door, and more than ever Helene felt like a middle-schooler with a crush on a boy, being watched by all the adults.

"Come in," she said.

They took their plates to the screened-in porch, overlooking the backyards of the neighboring houses. The porch contained a card table, temporary, to put the food on, and a couple of folding sports chairs, not uncomfortable but hard to get out of gracefully. Since Noel had finished the porch, she had put up hummingbird feeders right outside, filling them with sugar water. Now the place was full of hummingbirds, coming and going at top speed.

"Well," Helene said, swallowing a last bite of chicken salad. "Since I don't have a car, I'll have to rent one until I can get mine back from Vermont – and that means another driver to go up and bring it back."

"Convenient for you, that's what I do." A few tomato seeds had fallen on his otherwise clean shirt, and droplets of lemonade adorned his mustache.

"It would be an overnight, most likely," Helene continued. "We could stay at the cabin."

Erik dabbed his lips with the cloth napkin. "OK, then, problem solved."

"There's something else. I have to make another trip back to Boston to pick up more clothes and things – at least something for when the weather turns cooler."

His placid expression turned puzzled. "And you need my help for that?"

"No, just your understanding. I will be seeing Kenneth. I have to. We have more things to discuss."

He nodded. Now that he'd seen Kenneth, she wondered what he thought. Kenneth had a presence, attractive and confident; he was well spoken and intelligent. An impressive rival, in another world. But not this one, as far as she was concerned.

"And the main thing," she said with a sigh. "Izzy."

"You got the story out of him?"

"A version. I think it's the truth, as far as he told me. He was assaulted by two men, who will probably get away with it if he doesn't report it to the police soon, before the bruises fade and evidence is lost." She exhaled. "I think it is probably a hate crime."

Erik blinked a couple times. "In general these folks don't like to get involved with the police. Mostly it doesn't go well. And Louis had a couple of bad run-ins with the last police chief. This new guy I don't know about. For the most part, there hasn't been any reason."

"OK. But there's still some responsibility, don't you think?"

"I'm not sure how much good it will do."

"I'm not sure, either. But I think it has to be reported. I told Izzy that. Of course he's reluctant. Not just because of feelings about the police. It's more than that. He says he wants to leave the base and move to the city. Live on his own for a while, or at least with a friend or friends." She waved a hand vaguely. "He wants me to help convince his family that it's OK, that he will be OK."

Erik sat back from the table, napkin in a ball, kale pushed to the side of his plate. "It can be a pretty shitty world out there," he said. "But I guess he has to find out for himself." He started to stretch, covering a yawn. "Is that it, then? Seems like plenty to think about." He glanced at her. "No? There's more?"

"Well, just about things here," she said. "With me, I mean. And, you, sort of. I don't know what's going to happen when the family comes back. I will have to talk to them and apologize for what I did. But I don't know if they will trust me again. Or if they'll let the twins stay here with me, like they did before. Or even if they'll want me to stay on here at all."

"But you want to stay?"

"I do. At least for now, for while I'm figuring things out. I don't know about long term, and I guess it depends how it goes with Neesa and Malvina and Noel. It's just…" She shook her head, oblivious to the hummingbirds at the feeder.

"What?"

"Louis. He seems set against me having a real role in Wishi-ta's upbringing, or Tana-na's. I understand some of the reasons he rejected my request for adoption, but things have changed, I've changed. And it's not fair that he judges me for certain ideas about how Indians have been treated, and doesn't see what I have to offer the twins, and the rest of the family. Like, if it's not his view, it can't be the right view."

"That's Louis," he said, nodding.

"There's no way he hasn't heard about what happened. But will he give me a chance to explain and consider what I'm truly like? And" – the words rushed out – "I'm not sure what Renee told him about me, exactly;

maybe some things that were not so good."

He gazed at her a long while. "My Lady of the Sorrows," he said finally. "It's not like I couldn't guess there's been something weighing on your heart for a long time. But that's your business, and I respect that."

"Thank you."

Suddenly the hummingbirds darted away, spooked. A rustle in the far bushes caught Helene's attention; she held up a finger. They looked into the dark thicket of brush, where a few leaves now flapped, maybe just the wind.

Erik pushed himself to his feet, peering. "Yeah, something's out there, just passing through, I'm sure."

Helene got to her feet too. "Red Cat, come back home, or to haunt us." She raised her eyebrows.

Erik looked back, smiling ruefully. "I'm afraid Red Cat's gone for good. Maybe a coyote? We've got those around here."

Helene's face clouded. "Oh, great, predators circling the house."

He gave her a curious look. "You're not afraid, are you? Being here alone. I mean, after what happened up north?"

"No, no," she scoffed. "Not afraid, just more jumpy, jittery over little things."

He took a step closer, putting his arms around her, nuzzling her neck.

"So is it loving you want, or just company out here on the porch?"

"Just you, here with me, like this. That's exactly what I need right now."

Chapter 20

Helene decided it was best to keep a low profile, while Izzy was recovering and before the family returned. She spent time with Izzy and changed his bandages, checking his wounds, which were healing well. Her own bumps and bruises were mostly gone, and she would go hours forgetting about the concussion, until a bright light or loud noise would cause a twinge in her head. Erik was working on a local carpentry project, but he mentioned a couple of upcoming truck jobs. Good money; the customers depended on him. Meanwhile, somewhere, he'd gotten his hands on a loaner car for Helene, a patched-up red sedan; it looked like some teen boy's "wheels" but drove well enough.

"A pinto," Izzy remarked, gazing out the front window.

"No, I don't think so," Helene said. "It's a Chevy Impala; doesn't look like much but apparently the engine is fine." She was trying to keep it light.

Izzy kept his post at the window. "I mean the speckling, the spots, like a pinto pony, not the old Ford Pinto."

She stared blankly.

He turned to her. "Indian humor. You know, car/horse, like the old days."

She looked again at the splotchy car and laughed. "That's pretty good."

Thelma called most evenings, checking on Helene's health and well-being, reporting on news in town. Jacob, her son, had returned from his summer program with an infected bug bite but was responding to antibiotics. He was leaving for college on the weekend – on his own, in his own car. Thelma had not seen Kenneth, although she had noticed more properties in her neighborhood with the telltale wooden pole supporting an electric line into homes that were going to be torn down. The name on the sign was "Brown and Bradford Redevelopment."

"Your scandal hasn't exactly hit the airwaves," she said. "It's not really news that makes the paper – what's going on with the two of you, and how you've gone away. You were away most of the summer, taking care of 'family business,' anyway. That's what I'm going to tell them when school starts." Then she went on to school news, staff meetings, new hires, all that. It looked like the former school nurse was coming back temporarily.

Helene laughed. "Yikes. There's a woman with no sympathy at all. But she is good in emergencies, I'll give her that."

She told Thelma about Izzy, and also talked about how she was continuing to spend time with Erik. Then she mentioned the borrowed car, and the planned trip north to get her own car, when Erik could commit to a time.

"Seems like you're taking on quite a bit."

"Isn't that good?"

"Hmm…well, Jacob leaves Sunday. After that I'd like to get up to the base to see you before school starts."

"That would be nice. But don't feel you have to…"

"Maybe I want to."

The second week after Helene's return, late in the afternoon, there was a knock on the screen door, left open for light and the breeze. In the kitchen Helene was preparing a chicken and apricot dinner for herself and Izzy. She looked up to see a short, familiar figure. *Bernice!*

Helene rinsed her hands, wiping them on a towel, and hurried to the door.

"Come in," she said. Although she was glad to see Bernice, a sheepish feeling lingered from over all that had transpired: leaving with Wishi-ta and goings-on with Erik, in spite of Bernice's cautionary words. Helene was taking the view that pretty much everyone knew everything at this point, except the details about Izzy.

"You OK?" Bernice asked, stepping inside with a berry pie in hand.

"Oh, fine," said Helene. "And you?"

"Me? There's nothing wrong with me except the usual. I mean about your head injury."

Helene touched her head. "Oh, that. I almost forgot. Much better, thank you. Only a little headache once in a while. I'm lucky it wasn't worse." And of course lucky that Izzy and Denis had found her and Wishi-ta when she was most incapacitated. But she didn't add that. Her hand went to her short-cropped hair. "And I got my hair cut shorter; it was easier to take care of the wound."

Bernice gave her a critical look. "Well, not too bad." She held out the pie. "Here. I made pies this morning. This is for you and Izzy; you can share." Of course. An act of kindness and community.

"Thank you, Bernice. I appreciate it. And you…well…coming here…"

Bernice didn't let her finish. "And to ask about Izzy, since you're helping him out." Oh, that, too. Checking up on the real story. "I understand he's been lying low. Elsa said he got hurt pretty bad."

There was the opening for Helene to say more, but she didn't. Instead she had a question of her own. "He's doing alright. So why are you still here and not at the Home Camp? Your daughter's family's gone, right?"

Bernice gave her a look, guarded and mysterious. "Well, yes and no. The older one is gone; now I've got Josie and her daughter.'

"How nice! They must enjoy visiting you."

"Hmph," Bernice said, and then, "She enjoys my dividend check is more like it."

This was mysterious business. "Dividend?" Helene asked. "You mean some kind of government....."

Bernice cocked her head, "Hand-out? Is that the word you want?"

"Uh, no. I meant payment of some kind. But Malvina said...."

Bernice shook her head. "Not government. It's business, Inupiaq business, and I'm a stakeholder in the corporation that manages our resources. And we made a profit – that's the dividend."

"Oh, I see. Sorry. I mean, that's good, so...."

"So, every few months Josie comes around, "'Ma, baby needs this, baby needs that'' The baby is almost three," Bernice said. "But I wish her mother would grow up." She blew out some air. "Josie; she was always my wild child. Lots of drama. Married, separated, back together two or three times, now they're getting divorced."

Helene nodded. Bernice did have a full family life, not always smooth. She recalled Bernice's remarks about her daughter's prior interest, or more, in Erik.

"Is he Native, the father?" she asked.

Bernice smiled. "Puerto Rican, from New York, and a long-suffering man, if you ask me. She's the problem, not him."

"I hope it all works out," Helene said sympathetically. "Anyway, I'm just about ready to put this chicken in the oven. If you give me a minute, we could sit out on the porch. A glass of wine?"

"No, I'm not staying. I just wanted to bring the pie, and tell you that on Thursday there's a potluck and a speaker, something about medicine and healing, the old-time ways. Indigenous knowledge," she pronounced carefully, followed by a meaningful pause. "That might be good to know."

"Oh." That was unexpected but rather interesting. Perhaps in reference to her nursing background? "Maybe. I mean, thank you for, ah, letting me know, I'll think about it. Thursday, you said?"

"Like always."

"Right."

"And bring Izzy too, if he'll come." Another pointed pause. "You can drive him if he can't walk the whole way."

Bernice spoke in the same matter-of-fact manner, but she was talking about the extent of Izzy's injuries and his need for assistance. Suddenly Helene's eyes were stinging over the brutality of Izzy's beating. No longer in the room with him, no longer a nurse in charge, she felt it like a blow. And so did Bernice, she could tell, but the answer was not to dissolve in tears, but to stay strong for him, for herself. She blinked the tears back.

"Thanks again, Bernice," she said at the doorway. "For the pie."

Bernice shrugged. "I'm here. You're here. Izzy needs something to fatten him up. Why not?"

"Maybe I'll bring you some of the chicken dish, later, if it turns out well," Helene said hopefully.

Bernice descended the two steps, waving a hand behind as she walked away.

The dinner was good and the mixed-berry pie was good, and Helene and Izzy sat out on the porch for a spell. Izzy couldn't yet play the flute because his lip was cut on the inside. But the "beak" was off now, and he looked presentable with his trimmed hair, since the bruises on his face had faded and those on his rib cage were out of sight. Helene put on an audiobook of *The Three Musketeers* she had gotten from the library, something to divert and entertain them both. Izzy listened with a small smile until his chin dropped onto his chest. Waking him gently, Helene said he could sleep in the twins' room, but he wanted to go back to his own bed and would allow no escort.

After Izzy left Helene had a restless evening, trying to read, working on some notes. Erik didn't come over until late. His building project was finished, and he had gone out for barbeque and beer with the guys; a celebration. But Helene was anxious to make plans now that he was free, at least temporarily, before the next trucking job. She met him at the door, turning on the overhead light, and could smell the alcohol on his breath as he stepped inside.

"Hey, there, sweetheart," he said, slurring his words a bit. She figured he was exhausted from the physical work, as well as the extra beers. It was maybe not the best time to bring up what was on her mind, but she pressed on, anyway. She returned to the sofa, clearing a spot for him, but he dropped down in the recliner with a groan.

"Do you think we could go north on Friday?" she asked. "I mean to the Home Camp? Just for the weekend, and then swing through Vermont to get my car. I'm up to it; it's not a bad drive from the cabin."

"Hmm," he murmured, not really answering. He was sunk into the chair, his legs splayed and his hands across his belly.

"I appreciate the loaner," she said quickly. "But I would prefer my own car. The air conditioning works, and it doesn't smell like turpentine."

That at least got a slow smile from him.

"It's just…" Helene started, then all the thoughts tumbled out. "I want to see the family. I have to face this, and apologize for what I did. I miss Wishi-ta and Tana-na, and the others. I'm sure that Wishi-ta misses me too, after all the time we spent together. She saw me in such bad shape. I can't stand to think of her worried, and feeling another loss. I want to make it as clear as I can," she said through gritted teeth, "that I want to stay on here, or in this area, and be part of her life, and their lives." She got up, starting to pace. "I need to know where things stand, and I have to do my best to convince them that I understand what I'm doing, and that I'm trustworthy." She stopped in front of him. "You understand that, right?"

He nodded without answering, and she wasn't sure he was following everything she was trying to say.

"I mean, the fact that Izzy asked for me, that means he wanted my help, and my presence here. But it's OK to go now. He's mending, and Elsa and Bernice will help him if he needs it. So the timing is good."

But Erik didn't agree right away. Then it didn't look like he was going to agree at all. He sat up with his hands on his knees.

"I don't think so, Helene. Sorry about the car, but you'll have to stick it out."

"It's not the car!" she exclaimed. "I was just teasing. We can skip that if there's not enough time. I want to deal with this uncertainty and fix the problem, so that we all can all move forward."

He sighed, not a hopeful sign. "I think it's better to wait. You can't just hurry them into this. It's not about proving something; it's about time."

"Time?" She made herself pause, shading her eyes from the overhead light that was hurting her eyes. "But how much time has to go by before I know if they accept me? And meanwhile, what about Wishi-ta's welfare, and starting school, all that? Now there's more of them, not fewer, and Izzy's, uh, out of commission for a while." She refrained from mentioning Izzy's active plans to move; that could wait.

"They'll manage."

She stared at him, willing him to wake up, react. "That's not good enough. Managing is getting by, not thriving. Can't you see how much better Wishi-ta has been this summer?"

"Yes, and they see that too."

Helene felt the agitation growing. Maybe this was the side of Erik that Bernice had referred to – his avoiding responsibility and hard decisions.

She came to stand right over him, noticing the sauce stains down the front of his shirt. And now she could smell the smoke and the beer emanating from him. Not appealing.

"I don't know why you're not supporting me in this – when I'm telling you how important it is."

He shrugged.

"OK, fine," she said in a strange voice that she would never have used with Kenneth. "I'll see if I can get someone else to take me. Or I'll pay someone if I have to." It was kind of a false claim. She could ask around, but who was free last minute like that? And she might pay someone at the garage to drive the car down from Vermont, but she was not likely to get anyone to drive her to the Home Camp.

And then, in a cold voice. "Are you really not going to help me?"

He closed his eyes, seemingly to gather energy, and then opened them again. "I don't think that's going to help." Then, with some effort, he got to his feet, swaying a little. A sad, shadowed look came into his eyes. "I'm sorry to disappoint you. There are other things I'm dealing with right now. I should know about my next job in a day or so. Maybe we can squeeze in getting the car; maybe not. But I don't have time to go to Maine, and I don't think you should, either."

Helene stood, stunned, unable to decide whether his objections were genuine or whether he was slithering away from a difficult situation.

"I'll think I'll go," he said.

She could have said something, but the words were stuck in her throat. Maybe better that he did go, for her and for him.

"OK, then. Good night."

"We'll talk tomorrow," he said softly. "When I'm better rested. You know how to reach me."

He left, closing the door softly behind him, walking slowly and carefully down the block where he let himself in to Elsa and Chief's house, like an overgrown boy.

The next morning Helene woke to a warm day, close and muggy. She rolled onto her back, gaze on the ceiling, trying out different scenarios about making the trip north. In her heart she knew she should not go alone; it was too big a risk. She would call Denis, just to see where he was, assuming he was not in the Northeast. She could try Thelma, who would welcome a road trip, ordinarily. But she still had Jacob with her, at least until Sunday. The truth was there was no one she could ask who would both retrieve the car and drive all the way to the Home Camp and back. She was stuck unless Erik came around. Maybe he had just been overtired and drunk. She rolled to her side, facing the window, and found herself still angry and upset. Maybe it wasn't fair to expect him to come to her aid; and yet he had pursued her, encouraged her. He was the one who'd found her at Thelma's and brought her back to the base. So why back away now? What else could it be?

She was not ready to call and talk to him, if he were even awake. Instead she dressed and went next door with a cup of coffee and the leftover pie. Izzy was at the table eating cornflakes and cinnamon toast. The radio was on, more or less a country station, with lively, upbeat music. His hair was tousled and the ripped, oversized T-shirt made him look even younger, but he seemed more comfortable, relaxed.

"Hey, lady." Izzy looked up with a smile. "What you got there?"

She was about to put the pie in the refrigerator.

"How about we have some of that?"

"Now?"

"Why not?"

She cut two slices, one for her, one for him, and poured him some milk, while she had her coffee.

"Can't beat it," he said happily, taking a bite. And then, glancing up:

"Something on your mind?"

"No," she said. And then, "Well, yes. Kind of. Anyway, nothing for you to be concerned about. I'm going to the library this morning, not too long. Do you want to come, just for an outing?"

"I can't."

She took the bait. "You can't? Allergic to books, or what?"

"No, I'm waiting for Denis's song to come on the radio – this is Bluegrass Hour." He smirked. "At least it's just an hour. I'm more of a hip-hop fan, myself."

"Denis's song! No way!" Helene exclaimed, slapping the table. She hadn't heard a word about it. "How did you find out?"

"Denis; he left a message on the machine. It might or might not come on. But I'm not doing anything, so why not wait and see. It's called *'Shenandoah Springtime.'*" He looked at her expectantly.

"Good for him," Helene said. And then, more to herself than Izzy, she added, "If my dad could hear this, wow."

Izzy had finished the pie, as well as cereal and toast, pleasing her with this sign of his appetite returning.

"Raj is coming by later," he announced, licking some crumbs. His best friend, tall, dark, slim, an Asian Indian clone of Izzy. When Helene had met Raj the first time, her jaw dropped: she had thought his name was short for Roger. "We're going to work on my bike," Izzy was saying. "Then an afternoon movie and McDonald's; I'm jonesing for a Big Mac."

Helene smiled briefly. This Raj, though raised Hindu, was not strictly vegetarian.

Another song came on the radio, also lively and full of fiddles, but it was an old bluegrass favorite, according to the disc jockey, "Fox on the Run" by Blue Heaven.

"I don't think I'll wait; I'm sure I'll catch it later," Helene said, rinsing the dishes in the sink. "You know about the Thursday potluck, right? Bernice told me the program is on Native medicine and healing. You want to go?" She paused, surveying his face. "You're ready to be seen: puffiness is gone, and under your eyes are just shades of gray now. Lucky for you to have that darker skin."

He rolled his eyes. "Yeah, lucky me."

A fair jab. "You know what I mean." She went on, in a tempting tone, "I'll make that fancy mac and cheese. What do you say?"

He smacked his lips. "I do like mac and cheese."

Helene spent a lot longer at the library than she expected to. In the computer room, the reference librarian helped her access some of the law websites, searching on guardianship and adoption, relative to a parent in jail. Of course it was easiest if the parent consented. She was ready to do everything in her power to convince Louis, all of them, that it was truly best for her to care for the twins. Even so, if a certain amount of time went by and there was no contact, the parent gave up some rights. She also looked up information on ICWA – the Indian Child Welfare Act, to keep Native children within their communities, but it didn't seem to apply since the Lopes and Marshall families didn't belong to a federally recognized tribe, and the intertribal community at the base was just an informal arrangement. Then again, some of the language wasn't clear to Helene; or, as Louis had said, things might be different in "Indian Country."

The rest of the time she spent looking up hate crimes and assault cases. There was a lot to learn, but she thought much of the information related to Izzy's case. Maybe he could be persuaded to act.

The day passed quickly. She stopped a couple of times for breaks, stretching her legs, eating an apple in the lobby. She thought about calling Erik, but the library wasn't an ideal place to talk on the phone. Late afternoon there was a tremendous thunderstorm, which she enjoyed from the safety of the library, one of those older brick buildings with winding passages and many small rooms, plus the modern addition in the back. She didn't leave until after five o'clock. By then she was hungry, with no plan for dinner. Izzy was out with Raj. She thought again of calling Erik, but some niggling doubt, pesky suspicion, kept her from dialing his number. It would be dinner alone.

At the base Erik's truck was not parked in front of Elsa and Chief's house, whatever that meant. She showered and changed into a T-shirt and shorts, taking out the file on adoption to review. She fell asleep on the sofa, lights on. It was almost two o'clock in the morning when she woke again, and got up to look out the window. No truck. Suddenly she was sad and mad, both. Why wasn't he there? Where else could he be? True, he had said, "You know how to reach me." But he could have called. She got out her cell phone: no missed calls or messages. It seemed like he was just gone. Impulsively, she pressed his number. Then, as suddenly, she ended the call, closing her eyes. Tomorrow. Maybe he'd call by then. Or, she could try again, calmly, no panic – just checking in.

The next morning, no truck. Then she did call him, but he didn't pick up and she didn't leave a message. She couldn't, she wouldn't, call Elsa to ask. She really wasn't worried. He had business to take care of, so he'd said. Maybe he'd gone on an overnight trip with a friend to fish somewhere; he did that sometimes. Maybe, possibly, he'd started on the trucking job, but it didn't seem likely.

When she stopped in to see Izzy, he was in the shower, so she didn't stay. He came by afterward, waiting for Raj again; they were going to Walmart. Helene started to ask about Erik, but she couldn't do it. After Izzy left she gave herself a pep talk, how silly it was to get upset about something so vague and up in the air to begin with: his plans, her plans, and their whole relationship. However, she was pretty sure that he would not be driving her up north; maybe that's what he was trying to avoid.

The previous day at the library, she had picked up a newspaper to search the employment pages; she could also look online for nursing jobs. She had already called the hospital where they'd taken Cree; it didn't handle major accidents or surgeries, but it was clean, well staffed, and fairly up to date. The Human Resources woman said they were not hiring permanent staff, but they could always use per diem nurses. Helene heard that a nurse at the nearby health clinic was going out on maternity leave, so she put in an application there.

Again the day passed quickly enough; still no call from Erik. And when she did try to reach him, the phone rang and rang but didn't go to voicemail. That's when she began to think he was back on the road, had taken one of those long-haul jobs. She could not in fairness be upset with him; only that he hadn't told her. Or perhaps he kind of did. She sat back on the sofa, squeezing a pillow in her lap, no longer mad except at herself, but more sad, recalling she had not been kind to him when he'd come over, tired and beat, and relaxed with the beer.

Again it was Bernice who appeared at her door, before supper, with bunches of basil, rosemary, and mint from her garden. Her long braids lay over a light summer blouse, and she wore a half apron.

"Thank you!" Helene said, taking the herbs. "Let me give you some of Neesa's peppers and green beans." A bowl of fresh-picked vegetables sat by the kitchen window. Someone else, maybe Izzy, had tended the garden while she was gone, but she was now back to watering and weeding, ever aware of her missing helpers, Wishi-ta and Tana-na.

"I wanted to tell you," she said to Bernice. "I'm planning to go to the potluck. Izzy too. I think he's ready."

"Fine," said Bernice, who was rinsing the herbs at the sink. "Is he walking OK?"

"Sure. The ribs are mostly healed."

"Then maybe you can help Elsa and Chief bring over some of the materials for the program. Chief's on a cane these days."

"Happy to." Helene said, glad for these openings, these signs that she was still included.

"Since Erik's not here," Bernice said neutrally, patting the herbs dry and wrapping them in damp paper towels. "For a while."

"Oh," Helene said. And then, "A while?"

"Back in a week or so, Elsa says. Maybe more." Bernice went on, speaking over her shoulder. "We'll have to do without him." By which she probably meant, *You'll have to do without him.*

Helene must have been frowning.

"What's the problem?" Bernice asked, turning to face her.

"Nothing," Helene said hurriedly. "It's just, well, I had asked him about going north with me to get my car, and he said he would try. But now I don't think so. You may be right," she said. "He's not the most reliable character." She tried to make it light. "Remember what you said: charming, but doesn't stick around?"

Bernice stood hands on hips, directing her gaze at Helene. "He has a good heart," she said, pointedly. "I think he means to keep his word." She came to a full stop, looking away. But she was not done. "He has some things to take care of away, personal stuff. And the man has to work, you know. That's considered a good thing around here."

Helene was taken aback. He had mentioned about seeing his son more often, working things out with the boy's mother. She had been too focused on her own concerns to remember. And she still didn't really understand how things worked around here.

"You can steep some of that mint in a tea for Izzy," Bernice said, taking a few of the vegetables from the bowl. "And for you too."

"Thank you, Bernice," Helene said. Humbly. Gratefully.

The next day, Izzy came to the house bearing news. Louis had asked Noel and Malvina to bring Neesa and the kids to the prison before they returned to the base. He was ready to see them, and to have them see him.

Helene had just poured the hot water for tea. Her hand jerked and she almost knocked over the cup. "All of them, the children? To prison?"

"Yes."

"He thinks it's OK for the twins?"

"It's time, I guess." Izzy shrugged. "They'll come back here afterward, to get the kids ready for school. Sometimes we go back a couple times in the fall, for special gatherings and celebrations."

"I see." Helene had so many questions – about school, health, adoption – but wasn't ready to share her thoughts. Wasn't sure how much to share. Carefully she placed the hot cup in front of Izzy, and then went to stand behind her chair, unable to sit.

"He wants to talk to them about you."

"Me?" Her stomach clenched. "You mean about what happened, and about where I am now?"

He nodded, leaning over to blow on his tea. "They are his children, and this is his house."

"I know! I know! But he's in prison, and may not be out for twenty years."

Again Izzy nodded. "The lawyers are working on appeals, but that may be true."

The wind had gone out of Helene's sails, and she just didn't have the desire or energy to pursue arguments with Izzy. She brought over her own cup and pulled out the chair. Maybe it was time for the twins to see their father; how would she really know?

"OK," she said at last. "Let them pass judgment on me. I deserve it."

She sipped her tea, still burning. "So, anyway, how is everyone doing – the twins, Cree, the new baby?"

"Good," Izzy said. "Everyone's good. Healthy again, having a great time up there with all the kids running around. Lots of swimming and eating, campfires, singing and dancing, all that good stuff. Neesa's trying to teach some of the old language, but that's not going too fast, I guess. No, all fine, sorry for summer to end, except..."

"Except what?"

He gave that slow, otherworldly smile. "Wishi-ta misses you, and asks for you. And the other kids want to you to see how they've learned to swim and dive – show off, you know. Every afternoon they're supposed to spend time working on regalia. Wishi-ta is making a bracelet for you."

Even bruised and battered, Izzy had a sweetness and light about him, and quality of acceptance and ease that Helene could not really describe or explain. She had nothing more to say. What he had told her was enough. She would wait until she saw them all again. Whatever Louis said, and his conditions and concerns. Izzy was telling her there was a place in the family for her. That it didn't have to be a fight.

"One more thing," he said, before getting up to leave. "Denis's song – I heard it."

"Oh." And then, mustering a bit of excitement: "Oh! Great. How was it?"

"Not bad at all, if you like that kind of thing. They say it's going to be a hit. His head will be so large he won't be able to fit into the room."

Helene managed the smallest of smiles.

Chapter 21

Helene went about her day with a degree of calm in her heart and a hope that things were going to work out. Erik should be back before long, with some reasonable explanation for his extended silence. Probably the family at the Home Camp would keep in mind the help and the goodwill she had already shown. It wasn't until Thelma called in the evening that she found her throat closed up, and she was unable to speak, until sobs started to come, and she managed to rasp in between, "I'm sorry. I'm sorry." There was a lot she was sorry for, pain she had caused, and pain she had not stopped, but she was also sorry that she couldn't say anything intelligible to Thelma.

"It's OK," Thelma said from her modest home three hours away, surrounded by her somber photos and brightly colored curtains and throw blankets. "It really is. And you're OK too. You're going to be fine. So here's the story. Tomorrow we'll talk and you can tell me what's going on. Call me first thing in the morning. I'll try to come the next day and stay overnight. Whatever it is, we'll work it out. OK?"

"OK," Helene croaked.

"And you'll rely on your inner strength until then. OK?"

"OK."

Helene was able to sleep through the night, waking to a bright morning, which made her feel foolish about the phone call, or not-call, to Thelma. She took her time through breakfast and showering, and then sat down with her phone at the kitchen table. That's when she noticed a voicemail from Erik. It had come in the night – sometime after the phone call from Thelma. She must have been soundly asleep not to hear it – or because it was in her purse in another room. But when she checked the message, there was only static and garbled words. Her impulse was to call back immediately, but she stopped herself. She would call Thelma first, not just because she was probably waiting, but also to prepare for whatever was coming next.

The phone rang only a couple times before Thelma answered.

"Ah, you," she said. "Is it a good morning?"

Helene chuckled, still a bit embarrassed. She twisted away from the slanting morning light, coming right into her eyes. "Better, thanks. Yeah, definitely better. I guess I was tired; I slept like a log."

"All that crying," Thelma said. "Sometimes it really does help. So…you want to tell me the cause of your present sorrow?"

"Well, sorrows," Helene said, and explained about the falling out, so to speak, with Erik, and then Izzy's announcement of the family going to visit Louis in prison.

"Hmm," Thelma said. Helene could picture her in the now-familiar kitchen, small but cozy, home for almost thirty years. "Prison? That's quite the family vacation. Anyway, that's got you upset?"

"Yes, he's going to get their side of the story, about what happened with me and Wishi-ta. And I'm afraid that will make him even less accepting of me, or even letting the twins stay with me in the house."

"Perhaps. Maybe that's not all bad; maybe that's a fairly responsible thing to do."

Helene wanted to argue that Louis had this negative, unfair view of her. But then she wasn't sure. She wasn't even sure if Malvina had initiated the first contact, about Wishi-ta's allergy crisis, or if it had been prompted by Louis. She tried to visualize the family driving to the prison and then waiting in the visitor's room – white, bright, and sterile, those few sad toys and books for children.

"I hate that it's prison," she said. "But I'm glad the twins will get to see their father – and he can see them and how well they're doing. Plus the cousins, of course. He said he wanted to wait until he was transferred closer; I guess he changed his mind."

"Sometimes things change," Thelma said, "in ways we don't expect. Not much you can do until they get back, anyway. Right?"

"I guess not."

"OK, then. That's that. And Erik, you think it's a serious split?"

Helene considered, running a hand through her newly short hair. It still felt odd, something missing. And a lot cooler. "No, not really. More of a misunderstanding. It's only a week or so, one of the women told me." She didn't want to say anything about the garbled voicemail. Yes, that had come from him; but he could have been saying anything, including. "Good-bye. Don't call me anymore."

"I'm sorry I was such a basket case last night," Helene said. The sunlight had illuminated smudges on the window ledge, small fingerprints and large. A place to wipe down, she thought automatically. And then, No, those are remnants of the twins, or Louis or my sister.

"I don't know what came over me," she said aloud. "Maybe it was the concussion; something short-circuiting."

"Or old grief, coming out for new reasons."

"Ah." That Thelma, she had a way of putting things that always seemed so likely and true; maybe that was her training. Or maybe it was just her. "Could be, I suppose," Helene said. "But really I am OK, just like you said. Are you still coming up?"

"You betcha. It's kind of a fun place."

"No dances, though. Just the health lecture."

Thelma was laughing at the other end of the line. "You make it sound dull. I'm actually quite interested. Anyway, I'll see you tomorrow about three or four."

"Thanks, Thelma."

Helene found herself more lighthearted after the call, happy about Thelma's visit. It was so much easier to face an uncertain future with a friend and ally at your side.

Still, no word from Erik; or an answer when she called him. Glancing out the window, she saw the Red Pinto Pony – and another car parked right behind it: her silver Acura! She leaned into the glass for a better view, unsure. It could be someone else's, the same make and model. But no, that was her license plate and her sticker for the dump. And the mirror right where it should be, and no damage to the bumper, from what she could see. She hurried out to the street. Who had dropped off the car and when? Not Erik; he was on the road. And not Denis, who was doing promotional events for the new CD. Who else? Unless, maybe someone had been paid to drive the car back? – but not by her.

She walked outside, looking over the freshly washed and polished car, then opened the unlocked passenger door. Completely clean and empty, except for the umbrella she'd left there, and a snow scraper. Plus a couple of CDs in a holder between the front seats.

Strange.

As she walked around the car, she heard her name being called: a male voice that she didn't recognize at first. Too deep for Izzy. She saw movement up the street, at the corner, and then she saw Chief standing on the sidewalk, waving. He was half dressed, wearing a kind of breechcloth and leggings, but no shirt, only a small red bag on a cord around his neck. He was hobbling across the street with his cane. The sight alarmed her a bit, and she walked quickly toward him, worried that he was in distress.

"Chief," she said, meeting him at the corner. "Are you OK?"

"Fine." And then he stopped, looking down at himself. "No, I'm getting worked on. My regalia."

"For a powwow?"

"Not today. But Elsa has to let out the waist; it's gotten a little snug somehow."

Helene saw that the breechcloth was pinned together where Elsa had adjusted it; she pressed her lips together not to laugh.

"I wanted to catch you," he said. "I was waiting for you to come out and see the car."

"Where did it come from?" she asked, sure it was part of the community knowledge that she was not privy to.

He lifted his hands. "I was going to ask you the same question."

Helene shook her head, staring back at the car. "I don't know. There's no note or anything. It just kind of appeared."

Chief nodded. "That's good kind of magic, anyhow. I wondered if Erik was behind it, but we haven't heard from him since he left – sometimes the phone service isn't good. Or sometimes he just doesn't bother. No matter. It's here; that's good. I want to ask you about something else."

Helene moved back a few feet into a shaded area, and made room for the Chief, but he stayed where he was. In the bright, hot August sun, the skin of his abdomen was smooth and glistening, except for a scar on his knee from surgery. He had almost no chest hair and still taut muscles over a rounded stomach.

"Sun feels good on this big belly of mine," he said, patting himself. "So, anyway, here's what I want to know. When you got that concussion, right, when you were with Wishi-ta up north, do you remember anything that happened – did you see anything or hear anything?"

Helene had not expected that question. And in truth, no one had ever asked her, not even the doctors.

"I thought I heard voices," she said after a moment. "Yes, I did, but I didn't really recognize them, or even if they were speaking English. No words, I mean. More like murmuring, coming across the lake, like a breeze."

"Hmm," he said nodding.

"It might have been my parents I was remembering," she said. "Or even someone speaking French. My father's Canadian ancestors built that cabin – maybe I imagined it was them."

"Voices," Chief repeated. "Some of us think that when someone is sick, or feverish, or unconscious like you were, sometimes their spirit wanders, or that spirits visit them."

"I don't know about that, Chief," Helene said with a smile. "I don't think…" Then she stopped. "Wait. There was this other thing, kind of silly, and I doubt it has anything to do with spirits. It was a dream; I was in my kitchen at home – at my other home." She gestured in the direction of the rising sun. "Do you want to hear it?"

"I came hobbling out of the house half dressed to hear it," he said, a mischievous twinkle in his eye. "And I doubt I have long before Restless Turtle comes after me."

Restless Turtle! Elsa, of course.

Helene smiled, closing her eyes to summon the details of the dream. "I was by myself at the kitchen table at home, drinking a cup of tea, everything very still and quiet. Then I heard this popping sound coming from the cabinets. So I got up to look, and it was my glassware – you know, drinking glasses – breaking and shattering and turning into piles of dust. And then my dishes started to do the same thing. My cabinets looked really old, warped and cracked, and then the granite counters began to crack into pieces and fall on the floor. Just a total mess." She paused, gauging his expression. "That's pretty much it; I told you it was silly. Maybe it was from staying at that old cabin – you know, the confusion. But in the dream it was my lovely new house, and everything falling apart."

"Good," Chief said, arms across his chest, sober like a judge. "No, that's good. It's telling something. In the future, all made things will fall apart and come to nothing. Only the living things go on, generation to generation. The granite is rock, and returns to rock. The glass is from sand."

Helene blinked, a little unnerved at his grave manner. Maybe it was the oversized mustache and black eyebrows that had made him always seem a bit of a character, not a serious, wise old man.

"You think that's it?"

He cocked his head; a few beads of sweat had formed on his brow. "Maybe. I don't know these things like the old people used to. But I grew up on a reservation deep in Canada. We were so far apart from the modern world, it was a shock when I saw a city for the first time. Then I joined the military, and I saw the world, the big world. But then I lost my way in that world, yet I couldn't fit back into the first world." He looked to see if Helene was following. "Then, eventually, me and Elsa, we found our way here."

Helene nodded, taking in his words – testimony of his personal journey, with its own confusion and missteps. Leading to here, and to now – with her on this sidewalk on this warm morning.

"We are not made things," he said, holding her gaze. "We are living things that come and go on this earth like all the two-legged, and four-legged, and wings in the sky. The fishes and the plant world. We live through each other, not apart from each other, or on top or below each other. That way is such a lonely way, and leads to death in life, which is worse than when we cease to breathe."

Helene felt her own breath quicken as she stared into Chief's eyes. She heard what he was saying, and was starting to understand the sense of it, what it meant for her.

Out of the quiet morning they heard a voice shout. "Chief!" *Restless Turtle, Elsa.* They looked over and waved. "Can we finish?" she said. And then, "I'm not going out there on the sidewalk."

"In a minute," Chief shouted back.

"No one wants to see you like that." Elsa's voice carried up the street.

"She's right." He laughed. "It's hard to look dignified with pins sticking out of your breechcloth. But I wanted to ask you about your accident, and what it means."

"What it means?"

"It all means something, if we choose that it does."

"What?" Her pulse quickened, as a slow smile crossed his face. "What does it mean? Aren't you going to tell me?"

"It's for you to ponder, and to learn from." He gestured toward the parked cars. "I'll be interested to find out who's behind this."

She smiled back. "Me, too."

He turned and crossed the street, walking toward his wife standing at the front door, watching. The Chief, and Elsa, had been looking for her or looking out for her. Helene went back along the sidewalk to her car and got in, just for the pleasure of sitting in her own vehicle again. With a brand-new air freshener hanging from the mirror: pine.

After lunch Thelma called to say that she had gotten a late start and would be arriving closer to five. Helene went to check on Izzy and found him on the back deck at Malvina's, dozing in a lounge chair.

"Sorry to wake you," she said. "Everything OK?" She pulled over one of the lawn chairs into the shade.

"Fine." He yawned. "Just waiting for my hair to grow back." He gave her that sweet, sly look she'd come to recognize.

"Right. Actually, that haircut is not half bad," she said. "Slightly pixie-ish." That did not elicit a response. "Or kind of metro-sexual. That's a new buzzword."

"Which means?"

She shrugged, leaning back into the chair. "So, Izzy, do you know anything about the return of my car? I found it parked on the curb this morning, no note, no explanation – and Chief and Elsa don't seem to know, either."

"Don't seem to know," Izzy repeated, in the voice of a wise man. "That may be key. Nope, not me, don't know anything about it." He attempted to wink. "Honest Injun."

She shook her head at his silliness. "It's a mystery, then. Erik or Denis might know – but they're both incommunicado at the moment." She wrinkled her nose; it was hard to be patient. "Anyway, are you still coming tonight to the potluck?"

He wagged his head inconclusively.

"Thelma is coming up this afternoon. You remember her, right? She's going with me. Plus Elsa asked if I could help bring over some of the crafting supplies."

"Um…" He wavered. "I suppose my peeps are looking for me."

"You look much better," she said. "Your nose is pretty much back to normal. No one will see the bandage on your ribs. And the black-and-blue under your eyes has faded, more like not enough sleep." She squinted, checking closely. "I could probably put a little concealer there."

"That does sound like fun," Izzy said, closing his eyes again, as relaxed as a cat. "But no thanks. I'll go as I am."

"So, ready about five thirty? If you want, I can drive you."

"No, it's fine. I'll walk." He let go a long sigh. "I miss my bike."

5. The Mascot Thing – by One Little Indian

Every year at my old high school, our sports teams used to play the Devils, the Wildcats, the Bandits, the Red Men, and the Tomahawks (now the Hawks). Notice the logos, banners, face paint, and T-shirts: wild animals, evil spirits, criminals, a weapon, and us Indians. All very scary.

Reds, Redskins, Warriors, Braves, Chiefs, Indians…war chants and tomahawks. You get the picture. Somehow we got saddled, as a people, with being school and sports team mascots. All in tribute to our brave, tough, hard-fighting reputations, right? So where's the problem? To begin, think of some of the company that puts us in: Pirates, Vikings, Marauders, Buccaneers, Crusaders, Raiders – all tough guys with brutal, uncivilized, even terrorist-type histories. What are Marauders known for except raping, pillaging, and murder? What does that say, anyway, about those choices to represent a football or baseball team? Not to be emulated, I say.

Or there's being lumped in with animal mascots – your Tigers, Lions, Bears, Cougars, Jaguars, Sharks – lots of teeth and claws. Not that we have a problem with animals, per se. No, we're good there. Total respect for the power of these classic predators. But we are one of the few two-leggeds in this category, except for the above-named bad guys. Instead, how about some other creature mascots? Crows and ospreys, snakes and foxes, groundhogs. That's the way to go – speed, skill, guile – these have all learned ways to survive and outwit their hunters – at least some of the time. Just like teams.

Reds and Redskins, though. Really? How is that OK, when there are no teams called blacks, browns, yellows, whites; or niggers, spics, chinks, and crackers? What's more, Redskins is an old term for Indians scalps brought in for payment, along with other kinds of "pelts." Missed that part in your history book? Or maybe it wasn't there.

Just old traditions, all in the past? Doesn't mean anything now? Does to me. Not lost on me that my ancestors were on the "defeated" team. Some Indians may be OK with this idea, preferring a more honorable kind of interpretation. Seems like a lot of glossing over to see it that way. But for a lot of us, when it comes to mascots, just leave us out, thank you very much.

Chapter 22

Helene tried once more to reach Erik. Once more the phone went right to voicemail, which the electronic voice said was full. So nothing there. She didn't even try Denis – not wanting to have one of those frustrating phone calls while he was trying to talk over the music and other voices. She didn't see how he could have retrieved her car.

She was almost teary again when she saw Thelma's blue Subaru turn down the road and park at the curb. She walked directly to the driver's car door, stepping aside as Thelma climbed out, staring not at Helene but at Helene's spiffy car.

"What the heck?" Thelma said. She had put her hair in a bun for the heat and wore a loose, sleeveless dress in lime green, bright yellow, red, and royal blue. "I thought you were stranded here – or driving some kind of derelict car."

"It just showed up this morning," Helene said, following Thelma to the other car. "A complete mystery. I don't know where it came from or how it got here."

"Well, OK, then." Thelma stroked the glossy exterior admiringly. "We'll just take it as a minor miracle until further notice. Another good sign."

Thelma turned, and Helene's arms rose of their own accord, open for a hug. Then tears started slipping onto Thelma's shoulder, until she said, "There, there, Helene; let's go in, shall we? I'll come back later for my overnight bag."

Helene shook her head and laughed sheepishly. "Yes, please, before I melt on the sidewalk. Let's go sit and I'll try to hold it together. At least I can show some manners, and ask about you too."

She fetched lemonade for them both and they sat on the porch. Thelma was silent a few moments, fascinated with the antics of the hummingbirds. In her bold tropical colors, she looked like an exotic bird herself, a parrot perhaps. She took a long sip of her drink, then placed the glass on the table and turned to Helene.

"OK, then. Me. Let's start with Jacob," she said. "He's driving back to school with a friend. The spider bite is a distant memory. He's ready to take on the world, God bless him, and prefers more action than our little town." She wiped the drops of moisture on her glass with a napkin. "Let's see. I've looked at three, no, four condos now. I'm working with a realtor to put my house on the market, but I've already called the office of Kenneth's developer." She took a long breath. "It's looking like a good deal for me."

Helene felt a jab of emotion, maybe anger? Or betrayal, that Thelma would want to do business with someone who was clearly not on Helene's side. That she would trust him, Kenneth, maybe more than she actually trusted Helene, when push came to shove. But she shook her head, not wanting to invite that kind of trouble. Very likely it was best for Thelma, and that's what she needed to remember.

She started to ask a question, but Thelma held up a hand.

"Let's hold off on that until I even find out what the story is, and get all the details. Maybe it's not right for me after all. I'm looking at it as a business matter, but also the big picture. We'll see." She closed her eyes a moment. "What else? I saw the new, or I should say old, former school nurse at a staff meeting. Hand sanitizer for everyone, and 'there will be no malingering in the nurse's office under her watch.'" Thelma's face showed mock alarm. "Other than that, I'm just great, and happy to be here. How about you?"

Helene launched into her current musings and state of mind, including the talk with Chief the day before. Her main worry was that she had burned bridges and created a difficult situation. She was anxious that Louis would limit her involvement with Wishi-ta or Tana-na and would never allow a formal relationship. As far as she knew, she could stay in the house for now, paying rent to cover the mortgage. The place was almost paid off, hypoallergenic, and had half belonged to Renee. Part of her wanted to stay, and another part thought she might be better off in a little apartment or condo nearby.

"There's this other thing," Helene said vaguely.

After a moment, Thelma teased, "Are you going to tell me, or am I supposed to guess?"

Helene knew holding secrets had done her no good. Still, it wasn't easy. "OK. Well, I think someone came into the house – while I was out. We were all out. They didn't actually take anything, but I think they went through my papers, you know, legal and medical documents."

"You mean, a break-in?" Thelma was dead serious.

"Not exactly. It was daylight, and the house wasn't locked. I guess people on the base sometimes just walk into each others' homes."

Thelma frowned. "No note?"

Helene shook her head dismissively. "It's probably nothing. Probably…"

"It's not nothing," Thelma said. "It's weird, and kind of scary. But you do lock the door now, right?"

"Yeah." There. It was out. It wasn't good. But it wasn't exactly urgent danger, either. "For now I just want to leave it alone. OK?"

Thelma hunched her shoulders. "OK, if that's what you want."

"I do."

"So, then," Thelma picked up the thread from earlier. "What about income for you? Or employment?"

Helene explained her plan to work after the family returned and the twins were in school, either per diem or part-time at the hospital. Besides that she would have the money from the sale of the Roy family house, which would be split with Denis, and also the twins as Renee's heirs. She hadn't changed her mind about Kenneth, and would eventually meet with him and lawyers to work out details of legal separation.

"The thing is," she said, putting down her glass, "I don't blame Louis and the rest of the family for their doubts, after what happened. I'm not completely clear myself why I felt so desperate." She looked down at her hands in her lap, skin starting to age, no wedding ring. "I wonder if there's something about me that's not supposed to have children, have a family. If somehow, because of all the pain and trouble we had in our own family, I just don't have the right to. The thing is… it's not just Renee who was damaged. Or Denis. It was me too. I've always known it; I just tried to hide it and pretend. There's something inside me as desperate as Renee was, and maybe as bad."

"Bad?" Thelma said gently, reaching across to put her hand on Helene's. "Oh, honey, I don't think so. Are you telling me that you've had the wool pulled over my eyes all this time and I didn't know?"

"There are things…you just don't know about."

Thelma shook her head. "And you know everything about me? About the sexual assault in college? Or the abortion I had because I was in college and my boyfriend dumped me? Am I broken and damaged – maybe. Or if I were a Christian, did I commit a sin? Probably. But Helene, believe me – you are not bad – not the kind of bad that goes out in the world to create pain and harm for others – with intention."

"Intention," Helene repeated softly. "I'm not sure…"

"Is there something you want to tell me?" Thelma said. Her voice was gentle, calm, but Helene knew Thelma was alert, always, to trouble and pain.

"There is something," Helene said, shaking her head. "But it's better you don't know. I can't tell you, I don't think, or everything will change."

Thelma glanced away, diverted by a hummingbird buzzing by like a bee. "It's probably going to change, anyway."

Helene slumped in her chair. "Maybe I deserve the way things worked out. No man in my life, really. No children, probably ever. A job that means only so much to me. And a family that fell apart. We just didn't have what it takes to overcome all the bad stuff."

"That's what you think?"

"Pretty much."

"Hmm…" Thelma said. "I'm not sure you're right. But it's your journey. I hope you don't forget that you have Denis, the twins, Izzy, me, and…other people that you are important to."

"Yes," Helene said, lifting her head. She too watched the hummingbird at the sugar feeder, until it darted away. "Yes, I'm starting to see that now. And I am grateful."

Thelma got up, stretching her arms over her head. "Let's leave this for now. It's a beautiful day in a nice place, sitting here looking out over the yard and the garden, the birds and the bees. And I'm getting hungry." She glanced at her watch. "There's a bag of food in the car. I brought hummus and pita chips for the potluck. I wonder how that will go over."

"Oh, good, I think. Everything seems to go."

They went inside, retrieving Thelma's bags, to get ready for the potluck. Helene mentioned she would be transporting the Chief, plus the food and craft bags to the Intertribal Center. At five thirty, Izzy appeared at the door, ready to walk. No flute.

"I can do it," he said. "Plus it's an image thing."

"I see," said Helene, looking him over. In his shorts and Native T-shirt, none of his bruises were evident. Yet there was still something about the way he moved, gingerly, not with his usual effortless grace "I can't go with you, though. I have to drive."

"I'll be your escort," said Thelma from behind her in the hallway. "You don't mind, Izzy, do you?"

"I'd be honored."

Thelma and Izzy started out down the street, moving at an unhurried pace. Izzy managed on his own, while Thelma chatted nonstop. Helene turned the car around and pulled up in front of the Chief and Elsa's house, getting out to pop open the back and help load. Elsa was, as usual, prepared and organized, and packed everything expertly into Helene's car for the six-block journey.

"It's so nice of you," the Chief said, with the crinkle-faced smile that made his eyes almost disappear. With his short, stocky build and full head of white hair, he was a brotherly counterpart to Thelma, in a strange way.

"It's nothing." Helene had a warm feeling, thinking back to their talk on the sidewalk. If nothing else Chief was a kind man, who cared about people's feelings and, apparently, their visions. A slow cooker of baked beans sat in a box on the front seat, while husband and wife got in back, the cane on the floor.

Helene executed a three-point turn and drove the short distance like a celebrity chauffeur, delivering them to the front door, where they were met by Thelma and Izzy, and a bevy of excited children. *Red carpet, indeed!* Only after she parked down the block and started for the door did she ponder the strangeness of giving a ride to the sister and brother-in-law of her recent and sudden lover, who was still MIA – their lover's quarrel, if that's what it was, still unresolved. And yet it was not a matter of acrimony in this community, just the way it was: this living without knowing all the answers and being OK with it.

The hall was abuzz with folks returned from summer trips, the kids excited about the start of school, and the first big gathering in weeks. No Malvina, Noel, or the family yet.

They took their usual seats next to Bernice, Robert, and Charlotte. The two dour sisters, Frances and Alberta, chose another table, along with Wilton and another young man, turning away as Helene said hello to others she had not seen in a while. Unmindful, Thelma sat next to Helene, introducing herself to one and all across the table. Izzy left for the front of the hall to help Chief with the microphone. A crowd of small bodies followed, chanting his name, reaching up for high fives or just to touch him. From the adults, there were a few long looks at Izzy's new, short hairstyle.

It was pretty much business as usual: first, announcements – that the Caron family had settled into their new digs with plenty of furnishings, and were planning to hold a special celebration, date to be announced. Izzy took the microphone; he did not speak this time about Louis, or his family, or his "accident." But he did say thanks for everyone's well wishes, and that he was feeling better. Around her at the tables, Helene could see some folks murmuring, speculating.

Chief continued with the rest of the announcements: a proposal to build a separate women's sweat lodge – where that would be constructed, and when. Upcoming powwows, and health updates on a few individuals, including – to Helene's surprise – her own recovery from a fall that had produced a concussion – but no details about kidnappings or visions. Her eyes met Thelma's and she smiled, touched and embarrassed.

The food was consumed, the children released to roam and play, and then the presenter, White Fox from the Sioux nation in North Dakota, spoke on "Native American Healing Arts" which, to Helene's second surprise, included ways to sobriety. Thelma was listening carefully, taking notes. For the first time, Helene had an inkling of what Renee had been referring to in her journals, what had helped her turn from a seemingly hopeless path. It was experiencing generosity and sharing, and coming to value what her family and community valued; sharing their respect for elders' wisdom, their belief in the importance of ceremony and of nature, and their belief in the meaningfulness of life, and in another world, of the spirit. The idea that healing came through community – through singing, smudging, sweats, and awareness, so that the troubled individual was not alone, and not shamed for the pain they lived in and caused to others.

Toward the end of the presentation, a cell phone began to ring. After glancing around Helene realized with chagrin that it was hers. She reached into her purse to turn off the ringer, glancing at the number. She didn't recognize it, but it could have been Erik – from a pay phone maybe. She scrambled from her seat, pressing the button to accept the call. She just couldn't miss him another time.

"Erik?"

"Yep, me. Can you talk?"

"Well, I'm at the potluck, but yes, I can talk. I mean, yes, I want to talk. Just let me step outside…" She was walking as she spoke into the phone, heading out the front door.

"OK, I'll keep it short," he said. "I'm using a buddy's phone. I have to leave a message for Elsa and Chief too. I'll be back on Saturday, in any case, so we can talk then. I just wanted to tell you – or really, to ask you – if you got your car back OK?"

"I did!" she exclaimed. "So, that was you? There wasn't a note or anything."

"Yeah. My buddy was on a pretty tight schedule, and I guess he got there late at night – didn't want to bother you."

"I wasn't sure," she said, through the door, shutting out the noise of the room behind her. "The way we left things. I thought you were mad at me, after what happened, what I said."

"No," he said. "Wasn't ideal, but I wasn't mad; a little preoccupied with some matters. I was waiting for you to get over being mad. But I knew you wanted your car back."

Helene felt her whole body flush with gladness, relief, and embarrassment. The late-afternoon sun held a lot of heat, and her palms got sweaty.

"I did. And I'm so grateful." She was gushing, in a hurry to get the words out. "And I'm not mad; I have no reason to be mad. I just…well…"

"Let's leave it be, then," he said. "Until I get there, Saturday. Might not be until late. But, just so we're straight, you do want to see me again?"

"I do. I really, truly do. Come to the house, anytime."

"OK. Until then."

Helene closed her eyes, inhaling, leaning against the wall to stay steady on her feet. All that useless, unnecessary suffering and worry. And how would she tell Thelma, after all her foolishness and panicked phone calls, for nothing, really. But Thelma would understand; she always did.

Helene returned inside to find the presentation had just concluded. The speaker was surrounded by several audience members with questions. Elsa, Alberta, Robert, and Charlotte were clearing the buffet table and packing up leftovers. It was like a well-oiled machine, finished in almost no time. Izzy was fiddling with cords at the back of the room, a collection of followers at his heels. Helene glanced from Izzy to Thelma at the buffet table, packing napkins and paper plates into a box, and then back. She headed toward Izzy, wading through the thicket of arms and legs. He was clearly buoyed with the attention, but still thinner than he should be, fragile-looking.

"Are you ready to go? I can take you anytime, and come back."

"Nah, I'll be here for a while. White Fox is going to work with me." It took a moment to realize he meant healing work, not music or some line of business.

"Oh, really? But what else can he do? Did the doctors miss something? Did I?"

Izzy wriggled his lips. "No. But it was like going to an auto shop for body work, you know? This is not really for the bumps and breaks and bruises; it's for the other stuff – the inside stuff. You know?"

"Yes, I think so. I hope it does help. But I still haven't changed my view about reporting what happened to the police..."

He held up a hand. "I know, I know."

She found Thelma, the other white head that fairly glowed in the darkening room. They finished up gathering containers and pushing in chairs. Robert and Charlotte were on the last rounds of wiping down tables and emptying trash. Elsa and the Chief had gone upstairs to the office, some bookkeeping stuff; Robert would get them back home.

"The phone call," Thelma said as they made their way toward the exit. She was carrying the hummus bowl, every bite consumed. "Anything important?"

"Well, yes – and no – I mean, nothing urgent."

"Erik?"

Helene stopped short, glancing around. There was no one in the immediate vicinity. "How did you guess?"

"Your face is different. Your eyes. So he's back?"

"He'll be back on Saturday."

"And you're glad?"

Helene tipped her head, beckoning Thelma to follow, stopping at the door. "Glad, but nervous – not so much about him – what will be, will be. But with the family, when they return, and what they talked about with Louis. Maybe they won't like it, it won't look right, and they'll hold it against me if I'm seeing Erik, when I'm not even officially separated from Kenneth."

Thelma put up a hand. "Stop right there." She pulled her to the side, making way for others to pass. "Do you hear yourself? Creating a problem where it doesn't necessarily even exist. Right?"

"Maybe."

"But things are OK with Erik – for right now, this minute? Never mind; don't even answer. I can see they are."

"Yes."

"And you have no idea what the family will say on their return."

"No."

"So let it go."

"I try! But it's so hard; how do you just make it go?"

"Practice," Thelma said archly. And then, pushing open the door with a hip, she turned to wink at Helene. "Our work here is done; let's go."

The next morning, before Thelma left, Helene went to Neesa's garden with a basket and a pair of shears. It was already hazy and warm, maybe storms late in the day. She entered Malvina's backyard and opened the chicken-wire fence around the garden. Thelma had followed, watching Helene snip cukes, tomatoes, peppers, and lettuce.

"Zucchini? Yellow squash?" Helene offered.

"Why not?"

Helene crouched down to select a few choice specimens. "I feel a little Peter Rabbitish robbing the garden like this. But it will otherwise go to waste." She filled a grocery bag. "Here, take this."

Thelma took the bag, holding it to her chest like a baby. "Still warm from the sun. How wonderful!"

As they walked to the front of the house, Thelma turned to Helene. "There is something else, before I go. Two things."

"Yes?" Helene's heart skipped; Thelma was in serious mode.

"I talked with Izzy yesterday while we were walking to the potluck, about his desire to move to the city. I said he could stay with me, initially, at least a few months. Minimal charge."

"Really?" Helene exclaimed, and then cocked her head, trying not to scowl. "You don't think that's running away, from, you know, his problems?"

"So let him run. For now. It's his decision. And maybe he needs to grow and change before he's ready to fight."

Helene stared, shaking her head. "You are so good. An angel." She paused. "Do Jews believe in angels?"

"We do, but I'm not one. The other thing…"

"Erik?"

"Kenneth."

Helene winced. "Ah."

"His name hasn't come up at all since I've been here. But he hasn't disappeared, and you can't avoid dealing with him. Hopefully in a fair and kind way. I don't think he's told anyone yet that you've left permanently. Maybe he doesn't believe it himself. But eventually he has to address it, and so do you."

Helene moaned. "I know, I know. It's just so much easier not to think about all that."

"But that's life, my sweet. It won't go away on its own. So if you need to see him, come stay with me, anytime, preferably before the house gets knocked down."

"No! Don't say that, I mean about the house."

"Helene." Thelma was reprimanding her, but softly, and her eyes glistened. "It's only a house."

Then Thelma was gone, with her bag of vegetables and steady strength and good humor. In the kitchen Helene poured another cup of coffee, but that was not what she wanted. She wanted the time to pass; she wanted to see Erik again.

Izzy. He probably wasn't up yet, but that was the next order of business, to talk to him again about going to the police. She understood his reluctance, but still. It was not right, what had been done to him. Yet he needed his sleep, and she needed him rested to have any further discussion.

After that she busied herself with laundry, washing up, and working on the ribbon shirt she was making for Tana-na. Carefully, she placed the red, white, yellow and black ribbons across the front, just over the chest line. He had picked out the material himself, black with a pattern of white feathers. He'd also asked for "fringed leather leggins and an apron", beyond her experience. When she asked Elsa for advice, she said, "Get it from Bullocks. They'll make it custom." For a dizzy moment, Helene pictured herself in the upscale department store, now closed, some small section of Indian regalia she'd never noticed.

"Bullocks?"

"Yep," Elsa said. "Go online. It's easy. I just ordered bone buttons and a turtle shell."

Not the same Bullocks...

It was strange to sit at the sewing machine, a vestige of time with her mother, sad but comforting, soothing. The machine was humming along when she heard a few tentative notes through the open window. She stopped to listen, first thinking radio, and then realized it was Izzy on the flute. She left the material in the machine and searched around for her sandals. As she walked out of the house, there was only silence from next door. She knocked on the front door, to no answer, and then went around to the back.

"Izzy?" she called. She stepped onto the patio where the flute lay across one of the chairs, but no Izzy. Like smoke, he had disappeared, leaving Helene with a pang of concern. But that was silly; he was just off somewhere.

She let herself inside and left a note on the kitchen table. "Dinner tonight – next door – six o'clock, chicken parm. Bring bread. We'll talk."

That should do it.

Chapter 23

A long morning followed by a dull afternoon. Waiting for Erik, and then for Wishi-ta and the rest of the family, was almost unbearable. Two whole days to fill up before Erik was expected, on Saturday night, if he made it by then. And then Wednesday when the others were due to arrive. Helene called the number of the employment agency that placed per diem nurses, telling them she would be ready to work in mid-September, looking for daytime hours a few days a week, while the twins were at kindergarten from eight until three o'clock. She did a thorough weeding in the garden, delivering some of the extra produce to the kitchen of the Intertribal Center, as directed by Elsa. At four o'clock, Izzy popped by to say that he would come for dinner.

As she was preparing dinner in the kitchen, Helene heard her cell phone ringing in the living room on the coffee table. *Erik? Malvina?* With a start she recognized her own number on the caller ID, from home. *Kenneth.* She almost dropped the phone. She waited as a message was recorded in voicemail.

"Helene, we need to talk again, in person," Kenneth's voice said. "I realize I was not making much effort to understand you and what was going on with you this summer, and that's my fault. And it was wrong that I didn't get there to see what was going on for myself. I'm thinking of driving up there this weekend. Please call me back and let me know if there's a good time."

Oh, no. That was just what Helene did not want, especially not this weekend. No. Thelma was right, she had to deal with it eventually, but she was just not ready. And certainly not for another scene like at Thelma's house with the two men standing there. Some part of her did not want to mix Kenneth with this place and these people – it was better to keep it all separate. She should call and say she'd drive down there, sometime soon, so they could talk. But she did not want to be convinced otherwise, or to hear his voice, or his pain. She put down the phone and went back to the kitchen, pounding the chicken breast. *No, no, no.*

Minutes later Izzy called out from the front door. "I'm here, and I brought bread."

He entered carrying a loaf of Sunbeam bread, making Helene laugh. "White bread! Really?"

"It's easiest to chew. And I like it."

The chicken parmesan was done quickly, and the pasta drained into the colander. They chatted through the meal, about some of Izzy's high school friends and Helene's college experiences and nursing career. After they were done, she brought out ice cream for dessert. It was time to ask Izzy about his plans: whether he had registered for more classes at the community college, and what he told his boss about returning to work.

"I'm not going back. I'm leaving," Izzy said, hunched over the ice cream bowl. "Haven't changed my mind. I don't want to break the momentum. My bike is fixed, I have some savings and some contacts." He looked at her sideways. "And a place to stay."

"I know," Helene said. "And I won't try to cast doubts. But..."

"Ah, the but."

"You have unfinished business here. I really wish you would talk to the police before you leave."

He shook his head, the hair already creeping down his neck. "It's only going to be a hassle, and nothing will come of it."

"You don't know that." Helene paused, thinking. "We have those pictures of you to show them. And I'll be with you."

Izzy's tone remained neutral, not angry, but his face was pained. "I really, really want to say, 'don't bother.' But I get the idea you're not going to let up, on some kind of mission here."

She half smiled. "True. Just go with me once, whatever happens, and I won't bug you again."

A breeze came through the kitchen window, bringing a hint of rain, and likely a thunderstorm. Something stirred at the back of Helene's mind, a memory of standing in the kitchen with her mother, helping to prepare a meal. Renee, a toddler, had her hands in the flour, making a mess, making their mother laugh, while Helene tried to measure everything just right. A perfectionist. And persistent.

"What would Louis say?"

There was a glimmer in Izzy's eye. "I doubt he would go to the police. Probably hunt those guys down, and get in some kind of trouble himself. He doesn't have much faith in white man's ways, as you know."

"But he married a white woman, and his children are half white."

Still not enough to convince him.

"What would Renee say, do you think?" she asked.

Izzy stared at the empty bowl on the table. "Good question. She was a fighter, for sure. But after a while, she changed, quite a lot."

"What would she do if it happened to one of the twins – or their cousins, when they were older?"

Izzy took a deep breath, wincing slightly as the air filled his chest. But then he raised his eyes and met Helene's.

"She would go there, and she would speak her mind."

"So will you?"

Finally he nodded.

"Good." Helene let her breath out. "OK, then. Monday or Tuesday. Let's just see what happens."

Saturday was rainy and blustery, and not much good for anything outdoors. There was a crafts program at the Intertribal Center, a woman showing how to make jewelry out of sweetgrass, porcupine quills, and other natural materials. Bernice had called to say she was going, mainly for the socializing. Jewelry was not her thing. Earlier in the summer, she had shown Helene some of her chalk portraits, which were beautiful. But not for powwow, and not for sale. Just for gifts, she said, or to satisfy herself. Then she turned those dark, twinkling eyes on Helene, urging her to find what she most enjoyed creating, what most suited her. Finally Helene said, "Sewing, I guess. I'm good at that and I love making things, curtains, clothes, comforters, stuff like that."

"So you sew me a shawl, something I can wear at powwow, and I'll make you a chalk drawing," Bernice said, challenge in her voice. "Deal?"

Helene couldn't find a reason not to agree. She said she'd go with Bernice to the program. Whatever others might be thinking, it was still good to get out and try her hand at something new.

As Helene got ready to leave the house, putting on her rain jacket, she checked her cell phone, and saw a message from earlier in the day – maybe when she was in the garden. Her heart thudded. *Oh, dear. Who?*

Kenneth was trying to reach her again: "Helene, if you're there, can you please pick up? Please? Or call back as soon as you can. I'd still like to meet in person, the sooner the better. Tomorrow, maybe? A meeting fell through, so I could try to get there early." A pause and a sigh. "I don't know where you might have gone, but I assume you can still get messages. Call me, please; I need an answer." She heard annoyance in his voice.

She couldn't make herself return the call. He seemed to have a lot going on, as always. That should tie him up for a bit. After that they could talk, or meet. Maybe.

Bernice was waiting for Helene at the door to the Intertribal Center, a basket of materials and supplies in hand.

"Oh, I didn't realize we were supposed to bring stuff," Helene said, caught once again unprepared. "Maybe I'd better not…"

"Helene." Bernice might as well have said, *Stop talking.* Instead she said, "Are you not getting this? We're not all about the rules here." Her voice went singsongy. "Just bring what you have, if you have it. If not, someone else might have something you can use, and you can bring something next time. Just come on, for heaven's sake."

It was not until they were inside, entering the crafting room with five or six tables set up, and a host of women and a couple of men already present, that Helene understood what was happening. The buzz of voices softened, and then petered out. Across the way Alberta and Frances stood with another few women who stared at Helene as she entered, not in a friendly way. The expressions of disapproval were impossible to miss.

Others were more neutral, but also not talking.

Bernice, however, carried on as if all was normal. Elsa was not coming, according to Bernice, and the woman who was leading the workshop was a guest from New Hampshire, oblivious to the tensions in the room. Bernice steered Helene by the elbow to a table with open spots, the other jewelry makers looking up only to nod before going back to their work. They laid out the materials in front of them, and waited for the demonstration to begin. Throughout the hour, Bernice kept to Helene's side, chatting in a low voice, but any conversation was about the crafts.

This was, Helene now knew, an accounting of her actions to the greater community – some of whom were clearly against her. Bernice had engineered this deliberately, even if Helene would have avoided it. As they worked, coming and going to the instructor's workstation, sharing materials, it became clear that the main antagonists were Alberta and Frances, who would not speak to Helene, ignoring a question or request, and would not look her in the eye.

"Troublemakers," she overheard one of the women say. Some of the remarks were directed against the Lopes family itself: "Got what they deserved: inviting outsiders into the community."

Strangely, it was the careful beading and the weaving of the sweetgrass that kept Helene focused and composed. And, slowly but surely, others in the room came by to look at her work, and speak a word or two. "Maybe more blue on that side." Or "It looks like the colors of twilight."

Only Alberta got in a direct attack: "I don't care what Chief says, or Elsa. We got a right to say who comes here. It's called the *Intertribal* Center, right? That means it's for us, any tribe, any nation. To get away from all that nastiness in the rest of the world. Whatever we have, it always gets spoiled by whites in this country. Why can't they just leave us alone?"

But it came across as a kind of tired, bleating complaint, and no one really picked up on it. The energy had shifted, more or less, and others were more interested, it seemed to Helene, in creating crafts and not more pain and conflict. She knew too that Bernice had set herself up as guard and shield, for reasons Helene could not quite understand. And finally she understood her part. To each person in the room who had spoken directly to her or helped her with the jewelry in some way, she said, "Thank you. I know I have a lot to learn, but I'm trying to do better." She was proud of herself for surviving the hours and the testing, and departed with a bracelet in hand and Bernice at her side.

Only then, as they passed through the dining room, darkened by the drooping, dusty drapes did Helene think about how they might be fixed – taken down, cleaned, and then sewn at her machine. Ambitious, but it could be done, if they were worth repair and she had the time.

Dinner came and went, reading and TV, the time for rest and relaxation. But Helene couldn't settle down. It was a restless, anxious evening of waiting, trying not to dwell too much on Alberta's words and on the hostility she'd felt at the jewelry-making session. She missed the twins in the house, the noise, the activity. Still no sign of Erik. Anything could have happened on the road, and Helene might not see him tonight at all. Maybe tomorrow instead. She reminded herself that he needed to come back eventually – this was where he lived the majority of the time, and he did have family here. And he had arranged to get her car back.

At midnight she was able to finish her glass of wine, put down the file she was reading, and close her eyes on the sofa. Sleep was fitful, at best, and at one point she startled awake, thinking she heard footsteps outside. And then she heard the noise again, a step, or crack of a twig, but farther away, toward the back. There had been no stories of recent break-ins. The community had few young adults who might be playing pranks; and, fortunately, not many current problems with addiction. Then she thought back to the messed-up papers, the law briefs and Renee's journal, and wondered. What reason could there be to sneak around this house, except to spook her or threaten her, or drive her away?

She didn't think she'd sleep again, but she was dozing on the sofa when she heard the rap on the door and a man's voice. "Helene," and then louder, "Helene."

She swung herself upright, blinking. Erik – he was here in the night, just as he said he would be.

She hurried to the door to let him in.

"Oh," she said, blinking rapidly, pushing through the fog of sleep. "You made it. Hi!"

"Hello yourself." He stepped inside the door, no different than before, except more whiskery, the beard a little bushier. But he smelled like soap and toothpaste, so he must have freshened up. "Didn't mean to surprise you. It's just me, running a little late."

She stepped back so he could enter, limping slightly – maybe from the hours in the truck.

"No, no, I'm just glad to see you, really glad."

They kissed, first lightly, then more deeply. Then he stepped back, taking her in with his eyes, a tired smile crossing his face.

"Come in, come in," she said, leading him to the sofa. "Would you like something? Food or drink?"

"Nah, I'm all set."

They sat on the sofa, and he stretched out his legs under the coffee table. "Well, that was an adventure – one thing and the other. First the truck, then the cell phone. All these things are great, except when they break down and it's a pain in the ass to fix them."

"The truck?"

"Yeah, problem with the muffler. Loud as hell, and then it had to be replaced – easier said than done on the road. And then the phone – as you know. Plus service isn't all that reliable in many parts of the country. But all's well that ends well, as they say – and I made it back." He rubbed his chin. "Not much worse for wear."

"And all your business," she asked. "Business and personal?"

"Ah," he nodded. "OK, mostly. Made some progress, I think."

"You mean with your son, in New York?" She had guessed that the situation might be problematic, some things he'd said, hinted at, before he left.

He gave her a shrewd look, and then nodded. "That mainly. A few things still up in the air, but I can tell you more later." He reached over to take her hand. "How about you? How are you holding up?"

"Me?" she said, getting the distinct impression that he had changed the subject. "Fine. Well, OK. Maybe not at my best. I had a little meltdown – over a few things, but Thelma came out one night and that helped a lot. Except..." How was she going to put this? "There are a few people here not too pleased with me. And Kenneth's been after me to get together, but I just keep avoiding him."

Erik shook his head. "I don't care to meet him again, myself. I'm sure I suffer in the comparison. But I do feel for the guy. He needs to be heard, and he needs some answers."

"I know." Helene placed a hand on his forearm, her heart full of woe. "What are you even doing with someone like me – such a mess? I'm not crazy, but I'm acting like a crazy person. I really was afraid you'd given up on me, for the way I acted." She sighed. "I was so relieved when we finally made contact, and I realized you were not actually mad at me, or at least, not that mad..."

He squeezed her hand. "You're a good woman in a tough spot. How could I be mad at that?"

"That's charitable of you. Not that good, I'm afraid. Taking off with Wishi-ta first of all, and then that scene at Thelma's with Kenneth. Chewing you out over the car and the trip to the Home Camp. You were right for me to not charge up there." She gestured with one hand, taking in the room, the base, the world. "All of it, it's like some stupid soap opera, with a sort of Native American twist. Honestly, I'm not sure of myself these days."

"Those who are sure are often deluding themselves until adversity comes down the pike."

She smiled, but not with gaiety. "That's rather profound."

"Ha," he said. And then, "But you and me, we're OK, right? Right here, right now?"

"I think we are."

He kissed her hand, holding it between his. "How's this for an idea – a nice day in the country tomorrow – a swim and a picnic?"

"I would love to, if…"

He rolled his eyes. "No ifs. I don't mind a little mess now and then. I've certainly created enough in my time. I see how hard you're struggling to do the right thing by Wishi-ta, and all of them. And how you want something different in your life than what you've always had. I get that. We're not so different."

"How's that?"

He released her hand, opening the palm and touching her fingers one by one with his own. "We're not sure where we belong. Our own families fell apart when we were young. Elsa and I were in foster care, you know that, right?"

"I heard something…"

"And we both have sisters that were more than sisters – right? Elsa was like a mother to me, just like you were kind of a mother to Renee."

"Hmm…" Yes, but he was getting to rocky terrain.

He was on the third finger. "We're both making a public spectacle of ourselves at the moment, with each other, I mean, in front of everyone here. A favorite topic of conversation."

She groaned, because it was true.

"Number four, when things get too hairy, one way or another, we both run away to cabins in the woods." That made her laugh.

And then the pinkie finger. "And now we have kids in our lives that we care about and it matters what we do concerning them."

"Ah, yes." She nodded, because that was a big thing, wide open and uncertain.

Erik was suddenly serious again. "I want to be more of a dad to Connor. Even before I met you, I realized I haven't done as much as I should for him, and it's time to step up. I love kids, that's not it. His mother is not eager to have me in the picture, and I can't really blame her, from my past history. He's almost a teenager, and starting to act out with her and her new boyfriend. He needs a dad in his life, who actually spends time with him. So there's that."

He looked her up and down, waiting for a response. "So the question is, do you still want me around, even with all my baggage, as they say? And all the unknowns?"

"I do. I do, I do, I do." She stopped, making a face. "Wait! That sounds like a wedding. I didn't mean it like that. But yes – I do want you in my life, starting right here, right now."

"All right, little lady," he said, rising from the sofa and lifting her to her feet. He scooped her up with a groan, carrying her with uneven steps toward the bedroom. "I do too."

"Just don't drop me."

Chapter 24

The picnic was tasty and the day was beautiful, clear and sunny with little of the humidity of the earlier week. They went to a state park with hiking trails and a spring-fed lake. In the broad daylight, Helene had a better look at the dings and scratches on Erik's body, including the more grievous ones from his long-ago accident and the subsequent surgeries. Plus his little pot belly. But she loved the red glint in his hair and the soft fur on his chest, speckled with gray, the telltale signs of a somewhat rough and fully lived life. She herself was pale from all that sunscreen over so many years.

Just after lunch and a few minutes rest, Erik announced he was due to leave again the next day, Monday, to return the rig to the depot in Albany, and then wait for another truck to Montreal. Just a short trip, he explained. Easy driving, good money.

Drowsing in the sun, Helene wasn't sure she heard right. Gone again, for another two days and two nights?

"Do you want to come with me?" Erik asked, turning on his side. "I'd love to have you along, see the world from the cab of an eighteen-wheeler. We'll dine at all the best truck stops, and an overnight in Montreal."

A nice invitation, romantic even. But…

"I can't," Helene said, twisting on the blanket. "I'm going with Izzy to the police station Tuesday. I had to beg him to go. And then the family is returning on Wednesday." Her tone was firm, determined. "I have to be here."

Erik cocked his head. "Have to? I don't think so. They know you're here. That's no secret. And Izzy won't mind putting it off until another day, I promise you. I'm quite sure we'd be back on Wednesday before the family arrives – if they're even here before nightfall."

Helene pushed herself up to a seated position, shading her eyes from the slanting sun. "No, I just wouldn't feel right. It wouldn't look right."

Erik was leaning back on his elbows; his knees did not bend so well. "Fine, if that's how you feel. I'm sorry to leave so soon, but I made a commitment too. I have to go." He shifted his weight. "But I do have to tell you, Helene, this" – and he gestured from himself to her – "it's not about appearance. It's about reality – what's real for you, that you can live with. Not about other people's judgments. Isn't that what you wanted to leave behind?"

"Yes, it is. But I screwed up, royally, and I have to make sure everything's OK now."

"Really? Can you do that? Can anyone?"

A cloud had crossed the sun, leaving Helene chilled. With the dry air and shorter days, the seasons were beginning to shift, fall moving in. She stared at Erik, willing him to understand, and agree.

"OK, then. Let's put it this way: I don't want Izzy to wriggle out of this, ah, meeting. That's important to me, as a nurse, as a friend, family – really. And something I can do to make up for, well…"

And then, to her surprise, Erik nodded. "You don't need to do that. But I'm glad you're pushing him to go."

Helene swallowed, touched. "You are?"

"I'm sure you'll be clear and forceful. I don't know what kind of reception you'll get." He wagged his head, considering. "But you're a mature, educated white lady, let's not forget that, not to mention attractive. I wish you luck."

"Thank you, I guess." Helene said, disappointment transforming into gladness. "I appreciate your support."

Monday dawned cooler yet. Erik had to depart at dawn, leaving Helene alone in the warm bed, looking up at the ceiling of stars under the big wolf blanket. She had arranged to meet Izzy after breakfast to go over the pictures and make some notes – they needed to create a clear narrative of what happened, with as much detail as he could remember.

On the kitchen table, Erik had left a map of his driving route, showing when he expected to be at each stop. And then, at the end of the loop, a little rectangle with a heart inside – Renee's house, on the base – with the inscription, "Final stop – back to you." And then, in chicken scratch, "I'll be at your side when they return, or stay out of sight. Just let me know what you want." This was more than she deserved – a strange new kind of happiness that flowed through all the other troubles and worries.

After a cup of coffee, she went through Renee's bins, searching for material she could use for Bernice's shawl – fairly straightforward cutting and stitching with some embroidery – traditional, not fancy with all the satin ribbons. She would use Renee's shawl as a pattern – it looked to be the right size.

By nine thirty she was ready to meet with Izzy and run through the plan for the next day, rehearsing their points and arranging the "evidence." It took less than an hour to go over their strategy. By the end Helene was confident they were ready to present a strong case, one that would be taken seriously, including the possibility of a hate crime. They had to finish by eleven, when one of Izzy's friends was coming to pick him up to take care of unfinished business at Costco, and un-enroll from the courses he'd registered for at the community college, collecting a refund.

After lunch Helene had a long afternoon of waiting. She had cleaned Renee's house, and spruced up things at Malvina's. She'd tended the garden and done all the shopping – planning to cook lasagna for the family's return. She was as prepared as she was going to be for the trip with Izzy to the police station. The thing she hadn't dealt with was Kenneth. But she didn't call his number at work, or his cell. She called Thelma at her school office, leaving a message asking her to call when convenient. It wasn't much later that her phone rang.

"Any new developments?" Thelma asked, a small note of concern – or doubt – in her voice.

"No, all the same. It's this business with Kenneth." Helene could hear that her voice sounded whiny.

"Yup. You could help him understand a little better, why you're doing all this."

"I have tried."

"Maybe try a little harder."

"I told him it was all my fault. What else can I say?"

"Tell him the truth. That way of life wasn't working for you, for whatever reason. You can acknowledge how hard he worked to make a nice home and life for the two of you – that's still true. But you might say that you are searching for some other, ah, aspects of life – meaningful, creative, spiritual – something like that."

Helene closed her eyes. "Then he'll really think I'm a mental case," she scoffed.

"But it's not true. Your reasons are valid, even if your method was wrong. Maybe he realizes it too. Who knows? After a lifetime of more, bigger, better new houses, he might notice something lacking." She paused. A brief sip, a small hiccup. "Or not. But, Helene, do you really think he wants to say, 'My poor wife, she had a mental breakdown and went off'? Better that he says, 'She's on some spiritual quest that I don't really understand.'"

Helene's heart was beating a little faster, a kind of momentary panic. The afternoon was lovely and mild, windows open wide, birds chirping away. Yet she felt a kind of dread.

"I can't go back now, never. I can't live that lie; I don't have it in me."

"Yes, honey, I know. But don't dismiss those things altogether. It's not just the security and the comforts; it's having choices. The opposite can be very challenging, let me tell you. Making your way as a single woman in the world can be hard. It's nice when someone has your back."

Helene felt tears slide down her face. "I think I've always been alone. In my own family, dealing with Renee, in my marriage. Even here it looks like I'm on my own, until they decide if they can trust me – whether or not I keep seeing Erik. My own brother," she struggled to keep back a sob of self-pity, "has kept his distance all these years." Then she stopped. "There's just you," And that started her crying harder. "Thank goodness for you. What have I ever done for you, except bring problems to your door?" She stopped to grab a tissue and wipe her nose. "I don't know what

I'd do without you. That is the truth."

"Oh, come on," Thelma said mildly. "I like you better this way, well, mostly. It hasn't been dull." She chuckled softly. "I'm starting to feel I have two children leaving the nest…"

6. Freedom from Religion – by One Little Indian

I know, it's "Freedom of Religion," but not really. Lots of, but not all, Natives belong to some kind of organized church, mostly of the Christian types. This would include my mother, a devout Catholic in her own way, which is pretty flexible. That's the thing. Natives can pull in parts of other religions alongside ancestral beliefs and values, and it works for them, even if it doesn't work with the "our way or the highway" types. The Jesus story is great, I have to say, and Mother Mary has a big following too.

It's the other stuff that can be hard to take: rules and regulations and bigwigs in charge. Who likes having religion forced down their throats? In Canada, in the early days, the Jesuits, "Black Robes," were all about baptizing, aka "capturing souls," as if there were a bounty on those too. Then came all that stuff about devils, shame, guilt, damnation, and other ways to take the joy out of life. Never mind the sex stuff. Here in New England, the christianizers put the converted Indians into praying villages – so it wasn't just the religion, but the whole white man way of life, which was mostly not a good fit: those tight, scratchy clothes; cold, square houses; and living next to chickens and pigs. So unnatural to us.

In my view, Native spirituality is a big, fat, wide-open thing. Not so much about The Rules. Traditions, yes, but even those are pretty flexible and change over time. The whole setup of priests, bishops, cardinals, and popes doesn't seem much different than a big, multinational business, with its HQ at the Vatican. And what about those ministers who rake in lots of dough? Yes, shamans and medicine men are powerful leaders, also. They are respected for what they do for those in spiritual and medical need, not for how they judge and rule. And it's not just the bishops and popes who wear spiritual clothing; we, all of us Native peoples, wear regalia at powwows and ceremonies, to show that we too are sacred beings.

The part I really don't get in these Western religions is this whole idea of man on top, like humans are so special and supposed to use up everything in order to make some kind of heaven on earth for a few elite types – while others go without, and the earth and water get crapped on, excuse the language. There's no honoring of other living beings – animals, fish, birds, and plants. Nothing to say that they're important, too – that we need them and appreciate them. Natives call them relatives, because we are related – and that's way before Darwin and evolution showed it. Transforming from animal to human makes sense, when you think of the gene memory over so many years. Some old dude from Canada told me Natives in the cold, cold places considered polar bears their older, wiser brothers – they lived together in the same environment, facing the same challenges and using the same ways of catching fish and seals. Buffalo, deer, and whales – these creatures are honored for their strength and for providing so much for the people to survive on. Animals are thanked for their gifts. Why shouldn't they live free too, not penned up or factory-farmed only to be slaughtered? Western religion hasn't done too well by our animal relatives, or by our plant relatives, either. But it's done a number on humans, at the worst making them believe they are next to angels in the great pecking order of the cosmos, second only to God. Then there's evil – Natives have that concept too – those who desecrate what is holy. But hell, that's such a classic invention of Western religion – yet, not seeing that it's a place they've created here on earth.

Chapter 25

Helene was up half the night working on Bernice's shawl, and fell into deep sleep around dawn. The alarm for seven o'clock woke her with a start: *the trip to the police station with Izzy!* She stretched, her neck and shoulders stiff from the sewing. But she got up, started the coffee, and looked over the notes and photos again. Really, they were awful, Izzy's injuries, the broken nose and ribs, as well as the demolished bike. He was so slender to begin with, and kind of fragile. The ugliness of the bruises and the hacked-off hair marred Izzy's good looks – his beauty. And that was what could be seen, from the outside. Never mind the loose teeth and the bitten inner lip. Or the act itself – meant to hurt, diminish, humiliate – over a dent in a truck. She found her breath coming fast and shallow. And yet. It would be hard to say how these physical injuries were much different from falling off a bike being ridden at fast speed. Except the hair.

She was at Izzy's door well before nine. The door was left open, so she let herself in. He was up and finishing his breakfast. It wasn't like they had an appointment at the police station; she just wanted to catch someone, anyone, before they went off on their various duties.

"Ready?" she said, when he drank down the last of his juice.

"I have to brush my teeth," he said, straight-faced.

"After that?"

"As ready as I'm going to be." Not exactly hustling.

There were no other cars parked in the visitor spaces at the station. It had been renovated in the last five years or so, quite the model of modern design and, hopefully, operation. More like an office than a fortress of law, Helene thought, as they approached the building. In the front hallway, they passed bins for collecting old prescription drugs, syringes, and instructions on how to turn in firearms. All to the good.

As they waited for the secretary to get off the phone, Helene whispered, "You should do most of the talking. I'm here for support." He nodded, unenthused.

"Can I help you?" The secretary was a middle-aged woman, comfortably dressed with serious glasses, probably on the job a long time, probably seen all kinds of misdeeds.

For a moment, Helene didn't think Izzy was going to say anything. Then he heaved a sigh and began, "I'm here to report an assault. On myself, and my bicycle. About two weeks back. On Route 147."

The secretary nodded, registering no surprise. "OK. Then you'll need to talk to one of our officers. Why don't you take a seat, and I'll see who's available."

Helene piped up. "We'd like to talk to the chief. I think it may be a hate crime."

Izzy looked confused, until she realized that "chief" here was not the same as the Chief he knew. She meant, of course, the chief of police. "I assume the chief of police is in today," she added, to clarify.

The secretary looked over her glasses. "Take a seat. I'll be right back."

The chief of police, in uniform and name tag – Robert McMurray – returned with the secretary and introduced himself. He gave Izzy the once-over, subtly, before turning to Helene.

"Let's go in here," he said, indicating a room off the lobby. "Just brewed some coffee, if you'd like some."

"No, thank you." Helene said, and then poked Izzy gently with her elbow. It wouldn't do to clam up now.

"No, thank you," he said.

Chief McMurray looked to be in his mid-forties, just starting to gray, with a neat crew cut and bright blue eyes that didn't miss much. They took chairs across the table, and the chief settled back in his chair, no papers in hand, nor computer. He was just there to listen. The room held nothing personal, nor dangerous, no statues or trophies: a room for interviews, just the objective facts. They introduced themselves, saying where they lived. After a moment of silence, Helene began, "Isidore here – we call him Izzy – can tell you what happened. And I have a few notes and pictures that we thought might help."

"OK, then," Chief McMurray said, nodding. "Let me hear it."

Izzy gave a basic, bare-bones account in just a few minutes, Helene interrupting a few times to add details. He did not elaborate on the beating, but the recap of the event was clear and mostly complete. The chief put his hands together on the table as he listened, nodding once or twice.

"I'm sorry that happened to you," Chief McMurray said. "And an assault like that is a crime. Plus battery. It's too bad you waited, since that will make it harder to track down the assailants, but I think you've conveyed all the necessary facts."

That seemed to be it.

"Well, what now?" Helene said.

"I'll have one of the officers write up a report, pretty much just what this young, ah, fellow, has told me. We'll see if we can find any video surveillance along that route that would show the truck or the bike during that time frame. And we'll send out a report to other stations with the descriptions of those two men and the truck to cross-check against any information they have."

"And that's it?" Helene had thought a detective would be put on the case, someone who would go out and do an investigation, interview people – whatnot.

"You haven't given us a lot to go on, I'm afraid," the chief said, firm and sincere. "And as Izzy here says, there were New York plates on the truck – and that's a big state." He looked at Helene, not Izzy. "We'll enter the information on the computer, and have it on file, so that if those assailants do something else, we'll get flagged."

Helene could feel agitation rising, which would not help. She had to stay calm. Izzy was starting to slump in his chair, looking like some kind of long-legged bug, fairly squashed.

"But there's more to it than that," Helene said, speaking slowly. "I think it's a hate crime, and it needs be investigated."

The chief looked at her with some interest. "What makes you think that?"

"The hair," she almost yelled, but managing some restraint. "Look," she said, pushing the photos across the desk at him. "This is Izzy before, with his hair long, as he usually wears it. And this is what he looked like right afterward, with those fresh bruises. You can see the difference. And" – she paused dramatically – "they cut it with a knife. That's a weapon."

He looked awhile at the pictures. "So, against him as being an Indian, you mean or, well, ah, effeminate?"

"Well, yes, either, both. Or just being different."

The chief shrugged "Or being a hippie, maybe, a longhair. Some kind of an old country-boy joke. There isn't actually a law against cutting someone's hair without permission."

"Are you sure?"

"I can check it out, if you want. But I doubt we'll find much."

"But they beat him up!"

Now his face was closing, going into official role. "I hear what you're saying, ma'am. But, sorry to say, this is not entirely clear. He was riding his bike at a high speed, and these injuries could have come from falling off the bike – even if they did rough him up a bit."

"Rough him up? They broke his nose and his ribs – that was from a work boot, not a fall from a bike." What had seemed so clear and straightforward to Helene was now murky.

Chief McMurray held up his hands, tamping her down. "Listen to me, please. If we did find these guys, and if we did charge them, it's still a question of how the injuries were sustained – from a bike accident, or from a confrontation. In terms of intent, that's even harder to pin down. I'm just telling you, you're not going to get much satisfaction out of spending a lot of time and energy on this. If we hear anything about behavior of this kind, we'll follow up and let you know. But I can't hold out a lot of hope."

Izzy was right. And Erik too. Not much of anything was going to come out of it. From the police point of view, it was merely young men tangling over some perceived affront. Anger sprang from some unknown well; Helene was not ready to give up.

Erin McCormack

"You do see, don't you, that a hate crime affects the whole community, not just an individual?"

The Chief's jaw tightened, the end of his patience. "We can't even say what kind of hate they were supposed to be directing at him, can we?" He gestured at Izzy. "And, if we took up a campaign against every thick-headed kid who picks on someone, we'd never be done with it. They'll say they were provoked; damage was done to them. They just reacted."

"But – but –"

The Chief had had enough. "If you had more recent information, and better, clearer evidence, or witnesses, we might have a chance of getting these guys. But for now I'd say you've done your duty to report the assault, and it's now in our files. We'll do what I told you, but we can't devote a lot of time or resources on something like this."

Fat lot of good, she heard in her head, from somewhere, some time ago. She pushed the notes and photos at the Chief. "I made copies of all this," she said. "This is for you, for your files. In case it happens again, to someone else, who may need more of your attention."

He was making an effort now, to keep the professional tone. "Well, OK. I don't think it's likely…but we'll hang on to them."

Helene was too put out to even muster a "Thank you for your time." Izzy was already out the door as she hoisted her bag on to her shoulder, getting ready to leave.

"Ms. Bradford," the chief said, coming to her side. "I'm sorry not to be of more help. I see you're trying to help that young person, and that's very good of you. I'm not sure how well you know him, and if you can even be sure of the accuracy of the story…"

"He is my brother-in-law," she said coldly. "And this is important to us, to our family, and to anyone Native American who lives around here." And then she tossed over her shoulder, "Or longhair."

It was utter defeat, just as Izzy had said. *Yes, yes, yes.* Maybe they were late to make the report and maybe there wasn't a lot of information to go on. But it was a crime, and should be investigated. What else were they so busy doing, anyway? And then, as she got into the car and reversed out of the parking lot, she had another thought. *They just don't want a hate crime, not here, not now, in this peaceful little place.*

Her knuckles were white as she drove down the road. Finally she took a couple of deep breaths – another accident was the last thing they needed.

"Well, Izzy," she said. "You were right. And I was wrong. I'm shocked and disappointed."

Clearly he was not.

"I appreciate what you were doing, Helene," he said. "And it was the right thing to do. I'm sorry you're so disappointed."

"Not in you."

"Well, no. I did OK. But you had more hope than I did."

"Yeah, silly me."

"You tried."

"I guess my next career will not be a lawyer," she tried to joke.

"Me, either."

They parted with no further plans about the assault. The next morning, Wednesday, Helene sprang awake in bed well before her usual time. Even before her eyes were fully open, her thoughts were racing: a big day, no matter what. Erik was returning from the road, and the family from the Home Camp. At the same time, she was feeling the sting of yesterday's meeting at the police station. She had not been able to do what she'd hoped for Izzy; the wheels of justice were not turning in their favor. But neither was she ready to admit defeat.

After breakfast, at the kitchen sink, she heard melancholy piping next door. Was it Izzy's manner of playing or the songs themselves that were so sad? She kept herself busy with the lasagna and more sewing, until around noon there was a knock on the door: a petite young woman with a short, buzzed haircut in a sleeveless tank top and black jeans. She introduced herself as Casey, one of Izzy's friends; did Helene want to join them for lunch? She'd picked up some sandwiches at the sub shop.

"That would be nice," said Helene, sizing up her visitor with interest: a Celtic tattoo on her arm and a fondness for chain-type jewelry, including rings along the tops of her ears and one through her eyebrow. Behind her dark-framed glasses, she had sharp blue eyes, full of energy and intensity.

"Give me a minute and I'll come with you," Helene said.

On the way over, Casey explained that Izzy had told her most of the details of the assault, and she was interested in what had happened at the police station. She and Izzy had gone to high school together and she was majoring in journalism in college. A fellow video gamer and Star Trek fan. *Was there more?* Helene had seen the kind of adoration Izzy inspired, although it was not always clear to her of its nature.

In Neesa's kitchen Casey offered her opinion as she handed out sandwiches around the table. "That's the problem with hair. Sometimes it's hard to know what it means. Or the meaning changes across cultures. Still, it's wrong what they did. I know it, you know it, and that police chief should know it. I read something about some Amish dudes who had trouble with rivals, and the guys cut off their beards."

"Was it a crime?" Helene wanted to know, pouring herself an iced tea.

"That I don't remember. But they didn't break any bones, I don't think. I'll have to look it up online." The investigative journalist at work.

"It's not right," Casey pronounced. "I'm going to ask my criminal justice professor what she thinks. This is definitely hate-based."

"Hmm..." Helene took another bite of her tuna sub and chewed mechanically, still deflated from the previous day's outing.

"I think we're on to something; I really do. I am not dropping it."

Casey looked from Izzy to Helene for a response.

"Let us know," Helene said vaguely. She had caught Casey's unguarded look of devotion, of whatever kind. But she couldn't manage to sound enthusiastic, even in the face of such fierce commitment.

After she finished her food, she left them to catch up on their young adult talk of work and friends, video games and movies, and let herself back into a quiet house. She was starting to get restless about the return of Erik – and the family. Erik had expected to be back by four o'clock, five at the latest – unless something happened on the road. When he'd called the previous night, she gave him a brief account of the meeting at the police station. He was not as pessimistic as she would have thought, and said, "Give it time, and see what might happen."

It wasn't even three o'clock when Helene heard an engine turn off outside the house.

She leaned back to glimpse out the window. Erik's truck!

She put the needle she was using into the pincushion and rushed outside to meet him.

"Early!" she said, as he approached. But rather than hug and kiss on the doorstep, she pulled him inside, catching a manly whiff of food and fuel and clothes that had been lived in.

"Haven't even stopped to wash up yet," he said, almost shy.

She pulled him close and shut her eyes to kiss him, inhaling deeply. "You're not kidding. I guess you really wanted to see me."

"I did. And check in with you before the parade arrives."

"They're not due until suppertime, or later," she said. "I made lasagna; I could heat some up for you."

"Not now, thanks." He put a hand to her face. "I just wanted to feast my eyes on you."

She guffawed, but part of her was touched. "That's so corny, but I love it. More, more."

"Well, that's it. But I do have sort of an addiction to you, I believe. I can't explain it otherwise."

"Is that what it is? You're attracted to the drama?" She shook her head, somewhat sadly. "I don't like to think of the things I've done lately."

"It's a tough life, sometimes."

"It is."

"Like yesterday, with Izzy." She sighed. "What a disaster. Well, not a disaster. But we were pretty much completely shut down, like I said on the phone."

"Do you want to talk about it?"

"Not now. It won't make me feel any better." Then she added hastily, "But seeing you – that makes me feel better. I'm fine, really."

He lifted her chin. "Of course you are. It's all good." Then he stepped back. "Anyway, I know you have lots to do, getting ready and all. And I'd better get to Elsa's and take a shower." He raised his eyebrows. "Then, should I return, or do you want me to lie low?"

She took his hand. "Oh, don't go. I want you to be here when they get here – if you don't mind."

"Of course not. Right at your side. But I do need a shower."

"Take one here," she said.

"Really?"

"Really. In fact…" She traced the outline of his chin and neck with a finger. Everything was surging inside her – blood, warmth, affection, desire. He was still waiting for her to finish.

"We have a few minutes," she said, "unless they surprise me too."

"I've never had a more romantic invitation," he teased, pulling her close. "But I thought you were, ah, concerned about, ah, things."

She smiled. "Like you said, it's not just about appearances. If I can't be genuine, I'm not much good to them or me, come what may."

They embraced again, both bursting with energy and passion, like teenagers, until she pulled away, breathing fast and shallow.

"Maybe don't bother with the shower, until afterward," she said. "I kind of like that meaty smell."

"I'm in no position to argue," he answered, big and bearlike, equally breathless. "But then I'll have to go back to Elsa's for clean clothes."

"Chop, chop," she said. "Let's go."

Erik went back to Elsa's to change, and then returned to wait with Helene. They sat on the back porch, Helene wearing a sweater for the cooling night. The slider to the kitchen was open, and then the one to the front door, just a screen to keep the bugs out. They'd be able to see and hear any vehicles pull up at Malvina's house. The night was especially quiet, and bats flitted about in the twilight between trees. Finally, just after eight o'clock, the lights of a vehicle came down the street, and they heard it stop next door, and the engine turn off.

In a second Helene was on her feet, flying to the front of the house and out the door, Erik somewhere behind. She saw Noel getting out of the driver's seat, and then Neesa climbing out from passenger side, followed by Pawnee who'd been sitting between them. A door slid open to reveal Malvina in the middle row, next to the baby in its carrier, and Kiowa on the other side. In the back were impatient, excited voices: Cree and the twins, trapped until their mother and sister got out.

Helene felt Erik behind her on the sidewalk, and reached out a hand to draw him closer. Kiowa jumped out first, turning back to fold down the seat back. They waited while Malvina unlatched the baby carrier, putting the diaper bag on her shoulder. When the smaller children were finally released, they spilled out with shrieks of joy.

"We're here!" Tana-na shouted, to no one in particular. He was inches taller, it seemed to Helene, and brown as a nut. Cree bounded out, certainly recovered from his bout with Lyme disease. And finally, more carefully, Wishi-ta stepped out, in an outfit that was part princess, part wood fairy, and went straight to Helene.

"You're here, you're here!" she cried, in a voice louder and more forceful than Helene remembered. "I have something for you."

Noel had called the children over, except Pawnee, who let himself into the house, apparently on a mission.

"We say hello to family first," Noel said in his mild, firm way. The children scrambled to his side and looked toward the house where Pawnee had reappeared and Izzy behind him. The children fell quiet, subdued by the change in Izzy, his new hair style. But he smiled his broad, familiar smile and walked down the steps next to Helene and Erik, as if forming a receiving line. Around them Helene could hear the opening of doors, and a slight buzz of voices. The Chief had stepped outside, with Elsa at his elbow. Then Malvina and Kiowa were there with baby Tewa.

Noel gave Izzy a close look, and then a one-armed hug, heart to heart. Then Malvina and Neesa were at Izzy's side, with tight lips and close hugs. Noel walked up to Helene. "Good to see you," he said, and extended his arm over her shoulders, giving a warm squeeze. After that Malvina and Neesa each said "Hello," with a nod before moving on to Erik. The kids had come up in a circle, pushing in to get their hugs. Except for Wishi-ta, who had her arms around Helene's waist, and would not let go. She stayed firmly in place, only giving Erik a high five.

Helene greeted each child warmly, all the time keeping a hand on Wishi-ta's back. She saw Noel's eyes take them in, and then Neesa's, without saying a word. But it was clear the bond had held.

Only after they'd had a chance to say hello to Elsa, Chief, and some of the neighbors did the family go inside. Helene offered the lasagna, which was still warm, and Malvina said, "No thanks. We stopped at Burger King." But Izzy said he was hungry, and then Pawnee, and even Kiowa said she wanted some. So Helene and Erik brought it over, along with the salad and some rolls, placing them on the table next to the big basket of vegetables from Neesa's garden. The kids had found their friends and were running around the backyard in the near dark. Helene encouraged Wishi-ta to join them, saying, "We'll have plenty of time together, don't worry." Erik came in the kitchen to say good night. They had already agreed he would not stay with Helene.

"Go ahead," she said to Erik, placing a hand on his arm. She surprised herself. There were so many questions: *What did Louis say? Where will the twins stay, with me or back with the rest of the family? Who will feed them and get them to school? What do they want from me now?* But suddenly she'd found a patience she didn't know she had. Tonight, tomorrow, the next day; whenever they were ready, she would also be ready. Malvina still had so much to manage, and the baby first of all.

From the kitchen, Noel took Helene aside, into the living room, flipping on a light. Neesa had left for her side of the duplex with Izzy, and Malvina went to change the baby. The living room was a hushed place, not often used, with its curtains drawn most of the time to keep the furniture from fading. For the first time, Helene noticed shelves full of books by the window – books on Indian life and culture, history books, and books on law. Noel invited her to sit next to him on the worn, sturdy sofa.

"I'll be brief as I can, for now," Noel said, his voice calm and normal. "We're glad you're here and we want you to stay. We talked with Louis about what happened, before and after you left with Wishi-ta, and what we know of your actions and your motivation. We are concerned about you, and we want you to be well. Wishi-ta made it clear to her father that she wants you near, and Cree also told him how much you had helped him, and us, when he was sick. Neesa told him that Izzy asked for you after his accident. I can tell you more later, but the outcome is that you are welcome to stay in the house – next door – and for the twins to stay with you, as before. But Neesa will also stay there with you for a while."

Helene swallowed. That was probably right and fair, but she still felt uneasy. "Because they don't quite trust me?"

"Because the twins are precious to us, and because you went away with Wishi-ta without telling us, and because you also had an injury..."

"But I'm fine. I really am."

"That's good. In the meanwhile Neesa can help you with getting the twins ready for school, and anything else that comes up. She will help Malvina with cooking and laundry during the day, besides her own home, of course."

Helene nodded, taking this in, the meaning, the ramifications. She was excited, thrilled. But still unsure if this was a decision, or just another trial.

"Whose idea was it – Louis's?" It came out sharper than she meant. Noel had been nothing but kind to her; easier than the women to communicate with. Maybe that's why he was chosen to deliver the news. His background, she knew, was Pemaquot, also; and as far as she knew, he was full blood on both sides, without a drop of European or African, like Louis's own family.

"It seemed a good idea to all of us," he said – weighing his words.

Helene forced herself to take a deep breath. It was what she would do if she were in their shoes.

"I don't think Neesa really likes me," she said, finally. "Or that she'll ever really accept me."

Noel's eyes widened, perhaps surprised at her frankness. And then just the slightest twinkle – of fun, of all things – appeared in his eye. "No, it's not always easy." In a flash Helene knew that Neesa could sometimes be hard on him too, Indian or not. "But she might surprise you. She does appreciate your care for the children, and your medical knowledge. And I know she admires your sewing." His eyebrows went up. "Maybe if you made her a shawl…"

Helene laughed. "If only it were that easy." But it was not a bad idea; that was something she enjoyed doing, and she had such clear images about Neesa – her baskets, her vegetables, her love of birds, her Catholic faith, and of course all the children around her. She wagged her head. "Maybe…"

Noel stood to go. "I can tell you more later, about the children, and about our time with Louis. For now I need to know if you are OK with this plan."

"OK?" she repeated. "What choice do I have, really? No, I'm sorry. Please, I don't mean to sound negative. I do understand. And I thank you for telling me. I guess it's the best for now. I'm sure it is."

"Yes, for now. Things can change. But one more thing…" He was on his feet, headed for the front door, and the van, and all the things that still needed to be unpacked and put away. From the kitchen they heard the slider to the deck open and close, breathless steps crossing the kitchen to the bathroom.

"Louis wants to see you," he said. "I mean, for you to visit up there. Not this weekend but the next."

"Oh!"

"And Izzy too. He wants to talk to him."

"But not the children?"

"Not this time." He offered no further explanation. "Izzy can call to register your visit. You'll probably want an overnight at the hotel. Robert and Charlotte are willing to drive, if you're not able; they have the time and they like to travel."

Again Helene had to fight her first reaction. She decided it was better to hold off on more questions for now. But they still swirled through her mind: *Why so soon after the family's return? Why can't we talk on the phone? What else does he want from me? Or from Izzy?*

"OK," she said. Noel nodded, and then lifted a hand to cover a yawn. Helene guessed he had done most or all of the driving.

She followed him outside to the van, where he began to pull out bags and laundry baskets from the back. There were duffel bags full of clothes and shoes, labeled with each child's name. Plus a tote with Wishi-ta's medicine. Helene took the bags for Wishi-ta and Tana-na, crossing back to Renee's house. She caught glimpses of the children in the backyard, with Yellow Dog racing excitedly between them.

Inside the house she pondered how the new arrangement was going to work – would Neesa sleep in the twins' room? And what did it mean for her and Erik? Probably no more late-night rendezvous on the sofa or the back bedroom. But then what, or where? Not at the Chief's house, either. It was like being demoted to teenager again. Or more like Babysitter in Charge. But another part of her was happy and relieved, at least for the moment. She wasn't being ousted. She would remain here, and be part of this life. Any inconvenience was her doing – for taking Wishi-ta away in a panic, as she had. Things would change in time, no doubt.

She put the twins' bags on the bed in their room. The beds were pushed together but they could pull the beds apart, one for Neesa. She didn't think Neesa would want to stay on the sofa. Wishi-ta could sleep with Helene in the big bed tonight, and then they'd figure it out.

As she finished putting the clothes away, the phone starting ringing. She smiled – *Erik*, wondering what was happening. But it was Denis.

"Quick pit stop," he said. "We're heading back, finally, and I wanted to check how you are doing. What am I going to find when I get there?"

Helene sat on the sofa, stretching out her legs. "Hard to say. Everything is actually OK for the moment. I'm still in the house, and the twins will be here too – and Neesa. But I got a summons to see Louis at the end of next week. I guess he's going to lay down the rules – that is, if I want to stay here and be part of family life."

"And do you?"

"More than anything. I can't quite explain it."

"And Kenneth?"

She groaned, a hand to her temple, that tiny twinge of headache. "Don't ask me that. I owe him a call or a letter or something. I just haven't been able to make myself do it. We do have to meet with him, though, you and me – about the house."

"You mean, selling it?"

"Right, because you get a third. You have some say about the listing price, all that."

Denis laughed. "Oh, please. Like I care. That is some kind of sweet, sick karma, you know. For the first time in my life, I don't actually need the money. Or at least I don't need it tomorrow, or yesterday." He laughed again. "But I may actually need it in the future."

"I don't know what you're going on about." Helene said. "But to the point – I'll see you – when?"

"I can't say exactly, but in the next few weeks. I've got to stop and see Kiko and the dogs first."

"So Kiko. Something going on there?"

There was a rueful smile. "Maybe. I have to see if I can patch things up. She says she's done with me -- I can never be reached."

Helene stifled a *Ha!* "Seems only fair."

"She's very good to my dogs," he said, seriously.

"And that's important."

"You have no idea."

Chapter 26

The next few days were full of back-to-school business, the start of kindergarten, and follow-up appointments for both Wishi-ta and Cree. They scheduled both appointments for the same morning, and Helene and Noel went together, with Tana-na along for company. In spite of bruises, scratches, and bug bites, both children were doing well, and had gained height and weight. As a nurse Helene could see that all three children were cared for and growing properly. In spite of all the sadness and troubles they had been through, they played well with the other children in the waiting room, polite and even helpful. Good kids, not mean.

After that school began, and they settled into a routine that involved some coordination between Helene and Neesa. After waking at six, Helene made the coffee, got breakfast ready, and packed food for the children. At six thirty, Neesa would prod the children once before heading out to help Malvina. She returned forty-five minutes later, as the twins finished their cereal and juice and started getting washed and dressed. When they were ready for the walk to school, Neesa kissed them on the head and left for her own house, not to be seen again until after dinner, usually with food in hand, leftovers, or one of her pies, sweet or savory.

During the evenings Neesa was mild and circumspect, which surprised Helene. At night she sat in the living room, working on one of her projects, or watched TV in the den with the others until it was bedtime for the children. She also retired early, soon after the children's voices had quieted from the other room. After washing up she reappeared in the living room in her nightgown, and Helene would get up and follow her to the twins' room, where Helene scooped up the sleeping Wishi-ta and carried her to the back bedroom for the night. If she roused at all, it was only for a minute, and then to ask Helene to stay with her in the bed.

The start of kindergarten was not difficult. The building was close by, part of the elementary school where the children's cousins went, except Kiowa, who was now in middle school. They already knew many of the children from the Intertribal Center, and some of the teachers too. Plus they had each other in class, by request. Kindergarten ran from eight thirty until three o'clock, a pretty full day. Helene had already been to visit the teachers and classrooms earlier in the summer, before the big "escapade," and wondered what, if anything, they knew about it.

In all, the first, abbreviated week of school went smoothly, and Helene felt she could relax a little. And see Erik. The weekend weather was hot and sunny, and the children were outside playing with the hose, while Neesa had gone next door. There was housework to do, and laundry, but nothing pressing. Helene had seen Erik once, when he pulled his truck to the curb to talk. He had a couple days of carpentry work lined up, and then a trucking job in another week.

"So Neesa's there at night, right? Well, that's a romance killer. Would she mind babysitting if we go out?"

At first Helene thought he was joking, but he wasn't.

"Probably not," Helene said, after a minute. "She's got nothing against you, anyhow. But let's wait another week or so, until after I meet with Louis, just to be sure."

Erik made a wry face. "And then what? Dinner and drinks, and making out in my truck? Only for you, babe."

"Or you could come by after lunch," Helene teased. "At least for now, before I start working. No one's around until three. Unless, of course, someone happens to drop by."

"I'll never get back to work," he complained, hangdog. A car came around the corner, and they stopped to look. It was a neighbor of the Chief's who gave a friendly toot, and they waved back.

Helene blushed, flattered, and somewhat aroused thinking Erik desired her that much. Well, their time together was fun, and good, and very, very pleasurable. But there was a lot at stake and she didn't want to make things harder. They would have to figure something out.

"Well, unless you come up with a better plan."

He put a hand to her face out the open truck window. "Give me a chance. I'm pretty capable when I'm sufficiently motivated. Besides, I have an idea…"

"Tell me!"

"You'll have to wait, in case it doesn't pan out." He glanced at the dashboard clock. "I've got to go. Late for work; it will never do."

"Right. Of course."

"But I hate to leave you. I really do."

He was so corny, it was sweet. Or the other way around. Either way, Helene appreciated it, because Kenneth had never said things like that. It was always his time that was so valuable, and so many other, important things he had to take care of.

Their kiss was light and swift, and then he was away down the road. Helene wondered who else might have seen the two of them. And yet it was beyond her now to hide or control. Still, first things first. And that meant a right routine and right behavior, in preparation for meeting Louis – nothing that would alarm him, or others.

Helene was as good a "wannabe" Indian as she could be, gleaning hints from those around her in the base community, supplemented by a couple of books from the library. Expectations in this new culture were different – not about appearances and economic status, but how she handled herself and the twins, and how she interacted with others. It made a certain sense to her now, this way of life, leaving behind the hustle and worry and propriety of that other, upper-middle-class suburban life and all its aspirations. Yet she was not sure about the guiding principles of Native American spirituality, either. Leaving behind the old, bearded God of the Bible was easy enough; but the idea of the Great Spirit eluded her – the purpose and nature of all the traditions and rituals.

But then, the children. What she observed while spending time with them was a convincing argument. They seemed to come around to better behavior through gentle words and modeling rather than guilt, shame, or mindless bribes and treats; they saw themselves as welcome and important in the greater community, where they were treated as full persons, and spoken to with fondness and tenderness. The difference between them and the children at her former school, so many of whom were worried and anxious, or spoiled and mean. Not that they didn't have real problems, and adversity. But these children, the twins included, had an inner sweetness and self-possession, like Izzy.

Helene couldn't deny there was still so much uncertainty, especially regarding Louis. But she had to admit she was feeling stronger, sharper, more confident. What soothed her most was losing herself in sewing the regalia – perhaps just the benefit of any creative endeavor. For the time being, she put aside the research and legal documents on adoption; too upsetting and confusing. In quiet moments she read Renee's journal musings without the same dread of encountering all that was ugly and sad in their shared past. Mostly she was able to enjoy Renee's accounts of her life and came to appreciate her sister's sharp wit and hard-earned wisdom.

It surprised her when the nightmares started, especially when she was fast asleep in the bed with Wishi-ta at her side. Chase scenes, angry words, and violence. Some from childhood, and some from afterward. Almost all of them with Renee, at different ages – begging, demanding, crying for help from Helene.

At first she thought maybe the concussion had triggered some part of her brain that had been dormant for years. Her next follow-up appointment with the neurologist wasn't for another month, and there had been no other symptoms – no dizziness or headaches or confusion. Just these nightmares.

One night she woke in terror, her hands covering her mouth. She didn't want to make a sound and wake Wishi-ta, or Neesa. She swung her legs over the side of the bed and sat up, taking deep breaths, trying to remember, exactly, what the bad dream was about. And what did it mean?

In the dream Renee was still a child, but their mother had already died. She was in the kitchen with Helene, begging for a treat. At first Helene gave her cookies, and then, when Renee started crying because she didn't like them, some cake or a pastry. But it was spoiled. Helene tasted the cream on top and it was sour.

"It's no good," she told Renee, but Renee wouldn't listen or stop fussing. Helene rifled through the pantry, through the refrigerator. She found a Christmas log, a *Buche de Noel* her mother used to make, sitting on the counter, although her mother was dead and could not have made it. It was already cut, the knife smeared with a black goo oozing from inside. Helene, in desperation, tried to feed it to Renee, who was no longer a child but a young woman. She knocked it away in anger, and they started to struggle. Helene grabbed Renee by the wrists, trying to keep her away from the knife, starting to yell for help. But no one came, and the fighting continued, the anger escalating, until Renee's eyes had the red glow of a demon. Helene hauled back and struck her hardest blow, and Renee fell to the floor. As Helene leaned in, Renee growled and reached a hand to claw Helene on the cheek. Then Renee was gone, and Helene sat back on her heels in the kitchen, alone, feeling blood drip down her face.

Helene sat wet-faced and clutching her chest in a deep grief, undiffused, unabated after all these years. *Renee. What did she want?* If her soul could come back from the dead to give a message, what would it be? Helene was only doing what she could for Renee's children, helping out once again, doing what was expected, what was proper. Why should she be punished for that?

That was the first nightmare, and then there was a lull. Helene did not want to tell anyone about it – what was the point? And certainly, she did not want anyone to question her well-being. She was fine, she was fit; she could manage the twins. In a couple of weeks, she would start her new job at the health clinic, and really, then, her new life. Thelma had given her the name of a divorce lawyer – her own – and said it was time to start proceedings. A formal separation. An acknowledgment of how things had changed.

"All right," Helene breathed over the phone to Thelma. She had pen and paper at hand to take notes. Instead she was doodling, small, curly animals. "I'll make an appointment with the lawyer, for the end of the month. Will you go with me?"

"Yes. Not during school hours."

"And I can stay with you?"

"Of course."

"I really don't want to deal with it."

"No one does. Did you call Kenneth yet, or write him?"

"I can't. Honestly. I started a letter probably five times, but I can't get anywhere. I don't know what to say."

"Hmm..." Thelma cleared her throat at the other end of the line. "Well, I've seen him twice – once at the store and once when I was having lunch out with some friends. He seems OK. Bright enough, you know. Smiling. But kind of brittle, if you know what I mean."

"Not really."

"Let's put it this way. I think it's an effort to put on a good face. But he's certainly a popular guy."

Helene felt a jolt to the gut. Possessiveness? Jealousy? Or, was it envy, maybe? "Do you mean with women?"

"With men and women, both. He's at his prime: he's handsome, successful, pleasant, and basically a good, honest guy."

It was true, of course. Helene drummed the pen on the pad a few times. Was Thelma suggesting that Helene reconsider? No, she was just being fair and honest.

"Unlike me?"

Thelma made a sound. "I can't judge you. I'll just say that you were deceptive, on some accounts."

Helene was scratching out all that she had drawn, the cartoons, the silly stuff. But not the lawyer's name or phone number.

"But not dishonest. I didn't lie."

"OK, I'll give you that. Anyway I'm here for you, whenever you're ready. But you're OK, though, aren't you? I mean, recovered from the concussion, and all."

Helene had to think before she answered. No lying. "For the most part, yes. An occasional twinge. And of course it's not fun knowing that some people dislike me. Not the family – other people. I don't know why it's their business, but I see how they look at me, and hear some things they say."

Thelma tut-tutted. "That's life, my dear. Not everyone is going to like you or what you've done. It's not all about being nice, remember?"

Helene did know that. And she understood and accepted. Except for when she occasionally felt she was being watched, or even spied on. Those strange sounds outside the house; the ruffled papers when she was out. But no, that was starting to sound a little paranoid, over the top.

Instead she blurted, "I have these crazy dreams sometimes – sort of nightmares."

"Oh, really?" There was a note of professional interest in Thelma's voice. "About what? Do you want to tell me?"

"Oh, no. Nonsensical stuff. Nothing important," Helene said quickly. Inky zigzags and crosshatches covered the paper, which was starting to rip. "I'm sure it's to do with seeing Louis – honest to God, it feels like meeting the Great Oz hiding behind his curtain."

"Not exactly hiding. But I know what you mean. Sure, you're anxious, but I also think he's smart enough to understand your motivation, and to value what you've done for the family, and want to do."

Helene felt such a rush of emotion, she could hardly speak. "You do? Really? That's so kind of you."

"Only true. Just deal with it, go forward, not around it. Soon enough it will all be behind you. And the bad dreams too."

In spite of Helene's confession, the nightmares continued, and picked up. Almost every one of involved Renee, until Helene no longer felt comfortable sleeping in Renee's bed, or even in Renee's room. In every dream Renee was asking for help, and then angry and acting out – just like those terrible teenage years. But sometimes she looked like Wishi-ta, which was very confusing. And then she was sweet and loving. A couple of times Helene got up in the night and moved to the sofa, bringing a pillow and a light blanket. Once Wishi-ta appeared at her side, touching her cheek, and making Helene startle, frightening the child. The next time she awoke in the morning on the sofa to find Wishi-ta curled up on the rug in front of her, having dragged the wolf blanket from the bed. After that Helene stayed in the bed, turning on a light to read.

On the following Saturday, all of the family made a day trip to New Hampshire for the birthday party of an aunt, or great-aunt, their father's sister, who was turning eighty. Helene was not invited, nor did she expect to be, but she missed the twins' presence, and even to some extent Neesa – the warmth and energy of other living beings in the house.

Erik was working until midafternoon, but he said he would come by after he showered and changed. He was waiting to hear back on another driving job, always on the lookout for something that would take him through upstate New York so he could see Connor, his son.

Helene had cooked a pot of chili for their supper, and took him to the back porch to sit and relax. She offered beer, but he said he'd take an iced tea.

"I've got an idea where we can meet," he said. "But I'm not sure how you're going to like it."

Helene's eyes widened. "Not here? Now, while the cats are away?"

"Well, yes. That's a nice opportunity. But for going forward, when they are here." He gave a corny wink. "A private getaway."

"Which is...?"

"Close by, quiet, kind of comfortable, and, uh, free."

She shook her head. "Tell me, I can't imagine."

"The office at the Intertribal Center. Actually the lounge outside the office – there's a nice comfy sofa, a table and chairs, and even a TV."

Now she was smiling. "You're kidding me."

"No, the Chief is OK if we keep it on the QT." He fished into his pocket and produced a set of keys on a key ring. "I got this from him."

Helene buried in face in her hands, trying to stop the laughter and the embarrassment of it all. "Oh, my lord," she said. "What have we come to? What if we're discovered?"

"Oh, after ten or so most nights, there's no one there." Erik beamed. "Our best option, for the moment." Which it probably was. "You're not going to say no, are you?" He reached for her hand.

She rolled her eyes. "How could I resist?" Part of her was tickled – a bit of an adventure – temporarily at least. And maybe better than Renee's room. "I can't believe the Chief's in on this…"

"He's a guy too."

"That explains it."

"And he likes you. And me too, most of the time."

Helene sighed, leaning back in her chair, watching bugs flying outside the porch screen. Yellow jackets, it looked like, quiet and slow at this time of year.

"If only…" she said, not meaning to sound so downcast.

"What?"

"This business with Louis. If I could know that he was really going to accept me, and accept things, we could carry on like normal people."

"You don't know what he'll say."

"It feels so…I don't know. Like I'm being summoned to court, being judged like this."

Erik tipped his head side to side. "These are important matters, and I guess he thinks face to face is the best way to communicate."

Helene had to admit that Erik knew better than she did how things worked around here – the sometimes unspoken dynamics between individuals and groups.

"If he is against me, he's not the only one," she said darkly. "You know, Alberta, Frances, that grandson, some of those people. Not exactly my fans."

"Not my fans, either. They're not the most enlightened folks. And they're tough on everyone, generally, not just white folks." He paused, considering. "They come from some tough places; you truly do not know some of the shit they've dealt with. But it's not up to them. And you can't please everyone."

"Good points," she said finally. She released his hand, getting to her feet. "Any more iced tea – or anything to eat?"

He did not want those things. But he was also getting to his feet, and stepped closer to pull her into his arms.

"If I'm here, and you want me to, I'll drive you to see Louis. I won't take the trucking job."

She raised a hand to his cheek. "You would do that?"

"If it will help you, I will."

She buried her face in the hollow between his shoulder and his chest. "Thank you."

The call came – the summons to see Louis – for the following weekend at nine in the morning; they would have to go up the night before. Helene told Izzy that Erik would drive, so that he would include him on the visiting order. By this point Erik had told her the history between him and

Louis, going back to their younger years, and that Erik had not been particularly welcome at the start of Louis and Renee's marriage. After the twins were born, things were on better terms. And then, when Renee got sick, Erik had run errands for the family, and had time to sit with Renee, since he was often there anyway staying with Chief and Elsa.

At night, after the twins were in bed, Helene called Erik. "I can meet you at the place," she said, whispering like it was top-secret espionage.

She had told Neesa she was going out for a little while – but not where. She deliberated starting the car and driving around the block to park out of sight but didn't. She wasn't good at being sneaky. Even in an effort to preserve appearances and not to confuse the children, she wasn't going to waste her time or gas. She walked over to the Intertribal Center around ten, where Erik met her in front, unlocking the door to get in. They walked silently in the dim ambient light to the second-floor lounge outside the office. On the way, the pictures of Native leaders, men and women, on the Wall of Warriors glared fiercely but silently.

Erik had brought a heavy-duty flashlight, which made Helene smile. "How about a candle next time?"

They moved the back cushions from the sofa and sat down, beginning to kiss.

Helene pulled back, looking up. "So, we're still on, right, for Saturday?"

Erik blinked, confused. "What?"

"To see Louis."

"Yes, sure, all set. But what does that have to do with us, here and now?"

"Just double-checking. And, besides, I'm in a good negotiating spot."

"The lounge?"

She tapped his chest, and then let a hand run down to his belt. "No, silly. I mean this."

It was a long week, getting to Saturday, although the weather was beautiful and the twins had made a promising start at school – seeing their friends, doing projects, and taking part in the Talking Stick circle, where each had a chance to hold a stick that meant it was their time to talk. Plus a lot of music and outside time. A classroom aide kept an eye on Tana-na, and reported that his extra energy had been channeled in positive ways – handing out paper and markers and setting up a habitat for the classroom turtle. Yet every day, when Helene showed up to walk them home, Wishi-ta grabbed her around the waist for a long hug and would not release her hand on the way home. Even Tana-na never wandered far, coming and going like a puppy exploring his territory. After their return from the Home Camp, they had answered a few questions about the visit to their father, but they didn't bring it up otherwise. They seemed to prefer what was happening in the present, or things they were looking forward to, like powwows and turning five years old.

The twins' birthday was fast approaching on the Saturday after the Saturday of the prison visit. It happened to be the same date as Erik's birthday. He was turning forty-eight, younger than she'd thought. Helene had already told Malvina and Noel that she wanted to have a party for the twins in their adjoining backyards – more or less an open house for the neighborhood, anyone who wanted to stop in. The theme was animals of all kinds, with a few party games. And food, cake, and balloons. A crafting table: braided bracelets or armlets.

Wishi-ta wanted a pony, which she could not have; and Tana-na wanted a gun, which was subject to debate. The older boy cousins had toy guns of all kinds; and of course, their relatives at the Home Camp had hunting guns. Even Noel had a gun, which surprised her, but he left it in Maine. So water guns or maybe the foam-bullet kind for Tana-na. As for an actual pony – that dream would have to wait for some time in the distant future, if it survived. In the meanwhile Wishi-ta was not interested in a stuffed horse, or even a detailed molded-plastic horse – which Helene had pointed out at Walmarts. The solution came to Helene one night in bed, after waking from a bad dream, unable to get back to sleep. She would ride out to a neighboring farm, with horses, and see if they could "adopt" one as a special friend – bring treats, help to rub it down, and so forth. That might suffice – along with some other gift that Wishi-ta could actually open.

So there were birthdays to plan for, and the letter to Kenneth, after many false starts. Finally Helene completed a shortish one that she read over the phone to Thelma. She was still her night T-shirt, unwashed, out on the porch. Thelma had said to call early or late; this was early. Already the day was sticky with humidity and a coming storm.

Dear Kenneth,

How are you, etc.
I'm doing pretty well, etc. Brief news update.
Then*: I appreciate how hard you've worked and all that you've done for me personally. You have been a great provider. However, I find that I'm just not interested in so many of the material things of this world anymore. I don't see the need or reason for big houses, fancy meals or cars, or any of the luxury items. I have come to understand that all these things pass away, and they don't mean as much as human connections. Also, that it's not right for some to enjoy so much when others have so little. Therefore I am choosing this other life…*

Thelma stopped her. "No. Sorry. That's not doing it."
"But it's true!"

"Right. Kind of. Really, it sounds like some communist/socialist apology, or a rant against the bourgeoisie – is that what you're going for?"

Fanning herself with a file folder, Helene moaned. "No...it doesn't really, does it?"

"Well, it doesn't sound like you're addressing your husband of ten years on the breakdown of your marriage."

Helene went over the text again. Ink smudged her fingers with streaks of blue.

"I guess you're right." She sighed. "It's so hard."

"Yes, because it's hard." Then Thelma relented. "But you tried. At least it's a start. Don't give up; it will come to you. But you have to set aside some time, not just put it off."

"I know, but this prison visit is coming up, like I told you."

"Still having those bad dreams?"

Helene hesitated. "Oh, once in a while, now things are getting a little more routine, more normal. Nothing to worry about."

Sort of, kind of, true. She didn't tell Thelma that she worried about having Wishi-ta in the bed with her at night because of the dreams. Or that she'd asked Neesa whether she had heard anything – needing to know.

One morning she'd stopped Neesa after the twins went to school. "Can I ask you something?"

No answer. Just ask.

"Do I...have I been waking you in the night? With dreams, I mean?"

"Yes, I hear you. But then you are quiet, I go back to sleep."

"And am I talking? Yelling?"

After a moment Neesa said, "There is crying out. I hear you say 'Wishi-ta,' and I hear you say 'Renee.' That's all."

"I'm sorry," Helene said, but Neesa waved it away.

"I'm afraid that I'm going to wake up Wishi-ta too – and scare her. What do you think?"

Neesa considered. "No. If she wakes, you can give comfort; then she goes back to sleep. But she wants you next to her, for now. That is what she needs."

Helene felt tears spring to her eyes, surprised at Neesa's supportive words. "Yes, that's right. She should stay with me in the bed, for now."

That's what Helene wanted too. And she didn't want to give that up. That was all Thelma really needed to know.

When Helene and Erik met next at the lounge, Helene had wine and pretzels, and Erik had brought candles and CDs.

"Now it's shaping up for a real date," Helene teased.

"You know, it's not like we can't go out for dinner once in a while," Erik said. "Now I'm making all this money, I'd like to show you a good time."

"So sweet; so, so sweet." She poked him in the chest. "But, as you know, I'm just waiting for things to settle down. And also I am a working lady myself, as you know, or will be shortly. So I don't need the wine-and-dine treatment. Just you, being you. And me, being me."

"Great, that's settled. Let's bring out the wine."

They lit the candles and took their time to undress and explore. Helene was surprised how much she liked Erik's life-worn body, scratched and scarred, with strong arms, legs, and shoulders, but a little extra padding on his torso. His face and forearms were deeply tanned, with fine wrinkles, but not so his tender thighs and buttocks. He was no product of the gym or triathlons, but weather and labor. And his lovemaking was boyishly enthusiastic, knowing and humorous. He was not so much the brash fellow who had stopped her in her tracks at the entrance to the Intertribal Center all those weeks ago, or the one who kissed her in the back hallway, but a more patient, less impulsive man.

"I was thinking…" Helene started.

"No more thinking. Not right now.." His manner was surprisingly firm.

No thinking, no planning, no questions. Just being. It didn't come easy, but Helene would try.

"Just us and the candles," she said.

"That's all we need."

Afterward Helene dozed next to Erik, as calm and at peace as she'd been in a long while. When she woke, it was to pee; unfortunately, a trip to the downstairs restroom. She made her way with the flashlight, stepping carefully, coming into full wakefulness when she stubbed a toe. After she washed up and returned upstairs, she found herself restless, unable to snuggle in next to Erik on the couch. The candlelight was dim, and most of the room in shadow. It wasn't late; she could let Erik sleep a few more minutes.

She sat a while in one of the guest chairs, contemplating another glass of wine. Instead she got up, taking the flashlight and looking over some of the photos and notices around the office, coming around to the Intertribal Center's calendar hanging on the wall. Most of the meetings and powwows were printed in neat handwriting, probably Elsa's. For the following afternoon, there was a time set for "Alberta and Wilton," followed by a note: "Confirm with Marshalls."

Initially Helene smiled, picturing the complaining Alberta and the forbearing Malvina and Noel. Maybe a little intertribal tension, she thought, related to the Marshalls' large and noisy brood, which had a tendency to roam the neighborhood. Maybe someone had broken a window or fence, although she hadn't heard of it. And then another thought gripped her like a vise – it was her, Helene, they were meeting to talk about. That could be it, might well be it. Alberta still disliked her, for whatever reason – or for many reasons. That had not changed. And the grandson, Wilton, he wouldn't even look at her. And that was from even before she'd gone away with Wishi-ta; that was just her being here, and being white. Vividly she recalled the bumper stickers on his truck, so many, so angry. That terrible T-shirt he wore: "Kill the White Power; Save the Man." What was that all about? And why, for God's sake, couldn't he just get over all that past history? What did it have to do with anything going on now, especially anything with matters between family members?

Erik stirred and reached out a hand for her. She shook her head, trying to rid herself of the ugly words, and all her own negative speculations. The meeting could be about any number of things, including her. But she was quite sure there was nothing at this moment that would compel Malvina, Noel, Neesa, or any of the family to turn on her. If anything, the upcoming meeting with Louis was a way of formalizing the conditions and guidelines of Helene's care of his children.

"Don't shake your head," Erik laughed. "If we go another round, I'll be down for the count. I just want you near me. Is that too much?"

She snuggled in again, relishing the comfort of his body next to hers.

"No, just right."

There in the candlelight, in his arms, the swirl of emotions abated a moment: the dreams, the attack on Izzy, the letter to Kenneth, seeing Louis, new job, new school, new man in her life. And, potentially, the outcome of tomorrow afternoon's meeting. There was, she knew, so much at stake. So much to face, like it or not. And she needed to be ready, to draw on her own strength, all of it, as much as she could muster.

Renee's journal – 17

Since the diagnosis, I've been thinking a lot about home – about Mom and about Helene. It should have been obvious – the tenderness and irritation that didn't go away. My body's been so beat up over the years, I allowed myself to think for a while it might be something else. But when the biopsy came back "invasive breast cancer", all I could say was, "Of course." And when the doctor said, "We have a lot of different options to try," I thought to myself, Don't bother. Mom tried them all, but it was already raging out of control. So they've been keeping me busy these last couple months, trying this and that, the chemo and the radiation. Still it spread, and now it's in the lymph nodes and in the lungs. It's almost exactly like what happened to Mom. Whatever progress they've made in treating cancer, it wasn't enough for her. And not for me, either. I don't care what the doctors say; I know what I know.

I can't say I'm totally accepting of the whole thing, dying – it's a strange journey full of twists and turns. In some ways it's like I'm away from myself, watching. Like a movie, I guess. But not such a tragic story, at least not to me. Yes, I'm leaving behind my children, husband, family, and friends who are around me now. How can I not worry that sadness will fill the void, like it did with me and Helene and Denis? Except that it's not the same; it doesn't feel the same. Maybe it's because my life was such a wreck for such a long time. I'm still so surprised that I should have gotten to experience this new life at all – shocked, really – that I can't help but be grateful that it happened, even if it isn't going to last. As for my children, they are not alone, like we were. Louis is a good father to them. Neesa will fight for them, the best she knows how. Malvina and Noel will share whatever they have, even if it's not a lot. They'll find a way. Izzy means so much to them; he will lead them toward the light and beauty Denis will show up; I know he will. The community here, they don't turn their back on someone in need. I know this. I've seen it. Even me when I lapsed that time, they picked me up and brought me back. And they are good to me now, coming and going in the house, with the kids, so matter-of-fact, without drama.

Maybe I'm a chicken, but I'm glad the kids are too young to really understand. They know that Louis comes and goes. When I'm gone they will think I'm just in another place. With the ancestors – in a place not so different from this – full of trees and water and animals, where they will eventually go, after they've done what they can here on this earth.

But I think about Mom, how she went through this with so little support – not Dad, who was always working or in another part of the house. Not her family or friends, either. They had broken away from that, and never really found something to replace it. They thought they had each other and that was enough. But it's not enough; I can see now. Not when one dies and the other is left alone, and in sorrow that is like a disease.

Helene. I dream about her. At least how she was when we were younger. She's probably so different now, from what Denis says. All the things she wanted, now she has – the big house and well-to-do, successful husband. A good job and peace. Maybe that's what she wanted more than kids. Anyway, I want to see her, but I don't. I don't know how I can tell her about the cancer, without breaking her heart. I was only ever a burden to her, and I can't do that again. But...if only. If only I could let her know about the happiness I've found, like a miracle. And peace, another kind of peace, that is far beyond my ability to ever explain.

Chapter 27

The next morning dawned with a downpour so long and steady, Helene crept out of bed, anxious about leaks in the ceiling or around the windows. Although rain pooled on the front step and sidewalk, nothing came into the house. During the worst of the shuddering rain, she threw a small tarp over her laptop and boxes of papers and files, including Renee's journal pages, just to be safe. Then she returned to bed with Wishi-ta, passing the room where Neesa and Tana-na slept, all of them cocooned inside the little house. An hour later when everyone was up, the clouds were moving high and fast, and sunlight began to break through, sparkling on the grass. The children wore their boots for the walk to school, stepping into puddles. Just as they got to the school door, Tana-na shouted, "Rainbow!" pointing to the sky. Helene looked up, amazed; she couldn't remember ever seeing such an early morning rainbow.

Her mind was on a shopping list for the store and reworking the letter to Kenneth when she approached the corner to her street and saw Alberta out in front of her own home, sweeping the walk. Helene's hand rose, waving, and she called out, "Alberta" before she remembered the note on the Chief's calendar. Maybe that wasn't her business, but she had to know.

"Good morning, Alberta," she said.

Alberta looked up. "It's all right now. But the rain took all the blossoms off my flowers." There was a small pile of wet dirt and red petals at her feet.

Helene wasn't sure how to continue.

"Well, what do you want?" Alberta asked.

"Yes, well, here's the thing. I saw something…I found out about your meeting with Malvina and Noel this afternoon. And so…" She stopped, uncertain.

Alberta had stopped sweeping, her hands resting on the broom handle. Her lips were drawing together and her look was guarded.

"Yes," she confirmed. "So?"

"Is it about me?" Helene got out, flicking a drop of water that had landed on her cheek. "That is what I'd like to know."

Alberta looked right and left before answering. No sister, no grandson, no one nearby them on the sidewalk in the humid morning.

"We know what you're up to," she said at last. "And it's not going to work. You're not taking that girl away, or the brother, either. They belong here with us, with our people, not yours."

Helene blinked a couple times. "Well, you're wrong. That's not what I'm trying to do. What makes you think that?"

"You can deny it all you want," Alberta said. "We know better. There's evidence and everyone's going to know soon enough."

Evidence? "Alberta! What are you talking about?"

Alberta shook her head mutely and went back to sweeping. Helene let out a wry laugh. But it wasn't funny.

"I know you don't like me," she said. "And probably want to get rid of me. But that won't be so easy. I am family, you know. And maybe I am what's best for those children. Even if I did make a mistake to leave with Wishi-ta for a while."

Still no answer.

"You think I'm a troublemaker? Why are you trying to make trouble for the Marshall family? It's up to them, not you. And they know me better than you do, much better."

She was speaking to Alberta's back as she continued to move slowly but efficiently along the walkway. With a huff of breath, Helene turned on her foot and started to head away.

"They don't know everything," Alberta's voice came after her.

Helene spun around. Alberta was no longer glowering, just sure and matter-of-fact.

"They can't see it," she said. "But I can. You are not what they think you are. There's something you're keeping from them, whatever it is. That I know for sure."

It was such a personal attack, not even just about Wishi-ta. In spite of herself, Helene was so shaken she found herself hurrying to Malvina and Noel's house, although Noel had already gone to work. She hated to bother Malvina, with everything else she had going on, but she needed to get to the bottom of Alberta's murky accusations, her threats.

There was no answer at first at the Marshalls' door. Helene knocked louder, opening the door to call inside. A voice answered from deep in the house.

Malvina was in bed, resting with the baby at her breast. Probably the quiet after the storm, literally and figuratively: the rainstorm and the routine of children getting ready for school in the morning. At the door Helene hesitated, apologizing for disturbing them. But Malvina pushed herself upright, beckoning her into the room to sit in a chair near the bed.

"Go ahead," Malvina said, yawning a little. "What is it?"

Helene didn't realize how much the agitation must have shown in her face.

"Alberta," she began.

Malvina's eyebrows went up, but she didn't look completely surprised.

"About this meeting, your meeting…this afternoon. I know what it's about. Sort of."

Malvina nodded, with a tired smile. "How news gets around. Yes, we're meeting at the Chief's office, around four, after Noel gets home."

"So what do they want, Alberta and her grandson, what's his name...?"

"Wilton." Malvina shifted Tewa to the other side, smoothing the sheets. "I don't know, exactly. The Chief said that Alberta went to him with information that she found, or Wilton found, actually, and he wants to talk to us about it."

"About me?"

"I guess so."

"You mean to discredit me with the family?"

Malvina shrugged. "Chief said it was serious enough that we should meet."

Helene's heart was racing. "No! It can't be. There's nothing...nothing I can think of. I mean, I saw a therapist for a while, but that was a long time ago. There's nothing..."

Malvina was shaking her head. "No, nothing like that." She closed her eyes a moment, thinking. "Adoption laws. She says that you've been researching at the library, and that you went to a lawyer in town to get advice, in case Louis wouldn't agree to it."

Ah, that was it. But that was before, a while ago, not any more.

But there was more. "She said you had dug up Louis's criminal record, in order to make a case against him, if he didn't go along with you."

"Oh, that – that –" Helene sputtered. "So it was him, Wilton! He did go through my files while I was out. I was sure that someone was in there. I can't believe it, he broke into the house, went through my stuff."

Malvina wasn't done.

"And that you got an application for a passport for Wishi-ta..."

The women locked gazes, until Helene held up a hand. "It's true. It's all true, I'm sorry to say. From before, not now. From before I went away with Wishi-ta, when I thought I'd have to fight Louis to take care of the twins, and that she...they...could have a better life with me, somewhere else." She paused. "Not now, none of that is how I feel now. I won't take them away from here, from you."

Malvina nodded slowly.

"So that's it?" Helene went on, shifting in the chair, feeling how stiff her shoulders had become. "What they're going to tell you? And show you?" To herself, she muttered, "He didn't take anything that I can tell. Maybe he copied it? Or took pictures on his phone?" And then to Malvina, who was watching closely. "Let me go to the meeting, too. I can explain...."

Malvina shook her head, stopping her. "No, that's not the way. They need a chance to state their problem, and we must listen. Then we can decide what to do." Her head dipped. "Or if we need to speak to you."

Helene was dismayed. "I am sorry about what I did. I know it was wrong to take Wishi-ta away without letting anyone know where we were." The words rushed out. "I didn't know there would be no cell phone service – although maybe I should have. But...but they were wrong, too. Right?"

Malvina gave no indication of her thoughts, and no particular encouragement.

"Please...." Helene's voice was rising. "Please don't believe him, or them. There is no plan. I won't do anything. I'll destroy the papers, or give them to you, if you want."

They heard noise from the adjacent side of the house: Neesa in her kitchen, most likely. Or even Izzy rattling around, as he was still physically limited and only part-time at work. Helene glanced at the door, but there was nothing further.

Finally, Malvina nodded. "I understand what you are saying. There is error on both sides."

That would have to be enough.

"Why, though?" Helene asked, a plaintive note in her voice. "Why does it matter so much to them? And why are they so set against me? I don't really get it."

Malvina sat upright in the bed, moving the sleeping baby to one side on the mattress, and picked up her phone to text.

"I'll get Izzy," she said. And like that, it was clear that he was the spiritual center of the family, young as he was, and that it was his say, at least as much as Louis's, that mattered.

Malvina's phone buzzed back in a moment, and she looked up. "He'll be here in a minute."

In no great hurry, Izzy appeared at the doorway, foam on his lip, where apparently he had been shaving. He was still moist from the shower, and his hair hung loose, almost now to his shoulders, none of his bruises or scars showing under the T-shirt.

"Helene," he said pleasantly. "Are you working on Malvina now, too, about my case? That's not really fair, since she can't get away from you. Plus she agrees with you anyway, that I should be –"

"Nope," Helene said, shaking her head. "Wrong tree, Izzy."

"Oh." He sat at the foot of the bed. "So, then, what up, ladies?" He looked to the baby. "And I'm including you here, Tewa."

He was so easy in his nature, Helene found him almost comical at times. But this was a serious matter. She looked to Malvina to begin.

"Helene wants to know about Alberta and Wilton," Malvina said briefly.

"Ah." Izzy already knew, she was sure.

"So, to make it short," Helene said. "I found out about this meeting with the Chief to tell your family that I'm planning some kind of legal ploy to get the twins away from here. Which I am not. And, furthermore, I believe Wilton actually came into the house, Renee and Louis's house, and went through my private papers, as well as apparently spying on me."

"Really?" Izzy was interested. Maybe he hadn't heard that part.

"Really!" Helene said. "Isn't that trespassing, at the least?"

Izzy wagged his head. "Not necessarily, not around here. Most people don't lock their doors, and if someone comes by, and knocks and calls, but there's no answer, it's fine to go inside if you need something." He smiled. "The local custom."

"Seriously?"

"Yeah, for the most part. It's changing, but still common."

"I don't know about that. But in any case, why are they so against me? I've done nothing against them. Just because I'm white? Is that it?"

Brother looked at sister, and then back to Helene. "Part of it. But not all of it."

Helene laughed bitterly. "Why is that OK? Isn't that just being racist?" Now she was getting heated, and she could see them readjusting their faces. "Have you seen that T-shirt he wears, Wilton? The one that says, 'Kill White Power. Save the Man'? I mean, they're so set against me, no matter what I do."

Izzy was no fool. She knew that. He was thinking about what to say, and how to say it. In a lightning flash, Helene knew that he might be, would be, the leader of this community someday. Not his brother, Louis, but Izzy, the homeboy with city yearnings, of indeterminate sex, who knew these things, who understood.

"Racist?" he said. "Good question. No doubt, they are down on white people generally, and also specifically." He squinted one eye. "Can you be racist, if the race you are against is the one that mistreated your race for centuries? That I'm not sure of. But I do think they have other motivations."

"Like what?"

"Well, besides being general pain in the asses, you mean? That's also their role, somehow. But yeah, they've got their reasons."

"Like what?"

"Alberta's father, he was sent to an Indian boarding school run by Christians against his wishes, and against his parents' wishes. You've heard of the boarding schools, right? Or maybe not. Anyway, they cut his hair, forbid him to speak his language, wouldn't let him wear his medicine pouch or smudge. It was a bad experience, and he never got over it, I guess. He was a drinker, and he never got sober. That's what Alberta knew growing up, and that's what she's told Wilton all his life."

OK. Helene could see that there was something to that. Not just long-past history, but in-memory history. A reason, if not a good choice, to be bitter.

"That's what it refers to, his T-shirt, literally. It was the slogan of the man who supported the Indian boarding school in Carlisle, Pennsylvania. 'Kill the Indian, Save the Man.' You get the idea?"

How awful. Terrible. Still.

"All right. Maybe." She was stumped how to go on. It did make sense, but it was still so wrong, how they applied it, how they made her suffer for all that stuff she didn't do, or her family.

Izzy was watching her closely. "Wilton has another T-shirt too, but he doesn't wear it anymore."

"Oh, yeah? A good one, I'll bet."

"It says, 'White Christian Terrorism – No One Does It Better' with a picture of a burning cross." Izzy laughed. "He wore it once here, I think." He gestured to the other half of the house. "Until Neesa gave him the business. No one goes against the Virgin Mary or her son, no one."

Helene was still puzzled. "That's really reaching, don't you think? I mean, I know the Native Americans didn't appreciate all the missionaries interfering, but they brought some good stuff too, didn't they? Schools, charities, all that. I don't really understand what he's referring to."

"Ah, well." Izzy sighed; it was like a trail of clouds had crossed his vision. "I think, in a nutshell, he means the Crusades, the Inquisition, the Holocaust, American slavery, the Trail of Tears, lynching – that kind of thing, generally. Not just Native stuff." He pursed his lips, like one of Helene's former nursing instructors: *how to make this clear.* "Let's put that aside for the moment. I think they were afraid you would try to take the twins away. They truly think that white American power, money, and know-how would win the fight, and those children would be lost to us, in danger of losing their sense of identity and knowing where they belong."

Izzy, slight and battered, handsome and childlike, was unrelenting. "Most Natives see things differently regarding children. Not to say there isn't abuse, especially with drinking and poverty. But to us taking a child away from home and family and culture is a kind of terrorism; it makes them terrified, bad dreams, you know." He paused, waiting.

"Yes," said Helene, her voice catching, "I do." She knew all about sad childhoods and bad dreams. "I get it, I really do. I won't do that to them, the twins. I promise. You believe me, right?"

"OK," Malvina said, simply.

"But you're still going to the meeting?"

She shrugged. "We agreed. We should respect their request."

"But...but..." Helene stammered. "You understand how things stand with me now, right? How I've come to see the harm in what I did, and why it was not the best for Wishi-ta, no matter what I thought at the time?"

Malvina stood silent, unblinking.

Helene shook her head, as if clearing away old cobwebs of confusion. "It wasn't right for anyone: Tana-na, the family, Kenneth, not even me."

Finally Malvina stirred, the slightest nod of her head. "We have no thoughts of changing our plans."

Helene took a deep breath and exhaled. "Thank you."

For a long moment there was no sound, all eyes on the sleeping baby on the bed. Suddenly she blinked open her eyes, not crying. Then her arms and legs started to propel the air. Malvina's lips curved up. Then she pushed herself to the side of the bed, getting to her feet. She scooped up the waking baby, and stood in front of Helene.

"Can you hold her? I have to pee."

Again the eyes of brother and sister met, and Malvina left the room.

Tewa had come to full wakefulness now, her hands opening and closing like flowers. Helene thought she resembled Noel – the large features and gentle expressions. A big girl, likely, bigger than her sister or her mother. All of her Native, as far as Helene could see, except maybe the lightness of her eyes. She was a warm bundle against Helene's chest on a warm day, the fan only slightly moving the air in the room.

"So," Izzy said, after Malvina had gone.

"So?"

"There could be another reason why Wilton's pursuing this whole thing."

"Oh, God." She made a face. "Don't keep it from me, please."

"Yeah. So he's always been jealous of Louis; everyone knows that. And this might be his chance to make a little thunder."

Helene couldn't help smiling. Something so basic as human jealousy? "Oh, really?"

"It's a thought."

Helene was gazing down at Tewa. So innocent yet of all the different kinds of human folly.

"So that's an excuse? A reason?"

"Possibly. Like so many things, it's simple and it's complicated. Just remember that if you cross paths with the man, and you're tempted to tell him off."

Helene shook her head. "I don't know. He came into the house without permission, looking at my private property."

"He thought it was for the good of the children."

Helene snickered. "Right."

"Like you thought it was for Wishi-ta's good to go away."

She caught her breath.

"And the man who opened the boarding school thought it was for the good of the Indian children to make them assimilate."

Helene's mouth hung open, and the only solace she could find was in the face of the baby in her arms.

Chapter 28

The result of the meeting with Alberta and Wilton and the Marshalls was that nothing changed, except the Chief asked Wilton to meet with Helene at his office and show her the information he had gathered – mainly photos of papers from both the library and the house. It was all just as he said, except that the dates showed that the research documents had been printed before Helene left with Wishi-ta, and the application for a passport had only Wishi-ta's name and nothing more.

Alberta had indeed seen Helene's car at the lawyer's office; a friend who worked there told her that the lawyer had requested a couple of cases on custody and adoption for children whose parents were in prison. That was also earlier in the summer – just as Helene had said. Then Helene showed Wilton her current research on assaults and hate crimes. It was true she still spent hours at the library looking up legal information, but not on adoption. Wilton made a stiff apology to Helene for going through her belongings behind her back. Then, courtesy of Alberta, he brought out a framed photo of his great-grandfather as a young man in a boarding school uniform. Almost the same unhappy face as his daughter and great-grandson in faded sepia tones. Helene looked at it and handed it back, more relieved than any of them could have imagined; she was not crazy or haunted or stalked by a madman. She managed to get out, "I'm sorry to have caused you concern," to which Wilton nodded. The air seemed so much brighter when she stepped outside. The hurdle was cleared, and now all that remained was meeting with Louis.

Then, finally, on Saturday morning, they were set to depart at five a.m. for the six-hour trip to the prison. Helene's car was the most comfortable, with the best air conditioning on a warm September day. Erik wanted to drive; no argument from Helene or Izzy. Neesa had prepared a cooler of drinks and sandwiches, and Helene had pictures and artwork from the twins to give Louis. Izzy was in a T-shirt and shorts for the trip, but had put on some Native American jewelry, including a turquoise ring.

The trip was uneventful except for a shower crossing through the White Mountains of New Hampshire, and Helene had to tell Erik how to put on the windshield wipers in the sudden downpour. But shortly after that, a rainbow appeared in the clearing sky, and Helene said, "Can we take that as a good sign?"

"Why not?" Erik said.

"I see rainbows all the time," remarked Izzy from the back seat. "It seems like wherever I go, there they are."

"I don't doubt that," Helene said, not really teasing.

As they got closer to the prison, Helene sat up straighter, fiddling with her thumbs in her lap. She was as prepared as she was going to be for facing Louis; and yet the shadow of her recent nightmares lingered, and all that went before.

"I've been having dreams about Renee lately," she said aloud. She hadn't mentioned them before to Izzy. "Not very good ones. She's trying to tell me something or ask me something. Pretty much screaming at me, like the old days."

"That's funny." Izzy said, leaning forward. "I had a dream about her too. But it was a good one. She packed me a lunch for the trip to the city, and said she would tell Neesa I had gone up to the Home Camp on some spiritual quest. Covering for me, you know."

"Interesting," Helene said, looking back over her shoulder. "I could see her lying for you – she was pretty good at deception. But would Neesa buy that, do you think?"

"Probably not," Izzy agreed. "But she'd go along, anyway."

At the prison Helene felt her steps slowing, a weight on her shoulders that she could not shift. This reckoning. How Louis would sum up her life, her role in the twins' lives, and her credibility. Even the part of her that was eager to argue for Izzy, to support his desire to leave and try life in the city, had been subdued. Unbidden, images appeared to her of Izzy beaten up on city streets. Was it right to support his 'escape,' going to test himself in an environment that would not always be friendly? And yet bad things had happened to him near home; and even, she recalled, the incident at the gas station on the way to the prison earlier in the summer, on a remote stretch of highway.

Just as they turned onto the long driveway that led to the prison, Helene spotted a deer and two fawns grazing in a field, with the glint of the lake behind them. They lifted their heads to look as the car passed, but didn't run. Instead the doe seemed to hold Helene's gaze, as long as she was able to see them out of the window. Only then did they resume their leisurely way toward the woods, an unexpected sight during the middle of the day.

The guard in the visitor room said the three of them were cleared to meet with Louis in a reserved room, away from the family groups. Helene followed wordlessly, assuming that after the general visit he would meet with her and Izzy separately to discuss their more private business.

But she was wrong. He was brought to them in the room, where they sat around a small, round table with chairs for four, and a guard in the corner. There were paper cups for water, and almost nothing else. This room too was painted white, with high windows framing the tips of the fir trees, dipping occasionally in the wind.

Louis looked no different from the last visit, clean shaven with his long hair in a braid down the back. Izzy had explained to her, after the initial head shave and inspection for lice, they were allowed to wear their hair as they liked. But they could not wear the medicine pouch – a strangulation hazard, apparently. So much for religious freedom – according to Izzy.

After the initial greetings, Louis turned to Izzy and Helene for their reports. First he wanted an update on the injuries they had both sustained. Then he wanted to know about the transition of the family back from the Home Camp, and the children starting school. He wanted to know too about Izzy's situation with work and school, and what kind of timeline he had in mind for his move.

Helene could not relax, and the feeling of oppression was with her still – some kind of foreboding. Why did she anticipate bad things, when she had reason to think that Louis was inclined to want her as part of the family, in spite of the trip to the cabin in Vermont? It showed, on some level, Helene's devotion to Wishi-ta and concern for her welfare. Perhaps wrong-minded; perhaps biased in a certain way; but genuine nonetheless.

Louis seemed unconcerned about that now. He said he'd been talking to a Native American lawyer, and had been praying to the Creator and the ancestors about his children.

"The problem is," he said, facing Helene, "we don't know you, your real character. We don't know what to expect. Your other life was so much different from how we live. How can we know your true spirit?"

"I…I don't know. How do you know anyone's?"

"We see, we observe, we watch people grow. That is part of it. Or, in the case of Renee, your sister, she wore her soul on the outside so that anyone could see it. She was a woman in the midst of survival, and her most basic nature was clear – what she would do, or wouldn't do, in extreme circumstances. But you are still a mystery; there is much that isn't clear."

Helene looked around the table – the sympathetic but unhelpful gazes of Izzy and Erik – they could not speak about her, except for the little time they had known her, including the "great escape."

"What can you tell us, so that we can believe and trust you?" Louis asked. The way he looked at her, she felt he was someone else, someone apart from the family. He had come to a position of power and authority, and his judgments extended far beyond everyday matters. His face had become fuller with age, and his lips were more tight and drawn than Izzy's – his features lined with years and experience. And suffering.

She let the words come, unthinking. "I know that my behavior this summer must have seemed strange – and unacceptable, taking Wishi-ta away with no explanation. But I hope you understand why I left, and what I hoped for – to be sure that her life would not be in danger. I see now that I could not provide all the safety and security that she needs. Or I could provide much of it, but at a loss of what she loves and cares about. At the time I considered it a crisis, and something temporary. I would never have kept her from her family long term. I needed to think about things – and to see things more clearly."

Louis nodded. "But what about before – the life you had, and your husband and job, all those connections?"

Helene sighed. "It was not real, I'm afraid, although I was good at it, and I convinced myself that those kinds of things were valuable and important. But the truth is, I was never honest with my husband about how I really felt, or myself, really. And I only had one friend – Thelma – who is still my friend, even now that I have moved away. I am a good nurse, and I expect to continue in that – since it is a way to earn money and to help people. But I see now I needed other things too – other connections."

"You have your brother, Denis."

She nodded. "Denis." Then blew out a long breath. "We were never there for each other. We have always just been trying to get by, in our own way – which was not the same way."

"And what about Renee?"

For a moment the question hung in the air. Obviously, Renee could be no real family to her now – or support. "Renee?"

But he would not elaborate. Helene saw the treetops stirring mightily, and pictured the waves on the lake, and then the deer in the field. The room was stuffy and still, with Erik and Izzy sitting patiently, but also expectantly. And then the heaviness of the dream, of all the recent nightmares, was with her. Along with Renee, her pinched face and lank hair. And her voice:

Please. Help me. Let this be over. I can't go back. I can't go through it all again. I don't want to leave this bed, this house. Help me.

Helene tried to explain how hard it was at the end, dealing with Renee. That the early years were the best, when she was like Renee's little mother, helping their mother, even through her sickness. Then, after their mother died, Helene had gotten so busy, trying to help her father run the house – the cooking and shopping, getting Denis and Renee to school – all the while waiting, longing for her turn to leave and go to college. With all that going on, and their father's depression and his drinking, Renee had gotten wild, unpredictable, craving attention and then escaping, running away, again and again.

And then the long course of addiction – drinking and pills and pot, and at the end, heroin. It had been exhausting.

"We were close, but not close," Helene said. "She tried me and tested me every way she could, but I did not want to be the parent. I wanted my own life."

They were all listening, and looking not at her but past her.

Her words were brittle, full of bitterness and pain. "At the end, the last couple years, she was out of control – in and out of the hospital and detox

and the police station – for drugs, of course, and petty theft. Until the last
time…" Helene's voice sounded far away, like someone else. She had
gotten to a place she had not intended to go, but she could no longer stop
telling the story.

"And the last time." Her voice was hoarse now. "She'd been gone
awhile, a halfway house on the South Shore, I think, or the Cape. She
called, late at night from a party, somewhere in the next town over. She
was in bad shape, and I said I'd come get her. But she wouldn't let me,
said she'd get a ride. I waited and waited, but she never came. So I went
out looking. I drove all the side roads until I finally found her, sitting in a
snowbank, almost frozen. I got her home and put her in bed, our parents'
bed, the big one. She begged me not to take her to detox – only to get out
and start it all over again. I said we would talk about it in the morning.

"She was quiet for a while. I thought she was sleeping. I got into bed
next to her, to warm her, and dozed off. Around dawn she got restless,
shivering and sweating. Tears were running down her face but she wasn't
really crying, not from pain, I mean. That's when she asked me to stop it,
begged me."

Helene's tongue was dry, the words forced out of her mouth.

"She put my hands on the pillow, and said she needed me to keep it in
place and make sure it was finished. 'No one will know' she said. 'They'll
think it was an overdose, while you were sleeping.'"

Still no emotion showed on the faces of the men around her, only their
silent, still listening. Outside, the tips of the trees thrashed and whipped in
the growing wind.

"So I did it. Renee put the pillow over her face, and I knelt on the bed,
pressing down. I tried hard, as hard as I could, to do what she asked, put an
end to it all, the misery and the helplessness. I believed her that she wanted
to die. And I was so sick and tired and angry at trying to help her and never
succeeding."

She stopped, until all three men looked at her, waiting.

"I tried to kill her, I tried."

The truth was out, the admission of the worst, the ugliest, the hardest
secret a person could have. Not a nice person, a good person, but one who
would knowingly kill.

Now only the conclusion remained.

"Eventually, her hands dropped away and she was still. I thought it
was done. Truly, I did, and I could give up the effort, stepping away to
catch my breath. And then, her foot twitched and her fingers, so I wasn't
sure. And I heard a sound from under the pillow, so I knew. I hadn't done
what she asked, or what I wanted to do myself – to see her dead so there
would be no more struggle."

Helene's head tipped, remembering.

"Of all things, right at that moment, a dish fell in the cabinet, or a glass. Or maybe the cat. Something – a crash, not big, nothing broken. Just a slip in space, from one position to another. But I felt this jolt, seeing myself like someone watching from another room. I got off the bed and pulled the pillow away from her. She was still, and her lips were blue. I slapped her face. Then I tried what I could remember from first aid: pressing on her chest and blowing into her mouth until I could feel her breath coming back. In a few moments, her eyes had opened, and she was gasping for air.

"I said, 'I couldn't do it. I'm sorry. I tried. We'll find another way to help you.'

"She turned away from me and said, 'There is no other way.'"

Helene looked up in wonder, back in that room, on that day with her sister.

"I lay down next to her to hold her and stop the shaking. And I stood next to her in the bathroom when she vomited and lost control of her bowels. I never left her side for the next three days – only to go to the bathroom, or clean up or change, get something to eat. I called in sick at work. Finally, the fourth day, she seemed better, drinking a little, letting me give her a sponge bath and comb her hair. When I went out for groceries, I asked if there was anything she wanted. She said, 'coffee ice cream.' And I thought that was a good sign. But no, just another ruse. While I was out, she left." Helene paused, taken again by surprise. "I didn't see it coming; I thought we'd turned a corner. She took some cash from my bureau drawer, where my mom used to keep it. And a jacket. That was the last I ever saw of her."

She looked from Louis to Izzy and finally to Erik, who had closed his eyes.

"Me, a nurse. That's what I did, that no one knows about, not Denis, not my husband, not the therapist, not my best friend."

A long quiet followed. Helene looked first at Izzy and then Erik, both of them blank, faces like masks. She heard a voice inside her head: *You don't know me; no one really knows another person.* Perhaps her story had been too much for them to take in, to reconcile with what they had thought of her. Maybe this was it, the end of her quest, brought here to be rejected. For a moment they sat, as in a tableau. Then something stirred again, the silent branches outside the window, bringing breath back into the room.

Izzy looked past her, his face full of sweet sorrow, like a Madonna. Erik's rugged face contracted into something beyond shock; nearer grief.

"I knew this," Louis said into the empty space. "Renee told me."

Helene thought she had misheard him. Of course Renee might have said something in the course of their marriage, but then how could he have allowed Helene to live with his family, take care of his children, their children, knowing that?

But there was no mistake; his voice was not loud, but his words were

clear. He sat calmly as Helene felt again that disorientation of being in the
dark while everyone else around her knew things. Herself, exposed, for
being something terrible, not who they thought she was, not at all.

Louis continued. "I have known for a long time, well before Malvina
and I spoke about writing the letter to ask for your help."

Helene startled. *The letter!* That letter from Malvina, the very first
communication about Wishi-ta and her allergic condition. The one with the
photo of the children. The family was at a powwow, wearing regalia; this
was the family Malvina had been writing about; Renee and Louis's family.

Louis was still speaking. "I knew this about you, and how it had taken
place. The story almost exactly as you have told us. After the children were
born, Renee wanted to see you, to talk to you. She loved you, and she
wanted to ask forgiveness for what she put you through."

Helene's throat closed; there was no air to carry words. *Ask
forgiveness? But how? I failed her from beginning to end.*

"That is all I needed to know," said Louis, finally. "The truth, what is
real. For you to reveal, not me. And now you have told it, here in front of
these men. This is our business only, for the time being. Without this
admission, how could I allow you in our lives, no matter how caring and
helpful you might be? It was a secret that could hurt you, and harm us. The
others don't know. They want you to stay and be part of their lives. They
have said so. But it was my responsibility to find out your true nature."

Helene's hands were clutched in her lap like her mother had clutched
her rosary beads – for endurance of the unbearable.

"Helene," Louis said. "There will be no adoption. As long as I'm
alive, I will be the parent to my children, the one who is ultimately
responsible. However, if you can accept that, you may continue to live in
the house and to raise the twins while I am in prison. I can make you their
legal guardian, in charge of their health, education, and welfare – most
everything, except that I want them to be raised in their Native American
culture, to the extent possible, and to follow Native American ways in the
life of the spirit. When I am transferred closer, I want you to bring them to
see me, as well as coming yourself to keep me informed on your lives
together. If you agree to this, we can sign the papers. But you must take
time to think about it, to really know your own mind."

Then he turned to Izzy. "What do you say, younger brother? You've
been on the scene more than I have lately."

Izzy pressed his lips together, his forehead furrowed in concentration.
"I think if Renee asked forgiveness for her part in what happened, then it's
OK with me too. Helene took care of me when I had that bike accident –
well, incident – and she went to the police station for me. Even though it
didn't work, she tried."

Louis nodded. "And you, Erik, as a friend of our family for many
years, and part of the community. I know you have a sexual relationship

with Helene. What do you think of this idea, how I should proceed?"

Erik looked not at Louis, but at Helene. "Who am I to judge? I can only say what I know of Helene now, and how much I see that she cares about the twins, and is willing to change everything in her life for them."

"OK, then, we'll wait until you have made your decision, Helene. This is not easy for me, either. Already you have made a place in their hearts, and I'm reluctant to be the cause of another loss. So now it is up to you."

Helene shook her head emphatically. "I don't need time to decide. This is all I want, to help the twins and be part of their lives. And I understand, now, your wishes and Renee's wishes that they stay part of the community at the base and at the Home Camp. I'm ready to do that, and to be part of it, to the extent that I can."

"No, we must wait," Louis said. "If you decide not to become legal guardian, Malvina and Noel can manage, now that the baby is born and Wishi-ta's allergies are being managed. You must fully understand what it means, for your life as well as theirs; what the commitment is, and how long it might last."

Suddenly he looked like an older man than he was, older even than Erik – weathered with his own cares and responsibilities, and loss. Helene could see now something of what Renee had seen in him, even though it took him away and placed him, and also his family, at risk.

There was a clap of thunder outside, so loud that it penetrated to the small meeting room; even the guard blinked and glanced out the window. The lights wavered, and exclamations erupted from the large open visitors' area next door.

Helene felt a surge of something more than relief; almost gladness. The terrible secret was no longer secret. That long-carried shame and fear had been lifted. Where she expected a trial and condemnation, she found counsel and acceptance. How had she deserved this grace?

And then, another shift, from light to shadow to light again outside the prison walls; clouds breaking up here and there. The focus was no longer on her, but on others and life going forward.

Louis looked across the table at Izzy, his lips turned wryly. "I know you want to get away – to move away from the base and see what it's like in the city. I understand that feeling, which I had too when I was younger, and I wish you well. But you are uncle to my children, and I want you to be part of their lives now and as long as you can be. You too will be an instructor in how they live in this world, and what they will do in their future lives. Even if you make another home, always come back to this home – at the base and at the Home Camp – to be with family."

Izzy nodded, no questions, no remarks.

"And I think you should pursue this crime with the men who beat you up. I know it seems useless, and that you'd rather just forget about it. I have experienced very little benefit of the law for myself or for Native Americans, but I still have a hope and belief that justice comes in the long run, maybe beyond our own years. It's for my children, Malvina's children, and anyone else who's assaulted because of something different about them. Maybe Helene can help, but it's on you. Do you understand?"

Izzy blew out a breath. "Yes."

Louis stretched his neck side to side, releasing some of the effort of being still for so long.

"Erik," he said, shifting his gaze. "You are part of this circle, like it or not. My children have always liked you, and eventually, my wife. I don't want you to live in my house, or at least not unless you marry Helene, and are bound to each other. You have no responsibility to the twins, except as a man and an adult. But I hope that you too will help them learn about living in this world, and show them how to be part of the community as well as looking out for themselves. Will you do that?"

"I would do it even if you didn't ask me."

Then Louis dipped his head and smiled briefly, privately. "Then I think we are done here, at least for today. Maybe we can get a coffee before the hour is up." His face changed, a sudden wistfulness and vulnerability. "What I wouldn't give for Neesa's strong brew."

On the return trip to the base, Erik was at the wheel and Izzy in the passenger seat. Helene had said she'd like to sit in back. The radio was on for a while, and then Erik and Izzy began to speak, first of music, then sports, and then what Izzy might do in his life. Helene dozed on and off, and for a while there was silence in the car. No one was ready to talk of what had just passed, or how things might be now between them.

Just after they got back to the base, after dusk, Helene turned on the kitchen light and sat at the table, a pad of paper and pen in hand. She knew, now, what to write. Kenneth needed to know this, to know all, so that he could see things for what they were too.

Dear Kenneth,

I just got back from the prison to meet with Louis about the twins. He will not allow adoption. He hesitated to entrust me with legal guardianship of the children, because he was unsure of me as a person, my character and my motives. That's when I told him, what I'm telling you now, the truth of what happened with Renee, during those last days she was with me before she went away. You need to know that I tried to suffocate her with a pillow, at her request, and I almost succeeded.

She was going through withdrawal, weak and unwell. I wanted her go to the doctor's or to the detox center for medical attention. She begged me not to take her, and to help her end her life then and there at the house, persuading me that everyone would think it was an overdose. She put the pillow over her face and I held it down until she stopped moving; and I thought, then, that she was dead. Her addiction made me do a thing I did not think I would ever do, or could do. The fact that she didn't die, and revived soon after, also with my help, doesn't change that fact.

When I told this to Louis, in front of Izzy and Erik, I expected disgust and condemnation. But Louis already knew about it, from Renee. What he wanted was for me to be honest, and said that he was willing to accept that part of my past, for Renee's sake. The others, I suppose, will need more time to think it through.

And to you, I apologize for marrying you under pretense, for not being open and truthful with you, and for taking up with Erik while still married to you. I have been a fraud to you as a wife. But I was also a fraud to myself, that I could be a happy person while I harbored this secret knowledge. I cannot change what I have done and what I now feel. I can only ask forgiveness.

I need nothing more from you, beyond your cooperation in the separation and divorce arrangements. I hope you will think too about how long and hard I tried to be a good wife, and what people wanted me to be. I found the letter from Renee and I understand why you kept it from me. But in your effort to protect me, I lost a chance to reconcile with my sister, and that will never come again.

It won't be easy to explain to your family, and others, I'm sure. Perhaps the best explanation is the truth: that I felt so obligated to care for my sister's children that I agreed to be part of their Native American upbringing, even though it took me away from you. They may think it was my frustration over not having children; or those who knew about Renee may think it's out of guilt for her mixed-up life. It's those things, and more, but perhaps that's enough.

I had to find another way. I can no longer live in a false skin. Your instinct was right, that I have been deeply troubled. But I am hopeful that I can make a life for myself here, and live with the truth about myself. It has been a burden lifted from me.

You deserve thanks for your kindness and generosity to me over these past ten years. I can only hope that you will someday not think badly of me.

Helene

7. Bows and Arrows, Arrows and Bows – by One Little Indian

I was thinking about guns the other day – don't ask why. My father had a hunting gun that he kept in the back of his truck, alongside a tackle box and fishing rod. Naturally he wanted to teach his children how to shoot and how to fish. In his mind those were ways to provide food for a family, along with nets and traps, even long after my mom was sold on the grocery store. I suspect it was also his "get out of the house time", especially during those epic battles between my brother, an excellent arguer, and our mother, who is small but fearsome. Anyway, my father liked to talk about the healing nature of silence and the outdoors. And he said it was a way to learn about the ways of plants and animals – our other, quieter relatives.

I was good with the fishing; some might call it boring, but I called it an excuse to daydream, and to be with my father when he rambled on about old days and faraway places. But I hated that gun, the very first time I heard it go off next to my ear, when I was maybe seven or eight. Dad said it would sound like thunder, and I told him afterward, when I threw it down, it sounded like the Great Spirit was shouting in anger. I was right; maybe that gun put some rabbit and venison on the table, but it turned out to be a troublemaker after all.

So you may be wondering about the bow and arrow. As I did when I was a little boy. My father was not a fan. "It's been too many years since we used those; no one makes them anymore. I don't like the new ones. Anyway, time is food, and I don't have time to waste." That's what he said. In any case, this Little Indian grew up without a bow or an arrow; never held one until I took archery in gym class.

For sure, I had seen a whole lot of pictures of Indians with bows and arrows – somewhere, even though I grew up more with Sesame Street and Mr. Rogers' Neighborhood. Movies, books, magazines, museums gave me the idea that those old-time Indians were born with bows in their hands. What I didn't see were Indians building homes or mending nets or making drums or playing with their children – just bows and arrows, war clubs and tomahawks, face paint and war cries, and frenzied dancing around the fire. Always in preparation for battle. Never, ever singing, praying, resting, or relaxing. I got the idea of the "bloodthirsty savage," not the "noble hunter."

No question, there were warrior cultures, with lots of skirmishes and honoring the bravest. But it wasn't generally meant to wipe out whole populations and take their resources – maybe battle over prey or a good fishing spot, but not territory per se, being nomadic and not property owners. Sometimes, after a bad season, there were raids for people to replace those who had died. Women might be taken, or children, making slaves, but total wipeout was never the goal.

All that face paint and drumming and war cries made great theater – intimidation tactics – warnings to "move on" or "engage us at your peril." And what about the idea of counting coup (status points for touching the enemy, not killing) – isn't that a show of strength and skill rather than outright slaughter? Maybe "sneaky Indians" were just practical-minded people who didn't have the numbers or interest in drilling, marching, and training militias. Raiding and stealth were more economical and efficient. There were lots of other things to do, and lots of room to do them. Fighting might be an art, or a matter of necessity, but not a pastime.

There's another reason, too, besides the war-making. Hunting: we're stuck forever in the stone-age technology of wood, flint, stone. Bows, arrows, spears and nets, about the extent of our technology. As a science-fiction minded Indian, I object. We're just now getting credit for our science and inventions. The Inca and their engineering and road building. The Maya and their mathematics, calendars and astronomy. Plant husbandry – the potatoes and corn that feed the world today. Land management, like burning the prairies to sustain the buffalo herds.

Sometimes, I think about those images of Indians and I have this fantasy of airbrushing away the boys and arrows, so their hands could be free to hold something else: a golf club, a spatula, maybe a flute. Wouldn't that be nice?

Chapter 29

Helene knew that Erik would be leaving again on another trucking job within a couple of days after returning from the prison. She didn't expect to have a serious talk or to spend a night together until after he got back, even though Neesa was no longer staying at Renee's house at night. She didn't even know if that was what he wanted to do.

After the prison trip, they had said good-bye in the dark on the sidewalk, next to the parked car. Izzy had slipped off home, where Neesa's light was on in the living room where she worked on baskets once the weather turned cool.

"I guess there's something to think about," Erik said to Helene, just before they parted. But he put his arms around her, holding her lightly and patting her back like a child.

Helene stepped back, nodding.

"Just take it easy on yourself," he added, and "One day at a time," which was ironically one of the sayings from AA that Helene had learned from Renee.

The next morning she saw him leaving in his truck from Elsa and Chief's house, maybe for coffee, or maybe to the construction sites he'd been working at. She did not see the truck return.

Even with the twins at kindergarten and an afternoon program of gym and ball games, the day was full of business to take care of, including a review of all the current medical appointments for herself and Wishi-ta, insurance questions, and some paperwork for the job at the clinic that Helene was set to start shortly.

It must have been when she went next door to visit Malvina and Tewa that Thelma called and left a message on the answering machine:

"Haven't heard from you, so just checking in. When you're ready, let me know how things went on the visit. I'm cautiously optimistic, but I'd like to hear it from you. Also I'm ready for Izzy anytime he wants to come. But, and this is kind of important – he needs to know I will be moving fairly soon – in the next few months, anyhow. There's a condo I've looked at in the new development, in my price range. I'd like to make an offer. But – this I need to talk to you about directly – it's one of Kenneth's projects and I'd be working with his office, maybe with him. Anyway, call me, but not tonight – I have a meeting. The weekend is best, unless it's urgent. Otherwise, all is fine here."

Helene wiggled her lips. Weird, the idea of Thelma and Kenneth doing business together. Aside from her own situation, though, it made sense: good reputation, reasonably priced. Kenneth had not yet had time to respond to own her letter, so she wasn't sure of his reaction. How would he and Thelma manage to avoid the elephant in the room? Yet she was ready to shake it off; not her problem to solve.

Then, in the afternoon, returning with the twins from the Intertribal Center, Helene just missed another phone call. She caught the last of Denis's words just as she let them into the house. Tana-na had to make a quick run for the bathroom, and Wishi-ta was eager to tell her about a new game, something with mats and balls. So she left it until the twins had finished their juice and rice crackers, and then some Play-Doh time. Not that she would catch Denis, anyway. Always on the run, on the road, maybe more so since the band's music had hit the airwaves.

She pressed the playback button:

"Helene, yeah, me, Denis. Hey! Sorry not to catch you. It's about, uh, what time is it, anyway? Two or three, maybe? No worries; everything's fine; everything's good. But I want to give you a heads up; I'm headed your way. Should be in Boston by the middle of next week, and I'll get to you sometime after that. Also I'll have someone with me. But not the dogs. I bet the twins would love them, but I know what you said about the allergy stuff. Anyway, soon. I'll call you before we get there. At least, I'll try!"

Helene sat on the sofa, listening to the twins in the kitchen, that special twin language, not always comprehensible to others. Maybe there were a few Native words thrown in, from Neesa or the time at the Home Camp.

So, Gypsy Denis, her traveling brother. On his usual touchdown before taking off again. It would be good to see him. This friend, though – that was not the usual. Another musician, maybe, or perhaps the lady dog sitter? She was touched that he remembered about the allergies at all.

She glanced at the shelves on the wall that had been water damaged. Still empty. Noel had done a nice job; and surely, the primer and paint were dry by now. But he wasn't going to replace the files and notebooks, and photos and knickknacks himself. That was left for Helene, who had so far made some headway through Renee's writings, sorting and grouping drafts of stories and her journal entries. But for what purpose? For whom? Her children, perhaps in the future – some of the stories. The rest – her hopes and worries, addiction and recovery. But *the* secret? Was that in there, also?

Denis didn't know about the last hours of the last day that Renee was with Helene. Helene was certain. If he had known, would he ever have come around to see her and Kenneth in that dream of a designer house? Could he have stepped inside at all, knowing that?

And, more to the point, was she going to tell him?

"Uh-oh…" she heard Wishi-ta say. Helene started to get up.

She would tell him. She knew she would; just not exactly when.

In the evening, after the twins had gone to bed, there was a knock on the door. From where she sat at the sewing machine, Helene could see the outline of a man's head and shoulders: Erik. Her heart gave a little thump of joy and of dismay. She pushed the material from her lap, getting to her feet.

"Erik," she said, opening the door. He stood under the front door light with a half-bushel bag of apples and a tense look. "Come in."

"No, not tonight. I'm not here to pressure you in any way. But I did want to give you these apples. The second grade had a field trip to the orchards today, and I drove the bus." The briefest smile passed his lips. "My ears are still ringing. But I picked a bunch, and these are for you."

"The school bus, huh? Oh, boy. Well, thank you." She took the bag from him, resting it against her front. "That's very thoughtful. And you really can come in, you know, anytime. I'll make coffee." Now he was here, at her door, she wanted him to stay. The children's room was quiet, and her core was beginning to thrum.

He shook his head. "No. But there's something else. Something I have to tell you."

"Right here, on the front steps?"

"It will just take a minute."

"OK, then." Helene put down the bag of apples and stepped outside, wrapping her sweater a bit closer, the door left ajar.

Erik looked at the overhead light, his mouth working. "There's some, ah, development, that could be important."

"Yes?"

"That business I've been taking care of – it's partly to do with my son, yes. But there's something else too. Something I just recently found out. I was waiting for a good time to tell you."

Helene couldn't help herself. "You're sick?" It was a devastating thought, but not totally surprising.

He shook his head. "No, I'm fine. At least, same as usual. It's…well…I may have to take a paternity test, DNA. There's a little girl who could be mine." He paused, but Helene just blinked at him. "Possibly," he said. "Or not."

There was silence. Then Helene opened her mouth to speak, but Erik held up a hand.

"I know it's a shock, but I don't want to talk about it now. I just wanted you to know."

"OK, all right," Helene said, wanting to say something, anything. She shook her head; yet she was not actually shocked. "That I did not expect to hear tonight."

She watched him walk away, over to Chief's house where his truck was parked, and let himself in the door. She put the apples in a bowl in the kitchen and went back to her sewing, but she couldn't see straight, couldn't lose herself in the pattern and the stitching as she usually did. Eventually she gave up and went to pour herself a glass of wine, sitting on the couch, looking around the room, imagining her sister's life there: the sights, sounds, and smells. The voices and activity of daily living, all of it more real from Renee's journal pages.

She thought about getting up and going to Chief's house, as she had once before. By now she knew they would not argue or judge, or be anything but polite and accommodating. But she wasn't sure if it was right to go forward with Erik, both of them so caught up in matters and confused. It just seemed too complicated to take on more. It wasn't like they had so much time or history invested in their relationship. And not even like they knew each other all that well.

Then there was another knock on the door. It had to be Erik. Who else, at ten o'clock? Unless, possibly, Denis. But she wanted it to be Erik; she really, really did.

He was there again, in the same clothes, but with no apples.

"Whatever is going to happen," he said, "my feelings haven't changed. I want to be with you."

"Oh, just come in," she said, tugging gently on his arm.

"No, not yet. The thing is," he said apologetically, in the open doorway. "I know I said no pressure, but I love you."

She smiled and frowned and smiled again. "You do?"

"I'm pretty sure that must be what I'm feeling."

"Have you ever felt it before?"

"Not like this."

"And have you ever said it before?"

"I might have, once or twice. But I didn't mean it. Or maybe I did at the time but I didn't know what I was talking about."

"Well." There they were, again, stuck in the open doorway.

He tried again. "What happened, to both of us, it's in the past, right? This, uh, other woman, it wasn't love. The girl, if she is mine, that's from almost four years ago. There are two other…ah…guys who could be the dad, not just me. She's not looking for anything from me. Just to know for sure, I guess."

Helene stared a moment longer. "Would you just come in? Please, for my sake, so I can close the door and get out of the spotlight."

This got a small smile out of him. "Aren't you angry?"

"Angry?" she repeated, deliberating. "I don't think so. It's just a maybe, right?"

He nodded.

"And if it's true, it's not a terrible thing, not the end of the world. It's a life, anyway – not, well, attempted murder." She raised an eyebrow. It wasn't funny, at all, but the comparison was clever. So what, another complication? "Bring it on, I say."

So he stepped just inside the doorway. But that seemed to place further obligation on him. His face was flushed, his words slow and labored. "Thing is...maybe it's you. Maybe it's me finally getting old enough or smart enough. It's like we skipped the first steps right to the messy stuff, and all the real and important stuff. I really can't explain it."

"Me, either. I can't explain how this whole thing came about, really, never mind you and me."

He looked hopeful. "There is a 'you and me'?"

"I think so. But I'm just as ignorant as you when it comes to love, I'm sorry to say. However, possibly, this might be it. Come here," she said. And then louder, more insistent when he didn't move: "Come here so we can see how it feels."

They were back together, in full embrace. Only this time there were tears along with the gladness – the grief, the hope and fear, the uncertainty, all of it. Moment by moment, breath by breath, Helene felt calmer, more sure of what was in her heart. They went into the bedroom, taking their time to undress and to find each other, touching each other's animal skin and hair, making love slowly and deeply on top of the wolf blanket – everyone, all the family members, and friends and lovers with them and in them, one big jumble.

Helene kissed Erik's face and chest, his scars from that long-ago car accident. The doubts were still there, somewhere. But life, she realized, wasn't about the doubts, but living with the doubts. And holding open your arms to good, or the possibility of good. There was no immediate cure to the long history of pain and disappointment, but being restored a bit at a time, piece by piece. And, Erik, this man with her, was a pretty big piece, as broken as he may have been himself.

"You'll be back?" Helene asked sleepily as Erik got up to leave the next morning.

"Tonight, yes. But tomorrow I'm on the road again. Remember?"

"I do."

"I'm going to try to change my schedule and get more day trips, or pick up a few more cabinetry jobs, now that there's so much renovation work going on. This current job, they're going to start on the interior work soon."

"Good."

"I can't stay here, though. Like Louis said."

"Right."

"I'll be trotting back and forth across the street, under everyone's noses."

"Yup."

"But I may leave a toothbrush here."

"I think that will be OK."

"I might have enough time, this morning, for you and me..."

But just as he spoke the words, Tana-na's face appeared the doorway.

He didn't say a word, but launched himself onto the bed, next to where Erik was sitting.

"I knew it was you," Tana-na said.

"Right you are."

"I knew it." Tana-na climbed on his back, trying to wrestle him down. Erik gave him a minute and then flattened him like a bug.

Just as quick, Tana-na was off the bed, scampering to the other bedroom. "Wishi-ta! He's here, in the room with Helene. Come on, get up. But I saw him first."

So the day began.

In the afternoon, before it was time to collect the twins, Helene was on her way to Malvina's house with the small blanket she had sewn for the baby. She hadn't gotten to the sidewalk when Izzy bolted out the door, on a beeline to meet her.

"Helene," he said. "You are needed."

"Right now?"

"Can you come? Casey is here, my friend. You met her. We need to talk to you."

"Really?" Helene considered whether to run by Malvina's first. But that could wait. She had already conveyed Thelma's message to Izzy about moving, but she knew he was making plans, at his own pace, with a lot of phone calls back and forth to Raj in the city. Maybe it was something to do with that.

"OK," she said. "Let's go."

Helene remembered Casey from before, soon after the incident: serious, intense, heavily decorated with body art of different kinds. She was a tough-minded little thing, quick and scrappy, passionately devoted to Izzy. They were at Neesa's kitchen table, where Casey sat with a tape recorder, a small camera, and a notepad, which she'd been writing on.

"Hi, Casey," said Helene. "What's going on here?" It hadn't yet dawned on her that it was an interview.

"I write occasional articles for the Sentinel," Casey said, flicking her pen. "I'm doing a story about hate crimes. You know, like what happened to Izzy."

Helene's eyebrows arched with interest, but also anxiety. "I see."

"The assault," Casey clarified, narrowing her eyes, circled in thick black liner. "I'm also talking to a family in town, a Jewish family, who had swastikas drawn on their car windows."

Helene nodded, picturing for a moment Thelma's face – and her family pictures. "Oh, dear, dear. That's no good. So you think they're related?" She looked from Casey to Izzy, who shrugged.

"Could be," Casey said. And then less dramatically, "Well, maybe not the same people, but the same attitude, anyway. The idea that it's OK to threaten or intimidate people because of their differences."

Helene looked then to Izzy; after all, he wrote posts for the online Native paper. "What do you think?"

"Guess so. Could be a connection. We were talking about it, and Casey thought it would be a good idea to investigate further, and maybe tie things together."

Helene was intrigued; it might be worth publishing to see what kind of response, if any, an article might get. And, if the assaults were part of a pattern. There had been no follow-up from the police that she knew of, which might be part of the larger pattern of indifference.

"The thing is," Casey went on, "I have pictures of Izzy from before; you know, when he looks like his normal self, like at graduation, and then at this year's powwow, when he's dancing. You can see the date on the sign, and he's wearing only a breechcloth, so you can see pretty much everything else. And then I took some pictures today, to show his short hair. But Izzy says that you have pictures from right afterward, with bruises and bandages and everything. Especially how his hair looked before it was trimmed."

"Yes," said Helene, with a sigh. "I did take pictures to show to the police, so they could see the extent of his injuries."

"Can we use them?" It was Casey who was leading the charge now; all fired up on behalf of her beloved, even if he didn't know of or return that passion.

In her mind Helene could see the purples, blues, and greens of the swollen flesh, still-raw cuts, the jagged hair, and the bright white bandages. The pictures in the paper might not be in color, but still.

She turned to Izzy. It was his face and body and hair on display. "What do you think, Izzy? The pictures are pretty disturbing. Even in domestic assault cases, they usually don't publish pictures out of deference to the victims – once they're seen, they're hard to forget. People will remember those images, if the paper even decides to publish them."

"They'd better," Casey said, pink rising in her cheeks. "Or I'll send them to the Boston Globe; you know, their Spotlight team."

This was one ambitious young journalist, Helene thought – in love with her subject and her story.

"Izzy?" Helene prompted.

He looked like a man with indigestion, like he'd rather be elsewhere, even the Home Camp with no cell service and no Internet.

"Yes, I guess so." He turned an accusing eye on Helene. "What you said about the twins and Malvina's kids. And what about that Jewish family? They have kids too, right?"

Casey nodded.

"And what Louis said." Izzy set his face. "So that's what we're doing here. Whatever else happens, at least we tried."

He was right, Helene knew. But she hated to think of him exposed in that terrible way. His unique beauty made him even more susceptible to negative comments from letter writers who didn't like the story.

"But you should be prepared," she spoke slowly, deliberately. "Some people won't like what they read or somehow will blame it on you."

And then Izzy turned to her, his face both childlike and full of wisdom. "Helene, really? Like, I don't I know that already?"

Of course this was not new to him – being adored for his exotic, ethereal appearance, and also reviled.

Casey tapped her pen impatiently; she wanted the story, she wanted the fight, and she wanted those photos.

"OK," Helene said. "I'll get them. But please be mindful what you say."

Casey's eyes flared. "I'll present the truth; let other people deal with it. I guess we'll just see what happens. Anyway, the deadline is tonight by five o'clock, for next week's issue."

As Helene crossed back to Renee's house, she heard the murmur of voices, as they resumed the "interview." She had doubts about how this would go over, but another part of her said, *What will be, will be*. It might be another futile gesture, or it just might be the small thing that leads to bigger things, the cog that turns the wheel.

The next days went by quietly in a kind of golden shimmer Helene would no longer call Indian Summer, but the clear and dry air of early autumn. Erik was on the road, and the twins were noisily off to school. These were the last days before Helene was due to start work at the clinic, with a couple of orientation meetings and a trip to the department store in Pittsfield for new scrubs. She felt ready for the work, the routine, the new normal.

There was another Thursday night potluck with a Wampanoag storyteller, telling of Moshup the Giant who created Nantucket and Martha's Vineyard with the sand from his moccasins; and Granny Squannit, continually on the lookout for wandering children. Afterward Helene returned home in the cooling evening with the twins at her side, content for life to go on like this indefinitely. Although so much was still up in the air – the letter to Kenneth; what she would say to Thelma; Erik's DNA test; Denis's arrival; what would happen with Izzy after the article came out – it all felt distant from her this evening, and she had no need to hurry time, to find out answers. They would come soon enough.

Friday morning she called Thelma at her home number, knowing that she was at work, any one of the three schools that she covered.

"Hi, Thelma. It's Helene. You know what, it's fine whatever you want to do about the condo. This is important, and Kenneth probably is the best

person to work with. Whatever project he is associated with will be tasteful, good quality, and done on time. He's not going to gouge you; he's not that way. In all honesty I don't think he'll give you a hard time, no matter how unhappy he might be with me. But..." Seconds went by on the answering machine. *"There is something I really have to tell you, before you talk to him."*

Then the weekend was upon them, and the twins were at home, with shopping and errands and a trip to the park on another one of those sparkling autumn days with red and yellow leaves floating leisurely to the ground. Helene was surprised when she saw Thelma's number come up on her cell phone; she hadn't expected to hear from her until the end of the weekend.

"Thelma," she said. "You got my message?"

"I did," Thelma said from three hours away, probably in one of her colorful leisure-wear outfits. "Is this a good time to talk?"

Tana-na was near the brook, but not in it. Wishi-ta and another girl were collecting acorns and pinecones and creating tiny homes for tiny creatures.

"We're at the park. All's well at the moment."

"You know what," Thelma said, "let me call you later, when you're home, maybe after the twins are settled for the night. Is Erik in town?"

"No, gone until Tuesday. But you are still planning to talk to Kenneth?"

"Already did."

"What! Already?" Helene jerked; she couldn't help it. But no one was there to see. "That was quick."

"He returned my call right away." There was a pause, building anticipation. "He wanted to talk – about you."

"Oh, boy." If Helene hoped to dodge the news, she could think of no good excuse off the top of her head. "I'm sorry. I thought he'd try to keep work and personal stuff separate. I hope it didn't spoil things for you."

"No, not at all. He's happy to work with me, and we have an appointment for tomorrow afternoon at his office. But I guess he wanted to clear the air first. He said he'd gotten the letter, and that it did help explain things. Then he said he was glad I'd called, because he wanted to ask me something. It was a bit strange..."

Helene's heart was racing. She scanned quickly for the children, still at play. The sun glared off the water, hurting her eyes a little. No harm or danger; everyone as they were before.

Had Kenneth told Thelma about Renee, before Helene had a chance?

Thelma's voice continued at the end of the line. "He asked me if I felt you were making these decisions in your right mind. If you were healed from the concussion, and that it was truly what you wanted."

"Ye-es?" She could barely eke out the word.

"I said 'Yes,' of course. That is what I truly believe."

Ah, maybe that was it. That was all he wanted to know. "Oh, thank you, thank you…"

"And I think it reassured him. Anyway, he said that he could see things now, about you and how you were, that he couldn't understand before."

Full stop. No further detail or explanation forthcoming.

"So, he's OK with it?" Helene could hardly believe it herself.

"OK as he can be. I mean his heart has been broken, and naturally he feels rejected. But I think it's clear that what you had is over, and there's nothing that can be done to fix it. And maybe, just maybe, he's a little relieved."

"To be done with me?"

"To be done with the drama, I think. And the, well, mystery of it all."

"Well," Helene murmured, suddenly a little light-headed. "What do you know about that? Another battle I may not have to fight after all…" Her gaze was attracted to a spray of water, and then a shout of surprise and excitement: Tana-na in the brook.

"Oops," Helene said, "Thelma, sorry, I've got to go. I'll call you tonight after the kids go to bed. OK?" She was walking toward the brook, still talking. Tana-na was soaking wet, a big grin on his face. That wouldn't last long once the chill set in.

"Fine."

"Yes, I've got something else to tell you…" But the call was ended. Helene put the phone in her jacket pocket and hauled Tana-na out of the water, still splashing and merry, a water-skimmer in his hand, its little bug legs racing in the air.

Chapter 30

Erik was back in the afternoon on Tuesday, and said he'd come for dinner. The twins were excited, helping to set the table and put out the rolls and butter. Wishi-ta wanted to make cupcakes, but there wasn't time. However, there were ice cream treats in the freezer.

He arrived freshly scrubbed and playful. He clowned around with the twins in the backyard while Helene finished preparations for the meal. They loved that he was big, and could be loud, and pretended to be scary. He enjoyed throwing a ball and giving piggyback rides. It was those childlike qualities that made them love him; but did he have it in him to be the "heavy," to teach and to discipline when necessary?

She was on pins and needles waiting for a chance to talk to him alone, wondering if he knew yet about the paternity test, and what that might mean. After the meal, Helene put on a video for the kids in the den, and sat over coffee with Erik at the kitchen table. The ice cream was for later.

"Any news," she asked, "about your, ah, situation?"

He nodded. "I guess so. What I can tell you" – he pointed his chin toward the den – "if we're not interrupted."

"Will it take that long?"

"No. But I don't want to get you upset, or me."

She laughed. "I think that horse has left the barn."

He shook his head, not really smiling. "But maybe not the horse you thought."

That was cryptic. "So…details?" she prompted.

His lips twitched, almost a smile. "So, you really don't know? Bernice hasn't said anything?"

"Bernice!" What would Bernice have to do with anything? Oh, but, her younger daughter…the wild one…"Oh, no, no," she said without thinking. "Not Josie?" She covered her mouth to keep from yelling.

Erik closed his eyes.

She took her hand away, speaking in a low voice. "It is her, isn't it? Josie." Helene was sure of it. All the clues added up.

He nodded, and after that every thought left her head; she had no words at all to say. As crazy as everything had been, she could still be stunned.

"You're mad?" he asked anxiously. "Yeah, I can understand, but we don't even really know…"

She held up a hand, shaking her head.

"No," she stopped, still trying to get her breath back. "Not mad."

"You think I'm an idiot, for getting into this kind of situation?"

"Wait," she said. "Wait." She closed her eyes to keep the room from spinning, a tiny bit of that head wound acting up.

"Are you OK?" Now he was just anxious.

"Yeah, I'm OK. I'm just so surprised. I'm not mad, and I don't think you're an idiot. How am I in any kind of a position to judge you, anyway, after what I've done? No, I'm just trying to make sense of it."

Erik had just opened his mouth to speak when suddenly Helene burst out laughing, a deep belly laugh that took over her body until she had to cover her mouth and her face – *the cosmic absurdity of it all!*

But Erik wasn't laughing; his face had clouded over, the overhead light turning his whiskers to a whitish bristle. "What's so funny? I don't think it's funny." He lifted a hand, defensively. "It was sort of a bad time for both of us, just plain old loneliness and bad decisions. That's not something to laugh at."

Helene wiped her eyes with the heel of her hand. "No, I'm sorry. It's not funny. It's just that now…do you realize…there's this connection, I guess, with Bernice – whom I've always liked, by the way, from day one. But, lordy, could it be more unlikely? All the way from Alaska – Eskimo, for heaven's sake. Or, Inupiaq, I should say."

He shrugged. "So what? What's that supposed to mean?"

"So you could be the father of a Native American child – or indigenous, right?"

His face relaxed slightly. "I suppose so." And then he added. "If that's true. We don't know yet. And, I'm still crossing my fingers it…she's…not mine. There are two other, ah, candidates, as I told you. Josie's a great girl, woman, but she's not the easiest to deal with. I don't know what kind of role…" He trailed off, looking at the floor.

"Hey," Helene said, placing a hand on his forearm. "One day at a time. Isn't that what they say? AA and all? All about patience and knowing what you can and cannot change. Come on, the twins are going to be here in a minute, looking for their ice cream."

He straightened, gazing at her. "It's hard to think, what…"

"Shush. We just have to wait and see."

She could hardly believe it herself, that such things could happen in a life that had been so calm and orderly for so long. She stepped away, calling into the den.

"OK, guys. Ice cream and stories. Erik can read you a scary one, if you want, but not too scary."

The twins *were* tired and quiet after only a few minutes of *James and the Giant Peach*. It had been a full, active day. No protests at all when it was time for brushing their teeth and going to bed. Not even twenty minutes into the TV news, Erik was nodding off. Helene wriggled next to him on the sofa, full of a strange kind of excitement. All these new things to think about, good or bad; who was to say? Certainly made life interesting.

"Hey, time for us," she said, getting up and tickling him under the arm. Ice cream bowls remained on the coffee table; there were dirty dishes in the sink. Jimmies on the floor. They could wait.

He lumbered to his feet. "Really?"

"Oh, yes. I have to admit, you are good at this. Lots of practice, I suppose."

He looked a bit hurt.

"Erik, we've got to laugh at some of this stuff, if we want to get through it." Then she kissed him, and he had to respond. "It's not a bad thing that you're good with women," she said.

"I've always tried to please," he said, in all seriousness.

"I'm sure you have."

"It's just the follow-through and expectations I have a hard time with."

"I know that too. As for me, I stayed around long after I should have gone. Maybe we can help each other." She was nipping him with kisses, teasing.

He was getting worked up now, red and hot. "We can," he said. "We can."

After the weekend Denis called to say he would be arriving on Tuesday with Kiko, the on-again, off-again girlfriend and dog-watcher while he was on the road. Also a massage therapist and Reiki healer; that's about all Helene knew.

"Kiko's friend is watching the dogs," Denis explained. "But I really want you two to meet and get to know each other."

"Sure," Helene said. "But I thought that was over. That is, she dumped you since you were never around."

He kind of laughed. "True. But I turned over a leaf; she came around. It's all good. You have room for us?"

"Sure. The twins can sleep with me, or at Neesa's, since Izzy's away. I'm sure that will be fine."

"But Izzy, will he be around at all? I was hoping to get in a little music with him – I have some ideas for fiddle and flute."

"I don't know. He hasn't played much since the incident with his bike. Waiting for his lips to heal, I guess, or his teeth."

"Or his soul," Denis put in, unexpectedly.

"Yeah, maybe that too." She cleared her throat. "Anyway, he's on an exploratory visit to Boston, to see how he likes the city. Not sure when he'll be back."

"Ah. Then, Tuesday it is. We'll be there by dinnertime. I can pick up a pizza if you want."

"No, no, just come. But call if you're going to be late."

"I can do that."

"We'll see." He wasn't too old for some sisterly jazz.

But Denis was on time, and Kiko hopped out of the truck, not quite what Helene had expected: short but sturdy and muscular, in loose pants and a tunic, long black hair. Asian, at least in part. Japanese, maybe. Kiko, right? And Helene had thought that was a New Age name. Well. Kiko looked maybe late twenties, and wore some unusual, likely handcrafted jewelry with richly colored stones.

"Welcome," Helene said, hugging Denis, then stepping back. "Long time on the road, brother. Nice for you how everything's worked out so well with the music." If there was a little edge to her words, she tried to hide it. "I heard your song on the radio. Wow!"

"I know, I know, it's beyond crazy," he said, and then turned to wave Kiko forward. "Kiko, come meet my sister, Helene." The women shook hands, and Kiko said "Nice to meet you," in an accent that was neither Asian nor Bostonian, just somewhere middle America. "I've heard a lot about you."

Helene could not say the same. Guiltily, she recalled not asking, not wanting to know about Denis's women, assuming there were plenty here and there, none of them serious. But this one had been around longer than most. And she had been entrusted with Denis's dogs.

"Well, we'll have a chance to catch up now," Helene said. "Hey, I made a casserole and a salad. You're hungry, right? And how about a drink? I can offer you beer or wine."

A look went back and forth between Denis and Kiko.

"That's great, Helene," Denis said. "We'd love to take you up on the offer. Only, well, Kiko doesn't drink, so water is fine. And we're practicing a more or less vegetarian lifestyle, so the salad will be great. And bread, maybe?"

Well, that was a change. Good for them, Helene thought. "Whatever you want. You can –"

"But…" Denis jumped in. "Not just yet. There's something we want to show you before it gets dark. Won't be long, maybe twenty, twenty-five minutes from here. And back, of course."

Helene looked from one to the other, and at the truck. Packed to the gills.

Denis laughed, catching her look. "I was wondering if we could go in your car. The truck is pretty stuffed, and it's a little tight in the front seat."

"Yes, I see that." She nodded, slightly puzzled. Perhaps they were on their way somewhere else after this. "How about the twins, should I get them? We can squeeze." She cocked an ear, listening for that sound: children. "I think they're still out back. They've already eaten. Or, I can ask Neesa or Malvina to keep an eye on them."

Another look between Denis and Kiko. Denis was bursting with some kind of excitement, while Kiko looked far more relaxed – probably how she was with the dogs.

"No, better not bring them," he said, working hard not to contain himself. "We won't be gone an hour. Is that OK?"

"Fine," she said. Something had come over Helene, where none of the shoulds or shouldn'ts, or what was best and proper, was troubling her. So what, the casserole got cold? So what, no one except her was going to eat it after all? The kids had had fish sticks at five o'clock; good thing she'd nibbled a few. She was still a bit shocked that Denis had arrived on time; that he hadn't canceled last minute.

"Let me tell Malvina. But don't let the kids see you, or we'll never get away."

She fetched her purse and keys from the living room and went to Malvina's to let her know.

"Who's driving?" she asked on her return.

"I'll drive," Denis said. "So you can focus on the scenery."

"The scenery. Of course." She was getting a bit excited too, wild with speculation: a new dog? A horse? Maybe some mystery sacred grove?

They drove off the base onto the main road heading east, eventually connecting to the turnpike that ended in Boston. Maybe five or six miles after passing the town center, Denis took a left turn. The road narrowed, winding through a river valley, dotted with a few small farms and abandoned houses and barns. They passed an apple orchard and climbed a hill to a level opening in the trees overlooking the river. A lovely, rustic spot not very far outside of town – another world, maybe another time. What struck Helene first was a yellow barn, complete with a silo standing sentinel on the hill. It had a wide, bright-red door and many tall windows, certainly more recent additions. Only afterward did she notice the modest white house to the side, smaller and somewhat weathered, maybe from the 1940s. Cute in its way; homey.

"This is it," Denis said, coming to a stop on the gravel driveway. The barn loomed golden up ahead of them in the late sunlight. "What do you think?"

They got out for a better look.

"A recording studio?" Helene guessed. It could have been some kind of artist's retreat, and that barn was certainly meant for something special, big enough for rehearsals or for an audience even.

"Perhaps someday. But not right now."

"You better tell me," she said. "Because at this point in my life, I'm thinking just about anything is possible."

"Yes!" Denis cried, pumping his fist. "That's just how I feel. Right, Kiko?" Kiko didn't appear to be the type that smiled easily, but her gaze was set fondly on Denis.

"It's our new home," Denis announced. "Me and Kiko. Just as soon as the closing goes through. We made an offer, and it was accepted, and we should be in by the end of next month."

Helene blinked in astonishment. "Here?" She turned to him. "You're going to live here?"

"That's the idea." He smiled, almost bashfully. "I know, it's so close – to you and the twins." A ghost of the old sadness and insecurity flitted across Denis's face, and he stopped talking, watching her.

For a moment she was overcome with emotions: hope? Fear? Joy and pain.

"You're my only sister now," he said, his voice husky. "And they're my niece and nephew too, the twins, the only family I have, really. Helene, you know I needed to find my own way, and I didn't have any support, either. But I left you with that whole mess to deal with yourself…no choices, no freedom. That was wrong; I'm sorry." The words were sticking in his throat, but he pushed on. "I want to make it up to you, to help with the twins, whatever I can do." Again he paused. "I hope you're OK with that."

Her arms rose of their own accord and she stepped forward to embrace him. The laugh that escaped her throat came out like a cough or a bark. "Of course I am. I'm glad, really glad, that you want to be nearby and spend more time together." And then she thought to add, "You and Kiko. I'm just surprised you're ready to do this."

It was like a jolt of electricity went through him. "Right, so it's like this," he started, the waning light glinting off his eyes and hair. "With the money from the music, and the money coming from the sale of Mom and Dad's house, I have enough for a down payment. I'm getting a bridge loan until the other money comes through, but Kenneth says there are a number of interested buyers, offering over the asking price. And property out here is much less expensive, as you probably know."

Helene's mouth opened to an O. Then she realized Kenneth would be the logical one to market the house.

"And the best part," Denis went on, moving closer to Kiko's side. "Kiko can run her massage therapy business from the barn; it's completely renovated; heat and plumbing. And there's room to expand the business, if she wants, like other therapists or even a space for yoga. And I can soundproof the back part if the guys and I want to rehearse."

They were both looking at her expectantly, as if making a sales pitch – or waiting for approval. Most of the yard was in shadow now, with a few bright spots of red and yellow where the leaves had changed. Already the birds had roosted; the dark shapes of bats fluttered in the pale sky between trees.

"Great!" she said. "Just great. That's all I can say; it sounds like very good news all around." Oh, why not? Yes, there was still some question in her mind, about Kiko – her motivation, her stake in all this. But that was not Helene's concern; only theirs. Let the world, and time, judge as they would. Yet there was something else, another consideration from her side.

"There's one thing I should tell you," she said, "in all fairness. I'm not one hundred percent sure what my own role and plans are for the future. To put it simply, Louis decided not to let me adopt the twins, and I would be only legal guardian, with more limited say in what happens to them. I'm not quite sure how that will play out."

Denis's face dropped, the ghost of a sad, disappointed child. "But you won't leave."

"I don't expect to. But it is possible I'd relocate at some point after the twins are older, or if something happens with Louis's case and he's released early. It's possible he could meet someone new and marry that woman. So then what? Where does that leave me? Still the aunt, obviously, but not the one in charge. I'm just saying, it's not entirely clear."

"They're five now, the twins?" Kiko asked, quiet and thoughtful.

"Right. Still young. Don't get me wrong, I love them. And I want to be there for them. It's just that I'm not sure what my role will be or if I can achieve bringing them up in the Native way that Louis wants me to."

A cool breeze stirred the leaves, and a small sliver of moon appeared in the sky. Evening coming; season changing. Dinner calling. Time to go.

"You can tell me all the details at dinner," she said. "And if you want, we can stop at the new Thai place in town. I'm sure they have vegetarian dishes, something more than just salad."

They were all for that idea.

The twins were funny when they saw Denis. It had been a while, a long and very full summer, and they had seen a number of men coming and going in their world. But as soon as they saw him, they shouted his name and asked to see his dogs, sad that they had not come also. Standing at his side, Kiko let them check her out without saying a lot. She was at ease with them right away, more so than Helene, who still sometimes struggled with being the "nurse in charge." But the twins had loved her anyway, teaching her the joys of easy affection.

"Are you Native too?" Tana-na wanted to know.

"I'm Japanese, Irish and German," she said. "But you know we are related way back, thousands of years."

Tana-na nodded, too polite to respond otherwise. "But you have hair like mine."

"True. But Wishi-ta doesn't have hair like you, and she's your twin."

No one mentioned the new house. Not yet. There was time. And there were a few questions about how they would handle things. Like the fact that Denis and Kiko were not married, and did not appear to have a plan for marriage. Later, in the living room, after Kiko had retired for the evening, Helene and Denis sat across from each other, in the very place their sister had died. On the wall was a family portrait from soon after the twins were born, parents in regalia and the babies in naming blankets. In an odd way, the three of them together once again. Denis was finishing a bottle of the craft beer he had brought, examining the label thoughtfully. He had taken the easy chair.

"So," he said. "Erik, is he still in the picture?"

"He is." But she offered no more, for the moment.

"And Izzy, you think he's doing OK now, after the bike thing?"

The spot next to Helene on the sofa was still warm from Kiko's body heat. "He's well healed physically. But full recovery will take a while. We're still hoping there may be new developments with the case, but nothing yet. His, ah, friend, has written a story for the local newspaper."

"Hmm…OK." Denis cleared his throat. "And you? All better from the knock on the head?"

"I believe I am."

Denis was watching carefully, but he asked no more questions. "So, sister of mine," he began, "I know you have concerns. If I know you at all, you have, ah, concerns, about Kiko and me and the house. So fire away."

Helene shifted, sipping her glass of wine. For all the sadness and fear related to Renee's addictions, Helene found that wine in the evening helped her relax. And she wondered, not for the first time, whether if she let down her guard, and if life took an especially bad turn, that could happen to her too. Most probably.

"Maybe you don't know me as well as you think," she said. "Maybe I'm just fine letting you live your own life however you want to."

Denis smiled. "Right. But I have known you a long time. And you've always preached about consequences, consequences, consequences. I heard you. I just never did it."

Helene stretched her legs out on the sofa. "So let's hear these concerns, then," she prompted, playing along.

Denis sat up straighter, pitching his voice to imitate his sister's: "What's Kiko's motivation in this? She dumped you, right, for being unreliable? But now you have a house and a successful music career and money, now you're not so unreliable? Explain to me how you're not going to be gone, on the road?"

Helene had to smile. "That sounds like me – the old me, anyway." She had another sip of wine and was feeling very close to mellow. "So, then, how about some answers?"

"Now I have a schedule," Denis explained. "Published six months in advance, of recording and concert dates. I'll know, and she'll know, exactly where I'll be and when. And now I have a real place and somebody to return to."

There was a late-season fly droning slowly around the lamp. They had already shut the windows against the cool evening air. Tonight might be the first night that Helene turned on the heat.

"OK," she said. "So she's come around to this new, reliable, or at least more predictable, you."

"Well," Denis looked bashfully at his beer bottle. "After some sweet talk, I admit."

Helene saw the big brown eyes and expressive eyebrows of her brother at five or six, hopeful but prepared for disappointment.

"It's true, she got fed up with me; and she had a right to. But I think she loves me, and she says she loves my music. And I know she loves my dogs. What else could I ask?"

Helene's heart twisted a little in her chest: sorrow for her brother's long loneliness and at the appearance of this strange happiness. Like hers, when least expected.

"You know, Kiko is very strong," he said. "She's been on her own so long. I tell myself she can be strong enough for both of us, and I'll just try to do my best. I try to remember the good things that Dad did, before, well…"

A heaviness settled in the room, the light becoming thicker and dimmer. A picture of their dad, home from work in his recliner, a drink in his hand, stunned by a world that was just not right.

"They started out so well," Helene began, and then stopped, sobered by the thought that life could break people down in so many situations they couldn't prepare for. And it could still happen, to her or Denis, or anyone. Those circumstances, the combination of grief, hopelessness, disappointed dreams, could broadside regular people who might otherwise have prospered and thrived.

"He had the wrong idea, I think," Denis said, resting the beer on his lap. "I think chasing the American dream was not good for him. He got so close, and it was all taken away – losing Mom, losing his job, all the financial problems that came with the medical bills. And not to mention Renee, like a thorn in his side. He just couldn't seem to shake it, and adapt. Once he labeled himself a failure, he couldn't see the good in anything or anyone." And then, bitterly: "Especially me."

The wine in Helene's glass was almost gone. "Or me," she said softly, but not bitterly. "He hoped I could fill the void and rescue Renee. But I didn't, did I?"

Denis shrugged. "You did what you could. As much as anyone could. More. "Hélène knew it was time to tell Denis what had happened.

"You know she died here, Renee," she said. "In a hospital bed."

He nodded.

"She almost died before that, several times, as we know. But once, at home, that last time, with me…"

Denis and Kiko stayed only one night. They were headed back for the dogs, and to take care of other business while Denis was free from touring. Before he left he told Helene that he had arranged to take time off later in the fall. Also that Kiko said she wanted to go on the road with him, even if just once, to see what that life was like. No plans for marriage, however; at least not a conventional marriage, and not in the foreseeable future. They didn't want to rush.

"I see," said Helene, and no more than that.

"But we'll be working on the house now for the next few months, as soon as we have the closing. Maybe move in at the holidays."

"Good! Let me know if I can help: painting or wallpapering, light fixtures, curtains, those kind of things. And you know, Erik is a carpenter, he might help too."

Kiko waved at them from the truck – a good-bye to Helene, and a Come on, let's get going! to Denis. But she was smiling, and Denis was smiling too, like that same five-year-old boy who had some wish come true.

Renee's journal – 18

Homebound. Homebody. That's me these days, strange to say. In fact, I don't get much beyond the living room, except the bathroom, not even much in the kitchen these days. This from a girl who was never home, never wanted to be home. A runaway. That was me, truly. I think of Neesa's sister, who ran away and never came back. No one to this day knows what happened to her, but most likely bad. All that worry and sorrow she caused, that I caused. I can't offer comfort; I can only say that I ended up in an OK place, maybe she did too. I've been in touch with Denis, and he knows, but I asked him not to tell Helene until afterward, when it's over, not to force her back into my life because of this – more pain, more heartache, more trouble. I've come a long way, but no Hollywood endings.

Anyway, Louis is away again, three thousand miles or so away for the next week. In California, and then a trip to the Pacific Northwest, more water rights and fishing rights. So much is happening all at once; cases, suits, articles: a need for him and his advice. He didn't want to go this time, to be away from me and the twins. But I wanted him to go. Staying wouldn't help anything here, with me or my health. Me and the twins are cared for as well as we could be, by his family, and never lonely. It's not a lonely place or a lonely life. And now I know that was what ailed me most, even living in a big house with my father and a brother and sister. There was a loneliness there that no one could bridge. We all suffered – within feet of one another, but we suffered alone. Always, there is someone with me, if I want. Izzy is my constant companion, like Red Cat. And the women who come and go, and Noel checking in. Even Erik, who's become a regular visitor, and the one who asks about me, my own home and family, just making conversation, but interested. We have more in common that I might have guessed.

Sometimes I feel bad and scared, about Louis and the twins without me. I can't help it. No one could. I told Louis it would be good for him to marry again, and for the twins to have a mother, or at least some caring woman in their lives. And that after all the trouble I gave him, maybe a Native woman would be better – one who already knows the ways and the culture. With a serious face he said Native women could be just as much trouble.

"I doubt it," I said. "You dragged me across the country, helped me get clean, faced down your mother, and I still can't cook to save my life."

"Can't argue," he said.

"And what did I know about Native life? Next to nothing. Not even powwows or the Red Road."

"True that."

I took his hand and made him look at me. "So, what did you get out of being with me? Except I made you laugh and loved to go to bed with you."

"Hm." He was quiet awhile, thinking. "Well, you were a challenge," he admitted. "And not what I had seen for myself in my life, we both know that. But there was something..."

"Yes?" Our conversation was lighthearted, almost joking. But I wanted to know, at this moment, what there could have been of value to him in being with me.

"You speak truth," he said, wryly, "in your way."

"Me? I'm a world-class liar and an excellent actor, I've been told."

He smiled; I had that power too.

"There's more than that, I hope."

"You made me see," he said, serious again. "You made me believe that people could change, if they wanted to, and in the right situation, when they could understand what was at stake, and didn't feel judged or shamed."

"I know what you mean," I answered. "I've met some Natives along the way who can be very, very stubborn, or seem to have lost hope altogether."

"Yes," he said. "But white people too. Maybe they can change, if things are bad enough, or if they can see another way. There has to be another way." His eyes were dark and glittering with purpose.

"So I was a mission for you, a test case? Is that what you're saying?"

"No, you were a thorn in my side. I couldn't ignore it. Beautiful and fierce. Your suffering had made you hard as a diamond; strong, beyond fear, beyond pain. Like a warrior, who has given everything in the fight. It was your spirit that captured me, when I was not sure that the spirit world was even real. When I had doubts that all of our knowledge and traditions were not meant to die out. That is what I believe, why we are together."

I thought he was done; he clasped my hands in his, bringing them to his lips.

"I changed too," he said. "I am more fully Indian, and more fully human. This is human business I am about – these rights, these resources, the care of each other, the earth. You see that, don't you?"

I nodded. Because nothing makes us more equally human than addiction. I learned that, of course, from my own experience. But also from the four men and one other woman who met once a week in the lounge of the Intertribal Center, all of us in recovery, all of us equal in our struggles between pain and oblivion. It was never about happiness or joy, we agreed, but escape from the intolerable, until the escape was also intolerable, no escape at all. They coached me in the ways of "well-briety," and its daily discipline, full of effort, and its once-in-a-while rewards of peace and connection. We had each known those moments of transcendence, I guess you call it, when you are high – enough to torment. Mainly we were uneasy souls in a small lifeboat, only finally seeing we had a paddle and could use it, alone or together. They came to our house when I could no longer go out, and some said they were happy for me that I no longer had to wonder: the ways of addiction are so familiar, while sober life is so unsure. Here is a truth: to know I will die this way, from the cancer, means I will not relapse again; there is a kind of peace in that. Louis was not part of that world, but he recognized it for the medicine it was.

I ache now to think that I will leave him and this beautiful life behind. But how can I not believe in a world of spirits, beyond this one, when things have moved in ways to show me that it is so? That there is love, which is also invisible, but true.

8. Dance, Dancers, Dance – by One Little Indian

So, as I've probably mentioned, we dance. That's what we do. A lot. For all kinds of reasons and as often as possible. Pretty much anyone who wants to can join in – at some point. In the modern-day versions of powwow, there's special-event dancing: grass dancers, fancy dancers, jingle dancers – some of these are actual competitions, so you've got to be good and be prepared to exert some energy. It's not just jog-along time, if you know what I mean. Other times it's your basic social and community dance – everyone welcome, join on in! Old, young, wheelchairs, crutches, tone-deaf, rhythm-impaired, no problem. All dressed up or almost naked, it's all fine. Just come inside the circle, that's the idea.

We're not the only ones with this idea, I know. There are dervishes who whirl in the Middle East and the Shakers here in America, who, well, shake it up. That's the idea. Movement, mostly to sound and beat. That works for us, and for lots of other humans, as well. We're not the only ones with war dances, either, I've come to find out. But, like so much that's been misrepresented (sigh), it was never about seeking to leave our humanity behind to become killing machines. It was about courage; true. But also, all that bloody racket was a message to the enemy: we're loud; we're many; don't mess with us – maybe we can both avoid fighting. Or not.

Like everything else in our culture, dance is a work in progress, adapted to the times. Our fancy shawl dancers love to spin their satin ribbons; that's an innovation, not old school. The jingle dancers wear rolled up tin "bells" on their skirts, also not known pre-contact. So we like a little fashion and finery, splash and noise. Who doesn't? That's part of our regalia, our special, spiritual clothing. And it's not just about good looks, either. So much of it has meaning, of some kind, at least to us.

The most basic dance is our circle dance, joining hands, step to the left, step to the right. You get the picture. It's social; it's community; it's the great joiner and equalizer. It can be, I can tell you, great fun. And a good time to check out the girls and guys who might be interested in checking out you.

But there's a version of this circle dance which is not so jolly. The Ghost Dance, about as serious as a dance can be. From the old days, the late 1800s, although it continues today in some places. Not mentioned in most history books, because history writers don't relish the story. There was a prophet, Wovoka, out in the west, who had a dream during an eclipse: Native Americans would be taken up into the sky, while the earth opened up to swallow the whites, after which spiritual, right-living Natives would return in freedom to a peaceful, fruitful land. The way to bring this about was not guns and fighting but Natdia, the Ghost Dance. Wovoka spread the message and Indians all over began to dance this dance, seeking communion with ancestors who would come to help them to rid the land of white devastation. Instead the whites got nervous, and the Bureau of Indian Affairs sent in tribal police to arrest Sitting Bull – to force him to stop the Ghost Dance. The rest is history. Wounded Knee. Over two hundred men, women, and children, unarmed, impoverished, slaughtered. Because they wanted to dance.

So, things did not turn out as hoped for the Ghost Dancers. I did hear one old Indian guy going on, "Well, at least we got the browning of America. I hear by the middle of the century, there will be more people of color than white. At least above ground. Maybe old Wovoka was right after all."

And still we dance.

Chapter 31

Erik called from the road, checking in. Helene was alone in the house for another hour until it was time to walk the twins home, and the call had awoken her from an unplanned nap. Listening to his updates, she found herself yawning. Maybe she was still healing. Or else she was just fatigued from the roller coaster of emotions. When he finished his update, Helene delivered the news about Denis and Kiko.

"No way," he said. "Denis? Settling down? That's some crazy stuff. I met Kiko once, you know. She's got a backbone, that girl. I mean, woman. Not mean or anything, just tough; you know, firm. I guess anything can happen."

"Right," Helene said into the phone, blinking her eyes awake. "Like with you, right?"

It took a moment to register. "Oh, yeah." She heard his sigh. "Well, we'll know soon. By the way, it's the first and only paternity test I've ever taken."

"Duly noted."

"I really don't think there are any others out there."

"Do you want to put that in writing?"

"Hmph. Anything else on your end?"

Helene mulled it over. "Not really. Other than Thelma decided to go with Kenneth's office on the sale of her house; she's moving to a condo development he's involved with."

"Ah," he said. And then, "You mad?"

"No, not now. I was before, like she was picking the 'polished professional over the pathetic pal.'" She let out a short laugh. "But we talked about it, and it really is best for her. Kenneth is good at what he does; I'm sure he'll do right by her."

"Still." Erik didn't sound convinced.

Helene sighed. "He's not contesting the divorce, and I think that's something to do with Thelma; his regard for her opinion, generally. Plus I was the one in the wrong here, so to speak; at least, not keeping my end of the vows. So…"

"OK, then."

"Besides, he's already showing the Roy family house to potential buyers. He's the landlord, same as me. It seems the storm has passed, or maybe he just threw up his hands after all."

She could hear Erik's long intake of breath. "I really thought he was going to fight for you, Helene. I know I would."

"Ah…" That pleased and undid her. "But he would be fighting for a fantasy, a figment of his imagination, and I think he finally realized it. You've got the real deal, like it or not."

"Oh, I like it all right," he said. "I can't get enough of it."

"Three more days," she reminded him.

"Don't I know it."

And then, out of the blue, there was a new development concerning Izzy. The newspaper had run Casey's article with some of the pictures, before and after the assault. There was also a part about the swastikas drawn on a local family's mailbox, and one at the boys' lavatory at school. *"Hate Crimes in Our Town?"* the headline ran.

Bernice saw the article first and brought the paper to show Helene, who did not have a subscription. They stood in the living room among sewing projects, scissors, measuring tape and fabric on the furniture.

"Pretty bad," said Bernice as Helene was reading. *The news.*

"Well, it is bad," Helene said, skimming over the text, including a quote from the police: "Nothing conclusive yet."

"I only hope it doesn't make things worse."

Helene looked up at Bernice. "Not you too. So little faith. How will things ever change if they don't come to light and people are held accountable?"

Bernice held her eyes a moment. "That's a white person's view. We don't really see things that way."

That was the first time Bernice, or anyone, had singled her out for being white or for having certain views.

"That doesn't mean I'm wrong," Helene said heatedly. "What does Chief say, and Elsa?" She knew, positively, this had already gotten around to the rest of the community, like wildfire, and everyone had an opinion.

"Elsa says, 'Good luck to them finding out,' and Chief says, 'Could flush the fox out of the bush.'"

"Really?" Now that was interesting. At least Chief wasn't dismissing the idea outright.

"Probably not," Bernice was saying. "And now everyone sees how terrible he looked, Izzy, after this thing happened to him. Some people will say it was his own fault, riding so recklessly."

Helene looked back at the pictures. "They'll also see how beautiful he is, from before the incident." She tapped her finger on Izzy's photo face. "And will be again."

Bernice was looking over Helene's shoulder, past her. "Two spirits," she murmured.

"You mean his...?" Helene asked, remembering. "How he...uh..."

Bernice waved it away, offering no explanation, but remained standing at Helene's side, staring up at her.

"OK," Helene said, "I heard what you said, and we'll just have to disagree about this. OK?" Then, "Can I keep this?" The newspaper.

Bernice nodded once, but she didn't move.

"What?" Helene asked.

"Not that. The other thing."

And then Helene got it. "Wait. You mean Erik? And, uh, Josie? That thing?"

Bernice nodded. "Josie's husband decided one day that the baby wasn't his; she looked so white. And then he counted back to when they separated the first time. So they did the DNA test. It's not him, the ex – they're apart now. It might be Erik, but it might not. There are two other men, but one is gone, out of the picture. Actually, she doesn't remember his name." She paused. "Are you mad?"

A few seconds passed before Helene answered with a shrug. "Not really. I mean, we don't know who the father is, only that Erik might be the father."

"Will that make a difference?"

"Well, sure," Helene said. She had to be honest. "It certainly will add some, uh, complications if it is him."

"You'll part ways, then, if he's got to deal with all that?"

Helene shook her head, a smile at her lips. "I don't think so. I've never dealt with anything like it before, but it hasn't changed my feelings for him, the possibility. Why, Bernice? Do you hope they might still get together, Erik and Josie?"

"God, no," Bernice said. "Someone has to be the grown-up, if there's a child involved."

Helene laughed. "Come on, be fair. Erik is trying; I really think he is."

"Maybe." Then she added, to Helene's surprise: "He's better with you, anyhow." And then, to her greater surprise: "Who knows? We might be family one day."

"Bernice!"

Then, on Thursday morning, after the twins had gone to school, there was Neesa, standing in Helene's kitchen, after she emerged from the bathroom in her robe. Neesa had been growing her hair out, and had taken to wearing more of her Native jewelry, and even some of her Native-style clothing, along with the ever-present gold cross at her neck. Now Helene could see some of her in Izzy, never mind Malvina, her clone.

"Can you come?" Neesa said. "Quick. Police are on the phone. About Izzy."

Afterward Helene realized that Neesa could have told them to call Helene on her cell phone; she had given them her contact information. But the police had called for Izzy, who was now with Thelma, and Neesa wanted Helene to talk to them. Without even changing her clothes, she hurried to Neesa's house, picking up the house phone.

"Yes, Helene Bradford here."

"Officer Prisco. We have a new development in the situation we wanted to share with Mr. Lopes. This is the number he left for us to call. Is there another way to contact him?"

"He's away at the moment. But I can give you his cell phone, or try to reach him myself."

"His cell phone, please."

Helene looked at Neesa, who nodded consent, and then spoke the numbers to the officer.

"Can you tell me what the development is? I'm a relative. And I'm the one who went with him to the station to file the report."

There was a brief consultation at the other end. "Mrs. Bradford, you said?"

"Yes."

"OK, the story is this. We've met with a woman who is a credible witness to the incident. She did not see any assault or contact herself, but she did see a young man with injuries wheeling a broken bike, and also a white truck with a small logo going in the opposite direction. She recognized the logo – a company just over the state line with several employees. We have spoken to the owner, who says he doesn't know anything about the incident. But we are going to search the company trucks for signs of recent damage and repair, and interview the drivers."

"Well," breathed Helene into the phone. "At last, something." Then she thought to ask, "Was it because of the article that she said something?"

He hesitated. "I believe that's what she said."

"But she didn't think to say anything before this? Or maybe even to help an injured person she passed on the road?" Right then she knew she'd pushed it. But maybe things needed to be pressed.

"I'm letting you know the information we received." Helene could hear his radio crackling in the background. "That's all I can tell you."

"Wait," said Helene. "How about the other incidents, the ones in the newspaper, with the swastikas?"

"Still under investigation."

"Do you think it could be connected?"

"I really can't say more."

"Oh, come on."

There was a slight hesitation, but he couldn't seem to refuse her polite and pointed prodding.

"Well, that was probably more of a prank. Some kids, just looking for attention."

Prank? Helene could feel the heat climbing her neck. "Hmm...so what does that say about the climate in the area, that two such things should happen? Will they classify it now as a hate crime, what happened to Izzy?"

"I can't tell you at this point. As I say, we're working on it, and I just wanted to update Mr. Lopes on the situation. I'll call him now."

"OK, thank you," Helene said a bit stiffly, and then put down the phone, breaking into a smile.

"Making progress," she said. Neesa grunted. Helene could see the doubt in her eyes. She knew that Neesa was afraid to believe, but also ready to do anything for the sake of her son. And she had trusted Helene to take the call from the police. That was the main point.

At the next Thursday night potluck at the Intertribal Center, Chief announced that the men's drum group, Red Thunder, and the Gray Dove hand drum singers, had been invited to take part in a powwow at the state university campus about half an hour away. Neesa was going, with Malvina and her family, setting up the booth to sell baskets and jewelry, and Helene said she'd like to sell a few of her shawls. The twins couldn't be more excited, speculating on who they might see, what they would wear, and what they would buy.

"But why won't you dance?" Wishi-ta wanted to know, when they got back to the house. "It's not that hard; I can show you."

"You can wear Izzy's purple shawl," Tana-na put in. He disappeared into the back bedroom, where they could hear him rummaging, and returned with a sacred feather in a leather binding with fringe.

He held it out to Helene. "Hold this when you're dancing. That's what –" and then he stopped, looking at his sister. Wishi-ta was giving him a warning look.

"That's Mommy's," she said.

But Tana-na stood his ground. "No, it's all right," he said. "She wouldn't mind."

Wishi-ta looked doubtful.

"I asked Daddy, when we were there..." He stopped, looking at Helene.

"At the prison?" she finished for him.

"Yeah."

"OK," Helene nodded. "But did you really ask him, actually, about the feather?"

His face began to cloud with uncertainty. "I asked him...I asked him..."

"What?"

"I asked him if you were going to be our mommy."

Two small, pinched faces were focused on her every expression, every word. Helene sighed, reaching across the sofa to take Tana-na's hand, and then Wishi-ta's.

"I'm not your mommy," she said. "You know that."

"He said –" Tana-na got out. "He said you were not Mommy, but you could do things that mommies do."

"Yes, that's right; your father was right about that."

"And you'd like some of the stuff that she liked, Mommy. And she liked this feather. She used it all the time, for smudging. And when she danced."

Wishi-ta nodded gravely. "Yes, she did."

Helene felt she must accept the feather. "Kids, I'm not sure I'm ready for the dancing part, but I will certainly take the feather with me to powwow, and I'll hold it up when you are dancing. OK?"

How hard it was to know the right thing to do. Or what would bring them solace, yet not false hope for a mother who was never coming back. Helene had started on an outfit she could wear at the powwows, if she meant to attend regularly with the family. She had bought the materials and sketched a pattern for a dress from Renee's regalia hanging in the bedroom, only larger. She had no real vision of what she would make; just a general idea, something that would please the twins. Or maybe it wasn't a good idea after all, not appropriate. Meanwhile she was willing to hold a feather.

"OK!" they both shouted, and Tana-na pulled his feet under him and rocketed off the sofa in that way he had, no matter how many times Helene said not to.

Then, late at night, Erik phoned with news about the paternity test – from one of the other men who had taken it. Helene turned over the book in her lap, and finished the last of the wine.

"Nope, not him either," Erik said with a sigh. "So that leaves me and the mystery guy."

"She really has no idea who that man is?"

"Drinking, one-night stand. The same period as me." He sounded abashed. "I know. Pretty embarrassing."

Helene slipped a bookmark into the novel she'd been reading, by Louise Erdrich, about a family with its own host of problems, based in a Native American community in the Dakotas. She'd been trying to learn more about the culture and customs; much of it seemed linked to the legacy of pain and addiction.

"So, that means…"

"If it's not me, it's that guy, and probably no way to track him down. So the little girl grows up without a father."

"Boy," she said, "I don't even know what to wish for."

"Me, either."

The follow-up appointment with the allergy specialist in Boston had been put off until almost Halloween, and Wishi-ta was reluctant to go, especially without Tana-na. Helene broke the news one afternoon before supper. Wishi-ta was painting a picture of pumpkins at the kitchen table.

Tana-na was still at Malvina's, until he got the boot at five o'clock.

"We'll go to Wendy's, if you want." That was Wishi-ta's favorite place to eat out.

Wishi-ta worked carefully on the outline of some leaves. "We-ll…"

"We're staying overnight with Thelma, my friend. You remember that nice lady?"

"Thelma?" she pronounced it slowly, drawing out the syllables as she carefully drew the tendrils of the vine.

"With that turquoise necklace that you liked?"

"Oh, yeah. Her." Wishi-ta's voice was a little livelier. "She is nice, and *she* likes to dance at powwow."

"Yes, she does. And there's a cat, Misty, who used to be mine. You should be fine now that you're on the allergy medicine."

"A cat?" She was interested, an almost dreamy look on her face. That day in the future when she could share her life with a cat and also a horse.

"And Izzy is going to be there too. I think. I hope."

"Izzy!" Now Wishi-ta looked up, touches of green on her hands and her nose, where she had rubbed it.

"I'm not promising. He's working now, and he sometimes stays with his friends in Boston. But I left him a message, and he knows we'll be there."

"He better," Wishi-ta said with a bit of a pout. "Why doesn't he come home?"

"He likes it there," Helene said. "And we should be happy for him. Besides, he does come home once in a while."

"Not very often." Wishi-ta went back to her painting.

They drove to Thelma's after school, stopping as promised at Wendy's for the Junior Bacon Cheeseburger and fries. At Thelma's house there were signs of packing, and a number of boxes already closed and labeled. So, Helene realized, the big move was really happening, and before too long.

Thelma opened up the sofa bed in the living room for the two of them. "I'd say just sleep in Izzy's bed, but he may show up in the middle of the night. Or not."

"Does that drive you crazy?"

Thelma brushed the air. "Not in the least. Not my kid, not my worry. Plus my son pretty much came and went as he pleased. As long as he texted me when he would not be home."

"And you're otherwise doing OK with him being here?"

"Fine. He's such a sweet…ah…soul. Very thoughtful and easygoing."

"Noisy? He can be noisy."

"Not really. I mean, he's taken out the flute a couple times, but not for long. Plus I like that music. He's only had his friends here a few times, usually just stopping in when they drop him off. The only thing…"

"Aha, there is 'a thing.'"

Thelma checked that Wishi-ta was occupied with Misty in the other room. "He's a bit of a klutz, I'm afraid. So far he's managed to break a lamp and a chair – an upholstered chair. And he volunteered to wash up after dinner one night, and broke a glass – no big deal. But he cut himself, so I had to bandage him up, and after that he couldn't finish."

Helene laughed. "A bit accident prone. I've noticed that too. Which is surprising, since he's so graceful when he dances."

"Ah, well." Thelma shrugged. "I did tell him that my move date is February 1."

"What did he say?"

"I guess he's asking around. He's met some people at the restaurant where he's working. I'm pretty sure he'll find something."

Helene smiled, cocking her head. "Or come home."

"I don't think so, at least not for a while. This is where he wants to be."

After ice cream and cookies, Helene told Wishi-ta it was bedtime, since they had to get up early for the appointment.

"But Izzy's not here. I want to wait for him."

"No, it's too late. I'm not sure if he's coming back, or what time. He might be staying with friends. I said I'd call him after the appointment and maybe we can meet him before we go back."

"But I'm not tired. I can stay awake, for just in case."

"No, sweetie. We have a big day tomorrow."

"I'll just lie there with my eyes open."

"You do that. And poke me if he comes in."

Within five minutes Wishi-ta was asleep. Helene stayed up another half hour with Thelma in the den, catching up on school news and all the developments with Erik and Denis. Thelma was embarked on another knitting project, or was it crocheting? Something lacy that looked like it might be a girl's poncho.

"Don't you think it's strange," Helene said, relaxing on the sofa with Misty on her lap, "how six months ago I was like a normal suburban wife and school nurse, quiet as a mouse, and now it's like I'm living in the middle of a soap opera?"

"Strange?" Thelma tilted her head. "Probably more like most people's normal. That squeaky-clean kind of life usually has some cost; it's just not clear on the surface. Most lives are pretty messy, at some point."

"Messy, yes. I had that growing up and dealing with Renee. But I worked so hard to put it behind me. Whatever there was between me and Kenneth, I was comfortable and there were many things I enjoyed – nice food, nice clothes, fun trips, uh, tennis and museums, concerts and shows."

She blinked, a mocking note in her voice. "Big house, expensive jewelry, nice cars. And then, like that" – she snapped her fingers – "it's all gone, and I don't miss it at all. Except being with you, of course."

Thelma shrugged, back at her knitting. "The twins make a difference. Needing someone. And being family. Don't discount that."

"No, I know. It's just such a surprise to me."

"You might say it's a surprise to all of us."

"Oh, are they gossiping about me at school?"

"Eh, maybe a few tongues wagging. That you were always a bit reserved, private, stuck-up, even. And Kenneth was such a good catch; how could you give that up?"

It was all true, those perceptions. Only not true in fact. Helene could mount no defense. "Right. I know. It probably makes no sense."

"So who cares? Does it bother you?"

"Should it?"

Thelma unraveled another length of yarn, not looking up. "Well, would you care that he has a new woman friend?"

"He does!" Helene was shocked. A new woman in only a couple months, since their marriage had really fallen apart? He had found somebody? "Where did that come from?"

"I can't say. But she's a nice gal, pretty, divorced, two kids, and she owns her own business."

"You're kidding me."

"I'm not."

Helene reeled. It was one thing for her to roll along in her new life, on her new path. But Kenneth was meant to stay static, as he was, for just in case…the whole thing turned out to be a dream, and Helene decided to go back. Only now there was no going back.

"How old are the kids?" That was the thing that pricked her most.

"Maybe six to eight or nine? The girl is older. Cute kids; I saw them all at dinner. Then I asked him, when I saw him later. And, no, you don't know them. They go to private school."

That was something to mull over.

"Ah, well," Helene murmured, then added, "Good for him. It might make things easier, I suppose."

Thelma finished her row, and put the knitting needles down to get another skein of yarn, a deep purple-blue.

"What kind of business does she have, this woman?" it finally occurred to Helene to ask. *Fashion? Food? A spa, perhaps. Real estate?*

"She runs a yoga studio."

Helene's eyes opened wider." No way!"

"That's where he met her. It was a trial class, I guess, and he decided to go, you know, for stress, et cetera."

Helene slapped the side of her head." Now I've heard everything."

Thelma's sofa bed was not bad, but it was not good, either, with a support bar in the middle that pushed up the mattress. Helene contemplated taking Izzy's bed, but it would be an awkward moment if he did arrive back at the house. Besides, she was used to Wishi-ta and her occasional elbow pokes in the side, and relished her warm presence. She was tired from the drive, overwhelmed with all the news and developments. She took a pill for a headache, feeling tightness behind her eyes, and fell into a deep sleep until she woke around four, groggy and feeling like she'd had a lot of wine.

As she emerged from the bathroom, she felt a stirring in the air, like a draft from an open window or door. But she didn't hear anything, and she was sure the house was closed up with the colder weather. Returning to the living room, she felt before she saw a kind of apparition, gazing down at Wishi-ta, a disembodied face and shoulders, wreathed in the ambient light of the autumn night. At her entrance, the being turned toward her, eyes and lips, and the small dots of nostrils, outlined against a smooth face. Alien, expressionless, not of this world. Maybe there were spirits. Maybe they did appear to people. Or maybe there was something wrong with her perception.

Her head, the concussion, it must be. She blinked, trying to clear the vision. A hand rose and beckoned, and she wondered where she was being summoned to, and if she would ever return. And then the apparition moved again, the lips parted, and a voice reached her: Izzy's.

"Helene," he whispered.

Of course, Izzy. Not a phantom and not a cat burglar. At four in the morning, coming in from work, or partying, or some other part of his new, unknown life.

"This way." She motioned toward the den, where she closed the door and put on a dim table light.

Izzy, but not as she had known him. His hair was cut short, all the way, almost a buzz cut, except a bit longer on top. He was wearing a black T-shirt with some design, more Asian than Native American. And black pants, which was why he appeared to have no body out in the living room, out of the light. But the eyes, the lips – the unnatural intensity – he was wearing makeup. Not quite "Goth" or "Gothic," but starkly highlighting his narrow eyes, his angular cheeks, and beautiful lips.

They stood looking at each other, both familiar and strangers.

"I'm sorry if I woke you," he said, keeping his voice low.

"I went to the bathroom. But you did startle me."

Then he smiled, the old, sweet Izzy smile. "I know. The hair, the face. Right? I guess it's pretty weird. My mother hasn't seen me yet. She's going to freak."

Helene hunched her shoulders, but she was smiling. It was good to see him. She wanted to hug him, but was reluctant, cautious. They both had broken parts. They weren't there yet. "Hmm…well. Quite stylish, in its way. But certainly different from the old you."

"It's the new me. But the old me is still here too, somewhere."

"Glad to hear it." A pause. "And you're OK? And the city is what you hoped it would be?"

His whole face smiled. "The city is amazing. A lot of crap to deal with, of course, but so much going on. Besides, it's not the city I was coming to find out about, you know, all its pleasures and pains." He laughed softly. "It was me – you know, who I was when I wasn't" – he paused, frowning slightly – "twenty feet from my mother's side, if you know what I mean."

"I think I do."

He regarded her a moment, serious, no hurry. "I don't know how it would have happened, if not for you, Helene. And Thelma."

"Yikes, that puts a lot on us."

"No," he corrected himself. "It would have happened, I just don't know when. Or how it would have turned out."

Helene blinked a few times, not quite awake, dazed by the image before her.

"OK, let's leave it at that," she said with a yawn. "I'm glad to see you, but I've got to get some sleep. Can we see you in the morning?" She thought quickly. "Early, though. We have to leave for the doctor's office by nine."

"I'll be up. Promise. I'll set the alarm on my phone. Or just send Wishi-ta in – she knows what to do." He tilted his head toward the bathroom. "I'll wash up now. So she doesn't freak." He rubbed his face, smearing the eyeliner. "Good night."

"Sure." Helene started toward the door, and then turned back. "Oh, but also, I have some mail for you. Don't let me forget."

The lips parted into a wide circle. "Mail? Nobody ever writes to me."

"It's a bunch of stuff: notes and letters from the newspaper article, I think."

"Really?"

She let her eyes rest on him another minute. "Letters of support maybe, hopefully."

"That would be something."

"Yes, it would. We can talk, in the morning."

They said good night, and Helene crawled back under the comforter with Wishi-ta, but sleep eluded her. Izzy had spooked her, she couldn't deny it. He had a certain power, without even seeming to know it; she could see that now. Not so much for what he set out to do, but in the effect he had on people, including her. A lot was roiling under the surface, uncertainty in this changed life for both of them.

Wishi-ta squealed when she saw Izzy, now clean faced, and wearing his usual shapeless jeans and a sweatshirt.

He had taken a seat next to her on the sofa bed, where she remained asleep after Helene and Thelma had gotten up to get coffee and breakfast in the kitchen. From the doorway, Helene watched the reunion, holding her coffee cup close to her chest.

"Your hair!" Wishi-ta cried, pulling herself up next to him. She crawled onto his lap, placing her hands on his face, squeezing his cheeks. "Why did you do it?"

"I just wanted to see what it would look like."

"It doesn't look good," she told him. "Neesa won't like it."

"I know. But I have to make my own decisions now, and I wanted to do it. Besides, maybe it will be a little longer when she sees it."

But Wishi-ta was not placated. "Will you grow it back? Please."

"Why should I?"

"Because you have to. Because you're Indian, like us."

"I'm still Indian."

"So people will know," she insisted, "what kind of Indian you are."

Helene found herself holding her breath; the connection between the two was palpable. The seriousness of their talk and the warmth of their touch.

"What kind of Indian am I?" he asked mildly.

She looked at him like he was out of his mind. "You know. Our kind. Pemaquot, Wampanoag. Wolf Clan."

"So people will know I'm Indian by how I look. Is that what you mean?"

She shook her head, blond hairs sticking straight up with static. "By what you do. By braiding your hair and putting on regalia."

"Ah, that's what you're getting at."

Her face fell, closing with disappointment. "Don't tease."

"No, Wishi-ta, I'm not teasing. I would never be mean to you." His hand was smoothing her staticky halo. "I just wanted to know what you think."

"So you will grow your hair. Promise?"

"I will grow my hair. Promise. But" – he held her attention – "don't you want to see what it feels like?"

She let Izzy guide her hand across his head, until she squealed again, making such a funny face, Helene almost spilled her coffee.

"It's soft," Wishi-ta said. "Like a baby chick." She rubbed it a few more times, and then swung her feet over the side of the sofa bed. "But it's not very Indian," were her last words on the subject.

Helene gave Izzy the bag of mail, which he took to the kitchen table as she showered and dressed, leaving Wishi-ta to finish her breakfast. From the bathroom she heard a few exclamations and some laughter, prompted by the mail. By the time she had finished getting ready, Izzy had opened and sorted it. Along with the notes, he had received a few hand-drawn pictures: two with hearts and declarations of love. No surprise.

Thelma had already left for school, promising to visit the base soon, and telling Wishi-ta that of course she would dance with her at the powwow and wear her turquoise necklace. In the few minutes before they had to leave for the appointment, Helene went back into the kitchen where Izzy was sitting with his hands folded on the table.

"Anything good?" she asked.

"Oh, yeah, lots." But when he looked up, his expression was guarded.

"What?" she said.

"Take a look," he said, pushing over a paper. "Not a fan."

It was a handwritten letter, not very long:

You deserve no sympathy at all, you red asshole. You're the one that caused the accident and a thousand dollar damage to the truck. Now they're all over our place of business, and bothering people they shouldn't be. We have to see your face in the newspaper, complaining like a fucking baby. Someone needed to cut that hair of yours, so you don't look like such a pussy.

It took Helene a moment to catch her breath. "Wow," she said. "Wow." And then, almost to herself, "How awful...to think like that, to write those words."

After a shaking her head, she turned to Izzy and said, "I'm so sorry. It's so...wrong, and, and...ugly." She exhaled. "Izzy," she started again, and then stopped. She really didn't know what to else say, and she didn't have time to think it through before they left for the doctor. Yet how could she leave him here like this, comfortless?

"We'll talk again later. Maybe after the appointment?"

"Can't. I start my shift at eleven."

She thought fast, but what was there to offer? And then an image came to her, and some words.

"Wait. Listen, you know what Chief said? *Flushing the fox out of its den?* I think this is what he means. This gives the police something concrete to go on. Maybe even fingerprints." Her eyes traveled to the note, and then to the pile of envelopes. "There's all kinds of information in the letter – they'll be able to narrow it down."

She stopped to see if he was following, but his face was a blank.

"It's a good thing, really," she said. "You see that, right?"

Izzy's head tilted sideways. "They really hate me."

Helene tried to brush it away. "How can they hate you? They don't even know you. What happened was an accident, their fault as much as yours."

He was not consoled. "They hate something about me."

She couldn't argue against that.

"Let me have it, and the envelope it came in," she said, reaching out. "I know what to do. Do you trust me?"

After a moment, he nodded.

From Thelma's, Helene called the police station near the base to say she was coming in later in the day with a letter and envelope that might be evidence, along with other, separate letters. One of the others she had selected said, "Indians give nothing to this community except problems and handouts" – which didn't make sense. Another letter said, "Whites are having there (sic) rights trampled on, and losing there freedoms because of others coming in and taking over." That was ironic. And lastly, "Cowboys always win, you dumb Indian."

After dropping Wishi-ta off with Neesa, she waited at the police station, impatient – the matter seemed so insignificant to them, almost a bother, compared to other, more important problems. *Like what?* Then she reminded herself that things were progressing; the threats and actions couldn't be swept under the rug at this point. As she leafed through a magazine, she told herself there was much to be thankful for. Izzy was doing well, all things considered. Wishi-ta had a very good health report, and there was reason to hope she would outgrow many of her allergies. Tana-na had made a good start at school. Her own injury was healing, both inside and out. And Erik would be back the next day.

"You can do something with this," she said to Chief McMurray, who waved her into his office after a half-hour wait. This space was more personal: pictures on the bookshelf, young, gap-toothed white children who looked a lot like him. And a certificate of merit on the wall.

"Look." She pointed at the accusatory letter: "Thousand dollars of damage, bothering people at our place of business, see your face in the newspaper."

The police chief nodded. "Yes, that should help track them down."

"And you will call it a hate crime; the wording, the intention."

Chief McMurray looked disappointed. This was not what he wanted in his small town. Having to acknowledge that dirty, stupid stuff was always there in the background, animosity against others, especially newcomers. Not that Indians were new, technically.

"Yes, it's a hate crime."

"And you have some possible suspects."

He looked like he didn't want to tell her, but he did. "Yes, we do."

She handed him a plastic bag with the notes and envelopes she and Izzy had selected. Wearing hospital gloves, she had made copies to keep at home. But it was beyond her to test for fingerprints or check saliva for DNA; that they must trust to the experts. She included a summary that she had written up about how and when the letters were received, and her trip to the Boston area to share them with Izzy.

Helene was gathering her papers, ready to go; she'd gotten what she came for. Chief McMurray stopped her with a question.

"So you're the sister-in-law, you said, to Mr. Lopes?"

She nodded, holding the papers to her chest. "My sister married his brother. That makes us in-laws."

"So you're the family representative, then?" He looked interested. "Do you have some legal training?"

She held back a wry smile. Only on matters of adoption, divorce, and hate crimes. "No, nothing beyond some research online or at the library that anybody could do."

His fingers drummed on the desk. "So why, then..."

"Why am I helping?" she prompted.

"Well, yes, I suppose," he said, his face a little pink. "Or, rather, why isn't Mr. Lopes here himself on his own behalf, or his own immediate family?"

"Ah..." That's what he wanted to know. Big question. Maybe bigger than Helene could answer. But she'd try, at least, to be clear. "So you know that he, Izzy, Mr. Lopes, has given permission to share information with me, right? We addressed that the first time around."

He nodded. "Yes. But..."

Helene decided she might as well just say it: "He's not comfortable with the police. That is, he's doubtful he will get justice under the system as it is."

Chief McMurray seemed genuinely surprised, and affronted. "I don't know why he would think that."

Helene shrugged, silent.

"There haven't been any real issues or problems with those folks out at the base or at the Intertribal Center that I'm aware of."

"Ah," Helene said again. "Maybe that's it. You're not aware of them."

He scoffed. "Excuse me, Ms. Bradford. I can't agree there. I know most things going on in this town. I make it my business. But if they choose not to bring things to my attention..."

But Helene was done, no longer willing to stay in the discussion, so much bigger, wider and older than she had time for. She had things to get back home for: children, supper.

"Yes," she said, agreeable. "Do you ever wonder why that is?"

At that, she had her keys in her hand, files tucked under her arm, ready to be on her way.

Erik was back, catching up on sleep at Elsa's after an all-night drive from western Pennsylvania. He had called Helene to say that he would come by before the twins got home – there was "a lot to talk about."

Helene guessed that meant he knew the results of the paternity test; and that most likely it was positive the little girl was his. That would be a lot to talk about. On top of everything else: Denis and Kiko, Izzy and the letter, even Wishi-ta's good health report. Kenneth's agreement to the divorce. A lot. No question. She made herself breathe deeply, chanting, *one day at a time, one day at a time* in her head. Yet she couldn't help feeling that her life had never been so full and exciting, even with a certain amount of turmoil and uncertainty.

Erik let himself in the front door, still damp from a shower. The look on his face said everything. Even before he could open his mouth, Helene held up a finger, saying, "You got the news, and you have a daughter."

In spite of herself, a grin spread across her face – gladness to see him, and a certain thrill about the news, whatever it meant for him, or for him and her.

He looked a bit shell-shocked, from everything – including Helene herself, she suspected.

"Well, come on in," she said. She felt bad for him, facing how to deliver this kind of news to a new lover.

"Yes," he said, stepping in to the living room. "I guess so. She says so, and I don't think she's lying. She's sending me a copy of the results. But it seems to be true."

He sighed. "I know. Wow." He shook his head. "It's still hard to believe…all that time ago. Just the one time. Well, maybe twice. I knew right away that things were not going to work out between us, but it happened. I'm sorry…"

She waited to hear what he was sorry about.

"Well, sorry that it makes things more complicated between us. I have to deal with this, I have to. And I do want to be there for this child, more than I was for my son."

She watched him until she could see, too, his resolve. That's what mattered.

"Are you mad now?" he said, looking into her face. "Or upset?"

"Nope." Her hands went up. "Neither of those. Sort of amused, in a weird way."

"Amused?" He didn't seem to appreciate that.

"I don't mean funny, like a joke. I mean, kind of ironic, from my point of view. I wanted to have children in my life, longed for it, even though I was afraid. And now there are children all around me."

He frowned, trying to interpret. "And that's a good thing?"

"Why not?"

He closed his eyes, shaking his whole body like a bear. "Can you really mean that?" His eyes opened again. "You know I love you, Helene. I didn't really know what love meant until I met you. But now I'm sure. I want to be with you, and I hope to God you want to be with me. I know you aren't ready to talk about marriage. But I am; I'd marry you in a heartbeat. And we can still have children, you and me; it's not too late, I don't think. And I seem to be given many opportunities to learn how to be a father."

Helene laughed, a bit giddy. "That's four children between us. Don't you think that's plenty?"

"Four? Five? Does it make that much difference? And, not to mention, we're not the only ones in charge – for better or worse."

Helene smiled, and a strange, certain knowledge came to her. "Maybe. If it happens. But it doesn't seem to matter so much, anymore." She made a face. "And, since we're facing hard truths, there's another reality...."

Erik cocked his head. "Another secret from your dark, misspent youth?"

"The reality of the breast cancer that killed my mother and Renee, with some genetic link. One that I may share. And Wishi-ta. It's not impossible, and it could be....." She stopped.

"It could be something that we deal with if and when it happens. Right?"

She sighed. "I guess so. There are tests."

"Helene," He took her hand and kissed it. "It only makes you – and time – more precious. To live now, not in the future."

She didn't answer.

"Right now," he said. "In this moment. With you, me and all these...kids." He released her hand and his face crinkled in a smile. "So you want to meet her, my newest offspring? Her name is Aurora." And then he gestured toward the window and the night sky. "Like the northern lights."

"That's beautiful," she said, allowing herself to be taken back to the time she had seen the northern lights as a girl at the cabin in Vermont, shimmering ribbons of light. She had seen the little girl before, with Josie, but now it was all different. "Beautiful."

9. The Great American Indian Taco – by One Little Indian

Here's another one for you – Indians, like many other Americans, have some mixed-up gene pools. Go to a powwow; you'll see what I mean. There's the classic "Indian head nickel" look. Others look white, some black, some Asian, some Hispanic; some look Indian with a twist – blue eyes, freckles, red hair, curly hair; you'll see it. The DNA may say one thing; but Indians can look any which way. Mostly, Native nations have not yearned to assimilate into the good old American "melting pot", some new blend, or puree, if you will. Mixing is not so much a goal as history, welcome or not. That's why I prefer the "Indian Taco" – the base is fry bread, our traditions, basic, enduring, great just as it is. Yes, the meat can be varied and seasoned different ways. Tomato, lettuce, onions and cheese are nice additions. But please, some respect for the Taco.

Since first contact, there has been intermingling with all the major European groups – the Spanish and Portuguese mestizos all through Latin America and the Caribbean; the French and Scottish métis in Canada and the northern states; English and Indian unions on the frontier. And let's not forget the red and black combinations in Florida, Louisiana, the Carolinas, Virginia, and even up in New England, where black sailors intermarried with Natives along the coast. We're not talking just about individual families here, either, but often a whole community of mixed folks that developed for all sorts of reasons. In Canada the fur traders liked to have Native wives to help them conduct business; in many parts of the South, Indians married escaped slaves, sometimes living in secret communities. The frontier was short of white women in the early years; white men married, or at least had children with, Native women. It happened.

But I'm talking bigger than this when I talk mixed. First off, many tribes had a history of adopting captives, other Natives or Europeans, as replacements for lost family members. In the early days of New France, if the white settlers were not able to raise all their many children, some were adopted into Indian families. Likewise, European children and young adults who were kidnapped sometimes decided to "go Native" finding it a freer life. Even before contact, tribes moved about and intermarried. Disease, early battles, and the removal of Natives from their homelands – places where they knew the seasons, climate, plants and animals, even the bodies of water – the food and the medicine. All of these things displaced people and merged them into new groups, alliances of survival. Mixing – of cultures, traditions, and languages – and of genes.

That's part of why many Indians are skeptical of all these DNA tests. Only horses, dogs, and Indians are measured for "blood quantum" to prove identity or purity. For most tribes it's based on records of some kind – birth and census, or tribal rolls – to be considered a member. Not blood, per se. It's really up to each tribe to decide how to call it. Because these things matter, for statistical purposes, for getting federal recognition as a tribe, and for access to federal support that comes with it: money, power, survival. So what, really, do these genes tell us? Mainly that we're so much more alike, and mixed, than we are pure or different. You and me, we may be related – not so much on the Indian side, but the African or French or Portuguese sides. DNA and family trees could surprise you.

My brother, Louis, told me something after a trip to the Southwest with some of the Pueblo peoples, one of his favorite places to go. Every place he went he brought home stories and crafts, and there were none more interesting to him – and us – than those who had survived in the same dwelling places for centuries on end – in desert lands. Their kivas and kachinas – so different from anything we knew. He says that some Natives there don't want DNA testing, because they don't believe in what it shows. Not that science isn't true, but they question what the facts mean. They doubt that the theory of migration over the "land bridge" of Alaska is really the way, or the only way, that indigenous people came to this hemisphere. That's not what their creation story tells. It tells of emerging in this place through a hole in the ground where they became the people they are – that is why they are here.

Isn't that like the Bible story of Creation – seven days and seven nights? Science does not agree. And yet who's to say it's wrong – or what it really means? It's having a say in what things mean that matters, not the many contradictory possibilities of DNA. So say we. A-ho.

Chapter 32

And then all was strangely quiet for a couple of weeks. By November the birthday celebrations had come and gone. Helene's job had begun, and she found that she enjoyed being back in the health-care setting, using her knowledge and serving a population that was mostly in need and mostly appreciative. The twins were fine, better than fine; happy and doing what children everywhere did: growing and making mistakes and suddenly surprising you with their sweetness and wisdom.

Erik came when he could, on his irregular schedule that sent him throughout the Northeast for an overnight, or occasionally father south or west, which might take him away a few days. They agreed the only things he would leave at Renee's house were a toothbrush, an electric shaver, and some of his cholesterol pills. It still struck Helene as comical that he lived essentially across the street with his sister and her husband, coming and going to Renee's house in full public view. By then everyone knew about the paternity test, and that Erik was planning to help raise and support Aurora, Bernice's granddaughter. Helene had promised to go with Erik for a long weekend to Pennsylvania to see the house that he had decided to sell, to purchase something closer to the base.

They made plans for Thanksgiving, when he would bring his son in New York state back to meet her and the rest of the family. Thanksgiving was not celebrated in the conventional way at the Intertribal Center; instead, there was a "Day of Mourning" for all that had been lost and broken after the arrival of Western Europeans. However, the children had time off from school and there was a special dinner and potluck that featured "harvest foods," including cranberries, turkey, and pumpkin pie – not so different from the meal at Helene's childhood home.

During this period Helene enjoyed seeing Denis and Kiko, who had made progress on renovating the new house, and were set to move in before Christmas.

Izzy was also back and forth from his city life, now in an apartment share with three others, while he worked at a health food restaurant, returning to the base when he had a few days off, usually catching rides or taking the slowpoke bus. Exploring the city and the night life had given him a charge of energy that Helene had not seen before. His pal from home, Raj, was his partner in adventure, if not in more intimate matters. Who could say?

A date was set for Louis's reassignment to a federal prison closer to the base, less than an hour and a half away. Helene had told the twins, who were suddenly so much more serious and grown-up at five years old, that now they would be able to see him more often. She told them, too, that not everyone, including some of the students and teachers, would understand about their father being in prison, but many other people thought he was a hero and fighter for important things. In the meanwhile, Helene made a final trip to the prison in New Hampshire to talk with Louis about financial arrangements regarding the children and the house, those things she could manage in his absence.

After Helene's letter to Kenneth, and his decision to accept no-fault divorce proceedings, things had changed between them too. They were more distant, of course, but not combative or acrimonious. Neither of them mentioned his new lady friend or yoga. Even when Helene insisted that she didn't want more than her share of the proceeds from the sale of the Roy house, he said that he wouldn't feel right not to split assets from their life together – that some of his success had to do with her. The value of the property had increased, and even after taxes, there would be a tidy little sum. She should think of the future and the children, and what would happen to them if something should happen to her. She couldn't persuade him otherwise; and the truth was, he was probably right.

It was hard. She was grateful to Kenneth for his generosity and for not being vindictive. He was a good man, according to his own lights and the world's, and she wished him well, maybe to appease her own guilt. But it was like they now existed in different worlds, and it wasn't until she'd left the shelter of their home that she felt the weight lift from her chest. His protective instincts, with her complicity, had stunted her. He might never know how oppressive that had become.

On her return to the base from work, Helene had a few quiet moments before going to pick up the children from the Intertribal Center, and sat in the living room with a cup of tea. Something was still not right, not settled, holding her back from seeing what was to be done. She'd had a few dreams the last weeks, not nightmares, but situations where she had shown up late or was ill prepared for some activity, something to do with powwow or other ceremonies. Disappointing others; not doing things right; caught between.

Louis was right: there was still something going on with her, not the children or family. They were content where they were, except maybe Izzy, who was searching – not unusual for a young adult. But she was unsure of herself, her own path, wondering if it really was here with these people or somewhere else she hadn't even considered. Right now this was what she wanted, to be in this place. That she did not want to lose, or give up. But for the future, would it really work?

After her last visit with Louis, she still couldn't give him her final decision about becoming legal guardian. She could assist, and take responsibility for health and education. But the Native way of life? That she wasn't sure of. Could she truly act that way and be that way, knowing so little of the culture and values? For sure, she hadn't been a practicing Catholic for many years. Kenneth's family was Protestant, Congregational. But what about Jesus? She didn't think she could not believe in Jesus anymore. How did that go along with honoring nature and the Great Spirit?

She pictured Neesa with the ever-present cross at her neck, and the pictures of Mother Mary on her walls, like one of Izzy's aunties. Neesa straddled both worlds, picking and choosing the parts she liked – Native to her core, but a devotee of Mary and an admirer of Jesus, perhaps some invisible God, the Father. So did many others at the base. But Helene kept thinking about "Cafeteria Catholics," who picked and chose what they liked, not what faith required. After struggling so long to accept her own truth, who she was, what she had done, good and bad, and what she valued, she didn't think she could pretend anything anymore, or be a hypocrite in front of the children.

She got up from the sofa to bring her cup to the sink, and then to head out to collect the twins and their cousins. There was time, but she was restless and didn't want to sit brooding with thoughts circling and circling and going nowhere. She grabbed her jacket, ready to go.

At the door she met Chief, standing on her front steps with a bolt of material, a brown cotton with a white-and-gold feather pattern.

"Hello," he said. "This is for you. From Elsa. I don't know where she got it; I'm just the errand boy."

He had such a spark in his eyes, Helene had to smile. "Then should I tip you?"

"Sure. Who's going to win the next horse race?"

She laughed and reached out for the material. "It's lovely. Perfect for what I'm working on. I don't know how, but my projects seem to multiply like rabbits." She reflected that Chief always turned her into a chattering teenager. Was he a father figure, maybe? One who listened, and saw things.

"So," Chief said, planted on the steps. "Any more dreams, there, Helene? I see little clouds passing your brow now and then."

Helene sighed, clasping the bolt of material. "No nightmares or anything so vivid like I told you about before. It's more like worry dreams, anxiety, about doing the right thing."

"You're lucky, then," Chief said, nodding. "It's trying to work itself out."

Helene glanced at the clock. "Do you want to come in for a few minutes? I have to leave in a bit to get the kids."

"No need. We'll walk together, just go slow. That way I get my exercise too." He pulled at his waistband. "I'm working on it."

"OK, let me just put this away." Helene took the material to her sewing table, and returned to the front hall, stepping outside and closing the door.

"So check this out," Chief said, as they headed down the sidewalk. "See how good I can walk with my new hip." He dipped and swayed a few times to show his mobility.

"Very smooth," Helene said.

"You should see me on the dance floor," he quipped. And then, more seriously, "So tell me the dreams, and we'll see what comes to light."

Helene told him what she could remember, pretty lame, boring stuff for the most part, nothing ominous. Just annoying, more than anything. Except for the part when she mentioned that her mother had appeared and scolded Helene, lifting the small gold crucifix at her neck, the one she'd gotten at her first Holy Communion.

Helene looked at Chief to see if he knew what she meant. "Kind of like the one Neesa wears."

He held up a hand. "Stop there a moment. I think we're onto something."

"What?"

"You don't think you can wear the cross and the medicine bag at the same time?"

"Medicine bag?"

"I'm just giving you an example – symbols, say, of both faiths."

Helene nodded. "Something like that. The Catholics say, 'have no other gods before Me.'"

Chief nodded. "So, Catholic, then?"

"Not really, not anymore. But I was raised that way, and I know that's part of the deal."

"Well, good news for you, then. It doesn't say anywhere that you can't believe in other kinds of spirits, does it? I mean, the people who tell you what the Bible says? What about ghosts, souls, angels, and demons? Beliefs can exist side by side; in fact, they do whether we want them to or not. Our way is seeing spirit in all the different beings around us, including the Great Spirit of creation. You can call it Creator, Yahweh, God, whatever you like. That sounds OK, doesn't it?"

"I guess. Yes, I think so. But to be the children's guardian, to teach them Native ways, how can I do that? There's so much I don't know. And some of it I might not even believe myself."

"None of us know it all, or believe it all. So much is different from nation to nation. Native American spirituality is open to honoring all kinds of spirits in all kinds of ways, so you're in no trouble there. There's no real measuring stick of what a spiritual person needs to do. Whatever works, any combination, as long as it is honest and meaningful to the person."

"Oh, Chief," Helene said with a sigh. "Can that be so?"

He shrugged. "Why not?"

They trudged along further in silence, Helene seeing nothing in front of her. Could it be like that? Could there be a spiritual way not bound by exacting rules and an abiding sense of guilt? Could it be chosen, rather than imposed, and could that ever really hold together a community in a supportive, positive, even joyous way? She felt a kind of bubbling sensation, a buoyancy, giddiness almost. Such freedom: was it possible? Why not? In the next breath came new doubts: what did that mean for her and how she fit into this world? Unmoored from her old life, unable to picture the future, she was wondering blindly, lost. Her face clouded.

They had arrived at the Intertribal Center, a few minutes early. The Chief pointed at a bench that got some of the late-afternoon sun, starting to wane with the change of season.

"Sit with me. Maybe I can tell you something. Mind you, this is just the view of one old Indian, how I see things."

Helene sat, braced against what he might say.

"Maybe you belong here," Chief said. "Maybe your destiny has led you here for a reason. There is something here for you, more than taking care of your sister's children, maybe to do with your own healing. I understand from Renee that your own family had great troubles, from illness, death, money problems, drink, and drugs. All those things. But you were an ordinary family, no better or worse than others, and through no fault of your own pretty much lost your way, unable to help each other in difficult times.

"Well, that's pretty much what happened to us Indians. From the time of contact with the Europeans – the diseases, the land disputes, the violence – all of it leading to disaster, our own kind of apocalypse, the end of almost everything that came before. You know that character, Squanto, from the Pilgrim story?"

Helene nodded.

"He was a character, all right. But a real person too. And you don't always hear the part where he was kidnapped onto a ship and taken abroad for years. When he returned, his previous life had disappeared: his family was dead from disease, and his village deserted. No home to come home to. Likewise, all up and down the coastline, the survivors were left without resources or community. No one left even to bury the dead. It could not have been much worse, really, if a bomb had gone off. All the death, and the destruction of the land as our ancestors had known it – given over to livestock – not the hunting and gathering and gardens they were used to. The Christians tried to civilize us, believing our souls were in danger. And we began to think that we had offended the Great Spirit in some way not clear to us, and to doubt that our powwows, medicine men, had the power to help us.

"As you know, the story across the country was no better, and many of us were left isolated, hiding out from white settlement, and just finding our way blindly, as if in the dark, back toward each other and what we knew of our previous lives. Some resisted, and some remembered, and so some of the customs and culture survived, in bits and pieces. That's why, I think, the drum is so important to us, so necessary. It's like our voices calling out to each other, and the Great Spirit as we believed it was.

"So when we come together now, we use what we know and remember, and we make up whatever is needed to make sense of this new kind of life. It's a collaboration between people who share what they have, searching for meaning and beauty. So you can see there is no one right way, or really any wrong way, except what is done in harm to ourselves or others."

A figure appeared on a bike, and for a moment they looked up, thinking it might be Izzy, knowing it was not. He tipped his head in greeting, and sped on – a middle-aged man in spandex, on some kind of bike tour, perhaps. From inside they heard children's voices, excited, coming to the end of their game.

"But," Helene started, wondering if she had time before the children appeared.

The door started to swing open, a small face appearing first, and then a voice behind. "Wait for me!" The children were ready to come out, and the adults who had been there to supervise them. As soon as the little boy spotted them on the bench, he ducked back inside, yelling, "Chief!"

Chief smiled and said to Helene, "My mother would be proud. Chief of a very small nation of mixed-up tribes – that's me."

As the children and adults began to push out, Chief held up a hand, and they halted. "You can wait one more minute. Inside."

They retreated and the door closed again, muffling the high-pitched voices.

"But...what?"

"There was a time," Helene said, quickly, remembering how embarrassed she had been, "I was at a powwow, and a feather fell off a man's headdress, who was walking in front of me. I picked up it up and said, 'Excuse me, you dropped this.' He turned around and saw me, and his expression was angry. He said, 'You're not supposed to touch that. Now it's unclean. I'll have to smudge it again to cleanse it.' Something like that."

The Chief smiled briefly, and nodded. "Young guy?"

Helene shrugged. "Maybe twenty or so."

"Yes, well, it is a serious matter, Helene. For many of us, an eagle feather that falls to the ground represents a warrior going home – that is, dying. Some even think it means someone will die if the feather is not retrieved in the right way. There is a special ceremony that requires four veterans to be present, and that could stop the powwow right then and there."

"But I had no idea. How could I?"

The Chief was rubbing a hand over his midsection. "You might have learned ahead of time about what is most sacred, like an eagle feather," he said finally. Then he shifted his weight. "But it wasn't an eagle feather. And the young man, on that day, he might have done better to say, 'Thank you for your help or I might have lost the feather.'" He pitched his voice to a slightly lecturing tone. "'In the future, you might just call attention to it and not pick up the feather yourself. It was smudged earlier, which is our way of cleansing and purifying.'" The Chief's voice dropped to normal. "He could have said that."

"I need to be cleansed and purified," Helene said solemnly. "Do you think I could go in the women's sweat lodge when it's finished?"

The Chief's eyebrows lifted. "It's healing you need, Helene," he said gently. "A sweat is medicine, but it's not a cure. It takes time for healing, you must know that, especially when the suffering is old and deep." He hesitated. "Sure, you can do a sweat, but you don't have to wait for the lodge to be done. Say a prayer to the Creator, if you like. Or smudge when you're feeling bad. Just put a foot forward and keep on the path."

"The Red Path? I mean, the Red Road?" She knew of it from Renee's journal, that elusive place that seemed always far away.

"Whatever path is right for you."

There was more rumbling on the other side of the wall, like waves crashing, ready to splinter the door.

The Chief got up stiffly to rap on the door, pulling open one side to release a flood of youngsters. He spoke over the din. "I hope that was of some help. If you like, we can speak further. There is no deadline; only when you are ready."

The nights had turned colder, Denis's house was finally habitable, Erik was back for a long spell, and Christmas was looming. No one at the Intertribal Center had a problem with putting up a Christmas tree and stringing lots of lights. Even though it had become a commercial, secular celebration in many ways, that did not dim the excitement. Neesa put out a Nativity scene, carved in wood, with all the figures dressed as Native Americans, including the three magi and Joseph without a beard. Only later did she find out that a Winter Solstice celebration had also been scheduled, for right before Christmas on the longest night of the year. That was the community's occasion of feasting, drumming, and gift giving, while on Christmas day everyone was at home.

Helene had finished the shawl for Neesa, traditional with long, knotted fringe, awaiting the right occasion. When she heard that Neesa's sixtieth birthday was in March, she wrapped it in tissue and put it away. On a cool night in early December, Erik awakened her to come outside and see a fleeting show of the northern lights, so rare in Massachusetts. Inspired, she started on a child's shawl for Aurora, one of her most ambitious projects so far, laying ribbons of green and white in various shades and lengths, trying to re-create that play of light and color.

Still she had not given an answer to Louis; the urgency had evaporated as she settled into a new, busy routine. When he actually made the transfer to the closer prison, sometime in the spring, it would be a different matter. Logically, it all worked out so well for everyone, it seemed. And what Chief had said that day on the bench made sense, and his was an opinion she valued. But Alberta's words from early on still resonated: "She knows nothing of any of us, or our histories." There was also the matter of her own past, and her actions: having attempted to kill her sister; or, more properly, assisted her in suicide; having left her husband and taken up with another man; having kidnapped Wishi-ta and taken her from the only home she had known. Not to mention the risks she had taken with Wishi-ta and her own health and welfare – and a serious injury to the head. From the other side, she would have a hard time accepting someone like that to care for young children.

Sadly for the children, the early winter stayed snowless, the trees bare and the ground covered with brown grass. Even more disappointing, Izzy would not come back until after the solstice and Christmas, as it was such a busy time at work, and it was hard for him to get rides. Thelma assured Helene that they had enjoyed good food and festive gatherings with Izzy, his friends, and Thelma's son, who was home from college. They'd had an ecumenical-style get-together, borrowing from Hanukkah, Christmas, the solstice, and general merrymaking. That same crew showed up the following weekend to haul boxes from Thelma's house to the rented PODS container, going in to storage until she moved into her new condo.

"I know it's a busy time," Helene said to Thelma on the phone, Christmas Eve. "But would you have a chance to come up during the holiday break? The twins would love to see you, and so would I." She swallowed a small burp, tasting of eggnog and rum. "Plus Aurora's here, Erik's little girl. She and her mother are staying with Bernice a few days. You could see them. Aurora is awfully cute."

"There's nothing I'd like better," Thelma said. "Not that I don't enjoy my time with all these young...people." She laughed. "Men, women, I'm never totally sure. Anyway, they stay up too late for me. But I can't. There's so much to get done here. I'm being punished for hoarding all that yarn and material for so many years."

"Oh?" Helene's ears perked up.

"I've already put some aside for you," Thelma said. "Merry Christmas. Well, not really. You know I'm not a good Jew. Well, not a bad one, either. I'm OK with Jesus, for the most part, that is, his ideas, or ideas ascribed to him. And, of course, he was a Jew." It dawned on Helene that Thelma may have had a glass of wine or two. "But I can't buy into that fat guy with a beard coming down chimneys into people's homes."

"Oh. Yes, well. That."

"Anyway, I have a couple bags put aside with your name on them. And I'll bring them next time I'm up."

Helene had a thought. "Come in March," she said. "For the equinox celebration. They're planning a big to-do here, besides the usual – dedicating the women's sweat lodge. It's the twenty-first or twenty-second, on the weekend."

"I'll plan on it, if I don't get there earlier."

There was a rustling from the twins' room, even though it was after midnight. Helene thought it could be Tana-na, who was an active sleeper, or maybe Wishi-ta was still awake with excitement for the next morning.

"Someone's stirring," Helene said to Thelma. "I'd better go."

"Go, go."

"My best to your son, and to Izzy, if you see him."

"Certainly."

"I miss you."

"I miss you too."

Helene cocked her ear; there was muttering but no crying from the other room.

"You're the only one, Thelma," Helene said into the phone. "Well, besides Denis, who knows me from that other life and how I am now. It's been such a strange experience, I don't always know who I am myself. Thank you for...well, just thank you."

"You're welcome."

The winter school vacation week was fairly low key, with Tana-na down with a cold and the weather strangely mild and still unsnowy. Helene had taken three days off from work, with the idea of sledding or skating or other kinds of winter fun, but it wasn't meant to be. Fortunately Wishi-ta was happy to cook and bake with Helene, and spend time with Neesa and Malvina working on baskets and jewelry.

They were at Malvina's, in the kitchen with materials spread around the table, Tana-na in the boys' room watching a video, when they heard a rapid knock on the door. All three women stopped and looked at one another; most folks knocked and then opened the door, calling inside. The knocking came again, urgent and dramatic. All three got up to go the front door, Wishi-ta scurrying behind.

Malvina opened the door to a vision in head-to-foot black spandex, standing in front of an electric-bright neon-green bicycle. The rider was a tall, slim figure with a backpack, helmet, and mirrored goggles. Dark hair flowed from underneath the helmet, which was covered with decals: feathers, thunderbirds, wolves, rainbows, and Kokopeli, the flute player.

Then the smile widened, unmistakable – Izzy!

Wishi-ta screamed. "He's here! Izzy!" And then again. "Izzy!" until they heard footsteps in the hallway, the boys on their way.

"Thanks, God," said Neesa, who crossed herself quickly and whispered. "Mother of God protect us."

"I don't believe it," said Malvina, shaking her head and grinning. "Brother, you are too much sometimes."

Helene could not stop smiling: what a sight! Truly, like a messenger from another world, in the oddest-looking getup that only Izzy could make look wonderful.

"My new pony," he said, gesturing grandly. "The Red Streak." Which was kind of a funny name, as the bike was not red at all. Like a horse, it had a couple of saddle bags on each side, which looked full. Unlike a horse, it had a rack in the back and a basket in front, also packed.

"Expensive," said Neesa.

"Yup. I worked a lot of hours for this baby. But it rides like a dream."

By then they all realized that this was his mode of transportation from the city.

"You rode here from Boston?" Malvina asked.

"Took me two days. I had a stopover in Worcester with a friend. No problem at all," he said with a modest shrug. He gave Wishi-ta a kiss, which made her exclaim of the cold. "Well, a little chilly," he admitted.

"Too cold for standing here," Neesa said, waving everyone inside, including Izzy and the bike, which he leaned against a wall in the living room, away from the Christmas tree with its popcorn-and-cranberry garland. Even under Neesa's careful eye, he scratched the wall with the pedals and knocked a basket off the coffee table where the Nativity scene was displayed. Izzy released a duffel bag from the rack on the back, bulky but soft and light, and handed it to Helene.

"For you," he said. "Special delivery." Without opening the bag, Helene knew it was yarn, material, thread, ribbon, and trim, all from Thelma. Helene was warmed by her friend's kind gesture, especially because it wasn't necessary, or urgent in any way. Wishi-ta was right at her side, watching as she tugged the zipper open, pulling out pieces of cloth.

"Wait, there's more," Izzy said, taking an envelope out of one of the saddle bags. "There is something I have to tell you, tell everyone."

Behind the women the boys stood open mouthed at yet another incarnation of their uncle. Then he took off the helmet, shaking out his shoulder-length hair, and opened his arms to them; they came to him without a word, as solemn as Helene had ever seen them.

The adults looked at one another.

"Maybe later," Malvina said. "You can tell us. They want to see you, these ones."

Izzy stretched to his full height. "I want them to hear this too. It is for all of us, really."

He opened the envelope, which had a number of papers in it, and withdrew one, with a letterhead at the top.

"The police here called me, on my cell phone. They asked me to come back to the station to meet with them; that's partly why I'm here. But on the phone they told me they found the guys who..." – he paused, looking at the kids, choosing his words – "who punched me out and broke my bike last summer."

All eyes turned to Helene.

"Wow," she said. "My goodness. They actually did it. The police, I mean; they followed through. I'm amazed. Not that they couldn't figure it out, just that they stayed on it. Wow." She shook her head. "So, what then?"

"The guys admitted what they did. I guess their uncle, the guy that owns the business, suspected something and got the story out of them. He's the one that got them to go to the station. Plus they got fingerprints off that letter; the guy had been in a bar fight before, so they had a match." He stopped, like that was all there was to the story.

"And?" Helene prompted.

"I got a letter from their lawyers. It was supposed to go to my lawyer, but I don't have one."

Again he looked at Helene without much expression.

"Well," she said. "You can hire one too. I'm sure the Intertribal Council has someone they can recommend. Especially if it's a hate crime – that will probably increase the charges and the damages."

Izzy tipped his head, hesitating. He gave a quick look at his sister, and said softly. "Why don't you take the children now? We can explain things later. OK?"

She nodded, and the children filed out behind her without a word. Helene and Izzy were left on their own with the popcorn-studded tree and the miniature Holy Family with angels in buckskin.

"Izzy," Helene said, "You can't back down now. Don't you see? This is victory for you, and for all victims!"

"Yes, but..."

"If it's the money," Helene said, "or...finding good representation, I can help. My husband...my former husband...he can find a top-notch criminal lawyer, I'm sure." Then she stopped. *What was she saying, promising money, Kenneth's help?* Izzy was not persuaded, nor did he look particularly upset, except perhaps on her account.

"What?" Helene asked. "What is it?"

"The lawyers," Izzy started. "I'd rather not..." His voice petered out before starting again. "I think...we think...there's another way, something else we want to try."

She must have looked dumbfounded, because he went on. "I talked to Louis about this..."

Louis! Helene rolled her eyes; she couldn't help it. But Izzy was undeterred. "And he thinks we should try this other way...restorative justice." He paused, searching her face. "You know what I'm talking about? No? So the, ah, perpetrators and me, we meet with these facilitators, they call them; and other people, friends or family, volunteers who have some training. They meet with us by ourselves and together until we reach an agreement about what to do."

Helene was puzzled. "But why? What's the point of it?"

"To avoid going to court and all the fighting that goes along with it."

Helene felt heat rising, old anger, and perhaps fear. "But Izzy, you're clearly in the right here. And clearly deserve damages – by which I mean money, for medical expenses, lost work, all that."

"They can still decide those things; that's the restore part."

Helene shook her head. "I don't know. And they deserve...well, paying money is the least of it. Jail time, a criminal record. I don't think you should –"

He raised a hand. "No, Helene. I've decided. This is how I want to do it. You won't change my mind."

This time, Izzy held her eyes, the room around them silent and motionless, no kids, no pets, nothing but them and the holiday decorations.

"I know one of those guys who beat me." This time he did not mince words. "I recognized him from playing baseball against his team in middle school, and he was at the community college the same time I was."

"You knew him?"

"I knew who he was. Not his name, I knew his face. And I think maybe he knew me too. I'm not easy to miss."

Helene practically stomped her foot. "That makes it worse!"

Izzy was unswayed. "Yes and no. The same way I don't want to be a called a victim, I don't want him to be labeled a criminal for the rest of his life."

"He is a criminal! What they did was criminal, against the law."

"And the law offers this other thing – this form of justice. Helene, you can't know our experience with the legal and justice system in this country, but it's not good. And I would rather try this other way, if it leads to a fair outcome. Maybe, just maybe, they'll have some better idea of why they carry such anger in the first place."

Helene remained silent. She could only hope that this idea – this restorative justice – would work out in any kind of meaningful way. And then the words came to her, from Izzy and from Renee's letter, the one that had been hidden away from her. *There is another way.*

"Give it a chance, Helene," Izzy was saying, "It's closer to the Native ideas of justice, and I think it's a better in the long run for many people, not just Natives." He reached out to take her hand, holding it between his two. "Will you trust me on this? The way I have trusted you?"

Helene blinked, and then she knew: it was OK to try this, if Izzy felt it was right. As odd a package as he might seem at times, from the outside, Helene knew, because she could feel it, the power of his truth. And then came an unexpected flood of relief; that maybe she, and Izzy, and the family, would not be consumed in a trying battle that would take up time and energy.

OK, she nodded. No need for more words.

"This is good news," Izzy said, releasing her hand. "That they have come forward. So let's be glad. Now I'm home for a few days and ready to be with family."

Izzy was transformed into his old, sweet, light-spirited self. It was still there, under the pain and injury. His face had brightened with pleasure. "And show off my bike."

He shouted and the children soon reappeared in the room, crowding around him. They were excited not only about the bike but also the goggles and helmet. After a moment Wishi-ta went back to the duffel bag and the treasures within. She pulled out skeins of yellow and red yarn, cards of lace, and bundled scraps of materials.

"Helene, look," she cried, unfolding one of the bundles and holding it out. "Deers, for you." The material was printed with stylized animals against a winter landscape of pine trees, repeating every few feet. A buck stood within a full moon, and another deer bounded over a bush. Beyond was a doe with two fawns at her side. Wishi-ta looked up, smiling. "Twins, like us."

Helene nodded, fingering the cloth. "Very nice." She liked the material, good colors and not fussy. Was it chance, or did Thelma have a second sense? Had Helene even told Wishi-ta about seeing deer on the way to the prison, or dreaming of them? She must have.

Good news began to rain down upon Helene and all those around her and near to her heart. Wishi-ta was feeling well and putting on weight; Tana-na had settled in at kindergarten, with a couple of accommodations for his energetic nature. The sale of Erik's cabin in Pennsylvania had gone smoothly, and he was looking for another place near to the base with rooms for a girl and a boy. Thelma's house, too, was a thing of the past – literally, torn down with a new foundation in its place, for something almost twice the size. But she loved her new condo, and had no more worries about leaky roofs or snow to shovel.

Izzy invited Helene to be part of the restorative justice process, along with Noel. She was to sit with him through the sessions – on the condition that she not argue against the idea itself, but present the facts as she knew them and any changes she had observed in Izzy and his family. A couple of times she got hot under the collar, listening to the two young men try to rationalize their anger at the unintentional damage to the truck. But Noel stayed calm throughout and spoke in a soft, unhurried manner, making the

410   Erin McCormack

others listen carefully. The police department and the lawyers who were working with the case were still new to the idea, and it was not an overnight deal. As they met every couple of weeks, it looked like there might be a resolution by early spring. Through the Intertribal Center they created a roster of drivers to give Izzy rides to and from the city, including Helene, who used the occasion to stay over with Thelma.

They had a date now for Louis's transfer, and a nonprofit advocacy group at a university in the Midwest was thinking of taking his case to see if there was any room for further appeal or mitigating the sentence. The equinox celebration in March began turning into something larger, according to Elsa, who reported the news from Chief. The council had met and decided it would be a time of thanksgiving, for the many good things that had happened to their members, not only the Lopes family, but also the family whose house had burned, now in a new home. And the new sweat lodge, the women's hand drum group, and even Chief's successful knee operation.

"Why not?" Chief said when Helene asked him what had given him the idea for the celebration. "If not now, when? We know things will go all screwy again sometime for somebody, but the point is that we worked through these things with each other, more or less. Without a whole lot of grousing. Besides, we'll take any excuse for a good party."

She couldn't disagree. And some part of her was excited about it all. It hardly seemed possible that nine months come and gone since the letter had arrived from Malvina; and yet, it felt like this had been her life for a very long time.

"I think I need to see Louis again," she told Erik one morning after the children had been picked up for the walk to school. They were in snow pants for the first time this winter. She watched them plod along in their boots, joyous at this new marvel, fluffy, cold and white.

"Why?" Erik took another piece of toast. "I don't understand what's holding you back. Everyone is fine with things as they are. They want you here."

"Not everyone. There are still some naysayers."

"True. Well, it takes time. Do you blame them entirely for their reluctance, or suspicions? But the family is behind you, and lots of other folks. That's what counts."

Helene was on her second cup of coffee, savoring the warm liquid, the cozy house, and the time with Erik.

"I guess it's in my own mind, then. And now Louis will be much closer, more influence on the twins. He already has plenty of visitors, I know, other activists, some of them, women." She wiggled her eyebrows. "And if this group from the university manages to help him, it might take time off his sentence. So what then? Where does that leave me?"

Erik shrugged, but he nodded, understanding. He chewed a few minutes longer, and then swallowed. "Yeah, it's hard to know. But just for here and now. And just for the kids and you. What's best?"

She groaned. "I'm not sure, not completely sure."

"But Louis has agreed to you being legal guardian. And he agreed to it, even after he knew what happened with you and Renee. And what's happened since – all of it."

"Yes, under some duress, I must say."

Erik cocked an eyebrow, and she added, "It's not that he really wanted to, but without a lot of other options…you know, he really went off on me when I first brought up the idea of adopting Wishi-ta, and taking her back to live with me and Kenneth."

Erik looked at her squarely. "Because it was a bad idea."

"I know. But not everyone would think so, under the circumstances. Louis wanted the help, but he wanted it done his way, the Native way."

Erik sighed. "I know, I know, he can be so intense about it all, and in your face. But it's who he is, what he believes. For him, it's the worst thing to take away the traditions, and the community."

Helene put down the cup. "OK, yes, maybe. But even Chief says these traditions can be a little makeshift, whatever they remember from before."

After a moment, putting his napkin on the table, Erik said. "I don't think it matters. It's a matter of identity, and that's a big thing to take from someone, who they are, where they have come from, what they belong to."

"But she comes from us too. Our side of the family!"

He gave her one long, last look before getting up. "And what do you belong to?"

She had no answer. Erik put his dishes in the sink and went to wash up. She knew he was right, and Louis wasn't going to change what he wanted from her, what he wanted for the children. Then again, she admitted to herself, maybe she truly was not worthy to be more than a temporary custodian for these children, no matter how much she had come to love them.

Then another face came into her mind, and a voice – a motherly voice, although nothing like Helene's mother. Elsa: not Native. An outsider. Part of this whole setup for twenty or thirty years.

"I'm going to see Elsa," she said to a surprised Erik, who only nodded as she grabbed a jacket and walked out of the house. She didn't even know herself what she would say when she got there, if Elsa was even in. But she was. She didn't look as surprised as Erik that Helene had come. She was on the sofa sorting material on the coffee table, listening to country music on the radio.

"Come in, sit down," she said. "Chief isn't here at the moment."

"I came to see you."

"Oh?" Elsa looked up with interest.

Helene plunged in. "How do you do it? Do this" – she raised her arms – "take part in this community when you're not Native at all? How does that even work?"

"Ah, that question." Elsa put down a swatch of fabric and tucked a strand of gray-blonde hair behind her ear. "That's kind of difficult to answer. I didn't have a plan, and I never set out to do it. It just kind of happened; evolved, you might say."

"Because of the Chief's leadership?"

Elsa laughed. "Not so much. Well, not at first. We had a kind of regular, plain vanilla kind of home life at first, both of us, just regular jobs; he was in construction, and I was a social worker. We made a few trips to the reservation in Quebec to see family, and of course the naming ceremonies and other occasions, but there wasn't much going on in terms of Native culture around here, this part of the state, I can tell you. Very little. A few powwows in Maine and New Hampshire, and the Wampanoags down at the Cape and islands – those have been going on a long time."

This was not exactly the picture Helene had in her mind, that these gatherings were a relatively new kind of development.

"So, then, Chief got things going, the powwow and the Intertribal Center?"

Elsa considered, closing one eye, reminding Helene of Erik. "Really, a couple of others before him, who have passed on. We just kind of inherited the roles."

"We?"

"I'd say we're pretty much a partnership in this."

"It seems like it. But you're not Native at all, are you? Not one bit, even way back."

"Not born Native, no. But don't forget, my children are half Native by birth. The two girls are still very involved and connected in Native life. But our son, the scientist, doesn't have as much interest, or time. If anything, he's more enthralled with the Vikings, of all things!" She laughed again, and Helene had to smile. She'd forgotten the Scandinavian connection between her family and Erik's.

"So," Elsa continued, "I can say that we got more involved with the intertribal association while raising the children and then things started to pop up all around us. Until, here we are." She raised her arm in an open-handed gesture.

Helene breathed out, taking this in.

Elsa was looking her over carefully. "But as for me, first I just went along; then I tried to fit in as best I could. Then it became pretty much part of regular life and how we did things. And now, this is who I am, what is important to me, even apart from Chief. If he should pass away, this is still my community, as long as it lasts." She shrugged. "It works for me. And not just me. We have other members who were not born Native. Some married into Native families, but others just gravitated to the events and the community, and I suppose the cultural values."

Helene was quiet a moment, watching Elsa work.

"I know you and Erik had a rough start in life," Helene said, choosing her words. "And that you were kind of in charge of Erik, like I was in charge of Renee, whether or not we wanted to be. Did you…well, were you…looking for something, some kind of rescue, like Renee was, when you married Chief?" She blushed, looking down at her hands. But she needed to know.

Elsa sighed, and shook her head. "It didn't happen like that. Chief was a drunk in an alleyway when I first met him, in my early days as a social worker. He was a mess: young and lost and totally out of his element. He was homeless, without a place to shower, and he smelled terrible." The ghost of a smile came to her lips. "That was the beginning of our romance."

Helene was shocked; it was so hard to believe of the wise, robust, merry man she had met and talked with.

"But he cleaned up nice," Elsa said, her smile widening. "Handsome under all that grime. And he wanted to get better, find another way. Part of that way was going back to who he really was, his own traditions and values, as he could recall them."

She paused to remember, then continued. "I'd never met a man like him before, a person like him. So genuine and sweet in a way that lots of American men are taught not to be. But, more than that, he had a good mind and a good spirit, and he could put up with Erik – at least understand and care about him. Chief had traveled between these different worlds, looking to fit in somewhere. In the end, he decided, and I decided, to stay with each other and make our own world, being part of this community. So that's what we did. I guess you could say I rescued him from the alley, and he rescued me from a world of bad experiences."

So it was mutual, Helene thought, the give and the take between people, between cultures, looking for what worked in each of them.

"No regrets, then?"

"No regrets." Elsa laid her hands in her lap. "There is nowhere else I'd rather be, and no one else I'd rather be with. And I'm OK with who I am. What more is there?"

"Nothing that I can think of."

Helene sat another moment, hearing a truck pass outside, but not Erik's. She knew the sounds of Erik's truck by now. Elsa had gone back to matching fabric scraps, putting some aside.

"A new skirt for my new granddaughter," she said. "Pink and black, that's what she wants. Thirteen, the ideas they get!"

Still Helene sat, picturing the children at the powwows, so excited

Erin McCormack

with the new regalia, shedding the old pieces as they grew larger.

Elsa held out another folded piece of material, sort of neon green and yellow. "That might be something for my new niece," she said with a smile. Helene looked back dumbly. Was there more family than she knew about?

"Aurora," Elsa said simply. *Of course.* Then she smiled. "OK, then?"

Helene stirred but did not rise. "Yes, sure, thank you." Probably time to get going.

Elsa looked out of the corner of her eye. "Nothing you wanted to ask about Erik?"

Helene laughed. "No. Not today. Why? Is there something I should know?"

"Oh, lots. Erik's had many adventures in his life, not all of them good."

"I'm sure. But at the moment, I don't really care. I just want to be with him."

"I see that," said Elsa. And her eyes conveyed a certain pleasure that Helene had not expected to see.

Helene got up to leave, saying good-bye. She didn't head back to Renee's house, but turned instead up the walkway to Malvina's. She opened the unlocked door to call in. "Malvina? It's Helene."

"We're in the kitchen."

We turned out to be Malvina and the baby, Tewa, who was nursing. They sat at the kitchen table, where Malvina had opened a photo album to add more pictures, some from the naming ceremony, and some from the twins' birthday party. Helene stood behind to get a better look; there was one of her, Wishi-ta on her lap, huddled against the cold wind. And another of Helene and Erik, faces close in conversation. Malvina flipped through a couple of pages, looking for something, and there was the photo of all the children at the Home Camp – same as the one she had sent Helene last spring. And there, on the opposite page, was a picture of Renee with Louis and the twins, all together, happy.

"I've come to a decision," Helene said. "I know what I want to do."

"OK." Malvina adjusted her position, moving the baby to the other breast.

They heard a clanging of pots from Neesa's side of the house, and then smelled onions. "She's making stew," Malvina said with a smile. "We'll eat it for a week. And you too."

"I'm ready now to sign the papers for legal guardian. I'll call the lawyer today."

"OK." Malvina piled up the remaining photos, putting them away for another time. And then she said, "Good," nodding. Then to Helene's surprise, she continued, "You are wanted here. You are needed for Wishi-ta and Tana-na, as our friend and ally. Louis knows this. Treaties, agreements, protections – all of it can be taken away; mostly it has been. Even the ICWA, the law for Native children, that could be gone, and our children could be taken away again. It's good that you are with us."

Helene looked down at Tewa, all at peace, with a nose and mouth like Noel's. No matter the future trials, she had been born into a life of family connections and meaningful traditions – honorings, dedications, and celebrations, a sense of the sacred, and a circle of caring adults, including now herself, Helene. There was music, dance, fire, smoke, and water. There was regalia.

Renee's journal – 19

Not much more. Nothing important. Only, except, Helene. I dream of her. I told Louis. Forgive me, forgive herself.

I asked too much of her, she tried her best for me, at the end. At the end when I made her hold the pillow. Only her love was more than her anger. On the bed, next to me, she willed me back into life. As bad as it was then, to how good it is now. From hope of good, only. It was possible, this place, these people. I wish she...

10. The Circle and the Drum – by One Little Indian

This is who we are – our most universal symbols. The circle is everywhere – sun, moon, seasons, days, nests, drum, medicine wheel, hoop, home for many of us – not square and boxy. The circle is the beginning and end, inclusive, eternal, a way of belonging. We see ourselves in this way – always coming and going; tied often to a place or a point. Not a line headed off toward the future, or heaven, or anything like that. Just a circle.

The drum is the heart that beats – in all of us, human and animal relatives. The beat of the drum stirs all emotions, anger, fear, joy, and brings strength and energy. The drum calls us to sing and to dance, which is celebration, mourning, and honoring. The drum is a magnifier of our beings, our voices, our wishes to be heard. The drum calls us home to our sacred places, to one another. The drum connects our heartbeat with Mother Earth.

The other day, my niece was asking me about these things: she wanted to know who could be in the circle when we dance at the drum. I said, "Everyone who wants to be in the circle." But my niece, she's wise for a five-year-old; that answer was too easy, not enough. So I explained how special dances were for special dancers, who were prepared to dance in a certain way. And that sometimes the dance is for a certain reason, like medicine or victory or honoring. But the intertribal dance, according to our ways, is for everyone.

"Everyone?" she asked me. "But what about the rules? Don't they have to be Indian?"

"No, not for intertribal."

"Or American?"

"No."

"If some new ones come in, do the others have to leave?"

"There's always room."

"But what if there's too many?"

"The circle just gets bigger and bigger."

"How big?" Her eyes are big and blue, like those of her mother, who was not born Indian.

Hm…I had to stop and think about that one. And it had to be true, because she would know if I lied or fudged. You can't imagine how deeply she has thought about this.

"As big as the Earth, I think. Everyone in it. And maybe as big as the sky."

We are many nations, with many stories and histories. But these things, the drum and circle, belong to all of us, and show us we belong to the earth and one another.

Chapter 33

Everyone called it a "thanksgiving celebration," even though it was scheduled on the spring equinox in March. A bit confusing, Helene thought, but good, all good. There was a lot to do for the occasion, but when the hour arrived, Helene felt ready. Everything was done except waiting for the casserole to cool. The house was quiet; the twins were already gone, dressed in their regalia and walking to the Intertribal Center with their cousins. Helene could just see the back of them as they made their way down the sidewalk in the "parade" of folks headed for the celebration, avoiding puddles on the mild day.

Helene was in no hurry. For the first time in a long time, she did not feel the restlessness of something undone, out of kilter, a problem to be fixed. She was just one of a bunch of people going to a happy event, which was about as far into the future as she could see, or wanted to see. It was over, that strange and frightening and exciting transition from the old life to this new life. But she was still herself, same skin and bones, with a new scar on her head, but otherwise the same, with the same past life and experiences. They just appeared different now.

Out the window she saw Elsa and the Chief passing, steady and upright. No more cane. The Chief was magnificent in his full-feathered headdress. Elsa wore her Gray Dove singers regalia, and carried a basket over her arm – pie. They spoke a few words between them, and Helene saw a smile appear at Elsa's lips at some remark of the Chief's, always a kidder, even when he was serious.

She didn't expect to see Izzy or Erik until she got to the Center. They were setting up the new bike rack, and filling it with bicycles of all types and sizes – the restitution for the assault on Izzy from the previous year. Helmets too were part of the deal. And someone was coming to give a class on bicycle safety and maintenance, which Izzy was supposed to be part of, along with his cousins. Erik had no interest in vehicles without motors, but he was recruited for the jobs that required tools and building expertise. Helene hadn't ridden a bike in years, but she wanted to go on adventures with the kids – not too far.

She checked on the casserole, returning to the living room where she saw Denis's truck pull up and park in front of the house. Denis opened the tailgate to retrieve a bag, while Kiko climbed out with a dish, looking around. Most of the crowd had already disappeared inside the Intertribal Center. Helene opened the door to say hello.

"We're not late, I hope," Kiko said.

"No, the kids were just eager to get there."

"We'll leave the truck here if that's OK," Denis said to Helene. "Are you ready?"

"Go ahead." The casserole dish had cooled but she was not quite ready. "I'll be right there."

Kiko and Denis left, taking their time, Denis carrying a tote bag of food or drink. A kid on a bike passed them, ringing a bell. Maybe somebody trying out one of the new bikes, Helene mused.

A cluster of women and a couple men all in regalia were on their way, walking in the middle of the road. Alberta and Frances, the cranky sisters, were out front, probably scheduled to run the front table with Elsa; and still trying, as best they could, to adhere to the "right" ways, as they saw them. Yet they too had a bounce of excitement in their step, eager for the gathering and celebration. There was a lot to be glad about, not least that they were not isolated and alone, feeling alienated in their own land. Helene smiled to herself remembering their words against her, seeing her as a threat, when, instead, the community had managed to make a place for her too.

Half a block behind was Bernice and her clan: both daughters, a son-in-law, and all of their children, including Aurora in a stroller. Aurora's mother, Josie, was in regalia, but wore tall black boots, a fringed vest, and designer sunglasses, as well as bright-red lipstick. Bernice wore her Gray Dove shawl, and the older children were dressed to dance: jingle, fancy shawl, and grass dance, certainly new traditions for their Inupiaq grandmother.

The road cleared, and Helene got up to finish getting ready. In front of the hallway mirror, she surveyed herself in a long printed shirtdress, bound with a leather belt. She slipped on the silver-and-turquoise earrings that Thelma had given her, long and dangly. She put on moccasins, a gift from Malvina's family, wonderfully comfortable. Over her head she placed the beaded bluebird medallion which Renee had made. Finally she folded her own blanket, with a pattern of deer – bucks, does, and twin fawns, against moon, mountain, and lake. That was how she wanted to see the world, and the world to see her.

With the blanket inside the tote, she placed the bag over her shoulder. Inside the bag, also, was a note she had written, and a check made out to the Intertribal Community Association, money to purchase material for new drapes at the center. That she could afford, with the extra money from the house sale. And, now, she could see, it was all very doable – if she organized the project, directing how it should be done, and others could help cut and sew. Sewing, mending; it was her amends.

She picked up the casserole, ready to leave.

No one accompanied her on the road; they were all gone ahead, although she knew by now that they were not likely to start on the dot. They were on what they called "Indian time," which meant last-minute delays and necessary visiting. As she approached the Intertribal Center, she saw two figures working on the shed that housed the new bike rack in a grassy area outside the front door – surrounded by a noisy audience, laughing and heckling. From a distance she recognized Izzy and Erik, so different but connected in so many surprising, different ways. Two of the people who had become central to Helene's new world. Stars of this particular universe, which had a lot of light. Where everyone could shine, from youngest to oldest.

Elsa appeared at the doorway and summoned everyone inside. Izzy and Erik were putting their tools away when Helene arrived. Izzy's hair was in a short braid. He had put away his "more is more" regalia for a minimalist look: fringed leggings and a vest. In place of feathers and face paint, he had black eyeliner only, as striking as ever. Erik wore jeans and work boots, but there was a large silver buckle on his belt, and a bolo tie, which must have come from one of the powwows.

"Looking good, Helene," Erik said, straightening up. "It suits you, what you're wearing."

"Thank you," she said. "And the same to you both. Look at you in a bolo tie." Then she turned to Izzy. "Dazzling, as always."

"Not a fashion show."

"I know, I know," she said wagging her head. "And this is not really regalia. Not ceremonial, I mean. Just for the social parts."

Izzy shrugged. "Special clothes for special people on a special occasion – that's all. Creator isn't judging us on how fancy we are, or how authentic, no matter what some of these Indians think." He gestured with his chin toward the inside of the building. "It's the other clothes that are costumes, anyway. What we wear when we're being our other, everyday selves." He pointed toward Erik's belt buckle. "Check out the buffalo. Even Erik's getting with the program."

Erik walked over to kiss Helene. "It all makes more sense when you're here."

Helene had to laugh. "You must have been very confused, then."

"You have no idea."

Elsa was at the door, giving a curt wave to Izzy and Helene, before scowling at her brother. "Leave that alone for now. It's time for Grand Entry."

They heard another voice behind Elsa, high, female. "Wait, a couple photos. Please!"

One of Bernice's teenaged granddaughters had shown up with a camera.

"For the newsletter," the girl explained. "The new bike rack. We're trying to get everybody at the celebration. You too," she said to Helene, who squeezed in between the men. The girl snapped a few shots, and then showed the images to the group for approval.

"Handsome and beautiful, you two," Erik said. "I'm just background scenery." He made a last adjustment on the rack, leaving Izzy and Helene still posed, side by side. The girl ran off, followed by Elsa, who left with a warning look toward the stragglers.

"Look at us," Helene said to Izzy. "In-laws. Who knew such a thing was possible?"

"Anything is possible," Izzy said lightly. "Just about."

"I know, but not in my wildest dreams could I see myself being part of all this. If not for that letter from Malvina..." She shook her head. "I'm still so surprised that they thought to send it at all, her and Louis."

This time Izzy's expression was more serious. "That was my idea. Didn't you know?"

"Your idea?"

Helene could hardly imagine how that conversation had come about.

Everyone else had gone inside by now, except the two of them and Erik fiddling with the rack. They could hear static from the PA system, but neither stirred.

"When Renee was sick, really sick, near the end," Izzy said, "I was over there late at night, the twins were asleep. I thought she was too. But she said your name – "Helene" – and then, "Tell Helene." But when I asked her what she meant, what should we tell you, she had gone back to sleep. I tried again the next morning, but she was so out of it; she didn't remember anything. Then I thought maybe I'd dreamed it."

His mind was traveling back. Helene waited, still.

"When things got bad," he said, "after Renee passed and Louis was arrested, and Wishi-ta had those attacks, and Malvina was having problems with the pregnancy, that's when I remembered what Renee had said. And that's when I told them, Louis and Malvina. That's why they wrote you."

Helene nodded: like that, it had happened. Now she could picture it: how and why.

Elsa swung open the door. "Now."

Erik's head jerked up, and he turned from the rack. They followed Elsa inside, where the room was full, all the tables pushed to the walls, a drum set up next to the emcee's table. A circle of chairs made a wide ring around the dance area. A man was going around the circle, fanning smoke in all directions, the cleansing smudge. Helene stopped, scanning the room. Her eyes rested briefly on the display board, the photograph of Renee "Shooting Star," in regalia. In her mind's eye, Helene was in the back hallway to the kitchen by the Wall of Warriors with Sitting Bull, Geronimo, Wilma Mankiller, Louis Riel; and now, Louis Lopes – her brother-in-law, bound to her in mutual love and sorrow for Renee and the children.

"Line up, line up," came the emcee's voice, Robert, trying to be heard over the reverberations of sound. "Chief, where are you?" and then, "Do we have all our veterans ready to go?" It was a colorful chaos while the groups lined up – veterans; elders, male and female; dancers of all kinds, and then young people, and children; some family groups with babes in arms.

Wishi-ta arrived at Helene's side and pulled at her hand. She wore the fancy shawl in pink and blue that Helene had made, with shiny ribbon fringe, and a rather cuddly cat next to a butterfly.

"It's time," she said. "Come on."

Then Tana-na appeared, serious in his buckskin, with a suspicious cherry-red stain on his chin, which was not paint, Helene was sure. He said nothing but followed as Wishi-ta led them over to their cousins and Malvina and Noel, who held the baby. Neesa was with the older women, but glanced back, to see that her family was present.

"When the drum beats," Wishi-ta said loudly, looking up at Helene, "we'll start walking in, just little steps; we have to wait our turn. And then we go round and round until everyone is in there. Ready?"

The drum started. The voices stopped. The veterans led with the flags: the United States, state, and the different tribes that were present. The Eagle Staff was carried out – with its eagle feather honoring warriors who had given their lives for their people. Helene felt her heart starting to calm again and then find the rhythm of the drumbeat. The elders went in, the other adults, the dancers, and finally the children and families.

Wishi-ta held her hand. Tana-na gave an encouraging push from behind.

They stepped inside the circle.

The End

Made in the USA
Middletown, DE
20 April 2019